'I have never really fallen in love in my life,' he confessed.

'Not with a passion which has lasted, anyway. I can't say what I feel for you is love. I only know that it is different, and infinitely distracting. Desire for you has dominated my every waking moment since the moment we met. I can think of nothing else but touching you, kissing you, making love to you.'

Miranda Lee is Australian, living near Sydney. Born and raised in the bush, she was boarding-school educated and briefly pursued a classical music career before moving to Sydney and embracing the world of computers. Happily married, with three daughters, she began writing when family commitments kept her at home. She likes to create stories that are believable, modern, fast-paced and sexy. Her interests include reading meaty sagas, doing word puzzles and going to the movies.

Recent titles by the same author:

NIGHT OF SHAME
TWO-WEEK WIFE
A NANNY NAMED NICK
RED-HOT AND RECKLESS

JUST FOR A NIGHT

BY
MIRANDA LEE

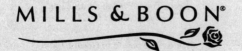

*First published in Great Britain 1998
Harlequin Mills & Boon Limited,
Eton House, 18-24 Paradise Road, Richmond, Surrey TW9 1SR*

© Miranda Lee 1998

ISBN 0 263 80730 4

*Set in Times Roman 11 on 12 pt.
91-9802-44134 C1*

Printed and bound in Great Britain

CHAPTER ONE

'I DON'T want you to go.'

Marina looked up from her suitcase and shook her head at the sulky expression on her fiancé's face.

'Please don't start that again, Shane. I *have* to go. Surely you can see that?'

'No, I can't,' he snapped. 'It's only three weeks till the wedding and here you are swanning off to the other side of the world on some wild-goose chase. There's no guarantee that your bone marrow will save that little girl's life. You're probably just getting their hopes up for nothing.'

'Firstly, I will only be away a week at the most,' Marina pointed out, impatience only a breath away. 'Secondly, I happen to be a near perfect match. Not only in blood, but in tissue type. Do you know how rare that is?'

'I'm sure you'll tell me,' he said sourly. 'You're the smart one around here.'

Marina frowned at his tone of voice, and at the indication behind his words. This was a side to Shane she'd never seen before.

There again, she considered slowly, she'd never crossed him before. After her mother's death a couple of months ago she'd been more than happy to accept the warm hand of friendship and support Shane had

5

offered, more than happy to have someone there to
make all the funeral arrangements and give her a
shoulder to cry on. Her usually decisive and strong-
willed character had failed her entirely during that
grief-stricken time. Shane had been strong when she'd
felt weak, kind and thoughtful when that was what
she'd needed most.

That his kindness had ended up in his bed had probably been inevitable. He was an attractive man and
she was, after all, so terribly lonely. Her satisfaction
with his lovemaking had not been quite so inevitable,
given her uninspiring sexual history. The pleasure
he'd given her had stunned her, so much so that she'd
believed herself in love at last. When he'd asked her
to marry him a month ago, she'd said yes.

Now she stared at him. His face was not so handsome as he scowled at her. His eyes not so kind, either. They were cold and angry.

'I had no idea how much you resented my being a
teacher,' she said, covering her distress behind a cool
tone. 'If you imagine I think you're in any way in-
ferior to me because you work with your hands, then
I don't.'

Shane had been her mother's right-hand man in the
riding and dressage school she'd run on the outskirts
of Sydney. Although a high school drop-out, Shane
was far from dumb. When Marina's mother had hired
him a good few years back, the then twenty-five-year-
old had known everything there was to know about
matters equestrian. He'd got along with Marina's

mother like a house on fire because they had a passion in common: the passion for horses.

Marina quite liked horses, and she'd learnt to ride adequately enough, but she'd never been obsessed by the showjumping scene, as her mother and Shane were. She'd always quite liked Shane too, but he'd been standoffish in her presence—till her mother's illness and death had changed the status quo between them.

After they'd become engaged, Marina had told Shane that the school and the horses were his to do with whatever he liked.

She wondered now if he loved the school and horses more than he loved her.

Or if he loved her at all...

'Maybe our getting married is not such a good idea,' she said quietly. 'We did rush into it a bit.'

He was around the bed and taking her in his arms before she could say boo. But his hard, hungry kisses left her cold. Shane stopped after a while and held her at arm's length. This time his expression was full of apology and remorse.

'You're angry with me,' he said. 'And you've every right to be. I was being bloody selfish. Of course you have to go. Of course. It's just that I'm going to miss you terribly, sweetheart.' He released her arms to cup her chin and lift her mouth for him to kiss again. Softly this time. And sweetly.

Marina had to admit to a moment of melting. These new sexual responses of hers could be very disarming.

And perhaps not always in her best interests, came the astonishing realisation.

'I'm really going to miss this beautiful mouth of yours,' Shane murmured. 'There again, everything about you is so beautiful. Your eyes. Your skin. Your hair. Your breasts.' His hands lifted to stroke them through her shirt and she was dismayed at the way they responded, as though they weren't connected with her brain.

'I've always wanted you, Marina,' he insisted, with a thickened quality to his voice. 'From the first moment I saw you. But your mother warned me right from the start that I could look, but not touch. Her little princess was not for the likes of me.'

Marina was not really surprised by this news. Her mother had been a very contradictory person. British-born and bred, she'd apparently defied her wealthy, upper-crust parents to run off to Australia with a colonial stablehand. She'd been told never to darken their doorstep again. Which she hadn't.

Her bitterness over their attitude had been such that she'd never spoken of her English ancestors to her daughter, and had forbidden Marina to ever seek them out.

One would have thought she'd bring up Marina to despise this kind of snobbery and hypocrisy. And she had, in a way. But at the same time, perversely, she'd tried to turn her only daughter into a right little madam, with all the associated refinements and manners. Marina had been given ballet lessons, piano lessons and speech and drama lessons, not to mention the obligatory riding and dressage lessons.

It hadn't really worked. Marina might look an elegant twenty-five-year-old lady on the surface, and she could hold her own in any company, but she was still Australian through and through—with a stubborn streak a mile long, an instinctive irreverence for authority and a pragmatic no-nonsense attitude to life.

She was also a chip off the old block when it came to defying parents, because when she'd gone to England on a backpacking holiday a couple of years previously she had tried to look up the maternal side of her family—her mother's maiden name being on her birth certificate—only to find that there were more Binghams in England than you could poke a stick at.

Without more information to narrow the field, or money to hire an investigator, finding the right Binghams would have been like looking for a needle in a haystack. Since she had never been all *that* curious about the English side to her family—they sounded horrible snobs to her—she'd given up the search without another qualm.

Shane's comment reminded her that she would be in England again soon. And this time she *did* have some money. Her mother's estate had been larger than she'd envisaged. It seemed she'd been a very astute businesswoman over the years. Now that Marina could not hurt her mother with a more in-depth search, she might just see if she could find her grandparents, plus any possible aunts, uncles and cousins.

And maybe she wouldn't.

They'd never searched for her, had they? Why should she care a whit for them? They'd probably only upset her by not wanting to have anything to do with her.

No, she would abandon that idea entirely. Best to let sleeping dogs lie.

'I never thought you'd look twice at me,' Shane was saying, 'with your private school education and your looks. But you did, didn't you, princess? And now...now you're mine.' He bent to back his claim with a long and very intimate kiss. It did set her heart a-thudding, but it was not what she wanted at that moment. All she wanted was to be left alone. Her head was absolutely whirling.

'Come back as quickly as you can,' he urged. 'Don't stay over there a moment longer than necessary.'

Marina didn't know what to say. She felt very confused. A couple of weeks ago she had not been able to wait to marry Shane. Now, suddenly, those heady feelings of being madly in love seemed to have disappeared and her thoughts were very disturbing.

Surely Shane could not be just marrying her for the horses. Surely he loved her. And surely she loved him back. Hadn't she quivered under his touch only last night? Hadn't she cried out with pleasure?

Her mental toing and froing led nowhere, but the urge to get away from Shane remained acute. The urge to get away all round was becoming even stronger.

The trip to London, which had loomed in her mind

as something of a trial, now took on a different perspective. It became a welcome escape, a time away from Shane during which she could think more clearly. By the time she returned, hopefully, she would know what to do.

It would not be too late to break her engagement even then. It wasn't as though they were going to have a big church wedding, only a simple ceremony in her mother's prized rose garden, with a celebrant and a few close friends attending.

This had been Shane's wish, not Marina's. She'd always wanted a traditional wedding, but Shane had argued the unsuitability of a big celebration so soon after her mother's death. She recalled Shane had also said it would be a waste of money—money better spent on the plans he had for building new stables and buying new horses.

Money figured a lot in Shane's arguments, Marina was beginning to realise.

When the phone call had come from the children's hospital, asking her if she could fly to London as soon as possible to be a bone marrow donor, Shane's first concern had been how much money it would cost and who was going to pay. He hadn't shut up about it till a follow-up letter had arrived, explaining Marina would not be out of pocket in any way whatsoever.

Shane *still* hadn't been happy about her going.

But in this case Marina had remained adamant, her natural tendency to stubbornness rising up through the uncharacteristic submissiveness which had been plaguing her. This had nothing to do with them as a couple and everything to do with herself as a decent and caring human being. She was prepared to go even if she had to pay for it all herself. How could she not, when a little girl's life was at stake?

Her name was Rebecca, and she was only seven. An orphan, God love her, but with a wonderful great-uncle, it seemed. An earl, no less. And rich as Croesus, thank heavens.

He'd sent a first-class return ticket for Marina, plus a written assurance that he would be personally responsible for all her expenses. His gratitude knew no bounds. He claimed he would be in her debt for the rest of his life.

Marina smiled as she thought of the letter and its incredibly formal-sounding expressions. The man was British aristocracy through and through, all right. But rather sweet, she conceded. For a blue-blood.

'Ahh, you're smiling,' Shane said, and bent to peck her on the lips. 'I must be forgiven.'

Marina could not trust herself to speak. She twisted out of Shane's arms and busied herself shutting and locking her suitcase. 'We'll have to leave for the airport shortly,' she said. 'If you're still going to drive me, that is?'

'Why wouldn't I drive you?' he said expansively. 'Don't be so sensitive, sweetheart.' He scooped the suitcase off the bed and placed his spare arm around her shoulders.

'I know why you're so touchy,' he said, hugging her to his side. 'You're just jumpy about the flight. And about your hospital stay at the other end. I'll say

this for you, Marina, you're damned brave, volun-
teering to have needles poked in you like that. I know
I wouldn't do it. Not for a perfect stranger.'

Marina frowned. She didn't think of herself as particularly brave. She'd been assured the procedure was
not painful, though there might be some discomfort
in her hip for a couple of days.

It dawned on her then that Shane was a very selfish
man. Selfish and ambitious and stingy.

Marina fingered her engagement ring all the way
from Bringelly to the airport at Mascot. Half a dozen
times she contemplated taking it off and giving it
back. But she didn't. And, in the end, she boarded the
plane still an engaged woman.

CHAPTER TWO

THE man holding the sign which said 'MISS MARINA SPENCER' didn't look like a chauffeur.

He wasn't wearing a uniform for one thing, like several of the other sign-carrying chauffeurs standing near him. He was wearing a black pin-striped three-piece suit and a crisp white business shirt whose starched collar was neatly bisected by a classy maroon tie. A matching maroon handkerchief winked from the breast pocket of the superbly tailored jacket.

Frankly, he looked like an executive. A very tall, very good-looking, very successful executive. In his early thirties, Marina guessed, he had straight black hair—impeccably parted and groomed—straight black brows, and an air of urbane superiority. She could see him sitting behind a desk, in one of those black leather swivel chairs. Or in a boardroom, at the head of one of those long, polished tables.

But the sign he was carrying placed him very firmly as the chauffeur she'd been told would meet her at Heathrow. So Marina set her luggage trolley on an unswerving path straight towards him.

His gaze, which had been staring rather blankly at the steady stream of arrivals, shifted abruptly to hers, and Marina found herself looking into deeply set blue eyes which widened at her approach. Clearly she didn't fit his idea of a Miss Marina Spencer any more than *he* did her concept of a chauffeur.

Admittedly, she probably didn't look like most Englishmen's idea of a girl from Sydney. Her bright red hair and very pale skin did not fit the clichéd beach beauties from Bondi, sporting honey-blonde hair as long as their legs and a gorgeous all-over tan.

At least I have the long legs, she thought, smiling ruefully to herself over her total inability to tan—inherited, possibly, from somewhere on her maternal side. Unless it came from her father's distant Irish ancestry. Who knew, where recessive genes were concerned? Luckily, Marina's mother had lathered her daughter's sensitive skin with sun factor fifteen her entire life, and she only carried a smattering of light freckles.

Marina stopped the trolley right in front of the chauffeur and smiled politely up into his by now frowning face.

'I'm Marina Spencer,' she informed him.

He gave her the longest look in return, one which left her feeling as poorly composed as the twenty-two-hour flight had. She'd hardly slept a wink, for one thing. And something she'd eaten had not agreed with her. All in all, the trip *had* been a trial, and she wasn't looking forward to the return flight, regardless of the first-class seat.

She'd done her best to resurrect her appearance in the Ladies just before disembarking, but despite fresh make-up her skin still felt dehydrated, and her normally vibrant red-gold curls hung rather limply around her face and shoulders. Her widely spaced green eyes, one of her best features, had dark smudges under them.

On the plus side, her jeans had survived the trip better than a skirt or a dress. And her favourite and thankfully crease-proof black jacket hid the wrinkles in the white shirt underneath.

But she still felt somewhat the worse for wear.

The chauffeur's thorough visual assessment irritated her somewhat. Finally, he bent to prop the sign against a nearby pillar, then straightened, still unsmiling, to hold out his hand to her in greeting.

'How do you do, Miss Spencer? I trust you had a good flight? I'm James Marsden.' The fingers which enclosed hers were firm and cool. 'My chauffeur had a problem with one of his knees this morning. Arthritis. So I came to collect you myself. He's waiting for us out in the car.'

Marina blinked her astonishment. *This* was James Marsden? *This* was Rebecca's great-uncle? *This* was the Earl of Winterborne?

Her first impulse was to laugh. No wonder he hadn't fitted the image of a chauffeur. But, my goodness, he didn't fit her image of the Earl of Winterborne, either. She'd pictured an elderly white-haired gentleman, with a handle-bar moustache, a walking stick and an Irish wolfhound at his feet.

'That was very kind of you,' she said, trying to school her mouth into a polite expression instead of an amused grin. She succeeded, but not before the Earl of Winterborne clearly spotted her struggle to suppress a smile. Those straight black brows of his drew momentarily together, and for a brief second she thought he was going to ask her what the joke was. But he merely shrugged and stepped forward to lift her suitcase from the trolley, swinging it easily to the ground at his feet.

'Is this your only luggage?' he asked.

'Yes, it is.' She was glad now that she'd brought only her best clothes with her. Glad too that she'd had a new suitcase to pack them in. The bag she'd brought to England on her previous visit would have proved a right embarrassment.

This one was an elegant tapestry model in smoky blues and greys which she'd bought from one of the chain stores during the after-Christmas sales at the beginning of the year. It had a roomy matching shoulder bag which was at that moment hanging fairly heavily on one of her slender shoulders, filled to the brim with everything she'd thought she might need on the long flight over.

'You travel light, Miss Spencer.'

She almost laughed again. He wasn't carrying her leaden shoulder bag. She smiled instead. 'Do call me Marina. Please.'

Now *he* smiled, if you could call a slight upward movement at one corner of his nicely shaped lips a smile. 'Australians have a penchant for using first names quickly, don't they?'

'We don't stand on ceremony, I guess,' she agreed, and wondered if she had offended him in some way.

There was a dryness to his voice which could have been sarcasm. Or disapproval.

The demi-smile disappeared as quickly as it had come. He was as stiffly formal in life as he'd been in his letters, she decided. But where his written words had seemed rather sweet, his blue-blood bearing and autocratic manner were not so endearing. Frankly, they were intimidating. Marina determined not to succumb to the temptation to kowtow and grovel, reminding herself he was just a flesh and blood man underneath the cloak of superiority he wore so arrogantly, yet so very elegantly.

'So what should *I* call *you*?' she asked. 'What does an earl get called, anyway?'

There was a minute lifting of his eyebrows, as though her casual attitude was to be expected but only just tolerated. 'My Lord, usually,' came his cool reply. 'Or Lord Winterborne, in my case.'

His pompousness sparked a touch of rebellion. 'That sounds awfully stiff. How can you stand it? At home you'd simply be called James. Or Jim. Or even Jack. Still, when in Rome do as the Romans do, I guess. I wouldn't want to do anything which wasn't appropriate while I'm over here.'

He gave her another of those highly disturbing looks. 'No, of course not,' he drawled, and his eyes dropped to her left hand and her diamond engagement ring.

Marina could not believe the thought which flashed into her mind. Immediately prickles of heat whooshed into her cheeks. When his eyes lifted back to her face, she hoped and prayed he could not read the reason behind her most uncustomary blush.

'Then call me James, by all means,' he said with starch-filled gallantry. 'Come.' He lifted her suitcase from the floor beside him with his right hand while he put his left at her elbow. 'You must be tired. I will take you to my apartment in Mayfair where you can have some decent food and a rest. Then, this afternoon, I will take you to the hospital to meet Rebecca.'

Marina felt guilty that she'd forgotten her mission for a moment. 'How *is* Rebecca?' she asked anxiously. This is what you've come for, she lectured herself sternly. Not to have unconscionable thoughts about the Earl of Winterborne.

'She's very much looking forward to meeting you,' he replied. 'I must warn you, though, she's very thin and she's lost all of her hair through the chemotherapy. So try not to look shocked when you walk in. Rebecca might only be seven but she's very much a girl, and very sensitive to her appearance.'

Marina's heart turned over. 'Oh, the poor little love,' she murmured.

The Earl of Winterborne gave a very un-earl-like sigh. It carried a weariness born of worry and grief, plus a type of resignation which came from feeling totally helpless. Marina understood perfectly what he was going through, because that was how she had felt while her mother had been dying of cancer. It was the reason why Marina had put herself on the bone marrow register. Because she'd wanted to give someone

else hope where there had been none for her
mother—or herself.

'Yes. Yes, that sums Rebecca up entirely,' he
agreed. His face had grown as bleak as his voice, and
his hand dropped away from Marina's elbow. The
suitcase was lowered to the floor once more. 'She's
had little enough love in her life so far. And little
enough luck. But that's been the way with things at
Winterborne Hall for quite some time.'

Marina found herself reaching out to put a comforting hand on his nearest sleeve. His handsome head
dipped slowly to glance down, first at her hand on his
arm and then up into her sympathetic gaze.

'Let's hope my coming will turn the tables, then,
shall we?' she said softly, giving his arm a gentle
squeeze before letting it fall back to her side.

He stared at her in silence for ages. Or so it seemed.
It was probably only a few seconds.

A thousand emotions seemed to flitter across his
face, none staying long enough for her to gauge properly. But she was left with the impression of a deep
distress, one which was disturbing him greatly.

'I would like to think so,' he said staunchly at long
last. 'But I have a feeling that might not be the case.
They say things are sent to try us,' he added in a
strangely bitter tone. 'To test our characters. I can see
that the next few days are going to test mine to the
limit.'

Marina was not sure what he meant. Had the doctors already given up all real hope for the child? Was
her own trip over here a waste of time, as Shane had

suggested? She wondered what other misfortunes had befallen his family lately. Marina suspected he had more on his mind than the health of the child. The Earl of Winterborne clearly had many burdens on his shoulders.

But they were very broad shoulders, she noted when he bent to pick up her suitcase a third time and began to stride off with it. She wondered if they would look as good without the suit. If they were mostly padding or real.

Marina frowned as she trotted after him. This was the second time in as many minutes that her mind had swung unexpectedly to the physical where this man was concerned. It wasn't like her to have thoughts such as this. Well, not till recently, anyway, and certainly not about any man other than Shane.

Not that she'd had anything to do with any man other than Shane lately. She'd taken compassionate leave from her teaching position after her mother's death and had stayed at home ever since, helping Shane with the administrative side of running the riding school. For the last few weeks her life had revolved around her fiancé and the astonishing things he could make her feel.

Her frown deepened as she tried to make sense of her unbidden responses to the Earl of Winterborne. Was her recent sexual awakening able to be transferred to any attractive man who came along? Had she turned into an ogler of male flesh? A female fantasiser?

The prospect appalled her. She'd never liked the

way some women talked about men and sex all the time when they were together, as though there was nothing else in their lives. Or the way they stared openly at certain parts of the male anatomy.

Marina's eyes drifted down from those broad shoulders to where Lord Winterborne's suit jacket outlined what looked like a nicely shaped *derrière*.

You're doing it now, that annoyingly honest voice piped in her head—the one which Marina could never deny.

And enjoying it, another sarcastic voice inserted slyly.

The first voice came to the rescue with a vengeance. *And what's wrong with looking?* it challenged belligerently. *There's no harm in looking!*

She wants to do more than look. She'd like to touch, too. She'd like to see if an English earl makes love like an Aussie stablehand. She'd like to—

'Oh, do shut up!' she muttered aloud.

'Pardon?' The object of her mental warring glanced over his shoulder, slowing his stride at the same time.

Marina almost cannoned right into him. She stopped herself just in time, rocking backwards and forwards on her toes as she hitched the tapestry bag higher on her shoulder for added balance.

'Nothing,' she said with a blithe and decidedly false innocence. There was definitely nothing innocent going on in her mind at that moment. 'Just talking to myself.'

'You do that often?' His drily amused smile did

wickedly attractive things to his mouth. Marina decided she preferred him dead serious.

'All the time,' she admitted, wrenching her mind back from the path to hell with great difficulty. 'I was an only child, and only children often talk to themselves. I used to talk to a tea-towel as well.'

'A *tea-towel*?' He laughed, and Marina gritted her teeth. Laughing did to his whole face what that smile had done to his mouth: transformed it from merely handsome to lethally sexy.

'Why a tea-towel? Why not a doll? Or a teddy?'

Marina pulled a face. 'It's difficult to explain. The tea-towel wasn't another person, or a pretend friend. It was me. Or another side of me. My...secret side.'

'Sounds fascinating. Do you still talk to tea-towels?' he asked as he walked on, more slowly this time, so that she fell into step with him by his side.

'Not since I was eighteen.'

'What happened to you at eighteen?'

'I left home to go to teacher's college. I didn't think my new flatmates would indulge my peculiarities like my mother did. Since then, any conversations with my secret side take place in my head.'

He slanted a thoughtful glance across at her. 'And how often do these conversations take place?'

'Not that often nowadays.' But she had an awful feeling they were about to pick up frequency.

'Do you tell anyone about them?'

'Lord, no!'

'Not even your fiancé?'

Marina hesitated a fraction.

'That *is* an engagement ring on your finger, isn't it?'

'Yes.' Marina had pretty well decided on the flight over that she'd blown the incident before leaving home way out of proportion, that of course she loved Shane and wanted to marry him. But her responses to the man standing before her had shaken that conviction anew. How could she possibly be in love with Shane and feel attracted to the earl of Winterborne?

It's possible because this is not love, pointed out her pragmatic side. *It's just...attraction. He's a very attractive man.*

Marina found comfort in that thought. Yes, of course. Any woman would find this man attractive. He was the stuff female fantasies were made of. Handsome. Rich. Enigmatic. I'm not being disloyal to my feelings for Shane. I'm just being normal.

'No,' she answered levelly, after scooping in and letting out a steadying breath. 'I definitely don't tell Shane about them. He thinks I'm a very sensible, level-headed girl.'

That disturbing demi-smile surfaced again. 'And you're not?'

'I do try to be.' But I don't always succeed, she thought ruefully.

'When is your wedding?'

'In three weeks.'

'Three weeks!' He sounded shocked. And almost disbelieving. 'You've come all this way...and your wedding is only three weeks away?'

'I would have come,' she said truthfully, 'even if

the wedding had been tomorrow. My mother died of cancer. I could not have lived with myself if I had not come. And now that I have...I can't tell you how much I'm looking forward to doing this for your Rebecca. As soon as it can be arranged, actually. Tomorrow if you like. You did say the sooner the better in your letter, didn't you?'

He stopped and stared at her, then began shaking his head. 'You are one special lady, Miss Marina Spencer. One *very* special lady. Tomorrow would be marvellous. But I thought you'd be too tired.'

'What's tired in the scheme of things? I can rest afterwards.'

'And you will, too. As soon as you can leave the hospital, I'll take you down to Winterborne Hall, where you can relax for a few days before flying home. It's out in the country and quite beautiful at this time of year.'

'But...' A host of terrible thoughts rushed into her head which had nothing to do with relaxing. Marina tried to think of these new fantasies as just normal, but their explicit nature was very perturbing. 'No, I'm sorry. I really can't accept. For one thing I should be getting home to Shane. Besides, I... I wouldn't like to impose on Lady Winterborne like that.'

He simply *had* to have a wife, a man such as this. Please God, let him have a wife, Marina prayed. I would never think thoughts like this about a married man. I know I wouldn't.

'There *is* no Lady Winterborne,' he informed her coolly, and something inside her fluttered uncontrollably. 'But there are a dozen guest bedrooms just dying to be used. And plenty of staff to see to your every whim. What's a few days?' he added temptingly, his eyes searching hers. 'Your fiancé surely won't expect you to jump on a plane straight out of hospital?'

'I...I guess not. But I wouldn't like to put you to—'

'I insist,' he broke in brusquely. 'I will not take no for an answer.'

Marina swallowed. It was the wrong thing for him to say to her at that moment in time.

An image filled her mind, of her lying on a magnificent four-poster bed in one of those undoubtedly huge and plushly elegant guest bedrooms...

It was night, but there were candles casting an intimate glow through the room. Her red hair was spread out against a mountain of pillows, gleaming gold against pristine white. Her nightgown was virginal white as well, but made of satin and lace, and it hid little. She was reading when he came into the room, dressed in a rich purple robe. His penetrating blue eyes clashed with her own startled green ones. He walked arrogantly to the edge of the bed and shrugged out of the robe. He was naked. He climbed onto the bed and pulled the curtains so the world was shut out and darkness enveloped them. The book was taken from her suddenly trembling fingers. She felt a hand sliding around her neck, and her mouth being slowly lifted.

'I will not take no for an answer,' he whispered against her lips...

Marina's glazed eyes slowly cleared to find the

main star of her shockingly life-like fantasy staring at her with unconcealed concern.

'What is it? Are you not feeling well?'

Marina felt decidedly shaky, for such was the power of her imaginings.

'I…I *was* feeling a little faint there for a moment. But I'm all right now.' She scooped in a deep breath and did her best to still her wildly hammering heart.

'You had me worried. I thought I might have to carry *you* as well as the suitcase.'

For a split second Marina contemplated organising a faint.

'Do you think you can make it outside?' he asked, worry on his handsome face. 'It's not far.'

'Yes, of course,' she said briskly, disgusted with herself for this ongoing and quite uncharacteristic weakness. She had to get a hold of herself and her head once and for all. This would just not do!

'Lead on, My Lord,' she said firmly. 'I'll follow.'

He frowned. 'I thought you were going to call me James.'

'I know, but somehow it doesn't feel right.'

He looked slightly annoyed. 'Surely I'm not that intimidating?'

'Well, actually, yes, you are, Lord Winterborne.'

In more ways than one.

'But I would *prefer* you to call me James.'

'Sorry, Your Lordship. No can do.' This unfortunate attraction might be one-sided, but Marina still felt it only sensible to keep him at a distance. Calling him James was just too intimate for her peace of mind.

His glare fell just short of scowl. 'You really have a mind of your own, don't you?'

'Well, why not?' she said in a challenging tone. 'Don't English women?'

He laughed, but didn't answer her, she noted. After one last shake of his head, he stalked on ahead with her suitcase, leaving her to follow as she'd said she would.

CHAPTER THREE

IT WAS raining outside—a light drizzle more like a mist than real rain. And it was freezing, by Marina's standards. After all, it was supposedly summer over here, unlike the actually warmer winter she'd left behind in Sydney. Of course it was still very early in the morning. Just going on six. The plane had landed in the dark, not long after five.

Still...

Marina thought of the clothes she'd brought and wondered if they'd do.

'Don't worry,' Lord Winterborne said when she glanced up at the sky. 'We have good heating inside. August can be like this. Very unpredictable. It will probably be fine and warm tomorrow. Ahh, here's William with the car.'

A large and stately-looking dark green saloon pulled into the kerb with a properly uniformed chauffeur behind the wheel. He looked about fifty, with a full, florid face and a few too many pounds around his stomach.

'Don't get out, William,' his employer called out, on opening the back door. 'Just hand me the keys and I'll put the luggage in the boot. This is Marina, by the way, all the way from Sydney, Australia.'

'How do you do, miss?' the chauffeur said, lifting

his cap in greeting as she climbed in and settled in the most comfy brown leather seat.

They exchanged a smile in the rear-vision mirror. 'His Lordship was over the moon when he found out you were coming, miss. It's ever so good of you to do what you're doing.'

'That's nice of you to say so, but I'm only doing what anybody would do, under the circumstances.'

'I wouldn't say that. I wouldn't say that at all.'

'What wouldn't you say, William?' the man himself asked, on joining them and handing back the keys.

'That not everyone would do what this pretty lady is doing for Rebecca. Or come this far to do it.'

'You're quite right. I wholeheartedly agree with you. Straight to the apartment, William.'

'Very good, My Lord.'

His Lordship stayed well over on his side of the roomy back seat, Marina noted, which was a relief. There was something about being confined in a car with him which was even more disturbing than ogling him from behind, or conjuring up erotic little scenarios in her head. Their enclosed closeness meant she could not only see him. She could smell him.

No matter how often Shane showered he still smelt slightly of sweat and horses. This man smelt of something very expensive. An exotic, spicy scent which teased the nostrils and made you think of crisp clean air and pines covered in snow, of cool white sheets and freshly washed bodies and...

Oh, my God, I'm doing it again!

Marina wrenched her mind back from the abyss, turning her head away from the inspiration of her erotic thoughts and that damned cologne he was wearing. She stared out at the suburban London street and the rows of identical houses, and tried to pull herself together.

'You mentioned your mother died of cancer...'

Darn it, he was speaking to her. She would have to turn her head back and look at him.

She did so. Slowly. Nonchalantly. 'Yes, that's right,' she said, and their eyes met. He really did have riveting eyes, she thought. The blue was as intense as their expression.

'Was it leukaemia?' he asked.

'No. She died from skin cancer. A couple of months back. Melanoma. It took her fairly quickly after it was diagnosed. Though it's never quick enough, is it?' she added, her heart contracting at the thought of her mother's suffering.

'And your father? How is he coping?'

'My father died when I was just a baby. A horse he was breaking in threw him into a fence. Snapped his neck. That's why I have no brothers or sisters.'

'Your poor mother.'

'Oh, Mum coped. Mum always coped. She was very strong. Very brave.'

'Her daughter takes after her.'

Marina shook her head. 'I wish I did. But let's not talk about me. I want you to tell me about Rebecca and her background.'

'What would you like to know?'

'Oh…everything, I guess.' She was very curious about the child, plus how she came to have such a young great-uncle.

'It's only a half-hour drive to Mayfair at this time of day,' he said a touch ruefully. 'I doubt I can fit the Winterborne saga into such a short space of time. But I'll try. Though I'll keep it down to the relevant details and leave whatever family skeletons I can in the closet. I want you to think well of us.'

'I already think well of you,' she said, before she could bite the words back.

But it was true. Aside from the unfortunate physical attraction, she *did* think well of him. This was no selfish man sitting across from her. A selfish man would not have personally taken himself in to Heathrow airport at five in the morning. A selfish man would not have given a hoot if his chauffeur had arthritis. A selfish man would not love a little girl as he obviously loved his great-niece.

His smile was ironic. 'You don't really know me, Marina.'

She shrugged. 'A man is known by his actions.'

He nodded slowly up and down. 'I'll try to remember that. Now where was I? Oh, yes. Rebecca…'

Marina soon realised she could listen to the Earl of Winterborne talk all day. He had a wonderfully rich voice. And perfect vowels. She would never have imagined perfect vowels could fascinate her, but they did. The whole man fascinated her, if she was truthful. As did his story…

It turned out that James had not been born to be

the earl of Winterborne. That honour had gone to his brother, Laurence, who was an amazing twenty years his elder.

This Laurence had apparently been a bit of a wild one, given to gambling and living the high life. Unfortunately, his father, the Earl, had dropped dead of a coronary soon after his elder son turned twenty-one, so Laurence had inherited the title at a young age.

Admittedly, Laurence had startled everyone by marrying almost immediately, but any hope that marriage would settle him down and make him face the responsibilities associated with his title, plus running the family estate, had soon evaporated—mostly due to his choice of wife.

Joy was the youngest daughter in a family of four daughters, all of them renowned for their wildly ambitious and social-climbing natures. With the high-flying Joy by his side, Laurence's life had been even more flamboyant and extravagant than ever. They'd gambled together, travelled abroad, skied, shopped and partied. They'd hardly ever been at Winterborne Hall, which was a relief to Laurence's mother, who was still grieving for her husband while trying to bring up a young son at the age of forty-five.

The birth of a daughter, Estelle, two years after their wedding, had done nothing to change the jet-setting lifestyle of Lord and Lady Winterborne. They'd merely installed their new-born baby at Winterborne Hall with a nanny and taken off again.

Because of their closeness in age, Estelle had been more like a little sister to James than a niece, and although he and his mother had done their best to fill the gaps of love in the child's life Estelle had grown up feeling neglected and abandoned by her parents. She'd always imagined it would have been different if she'd been a boy, and heir to the title, but James doubted it. His brother didn't give a fig about what happened to the title after he was gone.

Estelle had eventually left home and begun taking drugs, then, after her parents cut off her allowance, had paid for her habit through selling herself on the streets.

By this time James had been at university, at Cambridge, and Estelle would occasionally contact him when she was desperate for money. He would try to talk some sense into her but to no avail. It had only been when she'd fallen pregnant a few years later— father unknown—that he was able to talk her into going home.

She had, and, with her grandmother's help, had stayed drug-free till she'd given birth to her daughter, Rebecca. Less than a month later, however, she had died of an overdose of heroin. She was twenty-five—two years younger than her uncle James.

Rebecca's grandparents, who'd still been leading self-indulgent lives, had been no more interested in their granddaughter's well-being than they had in their own daughter's. A nanny had been hired and that was that. Unfortunately, when Rebecca was only one year old, her great-grandmother had passed away, and, with James leading his own life in London by then, little Rebecca had seemed doomed to grow up even more lonely and neglected than her own mother.

Fate had stepped in, however, when her grandparents were killed on the ski-slopes of Switzerland during an avalanche two years back, making James the new Earl of Winterborne. He'd taken over the reins at Winterborne Hall, plus the guardianship of his then five-year-old great-niece, and had just brought some real love and happiness into the poor tot's life when she'd been diagnosed with leukaemia.

Her existence over the last couple of years had consisted of nothing but doing the rounds of specialists, stays in hospitals, chemotherapy and sheer misery.

'So you can see,' Rebecca's amazingly young great-uncle finished up, 'she's been having a real rough time of it.'

'It goes like that sometimes, doesn't it?' Marina commiserated. 'It doesn't rain but it pours.'

Just then the rainclouds parted and a ray of sunshine pierced the passenger window, landing in Marina's eyes. She blinked, then laughed softly. 'I hope that sun's a good omen. I think it might be, you know. I mean...what were the chances of finding a near-perfect match with Rebecca? One in a million?'

She turned her head towards her co-passenger, and caught him staring at her with those intense blue eyes of his. 'I would say that just about describes you,' he said in a serious tone.

Marina's heart flipped over at the compliment. Her laugh felt strained. 'What a flatterer you are, My Lord. You'll turn my head if you don't watch it.'

He said nothing, and she found his silence even more unnerving than his penetrating gaze. What was he thinking? Feeling? Was it merely curiosity about her which made him stare so? Surely the attraction couldn't be mutual, could it?

She swallowed, and struggled to think of something to say. *Anything.*

'Are…are we far from Mayfair?' she asked, even when she already knew the answer. They were skirting a large park, possibly Hyde Park, and the streets were heavy with traffic even at this early hour. Some time back the rows of suburban houses had given way to impressive old buildings, mostly made of a greyish stone. Not a glass and concrete skyscraper in sight anywhere.

'Not far,' he said. 'I take it you haven't been to London before?'

'Actually, I have. A couple of years back. Came on a shoestring and did what touristy things I could afford. Saw the changing of the Guard at Buckingham Palace, and Madame Tussaud's and the Tower of London, not to mention all the museums and galleries. The free ones, that is,' she laughed.

'Did you go to the theatre?'

'Heavens, no. Too expensive.'

'I'll take you, if you like.'

She shot him a sharp look, but there was nothing in his face which suggested anything but politeness.

'Oh, I…er…I don't think I'll really have the time, do you? Not if I'm to go down to Winterborne Hall as well.'

His eyebrows lifted in surprise. 'You mean you'll actually come?'

'I...well...you said you wouldn't take no for an answer.'

His laugh did not sound particularly happy for some reason. 'But I never for one moment thought you'd succumb to that kind of male pressure.'

What a provocative expression, she thought. Succumb to male pressure. It conjured up the image of an attempted seduction and an almost unwilling surrender.

Marina could not help staring into his face again, for some hint of his feelings towards her. But there was nothing to go on. He had a habit of holding his facial features in that stiffly autocratic fashion which bespoke things like ancestral pride and honour and arrogance, but nothing of any personal emotion. If he was attracted to her on any physical level, his body language did not show it.

While some deep feminine instinct rang a warning that perhaps it was not wise to go down to Winterborne Hall, suddenly wild horses would not have kept her away. She wanted to see his ancestral home, wanted to see him in it, wanted to sleep in one of those dozen bedrooms—if only to spend the night fantasising over the Lord and Master of Winterborne Hall.

'It's not a matter of succumbing to male pressure,' she said firmly, 'but deciding for myself that I would really like to see Rebecca's home. Still, I can only spare a couple of days. I really need to be getting back to *my* home as soon as possible.' Back to the real world, she told herself ruefully. And away from this fantasy one, complete with fantasy man.

'You must be missing your fiancé,' he said. 'What was his name again?'

'Shane.'

'What does he do for a living?'

'He helped my mother run her riding and dressage school. He's quite marvellous with horses.'

'I see. But what is he doing now that your mother has passed on?'

'Just the same. It would be a shame to let all my mother's work go to rack and ruin. She built up a good business with plenty of clients. And her horses are simply the best.'

'But that's not what *you* do, is it?'

Marina was startled by his intuitive comment. 'Why do you say that?'

'Your hands, for one thing. It's also obvious you don't spend much time in the sun.'

She stared down at her soft, pale hands, which were resting lightly in her lap. She was unnerved by the sharpness of his observations. What else had he noted about her? Could he look into her mind as well, see all those appalling thoughts she'd been having about him?

Her fingers linked together and pressed down hard. 'You're quite right,' she said a little stiffly. 'I'm a teacher.'

'A teacher,' he repeated, and smiled a strange little smile. 'Yes, I can see you in front of a class. But not boys,' he added wryly. 'You would distract boys far too much. You teach at a girls' school, I gather?'

Marina was rather rattled by his comments. For, while the use of the word 'distracting' suggested he found her looks attractive, this fact seemed to slightly annoy him. Was this because she was an engaged woman? Would he perhaps have adopted a different attitude to her if she'd been free to accept...to accept...what?

A romantic tryst while she was down at Winterborne Hall?

Marina found such a thought breathlessly exciting. It was with difficulty that she reminded herself she had developed an overheated imagination since stepping off that plane. For all she knew, the Earl of Winterborne was just making idle and polite conversation to pass the time while in her company. His tendency to an occasional sardonic remark could be caused by boredom. It was a sobering thought.

'Actually, you're wrong this time,' she told him crisply. 'I do teach boys. Boys *and* girls. I'm a primary school teacher. I have a class full of nine- and ten-year-olds. Or I did. I've taken compassionate leave till next term.'

His smile was accompanied by a drily amused gleam in his eyes. 'Ahh. But boys of that age are not boys at all, just wild little savages. I was thinking of the slightly older species, which begins to appreciate the difference between boys and girls. And how old are you, exactly, Marina?'

'Twenty-five.'

He said 'ahh' again, as though highly satisfied with her age.

The green saloon turned down a narrow street at that point, angling between cars parked down one side, then turning into an even more narrow and slightly cobbled lane. The brick buildings on either side were three storeys high, with doors which opened straight onto the street. So did the windows. Only the window boxes spilling with brightly coloured flowers gave some relief to the austerity of the architecture.

'These are mews,' His Lordship volunteered, on seeing her glance around.

'Oh, yes, I've read about them. They used to be the royal stables, didn't they?'

'Not all of them royal, but certainly once belonging to London's wealthy. They've all been converted to apartments nowadays.'

'They must still be expensive, being so close to the city.'

'I dare say. This one's been passed down through the family. I inherited it when my father died. It might normally have gone to the eldest son but I think Father wanted to keep some of the estate out of Laurence's spendthrift hands. As it was, my brother did his best to bankrupt the estate.

'But I shouldn't be telling you any of this,' he muttered, seemingly irritated with himself for doing so if his expression was anything to go by.

He frowned and leant forward to tap his chauffeur on the shoulder. 'William, just let us out here at the door.'

The car stopped next to a large brown wooden door with a brass knocker and doorknob. Geraniums and petunias blazed from hanging baskets at eye-level on either side.

'And give me the key for a moment. I'll get Miss Spencer's luggage. No, don't argue with me. I know how painful your knee is. If I'd had my way you'd have stayed home in bed and I'd have driven myself this morning. Now, after you've parked the car, come inside for some breakfast. We don't have to leave for the bank for another hour at least.'

The chauffeur sighed heavily. 'You spoil me, My Lord. Your brother would not have—'

'My brother is no longer in charge, William. I am.'

Which, clearly, he was.

Magnificently and mercifully.

Marina saw then that it was not just the Earl's handsome face which had captivated her. Or his tall, well-proportioned body. It was the man himself. His whole person. His character. But especially his compassion.

'Wait there till I help you out,' he ordered her peremptorily, before climbing out himself.

But she didn't wait there. That wasn't her way. She was out of the car and standing beside the passenger door by the time he brought her suitcase around.

His smile carried wry reproach. 'I thought you said that when in Rome you were going to do as the Romans do?' he chided.

She shrugged, smiling. 'My mind is willing, but my flesh is weak.'

He stared at her for a second, then shook his head again. He seemed to be always shaking his head at her. 'I doubt anything about you is weak, Marina,' he complimented her, though in a cool voice. 'Like most Australians, you flout the old-fashioned ways and traditions for the sometimes foolish habits they are. But you haven't encountered our Henry as yet. Believe me when I warn you things in this apartment are done Henry's way, or not at all!'

CHAPTER FOUR

'WHO'S Henry?' Marina asked after the car had moved off.

'He's my valet. He used to be the butler at Winterborne Hall.'

'Oh? What happened? Didn't he work out?'

'He worked out very well for over thirty years. But my brother forcibly retired him when he turned seventy—packed him off to live out his days at the damned gatehouse like a broken-down racehorse banished to a far paddock.'

It was clear by his irritable tone that he had been furious at his brother for this action.

'Henry was still fit for service,' Lord Winterborne swept on. 'All he had wrong with him was the odd touch of gout. The poor old chap would have died through sheer neglect and boredom, so I brought him up here to London—told him I needed some company, plus someone of his experience to put some well-needed order into my wretched existence.'

'And was your existence really wretched?' Marina asked, thinking to herself how typical it was of this man to do such a thing, to care about a poor old retired servant.

'Lord, no. I was in my twenties and living the life of Riley! It was Henry's existence which was wretched. I quickly came to regret my foolishly generous gesture. Henry took me at my word and, indeed, put order into my life.' He rolled his eyes at the memory.

'How did he do that?' Marina was intrigued.

'You have no idea.'

'No, I don't. Tell me. I'm dying to know.'

His glance was drily amused. 'You have a compulsively curious nature, I think. But you're also very easy to tell things to, do you know that?'

'Yes, I've been told that before. Children come up to me in droves when I'm on playground duty to tell me their problems. And I'm always getting beseiged by little old ladies in buses and trains, and even supermarket queues. Maybe they're just lonely and need someone to talk to, but why it's always me they choose to pour out their hearts to, I have no idea.'

'It's your eyes,' His Lordship said as he looked right into them. 'You have understanding eyes.'

She flushed slightly under his compliment and his direct gaze. 'So...er...what did Henry do?'

'What *didn't* he do?' His Lordship grumbled as he reached out and rang the doorbell. 'Firstly, he converted my reading room into a gym, into which I was dragged every morning for a work-out. As a man whose only exercise before that had been turning on my computer and moving chess pieces, believe me when I tell you I was in agony for weeks. I nicknamed one particularly diabolical piece of equipment "the rack".'

'Well, it seems to have done you good,' she said. 'You look very fit.'

'I've suffered for this body, I can tell you.'

Marina thought the suffering well worth it. 'So what else did he do?'

'Changed my daily diet to a boring menu of low-cholesterol, low-salt meals. I hardly enjoy eating any more, except when I crack and go to a café and order the fattiest, most cholesterol-ridden pie I can find!'

Marina laughed while His Lordship scowled.

'But his crowning achievement was to bully me into giving up smoking. God knows how he managed that!'

'He sounds quite wonderful,' Marina said.

His Lordship finally smiled a wry smile. 'Oh, he is. But he took some getting used to on a daily basis. Now I wouldn't be without him. For one thing he plays a damned good game of chess. Of course, he *is* getting a little slow on the stairs,' he added, frowning at the still closed door. 'He turned seventy-seven last birthday.'

The door opened at that precise moment and Henry stood there, impeccably dressed in a butler's morning uniform of grey striped trousers, black jacket, white shirt and pale grey tie. He was even wearing white gloves. Marina noticed that his black shoes were polished as only a butler or a sergeant-major would polish them.

He had clearly once been a handsome man. And tall. But his back was not as straight as she imagined it had once been, and his steel-grey hair was thin and receding well back from his high forehead. He still looked a darn sight younger than seventy-seven.

Controlled grey eyes swept over her with a bland but all-encompassing glance which revealed nothing of his impression or his opinion. His coolly unreadable gaze returned to his employer.

'The plane was on time, My Lord?' he asked, somewhat starchily.

'Slightly early, Henry. And this is Miss Marina Spencer.'

Henry inclined towards her with a stiff nod, which could have been rheumatism or just his way. 'How do you do, Miss Spencer?'

'She will insist on being called Marina, Henry,' His Lordship said drily as he ushered her inside, depositing her suitcase by the door. 'So we might as well get that out of the way up front.'

'I see. Very well. How do you do, Miss Marina? Welcome to London. I have your coffee perking, My Lord, but have prepared a proper English breakfast for the young lady. You are not one of those impossibly modern young people are you, Miss Marina, who only drinks coffee for breakfast?' This with a sidewards glance of ill-concealed exasperation at his employer.

Marina only just managed not to laugh helplessly. He was so pompous and prim, he was adorable. 'Heavens, no, Henry,' she replied, the corners of her mouth twitching. 'Where I come from, some of us can eat a horse for breakfast.'

'I am most relieved,' he sniffed, and, picking up

the heavy suitcase with incredible ease, turned to lead the way.

It was a most gracious way too, Marina noted, following across a spacious black and white tiled foyer where, many metres above, hung a huge chandelier. Ahead curved an elegant staircase, covered in the middle by a wide strip of deep forest-green carpet whose pile was so plush it would be like walking on velvet in your bare feet. Sheer luxury!

Not that she'd expected anything less from a Mayfair apartment owned by an earl. Her eyes darted around as she mounted the steps.

The walls were wood-panelled up to a point, above which lay very English-looking green and gold striped wallpaper. The crystal and brass light fittings were splendid, as were the undoubtedly antique furniture pieces resting in various nooks and crannies.

'I have put Miss Marina in the Rose Room, My Lord,' Henry said on their way upstairs.

'Very good, Henry. Oh, and Henry, William will be along for a bite to eat shortly. Since I know he'll refuse to eat with Marina and myself, give him something in the kitchen. And make sure he's taken his medication. His arthritis is very bad this morning, poor devil.'

'I will see to it, My Lord. Breakfast will be served in fifteen minutes in the morning room. I thought Miss Marina might wish to freshen up first after her long flight.'

'Indeed I would, Henry,' she agreed, smiling when she realised she was talking like these two now.

'What's so amusing?' His Lordship muttered by her side as they trailed after Henry.

'Me,' she said. 'I think I'm beginning to do what the Romans do.'

'Not you, Miss Marina,' he teased drily.

'Oh, yes, me. Next thing you know I'll be taking tea in the afternoon and eating cucumber sandwiches.'

'And what do you usually have in the afternoon?'

'Just coffee.'

'I'm a coffee man myself. Especially in the mornings. I drink at least three cups.'

'So I gathered. What happened to the low-salt, low-cholesterol meals?'

'I can only tolerate so much of that. And definitely not first thing in the morning.

'I'll leave Marina to you now, Henry,' he said more loudly, once they reached the landing on the first floor. 'I'll see you in the morning room in fifteen minutes, Marina. Henry can tell you where it is. And don't be late or he'll be after you with a long stick.'

He turned and strode on, up a second but smaller flight of stairs which Marina deduced led to his private domain on the next floor.

'Very funny, My Lord,' the valet called after him in a droll tone.

'Don't take any notice of him, Miss Marina,' Henry continued as he led her down a wide hallway lined with massive gilt-framed paintings which looked as if they belonged in the National Art Gallery. 'His Lordship likes to rag me. It's a hang-over from his adolescent days when I was butler at Winterborne Hall and Master James alleviated his boredom by playing practical jokes on the staff—mostly on me.'

Marina found such a scenario impossible to imagine. Lord Winterborne surely had never been a boy, let alone a practical joker!

Henry stopped at a cream-painted door on their right. He opened it wide, then stepped back to wait for Marina to go in first.

She couldn't help it. Her breath caught as she walked through the doorway.

'Oh, Henry!' she exclaimed. 'This is the most beautiful bedroom I have ever seen. Why, it's fit for a queen!'

Her eyes were wide as they took in the delightfully feminine decor with its rose theme. Roses were everywhere, all of them in shades of pink. Tiny, pretty roses. They covered the wallpaper and matching curtains and bedlinen. They might have been overpowering if the room had been small, but it was immense.

Besides the sleeping arrangements, there was a cosy and intimate sitting area in front of a cream marble fireplace, with cream and gold silk-covered armchairs facing it. Fresh roses in pinks and yellows filled an elegant vase on the undoubtedly antique lacquered coffee table. The carpet was a deep cream, and the bed, though not a four-poster, was queen-sized with brass bed-ends.

The dressing table and matching stool in the corner nearest the bed were the epitome of feminine frippery, with their rose-covered throw-overs and exquisite gilt-framed mirrors. Fresh roses again filled an exquisite crystal vase sitting on the right side, while on the left lay a silver and crystal vanity set. In the middle sat three crystal perfume holders.

Marina's bedroom in her mother's house back home was very pretty, and mainly pink as well, but nothing compared to this.

Henry carried her suitcase over and placed it carefully on the cream-painted ottoman at the foot of the large bed. 'I don't think this room has ever had a real queen stay in it overnight,' he replied seriously, to her remark. 'But I do recall a countess or two. And Lady Tiffany always sleeps here when she stays overnight in London.'

'Lady Tiffany?' Marina asked innocently enough as she walked over to look through the window down at a small courtyard below.

'I'm sure you'll meet Lady Tiffany during your stay, Miss Marina. She comes up to visit Rebecca often. She's the youngest and only remaining child of the Duke and Duchess of Ravensbrook. His Lordship's next-door neighbours. Her poor brother, who would have been the next duke, was tragically killed in the Gulf War. He was His Lordship's best friend. His Lordship is very fond of the Duke and Duchess. *And* of Lady Tiffany. She's a dear, sweet girl.'

It finally got through to Marina that she was being told something very deliberately by Henry. When she looked around at him he was standing ramrod-straight at the foot of the bed and his gaze was steely.

'His Lordship and Lady Tiffany are planning to announce their engagement at Lady Tiffany's twenty-first birthday next month,' he stated, then just waited, as though expecting her to say something.

She found she could not for a few seconds.

Her dismay was out of all proportion to the situation and her feelings—which, after all, were just silly, secret feelings. They weren't really real. How could a girl like herself entertain real feelings about a man like Lord Winterborne? To do so was to waste both her emotions and her time. He was always going to be matched with someone like this Lady Tiffany.

Marina dredged up a smile even while her heart was not having a bar of her common sense reasonings.

'That's wonderful,' she lied. 'James is a fine man. And I'm sure Lady Tiffany is as sweet as you say. I must give her my congratulations if and when we meet. Actually, I'm going to be married myself next month, Henry.'

She could not help but see the relief in the valet's face. It both irritated and puzzled her. What had he been thinking? And why? He'd only known her for a few minutes and had only seen her with His Lordship for the same. What had passed between them which would make this old man think she was a threat to his employer's marriage or happiness? Had he overheard their light exchange on the staircase and interpreted it as a sign of growing intimacy?

Even if that were the case, did this starchy old gentleman's gentleman think she was a bold, amoral hussy, who would try to steal another woman's intended?

Whatever, she felt offended at Henry's judgement

of the situation. She might have entertained the odd
fantasy or two about her host in her head, but she
would never try to put any of them into action.

Pull the other leg, Marina, that awful voice piped
up in her head. *His Lordship could get you into bed
in no time if he put his mind to it.*

Enough! Marina's conscience intervened. *I am not
that type of girl!*

*Maybe, but is he that kind of man? Most men are,
you know.*

'That's good news, Miss Marina,' Henry was saying while this argument raged in her head. 'Very good
news indeed. I hope you'll be very happy. Now, I'll
leave you to freshen up. The morning room is on the
ground floor. Just take the hallway under the staircase
and it's the first door on the left.'

He bowed stiffly, then withdrew with a slightly
self-satisfied smile hovering around his mouth.

Marina glared after him till he shut the door. Then
she did the strangest thing. She slumped down on the
side of the rose-covered bed and burst into tears.

CHAPTER FIVE

'You do look tired,' His Lordship said as he started his third cup of coffee. 'And you've hardly eaten a bite.'

Marina gave him a wan smile across the six-seater circular table which was set as elegantly for breakfast as for a formal dinner party. The white tablecloth was starched linen, the cutlery silver, and the crockery fine white gold-rimmed china.

The whole room was not quite as formal as the rest of the house, however, and looked out onto the court-yard Marina had spotted from upstairs. Painted in creams and yellows, and with the sun shining through the tall windows, it would have been a bright and welcoming room if Marina had been in a bright and welcoming mood.

'You're not hungry?' His Lordship asked.

Marina stared blankly down at the breakfast she herself had selected from the superb sideboard buffet, which offered a huge range of hot food not to mention a choice of cereals plus freshly squeezed orange juice.

She'd sat down with a glass of the orange juice and a plate on which she'd unthinkingly deposited two poached eggs, two strips of bacon, a sausage, one slice of grilled tomato and several mushrooms. So far she'd only managed the orange juice and half a slice of bacon. The four slices of toast which Henry had placed on the table in a silver toast rack remained untouched, and she hadn't got round to the brewed pot of tea Henry had set before her.

Her appetite had totally deserted her, her earlier bout of irrational weeping leaving her feeling oddly fragile.

'I do think I need a sleep,' she admitted. Sleep would mean she could not think. She didn't want to think any more, about Shane or about this man opposite her. She certainly didn't want to think about the youthfully sweet and undoubtedly beautiful Lady Tiffany Ravensbrook.

'Are you sure you're up to being admitted to the hospital this afternoon?' His Lordship asked.

'Yes, of course I am,' Marina practically snapped. 'So, please, don't even *think* of putting it off. I don't want any delay in doing this. If I'm still asleep when you get back from the bank after lunch, just wake me up.'

He'd told her when she'd first sat down about his position as vice-president at one of London's largest merchant banks and how he had to go there after breakfast for a few hours. He also had a lunchtime appointment. 'Or, better still, have Henry wake me beforehand so I'll be ready when you come home.'

Marina could see by his frown that he was puzzled by her shortness. She sighed, and tried to remember that none of this was his fault. He'd not let her think by word or deed that he felt anything for her but an understandable admiration and gratitude for what she was doing for his great-niece. She was making a right fool of herself.

As for Henry...he was just a suspicious and dirty-minded old man!

'I'm sorry, James,' she said, then blinked her astonishment at herself. 'Oh—oh, I mean...Your Lordship.'

His grin was lopsided and heartstoppingly charming. 'So you've cracked at last,' he said, blue eyes glittering with amusement. 'I wondered how long it would take. From now on it will be James and nothing but James. And I will *not* take no for an answer.'

She couldn't help it. She smiled back at him, and melted all over. 'Very well...James.'

Henry *would* walk in at that moment, with her smiling with fatuous helplessness at His Lordship. And, *worse*, James was smiling back at her and looking at her for all the world as though he found her the most desirable, delightful and interesting woman. He then topped off the awkward and easily misunderstood situation by looking up at Henry and saying, 'Marina's finally consented to calling me James, Henry. For a minute there I thought I was going to have to put up with His Lordship for the next ten days or so.'

'Ten days or so, My Lord?' Henry echoed stiffly, a frown gathering. 'I booked Miss Marina's return flight for next weekend. I was assured by the hospital she would be ready to travel by then.'

'Yes, yes, no doubt she will be,' James said as he scraped back his chair and stood up. 'But I'm going to take her down to Winterborne Hall for a few days before she goes back to Australia. Don't worry, I'll have my secretary change the booking.'

Henry frowned some more. 'Have you forgotten, My Lord?'

'Forgotten what?'

'Lady Tiffany will be away in Italy around that time?'

James tossed his linen napkin down on the table. 'No, Henry,' he returned, with a sharp edge in his voice. 'I haven't forgotten. I am not taking Marina down to Winterborne Hall to visit with neighbours. I am taking her there to show her the countryside and Rebecca's home.'

Marina's swift intake of breath heralded her realisation that the Earl of Winterborne had no intention of telling her he was on the verge of becoming engaged, or of letting her path cross with his intended. Her shock was only superseded by exciting flashes of wicked speculation. Was this deliberate on his part? Did Henry know his employer better than she did? Did the Earl of Winterborne have a secret passion for redheads?

Maybe his marriage was to be one of convenience on his part? Marina speculated some more. A merging of money, breeding and titles. Maybe he meant to have women on the side, ones he momentarily fancied, ones he would keep secret from his naive young bride. It wouldn't be the first time such things had happened in those circles. And what better choice of a passing bed-partner than a woman who would return to a far-off land at the end of the affair—a woman committed to someone else...?

Marina stared up at James and wondered if his acutely observant mind had picked up on her unexpected but quite intense desire for him. Was he already planning her seduction? Plotting to have her while his fiancée was overseas?

It was obvious Henry feared as much. And he would know the nature of the beast better than herself.

Marina's emotions swung from a breathtakingly intoxicating excitement over such a prospect to an acute disappointment in the man she'd thought perfect. Perhaps she should not have put him on such a pedestal. After all, he was a human being, not a saint. A man, not a machine.

'But surely Lady Tiffany would like to meet Miss Marina,' Henry persisted.

With this reminder of James's intended, Marina decided with more reluctance than she would have liked to admit that she could not possibly be a party to any potentially sordid sexual games, if that was what His Lordship had in mind.

'Yes, and I'd like to meet *her*,' she tripped out brightly. 'Henry tells me you and this Lady Tiffany are getting engaged shortly, James.'

There was no doubting that His Lordship glared at his valet at this piece of news. But only for a second. Just as swiftly he laughed, but when he looked back at Marina, his expression was wry.

'You *did* say people liked to tell you things, didn't you? Believe me when I say it's not like Henry to gossip so. What will you tell her next, I wonder?' This with another caustic glance the valet's way.

'Possibly that you're the best Earl of Winterborne in a hundred years,' Henry volunteered, with a po-faced expression. 'That you're a good man, with a great sense of responsibility, loyalty and tradition. And that you love your niece's child, Rebecca, as if she were your own daughter and would do anything to make her future a lot happier than her past.'

'My, my, Henry. Do you think any mortal man could live up to such a glowing testimonial?'

'I think you'll try, My Lord.'

James nodded slowly up and down, a rueful smile pulling at his mouth. 'You are a sneaky old man, Henry. What alternative do I have in front of our guest but to agree with you?'

'I know that, My Lord.'

'You know too much, Henry.'

'I have lived a long time, My Lord. Your brother would have said too long.'

'My brother may have been right,' James muttered, before throwing Marina a parting smile. 'See how he browbeats me into behaving myself? Have a good sleep, Marina. I'll be back with the car to pick you up at two-thirty. Henry, make sure Marina eats some lunch before that. We don't want her relying solely on hospital food, do we?'

'Certainly not, My Lord.'

And then he was gone.

Marina stared at the empty doorway and wished her

heart was not beating so, despite feeling intolerably heavy.

'You haven't eaten much of your breakfast, Miss Marina,' Henry said as he gathered James's coffee cup and pot onto a tray.

'I...no, Henry. I'm sorry,' she said dully. 'I seem to have lost my appetite for some reason.'

'Perhaps you are nervous about what lies ahead of you in hospital, miss,' he said, with a gentleness in his voice she hadn't heard before.

'Perhaps, Henry.'

'Maybe you'll feel more like eating after a nap.'

'Maybe.' Her chin began to quiver and tears filled her eyes anew. Panic that she was about to disgrace herself had her rising abruptly from her chair and, in doing so, bumping the valet's arm. The silver tray he was holding slipped from his grasp and crashed to the polished floor, smashing the coffee cup and spilling the remains of the coffee from the pot.

'Oh, dear heaven!' she exclaimed, her face stricken. 'I'm so sorry, Henry. I'm such an idiot!' She squatted down immediately to help clear up the mess, but the incident seemed to have opened the floodgates of her very mixed-up feelings and tears started to stream down her face.

'Oh, God,' she choked out, when Henry's expression showed he was aghast at this display of emotion. 'I...I'm just tired,' she tried to explain through sobs. 'I'll be all right...in a...in a little while.'

Henry took the broken crockery from her shaking hands and placed it back on the floor, then he helped

her back upright. The arms he curved around her
heaving shoulders were incredibly gentle. 'You just
need a good sleep, Miss Marina. Come. Let me help
you upstairs.'

'Th-thank you. You're...you're very sweet,' she
said as he did so.

'It's no trouble. And you're the one who's sweet,
Miss Marina. I can see why His Lordship is so taken
with you.'

She blinked up at him through blurred eyes, halting
to dash away the remains of her tears and withdraw
from the valet's steadying arms. They were halfway
up the staircase and Marina leant against the mahogany balustrade, gripping it tightly with one hand.

'Why do you say that, Henry?' she demanded to
know, if a little shakily. 'There's nothing between His
Lordship and myself. Goodness, we only met this
morning. He's getting engaged next month, and, as I
said, I'm going to be married myself around the same
time. If you think for one moment I would entertain
the thought of some kind of illicit liaison with His
Lordship while I'm over here, then you're very much
mistaken!'

Henry seemed unfazed by her indignant outburst.

'That's as may be, Miss Marina, but I know what
I know and I see what I see. His Lordship *is* taken
with you. Make no mistake about *that*. Experience has
shown me that there are not many ladies who remain
indifferent to him once he turns on the Winterborne
charm.'

Marina didn't know what to say. She wasn't sure

if she was flattered by Henry's conviction or afraid of it. As for herself...it was pointless to deny the obvious: she was more than charmed by the Earl of Winterborne. It seemed crazy that such a thing could happen in such a short space of time. But it had. Her feelings for Shane seemed positively lukewarm in comparison to the feelings James could engender in her with just a look.

But that still didn't mean she was prepared to hop into bed with him.

'I have met plenty of Australians in my time,' Henry went on. 'I know they don't like people to...er...beat around the bush? So I hope you won't take offence over what I am about to say.'

Marina had a feeling she would. Henry might have met a good few Australians in his time, but he didn't seem to have much regard for the moral fibre of their women!

'His Lordship is going through a difficult time at the moment. He is under stress with what is happening to Rebecca. As I said earlier, he adores that little girl. On top of that, his relationship with Lady Tiffany is not the sort of relationship he is used to with his lady-friends. As such, he may be extra vulnerable at the moment to an undoubtedly real but ultimately passing attraction. Do you know what I am saying?'

Marina wasn't sure she did—till she recalled Henry telling her earlier that Lady Tiffany always slept in the rose room when she stayed overnight. Since this modern young woman was on the verge of engagement to James, wouldn't it be more natural if she spent the night in *his* bed?

The realisation that James was not sleeping with his soon-to-be fiancée should not have thrilled Marina.

But it did.

'I see you *do* understand what I'm saying,' the valet stated stiffly, his eyes not perfectly at peace with the pleased expression on her face. 'Maybe I have said too much,' he muttered.

Marina swiftly wiped the hint of satisfaction from her lips. 'No, no, Henry, you did the right thing,' she hastily assured the well-meaning valet. 'And I will give you the benefit of an equally straight-talking reply to your concerns. I promise you I have no intention of doing anything to compromise His Lordship or his coming marriage while I am over here. I *like* James very much. Okay. I *more* than like him. I think he's bloody fantastic. How's that for a good old Aussie expression? But I'm no fool. Neither am I a woman of easy virtue.'

'Miss Marina! I never meant to imply that—'

She waved him to silence. 'No, I realise that. But you do seem to think I have no will of my own in this matter. You seem to think James would only have to proposition me and I would forget my own fiancé back home and jump into bed with him. Not so, I assure you,' she insisted, and hoped valiantly that it was so.

'I also think you have overestimated James's feelings for *me*. Why should he be so taken with me? I'm not all that good-looking, for one thing. There must be plenty of ladies in James's social circle much more beautiful and glamorous. And *willing*, Henry,' she added pointedly. 'Do you honestly think a man as attractive as James could not indulge himself sexually any time he liked, if that was what he wanted?'

'I never said that was what he *wanted*,' Henry argued back.

'Then what *are* you saying?'

'Just that sometimes people get caught up in a combination of situations which work against their natural decency. I have *not* overestimated His Lordship's feelings for you, I assure you. I do think, however, that you *under*estimate your own attractions, Miss Marina. Aside from your delightfully feminine shape, you have a luminescent kind of beauty which shines from your face and your eyes. As for your hair...it has a touch-me colour and quality which any man would find hard to ignore.'

Marina coloured as her hand fluttered up to touch her hair. 'You exaggerate. Surely?'

'Not at all. About anything. I *know*, Miss Marina, what my Jamie-boy likes.'

She stared at the valet, aware he had deliberately used this old nickname to show her how well he *did* know his one-time boyish charge.

'You're frightening me, Henry.'

'I hope so, miss. For I would not like to see you go home with a broken heart. At the moment it is only beating as any woman's heart might beat faster when a man such as His Lordship flatters her with his attention. Take care not to let it beat faster for any other reason. Go down to Winterborne Hall with His Lordship by all means. But be on your guard against the temptation to forget where you are and who you are not.'

Marina drew herself up straight, her pride and self-esteem sending a gleam of righteous anger into her green eyes. 'I am as good as the next person, Henry.'

'I agree with you, Miss Marina. But you are not the lady whom His Lordship is going to marry. Even if you were madly in love with him—which seems unlikely at this stage—would it be in his best interests to ever acquaint him with that fact? Would you not show your love better by leaving him in peace to make a marriage he is not only committed to but which he will go through with regardless of his own feelings?'

'Are you saying he doesn't love this Lady Tiffany?'

'I am saying no such thing. Of course he loves her—just as he loved her brother. He also gave his word to that brother, Miss Marina. He promised his best friend as he went off to war that if anything happened to him he would look after his little sister. This marriage is a sacred duty, in His Lordship's eyes, and one which he was quite happy to carry out...till this morning...'

Marina felt very disturbed by what Henry was implying. 'But I haven't done anything!'

'Only been your lovely natural self, Miss Marina. I am not imparting any blame. I agree, things haven't progressed too far as yet, but I see the warning signs. Don't forget I have been His Lordship's valet for the past seven years, and I know his ways well. I can practically read his mind in matters of the opposite sex.

'He is not used to leading a celibate life, and his hormones may get the better of his conscience—especially if a lady whom he finds attractive is to be constantly alone in his company and will keep looking at him as though she thinks he's...what was the term? Bloody fantastic?'

Marina's sigh was as heavy as her heart. 'I get the picture, Henry.'

'Then you will stay out of the picture?'

Her chin lifted. 'I will do what is right.'

Whatever that was. She had no idea at that moment. She didn't think like these people. She didn't live her life by rules of stiff tradition and sacred duty. She went with her heart. And her heart at that moment told her she just might *be* madly in love with the Earl of Winterborne.

Stranger things had happened. If love at first sight did not exist then why had it been written about for centuries? Whatever her feelings for James turned out to be, she certainly knew that she could not marry Shane now. What she felt for him definitely wasn't love. He'd filled a need in her life when she'd been wretched and lonely, then confused her with his expert lovemaking.

Marina resolved to do the right thing and break her engagement when she returned home. She would soften the blow for Shane by giving him both the horses and the business name of the riding school he'd helped build up with her mother. Somehow she didn't think he'd be too upset with the arrangement.

As for doing the right thing at this end of things... That was up to James, wasn't it?

CHAPTER SIX

'YOU'RE looking much better,' James said as he handed her into the back seat of the green Bentley for the ride to the hospital, supposedly only a ten-minute trip—fifteen if the traffic was bad.

Marina had earlier secured Henry's approval for her choice of a plain black suit for the occasion, as well as the way she'd done her hair, its bright mass of red-gold curls held back at the nape of her neck with a plain black clip.

The valet hadn't actually said anything, but she was beginning to read his facial expressions, as subtle as they were. Approval rated the barest nod of his head on first sighting, plus the minutest gleam in his steely grey eyes.

Henry would not have approved if he'd been able to read her mind. Or her heart. She'd been breathless with anticipation for James's return from the moment she'd woken, hardly able to wait to see him again, to *be* with him again. Lunch had been stuffed down, not because she'd felt hungry but because James had ordered her to eat. Marina suspected she would do anything Lord Winterborne ordered her to do.

'You obviously had a good sleep,' he added when he climbed in beside her.

She tried not to stare, but she'd forgotten, even in

that short space of time, just how handsome he was.
Mindful of Henry's warnings, and her own infernal
conscience, she hoped nothing of her innermost feelings showed in her face, or her eyes.

But how wonderful it would be—just once—to feel
free to lean over and press her mouth to his, to look
deep into his eyes and tell him how her heart raced
whenever he was near, how heaven, for her, would be
to spend just one night with him.

Her mind drifted to such a scenario, but this time,
strangely, her fantasy was no longer of an explicitly
erotic nature. She saw them as just lying together,
naked, yes, but simply looking at each other and
touching each other tenderly, long, stroking caresses,
without tension, without the distraction of the flesh
aching for release.

And then she realised she was thinking about how
it would be with him...afterwards. Shane always
rolled over and went straight to sleep. Marina knew,
instinctively, that James would not do this. Not with
her...

'That's a most attractive perfume you're wearing,'
he muttered, the softly spoken compliment snapping
her back to the present. 'I don't recognise it.'

She simply could not look at him. Not at that moment. If she did, she would surely undress him with
her eyes and blush awfully. 'It's called True Love,'
she said, and turned her head to stare through the passenger window.

'Ahh. A gift from your fiancé?'

Her head whipped back to deny she had a fiancé

any more, not in her heart, and very soon not in reality. But she could not bring herself to say the words.
Marina found this distressing, because deception was
not in her nature. She wondered if she was deceiving
James for his sake, or hers. Henry's warning about
going home with a broken heart had been a fair one.
Men like James didn't break their engagements for
girls like her. They took them as mistresses, not
wives.

For all Marina's saying she was as good as the next
person, in the circles James moved in relationships
had different rules. Hadn't her own upper-crust
mother had to run away to Australia to be with the
man she'd chosen to marry, just because he was of
common descent?

'No, it belonged to my mother,' she said curtly, her
lips pressing together in annoyance at her thoughts.

He stared at her primly held mouth for a long moment, then turned his own head away. It was a slow
and rather arrogant gesture, his nose and chin lifting.
'I must buy Tiffany a bottle,' he said, the words a
dagger to her heart.

Idiot, came that sneering voice she hated so
much—mostly because it did not let her pretend.

He couldn't have spelled it out more clearly, came
a second, equally frank opinion.

Well, at least you know the score now, was the
third, and least scathing comment.

Marina tried to blank her mind, but it was impossible. The voices railed on, calling her all sorts of
insulting names and adjectives. Although emotionally

harrowing, Marina's mental warrings usually left her strengthened in will-power. Such was the case this time.

'I think, perhaps,' she said straight away, before she could change her silly mind, 'it would be better if I took that return flight Henry booked for me next weekend.'

That handsome head jerked round and their eyes clashed. His were furious, hers widening with shock at his instant and very fierce anger. 'What, in God's name, has Henry been saying to you?' he bit out.

Her guilty blush betrayed both herself and Henry. But the obscenity James muttered under his breath was even more betraying. For it outlined that James was, under his lordly manner, just a man, a mortal man with feelings and failings like any other.

'Interfering old fool,' he muttered. 'He thinks he knows it all when in fact he knows nothing. *Nothing!* What has he told you? Tell me! I must know.'

She didn't know what to say, for she was walking a minefield here. As she'd told Henry, there had been nothing between herself and James. At least, nothing spoken, and from what he'd just said about Lady Tiffany, and buying her a bottle of True Love, the valet might very well have jumped to all the wrong conclusions.

'He...Henry that is,' she began carefully, 'only has your best interests at heart...'

James snorted. 'He's living in the Dark Ages. That man has no concept of what life is like these days.'

Marina was startled when James suddenly slid

across the seat towards her and took her hands in his. She shrank back from him into the corner, her eyes rounding on his intense and far too close face. Her heart was immediately pounding. Her lips parted slightly as hot, panting breaths puffed from her lungs.

She was embarrassingly aware of William behind the wheel, just a couple of metres away, blithely ignoring what was going on. Was that because this type of thing happened all the time when His Lordship had an attractive woman in the back seat with him? Henry had implied James had once been a ladies' man. Maybe he'd never given up the tag. Maybe he'd merely moved his romantic rendezvous from his apartment to his car!

'My God, what *has* he said to you?' he rasped, on seeing her reaction. 'No, you don't have to tell me. I can guess. I never could hide anything from Henry.'

'H-hide?' She had begun to tremble at his nearness. His scent enveloped her, as did his powerful male aura. A yearning shuddered through her and she found herself leaning towards him. Closer. Closer.

His fingers tightened around hers. He stared down at them, then began to lift them towards his mouth.

'No!' she choked out.

He closed his eyes for a few seconds. On opening them, he sighed and placed her hands back in her lap.

'I do apologise, Marina. I got carried away for a moment. I didn't mean to, I assure you. But you are an incredibly beautiful woman. And so darned desirable! I told myself all morning that I would not, *could* not, entertain such thoughts about you. You're going to be married, as I am.'

'But I'm not,' she whispered, then gasped in self-horror.

His eyes lifted. Pained, beautiful blue eyes.

'You're not…what?'

'Not…not going to be married,' she confessed shakily. Having said this much, she felt compelled to elaborate. 'I was already having doubts before I came. The trip away has cleared my mind, and now…now I know I can't go through with it.'

He just stared at her, his horror almost as great as her own at this conversation. 'Not because of *me*, I hope,' he groaned, with a wealth of distress in his voice.

She said nothing, but his telling words sent tears pricking at her eyes. Henry had been so right. She would be going home with a broken heart. All she could ever mean to James was a passing fancy.

His fingertips on her chin turning her slowly back to face him sent a shiver of agonised desire all through her. It did things to her conscience which would afterwards shock her.

Yes, touch me, she willed wildly as their eyes met. Kiss me. Make me yours, at least this way. I don't care if you don't love me, I tell you. I don't care…

'Dear God,' he whispered, his face shaken as he stared into hers. His hand dropped away and he withdrew from her across the seat, his fingers raking his hair as he did so.

He fell broodingly silent, leaving Marina to her

guilt and her remorse. She wished now she'd never said a thing. It had been wrong of her. And wicked. She'd been warned, but she hadn't heeded that warning. She'd blindly gone ahead and as good as told James she was his for the taking. Henry had practically begged her not to put temptation in his path and what had she done? Told him she'd broken her engagement then looked into his eyes like a love-sick cow.

She felt sick with shame.

She had to *do* something—undo the damage which had been done.

'You're mistaken,' she said quietly into the thickening silence, hoping William was concentrating on the traffic. He seemed to be, as it was horrendous. 'My decision has nothing to do with you, other than that you showed me the kind of man I would like to marry. As I said, I was already having serious doubts about Shane before I left Sydney.

'I will not deny I am attracted to you. You're a very handsome and charming man, James, as I'm sure you are well aware. Henry sensed this...attraction...between us, and it worried him. But an attraction can stay just that, can't it?' she told him, with far more conviction than she was feeling. 'We don't have to act on it. We can just be friends, can't we?'

His eyes were sardonic as they turned to her. 'Not if you look at me as you did a moment ago.'

She swallowed, then steeled herself. 'Granted. But you were touching me at the time. If you give me your word as a gentleman that you will keep your hands off, I will give you my word as a good Aussie girl not to do anything equally provocative.'

His laugh was rueful. 'I've met some not so good Aussie girls in my day.'

'And I've met some not so gentlemanly gentlemen,' she countered. 'But they are other people and this is us. I would like to think we have a sense of honour. I know I have.'

He sighed. 'How unfortunate.'

'You don't mean that, James.'

'No,' he said wearily. 'I don't suppose I do.'

'And I think we will just forget my going down to Winterborne Hall. That would not be a wise move.'

'True.'

'Now I would like to put my mind and energy back on the reason I came over here in the first place,' she said as a large hospital came into view on their right. 'We seem to have arrived and I happen to be feeling quite nervous.'

He glanced over at her and his expression carried sincere regret. 'What a selfish bastard I am,' he murmured. 'Yes, of course you must be nervous—as must Rebecca. Yet here I am, consumed with my own pathetic needs. I am so sorry, Marina. For everything. Forgive me.'

'There is nothing to forgive. Things happen sometimes which have no rhyme or reason.'

'Do they? I'm not so sure. I have come to hold the view that things are written, that fate has plans for all of us.'

She wondered if he was talking about his brother's death, as well as his best friend's. Did he believe he'd been fated to become the Earl of Winterborne so that he would be in a better position to take care of his best friend's family? It was a romantic idea, but Marina held no such views on death. When you'd seen someone die of cancer it was hard to believe in anything like that.

James shrugged off a frown and leant forward, tapping William on the shoulder. Thankfully, the chauffeur had had the radio playing and did not appear to have been listening to them.

His head twisted round a little. 'Yes, My Lord?'

'Let us off at the front entrance, William, then go and find a park. I will be taking Marina in to meet Rebecca and staying a while to visit. Wait for me in the foyer and I'll find you when I come down.'

'Very well, My Lord.' If he'd heard anything of what had gone on, he gave no indication of it.

Marina popped out of the back seat, unaided, while James collected the overnight bag Henry had lent her from the boot. It was a snazzy little red leather number, and easily accommodated her nightwear, toiletries, plus some casual clothes.

When James joined her on the top steps of the hospital entrance and put his hand lightly on her elbow, she automatically shot him a warning glance. He rolled his eyes but took his hand off.

'This is ridiculous,' he muttered from beside her on their way through the huge glass doors.

'Maybe,' she returned crisply. 'But it's the way it's going to be.'

'You're a hard woman.'

'Not at all. I have a feeling you're spoilt where the opposite sex is concerned. Not enough women have said no to you in the past! But you're not that irresistible, Your Lordship.'

'Oh, my God, we're not back to that, are we?'

'We certainly are!'

He muttered an expression under his breath which she doubted would have found favour with Henry.

Marina almost smiled. There was something rather satisfying in taking the reins where this situation was concerned. She wasn't a teacher for nothing. Bossiness came naturally to her where little boys were concerned, and underneath she had a feeling there was still a little boy in the Earl of Winterborne.

Unfortunately, there was also a big boy. A very good-looking, utterly appealing and incredibly sexy big boy!

But she wasn't going to think about that, was she? And she wasn't going to listen to that awful voice in her head any more, the wickedly dark one which kept telling her she could have this man if she wanted to. That she could go down to Winterborne Hall and spend every night in his bedroom, then wing her way back to Sydney with no one the wiser—least of all Lady Tiffany Ravensbrook, whom Henry had kindly informed her would be in Italy!

CHAPTER SEVEN

THE first thing Marina saw when James directed her towards Rebecca's bed in the children's ward was not the small child propped up against a mountain of pillows, but the young woman sitting on the side of the bed with a book in her hands.

She was the most beautiful girl Marina had ever seen. Not just attractive. Not just pretty. Beautiful. Breathtakingly beautiful.

Straight, shoulder-length blonde hair. Skin like porcelain. A perfect profile. Full soft lips. A slender, fragile-looking body.

Marina knew at once who she was.

The girl looked up at their approach, and her eyes matched the rest of her. Large hazel eyes, thickly lashed and immediately smiling at James—as was her lovely coral-glossed mouth.

But it was the child in the bed who spoke first, the bald-headed, deathly pale, unbelievably thin child, whose big green eyes looked too large for her face.

'Uncle James!' Rebecca exclaimed, excitement bringing some colour to her hollow cheeks. 'Look, it's Uncle James, Tiffany. And he's brought my Marina with him!'

Marina was startled but touched by this term of endearment. And yet it was true, wasn't it? She *was*

Rebecca's Marina. They were going to become
bonded as few people could be. Her own flesh and
blood was going to save this brave little girl's life.
She just knew it would!

Marina came forward and held out her hands to the
child, who took them straight away, without hesitation. Out of the corner of her eye, Marina was aware
of the exquisitely lovely Lady Tiffany standing and
giving James a peck on the cheek. They also began
whispering to each other. She steadfastly ignored the
jab of jealousy and gave all her attention to Rebecca,
sitting down and giving her a big hug.

'Oh, Uncle James!' Rebecca cried afterwards.
'She's so pretty. And she has hair the same colour as
mine! When I have hair, that is,' she added, a little
self-consciously.

'You'll have hair again, my pet,' Marina said
softly, and took the child's hands again. 'In no time
at all, you're going to be feeling *so* well.'

'Yes, I know. Uncle James rang me this morning
and he said we're going to do it tomorrow. I can't
wait!'

'Neither can I.'

'The doctors said it won't hurt. Of course I'll be
fully asleep, but you have a choice. You can have a
general anaethestic, if you like, or just a local. I think
you should have a general,' she advised in all seri-
ousness. 'Then you won't have to worry whether it
hurts or not. You see, doctors *always* say things won't
hurt, but mostly they do a bit.'

Marina's heart twisted at this seven-year-old trying

to reassure *her*, the adult. She was like a little adult herself. But that was what pain and sickness did to one. It made you old before your time.

She'd seen it before in other children, when she'd gone to the hospital to visit her mother and stopped in sometimes at the children's cancer ward. Her heart had just wept for the poor, brave little darlings who'd seen more misery in their short lives than most people had in a lifetime.

'I think I'll be a coward and have a general,' she confided quietly. 'I'm not brave like you.'

Rebecca giggled. 'Did you hear that, Uncle James? Marina thinks *I'm* brave. Oh, that's so funny. I'm not at all brave. I cry all the time when they put those horrid needles in me. I *hate* needles,' she whispered to her new friend and confidante.

'Well, heavens to Betsy, of course you do!' Marina said indignantly. 'What self-respecting girl would *like* needles. Yuk! I shudder just to think of them.'

Rebecca crowed with laughter. 'Oh, but you *are* funny. And you talk funny, too,' she said, obviously referring to Marina's accent—though it wasn't as broad as most, due to her elocution lessons. Marina had always thought she sounded rather British. Clearly she didn't.

'But I like it,' Rebecca announced. 'And I like you too. She's smashing, isn't she, Uncle James?'

The arrival of a nurse wanting to do a routine check of Rebecca's vital signs gave James the perfect excuse not to answer. Unfortunately it also meant Marina had to finally face the girl he was to marry.

Gathering herself, she stood and turned, flinching at the sight of James's arm around Lady Tiffany's slender waist.

On second sight the girl was even more lovely. She was wearing cream cotton trousers with a cream and fawn striped vest-style top; the simple outfit screamed the sort of style money could not necessarily buy. The girl had class and elegance which had been bred into her. It was inherent, as was the way she held herself, so upright, and with a proud little tilt of her perfect little nose.

She was, for want of a better word, a lady.

'I'm so glad I had the opportunity to meet you,' the lady herself said, after James had introduced them. 'I think it's marvellous what you're doing. Rebecca is such a darling. I only wish I could be here for her tomorrow, but I have to fly to Italy this afternoon. In fact, I must be going shortly, James.

'Now don't go saying you'll come with me to the airport. That's silly. You stay here and visit with Rebecca. I've ordered a taxi. I only dropped in for a while on my way. I have to go to Rome to be in the wedding party of one of my cousins,' she explained to Marina with the sweetest of smiles.

Marina's own smile felt plastic. Why couldn't she have been a bitch? An upper-class snob with a snooty attitude instead of this softly spoken and obviously very *nice* girl.

'I don't really want to go, but I'm obliged. Worse, I'm having to go several days before the actual wedding to have my bridesmaid dress properly fitted. It's not even a nice dress,' she added laughingly. 'And it's purple! Can you imagine me in purple?'

'You'd look lovely in anything, Tiffany,' James complimented her.

Tiffany gave him such an adoring look Marina wanted to cry. This girl not only loved him, she was *besotted* by him. A quick glance at James's face showed more than mere affection for the girl in return. His gaze was meltingly indulgent and definitely loving.

They looked splendid standing there as a couple, she as fair and delicate as he was dark and strong. Marina could see why Henry was so protective of the relationship. Lady Tiffany would make a perfect Countess, the perfect partner for the best Earl of Winterborne in a hundred years.

'I agree,' Marina said quickly, to cover her dismay. 'With your hair and complexion, any colour would suit you. I would be a disaster in purple. Scarlet doesn't do much for me, either.'

Lady Tiffany laughed softly, and Marina tried not to pull a face. But there was just so much perfection she could take. Why couldn't the infernal girl have had yellow incisors, or molars full of metal, or an overbite? Why did her laugh have to show two flawless rows of immaculate pearly whites?

Marina herself had had to suffer years of braces to correct her own dental shortcomings.

Physical perfection in James she could admire and lust after. But not in this exquisite creature who was going to become his wife, but whom Prince Charming had not yet acquainted with his undoubtedly virile flesh.

Why *was* that? Marina puzzled all of a sudden, and with a vehemence alien to her normally pragmatic personality.

Surely she couldn't still be a *virgin*? Not in this day and age, not at nearly twenty-one and certainly not looking like *that*!

But the more Marina stared into those big hazel eyes the more she became convinced that Lady Tiffany was totally untouched by male hands.

Totally!

There was an unknowing innocence in her face, and in those eyes. The glances she sent James contained nothing of naked desire and everything of a blind and almost adolescent hero-worship. That peck she'd given him on the cheek bespoke the affection more of a sister than a lover.

What in God's name was James waiting for? For them to be officially engaged? Surely he didn't expect to hold out till his wedding night! That was archaic, and totally unnatural when two healthy young people were in love. He should be making love to her all the time. Good grief, if *she* were engaged to him then she would not—

Marina caught herself up short.

But you're not engaged to him, Marina, that awful voice piped up. *Whether Tiffany is a virgin or not is none of your business. The same applies to the current status of His Lordship's sex life. Or are you thinking of taking up the slack, so to speak? Of giving the poor dear chap some well-needed comfort while the ice-princess swans off to Italy, naively leaving her intended behind in the clutches of the evil Aussie seductress?*

'Look, Uncle James!' Rebecca said delightedly. 'Marina's daydreaming, just like me!'

Marina pulled herself quickly together and walked over to the bed again. 'Nothing wrong with daydreaming. I have a lot of fun in my daydreams.'

'So do I,' Rebecca replied happily. 'When I daydream, I'm all grown up and beautiful, with hair just like yours. I'm never ever sick. And I'm married to a wonderful man like my uncle James and I have lots and lots of children. I don't like being an only child,' she finished, her lips pouting.

Marina's heart turned over at the child's dream, which rather echoed her own. What she would not give to be in Lady Tiffany's shoes! 'Being an only child has *some* good points,' Marina said kindly, sitting down on the edge of the bed. 'For one thing it develops your imagination and your self-sufficiency.'

'What's self-suff...suffish...' Rebecca pursed her lips in frustration. 'What you said!'

Marina smiled. 'It means being able to do things all by yourself. It means being strong.'

'Uncle James says I'm strong.'

'He also says you talk too much,' James intervened. 'Now say goodbye to Tiffany. She has to go now.'

'Oh, does she have to?' the child wailed, for once sounding like a seven-year-old. 'She hasn't finished reading me the story about the princess.'

'I'll finish reading your story,' Marina offered. 'I'm not going anywhere. I'm sleeping here tonight.'

'Oh, goodie! You can go now, Tiffany.'

Lady Tiffany laughed good-naturedly. 'Such is the loyalty of the Winterbornes. But I'll bring you back a present from Italy anyway.'

'And will this Winterborne get a present too, when you come back?' James asked, giving his intended a darkly brooding look. Or so it seemed to Marina.

But the girl just laughed, seemingly unaware of the sudden sexual tension emanating from the man whose arm was around her.

'What could I possibly buy *you*, James?' she said. 'You have everything you could possibly want in that apartment of yours.'

'Not everything one wants can be bought, Tiffany,' he said.

She gave him a totally blank look.

'You'd better get going,' James said, though it sounded as though the words came through gritted teeth.

'Yes, I'd better. I'll be back next Monday. The morning flight.'

'I'll be there,' he said, with a hint of a sigh which perhaps only Marina heard.

Tiffany certainly seemed oblivious of her intended's strained state.

'You spoil me,' she said, and pecked him on the cheek again before turning to Marina. 'Goodbye,' she said with sweet politeness. 'I dare say I won't be seeing you again, which is a shame. I would have loved to find out all about you, and life back in Australia. It seems such an exciting country, and so different from England. I'd love to go there one day.'

'Then I'm sure you will,' Marina said, wishing with all her heart that she didn't like this girl so much. Then she wouldn't have to feel so guilty about the dark desires which still lurked in that treacherous mind of hers, ready and waiting to find a chink in her own armour. It was particularly perturbing that she could not wait for Tiffany to leave and fly away.

'Goodbye for now, poppet,' Tiffany directed at Rebecca. 'And good luck for tomorrow.'

'Bye, Tiffany,' Rebecca chirped back.

'Goodbye,' Marina said, guilt sending her forward to give the girl a kiss on the cheek. But when she glanced over her shoulder at James he stared at her, and his eyes carried a black frustration.

'When are you going to finish reading my story, Marina?' Rebecca asked as soon as Tiffany was gone.

'Right now, if you like.' And she picked up the book and sat down.

'Don't wear Marina out too much, sweetie,' James warned. 'Or yourself, for that matter. The doctors want you both bright-eyed and bushy-tailed tomorrow.'

Tomorrow, Marina thought with the beginnings of a nervous lump in her stomach. She wasn't really worried about anything hurting. But she did hope it would all go well. The last thing she wanted was to go home with a broken heart *and* a failed mission.

CHAPTER EIGHT

THE bone marrow transplant went well. More than well. It went perfectly.

Marina was discharged the morning after the procedure, with the doctors glowing in their optimism for Rebecca.

Although it was too early for their little patient to show signs of rejection, the specialists were unanimous in their opinion that she had the very best chance of a complete remission, since Marina was the best donor match that could be found outside of a brother or a sister.

Marina had learned on the evening she'd been admitted to the hospital just how lucky they had been to find a match for Rebecca outside of a relative, since her blood type was not a common one.

Marina had been surprised to learn that even if Rebecca had had a brother or a sister their bone marrow would not necessarily have been compatible. There was only a one in four chance of a perfect match between siblings. Even a twin was no good, because a twin, in fact, was actually *too* perfect a match. Only by having a register with millions of names on it could it be hoped to find a match outside of the family circle.

Having had all this explained, Marina had been

asked permission for the media to be brought in and a story told about their amazing match. That way, many thousands of others might be inspired to do what Marina had done.

She'd asked James about it, and while he hadn't been thrilled with the idea, and had vetoed any cameras being shoved in Rebecca's face, Marina *had* been interviewed and a story run on the news the following day and evening.

But when several news crews were waiting outside James's apartment when he brought Marina home from the hospital on the Wednesday morning, Marina saw the Earl of Winterborne in action, with all his arrogant, autocratic anger.

Henry would have blushed at his language, but Marina found herself on *his* side, totally. She had no time for the media when they started invading people's privacy, when they crossed lines which had been clearly set out for them. Marina had given permission for *one* interview and one interview only. If they were going to start hounding her she would have to jump on an even earlier plane than Sunday's.

Which was exactly what she told James after he'd routed the rabble and bundled her into the safety of his apartment.

'You will do no such thing!' he snapped.

Anger became him, she decided, looking at his flashing blue eyes and furiously stubborn jawline. The suit he was wearing became him too. It was pale grey and a silk blend, teamed with a crisp white business shirt and a blue-striped tie the same colours as his eyes, which were light blue in the centre rimmed by a darker navy.

Or so she'd found out after staring into them at length.

Every time they met anew now, they stared at each other, as though the time apart had been agony. Despite the distraction of her hospital stay and the media problem, Marina found her feelings for James were escalating rather than abating. And becoming intensely physical once more. Any admiration or respect for James as a person was being buried underneath an avalanche of desire for him as a man. She didn't know how much she could stand before the compulsion to touch him would overwhelm her.

He seemed under similar stress. During his several visits to the hospital he'd made a point of not getting too close to her, especially when she'd been in her nightwear. There had been no touching of any kind, no goodbye pecks, just an unsettling series of smouldering stares. Unfortunately, during the incident with the media outside, he'd had to take hold of her waist to shepherd her through the small crowd of aggressive journalists and photographers. His arms around her had rattled both her composure and his.

'You will stay the full week,' he ordered angrily. 'And you will let me take you to the theatre!'

'I will not,' she refused, sounding coolly firm even while her heart was racing.

They were standing in the foyer, facing each other at the base of the stairs.

'If you do not let me take you to the theatre,' he ground out, 'I will kiss you here and now.'

She just stared at him, afraid that he might, terrified that he wouldn't. For the threat, once voiced, conjured up the threatened kiss in her head. It would be hard and hungry. Not the sort of kiss she would normally like. But she would like such a kiss from him. She would like it much too much.

'Did you hear me, Marina?'

She clenched her jaw hard and prayed for salvation. 'I did, My Lord.'

He grabbed her shoulders and yanked her hard against him, scowling down into her instantly wide-eyed face.

'James,' he bit out. 'You will call me James or, by God, I will do more than kiss you.'

'James,' she whispered in a raw, shaking voice.

His face twisted as he fought the urge to do it anyway, to ravage her mouth *and* her body.

She saw the battle in his eyes and should have helped him out. But how could she when his body was pressed close to hers? When his mouth was a mere breath away from closing over hers and sending her to the hell she was beginning to ache for?

The sound of footsteps on the staircase sent them springing apart, James looking for all the world like a naughty schoolboy caught with his trousers down.

Which they might have been shortly, that ugly voice sneered.

Marina only just managed not to laugh hysterically. This was starting to feel like an Edwardian farce. But was *she* the heroine or the bitch? And was James the hero or the dastardly villain?

'Disgraceful,' Henry was muttering as he plodded down the last few stairs. 'Simply disgraceful!'

For a moment Marina thought he was talking about them.

'I tried to get rid of them earlier, My Lord,' he said apologetically to James, 'but they simply took no notice of me.' He turned to give Marina a small smile of greeting. 'And how are you feeling, Miss Marina? His Lordship told me everything went splendidly at the hospital.'

'The doctors are very optimistic, Henry. And I feel quite well, except for a tiny throbbing in my right hip. Nothing that some aspirin and a cup of your lovely brewed tea won't cure.'

'I will leave you in Henry's capable hands, then, Marina,' James said abruptly. 'William is waiting outside to take me on to the bank. I will get my secretary to make a booking for us on Friday evening for a show. Your hip should be better by then. Would you like to see a play or a musical?'

To argue at this point would be to tell Henry too much. 'A play would be lovely,' she said levelly.

He nodded and was gone in a flash, leaving Marina to stare longingly after him for a moment. She turned to find Henry watching her with those all-seeing grey eyes of his. Suddenly she saw red.

'Don't start, Henry,' she said rather sharply. 'And do stop worrying. I'll be gone soon. Then Your precious Lordship will be out of danger.'

She went to brush past the valet, but he stayed her with a soft but firm hand on her shoulder. Her eyes blurred slightly as she looked up at him.

'It's not just His Lordship I worry about,' he said gently. 'I would hate to see a lady as fine and lovely as yourself hurt in any way. His Lordship is a good man, but, as he said himself the other day, he is only mortal. And any mortal man could not help but find you desirable, Miss Marina.'

Marina might have coped with Henry's reproach. Or even some more of his dire warnings. But not his sympathy and kindness. 'Oh,' she cried softly, her hands fluttering up in a futile effort to stop the tears from flowing. 'Oh, Henry!' And she threw her weeping self against his broad but stiffly held chest.

For a second he froze, but then his arms went round her. Surprisingly strong yet gentle arms. 'There, there, Miss Marina,' he soothed. 'It's not as bad as that. Surely?'

'Yes, it is,' she sobbed. 'I love him, Henry. I love him so much.'

He froze. 'Don't say that, Miss Marina. Don't even *think* it.'

'I can't help thinking it. It's all I think about.'

'And you're all *he* thinks about lately, I'll warrant,' Henry said drily. 'But it's not love which spurs *his* mind, child. It's those blasted Winterborne hormones.'

'But I have hormones *too*,' Marina moaned.

'Miss Marina!'

Henry immediately put her aside, as though he was

in imminent danger of contamination after this appalling confession.

Marina blinked her astonishment—till she realised that men like Henry were not of the modern world. They were an anachronism. They actually believed sex was a male prerogative. A male flaw, perhaps, to be tolerated and hopefully controlled.

'I'm sorry to shock you, Henry,' Marina said, 'but it's not just James who thinks about sex. You might be surprised to learn that there are a lot of ladies these days who think about sex! So please, for pity's sake, don't worry so much about James taking me to the theatre. Or taking me anywhere in public. It's infinitely safer than our being in this apartment together, even if we do sleep on different floors and have you here as watchdog.'

Henry's spine straightened and his chest puffed up with indignation. 'I am no spy!' he protested.

'No, not a spy. More of an interfering guardian angel. Don't take offence, Henry. I do appreciate your good intentions. And I fully understand the predicament I find myself in.

'If it helps to put your mind at rest, I met Lady Tiffany at the hospital on Monday and I think she is one of the loveliest and nicest girls I have ever met. I would never deliberately do anything to hurt her, even if I don't think she's the right girl for James. She is far too young, far too naive, and far too sweet. James will walk all over her, which means he'll be bored to tears in no time flat.'

Henry was frowning, as though some of what she

was saying made sense, even if such thoughts had never occurred to him before. 'You don't think they'll be happy together?' he asked worriedly.

'No, I don't. They seem the perfect romantic pair on the surface, and they do look good together. But will it work in the bedroom, Henry? I ask you that. A man like James will not be satisfied with any girl who might be daunted—or totally dominated—by his Winterborne hormones.

'In the past, wives of this ilk might have tolerated their husbands dallying elsewhere, but not nowadays. Under the circumstances, I suggest you worry over the next woman to spark your esteemed boss's carnal desires, and not me. *I* won't be any danger to his marriage from Australia, will I? Even if I *have* decided not to go through with my own marriage, which would be a similar disaster!'

Wrenching off her engagement ring and clenching it in a tight fist, Marina marched off up the stairs, leaving a frowning Henry behind. She kept her chin up, but her heart had sunk to an all-time low. For, despite her bold and impassioned speech, she knew Henry was right about the most important factor. James didn't love her. He just wanted her.

Come next week, he probably wouldn't give her another thought ever again. He would go on to marry Lady Tiffany, and if they weren't happy then it would have nothing to do with a certain spinsterish teacher living out her days in Sydney.

CHAPTER NINE

JAMES finally settled in the roomy back seat of the white stretch limousine. William and the Bentley had been given the night off, it seemed, to be replaced by this huge luxury vehicle with its plush red upholstery, black windows and equally opaque privacy screen, which was at that moment sliding into place.

When they were completely alone—unable to be heard or seen by the driver—James turned to look at her across the seductively lit cabin.

'You look…stunning,' he said.

Marina's hair was up and she was wearing black again, the only outrageously expensive little black dress in her wardrobe, which had been a must to bring. Mostly because it did not crush. When she'd packed it, never in her wildest dreams had Marina thought she would wear it for a man.

But she was very definitely wearing it for James. It was cruel of her, she knew. For it could be a very provocative dress when worn with the minimum of underwear. And she was wearing it with *no* underwear other than a pair of sheer black Lycra pantyhose which had built-in panties.

The material was a silk crêpe and the style very simple. A basic sheath, it was severely cut in at the shoulder, with the front of the bodice gathered onto a round collar which was covered with black jet beads. The collar did up at the back of her neck with a hook and eye. There was no zipper, just a slit down the middle of the back from neck to waist. Mostly this slit stayed demurely shut, but just occasionally it gaped apart as she walked—or climbed into cars— with the expanse of bare back displayed shouting the absence of any bra or other undergarment.

Not that any man with twenty-twenty vision needed to look at her *back* to know she was braless. Marina was by no means a busty girl, but she had nice B-cup breasts, which were high and firm, with perky nipples which announced their naked state under the thin black material with all the subtlety of Henry's dire warnings.

'Thank you,' Marina said coolly. She leant back in the relative safety of her distant corner to survey James at her leisure. He was wearing a superb black dinner suit with a white dress shirt and a black bow tie. He looked magnificent. Dignified and handsome. A true lord in every way.

But, lord or no lord, he could not take his eyes off her. And Marina revelled in that fact.

I'm punishing him, she realised. For not loving me but for still wanting to take me to bed. I'm trying to make him suffer.

And he *is* suffering. I only have to look into his eyes to see it, to watch the way his fingers curl into tight balls when he's with me. And to see the dark rings under his eyes at breakfast every morning.

'Henry tells me you rang home today,' he began, after the limousine had moved off.

'Yes, that's right.'

She declined to say any more.

Shane had not even asked her how the transplant had gone, or how Rebecca was. All he'd wanted to know was when she'd be home and was she sure none of this was costing them any money. He'd never sounded more selfish or less loving. She'd also heard a girl laughing in the background who sounded awfully like Heather, the twenty-year-old who helped with the horses every weekend.

What had Heather been doing in the house, and on a weekday? she'd wondered for some minutes after hanging up.

The answers were not nice ones.

'Did you tell him you weren't going to marry him?' James asked curtly.

'No.'

'Why not? I notice you've taken off his ring.'

'I might change my mind back again,' she lied, and he shot her a look which made her want to laugh. He didn't want to marry her, but he didn't want her to marry anyone else. It would almost be funny if it wasn't so infuriating.

'My views on love and marriage have changed somewhat since being over here,' she continued icily, giving in to the compulsion to punish him further. 'I see no reason why us commoners can't operate on the same level as the upper classes. Marry with our heads and not our hearts. Shane will do very well by the horse business I inherited from my mother. And there is the added bonus of his being a more than adequate lover. You have no idea how talented a rider he is, in every way.'

'Don't,' James rasped. 'For pity's sake, Marina.'

Her shame was instant, but pride demanded she didn't back down. 'Don't what?'

'Don't torture me so,' he groaned.

'And what have you done to me these past two days?' she challenged. 'Avoided me like poison, even when I ran into you at the hospital when I went to visit Rebecca with Henry. You didn't even come home for dinner last night. Then you make an appearance tonight to take me out, looking like Prince Charming on his white charger, trying to seduce me with extravagant compliments.'

'They aren't compliments,' he said with a weary sigh. 'They're true. You *are* stunning. And I only stayed away because I could not bear seeing you all the time—just as I could not bear *not* to do this tonight.'

'What? Try to seduce me?'

He glared at her. 'That's the pot calling the kettle black, isn't it? I could accuse *you* of trying to seduce *me*, dressed as you are. Still, I'll recognise your right to dress as you please if you will recognise my right to react to the end result as any red-blooded male would.'

She laughed. 'What a pathetic excuse! Why don't you just say it, James? Spell it out. Tell me what you had in mind for tonight *before* you saw how I was dressed.'

His eyes narrowed upon her. 'I had nothing in mind,' he said tautly. 'I had become quite resigned this past week to being the complete gentleman till the bitter end.'

She laughed. 'Sure. That's why you ordered this little number.' And she waved her hand around the inside of the limousine. 'Blind Freddie could see that this is just a boudoir on wheels! What's the catch, James? Have you got a standing order for one of these whenever you take a girl to the theatre, or wherever else you take them? The ones you want to impress, that is.'

'I did not order this car,' he bit out frustratedly. 'Henry did.'

'Oh, sure.'

'It was either this or a taxi. William put the Bentley in for servicing and it wasn't going to be ready in time. You're quite wrong about my intentions, Marina. Now stop it, will you? I can't bear any more tonight.'

For a moment Marina felt guilty. It had been a hell of a week for him. She knew how worried he'd been about Rebecca. It was to be thanked that the early signs were so good. Rebecca had looked marvellous this afternoon. She'd been chirpy and cheeky, a very good sign. And the doctor had said her early blood tests were more than hopeful.

But, Rebecca aside, they really did have to sort this out.

'Well, if I'm wrong about your intentions, then tell me what's right,' she demanded to know. 'Tell me what you feel for Tiffany. And what you feel for me,' she added, her voice breaking a little.

He closed his eyes and shook his head. 'Dear God, you won't give me any peace, will you?' He opened his eyes to turn his head and look at her again, his face full of frustration.

'I am fond of Tiffany,' he stated brusquely. '*More* than fond. I have known her for years and we are well matched. The only reason I haven't slept with her is because she doesn't want to till we're married. She has been brought up in a very…old-fashioned…way. For reasons which are complex, I would feel duty-bound to marry her even if I didn't *want* to marry her!

'I admit I've been having trouble with living a celibate existence,' he confessed, combing agitated fingers back through his perfectly groomed black hair. 'But I vowed to myself I would remain faithful, come hell or high water! I just never dreamt that my hell or high water would come in the guise of a fiery, red-headed Australian girl whose spirit and beauty I have come not only to admire but to covet as I have never coveted before!'

He glared at her, as though this was all her fault. And she *was* beginning to feel very guilty over her dress.

'I convinced myself I could endure till you left England,' he went on, blue eyes glittering with desire as they roved down her body, then up again. 'And I might have succeeded if I, too, had not received a phone call today. From Tiffany.'

Marina's heart gave a nervous little leap. 'What...what did she say?'

'She told me she wanted to wait a while before getting engaged. She said she was worried she was too young for marriage at this stage. She said she needed some time and space to think things over.'

Marina was astonished. The girl she'd seen at the hospital had clearly been besotted by James. What had happened in Italy to give her last-minute doubts?

'And what did *you* say?' she asked James.

'I said I understood, and that she was being very wise if she was at all unsure.'

It immediately crossed Marina's mind that James had not told Tiffany in return that *he* was having doubts. The way remained clear for him to marry the girl, if and when she got over these last-minute nerves.

'How very...convenient for you,' she said, a bitter taste in her mouth.

James glowered over at her. 'There is nothing at all convenient about any of this, Marina, especially what I feel for you.'

Before she could protest, he slid over the wide red seat and forcefully gathered her hands in his. 'I have never really fallen in love in my life,' he confessed. 'Not with a passion which has lasted anyway. I can't say what I feel for you is love. I only know that it is different, and infinitely distracting. Desire for you has dominated my every waking moment since the moment we met. My sleep is similarly disturbed. I can think of nothing else but touching you, kissing you, making love to you.'

He lifted her hands and pressed her fingertips to his lips, kissing them feverishly. He turned over her right hand and snaked his tongue along its palm, then up the wrist, then along the soft, sensitive skin which led up to the elbow.

Marina's eyes were wide upon his dark head as it bent over her, his mouth working a shivery magic on her arm. She sucked in a shaky breath every time his hot, wet tongue trailed over a new and seemingly more sensitised spot.

She would never have believed an arm could possess such erotic zones. He was moving higher now, above her elbow, up to her shoulder and down around the deep armhole of her dress. Her breast seemed to swell as his mouth drew nearer, its nipple tightening. Oh, God! *Both* breasts were responding now. Her heart began to thud heavily and her lips parted to let the ragged breaths escape her panting lungs.

When his head lifted to look at her, her eyes felt glazed. He held them while he unhooked the collar on her dress and peeled it downwards, trapping her arms by her sides and baring her shamelessly aroused breasts to his sight.

At last, his eyes lowered to look straight at them.

'God forgive me,' he muttered. But it didn't sound like a prayer. More an expression of ruthless resolve.

His head began to bend and she just sat there, with her back pressed hard against the seat and her breasts thrust stiffly forward, her mind petrified but her flesh avidly awaiting his touch, and his tongue.

The first contact of his hands and lips on her naked flesh brought a rushing inward gasp of breath. She held it for several agonising seconds, disbelieving of the way it felt when he sucked on one breast while he caressed the other. Finally, she let the breath out in one long shuddering sigh of total surrender.

Nothing had prepared her for this, she realised dazedly. Not even Shane. For this was heaven and hell combined. Happiness, yet misery. Agony, and ecstasy. The sweetest pleasure, yet the most poignant pain.

For the man adoring her body, tormenting it, *enslaving* it, had just told her he probably didn't love her. Which was as good as saying he didn't. She would ultimately prove to be a passing passion, as all his other women had been passing passions. Only Tiffany had his heart. Tiffany, the innocent. Tiffany, the sweet. And it was Tiffany he would marry.

But it was *she*, Marina, he wanted to make love to right at this moment.

And she wanted him to. Oh, she wanted him to so much. There was an ache for him in her body and in her heart which was growing with each sweep of his tongue, with each touch of his hand.

She grew mindless with yearning, sliding slowly sidewards on the seat as he tongued her nipples into hard pebbles of exquisite torture. She moaned and writhed against the plush velvet seat, her restless legs screaming out for him to stroke them, *part* them. She ached to have him undress her further. She wanted to be naked for him. She would have done anything he asked. Given him anything he wanted.

So she was shaken when he abruptly yanked her upright. His hands felt angry as he dragged her dress up over her throbbing breasts and hooked the collar in place. Her eyes searched his for a clue as to what was going on. Why had he stopped? Had he had second thoughts? Didn't he want her any more?

Tears were just a second away when he spoke.

'Forgive me,' he said, poking a stray hair of hers back into place. 'I know how you must be feeling. But we're only seconds away from the theatre.'

Marina stared at him.

How had he known that? Had he kept an eye on his watch? Or was he a practised hand at this scenario, knowing exactly how much lovemaking he had time for beforehand, leaving his victim all primed up for the second act, *after* they came out of the theatre?

'Don't look at me like that,' he groaned. 'I said I was sorry.' And he bent to kiss her on the mouth. His first. But it was a mere apologetic peck. Not a kiss racked with uncontrollable desire. *She* was the one shaking with uncontrollable desire. James was very much back in control—of himself and the situation.

Oh, Marina, Marina, you fool. This man is a past master of such games. Didn't Henry warn you? Did you honestly think you could play with this kind of fire and not get burned?

No more, she resolved bitterly. No more.

'You're not at all sorry,' she flung at him. 'You planned this. I know you did.'

'I planned nothing,' he denied curtly. 'I give you my word. As a gentleman.'

'Then you have a strange idea of what constitutes being a gentleman. Or is it that you think I'm *not* a lady?'

His blue eyes blazed. 'What just happened between us has nothing to do with being a gentleman and a lady, and everything to do with being a man and a woman! God, if I'd planned this, do you honestly think I would be taking you into that stupid theatre at this point? I would be ordering the driver to go round in endless circles while I made endless love to you.

'I can't win, no matter what I do, can I? That's what's been so difficult about this situation from the start. Neither of us has been free to admit—and act on—how we feel. But I see now there are certain things beyond society's ideas of right and wrong. Beyond rules. What we feel for each other is one of those things. What will be will be!'

'What will be for *me* is what *I* decide!' she argued, though shakily. 'And I do not decide to be one of your passing passions! Come Sunday, I am going to fly back to Sydney, and Shane. And I'm going to forget you ever existed!'

'You think you can fight the fates, Marina?' he ground out, an angry bitterness in those beautiful blue eyes of his. 'I think not...'

She only had to recall herself a minute ago, lying half-naked and abandoned beneath him, to concede what he was saying was true. But that didn't make the truth any more palatable.

'You are not to touch me again in this disgusting car,' came her heated protest. 'You will get rid of it and take me home in a taxi. Give me your word. As a gentleman,' she finished challengingly.

He glared at her for one long, excruciatingly tense moment, then slowly turned his head away, his chin tipping up proudly. 'You have it,' he ground out.

The car slid to a halt as he spoke. The back door opened and the real world rushed back in.

Noise. Lights. Crowds.

Marina blinked and recoiled. No, she wanted to scream. No, close the door again. I take it all back. Tell the chauffeur to drive round in circles. Undress me. Make endless love to me.

Don't take me out there feeling like this! Don't make me sit next to you all night in a darkened theatre without being able to touch you. Don't torture me with this awful craving, this unacceptable, unendurable, unfulfilled desire!

But he did take her out there. He did make her sit beside him without so much as holding her hand. And he capped off the evening by taking her home in a taxi and not speaking a single word, let alone kissing her or touching her in any way.

She was in a terrible state by the time James silently opened the apartment door and waved her inside. She was on the verge of humiliating herself totally by begging him to make love to her right there on the black and white tiled floor...when Henry walked down the stairs.

'Good evening, My Lord, Miss Marina.' He nodded

sombrely towards her. 'I trust the play was enjoyable?'

The play? She hadn't heard a word of it, had no idea if it had been a drama or a comedy.

'It was excellent,' she said, and wondered how she could sound so normal when it felt as if ants were crawling all over her skin, when her breasts ached unbearably and a liquid heat scorched between her thighs. Never had Shane made her feel like this. She wanted to slap James's handsome face, rake her nails down his back, sob into his shoulder.

The valet nodded sagely. 'There is nothing like a night at the London theatre. I do apologise again for the limousine, My Lord, but it was all the hire car company could give me at short notice. William said to tell you that the car will be ready for tomorrow.'

'Tomorrow?' James echoed, frowning. 'What's happening tomorrow?'

The valet smiled an uncharacteristically wide smile. 'The hospital rang soon after you left this evening. They say Rebecca can go home for the weekend.'

'But that's wonderful!' James exclaimed.

'Indeed, My Lord. I spoke to the child herself and she was so excited. But she doesn't want to come here. She wants to go down to Winterborne Hall.'

'But of course! Anything she wants.'

'She...er...especially asked if Miss Marina could go too.'

Marina's stomach contracted fiercely.

'She can't, I'm afraid,' James said sharply. 'She has a plane to catch on Sunday.'

Henry looked a little sheepish. 'Er...I took the liberty of ringing the airline, and they are more than happy to exchange Miss Marina's ticket for Monday's flight. It seems the Sunday flight is always rather overbooked.'

James's expression was one of total exasperation. 'That's all very well, Henry, but I believe Marina is anxious to get back to Sydney and her fiancé. Isn't that so, Marina?'

Marina had to admire his ongoing fortitude. Clearly he *had* decided to fight the good fight to the bitter end, as he'd said.

But, perversely, his noble self-sacrifice only made her love him all the more. And *want* him all the more. Feeling as she did at that moment, his putting the decision in her hands appealed to her dark side, and that awful voice which would not be denied.

He won't be able to resist you, no matter what he's decided. Not away from Henry's watchful eyes. Not down there, in one of those enormous bedrooms he's sure to occupy. Maybe he'll even have a four-poster bed...

'I would dearly love to come down to Winterborne Hall with Rebecca,' she heard herself saying, with only the smallest quaver in her voice. 'You did the right thing about changing my flight, Henry. Don't make such a fuss, James,' she said, turning to him. 'It's only one night, after all. Shane can wait one more night.'

Their eyes locked and his widened slightly.

And then he knew. Knew what she was saying. She

would give him one night. And give *herself* one night. With him.

She watched him struggle with what she knew had to be a wickedly compelling temptation.

'It's your decision,' he said slowly, but his fists remained balled by his side.

'I've already made up my mind,' she said.

'So be it,' he said, and as he stared deep into her eyes his own were strangely cold, yet full of a dark triumph.

He was rationalising her decision, she realised. Seeing it for what it *wasn't*. A night of selfish, secret lust which would not stop either of them from forging ahead and eventually marrying others. He did not understand that she loved him with all her heart, that she would never marry any man but him, that she would go to the grave a spinster rather than settle for anything less than what she knew tomorrow night would bring.

And so the deed was done, and their fate sealed.

But was it fate? Marina wondered as she lay wide-eyed in the Rose Room bed later that night. Some kind of warped destiny which had thrown them together and forced them along this path?

She did not know. She only knew she had to do this. Call it fate. Or destiny. Or written.

Tomorrow night she would spend in James's bed.

Tomorrow night…

Her eyes slid to the bedside clock. Just after three. Would she never fall asleep?

No, she accepted with a small, dry laugh. There was no sleep for the wicked. No sleep at all.

CHAPTER TEN

'I'M GOING home! I'm going home!'

Rebecca was bouncing up and down on the back seat of the Bentley between James and Marina.

'Do be still, Rebecca,' James said sharply.

Rebecca pulled a face at Marina. 'Uncle James only calls me Rebecca like that when he's in a bad mood.'

James sighed. 'I am not in a bad mood. I'm simply tired. Marina and I went out last night and I was late getting to sleep.'

'I didn't sleep much, either,' Rebecca said, beginning to bounce again. 'I was too excited.'

'Yes, well, I understand exactly what you mean,' was her uncle's dry remark. 'I was pretty excited myself.' And he threw Marina a scorching look over the child's bobbing head.

'Were you, Uncle James? Oh, look. There's some horses. Can I go look at our horses when I get home, Uncle James?'

'Whatever you like, sweetie. Here, come and sit up on my lap for a minute so you can see better out of the window.'

She scrambled up onto James's lap straight away, hands and nose instantly glued to the glass.

Marina resisted the impulse to feel jealous.

'You have horses too?' she asked.

He shrugged. 'I inherited them from my brother, who was racing and gambling mad. They're not riding horses. They're thoroughbred brood mares. Laurence's wife, Joy, was also mad about jumpers, and she had a whole stable of hacks. I eventually sold them, because there was no one left who wanted to ride and they cost too much to keep properly fed and stabled for nothing. But I kept the brood mares as an investment. We have plenty of good grazing land and my estate manager said it would be foolish to sell them up. He said some of the foals would bring in a small fortune. And he was right, thank God.'

'Why do you say, "Thank God"? Was the estate in financial trouble when your brother died?'

'That's putting it mildly. Laurence had run up an overdraft a mile high, the house and land had a second mortgage and several of my father's prized paintings had been exchanged for copies—the originals sold to South American millionaires. A good number of antiques had also already found their way to Sotheby's—just to support two wastrels, flitting around the world.'

'What's a wastrel?' Rebecca asked, reminding them both that there was a child listening.

'A good-for-nothing person who spends money and doesn't work,' James answered bluntly.

'Well, you're not one, Uncle James. You're *always* working at the bank. And Marina's not one because she's a teacher!' The little girl frowned, then. 'I'm not one, am I, Uncle James? I mean, I don't work, and I know it costs a lot to keep me in hospital.'

James gave the serious-faced child a hug. 'Children can't be wastrels, sweetie. That's only for grown-ups. And I wouldn't care how much it cost me to make you well.'

'You won't have to pay much more, Uncle James, because I'm going to be perfectly well in no time.'

Marina's heart turned over. She prayed that would be so with all her heart. The thought that the transplant might *not* work in the end brought a lump to her throat. She glanced out of her window, willing away tears by concentrating on the passing countryside.

It was nothing like anything you would ever see in Australia. So ordered, and so very green, despite James saying earlier they'd been having a drought. Marina had smiled at that. She doubted the English knew the real meaning of the word 'drought'. Let them travel out into the outback during a drought and see what *years*—not a single season—without rain could do. Let them see bone-dry creek-beds and the bleached skeletons of long-dead animals on the banks. Or the rotting carcasses of newly dead ones.

She shuddered herself at the image, which had actually confronted her once during a camping trip into the red heart of Australia.

Not that Australia was all like that. It was only the interior deserts which were so merciless. The capital cities and large tracts of pasturelands along the coastlines came as a pleasant surprise to some overseas visitors, who thought Australia was one big outback.

Marina especially loved Sydney, with its many

trees, its beautiful harbour and beaches. Unfortunately, her mother's house and ten-acre property was right on the rural outskirts of Sydney, quite some way from the ocean which might have tempered the soaring summer temperatures. Bringelly reached the high thirties with regular monotony during the summer months.

Marina had to admit she was not fond of such heat. Now that she was more used to England's cooler climate, she much preferred it. She'd grown to like London, too. And she certainly liked what she was seeing of the countryside.

They were on the A3 something-or-other, travelling south-west of London at considerable speed, as were all the other cars, heading wherever they were heading for the weekend. Actually, they'd been on various A3 something-or-others since leaving the M3 motorway some time back.

'You didn't want to go and see Stonehenge while you were down this way, did you?' James asked politely from his corner.

She looked over and noted that he had sensibly refastened Rebecca into her seat belt. 'No, thanks. I saw it last time and thought it highly disappointing. Maybe if you could walk amongst the stones themselves in the moonlight, you might get some of the right atmosphere. But not in broad daylight from behind a roped-off section where you walk around like sheep in a queue longer than Pitt Street.'

James laughed. 'You'll never make a tourist if you don't like sightseeing queues.'

'I agree with you. That's why my last touristy trip over here was my one and only.'

'You haven't travelled anywhere else?'

'Not outside of Australia. I've been into the outback and down to Tasmania.'

'So you haven't been to Paris? Or to Rome?'

'No.'

'Would you like to go?'

She gave him a suspicious look. Surely he wasn't going to suggest he take her? Surely not!

His smile was wry. 'Just answer the question, Marina. It's not a trick.'

'I'd go if I could go first class,' she said truthfully. 'My days of economy travel are behind me. I'm very much a once-bitten, twice-shy girl.' And make of that what you will, Your Lordship!

'I'll keep that in mind,' he murmured, and fell irritatingly silent.

Marina scowled to herself.

See what you get for magnanimously planning to let him sleep with you tonight? came the predictable taunt in her head. *Now he thinks you're a cheap, two-timing tramp. No, not cheap. An expensive two-timing tramp who can probably be bought for illicit weekends in Paris and Rome and God knows where. Next thing you know he'll suggest you fly back to Australia via Paris and Rome with him as tour guide. But the only sights he'll want you to see are plenty of hotel bedrooms!*

You don't have to sleep with him tonight, her conscience piped up. *You didn't say you would in so*

*many words. If and when he tries to take delivery of
what he thinks you promised, you can claim he mis-
interpreted that look, that you had no intention of doing any such thing!*

Marina closed her eyes and shook her head. She
couldn't do that. The truth was that *she* wanted to
sleep with *him*. The extent of her desire had kept her
awake all night. Even now, inside, every nerve-ending
was tingling in anticipation of the coming evening.
Although exhausted from her sleepless night, she felt
more alive than she ever had before.

Did James feel like that? she wondered, and turned
her head just enough to look at him out of the corner
of her eye.

He was wearing the most casual clothes she'd seen
him in this past week. Pale grey trousers and a light-
weight crew-necked sweater in broad horizontal
stripes of grey and navy. His casual loafers were navy.
He still looked a million dollars—his black hair perfectly groomed and that tantalising pine perfume waft-
ing from his body.

She, herself, was wearing the tailored black trousers
which went with her take-anywhere black suit, teamed
today with a cream V-necked cashmere cardigan
which she'd thrown into her luggage at the last moment in case the evenings were chilly. Although the
sun was shining, Marina still found the air crisp.

Rebecca had insisted on wearing a rather tomboyish
outfit of white T-shirt and khaki overalls, completing
it with a white baseball cap.

She'd told Marina in confidence that she wasn't

going to wear girl clothes until she had hair and
looked like a girl. Marina could see her point.
Rebecca's bald head would have looked incongruous
above a frilly dress. And she simply refused to wear
a wig. She said they were hot and itchy and made her
look silly!

Marina glanced up from her survey of Rebecca's
clothes to find James watching her. For a moment the
air between them was fraught with a sizzling tension.
But then he smiled, and for a single marvellous moment Marina felt as she might have felt if they had
been a real family—husband, wife and daughter—going for a drive in the countryside.

Her heart swelled with a brief burst of happiness,
only to contract fiercely when she realised such a fantasy would never come true. It would be Lady Tiffany
who would sit here in future years. James's wife. The
Countess of Winterborne. Not silly slept-with-and-
discarded Marina.

Her face must have betrayed her thoughts, for
James's smile faded abruptly, to be replaced by a
troubled frown. They stared at each other and Marina
could have sworn that the misery in her eyes was
reflected in his, that they both longed for the same
thing, but both knew it would never come about.

'We're nearly there!' Rebecca suddenly shrieked.
'Look, there's the gates, Uncle James. Oh, just you
wait and see this, Marina. It's the prettiest place you'll
ever see!'

Marina dragged herself out of the black pit in a
valiant effort to respond to the child's enthusiasm. She

could not for a moment imagine that one of England's
ancestral homes would be 'pretty'. But then, a
seven-year-old girl would not have too many adjectives at her command. One only had to look at the
ancient wall and gateposts that the more modern elec-
tronic gates were attached to in order to get a hint of
what the house would be like. Dark and grey and forbidding.

They passed through the gates, which had opened
and begun closing behind them as if by magic, but
presumably by a remote control operated by William.
On one gatepost sat a small security camera, and below, attached to the post, was a black box with a big
black button which no doubt callers pressed so that
they could be vetted before the gates were opened.

Just inside the gates on Marina's side stood a simply awful old house, which looked dilapidated and
deserted. Although two-storeyed, it was small and
narrow and gloomy. It had tiny windows and two
black chimneys and ivy growing all over the walls.
There was no garden to speak of. Just rambling rose
bushes.

'That isn't the gatehouse Henry was sent to live in,
is it?' she asked, aghast.

James nodded. 'Now you know why I had to bring
him to London. The only reason I haven't had the
damned thing torn down is because it's protected by
a well-known charity. I ask you, what and who are
they protecting it for?'

'Not me,' Rebecca said, shuddering. 'It's creepy.'

'I suppose it has a long history,' Marina ventured.

'Undoubtedly,' James agreed. 'But it is *my* gate-house, isn't it? I should be able to do what I damned well please with it! I thank my lucky stars I've been able to pull the estate out of the red, or else I might have had to hand over the place to just such an institution, who would undoubtedly open the place to the public and have me spend every summer weekend standing on the front steps and smiling at those long queues of tourists you adore so much.'

Now she looked at him, *more* aghast. 'But you'd hate that!'

'Life can be full of doing things you hate,' he returned, and she had a feeling he was no longer talking about houses.

'I hate needles!' Rebecca piped up. 'And I still have to have them. Stop talking to Marina, Uncle James. We're coming to the pretty bit.'

The narrow, winding road dipped unexpectedly, plunging with amazing speed from open fields into a type of forest. Huge trees on either side stretched up and over, meeting in the middle of the road. The summer sun attempted to pierce the canopy of leaves but could only manage a dappled light. Fractured rays of yellow danced across the shadowy avenue, creating a magical and quite fanciful atmosphere.

Suddenly they were in another world, where it was possible to believe in fairies and elves, in Robin Hood and Maid Marion, in Prince Charmings and Sleeping Beauties and happy ever after.

'It's the enchanted wood!' Marina exclaimed.

As quickly as they had descended into the fairyland

they burst out of it, and there, on a rise at the end of a long straight driveway, stood Winterborne Hall.

It wasn't dark or forbidding. Not at all. The walls were made of a creamy grey stone, the roof of a shiny grey slate. It was three storeys high, with a very wide façade.

Not a castle by any means. But a most impressive mansion. Georgian in design, Marina guessed, with its clean lines and the symmetrical placement of windows on either side of the entrance.

'What do you think?' James asked as the Bentley moved with considerably less speed over the now gravel driveway.

'It's magnificent,' she praised.

'So it darned well should be! I've sunk a damned fortune in fixing up the place after Laurence didn't spend a penny on it for years. I had the ivy stripped off the outside and the walls sandblasted last year. You don't think it's too stark now, do you?'

'Oh, no. It's breathtaking! And so are the grounds.' As far as the eye could see there were rolling green hills, like parkland, with clumps of stately trees. Closer to the house, the wide expanses of lawn gave way to more ordered gardens, with beds of flowering bushes bordering the driveway—possibly hibiscus and definitely fuchsias and oleander—all of them in full bloom. They were covered in masses of gloriously coloured flowers in reds and pinks and white.

And then there was the fountain in the middle, where the driveway parted into two and went round in a circle. It was dominated by a great bronze statue of a chariot, horse and driver, and the circumference of the stone pond was rimmed with bronze archers shooting not arrows, but jets of water at the invading warrior, whoever he was.

'I simply love it all,' Marina praised, 'but especially that fountain. There again, I do so like water.'

'Wait till she sees the lake, Uncle James!'

'Lake?'

'The grounds roll down a slight hill to a lake at the back. There are swans and ducks, and we have a couple of boats you can take out. It's very pleasant down there on a summer evening. There's even a gazebo on a small point jutting into the lake.'

'I have parties with my dolls there,' Rebecca said. 'I'll show it to you after I've shown you the horses.'

'I haven't seen *any* horses yet,' Marina said, glancing around.

'They're not close to the house,' James explained. 'I have a motorised golf-cart we can use to get to them.'

'Don't tell me you have a golf course here as well?'

'No. Just the cart. But we do have an indoor heated swimming pool and an indoor tennis court.'

'And how many acres?' She might as well know the whole awful truth. Might as well let it sink in as just who and what she was dealing with here. It would keep her feet firmly on the ground.

'Around a thousand.'

Marina knew that was a *huge* acreage by English standards. 'My God, your next-door neighbours aren't exactly at leaning-over-the-fence-for-a-chat distance, are they?'

He smiled. 'No. Not exactly.'

'How ever do you get to meet them?'

'At polo matches and dinner parties and balls.'

'Polo matches and dinner parties and balls,' she repeated slowly, thinking this world was a far cry from a drink at the pub on a Friday night and McDonalds and a movie on Saturday. And yet, strangely, as she looked around she didn't feel at all like a fish out of water. If she hadn't known better, she might easily have pictured herself living here, with James by her side. In a weird kind of way her mother had prepared her for just such a life. She was well educated. She had an appreciation of art and fine things. She could ride...

She was almost tempted to tell him she was not totally working class, to say, Hey, half of me is Bingham blood. You know the Binghams, don't you? Smashing good family. They go back centuries. I don't know where they live, and they did give my mother the boot more than twenty-five years ago, but other than that I'm sure they're right up your alley!

'Uncle James doesn't like parties much,' Rebecca chimed in. 'Do you, Uncle James?'

'Not any more, sweetie.'

'Henry said you'd changed,' the child offered, giving additional information which had James's eyebrows lifting. 'He said you used to be a "right royal raver" in your younger days. But that nowadays you had "settled down nicely".'

Marina couldn't help a small laugh, for the child had imitated Henry's pompous manner to perfection.

'Henry said that to *you*?' James asked his niece in a disbelieving tone.

The child suddenly looked guilty. 'Well...um...no. Not exactly. He and William were having a cup of tea in the kitchen one day and I...I...'

'You eavesdropped,' James chided. 'You know that's not right, Rebecca.'

'I don't think it's so bad,' she defended herself. 'It's the only way I can find out interesting stuff. No one ever tells us kids anything!'

Marina struggled not to smile. And so did James, she saw. The corners of his mouth were definitely twitching. The car stopped at the front steps and Rebecca demanded to be let out immediately. William took too long to open doors these days, she confided to her uncle.

'All right, but don't run,' James warned, before he unzapped her seat belt and opened the car door. Rebecca jumped out and immediately raced up the front steps. Already a plump grey-haired lady was emerging from the house and holding her arms out to the child.

'That's Mildred,' he explained, sighing. 'She's been the housekeeper here for a hundred years. Or so it seems. She's actually only about sixty, and very attached to Rebecca. I don't know what she'll do if this transplant doesn't take. God, I don't know what *I'll* do, come to think of it,' he finished wretchedly.

Marina didn't stop to think. She simply reacted,

reaching out to touch his nearest arm. When he looked up at her with still sad eyes, she knew she would do anything to comfort him, regardless of the personal cost.

'You mustn't worry,' she said softly. 'And you mustn't fuss. Treat her like a normal child with a future. Have faith, James.'

'Faith?' He shook his head. 'I'm not a very religious person, I'm afraid.'

'What has that got to do with faith? Faith is simply believing. If you believe Rebecca will get better and you treat her as such, then *she* will believe she's going to get better and she will!'

He searched her eyes, with a type of wonder in his. 'Promise me you won't go back on tonight,' he suddenly urged in a low, husky voice. 'Promise me now. Say it!'

'I...I promise,' she whispered shakily.

'And not just for a short hour or two,' he insisted. 'All night.'

She shivered beneath the rather ruthless passion in his voice.

A nod was all she could manage this time.

William opened the passenger door at that precise moment, and Marina was relieved to turn away from James's disturbing intensity. But she knew it was only a temporary reprieve. Tonight she would place herself totally in his hands.

She hoped he would be merciful.

CHAPTER ELEVEN

MARINA woke with a start, as you do when you have fallen asleep not in your own bed. She half sat up, glanced around the dimly lit room, then sank back down on top of the bed with a sigh, her eyes sliding across to the form sleeping beside her.

Rebecca looked totally at peace in sleep, as most children did. She'd hardly moved since she'd drifted off while Marina read to her, having worn herself out with showing her visitor absolutely everything on the estate. The house, the pool, the tennis court, the horses, the lake and the gazebo, chattering non-stop all the time.

When his niece had begun to droop after lunch, James had put his foot down and insisted she have a nap. Marina had lain down next to her on the bed to read her Enid Blyton's *The Magic Faraway Tree*, and in no time Rebecca had travelled from Faraway Land to the Land of Nod.

James had settled in an armchair across the room while this was going on, listening happily. When Rebecca had dropped off and Marina had tried to stop reading he'd insisted she go on. He'd wanted to hear the end of the story—claimed he'd adored Enid Blyton as a boy and could not get enough.

Marina could not recall if she'd finished the story.

At some stage she must have closed her eyes herself and nodded off. The book, she noted as she rolled over and peered down, was lying on the carpet. And James was...

Marina's head jerked up and she stared through the gloom, surprised to find James still there, his head sunk sidewards, fast asleep. Goodness, she thought. What on earth was the time?

She struggled to see her watch, surprised again to make out that it was not as late as the faded light indicated. Only six. It was then she noticed the drawn curtains. Had James done that? Or Mildred? Maybe Talbot, the butler?

She would not have put it past either of those last two, who were the nicest people. Mildred was a real sweetie and Talbot wasn't nearly as stuffy as Henry. There again, he was not of the old school. He was a very modern style of butler. In his late forties, fair, shortish but fit-looking, he was efficient, courteous and attentive without being obsequious or too pompous.

Although Marina had become perversely fond of Henry's old-fashioned ways, he could do with lightening up a bit, she believed.

Dinner was not to be served until seven-thirty, so Marina decided not to wake anyone else just yet. She was loath to disturb the soundly sleeping Rebecca, and there was something far too intimate about waking James from sleep for Marina's liking. With the evening at hand, she knew it was imperative for her to keep good control of her nerves—and the situation.

She'd got herself into a right state last night and she didn't want a repeat performance—certainly not until they were safely alone together.

Rebecca was an intuitive child, and for all her kindness Marina doubted Mildred had come down in the last shower. It seemed likely the housekeeper had turned a blind eye to many a liaison under this roof, if the previous Earl and his wife had been such a swinging jet-setting couple. The same went for Talbot. Butlers must surely notice things like that. But Marina didn't want any blind eyes being turned towards herself and the new Earl. She wanted the whole household to be genuinely blind to their relationship.

Relationship? sneered that rotten voice in her head. *What relationship? You're having a one-night stand with him, Marina, that's all. Don't go giving yourself airs and graces, now. You are not the love of His Lordship's life. You are a very convenient passing passion while Her Ladyship is making up her mind.*

'Oh, shut up!' she muttered under her breath, and swung her bare feet over the side of the bed. Pressing her lips firmly together, she slid her feet into her black flatties and stood to walk over to the nearest window, gripping the heavy green drapes and pulling them apart just enough to look down at the rolling hill and the lake.

The water looked beautiful in the late afternoon light. Like liquid glass.

Marina was thinking how magnificent it would look under moonlight when James suddenly materialised behind her, his hands curling over her shoulders.

When she went to whirl around, his grip tightened and he pulled her back against him.

'Don't,' she croaked.

He turned her round and looked deep into her shadowed eyes. 'Don't what?' he asked, his voice strained.

'Don't...do anything. Not here.' And she nodded over to the sleeping child on the bed.

His expression was pained. 'God, Marina, you frightened the life out of me there for a moment. I thought you were going to tell me tonight was off.'

'And if I did?' she whispered, in one last crisis of conscience.

'Then I would have to set out to change your mind back again,' he vowed fiercely. 'By fair means or foul.'

'You...you wouldn't do that,' she said shakily. 'You have too much honour.'

'This is beyond honour, Marina,' he said, with a dark and bitter resolve. 'Beyond anything I have ever known before. Believe me when I say if you don't come to my room later tonight, then, by God, I will come to yours!'

The image of his battering on her bedroom door in the middle of the night was nearly as appalling as her sneaking along to his.

'You won't have to do that,' she rasped. 'I...I'll come to your room. But only if you promise to do nothing to arouse anyone's suspicions during the course of the evening. Don't flirt with me, or...or look at me as you are doing at this moment.'

'When will you come?' he demanded to know.

'When the house is quiet and everyone has retired for the night. I don't want anyone to know, James. That's very important to me.'

'Fair enough. In that case, don't knock. I'll leave the door unlocked and the key on the inside. Simply slip in and turn the key. That should prevent any disaster such as Rebecca barging in in the middle of the night. Not that she's likely to do that. As you can see, she sleeps like a log.' And he nodded to the still unconscious child.

'Yes, but she may have had the edge taken off tonight's sleep with this nap.'

'She still wouldn't come to me if she woke. She'd ring for Mildred. Look, what say I suggest Mildred sleeps in the nanny's room tonight? It's right next to Rebecca's. Just in case Rebecca wakes and wants something.'

'Yes, yes, that would be good.' *Good?* Marina thought, appalled. *Good?* Nothing about this was good. It was underhanded and tawdry and just simply awful! She wanted to cry, to scream at him. *Beg* him not to do this to her—turn her into something she was not.

'Marina, don't worry so,' he chided, making everything so much worse with his own apparent ease. 'It's a very big house with very thick walls and doors. No one will know. I promise you. Now...' He reached out and touched her cheek, his fingertips like licks of flame against her skin. 'Do you know where my room is? We don't want you stumbling around the corridors, getting lost in the dark.'

'I won't get lost,' she said, jerking her face sharply so that his hand dropped away. 'I know exactly where your room is. Rebecca and Mildred gave me the grand tour of the house. Mildred was especially proud of the master of the house's bedroom.'

It was hardly just a room. It was a suite, with a separate sitting room, dressing room and bathroom, all sumptuously furnished. But of course it had been the huge bed which had drawn her eyes earlier that day. A four-poster, which Mildred informed her proudly had once belonged to one of the kings of France.

It was truly magnificent, with an elaborate carved bed-head and a solid rosewood canopy. But what had sent Marina's heart racing were the blue and gold brocade curtains sashed to each bedpost with gold tasselled cords, similar in style to those in her fantasy.

It was the most glorious bed Marina had ever seen. And the most seductive in her eyes. She'd had to work hard not to let her mind fill with new fantasies, all the more arousing because she knew this time she could make them come true, every single decadent one. She had thanked her lucky stars at the time that Rebecca had been showing her the house in Mildred's company, and not James's. If he'd been with them, she would surely have blushed furiously and perhaps made the housekeeper suspicious.

Even thinking about it brought a flushing heat to her face. James saw it, and enclosed her in his arms before she could think to struggle. 'Stop getting your-

self all worked up,' he murmured as he moulded her
body to his.

Her eyes rounded at the immediate wave of desire
which swept through her body. It roared along her
veins, curled through her stomach, then crashed
against her thudding heart. A moan surfaced through
an ebb tide of longing and starkly sexual need. He
heard it and his arms tightened around her, making
her hotly aware of his own need, which felt as intense
as her own. But infinitely more powerful.

Panic-stricken, she pushed him away. Just in time,
too. For there came a sound from the bed and she
whirled to find Rebecca yawning and stretching.
Marina could feel her cheeks burning but the child
didn't seem to have overheard or seen anything.

'Was I asleep long?' Rebecca asked with a second
yawn.

'Not too long,' Marina said lightly, and walked
over to pick the book up from the floor. She didn't
dare look back at James. 'But you'd better get up
now. It's not that long till dinner.'

'Oh. I suppose we're having dinner in the dining
room, are we, Uncle James?' She didn't sound at all
thrilled with the idea.

'Yes,' he agreed. 'Why, would you prefer to eat
with Mildred and Talbot in the kitchen?'

'Oh, yes, please. I hate sitting at that silly long table. I can never see anyone on the other side through
the candles and flowers and stuff.'

James laughed and Marina's eyes snapped his way.
He looked superbly in control, she realised. No one

would have guessed that a few moments ago he had been so blatantly aroused.

'I can remember thinking exactly the same at your age,' he tossed over his shoulder at Rebecca as he strolled towards the door. 'Fair enough. I'll tell Talbot it's just Marina and myself for dinner in the dining room.'

'Am…am I supposed to get dressed up?' Marina asked, before he could leave the room. Privately, she was appalled at the prospect of having to sit in state with James over a lengthy formal dinner, knowing what was to come later.

He stopped with his hand on the door knob and turned slowly to face her. His eyes were superbly bland as they moved over her body. It was Marina who was a shambles, her heart racing as his gaze moved down over her breasts with their betrayingly hard nipples poking through the soft wool.

'No,' he drawled. 'Wear what you've got on, if you like. That looks lovely on you.'

His eyes returned to her face, where they remained fixed for a fraction longer than necessary. And, in that elongated and quite electric moment, she knew his composure was just a façade. He was still as turned on as she was. His need hadn't abated. Neither had his passion. He was just better at hiding it than she was, better at concealing his carnal desires behind a cloak of restraint and respectability.

Marina felt anything but restrained and respectable as she stared after his departing figure.

*   *   *

By nine that evening Marina was almost beside herself with tension. Dinner was proving to be the trial she'd suspected it would be, despite the food being as superb as the setting.

She supposed most females would give their eye teeth to be wined and dined in such a room, with its walnut panelling and gracious antique furniture. Most females would probably give their eye teeth to be going to bed with the Lord of the Manor that night, whether he loved them or not!

But it seemed Marina was not most females. She kept wishing with all her heart that it was love stirring James to look at her as he was looking at her across the table, and not those infamous Winterborne hormones.

So much for her warnings about his staring at her with lustful eyes! It seemed she'd unleashed the beast in the Earl of Winterborne with her promise of things to come. He was making Shane look positively civilised with the way his glittering blue gaze kept fixing on her mouth and her breasts, not to mention their sinfully erect nipples!

By the time Rebecca was safely tucked up in bed around ten-thirty—the child had been quite lively after her afternoon nap, as predicted—and Marina could reasonably say her own goodnights just before eleven, she was a mess. She could also no longer delineate between nerves and desire. Her stomach churned. Her hands were clammy. Her body burned.

Once safely in her own lavish bedroom, she fairly dived into the gold-tapped *en suite* shower, staying there at length in an attempt to cool down her whole system while gathering some much needed composure.

But composure had apparently fled to the far corners of the earth. She groaned her dismay at her utter inner panic. Her mind spun with self-reproach.

Giving her so-called word like this was the worst and the stupidest thing she had ever done! My God, she'd promised to deliver herself to his bedroom like a...a...whore! In a way, she wished she *were* a whore, instead of the basically very inexperienced bedpartner she was. With Shane, she'd simply lain back and gasped in pleasure and surprise at what he'd done. Before Shane she hadn't done anything either, her two earlier boyfriends wanting nothing but quickies, she now realised. They hadn't required her to do anything except not stop them.

But James was a difficult kettle of fish. He would surely be expecting a woman of the world. Instead, he was going to get *her*!

Marina emerged from the shower, shaking.

As midnight drew near she knew she could not delay much longer. She was physically ready, her body washed and perfumed and naked beneath her nightwear. The oyster satin nightie and matching robe covering her nudity were very pretty, though not overly seductive. Oddly, she'd left her hair up, perhaps in defiance of her fantasy about her hair being spread out on a snow-white pillow.

Pride alone propelled her out of the room. No way

did she want James coming to her room and making a scene.

The walk down the corridors and along to James's wing did not take nearly long enough. Before she knew it she was standing at his door, and before she knew it he was sweeping that door open as though some sixth sense had told him she was there.

'Where in hell have you been?' he snapped, and, grabbing an arm, yanked her into the bedroom. Just as swiftly he shut and locked the door behind him.

There were no lights on in the room, she noted shakily, yet it wasn't in darkness. The curtains at the main windows were wide open and an eerie silver moonlight was streaming in, making the blues in the room look grey and the gold like platinum.

James was wearing a darkly patterned silk robe, tightly sashed around his waist as though he had sashed and resashed it many times in the last hour. His obvious agitation made her feel a little better. Clearly he wasn't in the habit of making midnight assignations with women he had not promised to love and cherish, but from whom he'd exacted a promise of total sexual surrender for one long, mad, marvellous night.

Suddenly it was all too much for her, and with a soft sound of just such sexual surrender she threw her arms around his neck and lifted her mouth for him to crush.

He crushed it at first. Then adored it, tasting her tongue and licking at her lips, making her mouth feel not so much a mouth but an exquisite meal, to be savoured before being devoured.

She was melting against him when his mouth turned savage again as abruptly as it had gentled, making her moan beneath its onslaught, half in fear, half with a wild, mutual passion.

He must have heard the fear, however, for he dragged his mouth away and buried it in her hair, his breath hot and ragged. 'You don't know what you do to me,' he rasped. 'I've been in hell all week. But this last hour has unravelled me completely. I'm not going to be able to last.'

His confessed vulnerability was oddly reassuring and sweetly touching. She pulled back to cup his face and look up at him.

'James,' she said softly, and traced over his face and mouth with gentle fingertips. 'Darling James…we have all night, remember? It doesn't matter.'

He groaned and opened his lips to take one of her fingertips between them. Desire flashed like lightning through her, and without thinking she pushed the finger further inside his mouth, watching with wide eyes and pounding heart while he sucked on it.

Marina had read about women going weak at the knees over a man but had thought it a melodramatic exaggeration.

But it wasn't. As he sucked her finger she literally went weak at the knees, her legs turning jelly-like. Her head began to whirl. She had to take her finger out or risk collapsing!

She plucked it away with a low moan of regret and

he just stared at her. Her hands moved as in a dream, slipping the robe from her shoulders to let it flutter to the floor. Then came the nightie, one strap at a time, till she was standing naked before him.

She had never felt so desirable in all her life. His hungry gaze gobbled her up, especially her breasts which already ached for his touch. She felt their aroused heaviness lift upwards when she raised her hands to pluck the pins from her hair. She dropped them on the carpet, one at a time, letting the mass of red-gold curls tumble around her bare shoulders in erotic disarray.

'I don't think one night is going to be enough,' he said thickly, and bent to scoop her up into his arms.

He carried her over and lay her down in the softest of mattresses and pillows. The blue and gold quilt was already thrown back, she realised as she sank into snow-white linen. Her hands lifted languidly again, to rake her hair out onto the pillow. If she was going to live out a fantasy, then she was going to do it right.

'Are you going to close the curtains?' she asked, her voice sounding as thick as treacle.

'And block out such a sight? God, no.' He began unsashing his own robe. 'Do you know what you look like lying there in the moonlight? Have you any idea?'

He shrugged out of his robe and Marina snapped out of her dreamworld. For never had she seen a man so fiercely erect. Not even Shane, who was a very virile fellow. James was awesome in his need. Like a volcano rising up and ready to explode.

The sight unnerved her momentarily.

'Don't...don't forget to use protection,' she said in a breathy little voice.

'I'm well prepared,' he assured her, and pointed to a pile of foil squares on the bedside table.

'Oh...'

He reached to pick one up and Marina turned her head away. She didn't want to watch.

But what if he asked *her* to put one on him later in the night? She turned her head back, only to find the deed already done.

Now she felt a fool. James's need for her wasn't embarrassing. It was beautiful. *He* was beautiful.

She held out her arms and he joined her on the bed, kissing her hungrily. Her own need, which had receded with their separation, quickly raced back. Soon she could not get enough of his tongue in her mouth, or that hand which was stroking up and down her leg. Gradually it moved higher, then around between her thighs. Once there, it did not hesitate. It was focused and experienced and merciless.

In no time Marina was on the brink, and she burst from his mouth, gasping. Her back began to arch away from the bed, her flesh tensing in readiness for that electric moment when everything twisted even tighter before splintering apart. He immediately moved between her legs and surged into her, deep and hard. She caught her breath, and tried to stop herself from coming. But such was the burst of emotional and physical satisfaction at being one with him at last that her body refused to obey.

She cried out, her face grimacing in that strange

agony which was really ecstasy. And then she felt *him* coming, shuddering violently into her. Her mind spun out into a vortex where all those tortuous feelings he'd been evoking in her since they'd met sought to find total satisfaction.

She found herself raking her nails down his back and digging them into the taut muscles of his buttocks. But if it was pain she was wanting to impart, then she failed. The only sound he made was a long, low groan of raw animal pleasure.

It did wicked things to her, that groan. She vowed to make him groan many times during the night; she vowed to make him suffer for doing this to her—for making her love him even more than she had before.

CHAPTER TWELVE

'WHY is it,' James said softly, shortly before three, 'that the more I make love to you, the more I want to?'

He was lying on his side, propped up on his left elbow and trickling the tassel of one of the curtain cords over her nearest nipple.

Marina said nothing. She just clenched her jaw in futile denial of her own rapid resurgence of desire.

He started on the other nipple. 'You have such lovely breasts,' he murmured, and bent to lick the stiffened peak to an even greater state of acute sensitivity. After spending a full five minutes on this torture, he trailed the tassel down over her ribs and stomach, encircling her navel before moving down to her thighs, by which time Marina was breathing heavily and desperately wanting to part those thighs wide, to beg him to run that tantalising tassel over far more intimate places.

But a certain feminine stubbornness was creeping into Marina, an innate desire not to be so easy, she supposed. It was silly at this point, she knew, but she could not seem to help it. She kept her legs stubbornly closed, even when he drove her mad with that tassel trailing up and down her thighs.

Her resistance was perverse, really, because he'd

already kissed every inch of her, already reduced her several times to a quivering, mindless creature, unable to stop him doing whatever he pleased, wherever he pleased.

In the end, he stopped and frowned at her. 'What's wrong?' he asked.

'Nothing.'

'You don't want me to make love to you again?'

She said nothing. Wild horses were not going to drag the admission from her that she was dying for it already.

'Would you like to do it to me? Is that it?'

Her eyes blinked with the alien notion. For she had never ever made love to a man, not even Shane. He hadn't asked for it and she'd never offered, though she'd seen it often enough in the movies. It seemed the only position these days for sex scenes: the woman on top. To Marina it always looked choreographed, and frankly rather embarrassing.

'I...I've never done that sort of thing before,' she confessed.

His eyes showed surprise. 'Why's that?'

'I guess I...I never wanted to. And none of the men I've slept with have ever asked me to.'

'Not even Shane?'

'No.'

'I see. At least, no, I *don't* see. Damn it, Marina, must you confuse me even more than I am already?' He glared down at her with a mixture of exasperation and bewilderment. 'So tell me, exactly how many men have there been in your life so far?'

'Exactly how many women have there been in yours?'

The counter-question threw him. Clearly he could not even hazard a guess.

'Never mind,' she muttered. 'I get the point. I have technically had three lovers before you. But two of them were really just boys. I dated them at teachers' college. They were students, like me, with either limited experience or knowledge. I'm not sure which.'

She sighed at the memory. She'd been such a child at the time, yet thought herself so grown-up. All of eighteen and nineteen! 'I believed I was in love both times,' she said. 'But sex proved such an anticlimax on each occasion that I eventually decided what I felt couldn't possibly be love.

'That's why when sex with Shane was so unexpectedly good, I did the reverse and believed I *had* to be in love with him. Although, to be fair to myself, he was also very kind to me when I needed kindness. My mother had just died and I needed...someone.'

'I can understand that,' James murmured.

He idly resumed tantalising her with the tassel. Over her stomach this time. 'So you really haven't had all that much experience...?'

'No.' Her voice was as taut as her stomach muscles.

'That's a very exciting thought,' he said, trailing the tassel up over her breasts and up to her mouth, where he danced the ends of the golden threads over her softly quivering lips. 'Are you enjoying what I'm doing at the moment? You certainly seem to be.'

Her face flamed and she nodded, her tongue suddenly thick in her throat.

'If I asked you to, would you do it to me, Marina? Would you do all those things you have never done with a man before? You know what I mean, don't you?'

She nodded again, her heart pounding in her chest.

He stopped the torture with the tassel, and, taking her nearest hand, opened her clenched fingers and wrapped them tightly around the cord. Then he lay back on the bed beside her, his eyes shutting as he scooped in, then exhaled several very deep breaths.

Her stomach churned as she propped herself up on one arm and stared, first down at the cord in her hand, then over at his outstretched nakedness. She wanted to. Oh, yes. She wanted to touch him and kiss him all over, to trail the tassel over *his* flesh till he was groaning with passion. She wanted to make love to him better than all those other women, the ones he could not count.

But she had no experience to fall back on, and her mouth went dry at the prospect at making an utter fool of herself.

'You don't have to do anything you're not comfortable with,' he reassured her softly, even while his eyes remained shut. 'I'll love anything you do to me. Anything at all.'

Marina gathered all her courage and just began, her hand trembling. His chest quivered at the first touch of the soft golden threads, his lungs expanding on an inward gasp of pleasure. She took confidence from the

sound and started trailing the tassel over his broadly
muscled male chest. He sucked in sharply again when
she grazed over his nipples.

So she did it again. Then again, thrilling to the sight
of those small nubs expanding into twin peaks of expectant nerve-endings. Marina knew how they felt, for
she had felt the same thing herself. With the knowledge of her own experience in mind, she bent over
him and used her tongue on them in long, teasing
licks, and eventually he gave out a muffled groan, the
sound vibrating with tortured arousal.

A bolt of adrenaline raced through her as she discarded the cord and moved her mouth and hands
slowly downwards, over his ribs and onto his stomach. When she swirled her tonguetip in his navel, his
stomach fluttered wildly. When she moved on even
further, she felt every muscle in his body freeze in
anticipation of what was to come.

She didn't dare look up to see if he'd opened his
eyes. If she did, this new and intoxicating boldness
might fail her. As it was, she felt dizzy with an unexpected sense of power, and possessed by the most
incredible passion. She'd never realised how exciting
taking control of lovemaking could be, how much she
would revel in the feel of his hardness beneath her
hands and within her mouth.

'Don't stop,' he rasped when her head finally lifted.
'For pity's sake, don't stop.'

It still seemed the ideal time to do so, and to reach
for one of the foil packets. He groaned and grimaced,
his whole body as tightly strung as his face. She took

her time, partly because she'd never actually put a condom on before but mostly because underneath her seeming cool she was so hopelessly excited she couldn't think straight.

'God, yes,' he cried, when she finally moved to straddle him. When she began lowering herself rather gingerly onto his powerful erection, he took hold of her hips and pulled her down onto him more quickly.

Marina gasped at the feel of his flesh impaling hers, her mouth drying as her lips parted and hot, shallow breaths puffed from her panting lungs.

He reached up to knead her swollen breasts, crushing them together then drawing them down, down to his mouth. She bent forward in a type of daze, only dimly aware that she was no longer in control. *He* was.

He was suckling on her breasts and she was moaning, moaning and moving her bottom, writhing in her need. His own buttocks were rocking against the bed, setting up a frantic rhythm inside her. With a tortured gasp, she plucked her nipple out of his mouth and straightened so that she could match his movements with more uninhibited fervour. She no longer thought such an act embarrassing, or ridiculous. She no longer thought at all.

They came together like a thunderclap, and their cries echoed through the room. Afterwards she collapsed upon his chest, utterly spent. James clasped her close and buried his lips in her hair.

'God, how am I going to live without you?' he muttered.

The very real bleakness in his voice stirred Marina to hope as she had never hoped this past week. She waited breathlessly for him to say he loved her, to ask her to stay in England with him. But he remained silent. Clearly, no matter what his feelings for her, they were not strong enough, or deep enough, for him to change the path of his life.

Marina had not really expected him to. Men like him did not marry girls like her. A soul-sinking acceptance of the situation combined with her physical exhaustion, and she sighed a deep yawn.

'Don't go to sleep, for pity's sake,' he groaned. 'The morning will come soon enough.'

'It's almost morning now,' she told him drowsily.

'We still have a couple of hours. Talk to me,' he urged as he held her and stroked her spine. 'Tell me all about yourself. Tell me about your childhood, your teaching. Tell me what you do in a typical day. I want to know everything about you, Marina.'

It seemed pointless, but she did as he asked and told him of her upbringing, her school days, her wish to become a teacher—but not in her mother's riding school. She told him of her college years and how, after her unsatisfactory relationships with the opposite sex, she'd steered clear of boyfriends for a few years and filled her life with her career.

And as she talked that crushing exhaustion gradually left her. Just before the dawn it was James who fell asleep, leaving Marina to disentangle herself from his leaden arms. She crept back to her room, where she sat in an armchair and watched the sun rise. She dozed in the chair for an hour or so, waking when the mantel clock donged seven. With a sigh she rose and made her way to the shower, wondering as she stepped under the jets of hot water if James was still asleep.

She rather resented washing the smell of him from her. Making love with this man who she knew she *really* loved had been the most incredible experience she had ever had. She would never forget it. Neither would she regret it.

To know true love was a rare thing, she believed. That was why it had been impossible for her to turn her back on it entirely, to not grab the one opportunity she was given to consummate her feelings, even if having that one incredible night with him made her grieve over all the coming nights—and years—when she would never know his touch again.

Marina felt the tears come then. She lifted her face and let the water wash them away before she ended up with great puffy red eyes. There were too many intuitive people around Winterborne Hall for her to go down to breakfast looking as if she'd been crying.

It was while she was under the shower and had moved on to shampooing her hair that Marina suddenly remembered her hairpins, scattered all over the floor by the bed in James's bedroom.

She didn't know what to do. James was certain not to see them. Men like him, who had nothing to do with housework, would never notice a few hairpins lying on the carpet. But a housemaid would. And so would Mildred. They were very distinctive-looking pins, especially made for putting up long hair. Two and two would soon make four in the mind of whoever found them.

Marina knew she could not bear to go through this day fearing she was being looked at, and sniggered over, and pitied.

She had no alternative but to go and get them.

She dressed quickly, in the jeans and white shirt she'd worn over on the plane. She hadn't come with a whole swag of clothes for cooler weather and had little choice.

It was just going on eight by the time she was ready for her rescue mission. Drying her hair had taken some time, but she didn't want to waltz around the house at this hour with dripping locks. It would look suspicious. This way, if she ran into anyone in the hallways, she could say she was an early riser and was going for a walk.

Unfortunately James's room was not situated between her room and the staircase which led downstairs. Hopefully, being Sunday morning, not too many people would be up and about yet. She wasn't expected down to breakfast till nine, James having made this arrangement with Talbot over dinner the night before.

Rebecca was a worry. Children were notorious early risers. Then there was Mildred, who no doubt was of the old school who got up at the crack of dawn. Still, the housekeeper was more likely to already be downstairs. Or in church, with a bit of luck.

A peep out of the bedroom door showed an empty

hallway. Marina scooped in one last steadying breath, then made a determined dash in the direction of James's room, hurrying along the wide polished and carpeted corridors, not stopping on the way to admire any of the gilt-framed portraits and landscapes as she'd done during her tour the previous day.

Once in front of James's solid wooden door she knocked, before fear and panic got the better of her.

When Talbot opened the door, she almost died.

'Yes, miss?' he said, without turning a hair, as though it was perfectly normal for breathless ladies to call upon the Lord of the Manor at eight in the morning.

'I...er...I was hoping to have a brief word with James. Is he...er...in?'

'His Lordship is in the shower. Can I help you with anything, perhaps?'

'No. No, I don't think so.' She glanced past the butler and into the room, trying to see if the pins were still on the floor. The bed, she could see with a sinking heart, was already made. A tray with a silver coffee service and a newspaper was on the bedside table nearest the door—the same bedside table which the night before had held much more intimate items. 'Er...what time did James say breakfast was last night?'

'Nine, miss.' The butler frowned ever so slightly, then gave a small knowing nod, rather reminiscent of Henry's body language. 'Just one moment, miss,' he said, and disappeared for a few seconds before reappearing and holding out his hand. 'I think, perhaps, these are yours.'

She took the hairpins and wished with all her heart that the polished wooden floor would open up and swallow her.

'I won't mention finding them to His Lordship, miss,' Talbot added, without a hint of conspiracy and totally ignoring her wild blush. 'Or your little visit here this morning. It would only upset him.'

Marina was taken aback. She blinked, then glared at the butler through her own distress.

Well, we wouldn't want that, would we? scorned that brutally honest side of hers, which responded rather badly to hypocrisy and double standards. *To hell with your feelings, Miss Marina, as long as we don't upset His Lordship!*

'Thanks a million,' she snapped, and, whirling, she stalked off, the pins clenched in an angry fist.

What a first-class idiot she was to ever hope that what they'd shared last night might mean something special to James! Okay, so he might not love her as she loved him, but it was galling to find out she was probably one in a long line of ladies who'd left pins behind in his bedroom. Or panties. Or whole damned negligées!

As for Talbot—there were no flies on *him*! Clearly James had trained him better than Henry! Talbot probably had a whole cupboard full of ladies' leftovers somewhere! No doubt he'd even prepared the room for His Lordship last night beforehand, delicately leaving behind a ready supply of condoms in case His Lordship had an unfortunate slip of memory.

Can't have the Winterborne blood being contaminated in any way, can we? Can't go letting *common* flesh get too close to the purer strains. After all, commoners might have unspeakable diseases. Or, worse, they might actually *breed*!

Marina had worked herself up to a good head of steam by breakfast time. But once Rebecca joined her on the stairs, holding her hand and chattering away like the happy little girl she was, Marina resolved to put her bad temper aside. What would be the point in spoiling the day for Rebecca by being cranky? Or in spoiling the day for herself? She'd known the score, hadn't she?

But it was infinitely hard to hold her tongue when James came downstairs in a darkly brooding mood. He presented himself briefly in the morning room, saying he wouldn't be having any breakfast and that he'd already had coffee in his room. He then disappeared into his study with the excuse that he had estate business to attend to while he was down.

A most put-out Marina was left to entertain Rebecca, who didn't seem to mind. If Marina hadn't liked the child so much she might have gone and given James a piece of her mind. How dared he treat her so shabbily? As it was, she set to giving the little girl some quality time while they could be together. After all, Rebecca had to go back to the hospital that afternoon.

'I don't want you to ever go back home, Marina,'

the child said with touching sincerity, over the morning tea party they were having in the gazebo. 'Can't
you stay longer?'

'I'm afraid not, sweetie. I really must be going
home. Oh, dear!' she exclaimed as a thought struck.

'What is it?'

'I just realised. I...I haven't rung home to let them
know I'm catching the next plane. I wonder what time
it is in Sydney? I think there's ten hours' difference,
which would make it nine at night. I'll have to go
back to the house and ring straight away, Rebecca.
You'd best come with me.'

'Oh, do I have to?'

Marina had no intention of leaving the seven-
year-old unattended next to a lake. 'Yes, you do,' she
insisted. 'It'll only be for a few minutes. Come on.'

'Oh, all right. I'll go and talk to Mildred.'

Mildred directed Marina to James's study door,
then walked off with her charge already talking fifty
to the dozen. Marina knocked, and entered after a
brusque, 'Come in.'

James was indeed sitting behind a desk. But he
wasn't working. He was leaning back in a large wing-
backed leather chair and seemed to be contemplating
his shoes, which were propped up on the leather-
topped desk.

He's been avoiding me, Marina realised.

His feet dropped to the floor at her entrance, but
that wasn't as far as her heart had dropped. He
snapped forward, clearly agitated by her sudden appearance. 'I thought you were Talbot,' he said.

'No, it's just me,' she retorted coldly. 'Last night's lay.'

His eyes showed shock at her words. *And* her tone.

'I have to ring Sydney,' she went on curtly. 'I need to tell Shane to meet the following day's plane. Mildred said I could use the phone in the hall, but I'm funny about things like using other people's phones for long-distance calls. I worry about the money it's costing.

'Silly me!' She smirked at his still shocked face. 'I should have realised money means nothing to men like you. Sorry for interrupting your work. I'll just trundle on back the way I came and use the phone in the lower hallway, like Mildred said.

'Don't worry. I'll soon get the hang of doing in Rome as the Romans do. It's just that I'm not used to creeping into a gentleman's bedroom in the dead of night. I'm not used to a gentleman's gentleman secretly handing me my hairpins in the morning like it was the most normal thing in the world. And I'm certainly not used to my lovers—as pathetically few as they have been—treating me the next morning like I have a contagious disease. As I said. Silly me!'

She spun on her heels to leave, and would have done so if he hadn't grabbed her from behind, pulling her back against him and kicking the door shut with his foot. With an amazing burst of strength she wrenched out of his hold and whirled, her hand slicing across his face with incredible force. The sound of it striking his cheek was like the crack of a bull whip.

She stared, stunned, as the perfect imprint of her hand flared against his skin.

'Oh!' she cried, then stared down at her own stinging hand. She might have burst into tears if she hadn't been so appalled.

James just stood there, his hand lifting slowly to trace the red welts as they rose. 'Remind me not to grab you too often,' he said drily.

'James, I'm sorry!' she blurted out.

'Don't be,' he said. 'I dare say I deserved it. And it's I who am sorry. I didn't stop to think how my mood this morning might appear to you. Lords don't often have to think of others, although I honestly do try to.'

Which he did, she knew. She'd seen the evidence of his thoughtfulness. With William. And Henry. And Rebecca.

'You can make your call in here,' he said, and pointed to the phone on the desk. 'I think I'd best go and put a cold compress on this.'

Marina groaned once he'd left the room. She felt bitterly ashamed of herself. He hadn't made false promises to her. He hadn't treated her that badly. She'd had no right to hit him. She was acting like a melodramatic fool!

Sighing, she walked slowly over to pick up the receiver, having to stop and think at length before remembering the overseas codes and dialling.

Shane answered fairly quickly.

'Yep?' he said succinctly.

'Shane, it's Marina.'

'About time, too, madam. I was beginning to think you'd forgotten me.'

'Of course I haven't forgotten you,' she said carefully. She had no intention of breaking up with him over the phone and thousands of miles away. To do so would be cruel, and Shane didn't deserve that. 'The thing is, Shane, today's plane was overbooked and they've asked me to delay my flight till tomorrow.'

'What? With a first-class seat? You just damned well tell them that's not on. Insist on the Sunday flight.'

Marina sighed. 'I can't do that, Shane.'

'Women!' he scorned. 'How do you ever think you're going to get on in this world if you don't insist on your rights? Your mother would have told them what for, Marina. She was one tough lady. Still, I guess the airline pays for everything when this happens, don't they? But don't let them put you in some second-class joint tonight. Insist on a five-star hotel, with taxis to and fro.'

'I'm staying the extra night at His Lordship's apartment in London,' she explained. 'It's in Mayfair. And his car will take me to the airport.'

'My, my, how toffy! So what's the old geezer like, eh?'

The old geezer walked in at that point and stood there, watching her. Marina was somewhat relieved to see his cheek had returned to normal.

'He's very nice,' she murmured.

'And very rich.' Shane sounded envious. 'Has he

given you a gift in appreciation of your generosity in going over there?'

'Not exactly.'

'What do you mean by not exactly?'

'Well, he *has* put all he owns at my disposal,' she said, her chin lifting as their eyes met across the room. 'And that's been very…memorable.'

'Pigs! The least he could have done was give you something personal.'

'I must go, Shane. This is costing a fortune. Don't forget to meet the plane.'

'See yuh.'

She hung up and battled to stop her chin from quivering.

'You're not still going to marry him, are you?' James asked in a disbelieving voice.

She laughed the threatened tears away. But it was not a nice laugh. ''You're not still going to marry Lady Tiffany, are you?'' she shot straight back.

'But you don't *love* him,' he went on, as if he hadn't heard her counter-argument.

'And you don't love *her*!' she cried, and threw her arms up in the air at his obtuseness. 'For pity's sake, face it, James. Whether you love *me* or not is immaterial. You don't love *her*. If you did, you would have made love to her by now. Nothing would have stopped you. Not honour, conscience or some stupid sacred duty to her brother!

'You're a passionate man. For you, love and sex will never be separated. You might like and admire her. You might feel responsible for her. You might wish to protect and cherish her. But you absolutely do not love—'

A loud 'ahem' in the open doorway behind James stopped Marina in her tracks. It was the inimitable Talbot, doing a perfect imitation of Henry at his most formal.

'I'm sorry to interrupt, My Lord. But you have a visitor.'

James turned slowly. Stiffly. 'A visitor?'

'Yes, My Lord. Lady Tiffany.'

Marina threw a shocked James an equally shocked look.

'Lady Tiffany?' he echoed, his voice taut.

'Yes, My Lord. She's waiting for you in the drawing room. She wishes to see you…alone.'

There was a moment's fraught silence.

'Please tell Lady Tiffany that I will be along shortly.'

'Yes, My Lord.' The butler gave the minutest of bows and was gone.

Marina had to admire the swift way James had composed himself. But what on earth was Tiffany doing back in England a day earlier than expected? And why had she hot-footed it straight down *here*?

Her actions smacked of something suspicious. Marina wondered now if she had been told something about herself and James. Had there been some gossip which had led to that phone call on Friday about her having second thoughts?

Marina recalled the media had snapped more than a few shots of her and James together the Wednesday he'd brought her home from the hospital, one with his arm around her waist. It had been in all the morning papers. Maybe someone had also seen them together at the theatre and had hurried to inform Tiffany. People could be dreadful mischief-makers.

Another more horrible thought intruded.

'James, surely Henry would not have—?'

'No,' he broke in curtly. 'Henry would *not* have.' He came forward and took her by the shoulders, holding her firmly and forcing her to look him square in the eye. 'Before I see what Tiffany wants,' he ground out, 'tell me one thing. What was behind your tirade a minute ago? Dare I hope you really, truly love me, Marina? Or was there some other reason for it?'

'I...I...'

'Don't lie to me. I need to know the truth.'

Hope filled her heart at his passionately urgent demand. 'Yes,' she told him. 'Yes, I do love you. Really. Truly.'

'Dear God, why didn't you say so last night?'

'Why didn't *I*? Why didn't *you*?'

He looked bewildered. 'How could I, when I thought you were leaving me to go back to Australia, that all I could have with you was just the one night?'

Her breath caught. 'I...I only said that because I was so sure you didn't really love me, that all you wanted was sex.'

'Ahh.' He sighed deeply, then smiled the widest, most satisfied smile. 'Stay here, my love. I'll try not to be too long.'

Marina watched him stride out of the room, her heart already racing along with her mind.

His love…

He'd called her his love.

He loved her. He really, truly loved her—loved her more than he'd ever loved Tiffany.

Armed with that knowledge, Marina knew she would go to the ends of the earth for him now. He would never have to live without her. Never, for as long as they lived!

CHAPTER THIRTEEN

MARINA was pacing impatiently around the room when Talbot appeared in the doorway.

'His Lordship would like you to join him and Lady Tiffany in the drawing room, miss,' the butler announced. 'It's the second door along on your—'

'Yes, yes, Talbot,' she broke in agitatedly. 'I know where it is. Thank you.'

Talbot disappeared and Marina sucked in several steadying breaths. But to no avail. She was suddenly besieged by nerves, and the most undermining thoughts.

Why hadn't James come back to get her himself? Had Tiffany dashed straight home from Italy after the wedding because she regretted her phone call the other day? Was she at this very moment begging James's forgiveness, telling him she loved him and still wanted to marry him? Had he taken one look at her perfectly matched self and decided he could not possibly throw away the life he had planned with her in favour of a working-class Aussie girl he'd only just met?

Marina knew she was being ridiculously negative, but it was still with great reluctance that she stepped out into the hallway and headed towards the drawing room.

During her grand tour the previous day, Marina had thought the drawing room the most welcoming room in the house. The wallpaper was a soft green, with white flowers strewn across it. The drapes at the tall windows were gold and the carpet a toning pattern. The furniture, which was arranged in cosy groups, consisted of armchairs covered in green and gold brocade and various mahogany side-tables on which sat vases of fresh flowers picked from the gardens.

The whole room had a warm and friendly look.

But Marina felt anything but warm at that moment. Her stomach churned as she reached the drawing room doorway, then contracted at the sight before her eyes. James was standing in front of the fireplace, his arms around Tiffany. She had her head on his chest and she was weeping. Was that good news or bad?

'Don't cry, Tiffany, love,' James was saying in soothing tones. 'There's no reason to cry now, is there? You've done nothing to be ashamed of or feel guilty over. You're one of the sweetest, nicest girls I've ever known. And I still love you dearly. Don't distress yourself so. This is not the end of the world.'

Marina must have made some sound, for James glanced up and smiled an apologetic smile at her.

'Sorry to send Talbot for you,' he told her gently, 'but Tiffany was upset, as you can see. Though not about what you might be thinking,' he added. 'I haven't had the opportunity to explain about us. Tiffany has been telling me about this man she met in Italy. And fell in love with...'

Marina's eyebrows shot up as her heart leapt with a combination of shock and delight.

Lady Tiffany, who was looking beautiful and fragile in a pale blue dress, drew back from James's arms and shot Marina a confused look. 'Us?' she repeated, glancing from Marina back to James.

'Yes, Tiffany, *us*,' he confessed firmly. 'Marina and myself. Come over here, darling,' he said, and stretched out a beckoning arm towards her.

Marina's insides were trembling as she walked into its welcoming warmth, all her nerves and doubts disappearing as James gathered her to his side.

'We fell in love with each other this past week,' he told Tiffany gently. 'We didn't mean for it to happen any more than you meant to fall in love with your Italian. We tried to fight our feelings, but in the end fate conspired against us and we... Well I have to confess that our relationship has progressed beyond the platonic.'

Tiffany was definitely looking a little shell-shocked, but not at all shattered.

'But I want you to know,' Marina added, 'that till you rang James on Friday he was a perfect gentleman—and fiancé—in every way.'

'I'm quite sure he was,' Tiffany agreed sincerely, then smiled up at him. 'Oh, James, this is such wonderful news. You've made me feel so much better! There I was, terrified that along with losing your good opinion of me I might have broken your heart. But I can see that it is in very safe hands indeed. I could not hope for you to find someone any sweeter than

Marina, here.' And she came forward and kissed Marina on the cheek.

'And what a lucky girl you are too, Marina,' Tiffany continued. 'To have a man like James fall in love with you. I admire him more than any man I know. To be honest, I have hero-worshipped him since I was a little girl.'

'Come now, Tiffany,' James muttered. 'Don't go embarrassing me.'

'What is embarrassing about my saying I have always loved you? For I have. And I still do. But I see now it is not the sort of love a wife should have for her husband. Just as the love you have for me is not the sort of love a husband should have for a wife.'

'Tiffany, I—'

'No, no, James, let me finish. I think Marina should hear this too.'

Marina was all ears. She had never heard anything she wanted to hear more.

'I know about the solemn promise you made to Peter, how you vowed to look after me if ever anything happened to him. That was why you asked me to marry you in the first place, wasn't it? Because you thought I needed you by my side to protect me from this world. And I can understand why. I have been such a child. About everything. But I think I'm on the way to growing up a bit now.

'My Italian taught me in a single hour what twenty-one years of being the naive child of my hopelessly old-fashioned and starchily staid parents could never teach me. What true love was all about. What desire was. And passion!'

'Tiffany!' James exclaimed, shock in his voice. 'You haven't? You didn't? Not after one miserable hour with a man you'd just met?'

'Oh, dearest James, of course not. I couldn't change the habits of a lifetime that quickly. But I wanted to. Oh, how I wanted to. You and Marina must know what that is like, being in love yourselves.'

James was not going to be so easily mollified. Clearly he was also not about to forget that promise to Tiffany's brother. 'That's all very well, but who *is* this man? Where did you meet him? Does he love you back?'

Tiffany's smile made her whole face light up. 'He said he did. A hundred times. Oh, James, he is so wonderful. And so handsome. And so...so...'

'Sexy?' Marina inserted mischievously.

Tiffany's high colour and slightly flustered state transformed her from her usual cool beauty to a creature of startling sensuality. Her Italian lover might not yet have taken her virginity, but he'd certainly given her innocence a nudge.

'Yes, *very* sexy,' she admitted, and blushed even more furiously.

'But can he look after you?' James demanded to know. 'Has he a job? He doesn't know you're from a titled family, does he?'

Marina could only smile at this very male trait of looking first to financial matters. But she was glad James didn't seem to notice the change in the girl. He must truly love *her* not to be affected by Tiffany's blossoming sexuality.

'James, don't badger the girl!' Marina protested. 'When are you going to see your Italian again, Tiffany?'

'He'll be in London next week,' she said excitedly. 'His family are in fashion. The Ferruccis. You must have heard of them. They own an exclusive label, with boutiques all over the world, so I don't think you have to worry about Marco being a gold-digger, James, dear.

'Besides, we Ravensbrooks don't have that much money left anyway. My father's already frittered away most of the family's fortunes. Why do you think I have a job as a tour guide over at Bellham Castle? Any man marrying me certainly won't be marrying me for my money!'

James frowned. 'He's asked you to marry him already?'

'No, of course not. But he will,' she said, with all the confidence of the young and inexperienced.

Marina was not about to disillusion her by saying that men didn't always ask the girls they said they loved to marry them. They *made* love to them. But that was a different matter entirely.

Marina's thoughts suddenly struck closer to home. James claimed he loved her—and she really didn't doubt that—but his claim hadn't been accompanied by an offer of marriage. Of course he'd hardly had the opportunity, but maybe he never would. Maybe his loving her was not going to be enough to take them to the altar together. Not in *his* world.

A knot of immediate tension formed in Marina's stomach. Was it all too good to be true?

Tiffany stayed a little while longer, chattering away about her gorgeous Italian, who had been a guest at one of the pre-wedding parties and then at the wedding itself, where he hadn't minded her purple bridesmaid dress at all. Probably because his family's bridal boutique in Rome had provided all the clothes for the wedding party.

He wasn't a relative of the bride and groom. Or a personal friend. In fact the bride and groom hadn't been aware of his true identity. To them he'd been merely the man from the bridal boutique who was contacted when one of the dresses hadn't shown up.

The bride's mother had been so impressed with his helpfulness and charm that she had impulsively invited him to both the pre-wedding party that night and the wedding itself. It was Tiffany who was to later find out he was one of the famed Ferruccis, although he had modestly declined her wish to tell all and sundry. He'd said he was enjoying being treated like a nobody.

'I have heard the name Ferrucci,' James said, still not sounding happy. 'But I know nothing of the family. I'm also not sure your folks will be happy with your getting mixed up with some Italian, Tiffany.'

'They'll have to like it or lump it, I'm afraid. I'll be twenty-one next month. I think that's old enough to make my own decisions, don't you?'

Personally, Marina thought twenty-one was still awfully young. She'd been a right ninny at twenty-one.

And you're still a ninny, that perverse voice piped up. *Thinking that the Earl of Winterborne was going to marry you!*

'I'd better be going,' Tiffany said. 'But before I do I want to tell you how happy I am for you both. I think you're much better suited to James than me, Marina. You'll be able to stand up to him. And you're nice and tall as well. James always rather overawed me a bit.'

'And your Italian doesn't overawe you?' James asked.

Tiffany's laugh was a little self-conscious. 'Oh, yes, he does. Terribly. But in a different and rather delicious way. It…it's hard to explain,'

Marina knew exactly what Tiffany meant.

'You be careful with this Italian fellow, Tiffany,' James warned. 'Don't rush into things. Men of his ilk are used to girls coming across without their having to promise them anything.'

'Oh, Marco's not like that,' Tiffany denied. 'He's very passionate, but very sincere. He said he's prepared to wait for me for for ever, if necessary. But I don't think he'll have to wait as long as that.' And she winked at them both.

When James scowled, Tiffany laughed. 'Do stop worrying, James. I promise I won't do anything *you* wouldn't do with Marina. Now I simply must go. Walk me to the car, will you?'

They did, and waved her off. But once the car was out of sight Marina turned to him and voiced the mounting worry in her mind.

'Interesting observation about the male gender you made just then,' she began, matter-of-factly, even though she felt nauseous inside. 'So tell me—are you going to prove to be a man of that ilk you spoke of, who expects a girl to come across without him promising her anything? Is your so-called love for me just words, or are you going to put a decent proposal where your mouth is?'

'Ahh,' he said. 'Trust you to cut straight to the crux of the matter.'

'It's the nature of the beast,' she agreed, rather tartly. 'Well, James? Are you going to ask me to marry you or not? Because if you're not, then don't expect a repeat performance of last night. For all his miserliness, Shane at least gave me an engagement ring in exchange for my favours in bed!'

James glared at her for a moment, then took her arm and started propelling her down the front steps.

'What? Where are you taking me? Take your hands off me and just answer the question, damn you!'

'I will, when I'm good and ready,' he said curtly. 'Now, do please shut that very loud mouth of yours for a few miserable seconds, will you? I do not want William, who is just over there washing the car, knowing my private business.'

'No kidding?' she mocked. 'Since when do the aristocracy care about their staff knowing their private business? Talbot already knows exactly what went on in your room last night, and I'll warrant William has a pretty good idea too!'

'Be quiet, woman, or by God I'll make more noise than you—and in a way that will have William and the rest of the household scandalised for a decade!'

'Why, you're nothing but a bully!' she protested as he shepherded her across the lawn and down to the boatshed on the edge of the lake. Once there, he wrapped a solid arm around her waist, opened the door, hoisted her off her feet and carried her inside, then kicked the door shut behind him.

'Tiffany was right to dump you,' she huffed and puffed. 'Keep this manhandling stuff up and I'll dump you as well.'

'The only one being dumped around here is *you*, Miss Loud Mouth.' And he dropped her onto an old divan in the corner.

She stared up at him as he stripped his sweater over his head and tossed it aside, then began with breathless speed on his trousers. 'You wouldn't!' she gasped, despite her eyes being glued to his body and her pulse-rate accelerating like mad.

'I surely would. So get your gear off as well, my dear future wife.'

'Your what?'

'You heard what I said.'

'Oh!' she cried. 'You mean it? You really mean it?'

'Is this the body of a man who doesn't mean what he says?'

'I mean about us getting married, silly.'

'Of course I mean it. Would a peer of the realm lie to you?' He bent and began attacking the buttons of her shirt. Marina immediately found it hard to concentrate on anything but James's busy fingers, which were unhooking her bra in no time flat.

'Are you saying lords don't lie?' she asked, rather breathlessly.

'Not *this* lord.' The bra gone, he tipped her backwards again and started on the jeans.

'I...I didn't think lords married girls like me.'

He laughed. 'Wherever did you get such a crazy idea? Lords have been known to marry girls a lot more unsuitable than you, my darling Marina. At the turn of the century they went through a phase of marrying chorus girls and actresses—which, believe me, at that time were one rung above a woman of the streets. And then there was my own brother,' James went on as Marina's jeans joined the rest of her clothes. 'He married one of the notorious Bingham girls.'

Marina's head jerked up to stare at him. 'B-Bingham girls?' she croaked.

James took no notice of her horrified expression, his eyes focused on divesting her of her white lace panties while he raved on. 'I suppose you haven't heard of the Binghams all the way over in Australia?

'Their father was Sir Richard Bingham, knighted for his dubious contributions to trade and industry. An ambitious rogue if ever there was one. Still, he was filthy rich and spoiled his daughters rotten. A wild lot, the four of them, with little reputation left by the time they reached puberty. But damned beautiful. I'll give them that. All of them with names beginning with J.

'Joy, my brother's wife, was the youngest—though she was, in fact, a good few years older than Laurence. She had a twin sister who ran off with some stablehand barely a week before she was to marry some aging Italian count. Can't think what her name was. Jasmine? No, that was the eldest. And Janet was the middle girl. Oh, yes. It was Jocelyn.'

Marina gasped.

James pulled her up to his chest, their bodies already fused. 'Yes, I know,' he rasped. 'You take my breath away too. God, I've been thinking of nothing else but this since I woke this morning. Why do you think I was in such a black mood? And why do you think I avoided you like poison? One look at you and I was in agony. On top of that, I thought you were going to leave me and go back to Australia and marry that Shane person.'

'Never,' she choked out, her head whirling.

'We're going to have to get married soon, darling. I can't keep dragging you into boatsheds at inappropriate times. No, don't move. I can't bear it when you move. Oh, God, Marina. Yes, all right, move. Oh, my darling...my darling...'

CHAPTER FOURTEEN

'YOU'RE very quiet,' James said.

They were on their way back to London. William was busy negotiating the Sunday afternoon traffic, bumper to bumper in parts, and Rebecca was sound asleep again, with her head on a cushion in Marina's lap.

'Are you having second thoughts about my proposal?' he asked quietly.

'Are *you*?' she countered.

'Not at all. And if you're worried about being accepted as my wife then don't be. As I said before, that kind of snobbery is dead and gone. You saw the way Mildred reacted when I told her. She was very pleased. And Talbot, I assure you, was more than pleased when I told him. He said you were a lovely lady and wished us every happiness.'

'That's all very well, but what about Henry? I don't think Henry's going to be at *all* pleased.'

'Henry will get used to the idea.'

'Never in a million years. He had your life all mapped out, as the best Earl of Winterborne for a hundred years along with the perfect wife by your side. And it wasn't me,' she finished unhappily.

'I don't think you know Henry as well as you think you do. One of the reasons he was all for Tiffany was

170

because Rebecca liked her so much. Once he realises Rebecca's as crazy about you as I am, then you will have a new champion, I assure you.

'Frankly, I suspect you've already won the old coot over. I recognised the signs all last week. It was just his loyalty and liking for Tiffany that was getting in the way. After I explain Tiffany's change of heart, he'll feel free to grovel at your feet as I'm sure he would like to.'

'Henry, grovel?' Marina exclaimed, though somewhat soothed and flattered by James's assertions. 'Henry would never grovel.'

'Smiling is Henry's way of grovelling. Once he starts smiling at you, you're in.'

'He *did* almost smile at me once,' Marina remarked thoughtfully.

James bestowed a real smile on her. 'See? What did I tell you? You have nothing to worry about.'

Except that I haven't told you yet I'm one of those notorious Bingham girls, Marina thought ruefully.

Rebecca was teary at the hospital.

'You will come back?' she cried, clinging to Marina. 'You really are going to marry Uncle James, aren't you?'

Marina hugged the child to her. 'Wild horses won't keep me away from you, sweetie. Or your Uncle James.' And she glanced up at him through swimming eyes, before hugging the weeping little girl some more. 'I'll be back before you know it. But I have to go home for a little while to sell my mother's house and collect some more clothes. I hardly have a thing to wear, you know, and that's a dreadful thing in a lady's book. Much worse than having no hair.'

'Nothing's worse than having no hair!' Rebecca cried plaintively.

Marina pulled back and wiped the child's tears from her cheeks while she struggled to stop her own. 'You're so right,' she agreed. 'But in no time you'll have more hair than you'll know what to do with. And you'll be so well! Your Uncle James and I are going to take you home as soon as I get back, and you'll never have to come here again. Except perhaps for the odd check-up. But then I'll be with you, and I won't leave you alone for a second.'

Rebecca drew back to raise her big green eyes in the most heart-wrenching way. 'Promise?'

'Cross my heart.' Which she did with her finger.

The child threw her arms around her again. 'Oh, Marina, I love you!'

'And I love you too, darling. Now, let's get you undressed and into bed before I get into trouble from the sister. You wouldn't want to get me into trouble, would you?'

'You're so good with her,' James complimented her on the drive back to the apartment. They were sitting together on the back seat of the Bentley. James's arm was around Marina's shoulder and her cheek was resting on his chest.

Marina bit her bottom lip. She was feeling awfully fragile. What on earth would they do if Rebecca was not better when she came back? What if the transplant hadn't worked? What if the cancer returned with a vengeance?

Suddenly it all became too much for her. 'Oh, James!' she cried, and buried her face in his chest, the tears which had threatened in the hospital room flowing down her cheeks.

'Yes, I know,' he said quietly, holding her close and letting her cry. 'But someone quite wonderful recently told me that we must have faith. We must believe. And I do believe, Marina. I believe it was no rare coincidence that your name popped out of that register. Your being sent over here to save Rebecca's life was a type of destiny. It had been written. I'm not sure how or why, but it was. Rebecca is going to get well. She is going to live as surely as we're going to get married and live happily ever after. I know it.'

'Oh!' Marina gasped, and sat upright, wiping her tears away. 'Oh, I just realised! I didn't before. I was worried you might not be happy about it, but now I see how silly I'm being, because it's me you love, not someone's daughter. Yet being that person's daughter is why this happened, why I was a near perfect match. Oh, James, darling, you're so right. It *was* written. It *was*!'

He cupped her face and stared deep into her eyes. 'Marina, I don't have the foggiest clue what you're talking about.'

'No, of course you don't. And I wouldn't have—yesterday. But today, in the boatshed, you said something and I realised.'

'Realised what?'

'That my being a near perfect match with Rebecca was not a coincidence. You see, I'm not a stranger who just happened to have the right blood and tissue type. I'm a relative!'

'A *relative*?'

'Yes, my mother's maiden name, James, was Bingham! Rebecca's maternal grandmother—Joy Bingham—was my mother's twin sister. My mother was Jocelyn Bingham.'

'Good God!' he exclaimed. But then he laughed. 'Marina, that's just so incredible!'

'Yes, I know,' she said. 'Just think! You ended up with one of the notorious Bingham girls.'

He grinned. 'You mean one of those bad girls who married men for their money?'

'My mother didn't!' Marina defended. 'She married for love!'

'So she did. Just like her darling daughter. You do love me, don't you?' he asked as he gathered her to him once more.

'I love you so much,' she murmured, 'that it's positively indecent.'

'Mmm. Do you think you might sneak upstairs into my room tonight when Henry's asleep? I mean, if you're going to be away for three weeks, I'll need a little something to remember you by.'

'Are you sure I can trust you out of my sight for that long?'

'Are you sure I can trust you back there in sunny Australia with that Shane fellow?'

'Yes.'

'Give me your word.'

'You have it.'

'And you have mine.'

She sighed her contentment and snuggled into him.

'One thing you must learn about us Marsden men,' James told her as he stroked her hair, 'is that we have been notorious rakes down the years, but once we fall in love and marry it's for good. Nothing—and I mean nothing—will ever stop me loving you, Marina. That's the nature of *this* beast.'

'I like the sound of that.'

'We're just turning down the mews.'

Marina sat upright with a swift resurgence of nerves. 'Oh, dear God. Henry!'

James chuckled. 'Don't be afraid of Henry. He's a lamb in wolf's clothing.'

'I...I just want him to approve of me.'

'He *does* approve of you.'

'No, he doesn't. I think he thinks I'm a hussy.'

James grinned. 'You *are* a hussy.'

'And *you're* a rake!'

'See how well matched we are?'

'Oh, you...you...'

He kissed her, then helped her out of the car. William was pretending not to have seen or heard a thing, but Marina thought she saw the corners of his mouth twitching. And his eyes were definitely laughing at them. She found some comfort in that, for at least William approved of her.

Henry was waiting in the foyer to give them a welcome so un-Henry-like that Marina was rendered speechless. He smiled rather smugly at James, then flummoxed Marina by actually hugging her.

'I've just heard the wonderful news,' he announced, drawing back to stand with ramrod straightness once more. 'First from Lady Tiffany, then from Mildred. I can't tell you how delighted I am, My Lord, that everything has worked out so well.'

'Tiffany contacted you?' James asked.

'Yes, My Lord. To reassure me, I think, that she too was happy about the situation. I must admit I *was* relieved. I have always greatly admired Lady Tiffany, but there is something about Miss Marina, here, which is so hard to resist.'

'*Very* hard, Henry.'

'I could see that last week, My Lord. I did feel for you, and the dilemma you were in. I hope you will forgive me,' he went on, looking decidedly sheepish, 'but I…er…engaged in a little subterfuge myself in order to give you a push in the right direction.'

'Really? What subterfuge, Henry?' James asked, frowning.

'Yes, what subterfuge, Henry?' Marina echoed, intrigued.

'The Bentley was not really in for service last Friday night,' he admitted.

James sucked in a sharp breath. 'Are you saying your ordering that limousine was deliberate?'

'I thought you and Miss Marina could do with some time alone together. Away from here, and in more…romantic…surroundings.'

'Henry, you have genuinely shocked me!'

Me too, Marina thought.

'I find that hard to believe, My Lord.' Henry was back to his po-faced best. 'Being your valet over the years has broadened my mind considerably in matters dealing with the opposite sex. I merely thought of what *you* might have done a little while back, when your mind was not clouded by feelings of duty.'

'Yes, well, enough of past history, Henry,' James said briskly. 'I think we should move on to the present. Mildred rang too, you said?'

'Indeed, My Lord. She was beside herself with happiness for you and Miss Marina. She's so looking forward to Winterborne Hall being a family home again, with the patter of little feet to shake some dust off the portraits—especially those lining the staircase.' Henry's eyes twinkled in fond memory. 'Remember how you used to slide down the banister, Jamie-boy?'

Marina stared at Henry. Why, James was right! Henry was just an old fraud, with his stiff upper lip and his stuffy old ways. Underneath that starchy façade he was just a big softie, not to mention a romantic.

'My God, don't go telling Marina things like that, Henry!' James exclaimed, though laughingly. 'I'm already having enough trouble maintaining her respect. Now she not only thinks I'm a rake, but a rascal as well!'

'I think Henry's the rascal,' Marina said, and came forward to reach up and give him a kiss. 'But a lovable rascal.'

Henry actually blushed. It was a sight to behold.

'After James and I are married,' she said, 'whenever we stay at Winterborne Hall you're coming with us, Henry. And not to the gatehouse, either. You will have a room near the nursery. Talbot and Mildred are going to need all the help they can get once I start having babies.'

'But I know nothing about babies, Miss Marina.'

'Then you'll have to learn, Henry. Because I might have to have quite a few. Girls run in my family, and at least one boy is the order of the day, is it not? Now, I think we need one of your excellent pots of coffee, Henry.'

'Yes, Miss Marina.'

Marina gave an exasperated sigh. 'And no more of that Miss Marina stuff, either.'

Henry gave her request some thought before saying, 'Yes, I suppose Miss Marina really won't be appropriate, under the circumstances. All right. Would you like something to eat with your coffee, My Lady?'

Marina groaned. But then she shook her head and laughed helplessly. 'I give up. You both win. I'll be a good Roman.'

'Roman?' Henry repeated blankly. 'I'm sorry, My Lady, but I don't understand.'

Now James laughed. 'Don't even try, Henry. Don't even try. Just lead on to the kitchen.

'I must say I like the thought of our having lots of babies,' he whispered, after Henry had moved off. 'Having Rebecca with me has definitely sparked my fathering instincts. And I don't really mind if you don't have a boy.'

'Well, if I don't, then you can only blame yourself. It's actually the man who determines the sex of the child. But, knowing you, I'll have a boy straight away. In fact, it's quite possible that a little heir and Earl might be already on the way. You didn't use any protection in the boatshed, and today is right in the middle of my cycle.'

'Really?' he said eagerly.

'James Marsden!' she chided. 'Were you trying to make me pregnant on purpose?'

'Er...'

'Oh, James! You are worse than a rascal. You're a...a...'

'A man desperately in love,' he finished for her fiercely. 'Who doesn't want the woman he loves having any reason to change her mind.' He stopped and pulled her to him and kissed her soundly.

'I have only one thing to add at this point in time,' he ground out when he let her come up for air.

'What?' she asked breathlessly.

'I hope Henry goes to bed early.'

'You mean unshockable Henry?' Marina asked, smiling. 'The one who sent us off in that boudoir on wheels? The same Henry who saw you through all your wild years?'

'You're right!' James pronounced, and straightened his spine. 'Henry?' he called out gruffly.

'Yes, My Lord?' came the answer from the kitchen.

'Cancel the coffee. Marina and I are going to bed!'

There was only the minutest of hesitations in answering. 'Very good, My Lord.'

EPILOGUE

MARINA stood next to her husband in the small stone church, built over nine hundred years ago in Norman times, a far cry from St. Paul's Cathedral, where they'd been privileged enough to be married just over nine months previously.

At least I didn't disgrace myself by having a baby *too* soon after the wedding, she thought, smiling. Little Harry hadn't been conceived till after she'd returned from her trip back to Sydney.

It had taken her just on a month to tie things up in Sydney—slightly longer than the three weeks she'd promised James.

Shane hadn't been too broken-hearted when she'd given him his ring back, especially when it had come with the horses and the business name of the riding school. He *had* been shocked for a split second by her announcement she was going to marry the Earl of Winterborne, because he'd imagined James to be an elderly gentleman. When he'd quickly concluded—with smug predictability—that she was marrying for money, Marina had found herself letting him think so. It had soothed Shane's ego somewhat and amused her to death.

In the end Shane had taken out a bank loan on the

strength of his equity in the horses and riding school and purchased the house and property from Marina, which had meant everyone was happy. But the loan and the exchanging of contracts had taken time.

By the time she'd arrived back in London James had been predictably keen to show her his love in more than words, which he had done over the next week with overpowering passion and at odd times. Marina had been breathless at the chances he took. But when the urge overtook James, he could be very forceful. She would never be able to go into his bank building again without blushing madly.

Marina wondered idly whether Harry had been conceived in the lift between the ninth and tenth floors, or on the boardroom table. She rather fancied the latter, which, after all, had been the scene of many a merger. Though none quite so...exciting. Just thinking about it made Marina's heart beat faster.

Little Harry started to cry at that moment, snapping Marina back to the moment at hand. The vicar had started pouring the holy water over his forehead and Harry was not at all impressed.

Henry clucked and cooed the infant back to sweet silence with all the experience of six weeks being Harry's first emergency nanny, and now his godfather.

Marina leant over towards James. 'Henry's got a real knack with Harry, hasn't he?' she whispered.

'You won't be saying that when he starts imbuing him with all those starchy old ideas of his,' he whispered back. 'And when he insists on the boy being sent away to school at the tender age of eight.'

'A lot you know. Henry and I had a little chat the other morning—around two o'clock, it was—and we both decided Harry wasn't going anywhere for a long, long time.'

James sighed. 'Between the two of you, I don't think I'm going to have any say at all in the raising of my own son.'

'You chose his name, didn't you?'

'I chose Henry. And you promptly changed it to Harry.'

'Just to save confusion, old chap,' she said with a public school accent, then grinned up into James's startled face. 'Just being a good Roman.'

'Whatever am I going to do with you, Marina?'

'I'll show you tonight. The doctor's given me the green light.'

She loved the sound of her husband's intake of breath, plus the squeezing of her hand. 'Just in time, too,' he muttered under his breath. 'There are only so many exercises I can do to take my mind off things. Rebecca says I'm beginning to look like Arnold What's-his-name.'

At the mention of Rebecca, Marina's sparkling eyes shifted from Henry and the baby in his arms to the cute little girl standing next to him in the very feminine apple-green dress, her slender hand on the hem of Harry's long white Christening robe. She had grown so pretty, with her once bald head now covered in red-gold curls the exact colour of Marina's. The specialists had given her the all-clear some months back, although they would continue to monitor her for some time to come.

'Look at Rebecca's face,' James whispered when it came to the part where the godparents had to say something. 'She's so proud to be Harry's godmother. It was a lovely idea of yours to ask her, Marina.'

'She's like a *real* little mother to Harry. I've never known a child love another child so much.'

'She told me the other night she wanted you to have at least six babies.'

'Only six? She told me ten!'

'Er...I thought I'd better water the number down a little before you got ideas.'

'Me? Get ideas?'

'Yes, My Lady,' he whispered drily. 'Already you've swept through Winterborne Hall like a whirl-wind, with your radical Aussie ways, changing my normally sensible staff into doting, drooling idiots af-ter your making all of them part-time nannies to Harry! Now what's this I hear about you converting the gatehouse into a pre-school?'

'Well, there isn't one for miles and I rather miss teaching, James. I always did like infants better than older children, and I thought this was a way of killing three birds with one stone.'

'*Three* birds?'

'Yes. It will provide a valuable service for our chil-dren and others in the village. It will prevent my getting teacher's itch. And I'll be able to do something with that monstrosity. Brighten it up a bit. Maybe I'll paint it pink.'

'Pink!'

'Okay, I'll leave the outside up to you and your sandblasters. But inside there's going to be lots of colours. And I'm going to have a garden and playground out the back. What do you think?'

'I think you're marvellous.'

'I mean about the idea, silly.'

'I think it's marvellous too.'

'So I have your approval?'

'Go for your life.'

Her eyes danced up at him as she smothered a laugh.

'What?' he said. 'What did I say?'

'That was a very Aussie expression. You'd better watch it or you won't even be a Roman any more yourself. Now hush up. Henry's frowning at you, Jamie-boy.'

James opened his mouth to protest, then closed it again to smile wryly at his wife.

Marina was smiling herself. With happiness.

Thank you, God, she prayed, despite not having been brought up to be overly religious. But she'd come to have a great respect for the Almighty since he'd answered her other prayers regarding Rebecca.

Thank you for darling little Harry, who is utterly perfect. Thank you for keeping Aunt Jasmine and Aunt

Janet alive till I found them. They are much nicer than I imagined.

She cast a quick, smiling glance over her shoulder at the two handsome ladies a couple of rows back. They were dripping in diamonds and pearls, and both childless widows in their late fifties, after the elderly titled gentlemen they'd married in their twenties had long passed on. Despite being rich beyond belief, they seemed to be genuinely thrilled at meeting up with their long-lost niece and being drawn into such a happy—and more normal—family environment.

Marina's gaze shifted to the left and she exchanged smiles with Tiffany and her gorgeous Italian. They had been married for just on six months and were divinely happy, especially now that Tiffany was expecting.

Sighing her satisfaction with life in general, Marina turned back to face the front and resume her conversation with the Lord.

Thank you for Henry's continuing good health. And Mildred's. And especially Rebecca's. But most of all thank you for my darling husband, who truly does love me for the person I am and not for any other reason.

'Amen,' James said, and Marina's head jerked up to stare at him. Goodness, had he read her mind? Seen into her thoughts? She hoped not. Sometimes her thoughts were not quite fit for a husband's consumption.

'It's over at last,' he explained into her questioning face. 'The christening.'

'Oh.' Her eyes swept over her handsome husband and she thought of all those exercises he'd been doing and how marvellous he was looking.

Fervently she added her last prayer.

And please, Lord, please let Harry sleep right through the night tonight!

JAYNE ANN KRENTZ

Lady's Choice

Travis Sawyer has a plan for revenge. Juliana Grant has a
plan too—she has picked Travis as Mr Right. When
Travis takes over the resort in which Juliana has invested
her money, Juliana takes matters
into her own hands.

*"Jayne Ann Krentz is one of the hottest writers
in romance today."*—USA Today

MIRA®

1-55166-270-1
AVAILABLE FROM MARCH 1998

Catherine Coulter

Afterglow

Chalk-and-cheese lovers Chelsea Lattimer and
David Winter finally find happiness after a series
of disastrous relationships—thanks to their
match-making friends.

Afterglow is a wonderful romantic comedy from
New York Times bestselling author Catherine Coulter.

1-55166-472-0
AVAILABLE FROM MARCH 1998

JANICE KAISER

FAIR GAME

Dana Kirk is a rich and successful woman, but someone
wants to kill her and her teenage daughter. Who hates
her enough to terrorise this single mother? Detective
Mitchell Cross knows she needs help—
his help—to stay alive.

*"...enough plot twists and turns to delight
armchair sleuths"*—Publishers Weekly

1-55166-065-2
AVAILABLE FROM MARCH 1998

SANDRA BROWN

THE THRILL
OF VICTORY

Stevie Corbett's life is on the line, but her fate rides on
keeping the truth a secret. Judd Mackie's job is
to uncover secrets. After dogging Stevie for
years, Judd now has the story of the year.
All he has to do is betray her trust.

"One of fiction's brightest stars!"
—Dallas Morning News

MIRA®

1-55166-025-3
AVAILABLE FROM FEBRUARY 1998

HEATHER GRAHAM POZZESSERE

If looks could kill

Madison wasn't there when her mother was
murdered, but she *saw* it happen. Years later, a
killer is stalking women in Miami and Madison's
nightmare visions have returned. Can FBI agent
Kyle Montgomery catch the serial killer before
Madison becomes his next victim?

"...an incredible storyteller!"—LA Daily News

1-55166-285-X
AVAILABLE FROM FEBRUARY 1998

JoAnn
ROSS

❦ ★ ❦

NO REGRETS

Three sisters torn apart by tragedy each choose a
different path—until fate and one man reunites them.
Only when tragedy strikes again can the surviving
sisters allow themselves to choose happiness—
if they dare pay the price.

"A steamy, fast-paced read."
—Publishers Weekly

1-55166-282-5
AVAILABLE FROM FEBRUARY 1998

"Sorry about that display of temper," Seth apologized.

"Unfortunately you might be treated to more of the same for a while. When her mother left, Sooz was devastated. I'm afraid I spoiled her as a result. Now we're paying the price...I hope you hang in there."

Whenever she and Seth talked one-on-one, Margo felt as if they were the only two people in the world. He'd raised the girl who might be her daughter and, unable to stop herself, she imagined him as her husband.

Thank heaven her more sensible self remembered she wasn't in love with Seth. For one thing, she didn't know him well enough. And, for another, she couldn't afford to be. If she ever decided to pursue the subject of Sooz's parentage, they'd be on opposite sides of the fence. She'd just have to stop wishing he'd touch her every time they were together.

A rueful smile tilted the corners of her mouth. "Please don't feel as if I'm going to abandon you at any moment," she said. "Where Sooz is concerned, I've just begun to fight."

Suzanne Carey is a former reporter and magazine editor who prefers to write romance novels because they add to the sum total of love in the world.

Recent titles by the same author:

THE DADDY PROJECT

BABY
SWAP

BY
SUZANNE CAREY

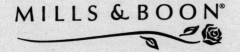

MILLS & BOON®

First published in Great Britain 1998
Harlequin Mills & Boon Limited,
Eton House, 18-24 Paradise Road, Richmond, Surrey TW9 1SR

© Verna Carey 1998

ISBN 0 263 80733 9

Set in Times Roman 10½ on 12 pt.
91-9802-52160 C1

Printed and bound in Great Britain

PROLOGUE

1983

THE tall, redheaded man with blond eyebrows was back. He stood looking through the double-glass pane like an overgrown boy peering through a toy store window, his gaze fastened hungrily on one small, downy head. His child was Baby Girl Danner, according to the pink-and-white card attached to her crib. She'd been in the nursery at Bayless Memorial since the first time Margo had put on her flowery quilted robe and walked down the hall to check on Beth Ann.

Funny, she thought. He's got a new baby and he obviously cares a great deal about her. Yet he looks as unhappy as I feel. Seconds later she conceded he was probably as ecstatic as a lark. He just hid it well. She was projecting her heavy load of conflicting emotions onto him.

Happy. Sad. Frightened. Loving. When it came to her inner woman, God knew, all those feelings and more were churning perilously near the surface. Too frequently these days, they spilled over in the form of tears.

At the moment, happiness was uppermost. Pressing her face against the glass, Margo focused with a rush of maternal affection on the tiny, perfect fingers of

5

Baby Girl Rourke as they fluttered like butterflies' wings at a sudden sound.

"Beth Ann Rourke," she whispered. "You'll never know how much you are wanted."

It was one of life's miracles that, though he'd already been fighting a rare form of cancer at the time of Beth's conception, Jim had given Margo a baby. Now Margo had reciprocated, returning to him one of life's most precious gifts.

Before it was too late.

Jim's cancer was getting worse. Though the doctors tried to hold out hope, Margo could tell they were somewhat discouraged. Little Beth Ann, so pretty and delicate looking now that the deep rosy flush of birth had faded, would be his immortality. His contribution to the next generation. And the one after that.

Unfortunately, he hadn't seen his daughter yet. He'd had to report for chemotherapy at Swedish Hospital's Fred Hutchinson Cancer Research Center the day before Margo's labor pains had started. A public relations staffer at Bayless before going on maternity leave, she'd gone there for the birth because of a sizable employee discount. As a result, they were stuck in separate hospitals a few blocks apart on Seattle's First Hill, sometimes called "Pill Hill" because of its heavy concentration of medical facilities.

Nell Hafner, who was one of Jim's regular nurses at Fred Hutchinson and a neighbor of theirs in the city's Ravenna district, was waiting for Margo when she returned to her room.

"How's my hubby?" Margo asked, anxiety regaining the upper hand. "I phoned him around lunchtime, and he wasn't feeling too well then."

"By the time I went off duty, a little better, I think. He's really anxious to see you and the baby."

Parking her purse on the floor, Nell sank into the squeaky brown leatherette visitor's chair. She'd brought a pen, a clipboard with some sheets of paper attached to it and a couple of paperbound books. The one on top was labeled *Ephimeris*. Both had faded blue covers.

Margo kicked off her slippers and got back into bed. She and Nell had become fast friends during the long months of Jim's treatment and she felt comfortable in her presence. Arranging her unruly dark curls so they wouldn't be crushed flat by leaning against the pillow, she smiled at the older woman. Life went on. You couldn't panic from moment to moment.

CHAPTER ONE

MARGO was tense, her nerves at the breaking point as she waited for private detective Harry Spence to give her the results of his investigation. She'd lost a lot over the past eight years—her husband, Jim in 1984 and, more recently, in 1991, her seven-year-old daughter in a school bus accident. But maybe, if the genetic study she'd allowed Beth Ann to participate in a few weeks before her death was valid, Margo hadn't lost everything. Maybe she still *had* a daughter.

The nationwide study, which would track its subjects for years, sought to determine whether there was an inherited predisposition to the rare form of cancer Jim had. With the slides of Jim's tissue long since frozen for their research, scientists had requested an infinitesimally small sample—a few cells, really—from one of Beth Ann's fingertips. It hadn't seemed much to ask. There'd been a quick prick, followed by smiles and a lollipop for Beth. Incredibly, though, the small act of cooperation had up-ended Margo's world.

As far from the movie stereotype of a gumshoe as it was humanly possible for anyone to be, Harry Spence shuffled some papers. "No guarantees, Mrs. Rourke," he said in his dry, sandpapery voice. "But I may have found what you're looking for. At the time of Beth Ann's birth, there was only one other baby girl of Caucasian ancestry in the Bayless Memorial nursery. She and Beth Ann were born on the same day, six hours and twenty-three minutes apart."

Margo stared. She hadn't expected the facts to be so cut and dried, so easily sorted. If there'd been several possible candidates...

"Her name is Susan Lynn Danner. Her parents were divorced a year and a half ago. She still lives here in Seattle—the Magnolia section, to be precise—with her father, Seth Danner. He's a custom yacht builder, in partnership with his brother."

"And her mother?"

"Remarried and living in Hawaii. According to the court records, she didn't seek custody."

Margo digested the information. Her skin was prickling with little shivers that had nothing to do with the temperature. "What else can you tell me about the child?" she asked. "Is she happy? Well?"

Sympathy flickered in Harry Spence's colorless eyes. "As for 'happy,' Mrs. Rourke, I couldn't say. From what I could tell, she seems healthy enough. However, there *is* something else that might interest you..."

A thousand thoughts competed in Margo's head as the detective explained that Seth Danner had placed an ad for a housekeeper. It had run in the previous Sunday's paper.

"He's looking for somebody to live-in a minimum of five days a week," he said. "Cook, clean, watch over the girl when she comes home from school. I had my secretary phone and pass herself off as a potential applicant. It seems they've had a parade of people in that post since Danner's divorce...most of them unsatisfactory. Currently, an elderly baby-sitter is holding down the fort in the afternoons. Danner's interviewing at his boat yard office. If you went, it's not likely you'd get a look at the child unless he was serious about hiring you.''

He passed a photograph across the desk. Obviously enlarged, it had the grainy texture characteristic of shots taken with high-speed film and a telephoto lens. The face that looked back at Margo from what appeared to be a school playground might have been her own when she was eight or nine years old.

But Beth favored me, she thought, still unwilling to accept the unexpected turn of events. *Not as much as this girl does,* her truthful inner self replied.

Shortly after Beth Ann's accident, the researchers had approached Margo again. To their surprise, the girl's tissue hadn't matched Jim's. As testing was 99.999995 percent accurate, they'd murmured, it wasn't very likely that she was his child. Had paternity ever been in question?

It most definitely had *not,* Margo had assured them. Still, mystified after she'd cooled down, she'd submitted a tissue sample of her own. And the result had been the same. The proteins in Beth's cell coatings hadn't matched hers, either. In their cool, detached way, the researchers had informed her that Beth couldn't possibly have been *her* biological daughter.

The researchers' findings had been quite a shock. If the unthinkable *had* happened and the child she'd borne Jim Rourke had inadvertently been switched for that of another woman, Margo wasn't sure she would be able to make herself believe it. To do so would mean Beth Ann hadn't really been theirs. It would be like losing her all over again.

Yet, what if the baby she'd carried beneath her heart for nine long months was living just a few miles away, growing up and celebrating birthday after birthday without her? What would she do? How could she find out if the girl Harry Spence had photographed really had belonged to her and her dead husband? She could hardly confront the man Susan Danner probably called Daddy and demand that his daughter's tissue be tested.

Meeting the child would probably be the strangest thing of all. Despite the distinct family resemblance, the face that looked up at her from the grainy print— impish, vulnerable, a bit strong-willed—was that of a stranger. If she *was* Margo's, except for the nine months of her gestation and the actual process of birth, they had no history together.

"Do you have an address?" she asked.

Harry Spence scribbled something on a piece of paper and handed it to her. His expression clearly stated that, while he disapproved of surveillance or any other facet of detective work being conducted by unlicensed individuals, it was entirely her own affair what she chose to do with it.

Not to be swayed, Margo folded the slip of paper and put it in her purse. "Were you able to find out anything at the hospital that might lead you to believe a switch actually occurred?" she asked.

The detective shook his head. "The records appeared to be in order, Mrs. Rourke. I'm sorry."

With a sigh, Margo got out her checkbook. "How much do I owe you?"

As she wrote out the stated fee, a strong desire to confirm or disprove the possibility that Susan Danner might be her baby drew up battle lines against the reluctance in her heart.

Margo had left the back door unlocked. Entering her Ravenna area craftsman-style bungalow through the kitchen door as she usually did, Nell found her sitting in a darkened living room. Perhaps because Nell dealt with distraught people every day, she knew better than to switch on a lamp.

"For heaven's sake, hon," she exclaimed, plunking herself down on the sofa and putting one arm about Margo's shoulders. "What's wrong? It's not like you to mope around this way."

There was a small silence. "I saw the detective this afternoon," Margo admitted at last.

Nell rolled her eyes. "Oh, geez. I forgot."

The two of them sat there for a moment, not saying anything further. Then Nell asked, "Have you eaten?"

Margo shook her head.

"Let me fix you something."

"I'm not very hungry."

"Well, *I* am." Giving her a squeeze, Nell took off her raincoat and strode back into the kitchen. Additional light seeped into Margo's sanctuary via the dining room. Before long the aroma of tomato soup and toasted cheese sandwiches filled the air.

It turned out that Margo was hungry after all. "I

don't know what I'd do without you, Nell,'' she maintained as they settled at the small table in the breakfast nook.

Grayer than she'd been when Beth Ann was born but still pink-cheeked and hearty, Nell beamed. A naturally caring person, she'd been Margo's staunchest ally during crisis after crisis with Jim, and had fussed over Beth Ann as if the child had been her own granddaughter. "That goes double,'' she replied.

"You have Bert.''

"Yeah, well. He's okay, I guess.'' Long divorced, Nell "kept company'' with a local widower. But to date she hadn't expressed much interest in marrying him. "Want to tell me what the detective said?'' she asked.

By now Margo was ready to talk. Quickly she outlined the essentials of her meeting with Harry Spence, including Seth Danner's advertisement for a housekeeper.

"I'm not sure what I want to do about it,'' she confessed with the soul weariness of someone who'd already wrestled with the problem for hours. "I know it's probably ill-advised, and might result in heartbreak. But I'm thinking of calling him…''

Nell was suddenly very quiet. "Sure you want to do that?'' she asked skeptically.

"Surely you can understand that I have to *see* her…for Jim's sake as well as my own.''

Nell's softening expression acknowledged that she did. "And if you think she's your daughter?'' she prodded. "Or aren't sure? What then?''

"I might take the position if it's offered to me. It

wouldn't have to be forever...just a couple of months.''

''You'd actually give up your desktop publishing business to keep house for someone, now that you're doing so well?''

Margo shrugged. ''In my line of work, you tend to have as much or as little business as you're willing to go after. I could cut back. Turn out the essential stuff on weekends. But that isn't the point, is it? You think I should let sleeping dogs lie. That I'd be making a big mistake.''

Nell was silent for a moment. ''Not a mistake, hon,'' she said at last. ''More like a step into shark-filled waters. If you decide to take it, there'll be great risk attached, as well as a great potential reward.''

''Do you have any advice to offer?'' Margo asked.

''Just to tread carefully,'' Nell replied. ''There are three lives at stake here...four, if you count the girl's mother's.''

Margo sighed. Nell was right, of course. The action she was contemplating really did involve a big emotional risk for everyone concerned.

''I plan to be careful,'' she reassured her friend. ''Don't think I haven't agonized over this. But I have to check on her, don't you see? Even if the whole thing's true and she *is* my daughter, I might never seek custody, or breathe a word of it to anyone. I just have to find out if she's happy, well cared for, and...'' She paused, struggling for control. ''I want to make sure...that she's truly loved.''

Seth Danner had a nice telephone voice—warm, deep and resonant. He sounded like a big, thoroughly masculine man, with a well-developed sense of who he was and what he was doing in the world. As a yacht builder, Margo guessed, he'd be casual, muscular and outdoorsy. She sensed vitality and drive, a determination to master circumstances rather than let them master him.

"Can you tell me a little bit about your background, Mrs. Rourke?" he asked. "For instance, have you worked in this capacity before? Particularly where there's a child concerned?"

Usually quite adept at ad-libbing, Margo found she wasn't sure what to say. "I...yes," she answered. "That is, not exactly. But..."

The wariness Seth Danner had acquired in dealing with his parade of housekeepers quickly became evident. "Mind explaining yourself?" he inquired, polite but terse.

Truth was definitely called for. Or the interview would be over. "I'm a widow," she replied. "My only child, a daughter, died last year. I'm very good at caring for a home and looking after a little girl. It's just that I haven't done it for a salary before."

If it occurred to him that she might be trying to fill a void in her own life by seeking employment with him, he didn't say so. Nor did he give her any other clue to his thoughts. Instead, he excused himself for a moment to instruct someone about how he wanted something done. He was patient but definitive—clearly the boss of his operation.

Apparently something in her words had hit a positive note. "I'd really like to find someone as quickly as possible, Mrs. Rourke," he said, coming back on the line. "I'm interviewing at the boat yard. That's Danner Yachts, Inc. We're situated on the north shore of Lake Union, at the foot of the Aurora Avenue overpass. Could you come by tomorrow? Or, better still, this afternoon? With the names of several references?"

It was now or never. Margo decided to take the plunge. "Actually, this afternoon would be convenient," she said.

For the interview, Margo dressed conservatively in a heather-gray turtleneck, matching slim wool skirt and flat shoes that added nothing to her five foot three inch height. But she couldn't seem to stifle the flamboyant side of her nature altogether. Unaware of the pizzazz they created, she fastened on a chunky gold necklace and topped her somber outfit with a swingy, bright gold, three-quarter-length wool coat that made a splash of color against the chilly, rain-soaked gloom.

As she parked her vintage M.G. Midget in the cindered lot outside Danner Yachts, Inc., a steady stream of cars, trucks and giant sixteen-wheelers roared across the soaring overpass. The lake was unpolished pewter, stippled by rain. Beyond the boatworks' roof, a forest of slender, white masts pierced the drizzle, swaying gently. In the distance a tug's horn bleated mournfully.

Not stopping to open her umbrella because she didn't want to risk having the time to pause and reflect, Margo ran the short distance from her parking space to a low annex marked Office. The reception area featured threadbare carpet, framed photographs of yachts and a cheerful pot of rust-colored mums.

"May I help you?" a secretary asked.

Margo swallowed. "I'm here to see Seth Danner."

The woman gave her a friendly smile just as the phone started to ring. "He's in the finishing shed... through that door and down the stairs," she said, reaching for the receiver. "There are cables all over the place...don't forget to watch your step!"

A bit apprehensively, Margo went in search of the man who might be raising her child. As she descended the rickety staircase, she couldn't help staring at the cavernous, unfamiliar surroundings in which she found herself. The boatworks was vast, much larger than she'd expected. Its high, corrugated fiberglass roof, which admitted a filtered, grayish light, began to ping gently when the rain came down a little harder.

At one end, huge doors opened to the marine ways, where some men were testing a medium-sized yacht with gasoline engines. Margo's nostrils flared at the mingled scents of motor oil, paint fumes and solvent. Somewhere a generator chugged steadily. Sanders whined in counterpoint to the creaking of an overhead crane's massive winches and the voices of men calling back and forth as they worked.

A laborer of about twenty or so, with a purple cap and spray paint on his dungarees, directed her to the finishing shed. Bulking in its slip was a large yacht in the final stages of completion. Margo guessed it to be at least sixty-five feet in length.

She didn't notice the tall, redheaded man in jeans and a nubby gray sweater right away. But he noticed her.

Who's that? Seth wondered, with more than casual interest. Not your typical yacht customer, that's for sure. I'll bet she's lost. She was just the sort of woman who appealed to him, though: slender, on the petite side, with a halo of naturally curly dark hair that had contracted to ringlets from all the humidity. He watched her closely; her movements were like quicksilver.

As Margo reached the finishing shed's lower level, a phone rang. One of the workers answered it. "Mrs. Rourke is here for her appointment," she shouted out.

Seth felt a lurch of surprise. It was quickly followed by the odd sense that somehow their meeting had been predestined. A fairly logical man, he decided he must be losing his grip.

"I'm Seth Danner," he announced, stepping forward to meet her. "Thanks for coming over."

He was about six foot two, and he had blond eyebrows. His tousled red-gold hair looked as if it had been raked back carelessly from his forehead. The sights, sounds and aromas of the shed seemed to recede as he held out one big, neatly manicured hand and Margo took it. I *know* him from somewhere, she thought as she gazed up at his broad shoulders and ruggedly handsome features. She could almost feel the vibrations of some past meeting connecting them.

Her fingers felt delicate wrapped in his. "Nice meeting you," she said.

For a moment, they just continued to look at each other.

"Let's go back upstairs to my office," Seth suggested, breaking the silence. "You'll be more comfortable there."

Seth's office had the same worn carpet as the reception area and a big, comfortable looking desk littered with blueprints and paperwork. Standing a little too close for comfort, he offered to take her coat.

Reluctantly, because she didn't expect to be staying long, she shrugged it off, revealing a slim but shapely figure. Probably the best policy would be to forge straight ahead—get things over with as quickly as possible. She extracted several sheets of paper from a waterproof portfolio.

"The bottom sheet lists my references," she explained, perching on a high wooden stool in lieu of the only guest chair his working space provided.

The choice of seating emphasized her pretty legs. Yikes, thought Seth, trying not to stare at them as he took cover in his usual spot. *She's much younger than the sort of woman I envisioned. If I hire her, the neighbors will have a field day.* Yet he felt inexorably drawn to the warmth that sparkled in her lively dark eyes. *He and Sooz desperately needed some of that.*

"You'll note they stem from my work in public relations at Bayless Memorial eight years ago," she was saying.

"The references?"

"Yes. Since leaving there, I've worked out of my home, designing brochures and publications...that kind of thing."

He was definitely interested in her. "Why the contemplated switch to housework?" he asked, unconsciously turning on his heart-stopping smile.

Though she'd barely glanced at another man since Jim's death eight years earlier, Margo realized to her consternation that she wasn't immune. He was gorgeous—like some big, tawny king of the jungle with that coppery-gold hair, those topaz eyes. In addition, he *felt* solid. Eminently trustworthy. I wonder if he has a temper? she speculated with sudden insight. Something tells me he can be pretty awesome when he's riled.

Under the circumstances, she couldn't afford to get all moony over him. "I guess you could say I need a change," she responded. "Having people around, especially since my daughter's death. I miss her... very much."

Though she tried to maintain control, he caught the slight quiver of her lower lip. It brought out his protective instincts. Losing a child had obviously been hell for her. As a father who doted on his own charmingly problematical little girl, he could only imagine how terrible her grief must have been. If she could cook, and she was reliable...

"You say you've worked out of your home for the past eight years," he observed, striving to be practical. "Does that mean you own your own house here in the city? The person I hire must be willing to live in five days a week, from Sunday evenings through Friday afternoons. Would that present a problem?"

No doubt he'd had a steady stream of girlfriends since his divorce, as well as a parade of housekeepers, and wanted a built-in baby-sitter. A man who looked like that wouldn't find it difficult to avail himself of female companionship.

So what? Margo thought in annoyance. *You* won't be dating him. She shrugged. "I don't see why it should, provided my weekends were my own."

"Of course, you'd have your own room and bath, as well. You could decorate them any way you wished."

Though she nodded, she didn't comment.

"What about salary?" he continued, naming a figure. "Would it be sufficient to meet your needs? For instance, would it cover your mortgage payments?"

In Margo's opinion, the wages he was offering were more than generous. But she knew what he was driving at. The cost of housing in Seattle had skyrocketed during the past several years with an influx of buyers from California. If she couldn't make ends meet, she wouldn't stay; and he'd be looking for a housekeeper again.

"I don't have a mortgage," she told him. "My late husband and I bought the property in 1981. His life insurance paid off the balance we owed. I just have to worry about taxes, which admittedly have jumped. In answer to your underlying question, I can afford to take the job."

Glancing at the cut of her clothing, which was simple but elegant and probably expensive, he decided she probably could. Yet she didn't seem to need it. Why was she giving his offer serious consideration?

"Sure it's the sort of thing you'd enjoy?" he persisted. "I'd like to find someone competent and reliable who'd feel comfortable, even fulfilled in the position, and wouldn't leave us after a month or so.''

For the first time Margo wondered if Susan Danner was a brat. Maybe Nell was right. She *should* have thought things through with more deliberation before phoning for an interview. Well, that was a moot point now. She was *there,* in his office. I hate to waste his time, she thought, or deceive him, but I've got to get a look at her.

"If I agreed to take the position, I'd stay for at least six months," she volunteered. "But before I could make that kind of commitment, I'd have to see your home. And meet your daughter. Could you tell me a little about her?''

Seth was well aware that she'd turned the tables and had begun interviewing him. But she'd done it so forthrightly and gracefully he felt as if he were being stroked. "I have a picture of her right here," he said, picking up a brass-framed portrait from his desk and handing it to her.

The girl in the photograph resembled Margo's whimsical eight-year-old self even more than she had in the grainy black-and-white shot Harry Spence had taken. So? Margo thought. It's hardly conclusive evidence. People always insisted Beth Ann looked like me, too.

No matter how much you loved her, Beth wasn't your biological child, she reminded herself brutally. The tests proved that. You have to accept it, even if it hurts. Meanwhile, *this* girl might be yours. Would she be able to tell if they met in person? she won-

dered. Or was she kidding herself? Abruptly, she realized she was staring.

"She's very pretty," she said, glancing up into
warm hazel eyes lit by tawny specks that resembled
a sprinkling of gold dust trapped in amber.

He smiled that remarkable smile again, clearly susceptible to flattery when it focused on his child. "Naturally *I* think so," he answered. "But then, I'm bi-
ased. I might as well admit it up front...she can be a
handful at times. Her mother and I were divorced a
year and a half ago and she hasn't taken it very well.
Sometimes I think she blames me. Yet we continue
to be very close. I'm afraid I spoil her. I will say she
responds to attention. Honesty. And lots of love."

He might not realize it, but he was asking Margo
to care about his little girl—the selfsame sprite who
might turn out to be her daughter instead of his. She
could almost feel the sharks Nell had mentioned
swimming around her ankles.

She placed the framed picture back on his desk
with deliberate care. If she was going to finish what
she'd started, she'd have to be tough. And steadfast.
The alternative was to spend a lifetime wondering.

"When can I meet her?" she asked.

"Would you have time now? It's already past four-
thirty. I'm not likely to get much more work done
here today."

They were standing very close now, so close Seth
could inhale her lily of the valley perfume. In his
opinion, the fresh, delicate scent suited her perfectly.
Was it possible this will-o'-the-wisp, pixieish female
would be content to cook their meals and wash their

dirty laundry? He felt like a cad asking her to perform such mundane tasks. Yet, incredibly, she seemed interested.

"We live in the Magnolia area," he added. "I'd be happy to drive you there. Or..."

Meeting Susan was why Margo had come. In the process of accomplishing that, though, she had to admit she wouldn't mind spending a little more time with Seth Danner. He had a lot of personal warmth and appeal.

"I suppose I could go over for a few minutes," she said, firmly quelling doubt and reservation. "I know the Magnolia section fairly well. If you'll give me your address, I'll follow you in my car."

It was November. Rush hour, and early dusk. The drizzle continued unabated. Consequently, traffic was heavy as Margo followed Seth's honey-tan Mercedes across the Fremont Bridge and around Queen Anne Hill to West Garfield Street. As she followed his distinctively patterned taillights, she was overcome with guilt. Put it any way you like, she thought, I *am* taking advantage of him.

He'd be furious if and when she ever had to tell him the truth. Yet, if she'd approached him at the outset with her mind-boggling suspicions, she felt certain Susan Danner would have been placed off limits to her immediately. If the girl was hers, she deserved a look.

Seth swung around to the left when they reached the intersection of Cliff and Magnolia. His home— gray-shingled and ultra-modern with black metal decking—turned out to be one of the favored few, with an unimpeded view of Puget Sound and the sparkle of downtown skyscrapers from a cliffside, waterfront setting. Its color blended into the twilight, misty and appropriate.

"You'll have to excuse the decor," he warned, getting out of the Mercedes. "It's post-divorce. Whatever my ex-wife *didn't* want, plus some pretty basic, utilitarian purchases I've made since. I'm not much of a decorator."

The foyer and large living room, with its stone fireplace and breathtaking wall of windows, were furnished mostly in gray and eggplant. Though the setting was fabulous, there were few homey touches.

"Sooz?" Seth Danner called out, doffing his raincoat. "Baby, I'm home."

"Daddy!"

Seconds later, he was enveloped by slender, little-girl arms. Margo watched with a lump in her throat. Susan and Beth had shared the same birthday. But by now, the child Seth had raised was almost two years older.

Wriggling free, Susan gazed up at her father. "Jill's mom and dad are taking her to the movies and they said I could come if it was all right with you," she announced in a somewhat wheedling tone. "They're leaving in fifteen minutes so they can catch the early show. Can I? Please! I already did most of my homework!"

Like a lion playing affectionately with its cub, Seth ruffled her curly dark hair. "What about the rest of it?" he asked. "And supper? You can't live on candy bars and popcorn, you know."

"Mrs. Johnson could make me a peanut butter and jelly sandwich before she goes."

Seth gave a helpless shrug. He seemed to be no match for Susan's wiles as long as she deferred to his basic rules. "There's somebody I'd like you to meet," he said.

For the first time, Susan glanced in Margo's direction. Her keen, dark eyes took on an expression of instant hostility. "Who are *you?*" she demanded bluntly. "Another one of Daddy's girlfriends, I suppose?"

CHAPTER TWO

COULD this unfriendly moppet actually be her child? The abrupt frontal attack only strengthened Margo's resolve to find out. With effort, she managed to keep her disapproval under wraps. At the moment, she guessed, the better part of valor would be to keep a low profile.

Seth was both embarrassed and annoyed on her behalf. "For heaven's sake, Sooz!" he exclaimed, a paternal frown drawing his blond brows together. "What kind of welcome is that? Mrs. Rourke isn't my girlfriend. But she might turn out to be our new housekeeper if you haven't already driven her from our door!"

Sooz, as her father called her, seemed anything but contrite. "We don't *need* a housekeeper, Daddy," she reasoned, like some pint-sized attorney warming to her case. "Mrs. Johnson takes care of me after school. And I look after you. I like things just the way they are!"

Seth and Margo glanced at each other. "Please... give us a chance," his beautiful eyes seemed to say. Just then, a gray-haired woman who was probably in her early seventies poked her head into the living room.

"I hate to interrupt, Mr. Danner," she said, clearly oblivious to her bad timing. "But I was wondering...will you be able to take me home now? Or should I call a cab?''

Margo's M.G. was parked behind Seth's Mercedes in the drive. If he had to take the baby-sitter home, it was going to require a bit of a shuffle. But that wasn't what caught Margo's attention. Thoughtfully, she considered the fact that she'd be left alone with Susan until his return. She found the prospect daunting yet rife with possibilities. What would they talk about? It was difficult to take her eyes off the girl's dusting of freckles, which reminded her of Jim's. The shape of her jaw was also reminiscent of his.

But apparently Seth wasn't ready to abandon her to his daughter's slings and arrows just yet. ''If you don't mind, a cab would be preferable,'' he told Mrs. Johnson as he reached for his wallet. ''I'll be happy to pay for it.''

Accepting the money plus her daily fee with thanks, the baby-sitter retreated to the kitchen, where she could be heard dialing a phone.

''Now then,'' Seth told his daughter. ''I think you should apologize to our guest.''

Though his tone was kindly, there wasn't much doubt that he meant business. Sooz seemed to realize it at once, and responded. She turned to Margo with what seemed like real concern.

''I'm really sorry if I hurt your feelings,'' she said. ''I didn't mean to. Honest. It's just...''

''That'll do.'' Seth gave the girl's hand a reassuring squeeze, which also served to silence any further explaining that might veer off in the wrong direction. ''What do you say we show Mrs. Rourke around?''

Suddenly Sooz was all cooperation. "Of course, Daddy. But could we please hurry? And can I call Jill first? If we're going to the movies..."

Seth had decided not to relax the rules. However, he'd learned it was easier to deal with situations like this one if he negotiated a settlement.

"I'm afraid that won't be possible tonight, sweetheart," he said with genuine regret. "You know our agreement...homework and an early bedtime on school nights. I have an idea...why don't the two of us go tomorrow night instead? On Fridays, you can afford to stay up late. I'll take you out for pizza first."

Sooz's eyes lit up. "Super, Daddy! It's a date!"

Mollified, she skipped off to the kitchen to press chocolate-chip cookies on Mrs. Johnson, who was rustling about, getting her things together. Seconds later, Sooz could be heard chatting on the phone with her friend. She seemed to have forgotten her father's request that she help him give Margo the grand tour.

Maybe I'm riding for a fall once the truth sets in, Margo thought, but she didn't feel particularly maternal toward Sooz. At first blush, the child who might well be her flesh and blood—as well as Jim's—came off second-best in any comparison with Beth Ann. Though she seemed to possess twice Beth's energy and drive, Sooz certainly didn't share her counterpart's angelic nature. Still, there was something inherently likable, almost touching, about Sooz, despite her prickly outspokenness.

"I warned you," Seth reminded with a grin, throwing up his hands. "She can be quite a little gremlin sometimes. C'mon... I'll show you the quarters that'll be your private turf if we can reach an agreement, as well as the basic layout. The house has three stories, including an exposed basement. And, in case you haven't noticed, some pretty spectacular views.''

The rooms Margo would call her own, if she decided to take on the challenge of keeping house for Seth Danner and his daughter, were pleasant indeed. In addition to a generously sized bedroom and bath, there was a small sitting room with a panoramic view of the Sound. As in the rest of the house, the furnishings were modern, bland and rather basic. But they seemed comfortable enough. With a few plants and pillows to brighten things up...

Margo hauled herself up short as Seth offered glimpses of Sooz's room—messy, with a stuffed teddy bear in the place of honor on her bed—and his own—masculine and lacking in personality, with blond oak furniture. Watch it, she reminded herself. Your purpose here is to check out a child who, through some trick of fate, might be yours from a biological standpoint. Beyond that, you don't have any legitimate business, or commitment.

As they headed downstairs, she reflected that at least the question of love had been resolved to her satisfaction. Seth Danner might be a single parent struggling to provide the kind of upbringing a mother and father acting in concert could have managed with more finesse, but he plainly showered the girl he'd nicknamed Sooz with affection. Despite any lingering unhappiness over her parents' divorce, she seemed relatively secure.

The basement contained laundry facilities, a storage area and a large recreation room that also had a stunning view. By the time they returned to the well-equipped but unremarkable kitchen, Sooz was off the phone, finishing her homework at the kitchen table and nibbling at the chocolate-chip cookies she and Mrs. Johnson had doubtless made together. And from the expression on Seth's face, Margo got the distinct impression that Sooz was violating a prohibition against spoiling her supper.

With a casual air, Seth opened the oven door and peered inside to see what the baby-sitter had left for their evening meal. "Tuna casserole," he mused, giving his daughter a sidelong glance. "I guess we're having it for dessert."

Sooz had the grace to look abashed.

A few minutes later Seth was walking Margo to her car. "Well? What do you think?" he asked, standing bare-headed in the drizzle as she rested her hand on the M.G.'s convertible top. "Sooz isn't always such a terror. At times, she can be rather sweet. Do you find the prospect of working for us just too much?"

Awash in conflicting emotions, Margo didn't answer him right away. Now that Sooz wasn't on the scene to distract her, she could feel the tug of Seth's masculinity a hundredfold. The man exerted a sensual pull on her like nothing she'd ever experienced. And she could ill afford the complication. Still, she knew she'd regret it if she never saw him again.

She also wanted to see more of Sooz.

"Does that question mean you're offering me the job?" she countered.

It was Seth's turn to appear thoughtful, but he'd already made up his mind. Pixie that she was, Margo Rourke hadn't allowed Sooz to bully her. Nor had she appeared to take the girl's bad manners personally, though she'd almost certainly disapproved of them. It was anybody's guess if she could cook or clean. But suddenly those skills seemed secondary. He had a strong feeling she possessed exactly the right bag of tricks needed to manage his daughter.

Regarding her from the eleven-inch disparity in their heights, Seth recalled Sooz's characterization of Margo as his "girlfriend." I wonder what would've happened if we'd met in some other way, he thought. It's a foregone conclusion that I'd have asked her for a date. And I have a feeling it wouldn't have ended there. Yet if she agreed to take the job, they'd have to keep things on a business footing.

Slowly but steadily, soft rain was soaking him to the skin and depositing tiny, jewellike beads of moisture on Margo's lashes. As she gazed up at him, they were clumped together like the points of stars. Her mist-drenched hair was as curly as a gypsy's, a sensuous tangle about her face.

With difficulty, Seth kept his hands to himself. She was waiting for an answer.

"It seems that I am," he acknowledged at last. "But I don't expect you to give me your answer right away. Maybe you could think things over tonight and call me at my office...say tomorrow afternoon?"

Though Margo fully intended to spend the evening at her computer catching up on missed work, she found it impossible to concentrate. You'd be insane to move in with Seth Danner and go to work as his house-keeper, she thought, pushing her chair back from the desk and heading upstairs to run herself a bubble bath. The job's far beneath your capabilities. Yet if she told him no, it was doubtful she'd see him or his daughter again.

And she wanted to. She had to admit that much.

You won't learn anything more by cooking his meals and washing his windows, she reminded herself as she poured out a glass of wine, lit a candle and sank down into the suds. You'll just grow fond of the child despite her bratty ways. And maybe of him. The only way you'll ever get a concrete answer is to talk him into submitting her for a tissue test.

But, after meeting Seth, she guessed she didn't have a snowball's chance in hell of convincing him to do that. She couldn't even think of a way to broach the subject. Though he seemed the most amiable of men when things were going his way, her intuition told her he was more than capable of a blowup. He was a redhead, wasn't he? And he'd have every rea-son to be angry if he ever learned what her real pur-pose had been in contacting him. God knows she'd feel the same if the situations were reversed.

What on earth was she going to do? She'd prom-ised him an answer. And the moment of truth was less than twenty-four hours away. As rain fell softly against her windowpane, Margo soaked and pon-dered.

Seth had given up hope of hearing from her by the time the phone rang in his office at 5:02 p.m. the following afternoon. Already half into his raincoat, he reached for the receiver.

"Mrs. Rourke on one," Josie informed him in a tone that indicated she was on her way out the door.

He could barely control his relief, or the surge of eagerness he felt as he pressed the flashing red button on his console. "Hi," he said. "I'm glad you caught me. After the way Sooz behaved yesterday, I'd all but decided you wouldn't phone."

"Was there ever any doubt?"

There was a smile in her voice. His hopes shot up a notch or two, revealing just how much he'd been counting on her acceptance. Something told him that if Margo Rourke came to live with them, they wouldn't be looking for a replacement in six months. What was more, the dramatic but somehow lifeless house where he and his little girl rattled around together would become a home.

Hell, he thought, trying not to jinx things. She's probably going to let me down easy. And I wouldn't blame her. We're not the plummiest of prospects.

"So," he said, taking the initiative. "Do I dare ask what you've decided?"

Though the decision had been a tough one, Margo didn't hesitate. "If you like, I can start on Monday," she answered. "At the agreed upon salary. And with the six-month proviso I mentioned. I believe we discussed the fact that I won't be available on weekends. I'll be spending them at my place."

Seth was stunned. She was really going to do it! He wanted to jump for joy. If she'd been present in his office, he'd have waltzed her around the room. I've got to have a serious talk with Sooz, he thought. This time, she can't be allowed to screw things up.

"Mr. Danner?" Margo prompted. "Are you still there?"

"I'm here. Please...call me Seth. I guess you could say I'm bowled over. And very pleased. I noticed your car is about as small as they get. Can I help you move anything? A television and linens are provided, of course. But you may want to bring some of your own things to make the place more habitable..."

He realized that, in his excitement, he was rambling.

"Thanks, I would like to bring a few things from home," she answered. "But you don't need to worry about hauling them. I have access to a station wagon. If you'll leave a key under the mat, I'll let myself in Monday morning...after Sooz has left for school."

Seth agreed her plan was probably best. With her strong territorial instincts, Sooz might prove a sullen onlooker were Margo to move in while she was present. But if Margo appeared firmly entrenched, already a fixture of the household on his daughter's arrival from school, it might serve to ease their initial confrontation. For his part, he was definitely looking forward to having a dark-eyed angel of mercy under his roof.

"Sounds fine to me," he assured her. "Again, I can't tell you how happy this makes me."

If you only knew what my reasons were, Margo thought guiltily, you wouldn't feel that way. The truth

was, she liked Seth a lot more than was advantageous
for either of them. She hated deceiving him.

"Well, see you Monday," she said as casually as
she could. "Feel free to phone me in the meantime
if you think of anything. Enjoy your movie tonight."

Stopping by to pick up Margo for a planned evening out, Nell had arrived in time to catch the last
half of her conversation. "So you're actually going
through with it," she observed after Margo and Seth
had said goodbye.

Margo nodded. "I'd never forgive myself if I
didn't. Sooz Danner may be 'quite a handful,' as her
father puts it, but she might also be my daughter. I
need to know her a whole lot better before I decide
whether or not to reveal the set of circumstances that
led me to her door, or relinquish any claim I might
have to her."

She couldn't bring herself to confess that her attraction to Seth Danner had also been a significant
factor in her decision-making.

Clearly aware more was going on than met the eye,
Nell regarded her with a questioning expression.
"There's something different about you," she remarked at last. "Something that can't be attributed to
meeting this child."

Though she didn't enlighten her friend, Margo
knew just what that something was. For the first time
since Jim's death, she felt like a living, breathing
woman—one with sensual desires. And needs. A man
who towered over her like a giant oak, with red-gold
hair and eyes like topaz, was responsible.

"C'mon," Margo urged, nudging her off the scent.

"We might as well get going if you want to have a bite of supper before the concert starts."

Determined not to submerge her identity in the role of housekeeper, Margo borrowed Nell's station wagon to convey an assortment of books, pillows, plants and framed pictures to the Danner residence. She even brought over the hand-quilted bedspread and shams from the room that had once been Beth's.

Returning for her M.G., Margo left Nell's vehicle in her own regular parking space at home so her friend could pick it up after work. Though she clearly had misgivings about what Margo was doing, Nell was being supportive, as usual. She'd even arranged a ride with a friend so she could pick up her ancient Volvo without Margo having to be involved.

Returning to the house on Magnolia, Margo went to work on her personal space. Using special hooks that wouldn't damage the walls, she put up some of her favorite prints. Books she'd been planning to read lined an empty bookcase. Toss pillows and an afghan materialized on the couch in her sitting room. When she was finished, her quarters were the most attractive in the house.

There wasn't much time to whip up a spectacular meal, thanks to the move. The Danners would have to settle for an old-fashioned, everyday supper.

She was in the kitchen, putting the finishing touches to a meat loaf and a casserole of baked beans when Sooz walked in the door. The dark-haired sprite who looked so much like Margo's childhood self didn't speak as she headed first for the refrigerator and then to the cookie jar.

"Hi, Sooz," Margo said, glancing up from her work but not making a big deal of it.

There wasn't any answer. Helping herself to a glass of orange juice and a handful of cookies, Sooz flopped down at the kitchen table and turned on the television set. Thoughtfully she munched and sipped, ignoring both Margo and the school books at her elbow.

"Don't you have homework tonight?" Margo asked.

In the blink of an eyelash, Sooz switched from seeming indifference to absolute fury and loathing. "You're not my parent! You can't tell me what to do!" she huffed. "Where's Mrs. Johnson? I'd rather have *her!*"

Margo shrugged. "Now that I'm here, she isn't needed. I asked you about your homework."

Sooz folded slender arms across her chest, telegraphing all the classic signs of resistance. "I don't want you here! I'm sick of housekeepers," she said. "All they ever do is boss me around. And leave, the minute I get used to them. I'd rather have Mrs. Johnson. At least she can cook."

Margo tried not to smile. "I guess you must hate meat loaf and baked beans," she commented, taking a boxed mix down from the cupboard. "Not to mention chocolate cake."

In answer, Sooz stuck out her tongue.

Seth came home with anticipation written all over his face. Once again, he was dressed in jeans and a sweater, as if he'd spent another day in the finishing shed. This time the sweater was gold, with a rolled collar. A little more form-fitting than the one he'd worn the day they'd met, it hinted at the well-developed muscles of his chest and upper arms. In Margo's opinion, jeans didn't have any right to fit a human body the way his did.

"Hi, sweetheart," he said, giving Sooz a squeeze, which she rewarded with a stingy peck. "Hello, Margo. Something sure smells terrific."

Somebody looks terrific, too, he thought, though he didn't dare say so. Trim and shapely in her forest green sweater and ivory corduroy trousers, with her hair curling from the heat of the oven, Margo was a vision of domesticity and sexiness. On her, an apron was almost as enchanting as a negligee.

The idea that both qualities could exist so harmoniously in one woman fired Seth's imagination. He suddenly wished her duties included giving him a welcome-home kiss.

"Meat loaf, baked beans and chocolate cake." She smiled. "Plus a salad. I'm glad you're hungry. Apparently I managed to pick everything Sooz detests."

Seth glanced at his daughter in surprise. "But that's nonsense," he averred. "Sooz loves meat loaf. Why, only last week…"

He paused as he caught Margo's wink. So Sooz had been giving her a hard time already. Well, he'd see about that!

Uh-uh, Margo signaled with a slight shake of her head. *Let me handle it. Everything will be all right.*

Wonder of wonders, Sooz hadn't terrorized her yet.

It seemed he'd struck pay dirt. Excusing himself with what he suspected would be the first of many contented grins, Seth went upstairs to wash.

They ate in the dining area, in front of a window that spread the glitter of downtown and the muted sparkle of Alki Point at their feet. Though the meal was simple, Margo had lighted a couple of candles and arranged some yellow mums from her garden at home in an oversized mug for a centerpiece. Taking his place at the head of the table, Seth began to believe his beleaguered personal life was finally straightening out.

His sense of well-being notwithstanding, dinner was a somewhat uneven affair, with Sooz sulking and uncommunicative, though she was too hungry not to eat. He and Margo made the best of it, chatting amiably about books they'd read and upcoming events. Afterward he suggested Sooz help Margo with the dishes while he fixed the faucet in the laundry room.

"Why do I have to?" the girl protested at once, giving Margo a hostile look. "She's getting paid, isn't she?"

"*She* happens to have a name," Seth replied, in no mood to put up with his daughter's shenanigans. "It's *Mrs. Rourke.* I suggest you use it whenever you refer to 'her.' As for helping out, that's expected of everyone in this household. Understood?"

"Yes, *sir.*"

Obviously still rebellious, though she didn't dare go against her father's wishes, Sooz began clearing the table with the ferocity of a whirlwind.

Seth shook his head regretfully as she disappeared

into the kitchen with a stack of plates and silverware. "Sorry about that display of temper," he apologized. "Unfortunately you might be treated to more of the same for a while. When Cheryl left—Cheryl's my ex-wife and Sooz's mother—Sooz was devastated. I'm afraid I spoiled her as a result. Now we're paying the price. I want you to know I'll back any reasonable disciplinary measures on your part. And that...well, I hope you'll hang in there."

Whenever she and Seth talked one-on-one, Margo felt as if they were the only two people in the world. He'd raised the girl who might be her daughter and, unable to stop herself, she imagined him as her husband. In her opinion, his ex-wife had been crazy to walk out on him.

Thank heaven her more sensible self remembered she wasn't in love with Seth. For one thing, she didn't know him well enough. And, for another, she couldn't afford to be. If she ever decided to pursue the subject of Sooz's parentage, they'd be on opposite sides of the fence. She'd just have to stop wishing he'd touch her every time they were together.

A rueful smile tilted the corners of her mouth. "Please don't feel as if I'm going to abandon you at any moment," she said. "Where Sooz is concerned, I've just begun to fight."

CHAPTER THREE

ALONE in her sitting room after packing Sooz's lunch, setting the coffeemaker to timed-brew and drawing up a marketing list, Margo finally realized what had been nagging at her since she'd first contacted Seth. She'd been concentrating on only half of the equation.

Genetic tests had proved Beth didn't belong, biologically, to her and Jim. It followed that, if Jim had been Sooz's dad and she was the girl's mother, then Seth had fathered the child she'd raised. With Sooz and Beth the only two female Caucasian infants in the Bayless Memorial nursery following their births, no other conclusion was possible.

In other words, Margo thought with a stirring of gooseflesh as she curled up beneath her afghan and listened to the rich chords of Ralph Vaughan Williams's "Theme from Thomas Tallis" play at low volume on her portable stereo, I've nursed his child at my breast. Kissed her good-night and wished her sweet dreams from her first day on this earth until she died in that accident.

It seemed she and Seth were connected by bonds that went far deeper than the schoolgirl crush she'd begun to develop for him.

Nell had confided that she supported the theory of karma and reincarnation. It was her stated belief that people who were important to each other in past lives often reincarnated together. Supposing there was some basis in fact for those beliefs, Margo thought. Could experiences in another lifetime have drawn Seth and her together?

Margo was eager to share her thoughts with her friend and ask a few questions. She wished it weren't too late to call.

Reaching for Beth Ann's picture, which she'd placed on a nearby table, Margo studied the elfin, heart-shaped face she loved so much. But, try as she might, she couldn't detect any resemblance between the dark-eyed child she'd lost and Seth with his hazel eyes and red-gold hair. In the past, she'd always believed Beth had inherited her coloring. I wonder what Cheryl's like, she thought now. Maybe she has dark hair and eyes, too.

She glanced up at a knock on her door.

"Margo...are you awake?" Seth called.

"Yes. Come in." Replacing Beth Ann's photograph, she reached for the stop button on her stereo.

Seth paused just inside the door. "Don't turn it off. That's a lovely piece of music."

"I'll just lower the volume so we can talk."

Seth glanced around the transformed sitting room. "I can't believe this is the same place I showed you just a few days ago," he said with a shake of his head. "With a little of this and that, you've made it very inviting. I wish you could work the same magic on the rest of the house."

Margo shrugged, embarrassed by the praise. She'd hardly done anything. Yet she knew what he meant. Beautiful as it was architecturally, his house was crying out for the personal touches that had given her quarters such a comfortable look.

"I suppose I could tackle it in my spare time, if you don't mind footing the bill," she offered. "You wouldn't need to spend a lot of money. You already have the basics. Besides, it's the little things that count."

What a contrast she is to Cheryl, Seth thought. A year and a half after his divorce, he was still paying off his ex-wife's credit card charges for, among other things, costly but somehow impersonal objets d'art that now graced his successor's million dollar Hawaii condominium. Meanwhile, orders at Danner Yachts, Inc., had fallen off, thanks to the 1991 federal luxury tax that had increased the price tag on the firm's top-of-the-line models by ten percent. He'd had to lay off a few people. And that had hurt.

Despite his financial concerns, though, he was still in the black, and he considered Margo's services a bargain. He believed that, in time, she'd bring Sooz around and establish peace and order in his home. The prospect was worth a great deal to him.

Before she'd walked into his life, he'd been convinced he'd never marry again. Now he wasn't so sure. Though Sooz seemed to hate every unattached woman he introduced, an inner voice kept whispering it was too bad he and Margo hadn't met in some other way. If they had, he most certainly would have romanced her—maybe even offered her a more intimate and permanent place in his life, provided she and his daughter could manage to get along. But now that she was his employee, he didn't feel comfortable making romantic overtures.

With a start, he realized she was studying him.

"Won't you sit down?" she asked. "That little rocker doesn't look as if it would hold you, but you're welcome to the opposite end of the couch."

Seth wished he felt free to accept—her smile, her warmth, were getting to him—but he couldn't.

"No, thanks," he said. "It's getting late. I just wanted to tell you again how much I appreciate your taking this job, despite its obvious drawbacks. And to say you needn't spend your evenings cooped up in here if you'd rather not. I want you to feel like part of the family. As far as I'm concerned, you have the run of the house."

For Margo the next few days were hectic as she organized the Danner household and established a routine. She didn't have time to phone Nell right away.

Bit by bit, Sooz's overt hostility faded; perhaps she'd concluded it wasn't having much effect. In any case, Seth had left her with little doubt. He wasn't prepared to stand for it. Yet Margo knew the battle hadn't been won by any means. Sooz's refusal to accept her had just gone underground, to manifest itself in more subtle ways. On one occasion, she'd "accidentally" slopped chili all over the range top, creating a burned-on, sticky mess. And one of her favorite tricks was pretending not to hear when Margo asked her a question.

More stubborn than she'd realized she had the power to be, Margo refused to let the girl provoke her into an argument. Instead she repeated herself a lot, calling on every shred of patience she possessed. When Sooz made a mess, she simply handed her the cleanser. Or a broom. Stubborn hearts aren't won over in a day, she told herself firmly. It'll take time to make friends with her. In the meantime, she'd keep a low profile. And wait.

That week Danner Yachts received a lucrative rush order. With Margo in command of the home front, Seth felt free to put in extra time at work. On Thursday he barely made it home in time to kiss Sooz good-night. Afterward, he hung around in the kitchen, chatting with Margo as she reheated his supper, then asked her to keep him company while he ate it at the coffee table in the living room in front of a crackling fire. The feeling was incredibly cozy, as if he'd been coming home to her for years.

Her every logical thought and instinct crying out that he was Beth's father, she found it easy to imagine Seth as her husband. You can't let yourself think of him that way, she warned herself. He'd be outraged if he knew your reason for being here. Since you might have to tell him the truth someday, getting emotionally involved with him would be a big mistake.

Yet she couldn't help the spontaneous attraction she felt. Or keep from wondering if it was reciprocated. She wanted to melt every time she looked into tawny eyes shaded by impossibly boyish, straw-colored lashes, and felt the strong physical tug of his presence.

*   *   *

Friday was Nell's day off. Margo had planned to have dinner downtown with her and do a little shopping after Seth returned home from work and she was free to leave. Around eleven o'clock Friday morning, with the initial backlog of housework out of the way, Margo dialed her friend's number.

Nell was waiting for her in the sedate but elegant Frederick and Nelson Restaurant, which was situated on the eighth floor of the department store of the same name. She'd managed to secure a quiet, out-of-the-way table beside one of the potted palms. Though their view of the piano player was blocked by a square, mirrored column, they were right beside one of the sweeping windowed walls, that offered a sparkling evening panorama of the surrounding buildings.

Margo rolled her eyes. "I really need some advice abut Sooz. Is there any hope do you think?"

"Oh, definitely." Nell took a sip of her wine. "I suspect that, every time she hits you with one of her zingers, it hurts her twice as much."

Margo had guessed at Sooz's hidden vulnerability herself. As her first week in Seth Danner's employ had drawn to a close, she'd found herself wanting to hug the girl when she was being her most obstreperous.

"Go on," she said.

Nell smiled. "Only by convincing her that your presence in the household is right will you persuade her to call a truce. You'll have to do it with tact and delicacy. She probably wouldn't want anyone to second-guess her. Or have her pegged."

Just then the waitress brought their salads. Since

neither of them had bothered with lunch, they munched contentedly in silence for several minutes. At last Nell put down her fork.

"What about your big, handsome redhead?" she asked with obvious curiosity.

Margo almost choked on a radish.

"I wouldn't be surprised if there's a strong physical attraction between you..."

Margo could feel herself blushing. "I have to admit he's quite a hunk," she conceded. "But you know the situation's an impossible one."

Nell didn't agree or disagree with her statement. "He probably has women falling all over him," she said.

So far, Margo hadn't seen any sign of the harem she'd expected. And to be honest, she didn't want to. She pressed her wineglass against one burning cheek in an unconscious gesture.

"He's likely to be one heck of a lover," she said. "Plus, he's likely to be the sort of man who gets under a woman's skin, redheads supposedly have a temper though. I trust you haven't seen anything of that yet."

Saved by the chicken pot pie, Margo thought with relief as their waitress deposited identical specialties of the house in front of them. "Actually, no," she reassured her friend. "So far, he's been more of a lamb than a lion."

Margo was removing a sheet of perfectly browned peanut-butter cookies from the oven Thursday afternoon when she caught sight of Sooz slipping into the house with a tear-stained face. I wonder what's wrong? she thought, wiping her hands on her apron. Has she skinned her knee or something? Without warning, the maternal feelings that had largely eluded her thus far crept into her heart.

Following the girl upstairs, she found Sooz's door firmly shut. "Sooz? Are you okay?" she asked.

There wasn't any answer.

Sooz would be nine in just two weeks. But that wasn't very old in the overall scheme of things. Deciding to butt in, Margo tapped lightly and opened the door.

"Go away!"

Sooz had flung her schoolbooks on the floor and flopped down on her stomach across the bed with one arm around her stuffed teddy. Every line of her body spelled misery.

"I will if you really want me to," Margo promised, "*after* you tell me what's wrong. If you're hurt, it's my job to apply disinfectant. And a bandage."

For some reason the bland, unemotional approach got through. "I'm fine," Sooz insisted, affording Margo a glimpse of her puffy, reddened face. "I got into trouble at school, that's all. And it wasn't my fault!"

"Want to tell me about it?"

"No! You're just the housekeeper here."

Margo stifled a flash of temper. Though Sooz had just shot her another barb, she thought she perceived an opening.

"Okay," she said, sitting down on the end of the

bed. "I'll tell you about something that happened to me instead."

Sooz kept her back turned and her face hidden as Margo began to relate an episode that had taken place when she was in the second grade. But she didn't demand again that Margo leave the room.

"I put pepper in another girl's milk one day after she grabbed my cupcake," Margo recalled. "Of course, she told the teacher, and that teacher wasn't very nice. She did something a teacher should never, never do. Everyone who got in trouble that lunch hour had to take a turn wearing toy handcuffs. There were a lot of tears, I can tell you. It was very embarrassing for all of us."

Slowly Sooz turned over. "What did you do?" she asked, surprise and interest in her voice.

Margo pretended not to notice that Sooz was softening. "I was last in line," she said. "Watching the other kids bawl, I decided I wouldn't give that teacher—or the rest of the class—the satisfaction of seeing me do the same thing. When my turn came, I rested my chin on my hands and stared at the clock until my twenty minutes were up. Guess I'd make a pretty unrepentant jailbird, huh?"

By now, Sooz was sitting up, facing her. "So...you didn't cry at all?" she demanded, obviously wishing she could make a similar boast.

Margo wanted to hug her. She managed to restrain herself. "Ah, but I did," she admitted, "after I got home. When I told my dad about it, he laughed. It made me feel terrible."

"*My* dad wouldn't laugh," Sooz vowed, quick to

seize an opportunity for one-upmanship. "He'd get mad at me if he thought I did something bad. But he wouldn't make fun of me."

"I don't think my dad meant it. That's just how he was. My mom fixed me hot chocolate. And that made me feel better."

Sooz was silent a moment. "Did you ever ask your dad why he laughed?" she asked finally. "I mean, after you were all grown up?"

Margo shook her head. "No, I never did. You see, he died the year after the handcuff incident, when I was your age. He and my mother were killed in a plane crash. So I never had the chance."

Sooz's eyes widened in pity. "Wow," she exclaimed in a hushed voice. "That must have been awful for you, losing both your parents! I have my dad. And I get to talk to my mother sometimes. She lives in Hawaii, you know."

"Yes, I did know that," Margo confessed. "Whatever happened today at school, I'm sure that, if it needs to be straightened out, your dad will take care of it. What would you say to washing your face and coming downstairs for a few peanut-butter cookies and some hot chocolate with marshmallows on top? We might be able to arrange a dispensation from homework until after supper."

When he walked in the door that night, Seth found phone-order pizza on the menu instead of lovingly prepared comfort food. But he didn't mind. To his amazement, Margo was seated at the kitchen table with Sooz, sketching the girl a set of homemade paper dolls. Clearly charmed by her creative ability, his prickly daughter was chattering away like a friendly monkey.

His amazement only deepened when Sooz mentioned her run-in at school—she'd pinched another girl who'd played keep-away with her lunch box— and retold the handcuff story that night at the dinner table. Had she and Margo progressed to the point of sharing confidences, then? Never in his wildest dreams had he expected the transition to friendship between them to be that easy.

When it was cleanup time, Margo gave Sooz an added break. "Go up and do your homework, babe," she said. "There aren't that many dishes. I can handle them by myself."

Always pleased to get out of chores, Sooz didn't have to be told twice. She ran lightheartedly up the stairs.

"You don't need to," Seth remarked in a husky voice, following Margo into the kitchen.

"Need to *what?*"

"Do the dishes by yourself. I'll be glad to help."

"Thanks. But it's really not necessary."

"I insist."

As usual, strong sensual vibrations crackled between them. Seth was looking down at her as if he planned to have her for dessert. It made Margo feel unsteady on her feet.

I'll bet Nell was right about his lovemaking ability, she thought, thoroughly smitten with him. He's probably like some great passionate archangel in bed.

Shivers swept over her when he leaned down to kiss her lightly on the cheek. "That's for being so

good to Sooz,'' he whispered, his hands lightly framing her shoulders. ''I want you to know, I love you
for it.''

CHAPTER FOUR

THEY were standing very close—little more than a breath apart—and the attraction between them was too powerful to resist. Circumstances and Seth's sleek but nondescript kitchen with its pizza remains and after-dinner clutter receded, until the two of them were marooned on an island in time and space. Like one bemused or bewitched, Margo felt Seth's arms come around her. The palms of her hands settled against the soft, nubby texture of his sweater as he lowered his mouth to hers.

From the moment they'd met, amid the damp and paint fumes and bustle of Danner Yachts, Inc., she'd had the uncanny feeling that he was someone she *knew*—a missing piece of her life's puzzle. Thanks to Sooz and Beth, she was convinced their destinies were intertwined like lovers. With a little sigh of surrender, she shut her eyes.

At first he nuzzled her with tentative ardor, his mouth barely brushing hers, though it was hot and sweet. Hushed and bursting with promise, the moment couldn't last. Margo caught her breath as Seth drew back, hesitated, and then kissed her again with more blatant hunger, questing and tasting as if she were some hitherto untried delicacy that he planned to savor to the utmost.

Overcome by the splendor of what he was making

her feel, she wanted to melt into him, lose herself in the wonder that he was. Caution and common sense abandoned her, and she parted her lips.

My God! Seth thought, going hard in an instant. She's incredible. Generous and nurturing, yet as volatile as a Gypsy. Her warm, wet mouth was like ambrosia to him as he probed its depths with his tongue.

In that passionate embrace, the extent of Seth's arousal wasn't any secret. Though Margo could keep her body's response hidden better than he could, she was helpless before the avalanche of need that surged in her blood. She longed to wrap herself around him.

Afterward, she couldn't have said how long they stood there by the sink, blurring and blending into the knowledge of how much they wanted each other. She only knew it was paradise to her. By contrast, she hadn't been fully alive for years.

It was like a dousing of cold water, then, or a sudden jolt of electricity when Sooz's little-girl voice rang out.

"Daddy? Can you come up and help me with my arithmetic?"

As if they'd been caught in some illicit, unpardonable act, they hastily jumped apart. Margo's heart was beating like a sledgehammer, but they hadn't been discovered. Sooz had shouted her request from the top of the stairs the way she usually did, rather than appearing in the kitchen to ask her father face-to-face.

The fire in Seth's tawny, king-of-the-jungle eyes was banked but far from extinguished. Margo had wanted him as much as he'd wanted her and it was too late for her to pretend otherwise. He didn't plan to let her off the hook, either. "Back in a minute," he said, giving her upper arms a possessive little squeeze before he left the room.

Shaken, Margo rinsed and stacked the dishes and her baking utensils as she tried to get hold of herself. Never, not even in her late husband's arms, had she felt so bonded to a man, so erotically stimulated. By now she knew what she'd only guessed at before. Making love to Seth Danner would be like burning to a white-hot ingot. A woman would emerge from the cauldron of his embrace even more herself, yet forever changed. Everything in her was aching to experience it. She couldn't remember wanting anything so much.

Yet how could she justify indulging herself? Love couldn't be built on a lie and she was an imposter in Seth's house—a stranger passing herself off as a single father's dream of a housekeeper, when in reality she was on a fact-finding mission that could forever change their lives. If and when Seth discovered her motive for agreeing to cook and clean for him, or once she was forced to tell him, they wouldn't stand a chance.

There weren't enough dishes to bother turning on the dishwasher and, with a sigh, Margo ran a sinkful of suds. In her opinion, Seth was the kind of impassioned, demonstrative yet sustaining and trustworthy man every woman dreamed about meeting and loving someday. Though she hadn't been looking for anyone in a romantic sense, she'd found him. And maybe, just maybe, he was genuinely attracted to her. Why not keep quiet and see what happens? she thought.

Seth's unattached, and you have a perfect right to know if Sooz is your natural daughter. You wouldn't be harming anyone if you let matters take their natural course.

As Margo scrubbed the cookie sheets, her conscience argued that getting involved with Seth would be disloyal to Sooz. She's the reason you're here, Margo reminded herself. All your focus should be on her. Later, if the truth comes out and you've kept your relationship with him on a business footing, at least he won't feel betrayed in a man-woman sense.

She'd have to reach an understanding with him—and fast—before they ended up in each other's arms again. "Back in a minute" had definite connotations of taking up where they left off. And she was hardly immune.

Margo was waiting for Seth in the living room when he came back downstairs. Perched nervously on the hassock that matched his black leather and teak Eames Chair, she got to her feet.

He could see at once that she'd thrown up barriers. "Margo, I..." he began.

She wouldn't let him finish. "What happened in the kitchen a little while ago was nobody's fault," she said, keeping her voice low so Sooz wouldn't overhear. "But it was a major mistake. It's part of my job to care for your daughter and I've just begun to establish a relationship with her. It's still fragile and I don't want anything to spoil it. If she caught us...*embracing* like that...she'd conclude I was trying to take over her father, that I had no real interest in her."

Standing there looking up at him from the downhill end of the eleven-inch disparity in their heights, with determination glowing in her dark eyes and her lipstick all but obliterated by the ministrations of his mouth, Margo was a tempting sight. Seth wanted her, damn it! Distractedly helping Sooz with her math, he'd been eager as a high school kid sunk in his first romance to taste Margo again and see if the delicious surrender she'd offered was fact or a figment of his imagination. The urge to sweep aside her objections and let passion have its way warred with reluctant understanding on his face.

Sooz will have to accept another woman in my life eventually. It might as well be now, he thought. Yet he had to admit Margo had a point. If he knew his daughter, Margo's assessment of her probable reaction to anything approaching an affair of the heart between them was right on target.

Because of the employer-employee relationship in which they found themselves, there was also the question of propriety. He didn't want to put Margo in an awkward position.

"You're right," he agreed, setting aside his own needs and desires. "I was completely out of line, coming on to you the way I did. Sooz and I need you here, and I don't want to do anything to drive you away. I promise I'll do my best not to let it happen again."

It wasn't an ironclad guarantee. Still, for the next few weeks, Seth made himself scarce, staying late at the boat yard almost every night and carting off his warmed-over supper to his office when he returned to the house on Magnolia Boulevard. In the mornings, he snatched his breakfast on the run.

Now and then, he paused to exchange a few words with her about Sooz. Whenever he did, the regret she felt over the wall that had sprung up between them intensified. He was sexy, caring, a man who radiated a special resonance all his own. Each time their hands accidentally touched, or they brushed against each other in passing, her attraction to him deepened. Apparently he planned to keep his word and his distance, but in her secret heart, where common sense played only a minor role, she didn't want him to.

At least she was making progress with Sooz. The girl had thawed to the point where she hung about after school most days, helping Margo fix dinner and begging for more paper dolls, unless she was doing homework or playing outdoors. Day by day, Margo's affection for the energetic, outspoken moppet grew. Though she continued to miss Beth Ann and regard the elfin, dark-haired child she'd lost as her own little girl, she had to admit Sooz was helping heal the hurt.

We're a long way from having a mother-daughter relationship, Margo commented to herself one rainy afternoon as she taught Sooz how to sew in the process of helping her mend her precious ''Bear's'' ripped taffeta vest. Yet, little by little, we're becoming friends. Though Sooz will never take Beth's place in my heart, she seems to be creating one of her own.

It was the Friday before Thanksgiving. Several hours later, as Margo was about to slip out the door and head home for a weekend of playing catch-up with her sadly neglected desktop publishing business, Seth laid a detaining hand on her arm. He was wearing a maize fisherman-style sweater that emphasized the natural highlights in his reddish-gold hair. The well-worn trousers in a nut-brown corduroy he'd chosen to go with it fit snugly. They did nothing to hide his narrow hips and powerful leg muscles.

Just to have him touch her again after yearning for heaven out of reach made her knees go weak. She could feel the sensual pull of him like a magnet.

"Yes?" she managed.

"I wonder if I could talk to you for a moment?"

Sooz was upstairs, getting ready for an evening out with him. She wouldn't overhear. Meanwhile Margo was keenly aware that, once again, Seth had invaded her personal space. He was so big, so warm and muscular, and he smelled so good. The tang of his aftershave and skin-scent teased her nostrils.

"What about?" she asked, concentrating on his disarming fringe of blond lashes to keep from getting lost in his eyes.

It's a lot to ask, Seth thought. I don't know anything about her life away from here. But, what the heck? I might as well give it a try.

He gestured with one big, beautifully proportioned hand. "About the coming holiday..."

"Yes?"

"Naturally, it's yours if you want it. But if you don't have any special plans, maybe you'd consider taking a different day off at your convenience and hanging around to fix a turkey for us. Sooz hasn't been part of anything like that for ages. I know it would mean a great deal to her."

Though it was equally accurate, he didn't add that it would mean a great deal to him, as well. To the best of his recollection, Cheryl had never fixed a traditional holiday meal, preferring that they dine at the home of relatives or in a first-class restaurant. He was charmed by the notion of turkey roasting in his own kitchen and Margo smiling at him over the assembled feast.

As she approached her first major holiday without Beth, who'd died the previous January, Margo hadn't been looking forward to much of a celebration. Hoping to stem the tide of painful memories she expected to assail her, she'd decided to prepare a capon at her Ravenna bungalow and invite Nell over, since her friend's beau would be out of town. But now that an opportunity had arisen to spend the day with Seth and Sooz, a little flame of anticipation curled to life inside her.

"To tell you the truth, it sounds like fun," she admitted. "If I hadn't planned to invite a friend over—"

Seth's light-colored brows drew together in a frown. I might have guessed she'd be cooking for a man, he thought, pushing down the prickling of jealousy he felt. "Say no more," he cut in. "You've been very generous with your free time already and we don't want to impose."

"It's just that her gentleman friend plans to spend the day with his family in Portland," Margo explained. "And she doesn't have any close relatives west of the Alleghenies."

Her *gentleman* friend? Wonder of wonders, Margo's prospective dinner guest was female. "By all means, ask her to join us, if that's the only thing stopping you," he said, flashing her a smile that was like the sun reappearing from behind a cloud. "I'd like to invite my brother and sister-in-law, as well. They've entertained us so many times I've lost count and it's time to repay the favor. Besides, I enjoy a houseful of people underfoot on holidays."

Eager to have Nell meet the Danners, Margo phoned her right away. As she'd expected, her friend snapped up the invitation. All weekend long, as Margo sat at her computer and struggled to pay attention to the brochures and newsletters she'd promised to get out as soon as possible, her mind wanted to focus on pumpkin pies and cranberry sauce. She kept daydreaming about stuffing the festive bird with Sooz's help, and watching Seth beam at everyone in that benign, masterful way he had from the head of his dining-room table.

When Sooz got home from school on Tuesday, Margo asked her if she'd like to go along to the market and help pick out the turkey. "It's quite a responsibility, you know," she added, "getting just the right one."

Sooz's eyes widened. "Could I really?"

Margo risked a hug. "I wouldn't ask if I didn't want your help. But I warn you…we have lots of other groceries to get. And my car's pretty small. On the way home, some of them might end up in your lap."

Seth wasn't due home for quite a while, and for once Sooz didn't have homework. If they got going immediately, they'd be back by dinnertime. Bundled up against the damp, chilly weather, they emerged from the house to find Seth's Mercedes pulling into the drive.

"Daddy! What are you doing home?" Sooz exclaimed as he turned off the engine and got out.

Playfully, Seth pulled her knit cap down around her ears. "I live here, remember? The question is, where are you two ladies going with such eager expressions on your faces?"

By now Sooz was literally bouncing up and down with excitement. "We're going to get the turkey! Please...*pretty please.* Come with us!"

Still smiling, Seth quirked a questioning brow at Margo.

"It might take quite a while," she said. "We've got a lot of stuff to get."

"In that case, you need a bigger car to haul it in. And an extra pair of hands. Allow me to volunteer my services."

Nothing about her experience to date had prompted Margo to view Seth as the domestic type. Yet he truly seemed to enjoy sizing up the plumpest, most promising birds at her favorite market, not to mention checking out the cauliflower, fresh cranberries, spices, homemade mincemeat and extensive wine selection.

Sooz was in seventh heaven. It was impossible not to smile as she dashed between her father and Margo,

touting this or that discovery and adding more selec-
tions to their already overflowing cart.

I know it's dangerous to think this way, Margo
admitted to herself, but we're almost like a family. I
can feel happiness settling into place around me. Well
aware that relationships built on deception had two
strikes against them from the outset, she was none-
theless tempted to hope, as Seth bought her and Sooz
each a bouquet of freesias on their way out of the
market, that the mixup that had drawn them together
might quietly resolve itself.

Thanksgiving dawned misty and overcast, a muted
watercolor of a day still glistening with wash. Not a
trace of unfiltered light—the equivalent of bright,
white paper—showed through. Puget Sound was like
blue milk, its islands mysterious blue-green shapes.
In the shipping lanes, a barge was running with its
lights on. The far-off mountains of the Olympic Pen-
insula were obliterated by clouds.

In an effort to counteract the gloom, Seth built a
fire and put some classical music on the stereo. To
Margo's surprise, a few minutes later he joined her
and Sooz in the kitchen. A domesticated lion that
morning, he offered to clean celery and onions and
run the food-processor while she and Sooz rinsed the
turkey and got out an assortment of spices and bread
crumbs for the dressing.

Margo didn't expect him to. Yet, once the bird was
stuffed, trussed, patted lovingly by Sooz and nestled
in its roasting pan, Seth stayed around, cleaning up
after them as they made pumpkin and mincemeat

pies. At Margo's suggestion, Sooz used the pastry scraps to fashion little jam-filled tarts, which she proudly rolled out herself. Blissfully flour-dusted, with assorted cooking stains on her apron and a streak of jam on her chin, the dark-haired child who'd initially been so unwelcoming to Margo was a model of friendliness and cooperation.

"Thanks," Seth mouthed behind Sooz's back as, with Margo hovering over her for safety's sake, Sooz pulled the cookie sheet with her finished tarts on it from one of the twin ovens.

"My pleasure," Margo's smile replied. She'd had some bad moments on awakening, over Beth's loss. Yet most of her emotions that morning were happy ones. Despite her fears over where it could lead, her feeling of connectedness to Seth and Sooz continued to grow. A strong affection for both of them was putting down permanent roots in her heart.

At last they adjourned to the living room to drink hot chocolate, watch Macy's parade on television and play Chinese checkers in front of the fire. Gradually the turkey began to permeate the air with its heavenly aroma. By the time it was at the point where it needed basting, Seth had settled back with a bowl of popcorn to watch football. Between trips to the kitchen, Margo and Sooz flopped cozily on the couch nearby to leaf through the Christmas catalogs.

Around 4:00 p.m., Nell arrived and was properly introduced. After a few minutes' conversation with Seth, Margo's friend gave her an approving look. The sparkle in Nell's eyes didn't diminish when her gaze rested on Sooz. It was easy to see that Nell agreed:

Sooz was a treasure in her own right and very likely Margo's missing daughter.

An hour or so later, they set the table. Since Seth's brother and partner, Bob Danner, and his wife, Joy, were childless, Margo barely gave it a second thought when she assigned them two places. No one had mentioned they might bring a guest.

In her room, changing from slacks and a sweater to her favorite emerald-green velvet holiday dress, Margo heard *two* unfamiliar female voices in the entryway as Seth welcomed them. She descended the stairs to find Joy's divorced cousin, Samantha, hanging flirtatiously on Seth's arm.

Though Samantha lived and worked in Bellingham, apparently she and Seth had met several times before. Throughout the meal, which earned raves from everyone, the pretty if somewhat jaded looking blonde seemed bent on ingratiating herself with Seth and Sooz—apparently with Bob's and Joy's blessing. Sooz responded warily, obviously scenting strong competition for her father's attention. Relaxed and affable, Seth gave every indication of basking in Samantha's regard.

Unfortunately, after making it clear to him that their relationship mustn't go beyond the casual friendliness of employer and employee, Margo was in no position to protest.

Saturday was Sooz's ninth birthday, just as it would have been Beth's. Expecting to spend the day at home, alone and depressed, Margo let Seth talk her into a boat trip that—thanks to warmer weather—

would culminate in a cookout-birthday party at a cottage he and his brother owned near the village of Friday Harbor on San Juan Island.

"We've already laid claim to most of your holiday...you might as well devote the rest of it to us," he said with a grin when Sooz got into the act and begged her to come along.

Provided they got an early start, it would be an easy day trip north of Seattle on Seth's thirty-foot power yacht, which he kept at the boatworks. Several of Sooz's school friends and their parents had been invited, as well as her Uncle Bob and Aunt Joy. Having learned Samantha would be spending the weekend with them, Margo wasn't too surprised when the pair arrived with her in tow.

Deciding it would be emotional suicide to compete, Margo turned her attention to getting Sooz and her friends settled in the stern as everyone boarded the yacht. To her chagrin, she was only partly successful in ignoring Samantha's blatant campaign. As they left Lake Union and the Lake Washington ship canal behind to pass through the massive Hiram M. Chittenden locks, she was treated to the sight of the seductively attired blonde fraternizing with Seth on the bridge while she and Bob tossed temporary mooring lines to the blue-uniformed attendants.

The trip up, via Puget Sound and the San Juan archipelago, was almost beautiful enough to distract her. San Juan and its sister islands, including Shaw and Orcas, were situated in the so-called rain shadow of Mt. Olympus and they were traditionally sunnier than Seattle. Before long the sun appeared, glinting off the snowcap on distant Mt. Rainier and sparkling on ice-cold water that foamed aquamarine in their wake. The islands themselves, humping like partially submerged whales, were the color of emeralds.

The Danner cottage, on San Juan's southeastern shore, had been built of redwood and sat atop a steep, forested bluff. Because of the disparity between high and low tide in that area, Seth had told Margo, it had a floating dock and ramp. These led to a narrow wooden staircase that zigzagged up the bluff face.

A stranger to everyone but Seth and Sooz, Margo did her best to serve as hostess, passing out snacks and soft drinks and making polite conversation as he cleaned up the outdoor grill for a barbecue. But she didn't *feel* self-effacing. Inside she was steaming. Seth Danner's too good for you, she told his sister-in-law's cousin silently as the woman teased and flirted with him.

As the afternoon wore on, it appeared that, for Margo, the only high point of the day would be Sooz's delight when she opened her gifts. Cuddling the rag doll that Margo had fashioned in her image, complete with miniature flannel pajamas that resembled the kind she usually wore, Sooz flung her arms around Margo and gave her a resounding kiss on the cheek.

"This doll comes with a special offer, you know," Margo said with a lump in her throat.

Open by now to considering almost any deal Margo cared to suggest, Sooz demanded an explanation.

"If you take extra good care of her," Margo explained, "on Christmas morning, you'll find more clothes for her under the tree."

Sooz's dark eyes danced with anticipation. "I will, Margo. I promise!" she exclaimed.

Flattered by Samantha's attention, though she wasn't his type, Seth watched his daughter and Margo interact with pleasure. In his opinion, Sooz hadn't looked as happy and secure since she was a toddler. Margo's been good for both of us, he thought, though it's impossible to live under the same roof with her and not want to kiss her until she melts. I wonder what it would take to change her mind about us....

Maybe he was imagining things, but he had the distinct impression that she wasn't too happy over Samantha's flirtation with him. And then there'd been that incident in the kitchen. She'd participated fully, no mistake. So she had to be interested.

It was an unseasonably warm afternoon, considering the month and the latitude. With Sooz's birthday cake reduced to crumbs and the children off to play a game of tag among the trees, the adults pitched in to dispose of the debris, then settled back in a motley collection of outdoor chairs for coffee and conversation. Clinging to Seth like a leech, Samantha claimed the place of honor beside him on an Adirondack-style wooden bench.

That tears it, thought Margo in disgust. I can't take any more of this. My voluntary duties as hostess are about finished and I need a few minutes to myself. Mentioning something about going down to the yacht to retrieve a sweater, she descended the wooden staircase that led to the water.

About halfway down, hidden by the bluff from the party above, she paused and leaned over the railing. Waves were washing to shore from the wake of the Anacortes-San Juan ferry as it made for Friday Harbor and she didn't hear Seth's footsteps on the weathered planking behind her. She jumped when he put his arms around her waist.

"You startled me!" she exclaimed, turning to face him.

"Did I?"

His murmur was husky and intimate, and—if she really wanted to keep him at arm's length—the maneuver had been a mistake. Desperately, she racked her brain for something to say.

"I was just on my way down to get a sweater..."

Seth lowered his head. She could feel his breath on her like a caress.

"So I understood," he said. "I came after you to say that you won't need it...not with me to keep you warm."

Any protest she might have voiced was forgotten as his mouth took possession of hers. In an instant the afternoon's frustrations were swept aside. Screened from the eyes of Sooz's birthday guests and lost in a green-and-blue world of fir trees and water, they touched and tasted. With each thrust of his tongue and heated response from hers, they moved deeper into a wilderness of passion from which ultimately there might be no retreat.

At last Seth drew back and looked at her.

"I thought...we weren't going to do that again," she whispered.

"So did I," he admitted, placing a light kiss on the tip of her nose. "But then I seem to be fairly weak-willed where you're concerned. Tell you what... I'm ready to break the rules whenever you are. I'll leave the time and place of our next infraction up to you."

CHAPTER FIVE

DURING the next few days, Sooz seemed to open like the petals of a flower under Margo's influence. Humbled by the girl's trust and aware she didn't fully deserve it, Margo realized she'd gone from curiosity and exasperation to loving her very much. Though she didn't dare ask for the genetic tissue test that would prove it, she was almost one hundred percent certain Sooz was hers, the child she'd carried in her womb.

Her feelings for the girl raised a question she couldn't avoid indefinitely—namely, whether to give Sooz up, tell Seth the truth and risk alienating him, or settle for something in between. She couldn't continue as the family housekeeper forever, even if she were willing to consign her desktop publishing business to the scrap heap. Ultimately, living on the fringe of Sooz's life wouldn't be enough.

There was also the problem of Seth. With each passing day, her desire and affection for the tall, redheaded yacht builder grew. His kiss on the wooden steps leading down to the water from his vacation cottage and the challenge of sorts that had followed it had done everything to excite and unsettle her and done nothing for her peace of mind.

If she'd understood him correctly, he didn't intend the interplay of sensual possibilities between them to end there. Though she'd escaped back up the bluff, deciding she didn't need a sweater after all, his tawny eyes had followed her. "When are you going to give up and admit we're fatally attracted to each other?" they'd seemed to ask as she'd moved self-consciously among his guests. "A divorced father shouldn't have to walk on eggs forever. Why can't you care about us both?"

The unresolved tension between them had only increased since they'd returned to Seattle. Every look, every unspoken comment from Seth prompted her to commit the next "infraction," as he'd put it. Soon, something would have to give.

As the weekend approached, Margo thought she might get a breather. Seth's ex-wife, Cheryl, and her new husband, Tom Magnuson, were scheduled to breeze into town on Saturday for a couple of days before flying on to Chicago. The inevitable awkwardness of their visit should take Seth's focus off *her* for a while.

During their stay, Seth had agreed to let Sooz sleep over with her mother and stepfather at a downtown hotel. Supposedly a belated birthday celebration was in the works. Though she hadn't worked for the Danners long, Margo had already guessed how the Cheryl-Sooz equation worked. Stingy with her time and attention, Cheryl gave lots of expensive presents.

As Saturday drew near, Sooz's excitement escalated until she was all but jumping out of her skin. There's no need to be jealous, Margo reminded herself with only partial success as she prepared to depart for her Ravenna bungalow. You can't expect to assume Cheryl's place in Sooz's heart any more than she could have supplanted you with Beth.

She couldn't help being a little envious, though, of the woman Sooz clearly loved so much. How could Cheryl have given up her daughter so easily, and settled for infrequent visits? According to Harry Spence, custody had never been an issue.

In fact, how could Cheryl have given up Seth?

Sooz rushed to answer the door Saturday morning when Cheryl and Tom arrived—fully two hours late. From his office, where he'd holed up to avoid the initial drama of the mother-daughter reunion, Seth could hear his daughter's fervent squeals of delight. They were accompanied by Cheryl's effervescent laughter and Tom Magnuson's affable, slightly nervous boom.

Seth had nothing against Tom, though the wealthy real estate magnate had been seeing his ex-wife while she was still married to him. The person he blamed for that blatant lapse of decency was Cheryl. As his wife, she had owed him loyalty and a certain amount of respect. The least she could have done was let him know before going out and finding herself another, wealthier husband.

It's my damn pride, Seth acknowledged ruefully, putting aside the estimate he'd been working on. He'd lived long enough to realize that the need to avoid embarrassment and ridicule was one of his biggest stumbling blocks. Maybe seeing Cheryl again would be easier if he remembered she'd done him a favor by leaving him.

His ex-wife and her new husband were ultra-polite when he entered the living room. About to offer his hand, Tom Magnuson apparently thought better of it and thrust it back into his pocket. Sooz, of course, was jumping up and down, hanging onto her mother. Though she had eyes only for Cheryl, Seth knew his daughter's keen ability in picking up unfriendly vibes between her parents only too well. She'd detect—and be upset by—the slightest hint of discord.

"Hi, Cheryl...Tom. How are you?" Seth greeted them, doing his best to be magnanimous. "You're both looking well."

After they'd gone, taking Sooz with them, he was at loose ends. Though Margo had enlivened its decor, adding a few colorful pillows here, and an afghan there, without her and his daughter, the house seemed empty. He considered finishing the estimate he'd started. Or putting in some extra time at the boat yard. Neither idea appealed to him. Throughout the week, the weather had continued unseasonably warm and clear. It was a fine day for an outing. Except for Sooz, there was only one person he wanted to spend it with.

Busy playing catch-up on her computer, Margo frowned when the doorbell rang. Darn, she thought, somebody trying to sell me something. Then she softened her irritation. Maybe her caller was a Brownie or a Girl Scout, hoping to land a cookie order.

Her eyes widened as she opened the door. "Seth!" she exclaimed, staring up at him in astonishment. "What are you doing here? Is anything wrong?"

He shrugged, not quite sure of his welcome. "Not

really. The house seemed kind of empty with Sooz gone. I got lonesome.''

For whatever reason, he'd turned to her. A warm little flame of pleasure curled to life inside her. At the same time, she shuddered as she took mental inventory of herself and the home that had become something of a weekend getaway.

Seth had chosen to arrive, unannounced, at her usually tidy bungalow on a morning when she'd barely combed her hair and had left the previous night's dishes soaking in the sink. Some housekeeper she'd turned out to be on her own turf! And some glamour girl—she hadn't even put on lipstick!

"Aren't you going to ask me in?" he said.

Head-over-heels crazy about him, Margo couldn't send him away, though she was well aware that being alone with him meant flirting with danger.

"Of course," she answered, stepping aside so he could enter. "It's just that you startled me, turning up out of the blue like this. Promise me you'll keep your eyes closed. Or at the very least, excuse the way I look. I'm afraid the house is a bit of a mess, too. I let things slide so I could finish up some work…"

If she expected him to keep his eyes shut, then she'd have to lead him around by the hand. Come to think of it, if she did that, he'd be justified groping in support. But while it was an entrancing idea, he wasn't willing to forego the satisfaction of looking her over from head to toe. She was positively scrumptious this morning in a baggy sweatshirt with no apparent bra beneath it, and form-fitting, faded jeans that were fraying at the knees. He ached to sweep her off her feet.

"I know I should have called first," he admitted with the beginnings of a grin as he glanced around her cozy living room with its white brick fireplace, multiple shelves of books and overstuffed couch upholstered in a rose-and-white tulip pattern, then back at her. "Of course, you might have said no. Have you had breakfast? All I managed this morning was a cup of instant coffee and a stale doughnut."

Margo realized he wasn't complaining. He was just being a typical man: semi-helpless in the kitchen and more than willing to let someone take care of him, preferably a woman. Distracted by his strong male allure, she tried to picture the contents of her refrigerator. Now that she was gone five days out of seven, its contents were pretty meager. She'd just been thinking she ought to do some shopping.

"I'm afraid I don't have much in the way of groceries on hand," she admitted. "If we're lucky, I might be able to rustle you up some scrambled eggs and toast."

It was nearly noon. And Seth hadn't driven across town simply so she could cook for him. He resisted the urge to pull her into his arms and place a warm little kiss on the tip of her nose.

"I thought we might go out," he answered. "For lunch. My treat. The weather's great and, afterward, we could bum around awhile. That is, if you have time and I wouldn't be taking you away from anything important."

Margo had turned out no work the previous week-

end. If she took Seth up on his invitation, she'd have
to beg for an extension on the Peterson project. And,
though she'd probably get it, there were other pitfalls.
The kind of "going out" he had in mind would permanently transform the nature of their relationship.

Well, what was life anyway but a series of risks?
If getting closer to Seth was a mistake, she'd pay the
price. At the moment, it felt exactly right.

"There's nothing I can't finish later," she decided,
running her fingers through her tousled mane of curls
in a preliminary effort to tame them. "If you don't
mind waiting, I'll run and change."

Seth had dressed casually in loafers, tan corduroy
slacks, a cream-colored cable-knit sweater and a
bomber-style leather jacket. Pouring on the steam,
Margo raced and shucked her disreputable working
clothes and pawed frantically through her closet. She
wanted to look her best!

Shifting his attention from a collection of family
photographs arranged on a table as she came running
back, Seth couldn't believe the speed or extent of her
transformation. For her day of "bumming" around
with him, Margo had chosen a schoolgirl tartan that
ended at mid-thigh. Its pleats swished flirtatiously
above shapely legs clad in demure red tights. A tailored white blouse left open at the throat and a red
wool-velour blazer completed her outfit. The flat
skimmers she wore only added to her youthful look.

She could be Sooz's older sister, Seth thought.
They even look alike. But he knew Margo's age;
she'd mentioned it when she'd applied for work with
him. She was thirty-one—just seven years shy of his

own randy and still youthful thirty-eight. No problem there.

"You look terrific," he said, meaning it.

So do you, she wanted to answer. Something about the way he stood gazing down at her, with his six foot, two inch frame taking up an inordinate amount of space in her tiny living room, made her heart turn over. It was like having a magnificent and only partly domesticated wild animal under her roof. Maybe even eating out of her hand.

At Seth's suggestion, they drove to Pike Place, Seattle's revamped covered market situated between the downtown skyscrapers and the port. By sheer luck, he managed to find a parking place for the Mercedes on a nearby street.

"I thought we might try the Athenian Café," he murmured, taking firm possession of Margo's hand and leading her inside, past crowded produce stalls where every apple was polished and every bunch of broccoli beaded with water droplets.

As usual, the stall keepers could easily have been mistaken for carnival barkers as they touted the quality and low cost of their wares. The hawkers of fresh seafood, including Dungeness crab and pink-hued salmon on beds of crushed ice, seemed even more intent on showmanship.

Joining the throng of shoppers and tourists who wandered the market's narrow aisles, Margo and Seth skirted T-shirt vendors and displays of exotic spices, a Chinese fast-food counter and racks of foreign magazines. A youngish, bearded man with a guitar was singing religious songs and accepting contributions. A woman passed out leaflets advertising a free peace concert. From his vantage point atop his father's shoulders, a toddler in a bunny suit stared at the shifting scene with solemn eyes.

The Athenian—bustling, smoky and somewhat dark except for a double tier of window booths overlooking the water—offered an oasis of sorts. It had an old-fashioned square lunch counter with round, chrome and red leatherette stools. Honey-soaked Greek pastries glistened on paper-lace doilies in domed and footed glass dishes. A huge copper samovar, no longer used to dispense coffee, was part of the restaurant's ambiance.

Seth tipped the hostess to ensure them a window seat. "This has to be one of the best views of Elliott Bay from downtown...at least from street level," he remarked, sliding onto the bench opposite hers though he'd have preferred to sit beside her.

Scarcely able to believe they were actually spending the day together, Margo smiled back at him. "You're right," she agreed, noting with pleasure the little laugh lines at the corners of his eyes and the generous proportions of his mouth. "Today you can see the mountains. With the sun on their peaks, they're just a shade darker than the sky."

Though the menu featured a variety of main dishes and accompaniments ranging from seafood fettucine to Jugoslav potatoes, they settled for Greek salads, conversation and a glass of retsina each. When they'd finished, Seth suggested they descend through the market's lower levels to the port and play tourist by visiting the city's famed aquarium.

They were employee and employer. Amateur sleuth and an unwitting target of her clandestine quest for information. The questions of Sooz's parentage and Margo's failure to tell the truth about her motives stood ready to separate them. But Margo didn't want to think about that. For a day, an hour, the next few minutes, if that's all she was destined to have with him, she wanted to live in the present.

"Sounds great," she answered, pushing guilt back into its subterranean hiding place.

Hand in hand, they scrambled down seemingly endless steps to emerge in sunlight. Across the trolley tracks and busy Alaskan Way was the city's popular waterfront promenade with its fish 'n' chip eateries, souvenir shops, harbor tour ticket booths and ferry docks.

"Did you change your mind?" Margo asked when Seth tugged her to a halt on the wooden decking outside the aquarium entrance.

His hands spanned her waist. "I know I promised to let you choose the time and place for our next infraction, but I can't wait."

They were in full public view—center stage with the city for a backdrop—as he took possession of her mouth. By now his warmth, the incomparable taste of him, had become as necessary to her as light and breath. Straining on tiptoe, she returned his kiss full measure. Time slowed, pouring out like honey as their tongues made contact.

How much deeper in each other could they get?

They both knew the answer: a *lot* deeper. At last Seth drew back and looked at her. A forest fire of need was raging in his tawny eyes.

"You know, don't you," he growled, "that you're habit forming?"

Still drowning in the exquisite morass of feelings he'd evoked, Margo wasn't sure how to answer him. She only knew she wanted them to go on touching.

Seth had similar aspirations. Though she'd failed to confirm what they'd just shared in words, her capitulation and the way she continued to let him hold her told him everything he thought he needed to know. "Let's go inside," he said gruffly, staking his claim with one possessive arm about her shoulders.

That afternoon, the aquarium's dim, underwater light, the echoing voices of children and tank after tank of exotic sea life took on a surreal quality Margo would never forget. It was almost as if the sharks, clown fish and sea anemones they viewed had originated on another planet.

All her real attention was focused on Seth. With a yearning that sprang from some primitive place inside her, she longed to kiss him again and again until they were both drunk with it. Yet it was magical, too, just being with him. Where before she'd existed separately in the world, for today, at least, the two of them were a couple.

As they stood in semi-darkness, watching sunlight filter through an overhead tank of frantically swimming salmon "fingerlings," Margo dared to slip an arm about his waist. In response, he drew her closer. Lovers come here, she thought. Later, they return as husband and wife to explain the sea's wonders to their children. If her suspicions were correct, she and Seth already shared a child, though they hadn't created her together in love.

From the aquarium, they took a streetcar to the International District, where they browsed through Uwajimaya, a huge Oriental grocery-hardware store, then crossed the street so Seth could purchase a mango sponge cake, the specialty of a bakery he knew.

"You don't seriously expect us to eat the whole thing?" Margo protested in mock dismay as they walked back to the trolley terminus.

"We could have a food fight with it when we get back to your house," he answered imperturbably, holding the cake box upright in one hand while making sure she stayed close beside him with the other. "But these cakes are pretty fabulous. If you've never tasted one, maybe you'd better sample it first."

The day was cool enough for his purchase to keep without refrigeration. When they reached the Mercedes again, Seth proposed drinks atop the Space Needle at Seattle Center. "We can make it coffee if you like," he said. "After spending most of the day at sea level, I have an overwhelming urge to lay the city at your feet."

In the Needle's revolving restaurant, they shared cappuccinos and held hands as the sun dipped in the west to disappear in a streak of pure beaten gold. Studded with more and more lights, the city's cozy, identifiable hills assumed their nocturnal glitter as the dusk deepened to indigo. Downtown, the cluster of

tall buildings that thrust skyward, was paved with diamonds.

Consulting each other's taste, they discovered they
both liked jazz. They wound up having a casual supper at Dimitriou's Jazz Alley and hanging around for
part of the show. At last they were back at Margo's
door.

It was the classic moment of truth. Should she ask
him in? Though the same troublesome caveats that
had bothered her earlier still applied, there wasn't any
real doubt in her mind. She couldn't let him go without another taste of what had pleased them both so
much.

"My fireplace isn't as elegant as yours, but I have
a few birch logs and some cognac left over from an
impulse buy last winter," she said. "Would you care
to partake?"

She didn't have to extend the invitation twice.

Unlocking her front door, Seth tossed his jacket
over a chair and set about building a fire while she
took off her shoes, stowed the mango cake in the
refrigerator and poured out their drinks.

Their fingers brushed as she handed him a miniature snifter, half filled with potent amber liquid, and
her inner glow of excitement deepened. "Any musical preference?" she asked casually, placing her snifter on the coffee table and going over to the stereo.

Seth had kicked off his loafers. He was padding
about in his woolly socks. "You choose," he replied,
taking a seat on the couch next to the one she'd staked
out. "Mind if I appropriate one of these throw pillows
and put up my feet?"

A warm little shiver of anticipation coursed through her. "Be my guest."

Selecting Ray Lynch's compact disc, "Deep Breakfast," which she set to repeat at low volume, Margo returned to his side. It seemed the most natural thing in the world that he should slip an arm around her.

There was nobody else about, no beloved but difficult Sooz to catch them and take offense. The lamp they'd turned on when they arrived had a three-way bulb and Seth had switched it to low. Its diffuse illumination didn't compete with the romance of the firelight as they sipped at their cognacs and set them aside.

Seconds later, they were in each other's arms.

"God, how I want you," Seth confessed, pulling her onto his lap and crushing her mouth with his. "Being so close to you all day...it's made me crazy."

Margo wanted him too—a thousand times more desperately than she'd known it was possible to want someone. "I know," she admitted when he gave her a chance to speak. "I felt the same way."

It was as if an avalanche had been set in motion. Fierce and tender, with the finesse of heaven's most accomplished archangel, Seth probed her mouth's moist privacy with his tongue in imitation of the act of love. Every ounce of fervor Margo possessed welcomed him. Encouraged not to stop at barriers, he inserted one hand beneath her blouse, then inside the lacy scrap of her bra. She moaned softly as he stroked her nipples to taut readiness.

Flooded though she was with mind-blowing sen-

sations, she knew what they were ready for: the sweet
marauding tug of his mouth. She wanted to give him
everything—every womanly attribute and soul-
satisfying pleasure that could take shape in her imagination. Poised on the brink of complete abandonment, she gloried in the hard sensation of his thighs
beneath her buttocks.

You mustn't do this, the voice of reason pleaded,
struggling to be heard. You have to think of Sooz,
and where your deception of Seth might lead. Do you
want to love him only to lose him? The woman who
lusted so hotly in her refused to be satisfied with
crumbs. Or logic. It's been nine years, that sensual,
reckless woman argued. You deserve a night of happiness. In the morning, you can work things out.

To her surprise, it was Seth who called a halt. Taking a deep breath, he removed his hand from beneath
her blouse and cuddled her head against his shoulder.

"Don't I...please you?" she faltered, her cheeks
going scarlet.

"Ah, Margo..." With a little shake of his head,
Seth tightened his hold. "I want more from you than
an hour of bliss, followed by your resignation in the
morning. That's why I won't make love to you so
precipitously. But, if you'll let me, I'd like to spend
the night."

CHAPTER SIX

RELUCTANTLY Margo had to admit Seth was right—
for reasons he knew nothing about. If they became
lovers, and she didn't offer him a full and immediate
explanation of her reason for accepting work as his
housekeeper, she'd be in an untenable ethical position. Since she wasn't ready to face that hurdle, she
had no business making love to him. Yet she didn't
want him to go.

Meanwhile, there wasn't much doubt what would
happen if they shared a bed.

"I have a guest room..." she offered uncertainly.

Seth brushed a strand of dark, curly hair back from
her forehead and replaced it with a kiss. "Thanks but
no thanks. I'm not willing for us to sleep that far
apart."

Ultimately they compromised by dozing off right
there on the couch, under a quilt Margo's grandmother had pieced together many years earlier. When
they woke, stiff and groggy from sleeping scrunched
together in their clothes, it was already light.

For several awkward moments, they seemed like
strangers. Determined to take advantage of Sooz's absence by spending as much time with Margo as he
could, Seth quickly moved to dispel the notion. Murmuring something about being creased in more places
than a road map, he gave her a gentle good-morning

kiss. She found the stubble of beard that had appeared on his jaw overnight intoxicating.

It was morning—time to expand the friendship part of their relationship. Slipping on his shoes, Seth volunteered to go after the Sunday paper while she put on the coffee.

Overnight, it had turned colder and started to rain. Still rumpled but relatively free of aches after exercising their necks and shoulders, they drank mugs of Margo's favorite hazelnut-flavored brew from Starbucks and ate wedges of Seth's mango cake in lieu of a more conventional breakfast.

Afterward, they spent a lazy morning passing various sections of the *Times* back and forth and mounting a joint assault on the day's crossword puzzle. Though they exchanged a few more kisses, Seth kept it light. Unless he was very much mistaken, Margo had begun to worry about what would happen when their stolen weekend had run its course. That evening, she was due to report back for work.

When it was time to part, they shared a lengthy kiss at her front door. It was soul-wrenching in its intensity.

"You needn't worry that I'll embarrass you in front of Sooz," he said when at last they came up for air. "I won't. But I have some very definite intentions where you're concerned. I don't plan to let you off the hook."

Seth had arranged to pick up Sooz from her mother around four o'clock, as the Magnusons planned to rest before attending a party that night. Returning to the house on Magnolia Boulevard a few minutes before seven, Margo got a warm but restrained welcome from Seth. Covertly squeezing her hand, he disappeared into his study. Sooz was moping at the kitchen table, trying to catch up on neglected homework.

The girl didn't respond by word or glance to Margo's greeting. "So...how was your weekend?" Margo asked with a shrug, getting out the makings of an elaborate school lunch. "Did you have a good time?"

Still Sooz refused to look at her. "It was okay, I guess," she mumbled.

Masked though it was by the noncommittal reply, Margo thought she detected a cry for help. Having learned Cheryl and her husband planned to depart for Chicago in the morning and, subsequently, to spend several months in Atlanta overseeing one of his real estate projects before passing through Seattle again on their way back to Honolulu, Margo was willing to bet she knew the reason for Sooz's distress. It was clear to anyone with half a brain that time spent with Sooz wasn't very high on the Magnusons' priority list. No dummy, the girl had easily figured it out. She was wounded to the quick.

About to ask whether Sooz had received any birthday presents she particularly liked in an effort to strike a positive note, Margo thought better of it. Kids knew the difference between money spent on them and genuine affection.

At the moment, she realized, a hug from her definitely wouldn't be appreciated.

"Know what?" she remarked, observing a strict hands-off policy. "The weather's turned cold and I could use some hot chocolate. But I hate to make it just for myself. I don't suppose I could talk you into having some…''

Early on in their acquaintance, she'd established hot chocolate as a remedy for emotional bruises and bumps. Subliminally, at least, Sooz seemed to make the connection.

"Maybe you could," the dark-eyed moppet allowed, perking up a little. "Are you any good at arithmetic?"

For the next few days, Seth didn't say or do anything to arouse Sooz's suspicions about them. Thanks to the looks they exchanged and an occasional brush of hands that seemed to come about by accident, Margo knew that it was just a temporary reprieve. Things had changed as a result of their idyllic day together and the cramped but cozy night they'd spent on her living-room couch.

In a sense, they were lovers already though they hadn't made love. Someday soon she'd have to face the music. Yet if she opted for honesty, she stood to lose the two people she cared about most.

Obviously still missing Cheryl and feeling betrayed, Sooz clung to Margo the way a drowning man might clutch at a life raft, though characteristically she made a show of maintaining her independence. In return, Margo tried to distract the girl and herself by teaching her to make clothespin angels for the Christmas tree and baking endless batches of cookies in cutout shapes, which Sooz meticulously decorated.

Margo was well aware she and Seth couldn't walk

an emotional tightrope forever, pretending nothing had changed between them. Though she suffered a little stab of panic, she wasn't too surprised when, late Friday morning, he phoned from the boat yard, catching her in the midst of putting away the weekend groceries.

"I've lined up Mrs. Johnson to baby-sit," he announced. "We're going out tonight."

Just like that? What would Sooz say?

"You make it sound as if I don't have any choice," she hedged.

"You don't," he agreed. "The Guarneri Quartet is in town and I've sprung for tickets. I refuse to let them go to waste."

Sooz was lying in the front of the television set with Bear, watching a video, when Seth got home and broke the news about their date. From her strategic vantage point in the kitchen, where she was nervously tidying up, Margo could tell the girl wasn't pleased. No doubt to her, their involvement seemed like one more rejection.

"I'm not hungry!" Sooz snapped when Margo dared to poke her head into the living room a few minutes later and offered to fix her a supper tray.

Scooping up Bear, she stomped up to her room in a blue funk. Despite her affection for Mrs. Johnson, she refused to put in an appearance when the older woman arrived.

Margo was torn with guilt. "Looks like we've done it now," she told Seth anxiously as they left the house. "We've got Sooz mad at us. And I noticed one of your next-door neighbors pulling back the curtains to observe our departure. Before you know it, our reputations will be in shreds.''

Seth didn't appear perturbed as he helped her into the Mercedes' passenger seat. ''To tell you the truth, I was planning to discuss that problem with you later this evening,'' he replied, his eyes telegraphing a message she couldn't seem to translate.

For Margo, the dinner they shared that evening at a Thai restaurant on the north shore of Green Lake and the Guarneri concert at the University of Washington that followed it, were fraught with conflicting emotions. On the one hand, she felt as if she'd re-entered the blissful, romantic state that had so captivated her the previous weekend. And on the other? Things were moving much too rapidly for comfort.

With Seth's announcement that they were ''going out,'' she feared that Sooz had begun to view her as his new girlfriend—competition for his affection rather than a stable, caring force. Coming as it did on the heels of Cheryl's de facto abandonment, the revelation had doubtless packed a double whammy. All of Margo's efforts to win Sooz's friendship and confidence would likely be thrown back in her face.

I never should have agreed to go out with him tonight, Margo thought, thoroughly upset with herself. Sooz is the reason Seth and I got together and Sooz has to be my first priority. Yet in a man-woman way, she loved him just as much.

The weather was nippy but well above freezing. Though Margo's raincoat and zip-in liner would have been adequate protection, Seth had proposed she wear her full-length woolen coat and bring a scarf. She understood why when, as they drove out of the parking garage beneath the university's Meany Hall, he remarked that a dose of wind and salt spray aboard the Bainbridge Island ferry would be just the ticket to clear their heads.

"If you haven't ridden it before," he coaxed, "it takes just a little over an hour, round trip. The view of downtown Seattle is breathtaking."

Since it was long past rush hour and winter in the bargain, the ferry wasn't crowded. Tired shoppers and commuters, who'd stayed in town for dinner or worked late, settled back to read in the brightly lit observation salon's blue plastic chairs. The more exhausted looking stretched out on black leatherette benches by the windows.

Only the hardy opted for fresh air. Though it was cold and damp outside, Margo and Seth chose a protected spot on the rear deck, where the view would be most spectacular. As the ferry separated from the dock and they retreated from the city's brilliance, she realized fully why he'd suggested they make the trip.

The panorama that spread before them was like New York at night. Or Camelot. Taillights from a steady stream of cars glow-wormed their way over the city's hills. Its skyscrapers were bands of diamonds set in concrete. Floodlights from the Kingdome poured gold onto the hiss and slap of the water.

A light plane, winking against the overcast, passed by on the left. Nestled in Seth's arms, with tiny pinpoints of rain and mist hitting her in the face, Margo could feel the thrum of the ferry's powerful engines radiating up through the deck into the soles of her leather boots.

The further they got from it, the more unreal downtown Seattle appeared. Miniaturized, it became a toy, the scene on a glitzy postcard.

"Beautiful, isn't it?" Seth whispered.

She lifted her face to his. "I never realized..."

A moment later they were kissing—hungrily, desperately. Built up during a week of longing and self-denial, the force of their need for each other had grown until it was like a tornado that threatened to destroy everything in its path. Aching to succumb to its passionate intensity, Margo struggled to maintain her perspective. She couldn't help worrying about Sooz. Or the secret she'd kept from the man she loved so much.

"Seth, please!" she protested when he gave her a chance to speak. "We can't go on like this..."

"Hush, sweetheart." He placed one loving finger against her mouth. "I planned to save this for the return trip, but you've forced my hand. I know it's sudden. But I've never been more sure of anything than I am about what I feel for you. I want to marry you, Margo. Make love to you every night. In that order, so Sooz won't be scandalized and the neighbors can't disapprove."

Margo was speechless. She wasn't sure if it was the biting salt spray making her eyes water so, or if it was tears of mingled happiness and regret.

"Oh, Seth," she moaned. "You know it would never work. Sooz..."

"Hasn't been this happy since Cheryl and I divorced. Oh, I know how she behaved tonight. She's upset and jealous...probably more over me stealing you from her than vice versa. Given time, she'll learn that we can share you, and adjust. In the long run, our getting together will be the very best thing that's ever happened to her."

Unbidden, the idea that she could have Seth *and* the daughter she'd lost at birth took root in Margo's heart. The only price she'd have to pay was silence. And the loss of her self-respect. She couldn't build their marriage on a lie.

"Say yes," he prompted in a husky voice. "I love you so much."

In the end, though she confessed she loved him too, she'd only agree to think about his proposal. They were subdued, exceptionally quiet with each other as they returned to the house on Magnolia Boulevard. At Seth's invitation, Margo accompanied him upstairs to check on Sooz before leaving for the weekend. The girl was sprawled on her stomach, one arm flung out in sleep to make contact with her precious stuffed teddy.

"Cheryl gave Bear to Sooz the last Christmas we were together," Seth admitted in a hushed voice. "She hasn't been without him since."

Gazing at the stubborn, vulnerable child who had almost certainly taken shape inside her body, Margo vowed never to knowingly do anything that would hurt her. She hoped that wouldn't mean giving her up, along with the chance for a life with Seth.

The weekend, during which she'd had her father to herself, didn't improve Sooz's perspective. Returning on Sunday night, Margo found herself facing the same uphill battle that had loomed when she'd first accepted employment with Seth. *No, that's not quite accurate,* she thought. *This is worse. Before I had a blank slate. Now Sooz views me as a traitor.*

In a quiet talk with Seth one night after the girl had gone to sleep, Margo asked that he give her time. And space. She couldn't possibly go out with him—or consider discussing his marriage proposal—until the situation with Sooz smoothed out.

"If we wait until she calms down, we'll just have to go through this all over again," Seth argued, feeling her slip away. "Calling a spade a spade will force her to get used to the idea. The sooner you and I wed, the sooner all three of us will be happy together."

To his amazement, though she was usually putty in his hands, Margo wouldn't budge.

"If we can't get married right away, or even date, at the very least, I want you here on Christmas," he replied, determined to make some kind of progress with her.

Slowly she shook her head. "If I stayed, Sooz would sulk. The holiday would be miserable. Besides, I need time to think."

True to her word, Margo spent Christmas Eve alone, with her memories of Beth and Jim. But she wasn't mired in the past. Instead she was aching for Sooz and the future Seth wanted to give her. All her energy had gone into decorating the Danner household and now she was drained. She couldn't make herself put up a tree. Her effort to light a few candles and put some Christmas music on the stereo fell flat. She couldn't seem to make the holiday exist, even in her own imagination.

On Christmas Day, she dragged herself over to Nell's for dinner and found herself ducking the concern she saw in the kindly nurse's eyes. With Nell's gentleman friend making it a threesome at the table, she managed to fend off any conversational forays into personal territory.

When she returned to work on December twenty-sixth, Sooz was so difficult it brought tears to her eyes. Maybe the best thing for everyone concerned would be for me to bow out, Margo thought. Still depressed from the holidays and afraid to tell Seth that she'd been less than honest with him, she decided to quit. Even if he could forgive me for not telling him the truth, she reasoned, he'd think I was trying to take Sooz away from him. Meanwhile, she wants nothing to do with me. It's an impossible situation.

Seth came home to find her packing. "What are you doing?" he asked, a thunderbolt of a frown drawing his blond brows together.

When she explained that she was leaving because it would be best for all concerned, she thought he'd explode. "What happened to our six-month agreement?" he demanded angrily. "And your claim to care about us?"

Sooz chose that moment to stumble onto the tense scene. "What's going on?" she asked, looking from her father to Margo and back again with a frightened expression.

"Margo's leaving us," Seth announced in a clipped tone. "She doesn't think you want her to stay."

"Oh, but I *do*..."

Betrayed into blurting out her innermost feelings, Sooz retreated a little. But Seth wouldn't let her get by with it.

"I've asked Margo to marry me," he told the girl bluntly. "If she says yes, she'll be my wife. And your stepmother. She'll live here with us permanently. I'd appreciate it if you'd let us both know—very honestly—how you feel about that."

There was a long silence during which Sooz searched their faces, then looked down at her shoes. Appalled at the way he was handling the situation, Margo could feel Seth willing her to keep silent. The male lion at his most regal, he wouldn't welcome any interference.

"I guess...that would be okay," the girl admitted at last.

Seth was relentless. "How about *more* than okay?"

Sooz bit her lip, then started to smile. "Yes, Daddy," she confessed.

With typical mastery, he drew them both into his arms. "Now you have to say yes," he told Margo triumphantly. "You don't have any other choice."

CHAPTER SEVEN

STUNNED, Margo found herself wearing Seth's diamond. It had all happened so quickly—Sooz's capitulation, his categorical statement that now there could be no impediment to their marrying, her own surge of hope that, out of a tragic mix-up, the heartache of divorce and death and her own weak-willed failure to tell him the truth could come a happy ending for everyone. Actual belief hadn't settled in for several days.

She hadn't said yes exactly. Just nodded with tears in her eyes. Seth had kissed her and Sooz, and pronounced it a done deal. The following day, he, Margo and the energetic sprite who'd drawn them together had gone to Friedlander's to pick out an engagement ring and two wedding bands.

The diamond they'd selected was pear-shaped, nearly two carats of blue-white fire poised above a plain yellow-gold band. Their wedding rings, which matched, were also fashioned of yellow gold. For Sooz, they chose a heart-shaped gold locket set with a tiny aquamarine.

Engraved on the spot, the locket's reverse side bore the inscription *Susan, Daddy & Margo*, and the date *January 15*. Before returning it to its velvet box, Seth explained that it symbolized the important role Sooz

would play in the three-way pact they'd made to love
and cherish each other.

"You'll be one of the three most important people
at the ceremony, pumpkin," he promised the entranced child. "When we finish exchanging wedding
rings, Margo and I fasten it around your neck."

That all important moment was just eighteen days
hence. Ironically, they'd chosen a date three days before the first anniversary of Beth Ann's death. Happier than she'd ever thought possible after such a
wrenching loss, yet increasingly guilt-ridden as her
wedding day approached, Margo wanted to believe
she'd have unburdened her conscience the day they'd
settled things if Sooz hadn't been standing there. But
she couldn't be sure. She only knew she loved both
the man and the child too much to risk losing them.

Surely love will carry us through, she told herself.
Why should a secret that doesn't matter anymore be
allowed to spoil things? Now that he was hers, that
she knew he loved her back, life without Seth would
be a desert. And though Sooz would never know the
truth about their biological relationship, she'd be Margo's daughter in every practical sense.

Margo couldn't hide her qualms from Nell, who
accompanied her to a well-known Sixth Avenue boutique in her search for a wedding outfit. Twisting and
turning before a three-way mirror in a marked-down
beauty of a pale aqua silk *duppioni* suit with pavé
rhinestone buttons, she kept meeting a look that was
part fondness, part worry in her friend's eyes.

"Okay…let's have it," she said, confronting Nell
face-to-face.

Perched on a corner stool in the dressing room with both Margo's purse and her own, as well as several packages, piled on her lap, Nell nodded. "It's perfect...glamorous but elegant. And very flattering to your complexion."

Margo agreed. The suit was exactly what she'd been looking for. Though it was expensive even on sale, it would be worth every penny.

"You know what I mean," she countered stubbornly.

Nell sighed. "I suppose I do. You're talking about the fact that you haven't confided in Seth."

The heightened color in Margo's cheeks offered silent confirmation that the older woman was right on target.

"Since you ask, I can't help wondering if you plan to tell him about the circumstances that brought you together before saying 'I do,'" Nell admitted. "Or if you plan just to go forward, keeping the facts unearthed by those cancer researchers and the detective you hired locked away in your heart."

"You think I should tell him, don't you?" Margo said.

"Don't *you*?"

Hesitating, Margo searched her own eyes in the mirror. They were bright with love and the excitement of a bride-to-be, yet they contained shadows of fear that she could lose it all.

"Half of me does," she said at last. "I hate the idea of founding our marriage on a lie...even one of omission."

"And the other half?"

"Is terrified. I let the chance to make a clean breast of things before our relationship got too hot and heavy slip away. Now I don't know what to do." Nervously she fingered one of the suit's buttons, which needed to be sewn on a bit more securely. "If I told Seth at this juncture," she added, "I'm afraid he'd lose all respect for me. All trust."

Usually so voluble with advice, Nell didn't offer a peep. This time, Margo was on her own.

"I guess this is the one," she murmured after a moment, taking off the sleek Italian suit and replacing it on its padded hanger. "Did I tell you a dressmaker is making Sooz's gown? We couldn't find the kind of dress she wanted."

Since their marriage would be the second for them both, Margo and Seth had decided to hold it at his house, with a minister from the local Unitarian church officiating. After all, the weathered cedar, architect-designed home was big enough, and it had a sweeping view of the Sound. They couldn't ask for a more breathtaking backdrop.

The ceremony itself would be held in front of the living-room fireplace. Seth had asked his brother, Bob, to be his best man and Nell had agreed to serve as matron of honor. In her teal velvet dress, which by happenstance harmonized beautifully with Margo's suit, Sooz would be child-of-honor and flower girl.

Seth had ordered enough flowers for a cathedral. Though just twenty guests or so would be on hand to hear them speak their vows, he'd arranged a catered buffet, too, with rare roast beef, smoked salmon, petit fours and gooseberry tarts, among other delicacies.

"This is us, getting married. I want to do things right," he'd replied when Margo had objected to the cost.

At last January 15 dawned, overcast but with a good chance the sun would peek through, according to the weatherman. It was a Saturday, the last Margo was to have as a single woman in her Ravenna bungalow. Instead she opened her eyes in the charming housekeeper's suite Seth had first shown her in late October. Though she'd fully expected to go home the night before and dress for the ceremony there, her masterful husband-to-be had refused to hear of it.

"We've been very careful to toe the line because of Sooz," he'd reminded her the night before, a hint of what that forbearance had cost flickering in his hazel eyes. "But, contemporary mores being what they are, I doubt most people would believe it. Since we'll be husband and wife tomorrow, what difference will it make if we spend another night sleeping apart under the same roof? I want you *here,* where I can kiss you good morning on our wedding day."

Agreeing to stay didn't give me the time and distance I needed to think, Margo moaned, burrowing deeper under the covers. I love Seth with all my heart and I want to marry him. Yet as the minutes tick by and our vows keep getting closer, it's like I'm on a speeding train, hurtling toward a mistake I'll never be able to put right.

Caught in a web of misrepresentation, though she'd never actually lied to Seth, she didn't know what to do. At this late date, bringing up the issue of Sooz's parentage and the way she'd deceived him was almost

unthinkable. Yet she found herself longing to do just
that. *I should have told him everything months ago,*
she thought miserably. *The day we met at the boat
yard, I should have been right up-front.*

You know what would have happened, her pragmatic self replied. *He'd have been upset. And angry.
The two of you would have ended up on the opposite
sides of a very high fence.*

Just then there was a light knock on her bedroom
door. Seth eased it open. Dressed in old jeans and a
plaid flannel shirt that made him look like a red-
headed lumberjack, he was balancing a tray loaded
with coffee, a basket of bakery shop goodies and a
bud vase containing a single mum. There were even
a place mat and two carefully folded cloth napkins.

"Wake up, sleepyhead," he exhorted, putting the
tray down on the coverlet beside her and leaning over
to give her a possessive kiss. "The caterers and the
florist will be here sooner than you think. And Sooz
is jumping out of her skin. You can't stay in bed
forever if you expect to snag a scapegrace stepdaugh-
ter and a thoroughly besotted husband."

Reluctantly Margo pulled herself up against the bed
pillows. "Oh, Seth..."

It was an unmistakable wail of uncertainty, seeking
comfort. Plopping down on the end of the bed, Seth
grinned and reached under the covers. "What's the
matter?" he teased. "Cold feet? Let me warm them
up for you."

"Seth, don't! You're going to spill..."

"No, I'm not. Just tickle the bride-to-be."

Margo was *very* ticklish. "No...no! Please stop!" she begged, letting out a squeal of dismay.

"Daddy, you're sloshing coffee on the napkins," Sooz reproved from the doorway, where she'd plainly been lying in wait for the opportunity to make an entrance. A moment later, she'd dissolved in giggles and joined the fray.

Following Margo's unconditional surrender, the three of them munched doughnuts and other assorted breakfast treats on her bed. Clearly thrilled to be in the center of things, Sooz hadn't uttered a single complaint about the prospect of staying behind in Mrs. Johnson's care while her father and Margo honeymooned in San Francisco. Meanwhile Seth was eyeing Margo as if he'd rather take a bite out of her than his favorite honey-dipped crullers. What more could a woman want?

This may not be anyone else's version of heaven, but it's certainly mine, Margo thought. The question was, did she deserve it? Like the runaway train she'd pictured, time seemed to be speeding up, making it more and more difficult for her to set the record straight.

Soon, much too soon, Sooz was offering to carry the breakfast tray back downstairs and Seth was dialing the airlines to check on their flight reservations. It was time for Margo to get up, shower, dress in jeans herself, and plunge into last-minute preparations.

They'd decided on a late afternoon wedding. Getting everything ready would be quite a task and Nell came over early to help. Her stomach queasy with guilt, Margo didn't have an uninterrupted moment to

talk with Seth. Though he was prowling about, supervising their efforts and doing his best to pitch in,
Sooz, Nell, or someone else, like the florist, always
seemed to be underfoot.

Nell's expression was pleased but guarded. By contrast, Seth was pleasantly wired. Sooz bubbled over
with excitement and self-importance. When the caterers arrived, she started issuing orders to them like a
miniature martinet.

Before they knew it, the hours had fled and it was
time to dress. Leaving Nell in charge, they went upstairs—Seth to his room and Margo to Sooz's, where
she helped the girl put on brand new, frilly underwear
and her teal velvet dress. Though Sooz's hair wasn't
quite as curly as Margo's, it coaxed easily into ringlets. Her legs were skinny, coltish in the white tights
they'd chosen to go with her black patent Mary-Janes.

Sooz is growing up fast, Margo realized. Her childhood's almost half over. She didn't want to do anything that would cause them to be separated again.

"You look gorgeous, honey," she said with a lump
in her throat.

"Do I really?" Sooz preened in front of the mirror
over her dresser, then turned to give Margo one of
her rare, spontaneous hugs. "Now you," she prodded.
"Daddy said we should get a move on."

Their guests would begin arriving in less than
three-quarters of an hour. Clinging to her like a lim-
pet, Sooz followed Margo into her suite.

"I wish you had a train and a veil," she chattered
when Margo emerged from her private bath in a lacy
bra, bikini pants and matching garter belt to draw on

sheer hose and slip into her chic Italian suit. "You should have let *me* pick out your dress. It would have been white, with a long, long train. I'm going to wear white when I get married someday. And have a great big wedding cake, with a little bride and groom on top and lots of layers and roses made of frosting."

As the girl rattled on, Margo could feel her crisis of conscience coming to a head. Could she make it through the ceremony without first telling Seth the truth? The closer their nuptials came, the more it looked as if the answer had to be no.

The doorbell rang and guests began arriving as she put on her makeup, Sooz in rapt attendance. A buzz of festive talk quickly filled the house. Margo recognized the voices of Bob and Joy Danner, as well as that of a good friend she'd worked with during her hospital public relations days. What would they think, she tormented herself, if I broke down and confessed the truth in the middle of the ceremony?

"You look kind of funny," Sooz observed, pausing in the midst of her monologue. "Are you okay? Mrs. Johnson says..."

For some reason, Sooz's awareness of the war that was raging inside her pushed Margo to the breaking point. "Sooz, honey, please go get your daddy and tell him I have to talk to him," she said in an anguished voice.

"You can't," the girl replied matter-of-factly. "Once you're dressed, he's not supposed to see you until you come down the stairs with your bouquet."

It was now or never. And, though they were hanging on by their fingernails, Margo's scruples had won the fight. "I *have* to, sweetheart," she begged. "Please…"

Something in her tone worried Sooz into obedience. With a backward glance at Margo, the girl ran off. Seth appeared a minute later, strikingly handsome in a dark gray business suit with a carnation in his lapel.

Before Margo could say anything, he enfolded her. God but he smelled good—like soap and shaving cream, his own special blend of skin scent and aftershave. He *felt* good, too. All warmth and reassurance. It was like having the world in her arms. If she lost him and Sooz, her life wouldn't be worth a damn.

"You're so lovely," he whispered, kissing her and then drawing back a little to repair her smudged lipstick with one gentle fingertip. "I forbid you to get cold feet again. Our guests will be convinced I'm torturing you if I have to reapply the tickle treatment. We don't want them to call the police."

Margo didn't laugh, or crack a smile. She felt sick all over. "I'm not getting cold feet," she said, drowning in the love she saw in his eyes and hoping it would still be there when she'd finished. "But you might…after you hear what I have to say."

He smoothed her cheek. "Isn't it a little late to reveal you already have a husband somewhere? Or that you're wanted for bigamy in three states?"

Resolute, she forged ahead. "This is serious, Seth."

Something really *was* the matter. He started paying attention. "All right, cupcake," he said. "I'm listening."

Now that she had his ear, Margo didn't know where to start. There didn't seem to be any choice but to meet the issue head-on. "Before we get married, there's something I think you should know," she told him. "I didn't lie to you. But I took the housekeeping job with you under false pretenses."

Seth frowned in disbelief. Was she flipping out, out of nervousness? "*What* false pretenses?" he demanded skeptically. "I didn't check out your references with the hospital where you used to work, but I'm sure they were first-rate. Your homemaking skills are everything an employer could want, though at this point I wouldn't care if you couldn't boil water. Best of all, you've charmed Sooz out of her emotional suit of armor and made me come alive again. So what's left to worry about?"

A *lot* was left. Margo chose her words with care. "When I called about your ad in the paper," she said, "it was because I wanted to find out more about Sooz, not because I was looking for a housekeeping position."

Confusion and bafflement registered on Seth's face. "I don't get it," he confessed. "You'd never met either of us before. Why on earth…?"

"It's a long story." Her words halting and painful, Margo described the rarity of Jim's cancer, Beth's tissue testing as part of a national research program and the mind-bending results.

His puzzlement only deepened. "No doubt you should have told me about this before," he admitted. "After all, we're about to be married and I have a right to know if something's bothering you. But I don't see how this changes anything. You mentioned when I hired you that you missed your daughter, and liked the idea of being around another child.''

''Not just another child. Sooz. You see, after I got over the shock that Beth wasn't Jim's and my biological child, I realized that the baby I'd carried for nine months had to be out there in the world somewhere. I became convinced she and Beth had been switched inadvertently. I had to find her.''

''And you think that Sooz... Margo, that just doesn't make sense! So what if your child and mine would have been the same age? There are thousands of female children born in Seattle every year.''

Having begun, Margo had to follow through. ''I know how this must sound...today of all days,'' she said. ''But I didn't fasten on Sooz out of thin air. When the hospital refused to give me any information because of privacy statutes and the understandable fear that a lawsuit might result, I hired a detective. I don't know how he found out, but he got back to me with the news that there were only two female Caucasian babies in the Bayless Memorial nursery at the time our Beth Ann was there...Beth and Sooz.''

Crazy as Margo's story about tissue tests and inadvertent baby-swapping sounded, it was plausible, Seth supposed. But to hint that Sooz might be her missing child was completely outlandish. Much as he loved her, Seth began to wonder if pre-wedding jitters had caused Margo's mind to snap.

Yet as she talked about hospital records and hammered home details, he began to realize her astonishing tale wasn't fantasy, at least in her own head. She'd actually set out to deceive him!

"So you answered my ad to do a little investigating of your own, is that it?" he asked, the Leo temper she hadn't glimpsed before putting in an appearance at last.

Terrified he'd reject her, Margo nodded. "I had to find out for myself, don't you see?"

It was all true—the tissue test on her daughter and the detective she'd hired. Her bald-faced masquerade. Well, he'd be damned if he'd accept the conclusion she'd drawn. Sooz was his child, his flesh and blood! She had absolutely no right...

Furious, he grabbed Margo by the shoulders, his strong fingers biting into her flesh through her suit's rich fabric. "Exactly what did you have in mind?" he demanded cuttingly. "Taking Sooz away from me if she came up to snuff? Or would you have settled for visitation rights? Did you plan to drag me and my ex-wife into court?"

Caught in his remorseless grip, Margo fought back tears. She wanted him to forgive her, not hate her. "I'm not sure what I thought would happen," she confessed, aching to rest her head against his chest. "I just wanted to make certain she was well cared for. And loved."

"How noble, given your methods! Too bad your scheming didn't stop there!" By now, Seth was shouting. He wanted to shake her. Instead he dropped his hands, clenching them at his sides.

"I don't know what you mean," Margo protested,

her desperation escalating a notch. "I fell in love with you..."

"Like hell you did. You only pretended to, in your obsession to get at Sooz. What a coup it must have been when I asked you to marry me! You had me so hooked you could keep me dangling while you thought it over. I have to hand it to you, lady...you deserve an Academy Award for your whole damn performance!"

His pride had been hurt. He felt threatened and humiliated. He was like a big, wounded lion, ready to go for the jugular.

"I wasn't honest with you," she admitted. "And I'm very, very sorry about that. But you've got to believe me when I say I love you"

"I don't have to believe any such thing."

Announcing her presence with a discreet tap, Nell poked her head in the door. "Sorry to interrupt," she murmured apologetically. "But your voices are carrying."

Though Seth quieted in a heartbeat, his anger became even more terrible. His friends were whispering about him. He'd have to face them and admit he'd made a mistake. As for his little girl, she'd be devastated. She might never trust anyone again.

"Seth, please..." Margo begged. "Forgive me..."

The entreaty didn't seem to register.

"Stay here," he ordered, his firmly hewn features as implacable as granite. "I'm going downstairs and call the whole thing off. Once everyone leaves, Sooz and I are going out. We won't be back for several hours. I want you *gone* by the time we return."

CHAPTER EIGHT

ON THE verge of collapse, Margo watched helplessly as Seth brushed past her friend on his way out. "Oh, Nell," she whispered. "I've lost them…"

Without a word, the older woman enfolded her. For a moment, they held fast to each other, Nell rocking her as if she were an injured child.

Then, "Come sit down…you're shivering," Nell urged, guiding her to the padded window seat of the pleasant sitting room she'd planned to turn into a sewing and craft area for herself and Sooz.

She was still wearing her beautiful Italian suit. But what did it matter now if the delicate silk fabric got wrinkled and crushed? There wouldn't be a wedding. Or a soul-consuming nuptial kiss. The photographs a friend of Seth's had planned to shoot would never be taken.

Like a whipped dog that wants only to retreat from the world and lick its wounds, Margo curled up under the quilt Nell spread over her lap. Taking a seat beside her, Nell drew Margo's head against her shoulder. "I'm so *sorry,* hon," she commiserated.

"We were perfect for each other, Nell."

"I know you were. You still are, dearest girl. His pride's hurt, that's all. Nobody likes being deceived by someone they love. Given time…"

"No. It's hopeless. Even if Seth could forgive me,

he'd want to protect Sooz. He's convinced...that I never cared about him. In his mind, all I really wanted was...was...to take her away from him.''

Her heart aching at the thought of what their change in plans would do the dark-haired moppet she'd almost certainly carried beneath her heart, Margo burst into tears. Emotionally abandoned by Cheryl, Sooz had blossomed under her care, despite an occasionally difficult period of adjustment. Once Sooz had conceded it would be ''more than okay'' for Margo and her father to get married, she'd seemed pleased and excited at the prospect.

Now those plans were shattered. It would be doubly difficult for Sooz to trust anyone again. I wonder what Seth's going to tell her, Margo agonized. The whole story? Or just that it's over between us? I hope I haven't hurt her too much.

From downstairs, she could hear the terse rumble of Seth's voice as he spoke to their guests, though she couldn't make out his words. Shocked murmurs and what were probably embarrassed condolences were followed by a general exodus, the syncopated slamming of car doors. Margo pictured Sooz crying, Mrs. Johnson comforting her.

When at last the house was quiet, and all the guests had gone, Seth returned for a moment. Though to all outward appearances he was in control, his gaze drilled into Margo's with a multitude of accusations.

''The coast is clear,'' he announced in a clipped tone, ignoring Nell. ''When I said I wanted you gone, I meant you *and* your possessions. There'll be no coming back for something you deliberately forgot.''

He hopes to erase me from his life as if I never existed, Margo thought. All the love I felt has turned to hate. "Is...Sooz okay?" she summoned the courage to ask.

Briefly the full power of Seth's fury showed itself. "Sooz isn't your concern," he ground out. "You're not to go near her again."

Her heart aching, Margo watched silently as Seth turned his back to her and walked away. Though she knew it would be a form of self-torture, she threw off the quilt and ran to her bedroom window, which overlooked the drive. She was just in time to watch as Seth led Sooz out to the Mercedes. The girl was still wearing her teal velvet dress and white tights. Because the day was chilly, Seth had seen to it that she'd put on her winter coat.

Margo caught only a glimpse of Sooz's face. Yet she could read intense hurt and bewilderment there. The last shred of her self-esteem withering, she buried her face in her hands.

Nell had come to stand behind her. As Seth backed the Mercedes out to the street and headed east toward the Garfield Street overpass at a high rate of speed, she rested a hand on Margo's shoulder. "I can imagine how you must feel," she said softly. "But maybe we'd better do as he says."

If she failed to vacate the premises as ordered, Margo believed Seth was capable of calling the police. He was *that* angry with her. "Okay," she responded numbly, turning away from the window. "I don't have any packing boxes. We'll have to stuff most of my junk in your station wagon as is, if that's all right.''

Functioning as if in a self-induced trance, Margo changed to jeans and an old sweater and started gathering her possessions together. But her seeming calm was a fragile one. As she and Nell descended the stairs with the first load, the reality of what had happened struck her afresh. More tears streamed down her face.

The wedding flowers Seth had ordered, so riotous in their profusion, had taken on a funereal air. Untouched and suddenly nauseating in its perfection, the lavish buffet their guests were to have enjoyed seemed to mock her. Apparently Seth had sent the white-coated waiters home. For all he cared, she supposed, the food could rot.

Aware that some of the neighbors had been invited guests and were probably watching her, Margo stowed her things in Nell's station wagon and her convertible as quickly as possible.

"That's it, I guess," Nell said at last. "Unless you've got stuff to load up from the kitchen, too."

Margo shook her head. "Nothing that matters. But there *is* something I have to do before I leave."

She'd thought of writing Seth a note. But there wasn't anything she could say that he hadn't heard already. If he was going to come around, he'd have to do it on his own. She doubted it would ever happen. When he'd ordered her out of his house, it had been goodbye in no uncertain terms.

Margo slipped into Seth's office. Their plane tickets to San Francisco were lying on his blotter. Touching them lightly, lingeringly, as if they were mementos of a long-lost love, she opened a side drawer and took out a plain, business-size envelope. Though every instinct in her cried out against it, she slowly drew Seth's diamond off her finger and dropped it inside, sealing the flap. Placing the envelope beside the airline tickets, she left the room without a backward look.

Somehow she managed to hold herself together sufficiently to drive as she followed Nell's well-traveled Volvo back to her Ravenna bungalow, which she'd planned to rent out after the honeymoon. But once she got there, she wasn't up to putting her things away in their proper places.

"Just leave everything in the hall," she told Nell despairingly. "I'll take care of it later. Right now, I..."

"Need to sit down and catch your breath."

Putting one arm about Margo's shoulders, Nell led her to the tulip-printed couch where she and Seth had spent the night. Though Margo had dared to dream otherwise, that night would be the only one she'd ever spend in his arms. If there was a bottomless pit in the world, she'd found it.

"After what happened, I feel a little shaky, too," Nell confessed. "I'll fix us each a drink."

There was a little cognac left in the bottle. Dividing it between two small glasses, Nell returned to Margo's side and handed one of them to her.

"I should have known better," Margo said, accepting it. "Keeping Seth in the dark about the way our daughters were switched was wrong. So was getting romantically involved with him. But if I hadn't done the former, the latter wouldn't have happened. And I do love him so."

Nell was silent a moment. "To be honest, I was afraid something like this would happen," she admitted as Margo forced herself to take a sip of the fiery amber liquid.

Margo raised a tear-stained face. "Why didn't you say something?"

"Ah, hon..." Helplessly Nell patted her shoulder. "You were pretty determined. You didn't want to be told."

In a downtown restaurant, Seth was trying to explain things to Sooz. The story he'd concocted—that he'd found out Margo wasn't such a nice person after all and decided not to marry her—didn't satisfy his daughter. To his chagrin, she demanded details.

"What did she *do,* Daddy? Was it something really bad?" the girl asked, obviously confused and frightened by the afternoon's events.

Heartsick over what the breakup was doing to his child, and unable to reveal the root cause of his anger without divulging Margo's stunning allegations, he repeated lamely that the marriage would never have worked.

In response, Sooz fiddled with her knife and fork. Always quick to note when one of her questions wasn't getting a direct answer, she appeared to be thinking things over. "You won't ever get mad at *me* like that, will you?" she queried after a moment, darting him a look.

"No, never!" Stung, Seth grasped Sooz's hands in his much bigger ones and held them tightly. "I promise, pumpkin. You'll always be my little girl. Nobody and nothing is ever going to change that."

Because of the amazing story Margo had told him, the words had a hollow ring. Worries over what she might try to do drifted through his head on the way home. As ordered, the space where she'd usually parked the M.G. was empty. He knew without having to look that her sitting room would be stripped bare of the plants, framed photographs and hand-woven toss pillows that had lent it such a comfortable air. The rest of the house, which she'd begun to decorate, wouldn't have changed, but it would be empty of her.

Incredibly he *missed* her. And hated himself for it.

I'll be damned if I'll forgive her...take her back, he thought, longing to slam his fist through the windshield. All she wants is Sooz. I was just a means to an end.

Before the gossip over their aborted wedding quieted down, there'd probably be a new and even more sensational rumor making the rounds. Once Margo recovered her equilibrium, she'd probably serve him with a court summons. He'd find himself fighting for his own child's custody!

To be fair, he'd have to tell Cheryl about the situation. As Sooz's mother, she had a right to know. Yet he shrank from the humiliation it would entail. Gritting his teeth, he promised himself to call her right away.

His insides eaten up with anger, dread and embarrassment, he walked into the house to face spoiling food, a semicircle of empty folding chairs and the travesty of floral decorations. Though ethically she'd been right to leave it, the white envelope he discovered on his desktop a few minutes later turned out to be the most telling blow of all. Tumbling out into his palm when he tore the envelope open, the beautiful, pear-shaped diamond he'd placed on Margo's engagement finger symbolized love turned to ashes. Seth had never been the sort of man to cry easily. Yet as he consigned the ring to the bottom of a desk drawer until he could return it to the jeweler's where he'd purchased it, he was very near tears.

Alone in her quiet bungalow after Nell left, Margo holed up in bed to cry her eyes out and live on ice cream and potato chips. After a week of misery, she couldn't take it any longer. I don't have any claim on Seth, she thought. But Sooz is my child. I have to make sure she's all right.

She didn't dare go near the house. Seth would have her arrested. But maybe if she drove over to Sooz's school...

Putting on a scarf and dark glasses in the hope she wouldn't be recognized, she drove over to the Magnolia section of town and parked a half block from the school grounds. The day was chilly and she huddled inside her turned-up coat collar as she waited for recess to start.

Sooz's school, Blaine Elementary, was situated cater-cornered to the hardware store, behind a tall chain-link fence and velvety green playing field. The beige-

and-brown brick building, with its prominent gym, was set among tall deciduous trees.

Suddenly a buzzer rang. A blue-painted door nestled between the gym and a classroom wing burst open. Children poured forth, their bright parkas and scarves and mittens dancing like leaves in an autumn wind.

Uncertain what she'd say if she and Sooz came face-to-face, Margo got out of her convertible and crossed the street. Standing beside a tree trunk close to the fence, she searched the crowd of darting, laughing youngsters for the strong-willed, outspoken little girl she'd come to love.

Her heart skipped a beat as she caught sight of a familiar yellow beret and white quilted winter jacket, skinny legs encased in flowered tights. It was Sooz.

At the same moment, the girl saw her. Plainly recognizing Margo despite her attempt to appear inconspicuous, Sooz took several steps in her direction, then hesitated. Moments later, she'd turned her back and surrounded herself with her classmates as if for protection.

When Seth came home that night, Sooz was seated quietly in front of the unlit living-room fireplace, with Bear hugged tightly to her chest. She didn't move as he gave Mrs. Johnson cab fare and wished her goodnight.

"Okay, baby doll...what's up?" he asked, sitting down beside her. "Did something go wrong at school?"

Sooz squirmed a little. "I, uh, saw Margo today."

Seth felt as if he'd been punched in the stomach. Simultaneously, his anger flared. "When and where did this happen?" he demanded.

"At recess. She was standing by the edge of the playground, outside the fence."

He winced, imagining the scene. It was starting already. "You didn't talk to her, I hope?"

"No. I didn't think you'd want me to."

"You were right, honey."

Sooz was silent a moment. "Daddy, why did you and Margo break up? Is she really a bad person?"

He'd never be able to tell her the truth. If she found out, it would give her nightmares. As for the heartache...

"Ah, cupcake." Seth hugged her close. "The reasons Margo and I called it quits are a bit too complicated for a nine-year-old to understand. Just trust me when I say it never would have worked. We're better off apart."

Though deep down Seth was grieving over the death of his relationship with the petite, dark-haired woman he'd grown to love, consciously he'd managed to convince himself that everything he'd felt for her had been a lie. He refused even to question whether Margo's story about an inadvertent baby swap might be true.

If it is, I don't want to know, he thought the following afternoon as he rode the elevator up to his attorney's office on the fifty-eighth floor of the Columbia Center building. And I'm damn well going to see to it she doesn't traumatize Sooz, or disrupt our lives again.

*   *   *

Though her heart wasn't in it, Margo was at her computer, churning out copy for an orthodontist's patient newsletter, when her doorbell rang. She didn't recognize the slight, balding man who waited diffidently for her to answer.

"Yes?" she inquired.

"Mrs. Margo Rourke?"

She nodded.

"Court order for you, ma'am." He handed her a flat, white envelope. "Have a nice day."

Was somebody *suing* her? Shutting her front door against the damp chill of a late January day, she tore the envelope open. To her astonishment, it contained a restraining order. Seth had gone before a judge to prevent her from attempting to see Sooz or contact her again. Apparently that included watching the girl through a playground fence.

Devastated, she sunk into one corner of her living-room couch with the court document on her lap and tried to think. Up to now, she'd rejected the idea of using legal means to determine if Sooz was her daughter. In part, that was because she hadn't wanted to upset the girl further. She'd also secretly continued to hope Seth might have second thoughts.

Now she knew he wouldn't. Instead he'd drawn up battle lines. He didn't appear to care whether or not her story had any validity. Or consider how he might have reacted if their situations had been reversed. Much as she loved him, she couldn't ignore the painful knot of anger and hurt that had formed in the pit of her stomach.

It was Nell's day off. Bent on taking some kind of

action, she went to the phone and dialed the older woman's number. "Seth's filed a restraining order to keep me away from Sooz," she announced when Nell answered. "All I did was go over to her school and look at her through the playground fence. I don't think I can stand to live the rest of my life not knowing whether I gave birth to her. If I sued to compel a blood test, with tissue testing to follow if researchers believed it was warranted..."

"Hon, I'm not so sure that's a good idea," Nell cautioned. "Perhaps it would be better to keep a low profile. If you gave Seth a chance..."

Regretful on the day she and Seth had parted company that Nell hadn't been more forthcoming with her advice, Margo was no longer in any mood to listen. "He's had plenty of time to think and this court order is the result," she replied, her determination crystallizing. "If I'm ever to know the truth, I've got to go ahead."

Tom McMillan, the attorney who'd negotiated damages for Margo following Beth Ann's death in the school bus accident, had an office in the Columbia Center building, too. Though at first he appeared to find her tale of switched infants a bit farfetched, the letters and accompanying documentation she'd received from research scientists involved in the cancer-heredity project seemed to impress him. So did the meticulously written report compiled by Harry Spence.

"You may actually have something here, Mrs. Rourke," he admitted at last. "Though the odds are against something like this occurring, it seems to be within the realm of possibility. I happen to know Jake Nauman, Seth Danner's attorney, rather well. If you like, I'll give him a call. Maybe we can avoid the expense and heartache of pursuing legal channels on this.''

Though she was willing to bet any attempt to negotiate with Seth would be doomed to failure, Margo agreed that Tom McMillan should give it a try. She wasn't surprised when, at Seth's insistence, his attorney refused even to discuss the situation.

"We'll have to file a lawsuit if you wish to proceed," Tom informed her after he'd phoned. "It's going to be costly, both in financial and emotional terms."

Seth's refusal to discuss things only solidified Margo's position. "I don't want to hurt Susan Danner," she said. "But if, as I suspect, she's my biological child, I have a right to know. We both have a right to some kind of relationship based on that unalterable truth."

A clerk from her attorney's law firm filed the lawsuit twenty-four hours later. Almost immediately, reporters got wind of it. They started digging for the identity of the child involved, though the judge assigned to the case had sealed the court records for Sooz's protection.

All they had initially was Margo's name, and she wouldn't talk to them. Learning from birth records at the King County Courthouse that Seth had a daughter born on the same day in the same hospital as her deceased child, they started dogging him with questions and struck a nerve. Ejecting them from the boatworks after threatening to call the authorities, Seth found more newshounds camped out on either side of his drive when he returned home that night. Promising they'd shield Sooz's identity from public knowledge, they pleaded to interview her and Seth.

As he brushed them rudely aside and vanished into the house, his fury at Margo knew no bounds. He'd have her hide for this if it was the last thing he ever did! Yet in one way he knew he was partly to blame for it. If he hadn't filed the restraining order, maybe Margo would have looked but not touched and left well enough alone.

Whatever the case, the hostilities had escalated. Though he had no intention of speaking to the press on the subject *ever,* he'd have to talk to Sooz. Reporters had already guessed her identity. If Margo's suit wasn't thrown out of court, eventually the story would surface in the media. Before that happened, Sooz needed to hear the details from him. That way, if her name and photograph appeared on television or in the papers, and the case was bandied about at school, she wouldn't be caught off guard, or hurt quite as much.

"Sooz, honey...come here and sit by me," he said, after warning Mrs. Johnson not to speak with anyone and seeing her to her cab. "We need to have a little chat."

Something in his tone seemed to alert Sooz that their discussion would be a serious one. "What is it,

Daddy?'' she asked, her dark eyes somber and brimming with questions as she nestled in his lap.

He didn't know where to start. How in the hell was he supposed to make a nine-year-old understand what was happening without scaring her half to death? I'll never forgive Margo for doing this to us, he thought as he hugged Sooz close.

"Margo has a funny idea that you're really *her* little girl, not mine," he said, forcing himself to proceed. "She thinks you and her daughter...the one who died...got mixed up when you were both babies in the Bayless Memorial Hospital nursery."

Sooz flinched. "No! That's wrong," she cried. "I've *always* been your little girl. You're my daddy..."

Seth wanted to weep. Or shout. At the very least to gnash his teeth. "Of course you have," he reassured with barely controlled anguish, smoothing Sooz's hair. "And you always *will* be. This is just a crazy idea Margo has. Unfortunately, she's asked a judge to look into it. Nothing's going to happen as result of that, but people might find out and ask a lot of questions. I only told you so you'd know if anybody mentioned it."

Clearly frightened by allegations she didn't comprehend, Sooz burrowed against him. "Margo really *is* a bad person," she decided. "She won't come and try to take me away from you, will she?"

In Seth's opinion, that was exactly what Margo had in mind. "Never," he vowed. "I promise, sweetheart...I won't let her do any such thing."

In the morning, Jake Nauman talked reason to him.

"If we let this case go to trial, your daughter's the one who'll be hurt most by it," the attorney counseled. "I know at this point it goes against the grain. But I think we should meet with Mrs. Rourke and her attorney. I know McMillan well, and he's a reasonable man. Maybe we can work something out."

At the mention of a possible compromise, Seth's redheaded temper got the best of him. "I don't want to see Margo Rourke!" he hurled back. "*Or* to work things out with her. There's absolutely nothing to discuss. Sooz is my daughter, and that's all there is to it."

A tall, thin man in his early sixties with a calm demeanor, Jake Nauman rested a hand on Seth's arm in an appeal for moderation. "It's my advice that we don't cut off our nose to spite our face in this matter," he said. "We'll never know how much ground there is to be gained until we try. What do you say we set up a meeting for sometime later this week?"

It would be painful beyond belief being in the same room with Margo, let alone discussing whether she had a right to Sooz. Yet maybe Jake was right. If he could get the monkey of her lawsuit off his back, facing her would be worth it. Though Seth continued to glower, he didn't object.

Interpreting his silence as a concession, Jake consulted his calendar. "Let's say Thursday," he proposed. "Here in my office, at 2:00 p.m. I expect you to let me do most of the talking."

CHAPTER NINE

MARGO got off the elevator at the Columbia Center's fifty-eighth floor with trepidation. A scant ten minutes early, she half expected to find Seth pacing there. Instead the plush reception area of Nauman, Gainsborough and Knight, Attorneys at Law, was empty except for a receptionist seated behind a semi-circular cherrywood desk.

"I'm Mrs. Rourke," Margo said, nervously clutching the strap of her shoulder bag. "I'm supposed to meet my attorney, Tom McMillan, here…"

"Ah, yes." The woman smiled pleasantly, no curiosity in sight, as if the firm handled baby-swap cases every day. "Mr. McMillan hasn't arrived yet. If you'd care to wait?"

I'd rather be boiled in oil, Margo thought, wishing now that she'd taken Nell's advice and given Seth a little more leeway. Yet she was convinced nothing would have been gained by it. Since she'd confessed the truth about her motives, the situation between them had gone from bad to worse.

Without replying, she walked over to a sweeping expanse of plate-glass windows that overlooked downtown Seattle. Out in Elliott Bay, a ferry chugged toward Bainbridge Island, trailing its miniature wake. Matchbox cars and buses plied the streets between jutting skyscrapers, which arose from their matrix of lower buildings like some exotic form of vegetation, a breathtaking study in smoked glass and concrete. There was the Mutual Bank Tower, there the First Interstate Center. Was it possible that, so high above the city, a saner perspective could be achieved?

She was startled by a light touch on her shoulder. Tom McMillan had joined her. "Hi," she said in a small voice. "I'm half sick to my stomach."

He squeezed her hand reassuringly. "Before we go in, I'd like you to think about something. Your former fiancé has been Susan's father since the nursery identification card printed with the words Baby Girl Danner was first attached to her crib. Whether or not he sired her, his emotional attachment to her must be tremendous."

Margo shook her head. "I realize that. But…"

"Right now, I'm willing to bet his greatest fear is that you'll try to take her away from him. If that isn't your objective, we might be able to convince him to allow the tests you want provided you agree not to seek custody."

"You mean…give her up in advance? Even if she turns out to be my baby?"

"Not entirely. Visitation would still be a possibility if Susan didn't object…"

The receptionist was motioning to them. "Mr. Nauman is ready to see you now."

Tom McMillan nodded. "Think about it, Margo," he said. "It could save everyone a lot of heartache."

Ironically, the room Jake Nauman had chosen for their discussion overlooked Pill Hill and the hospital where both Sooz and Beth had been born. Seth was seated beside his lawyer at a rectangular conference table, his back to the windows. Giving Margo a brief, flinty look, he stared down at his hands.

Pleasant but a bit austere, Jack Nauman welcomed them. Tom's response matched his, with perhaps a shade more warmth. Margo's was barely audible. For his part, Seth didn't say a word.

God but he's wonderful, Margo thought, unable to keep her eyes off the man she'd almost married and still loved. She longed to circumvent the expanse of polished wood that stretched like a mine field between them and throw herself into his arms.

To a degree she hadn't thought possible, she'd forgotten just how big, muscular and sexy Seth was. His red-gold hair was slightly mussed, as if he'd recently raked his fingers through it. His blond brows and lashes, features she'd doted on from the first, offered a disarmingly boyish contrast to the tightly clenched, furious man he'd become.

"Well, then," said Jake, glancing around the table. "Where shall we start?"

Margo's attorney aligned the pen and legal pad he'd taken from his briefcase before answering. "It's our hope that by meeting this way, we can spare the court and both parties a great deal of time and expense," he replied. "Since you and Mr. Danner have both had ample time to review your copies of the research scientists' findings and the highly suggestive report compiled by detective Harry Spence, I'm sure you'll agree there's sufficient evidence for a judge to look into the matter. Why not permit Susan Danner to undergo a simple blood test as part of a school physical or routine checkup? If it turns out to be negative, you've heard the last of us. No more lawsuit, uncertainty or heartache.''

Thoughtfully Jake stroked his jaw. "And if it's positive? Mind you, I don't expect it to be. But supposing it is?''

"Then I would think both Mrs. Rourke and Mr. Danner would want the confirmation or denial of a genetic tissue test..."

"The hell I would!" Shrugging off Jake's restraining hand on his arm, Seth leaped to his feet. "Sooz is my daughter, not Mrs. Rourke's...no matter what a bunch of researchers say! I'll leave town...abandon my home, my business and vanish before I hand her over to a conniving, dishonest stranger!''

Another second and he'd be out the door. Tom threw Margo an urgent look. *Say something,* he advised silently. Or we'll have a long, acrimonious fight ahead.

The word *stranger* had twisted like a knife in Margo's gut. Oh, Seth, she grieved. Whatever else I am, I'm not that. If I hadn't broken down and told you the truth, we'd be sharing a life. And a bed. Our little girl...

"Is Sooz all right?" she asked tremulously, the question coming straight from her heart.

For a moment Seth appeared nonplussed. Then, "She's fine," he snapped, grudgingly resuming his chair. "She wants nothing to do with you."

Silence reigned as Margo absorbed the blow. Even if I'm right and we win in court, I've lost them, she realized. But I've still got to know the truth. Leaning over, she whispered something in her attorney's ear.

Nodding several times, Tom gave her an approving look. "My client has just instructed me to offer a compromised proposal," he announced, glancing from Jake to Seth and back again. "If Mr. Danner will allow the necessary genetic testing to determine biological relationships in this case, she'll drop her suit and agree not to seek custody…even if the child known as Susan Danner turns out to be her natural daughter."

Jake and Seth exchanged a look. Astonishment and something else—regret at his estrangement from the petite, dark-haired woman seated across the table from him, perhaps?—flickered in Seth's eyes.

"Further," Tom continued, forestalling what Margo guessed would be their next question, "she'll be guided in any attempt to secure visitation rights by Susan Danner's wishes and the advice of a mutually agreed upon psychiatrist. Given the facts, I can't imagine any more fair or reasonable position she could take."

Jake Nauman clearly wasn't the sort of attorney to shoot from the hip. Or attempt to persuade a client of Seth's obvious temperament in front of the opposition. "If you'll give me and Mr. Danner a moment to confer in private," he murmured, "we'll get right back to you."

Giving Margo a sidelong glance that didn't reveal his thoughts, Seth followed his attorney from the room.

"That was a wise move," Tom complimented her

when they were out of earshot. "In actions of this
sort involving highly charged emotions on both sides,
sometimes a Pyrrhic victory is worse than no victory
at all. If Susan turns out to be your daughter, but
refuses to see you, all isn't lost. Children grow up.
They learn. Sometimes they change their minds."

Despite his praise and reassurance, Margo felt
chilled to the bone. If Sooz is mine, maybe someday
she'll seek me out, she thought. Not Seth. I've lost
him for good.

"Maybe." She shrugged. "I don't deserve much
credit. Practically speaking, I didn't have any other
choice."

Several minutes later Seth accompanied Jake back
into the room. Though he didn't show it, he was
deeply shaken. Margo's willingness to see his side of
things had caught him by surprise. Touched, and aching at the sorrow that stared back at him from her big,
dark eyes, he'd found himself agreeing to accept her
proposal.

If Sooz isn't my biological daughter, I don't want
to know about it, he thought fiercely. Yet with the
superstructure of his anger collapsing, doubt had begun to creep in. So had memories of how he'd felt
about Margo once. The memories hurt. Maybe once
the tests were completed, they could get on with their
lives—put the whole mess behind them. Given her
promise, at least he wouldn't have to worry about
custody. Or visitation. Now that he'd told Sooz the
reason for their breakup, the girl wanted nothing to
do with her.

He watched Margo from beneath lowered lashes as

Jake spelled out the terms of their acceptance, which were basically in accord with her offer. She looked pale and cold, as if she were freezing to death. Though he told himself not to be a fool, his heart went out to her. If only she hadn't deceived him that way.

They rode down in separate elevators, a minute or two apart. Emerging from Columbia Center's imposing lobby, Seth glimpsed Margo as she mingled with a crowd of pedestrians. Except for the set of her shoulders, she looked much as she had the afternoon they'd met in the finishing shed at Danner Yachts, Inc. Her movements were brisk and graceful, her bright yellow coat a stab of color against the dreary weather.

Two weeks later Seth was at the boatworks, overseeing repairs to a yacht he'd built, when one of his mechanics handed him the portable phone. Jake Nauman was on the line.

Holding the receiver to his ear, he waved to his assistant at the helm to cut the yacht's engines. "Okay," he said, tensing up despite an earlier vow that he'd take things in his stride. "Let's have the results."

As usual, Jake didn't mince words. "It's bad news, I'm afraid," he said. "Both the blood test and the tissue evaluation that followed it were positive. Genetically speaking, there's a better than ninety-five percent chance that Margo Rourke is Susan's natural mother."

If Sooz was Margo's child, she couldn't be his.

Seth felt as if he'd been kicked in the stomach. Helplessly he cursed medical science for mocking a father-daughter bond that had encompassed first steps, bedtime stories and countless jam-smeared kisses.

"Seth?" Jake asked, concern resonating in his voice. "Are you still there?"

"Yeah, I'm here." He was grasping at straws. But he had to ask. "Any chance *my* cell proteins matched Sooz's, too?"

The attorney sighed. "Sorry. But they were way off the mark. I know it's hard, but try to look at the positive side in this. Thanks to our written and notarized agreement with Mrs. Rourke, nothing has to change."

Getting a similar if more exuberant message from Tom McMillan on her answering machine when she returned home from delivering some work to a client, Margo didn't feel much like celebrating. Granted, the relief of finally knowing the truth had begun to seep into blood and bone. Yet she couldn't seem to think of anything but Seth.

All too well, she could imagine what a blow the news would be to him. God knew she'd found it traumatic when researchers had contacted her after Beth Ann's death. The urge to say or do something that would ease Seth's pain was overwhelming. Acting on impulse, she sat down at her computer. Words flowed onto the screen.

In her letter to Seth, Margo apologized again for deceiving him.

Seth,
When I first contacted you, I didn't know what kind of man you were. I wanted to make sure the child who might be mine was well cared for. And loved. Then I met you, and her. And began to love you both. I was trapped, by my feelings for you and my yearning to share your lives. I never meant to hurt either of you.

I know that's no excuse. It just happens to be the truth. I urge you not to discuss the test results with Sooz until you're comfortable with them yourself and you can focus on her feelings. Once you've told her and she's had time to think about them, I hope you'll ask her if she's willing to see me. If she isn't, there's no need for her to visit a psychiatrist unless you think it's advisable. I'm willing to drop the matter, at least for the next couple of years.

                                                    Margo

Closeting himself in his home office to read what Margo had written, Seth was astounded by her selflessness. She'd been right about Sooz's genetic heritage. Maybe she was telling the truth when she said how much she cared for him. I'm not sure I'd be so generous if our situations were reversed, he acknowledged, his anger collapsing still further. Without Sooz, she has no one. And I, for one, would find that difficult.

A shaft of regret pierced him when he thought of the life he and Margo might have had together. The diamond she'd returned to him was still in his desk.

Though he'd lectured himself several times about returning it to the jewelers, he'd never gotten around to doing the actual deed. Something had stayed his hand.

Unfortunately, a lot had happened since the afternoon he'd purchased it. At this point, retrieving what they'd lost seemed an impossibility. For one thing, the humiliation of being forced to call off their wedding at the last minute and the problems she'd caused him with the media were too fresh in his mind.

There were other factors, too. If he and Margo reconciled, he suspected, the press would have a field day. It would be tantamount to admitting Sooz was the child in the baby-swap case. Meanwhile, the girl in question wanted nothing to do with Margo. Whenever her name came up, she characterized Margo as a "bad person."

Sadly he put the letter away. Yet as the days passed, it continued to haunt him. Like Margo before him, he realized he'd failed to consider the opposite side of the equation. The yearning she'd expressed to be close to the daughter she'd lost at birth, had made him think of his own biological child.

Not once since Margo had first broached her incredible tale of switched infants had he asked about her. He'd never even studied her likeness, though he'd seen several photographs of her at Margo's house, as well as the one she'd kept in her sitting room. Suddenly aware at a feeling level that his child had lived and died without him, he began to obsess on the subject of Beth Ann Rourke, who'd survived to the ripe old age of seven before taking her place among the angels.

Had she looked like him? Or Cheryl? Had she been sweet and gentle, or a little gremlin like his beloved Sooz? One Friday evening, after driving Sooz to a slumber party at her friend Jill's house, Seth couldn't restrain himself any longer. Drawn as if by a powerful magnet, he found himself on Margo's doorstep.

Her knees almost buckled when she answered the bell. Unless her imagination was playing tricks on her, *Seth* was standing there. In his parka, heavy sweater and old jeans, he looked more than a little unsure of himself.

"Won't you...come in?" she stammered, opening the door wider.

After the way he'd treated her, he'd half expected her to slam it in his face. His voice was low and a little rough. "Thanks, I will for a minute if you don't mind."

Her mind reeling with questions, she showed him into the living room. Had Sooz agreed to see her? Or, please God, was it that he still cared for her?

Seth sat somewhat awkwardly on the sofa where they'd come so close to making love. He hadn't removed his parka and, as a result, he looked about as relaxed as a wanted man at a police convention. Though the legal issues between them had been resolved, it seemed their estrangement was still in effect.

"How's Sooz?" Margo said, attempting to break the ice as she tucked her feet beneath her in an easy chair.

"Doing okay. Mrs. Johnson comes over Tuesdays

and Thursdays. I found a college student to clean house three days a week.''

She couldn't help but feel sad about the ease with which she'd been replaced. Afraid to ask, she forced herself to broach a subject that had made for some sleepless nights.

"I don't suppose she wants to see me."

Sighing, Seth shook his head. A small silence ensued. In it, Margo tried to remember Tom McMillan's comforting words about children changing their minds. But they didn't take the sting out of Sooz's rejection.

"Then why are you here?" she asked.

Gold-flecked hazel eyes met hers. They were filled with pain. "I've been something of an idiot," he confessed. "I never even asked...about the child you raised. Since it stands to reason she was my daughter..."

He choked up, unable to get out another word.

It took all the self-discipline she possessed not to take him in her arms. Reminding herself she didn't have the right, she got up and took a leather-bound album down from one of the bookcases.

"I have quite a few pictures of her," she offered. "Would you like to see some of them?"

He nodded, not trusting himself to speak.

"Mind if I sit by you?"

"No...of course not."

Unsnapping his parka and tossing it over the back of the couch, he slid over to make room for her. Moments later they were side by side, engrossed in the events of Beth Ann Rourke's life and the many photographs that had documented them.

The girl's newborn pictures didn't tell Seth much. "I guess all babies look alike," he commented with a twinge of disappointment, studying a close-up Jim had taken.

Margo recalled several baby pictures she'd seen of Sooz, in particular, one Seth kept on the dresser near his bed. She'd spent several minutes studying it the first time she'd changed his sheets.

"I wouldn't say that," she disagreed. "But you're right, in a sense. As infants, Beth and Sooz must have resembled each other quite a bit. They were about the same weight, for one thing. And they both had dark hair. I can almost see how the mixup occurred."

On the next page of the album was an enlarged, professional-looking photo of Margo nursing Beth. Seated in a bentwood rocker with her blouse unbuttoned and sunlight streaming into the room, she'd cuddled the child she'd believed was hers with a look of absolute love and devotion on her face.

Focusing on her expression, the generous swell of her engorged breast and his daughter's hungry mouth, Seth almost lost it again. His baby had landed in paradise whereas, with Cheryl, Sooz had never received much lap time. A tireless socialite who hadn't wanted to be pregnant in the first place, his ex-wife had relied heavily on pacifiers and baby-sitters.

"Who took this?" he managed at last.

"My husband."

"He was a damn good photographer."

Margo nodded, keenly aware something precious

hung in the balance between them. "He did pretty well, considering how sick he was."

More pictures followed, including poses of Beth in the buff on a shaggy white rug, Beth with gobs of baby cereal on her chin learning to eat from a spoon. Turning a page, Seth suddenly found himself skipping to amateurish, overexposed shots of a sturdy eighteen-month-old, beating delightedly on a toy drum in her striped pajamas and waltzing Raggedy Andy around Margo's living room.

"What happened?" he asked. "These photos look different, as if they were taken by someone else. And there's a gap. You didn't record her first birthday."

"Jim's death happened."

Dummy, Seth taxed himself.

It was Margo's turn to endure a bittersweet moment. But it didn't last. Though she'd deeply mourned Jim's loss, it had taken place years earlier. She was over it now—as much as anyone got over such things. These days her heart was filled with longing for the living, breathing man whose muscular, denim-clad thigh was currently just inches from hers.

In Seth's opinion, the daughter he'd never known favored Cheryl most. But she'd drawn from his heritage, too. Abruptly, in a snapshot of the girl clutching a pair of Easter bunnies, he recognized his mother's smile. There was something of the late Margaret Mary Danner about her eyes, as well. Though they hadn't met in life, Beth and her paternal grandmother were together now. He brushed away a tear.

Pictures of Beth clowning around in her various Halloween costumes brought smiles, as did shots of her splashing in a backyard kiddie pool. Margo had many happy memories to relate. Yet even as she did, she braced herself. The last photo in the album, one of Beth in a brand new Brownie scout uniform, had been taken just hours before the school bus accident that had claimed her life.

When they reached that page, she couldn't help it; the tears started to flow. Not stopping to weigh the consequences, Seth slipped an arm about her shoulders. "Margo, I'm so sorry," he said.

To feel his warmth, his protectiveness surrounding her even for a moment was more than she'd hoped to experience again. "Beth was so young," she grieved, struggling for control. "When I kissed her goodbye that morning, I never dreamed it would be for the last time. Sometimes I think the place in my life where she belongs will never heal."

Yet she'd opened her heart to Sooz.

His hold on her tightened possessively. How had she managed to survive the tragedy of Beth Ann's death alone? If he'd lost Sooz under similar circumstances, he was convinced he'd have become a stark, raving maniac.

"I wish to God you'd told me about Beth and the tests up front," he said. "Maybe we could have avoided some additional heartbreak. Maybe..."

Margo guessed the words he couldn't bring himself to say would have been about the life they'd promised to share. "Would you have listened?" she queried softly. "And believed me? Or would you have been just as incredulous and upset?"

Though he didn't do so aloud, Seth had to admit

she was right. He'd have been furious, though without
the added twist of feeling betrayed by someone he
loved. If Margo had done as she probably wished she
had a thousand times over, they'd never have known
or learned to care for each other.

"I miss you," he said, his confession coming
straight from the heart.

It was as if a dam burst inside her. "Oh, Seth. I
miss you, too."

Seconds later the barriers were down and she was
in his arms. He was holding her so tightly she thought
her bones would break. Though they tried, they
couldn't seem to get close enough. At last he drew
back a little and tilted her chin with one finger so that
it was on a level with his.

"Let me stay," he begged. "Sooz is sleeping over
at a friend's. I promise nothing will happen. I just
need to be with you."

He hadn't said anything about loving her. Or trying
to piece their shattered plans back together. Probably
with Sooz feeling the way she did, he viewed marriage as an impossibility for them.

If that was true, it was risky letting him get close
to her again. She was bound to be hurt by it. On the
other side of the balance sheet was her love for him
and the fact that, in a way most people never did,
they'd shared two children. Ultimately she couldn't
deny him what she wanted so much herself.

"Okay," she agreed. "But I haven't been sleeping
well lately. I'm not sure I could deal with another
night on the couch."

She was inviting him to share her bed.

So grateful he felt humble, Seth pulled her to her feet. They went, arm-in-arm, to the bedroom he'd never seen. Turning back an heirloom quilt and the bed's top sheet, Margo got out one of her flannel nightgowns and went into the bathroom to change.

When she came out, Seth was already under the covers, his tall frame taking up most of the available space. Pausing to turn off the lamp, she got in beside him. His mouth sought hers and, for a hot moment, the union they'd denied themselves so long seemed inevitable.

Seth wished he could justify going ahead. But he couldn't. He'd made Margo a promise and he intended to keep it. Instead of taking advantage of her, he'd put his energy into finding some kind of answer for them. Kissing her again, this time with great tenderness, he drew her head down against his shoulder.

CHAPTER TEN

SETH awoke to hear the shower running. By the filtered, grayish light of another rainy Seattle morning, Margo apparently had decided the better part of valor was retreat. Well, he wouldn't push his luck. First he had to undo some of the damage he'd done with Sooz.

Throwing off the covers, he zipped up his jeans over the boxer shorts he'd slept in and padded to the kitchen to make them some coffee. Much as he wanted to, he couldn't remain at the bungalow for long. In an hour, he'd have to hotfoot it back to Magnolia and pick up his daughter.

Sooz is my daughter, he reiterated, testing a time-honored formula. But so was Beth. Funny how the word's meaning had expanded for him since Margo had led him through her collection of photographs the night before. For the life of him, he wasn't sure which dark-haired moppet was actually *his,* just that he mourned not knowing the one and loved the other more than life itself.

If I'd learned about the switch before Beth died, while I still had a chance to meet her, you can bet I'd have taken it, he admitted, filling Margo's coffeepot with water and pouring it through the grid on the top of her electric drip machine. His strong feelings about Beth had finally explained Margo's motives to him in a way that he could understand.

As a small apology for not getting the message before, he decided to try his hand at scrambled eggs. They were bubbling in the pan when Margo walked into the kitchen, wearing a white terry-cloth robe that tied simply at her waist. Her hair was a mass of damp ringlets.

"Oh, babe..." he said helplessly, desire curling to life inside him.

Passion took precedence as the eggs burned. When Seth drew her into his arms, she nestled closer. He wasn't wearing a shirt and, unable to resist, he unfastened her belt, causing the front of her robe to fall open. Though her arms and back were still covered, she was completely naked against him.

For Seth, the feeling of closeness was incredible. Her nipples had hardened into tight nuggets of longing against his chest. Reaching inside the robe, he ran his hands down the fluid curves of her back to grasp her buttocks. God, but she was exquisite! Her heated flesh was as smooth as alabaster. He wanted to make love to her right there, on the kitchen floor, with an encore on the countertop.

It wasn't any secret that she wanted it, too. Never since their first kiss, also consummated in a kitchen, had her body lied to him. To think he'd claimed her attraction to him was just a scam to get at Sooz! He should have known better from the start.

With Seth's hands on her body and his tongue deep in her mouth, Margo could feel her scruples weakening. His arousal was big and hard, pressing against her thigh. She wanted him inside her. What did it matter if she couldn't keep him for a lifetime? She wasn't proud where he was concerned. She'd take whatever she could get.

Once again it was Seth who stopped them. "I haven't earned the right to do this yet," he explained, drawing the front of her robe together. "First, I have a few things to work out. I know a lot has happened in the past couple of months that seems insurmountable. But there's got to be a way for us. Somehow, I'm going to find it."

Margo wanted to believe him so much that there was a hollow place inside her. But she wasn't sure he could. Sooz had her back up, and she was no pushover. After Seth left, kissing her goodbye at the door, she put the skillet, scorched eggs and all, into the sink to soak and phoned Nell.

"Seth spent the night with me," she confided, secure in the knowledge that her longtime friend could keep a secret.

Nell whistled. "You're kidding!"

"Nothing happened. That is, we didn't make love. But we slept in the same bed. Apparently it hit him at gut level that, if I gave birth to Sooz, then Beth Ann must have been his child. He came over looking pretty desperate and I offered to show him some pictures. One thing led to another, and we ended up in each other's arms."

Her friend was clearly delighted. "But that's wonderful, hon!" she exclaimed. "I know how much the breakup hurt you. By the way, where was Sooz while all this was going on?"

"Staying over with a friend. Nell...I think Seth

wants us to get back together. But I'm not sure he can pull it off, given Sooz's renewed antipathy to me.''

"Maybe I'm going out on a limb by saying this," Nell admitted, "but I'd like to bet that, deep down, she misses you. And cares about you very much."

Broaching the subject of a possible détente with Margo to the prickly, outspoken little girl in question, Seth hit a brick wall.

"Margo Rourke is a bad person," she declared in no uncertain terms. "She lied to us and made up a story so she could take me away from you. I don't ever want to see her again."

While he'd been fighting Margo's lawsuit and his own inner battles, it seemed, Sooz had been constructing an emotional fortress.

"That's not quite true, pumpkin," he countered, inviting her onto his lap. "I should have explained before, but her story about you and another baby being switched wasn't phony after all. It really happened. Remember the finger stick that was part of your checkup at the doctor's office? Well, some blood and a few tissue cells from that stick got tested, and they proved Margo right. Before you and her daughter were born, you were in her tummy, and her daughter was in your mom's. You got switched accidentally at the hospital."

A look of sheer panic came over Sooz's face. "No, Daddy! No! Please don't say that!"

Soothingly, he kissed her forehead. "Why not? It's true, sweetheart."

Tears welled in Sooz's eyes. "Does that mean... you don't want to be my daddy anymore?"

"Of course it doesn't!" The hug he gave her was fierce. "You'll never have to worry about that."

"I will if Margo comes back," she predicted darkly, burying her face against his shoulder.

Distraught, Seth didn't contact Margo for several days. Or tackle Sooz on the subject of a reconciliation again. He didn't want to hold out false hope, or upset his child needlessly. Yet without the woman he'd learned to love so profoundly, life was a basic shade of gray. In his opinion, doing without her might even be injurious to his health. Though he was almost never sick, he'd caught a cold, damn it. He couldn't sleep, or seem to concentrate at work.

After a great deal of soul-searching, he decided that, while parents owed their children love and the best possible upbringing, they weren't obliged unnecessarily to throw away their own happiness. Sooz was just nine years old. His divorce from Cheryl and aborted wedding with Margo, followed by the discovery that she'd been unintentionally switched with another infant at birth, had been extremely upsetting for Sooz. But with time and lots of affection, he believed, she'd adjust.

The sixth sense he'd developed as a single father told him that, in her heart, Sooz *wanted* him to set things right. After the way she'd handled the girl during her tenure as their housekeeper, there wasn't any doubt in his mind that Margo would be good for her. God knew she could use some of the luminous, selfless devotion that had flooded the photograph of Margo nursing Beth.

The conclusion he drew propelled him back to Margo's door. To his chagrin, she didn't seem to be at home, though her car was parked in the drive. Had something happened to her? Restlessly pacing back and forth on her front sidewalk, he began to arouse a certain degree of curiosity among the neighbors.

At last Margo appeared, struggling out of a taxi with several bags of groceries in her arms.

"Where have you been?" he demanded. "I've been worried about you. With the M.G. in the drive..."

Abruptly aware of how burdened down she was, he took the groceries from her and stood there waiting for an explanation.

"Sorry I didn't notify you my car was on the fritz," she replied tartly, unable to hide her amusement and relief at seeing him. "I didn't realize you'd volunteered to be my keeper."

"For your information, I have a strong interest in everything that concerns you," he answered. "I want you to be my wife, if you'll have me after everything we've been through. To be perfectly honest, I've never stopped wanting it...not even when I was at my most furious. Say you'll give me another chance."

They were still squared off on the sidewalk and Margo was suddenly afraid to move or take a breath. "What about Sooz?" she asked faintly. "I can't believe she'd approve. Or allow herself to trust me again."

At the mention of his favorite prickly pear, Seth shook his head in frustration. "Sooz is being opinionated and contrary, as usual," he confessed. "In my judgment, it's her way of fighting the fear that she'll lose me now that we've learned she isn't my natural daughter. I can't prove it. But I think that, beneath all her hostility, she still cares for you. I know for a fact she was much happier when the three of us were together."

It was uncanny the way his words echoed Nell's. "Do you honestly think so?" Margo said hopefully.

"Yes," Seth told her. "Most definitely *yes*."

Since coming to a decision, he'd had a one-track mind. It wasn't focused on practical things. Setting the grocery bags down in a puddle without giving a moment's thought to the fact that they might disintegrate, he took her in his arms. "If you're willing to trust me on this," he added lovingly, "don't you think it's time you answered *yes*? And that we sealed the bargain with a kiss?"

They were married a week later at the King County Courthouse, without Sooz's blessing, though Seth had insisted she be present. Held in the chambers of a judge who had known his parents, the brief ceremony was unlike the one they'd originally planned in almost every respect. The only exception was that Nell and Seth's brother Bob stood up for them. Because of Sooz's opposition, they hadn't asked her to take part.

Joy Danner, Seth's sister-in-law, held Sooz by the hand. Staring down at her shoes, the girl looked as if she wanted to make a break for it. When everyone had met downstairs, by the courthouse lobby's information desk, she'd refused even to speak to Margo. The immediate future looked bleak from the standpoint of establishing a mother-daughter relationship.

Nervous and not totally convinced that they were doing the right thing, Margo wore a plain navy suit and white silk blouse with a white orchid on her lapel. As she and Seth spoke their vows, she could feel Sooz's resentment enfolding her like a cloud.

It was difficult for her to believe the wedding was actually taking place. After giving up hope of ever seeing Seth again, she would be his wife, and her own daughter's stepmother. If only past traumas could be erased and they could start afresh, with full knowledge of their fatefully interconnected relationships, from the moment he and Sooz had tickled her as she lay in bed.

Both her wedding ring and the diamond she'd returned to Seth were on her finger as he drew her into his arms for a nuptial kiss. Suddenly, miraculously, everything felt right. With his mouth on hers and his hard, tall body pressed against her, she knew with the deepest kind of knowing that here was a man she'd always been destined to meet and love—one who had helped to integrate and complete her evolving self.

They weren't separated by any more secrets. He'd forgiven her for her deception and she'd let go of her prodigious hurt. Whatever their problems with Sooz, Seth would make her feel protected and cherished. She wouldn't have to face the girl's resentment alone.

Abandoning her need to take full responsibility for everyone's well-being and their capacity to recover

from what had been a very difficult situation, she let
herself merge with him. Hadn't he insisted they had
a right to be happy? And promised her everything
would be all right?

Her spurt of confidence faltered a few minutes later
as they entered the elegant lobby of the Westin Hotel,
with its mirrored ceiling, broad gold pillars and cocoa
patterned carpet. Sooz wouldn't look at her *or* Seth.
Her footsteps dragged as he ushered them into the
gardenlike Palm Court Restaurant for their wedding
lunch.

Seated directly across from Sooz at the round,
peach-linen-napped table they'd reserved beneath the
Palm Court's soaring glass-roofed gazebo and crystal
chandelier, the girl barely spoke when spoken to, even
by her uncle and aunt. She spent most of the meal
toying with the food on her plate.

Likewise, though they were painstakingly polite
and made lame attempts at jocularity, neither Bob nor
Joy Danner seemed to be enjoying themselves very
much. It was obvious they couldn't forget Seth's
aborted January 15th wedding and its painful aftermath. That afternoon he'd informed their assembled
guests, somewhat cryptically, that an impediment to
their marriage had come up. And it was clear to
Margo that her new in-laws still considered the tangled relationships caused by the inadvertent swap of
their infant niece a strong barrier. She got the strong
impression they thought Joy's cousin would have
been a far more suitable mate for Seth.

At last it was time for them to leave on their honeymoon. Bob and Joy offered to drive Sooz home,

where she'd be looked after by Mrs. Johnson until her parents returned at the end of the week. Hoping to distance herself from their earlier fiasco, Margo had insisted she didn't want a San Francisco wedding trip. She'd succeeded in convincing Seth she'd much prefer spending what time they had alone with him at his San Juan Island hideaway.

Beaming, Nell congratulated Seth. She hugged Margo as he went to fetch the car. "Relax, hon," she suggested. "Sooz won't be won over in a day. It might take a while. On the bright side, you've got a fabulous new husband you happen to be crazy about. And hopefully the worst is over, though there might be a few minor glitches yet."

"Related to Sooz, no doubt," Margo predicted.

Her friend responded with a helpless shrug. "I suspect she's going to be quite resistant, particularly over the next few days."

Margo groaned. "The next few days just happen to coincide with our honeymoon! If I thought anything bad would happen to her..."

"Spoken like a true mom." Nell patted her shoulder reassuringly. "The feeling I get is that she needs to learn a lesson here. And that you should go off on your honeymoon and let her learn it. If it'll make you feel any better, I'll look in on her and Mrs. Johnson..."

"*Would* you?" Margo was overcome with relief. "Oh, Nell... I'd really appreciate it!"

Just then, Seth drove up in the Mercedes. Putting it in park, he got out and came around to install his bride in the passenger seat.

"Bon voyage!" Nell called out, digging a surprise handful of rice out of her pocket and tossing it at them. "Have a wonderful time! Everything's going to be okay."

Locking up the Mercedes in the fenced storage area outside the boatworks, they changed into casual clothes in Seth's office and boarded his yacht. Everything was ready to go. To make sure of that, he'd stowed their luggage away, along with all the provisions they could possibly need, the previous afternoon.

Kissing her lingeringly and with love, he gave the order to cast off. With Margo performing the duties of first mate, they edged out into Lake Union, heading west toward the Lake Washington ship canal and Puget Sound.

It was a soft, silver-gray Seattle afternoon, with rain clouds dissipating and a moonstone glimmer of sunlight peeking through. The temperature was in the upper fifties. Though it was brisk on the water, they were dressed for it in waterproof parkas, jeans, sweaters and flannel shirts.

"Going up to San Juan was a great idea," Seth affirmed, tugging Margo close to him when she joined him on the yacht's flying bridge. "You...me...alone together. With no telephones and no responsibilities. Maybe we won't stop there. What do you say we head on up to Alaska? We could build our own igloo and make love for a month."

After so much unhappiness and frustrated desire, running away together for an extended period was lovely to dream about. But they both knew it was an impossibility. With Sooz in her current troubled state, a few days was the most they could snatch.

Having Seth would be enough for her. "It sounds like heaven," she answered, standing on tiptoe to nuzzle a warm kiss against his neck.

It was a slow day at the locks and they passed through with record speed. Wind whipped at their hair as they entered the Sound and turned north toward Admiralty Inlet and their destination. Seth pushed the throttles to three-quarters full. At that speed, he estimated, the trip to San Juan would take them five hours.

They reached his cottage near Turn Point at sunset. As they tied up at the floating dock and unloaded the essentials, lights winked on in some of the other dwellings scattered along the shore. The water was silver-blue with a delicate sheen of peach. Backlit by the waning glow in the west, a few clouds that had turned the deep purple-blue of iris floated overhead.

As she and Seth started up the dock's cantilevered steps, Margo's excitement grew. In a matter of minutes now, their provisions would be put away in the cottage's refrigerator. Seth would build a fire in the two-way hearth that separated its living area from the master bedroom. They'd disrobe by its flickering radiance, making love to each other first with their eyes.

Seth had been thinking similar thoughts all afternoon. Like Margo, he'd imagined a slow, exquisite seduction. Before entering her and driving them to their first consummation, he'd wanted to make her crazy with wanting him.

Now sheer lust to claim her was uppermost. As they gained the top of the wooden staircase that scaled the bluff and stood on the cottage's rustic deck while he fitted his key into the lock, he paused and turned to her.

"I hope you're not hungry," he announced, his voice harsh with barely suppressed emotion. "Because all I want is you."

They were entwined before they were halfway through the door—tugging at parka snaps and mauling each other with deep, intrusive kisses as they closed it. Exercising the right she'd given him that afternoon, Seth helped pull her sweater over her head. Her eyes darkening to pools of velvet, she reciprocated. With unceremonious haste, buttons were separated from their buttonholes.

In the picnic cooler at their feet, the perishables could wait. So could the fire, though the redwood-and-stone cottage was breathtakingly cold. Naked to the waist, they rubbed against each other, her nipples puckering against his reddish-gold mat of chest hair, his hips thrusting forward so that he could caress her with the bulk of his desire.

In response, a fire pit of longing opened between her legs. At the very core of her being, she was desperate to contain him. "Oh, Seth," she cried, the words barely above a whisper. "Please...take me to bed."

CHAPTER ELEVEN

THERE'D be no scruples, no barrier of clothing to separate them. With a groan, Seth lifted her off her feet. Her fingers meshed in his thick, red hair, she wrapped her legs around him. He was all man, solid as a tree trunk in her arms, and miraculously hers.

"God, but I love you!" he confessed, kissing her mouth, her nose, her eyelids with passionate urgency.

"Seth, darling...I love you, too."

Already she was part of him. Before they'd ever met, she'd nursed his baby. And he'd raised hers. Now they could make one together.

"Don't let's use anything," she pleaded, seized by an uncontrollable impulse as he carried her into the shadowed, unfamiliar room where they'd consummate their vows. "Now that you're mine, I want to risk it all."

Spontaneous though they were, the words echoed her dearest wishes. It's what I've wanted from the beginning, she realized, though the urge wasn't conscious until this moment.

Seth was stunned. His first wife had never said anything like that to him. Now the petite, dark-haired Gypsy he ached to possess would let him come flooding into her. She'd welcome the presence of his seed in her body without protection. The utter commitment

159

and deep surrender that entailed caused him to lose
the scattered remnants of his self-control.

Lowering her to the brass-framed bed, which was
spread with a down comforter, he unzipped her jeans
and dragged them down her legs. The lacy triangle of
her bikini panties followed, to be tossed on the floor
beside her shoes and socks.

Dropping to his knees, he lavished kisses on her
upturned breasts, the yielding vulnerability of her
stomach. Her skin was like cream, or velvet.

"Did you really mean it?" he asked, raising his
head from the coarse nest of curls that guarded her
feminine portal.

Her eyes glittered with love for him in the dark.
"I've been empty of you all my life," she whispered,
her hands claiming the broad, sweet shape of his
shoulders. "I don't know what would make me happier."

Neither did he, though he hadn't been planning
anything of the sort. Why *not* now? he thought, the
idea taking hold of him. We're both in our thirties.
There's no reason to wait.

Fired by the almost mystical connection they'd
forge, he parted her velvet folds. She was liquid with
wanting him. Hungrily he searched out the nub of her
desire, to tease it gently, then more emphatically with
a rhythmic, circular motion. Darting deeper, his
tongue returned to its loving task.

Margo writhed in ecstasy at the helpless blossoming of her desire. Like the petals of an exotic flower
opening in time-lapse photography, its ripples unfolded, each overlapping the next with greater and

greater fervency. With every breath she took, release moved closer within her grasp.

I want it to happen with him inside me, she thought frantically. With us fused together like one person.

"Oh, please..."

Seth was burning up with need. "Tell me what to do," he pleaded in a passion-drugged voice. "Do you want it this way? Or..."

Her hair was a tangle of curls against the puffy, channel-quilted coverlet. "I want...you and me... rocketing off together."

He didn't need a second invitation. Taking off his shoes and unzipping his jeans, he kicked them aside. Though the room was still icy cold, neither of them felt it. From her prone position, Margo ravished him with her eyes.

Lying there with her arms outstretched and her thighs spread apart like wings, she looked like heaven to him. Would the difference in their heights, his added weight, be a burden to her? He'd try not to crush her too much.

She wouldn't let him ride low, or rest the lion's share of his weight on his elbows. Instead, as they fitted themselves together, she shifted position so that her face was half buried against the hairy mat of his chest and she bore the full brunt of him.

"Sweetheart, you'll smother..." Seth protested, his hand between their bodies, coaxing her back to the heights.

"No, I won't." She moaned with pleasure, lifting her hips from the bed. "I want...you this way. I can *feel* you best."

Incredibly she was right. When they began to move, with Margo thrusting her lower body into him and Seth grazing the apex of her sensitivity on each downward stroke, the contact they made was electric. Each time he withdrew and entered, he seemed to go deeper. Her strong inner muscles grasped and released him in erotic point counterpoint.

Their profound need for each other and the unbearably exquisite pressure they were exerting wouldn't let them last. Though Seth tried to maintain their rhythm or even slow it, the radiance of their arousal seemed to grow until it was a halo surrounding them.

Suddenly they broke free, reaching their peak just seconds apart. As he filled her the way she'd begged him to, the tidal wave of sensation that engulfed them was almost global. Together his archangel brightness and her dark, feminine mysteries shook the universe.

They made love twice more before curling to sleep beneath the down comforter as, in the woods outside the cottage, a soft rain began to fall.

The following morning, the sun was out. Pleasuring each other again, showering and starting for the kitchen, they decided they wanted more and spent an additional half hour in bed. At last the craving of their empty stomachs for food drove them to make coffee and an omelet.

"You know, a honeymoon isn't supposed to be *all* sex." Seth grinned, utterly sated and content with his existence as he polished off a man-size portion of eggs with the appetite of a lumberjack. "What do you say we go into town...bum around a little after stopping by Harve Bjorn's place to see if there've been any calls?''

Harve Bjorn was an old friend of Seth's who owned and operated an art gallery in Friday Harbor. Since the Danner cottage didn't have a phone, when they'd decided on a San Juan honeymoon, Seth had called him to ask if they might leave the gallery number with Mrs. Johnson in case a problem arose.

"Do you think everything's all right?" she asked worriedly, a breath of apprehension ruffling the hairs on the back of her neck.

As close as they'd become during the past twenty-four hours, Seth didn't share her concern. "What could happen?" he replied. "It's probably safe to say Sooz is still steaming. A few days to cool down and think things over will be good for her. Besides, Mrs. Johnson's eminently reliable. Aren't you curious how we're going to get from here to civilization?"

They'd come by boat. "The yacht, I suppose," Margo answered, temporarily distracted from her fears. "Or should I put on my hiking boots?"

Seth's grin widened. "I have to admit they'd look pretty cute with my favorite white robe and what's underneath it. But they won't be necessary. Your tennies will do."

His mood reassured her. Dimpling, she tilted her head to one side. "What shall I wear?"

"How about your best black leather jacket? Bob and I keep a motorcycle in the shed."

The cottage was situated off a winding gravel thoroughfare known as Pear Point Road. Seated on the back of Seth's motorcycle, with her arms wound

tightly around him, the breeze disarranging her hair
and sunlight glancing through the trees, Margo felt as
if she didn't have a care in the world. With Seth as
her husband, she could handle whatever fate had in
store.

Rising steeply from its ferry dock, Friday Harbor
was a charming collection of little restaurants, gift
shops, bookstores and everyday emporialike hardware
stores and supermarkets. There was even a movie the-
ater.

Harve Bjorn's gallery was on Spring Street. Deciding that she'd been crazy to borrow trouble, Margo
was looking forward to enjoying its surprisingly fine
collection of paintings when Harve himself greeted
them with a relieved expression.

"Thank heaven you're here," he said. "I was
about to close up shop and drive out to your place.
Someone just called and left an urgent message.
You're to phone home right away."

"Oh, no…" Margo rested one hand on Seth's arm
for support.

He shook his head. "It's probably nothing." Yet,
as he dialed his Magnolia number, a concerned frown
drew his blond brows together.

Nell answered on the first ring. The gallery had a
speaker phone, and Margo was able to listen in on
the conversation.

"I'm sorry to have to tell you this," her friend said
over audible expressions of distress from Mrs. Johnson in the background, "but Sooz has disappeared."

She'd run away. Margo's heart sank. This is all my
fault, she thought.

Seth's expression was a blend of outrage and fear for their daughter's safety as he ground out a question.

"When did this happen?"

"Just this morning." There wasn't much doubt Nell, too, was upset. Yet she seemed to be keeping a cool head.

"Sooz didn't turn up at school," she elaborated. "Apparently her friend, Jill Lancaster, knew about it, got scared and told. The principal phoned Mrs. Johnson about ten o'clock."

Seth was looking more disturbed by the moment. "Did Jill say anything else?" he asked.

"When pressed, she mentioned something about your first wife passing through town on her way home from Hawaii. It seems she called just a few hours after you left and Sooz talked to her, though Mrs. Johnson didn't know anything about it. We think it's possible Sooz left to be with her. But we don't know where the Magnusons might be staying. Or even if they've arrived yet."

Damn Sooz, Seth thought. Doesn't she know how much we love her? Why can't she see Cheryl is *nobody's* refuge?

With a churning feeling in the pit of his stomach, he related the name of the hotel where his ex-wife and her new husband had stayed on their trip east. "Have you called the police?" he said, causing Margo to wince.

Nell had. She was keeping in close touch with them.

"I don't know how to thank you," Seth told her.

"Can you hang around until we get there? We'll be back just as quickly as the *Sea Wind* can carry us."

Romance was the furthest thing from their minds as they roared back to the cottage, Seth's motorcycle trailing a cloud of gravel dust. Within minutes they were aboard the yacht, slicing full speed ahead through the frigid blue water that separated them from Seattle. Half sick with guilt for what she believed was her selfishness in accepting Seth's proposal and allowing him to take her away on a honeymoon trip when Sooz was so upset, Margo shrank further and further into herself.

They were within sight of Shilshole Bay and the mouth of the ship canal when Seth couldn't stand it any longer. It had been heartrending enough to learn Sooz was missing. He couldn't bear it if Margo withdrew from him, too.

"Look at me," he ordered with fire in his eyes, momentarily letting go of the wheel and grasping her by the shoulders. "I want you to believe it when I say none of this is your fault. We have a right to each other!"

Sooz was still missing when, with a lurch of the Mercedes' brakes, they drew up at the house. There was an unfamiliar car in the drive. The police detective assigned to look for her had returned to question Mrs. Johnson and Nell further.

"Mr. Danner," he said, pre-empting Mrs. Johnson's tearful apologies. "I'm glad you're back. The hotel you mentioned has no reservation for your ex-wife and her husband. And we've checked most of the others. Can you think of any other arrangement they might have made?''

Seth wanted to kick himself. In the upset over Sooz's disappearance, he hadn't thought of Cheryl's widowed aunt, Roberta Kuhn, who lived a short distance from them on the north side of Magnolia, near Discovery Park. That is, she did when she wasn't supervising her ranch in the eastern part of the state. On at least one occasion, Cheryl and Tom Magnuson had stayed with her there.

A bit shamefacedly, he related the information.

The detective nodded. ''I think we should check with Mrs. Kuhn right away.''

Though they let the phone ring at least twenty times, no one answered at the Kuhn residence. Still, it was their only lead. Leaving Nell and Mrs. Johnson in charge of the home front, Seth and Margo got back into the Mercedes to follow the detective to Roberta Kuhn's residence.

Margo had laced her fingers nervously through Seth's, forcing him to drive left-handed. ''What if we don't find her?'' she whispered.

His reply was fierce. ''That simply isn't an option.''

Like many of its neighbors situated above the ship canal west of the locks, Roberta Kuhn's modern redwood home had been built on a steep hillside with several decks supported by pilings at the rear. Nobody answered when they rang the bell.

Peering inside the front windows, the detective decided to question the neighbors. ''Wait here,'' he instructed. ''I'll be back in a moment.''

Seth shook his head. "I'm going to check the back entrance."

"And *I'm* coming with you."

Slipping and sliding down the rocky descent, Margo scrambled after him. Thorns from some of the natural plantings that helped to protect the steep grade from erosion caught at her jeans, but she didn't notice. All she cared about was finding the precious but stubborn little girl she'd lost at birth and only just found again.

If Sooz won't forgive me and agree that we can live as a family, I'll bow out of the picture, she thought, fighting back the tears that threatened to obstruct her vision. Never mind how much I love Seth, or what we've come to mean to each other. We have to place our daughter's needs first. She didn't stop to think she might already be carrying another child.

Apparently the basement that opened from the concrete pad beneath Mrs. Kuhn's lower deck, was a laundry and storage area. Peering through its somewhat dusty windows, they could see an array of packing boxes and discarded tools. A washer, dryer and laundry tub were arranged side by side. There wasn't any sign of Sooz.

"Looks like we made the climb down here for nothing," Seth sighed. "The door and windows are locked. Even if she tried, Sooz couldn't possibly have gotten in this way."

Margo wasn't so sure. She'd spotted a dog entry, the kind of small, square opening with a swinging flap people sometimes used at the front of a house to facilitate newspaper delivery. It was too small for most adults to squeeze through. But a child? Or someone with Margo's petite, slender build? Either seemed a possibility.

"I know Sooz could be in a thousand different places," Margo admitted. "But something tells me this is the one. She might have crawled through that dog door. Maybe it's breaking and entering, but I'm going to investigate."

Seth grabbed her by the back of her sweater when he realized what her intentions were. "You can't, sweetheart," he protested. "It's too small. You'll get stuck."

"No. I don't think so."

Though it was a tight fit, by compressing her arms against her body, Margo managed to drag herself through the tiny opening. Getting to her feet and dusting herself off, she stood very still for a moment, just listening. She thought she'd heard a sound from one of the floors above.

Whatever the slight noise had been, it wasn't repeated. Unlocking the back door, she let Seth into the house.

Checking out the basement area and finding nothing, he started up the stairs. "Sooz," he called, "it's Daddy! If you're here, please answer me!"

The sound of a chair scraping against wooden flooring met their ears. *"Oh, Daddy..."* Sooz cried.

Seconds later she was scampering down the stairs and flinging herself into Seth's arms. Scooping her up, he held her as if he'd never let her go. Her feet dangled from grubby corduroy slacks in scuffed shoes and snagged cotton anklets as she buried her face against his neck. Margo watched from the step below them, tears of relief and sorrow for what she might be about to lose spilling though she tried not to let them.

Just then a car door slammed. After a brief hiatus, someone inserted a key into the front door lock. "What's going on?" Cheryl's voice said.

The detective was right behind her. "Mrs. Magnuson?" he asked.

They both stared as Seth gained the upper level carrying Sooz, with Margo following him.

"Mommy!" Sooz exclaimed though she continued to hold tightly to Seth. "You said you'd be here today. And you weren't. Neither was Aunt Roberta. It started to rain and I climbed down the hillside so I could get in through Tuffy's door and wait for you."

Cheryl didn't come forward to offer a hug or kiss. Instead she deposited her armload of department-store shopping bags on a nearby chair and rested expensively manicured hands on her slender hips.

"That's crazy," she said. "We might have been gone already. I *told* you we might not have time to see you this trip."

When nobody said anything in response to that, she looked at each of them in turn, her eyes narrowing slightly when they rested on Margo. "I want to know what's going *on* here," she demanded.

In a superficial way, she resembles me, Margo thought with a devastating flash of insight. But she doesn't have a heart.

Seth explained in something of a monotone. "This is my wife, Margo," he said. "And Detective Ryan, who's been helping us look for Sooz. Margo and I were married yesterday. We were on our honeymoon when we got a call that Sooz had run away. Once we learned you'd be in the area, we thought she might have run to you. Since you weren't registered at any of the better hotels..."

He'd already told Cheryl about the test results and Margo's agreement not to seek custody. But he hadn't gotten in touch with her since he and Margo had made up their differences. It was clear to him that Cheryl had no interest in the daughter she'd never known. In his opinion, his ex-wife had reacted to the truth about Sooz's parentage by distancing herself even further from the living child who loved her so much. He didn't have to add that Sooz was opposed to his remarriage. Understanding of that painful fact was written all over Cheryl's beautiful face.

She turned to the girl who, prior to Margo's revelations, she'd had no reason to think wasn't her natural daughter. "Running away was wrong," she said severely. "You must never do it again."

A tear rolled down Sooz's cheek. "I thought I could come and live with you in Hawaii, Mommy," she said in a small voice. It was apparent, though, that she'd all but reconsidered.

Obviously not stupid, Cheryl seemed to catch the girl's change of heart at once. "You know that's nonsense, Sooz," she said with a relieved smile. "This isn't even a good time for you to visit. You have school and, the minute we get home, Tom and I will be leaving for Australia and New Zealand. I want you to calm down and use a little common sense. People get remarried every day. The best place for you is here in Seattle, with your father.''

''Yes, Mommy,'' Sooz said obediently.

With a potential crisis averted, Cheryl began to behave a little more like an affectionate parent, though her range in that department was clearly limited. She still didn't hug Sooz. But she kissed her on the cheek.

''Maybe next summer...'' she murmured.

It was easy to see that, though the child Margo loved so much might wish to delude herself, she knew ''next summer'' would never materialize.

Margo drove the Mercedes on their way home, with Sooz sitting so close to Seth, she was practically in his lap. The girl stubbornly refused to look at her.

Nell and Mrs. Johnson were weak-kneed with relief when they walked in the door. Sending Sooz upstairs with the latter to wash and change, Seth paused to give Nell the particulars of how they'd found her.

''I want to thank you for all you've done,'' he added, shaking Nell's hand. ''You've been a wonderful help to us. I know you've got a life apart from my family's, but I wonder if you could stick around for a few minutes...keep Margo company. I've got to get upstairs and corral you-know-who for a father-daughter talk.''

Nell replied that she'd be happy to. ''I'm glad I have the time,'' she said. ''Tonight, I'm working the graveyard shift.''

Surrounding Margo with a brief, hard hug that promised *later we'll talk,* Seth ran up the steps and vanished into Sooz's room. Having supervised a quick sponge bath and change into pajamas, Mrs.

Johnson came down almost immediately and called a
cab. After she'd gone, Margo fixed herself and Nell
each a cup of tea. They sat across from each other at
the kitchen table.

"Okay, hon," Nell said, giving her an inquisitive
look. "Let's have it. Was it meeting Cheryl that's still
upsetting you so? Or Sooz's rejection? I told you…"

"I know. That it'll take time for Sooz to get over
everything's that's happened. I wish I could agree
with you. But I'm not sure she will. I hate to say this
because I love him so much…more than I ever
dreamed it was possible to love anyone. But I think
marrying Seth was a mistake."

For several minutes Nell listened quietly, allowing
Margo to vent her feelings. Then, "Why not be positive and see if you can't weather this. Even in the
middle of a crisis, a person can't look at you and Seth
together and not know your marriage is right."

By now it felt to Margo as if the two of them were
one person. But she didn't want to hurt him, or the
child they shared. "What if Sooz can't forgive me?"
she asked.

Nell reached across the table to squeeze her hand.
"I'm sure there's smooth sailing ahead if you can just
hang in there a little longer. I dare you to tell me she
and Seth aren't worth the effort!"

It was a long, long time before Seth reappeared. By
then, Nell had headed home to catch a nap before
going on duty at the hospital. The sun was setting
over Puget Sound. Exactly twenty-four hours had
elapsed since he and Margo had tied up at the dock
below his cottage with lovemaking on their minds.

He found her in the kitchen. Guessing he'd order Sooz to eat in her room, she'd prepared a dinner tray.

"I hope you're hanging in there with me, sweetheart," he said, echoing Nell's words as he put his arms around her.

"I'm doing my best," she answered. Already the survivor of too much heartbreak, she knew losing him would be more than she could take. But what if Sooz *wouldn't* relent?

When Seth took the tray upstairs, he didn't linger. A short time later, he and Margo shared wine and cheese in front of a crackling fire as he gradually filled her in on his conversation with the girl he termed "our daughter."

"For me, the turning point in the mess we made of things came when I realized at gut level that Beth was my child," he said. "I started wanting to know her, even though it was too late. This evening, some angel on my shoulder prompted me to explain that to Sooz. I emphasized that, while her biological father had died, too, you were still here, and loved her very much. I reminded her that you could tell her about Jim. She was awfully quiet after that. I think she's reconsidering."

Margo didn't dare believe it. Leaving their dishes in the sink, they went upstairs to the room where, previously, Seth had slept alone. Though she didn't expect them to make love that night, suddenly they were clinging to each other. Their adjustment as sex partners had been almost instantaneous and, though their coupling was brief, they both reached fulfillment.

Afterward Seth drew her head against his shoulder. "I love you, sweetheart," he said.

If only things were that simple, Margo thought. "I love you, too," she reciprocated, placing a kiss in the vicinity of his collarbone and adding silently, *I hope I get to keep you.*

As the rhythm of his breathing relaxed into sleep, she lay awake at his side, staring at the ceiling and wondering what lay ahead.

CHAPTER TWELVE

WHEN she woke, Seth was still sprawled beside her on his stomach. Always a bit unruly, his red-gold hair was wildly unkempt, as if it had been combed by a whirlwind. The straw-colored lashes she admired so much brushed the hard cheekbones of his man's face like a little boy's.

He'd turned toward her in his sleep. How I love him now, she thought. My feelings go deeper with every second. The simple act of lying here beside him under the covers is paradise.

For the second night running, they hadn't used birth control. She'd told him it would please her to have his child, and he'd taken her at her word. Apparently in his view the matter was settled. To hint that she had second thoughts now might inflict damage on their relationship that could never be reversed.

He'd never understand if she tried to explain her reservations. Yet during the past twenty-four hours she'd begun to believe a baby might exacerbate the problems they faced. When she'd told him she wanted to risk everything, she hadn't known Sooz would run away, or felt quite so pessimistic about regaining her child's friendship and trust.

Baby or no baby, the happiness she and Seth had been reaching for when they'd agreed to wed wouldn't materialize if he was forever torn between her and Sooz. Each time he backed up her authority or took her part, the girl would become more withdrawn and hostile. Ultimately Seth would lose what she'd already lost.

She didn't want that for him. Or to build a wall between him and the outspoken nine-year-old he adored. Yet a life without them didn't even bear thinking about. At the moment, the only thing she could do was to keep a cool head—try to hang in there, as Nell had said.

I hope Seth can sleep awhile, she thought, getting out of bed and putting on her robe and slippers. He's not expected at the boat yard for several days, and Sooz's disappearance was pretty rough on him.

With a lingering glance at his tawny head against the pillow, she headed downstairs to make pancake batter and squeeze fresh orange juice for their breakfast. Lining up the ingredients on the familiar island counter where she and Sooz had made so many batches of cookies and hot chocolate, she didn't see or hear Sooz come into the kitchen in her bunny-ear slippers and quilted robe, with Bear clutched tightly to her chest.

"Can I help?" the girl asked in a tentative voice.

Margo was careful to wipe the surprise off her face before she turned around. "Sure...why not?" she answered. "How would you like to break the eggs?"

Clearly pleased to be given a task that required manual dexterity, Sooz placed Bear where he could watch the proceedings and clambered up on the stool. "In the glass cup, right?" she asked. "How many do you want?"

Margo didn't have the heart to tell her to put on an apron. For several minutes, they worked quietly together, exchanging just the necessary information to carry out their task. At last the batter was made. The electric skillet ready. And the orange juice squeezed. Sooz had even set the kitchen table. There were three places, complete with place mats, napkins and silverware.

Can it be, Margo asked herself, that a *family* will sit down this morning to eat together? Though it had begun to seem like a possibility, she didn't dare hope too much.

Meanwhile, there wasn't any rush. She didn't want to wake Seth before he was ready. And, since it was a teacher's in-service training day, Sooz didn't have to hurry off to school. The day stretched before them, unmarked by conflict or harmony, a blank slate.

Not sure what her next move should be, Margo made a point of cleaning up every trace of their cooking clutter in order to give herself time to think. Initially, she knew, any balance she and Sooz struck would be a delicate one. She didn't want to make any more mistakes.

Watching her, Sooz twisted a lock of her hair. "When I talked to Daddy last night," she said slowly, "he told me you had pictures of your little girl. And the man those tests proved was..." She paused, obviously not ready yet to acknowledge a relationship that still troubled her. "I mean, the man who died, who used to be your husband," she finished instead.

Margo nodded, stunned she would broach the subject at all. "You understand, don't you," she replied after a moment, "that the mixup changed things? It made Beth mine, even though I didn't give birth to her. And it made you belong to your daddy. You always will."

Though she didn't answer Margo's question directly, Sooz seemed reassured. "I was wondering..." she began, exhibiting an uncharacteristic shyness.

"Would you like to see the pictures?" Margo asked.

In response, the girl retrieved Bear and hugged him close. "Yes, please," she whispered.

Longing to put her arms around Sooz but opting for a more casual approach, Margo led the way into the living room. The album she and Seth had gone through the night he'd turned up on her doorstep had already been installed on one of the shelves by the fireplace. He'd asked her to bring it several days earlier, pointing out that the history it contained belonged to all three of them.

Taking a seat on the couch, Margo rested the album on her knees. A bit awkwardly, Sooz settled beside her. As they began to turn the album's pages, they didn't start with Beth's baby pictures, as she and Seth had done. Instead they began at the beginning, with snapshots she'd taken of Jim during their courtship.

In particular, one taken at Snoqualmie Falls tugged at Margo's heart. The occasion had marked the first time they'd talked of marriage and the family they each wanted to have someday. Slim, dark-haired and witty, Jim had been a wonderful person. In a place reserved for him, she loved him still, though these days her tall, red-headed boat builder filled her heart.

Realizing that made it easier to describe Jim to Sooz.

"He was a police detective," she said. "Smart and funny and very courageous. He saw all kinds of terrible things in his work, yet he didn't bring them home with him. His faith in the essential goodness of human nature remained unchanged. Whenever I think of him, I remember his smile. It could light up a room…"

Sooz didn't comment. "That was a pretty veil and dress you had," she observed a few minutes later, poring over their wedding photographs. "What happened to them?"

"I kept them, thinking Beth might want to wear them someday. They're still packed away in the attic of my house."

Predictably, the girl clammed up when they came to the photos Jim had taken of Margo while she was pregnant. At five foot three, she didn't have much room between her breasts and hips to hide the extra weight an expectant mother gained. As a result, her baby-to-be had stuck out in front rather dramatically.

That was you, Margo wanted to say as Sooz flipped past several poses of her modeling a top printed with the word Baby and an arrow pointing to her area of widest girth. She longed to share the tender emotions that had washed over her when her infant daughter had been placed in her arms. During those fleeting, half-drugged moments in the delivery room, the child she'd held had been Sooz, not Beth.

It was much too soon to do anything of the sort.

They'd come a long way in just a few hours. But their truce was fragile yet.

They were about to turn to Beth's baby pictures when Seth came down the stairs in jeans and an old shirt. His eyes lit with incredulity and pleasure when he saw them sitting side by side.

"So...what have you ladies been up to this morning?" he asked.

Sooz's quick glance said she wasn't ready to talk to him about what was in the album yet. As Margo quietly closed its cover, she jumped up and gave him a hug. "We made pancake batter, Daddy," she said in her most self-important voice. "Margo says I get to cook the first batch."

At Margo's suggestion, Sooz made her pancakes silver dollar size. They were easier to turn and they browned to perfection. She glowed at Seth's high praise and chattered to him like a magpie as they ate.

Yet, though she was pleasant enough to Margo, something about the girl's attitude suggested she still viewed her as an interloper—one she expected to compete with for her father's affection. *I wonder if she'll ever accept me as a mother figure in her life?* Margo thought.

To her chagrin, as she was pouring coffee and orange juice refills, Seth mentioned their canceled honeymoon. "Though it wasn't completely scrubbed, we had less than twenty-four hours alone on San Juan," he pointed out. "I'm not willing to settle for that. It's my turn to choose, and I've thought of a completely different destination."

Margo wasn't at all sure they should leave Sooz

again, at least not for quite a while. She truly wished he hadn't brought up the subject.

"Don't I get a say in this?" she asked as tactfully as she could, reluctant to air a difference of opinion in front of their pint-sized audience.

The masterful man she'd married grinned and shook his head. "Nope," he answered, diving into his second plateful of pancakes with gusto. "Furthermore, I plan to keep our destination a secret. That way, nobody will be able to find us and drag us back if a certain little girl decides to run away from home again."

Already closing up like an offended mollusk at the word honeymoon, Sooz squirmed in embarrassment. "Oh, *Daddy!*" she groaned. "You don't have to worry about that."

"I sincerely hope not, pumpkin," he relented, his eyes twinkling as he ruffled her hair.

Later, while Sooz was out playing with some friends and they were going over redecorating plans that would incorporate some of Margo's furniture, they discussed the subject in greater detail. Seth confessed he'd been thinking about Paris.

"As in *France*," he emphasized. "That might be far enough to guarantee us some time alone."

"I really don't think we should leave Sooz for at least six months...if that soon," Margo countered. "Like the rest of us, she's been through a lot. And she's just a little girl. We need to give her ample time to adjust."

How completely unlike Cheryl she is in every respect, Seth thought, dropping a kiss on her nose. I can't imagine *her* giving up a trip to Europe because of a child's sensitivities.

"I was thinking about two weeks from now," he said. "But if you want to make it the first of April, you've got a date. You know, don't you, that after what we've been doing the past few days, if we put it off indefinitely, another little person's needs might intervene?"

They agreed on April. As the weeks passed, their combined household settled into place. Though Margo's things and Seth's were quite different, somehow they seemed to go together. The big silver-gray house overlooking the Sound had become more of a home.

Their private life went from glorious to ecstatic. Yet the close-knit relationship Margo yearned to have with Sooz continued to elude her. Polite, even friendly in a way that was hard to define, Sooz kept her distance. She didn't ask to see the album again, or mention the inadvertent baby swap that had woven their lives so intricately together. At times, Margo despaired of ever really reaching her.

At last it was time for Margo and Seth to leave on their trip. Back on the day shift at the hospital, Nell volunteered to sleep over at their house to help ease Mrs. Johnson's nervousness and both their minds. She and Sooz drove them to the airport in her station wagon.

Sooz clung tightly to her father when their flight was announced. Though she didn't offer Margo a hug, she didn't leave her new stepmother out altogether. "Have fun," she said with a quavery little smile.

Radiant in a jonquil yellow suit, Margo didn't let
Seth see her worry. She was a month and a half pregnant and he was being overprotective of her. Dying
to go, she still had doubts about their trip. Sooz
clearly felt deserted. When they'd told her about the
baby, she hadn't said very much.

Will Sooz ever really return my affection? she
wondered as they boarded the plane. During our absence, will I lose the ground I've gained? How will
she react when she's no longer an only child?

On their last afternoon in Paris, Seth and Margo lay
partially covered by rumpled sheets in their hotel
room bed. Though at the moment they were sated,
she knew they probably hadn't finished making love
yet. They'd have time for one more appetizer before
getting showered and dressed for an early dinner at
Maxim's on the Rue Royale.

Lazily Seth traced a pattern on her stomach. "It's
hard to believe there's a baby in there," he said.
"Your waist looks as tiny as ever."

Margo smiled fondly. "Just you wait."

A moment later, she'd turned pensive.

"What is it, sweetheart?" he asked.

"I'm worried about how Sooz is going to act when
the baby's born. I don't want her to feel displaced."

He sighed. "Neither do I. No doubt if we'd had
any sense, we'd have waited a while. But when you
asked me not to use anything that night on San Juan,
it was like setting me ablaze. I began to *crave* having
a child with you."

"Selfishly speaking, I'm glad you did," Margo replied.

Neither of them said anything more for several seconds.

Then, "Maybe we're borrowing trouble," Seth allowed. "Before Cheryl and I were divorced, Sooz used to ooh and aah over every newborn and toddler that crossed her path. She actually begged us for a little brother or sister. Maybe while we've been gone, she's had a chance to think."

They slept most of the way on their overnight flight from Paris to New York, where Seth had scheduled a meeting with a business contact of his who had numerous investments and a second home in the Pacific Northwest. The result was an order for a top-of-the-line yacht that would keep the boat yard fully employed through most of the summer. They went out to dinner to celebrate, although because of the time zones they'd crossed, it felt like lunch.

Departing John F. Kennedy airport at 7:25 p.m., they reached Seattle shortly after midnight. When they arrived home by taxi, the house was silent. A single lamp had been left burning in the entry hall. Glancing at each other as they unlocked the door, they went straight upstairs to their daughter's room.

Sooz was fast asleep. In the dim light from the hall, she looked almost angelic. Seth had a fleeting impression something was missing from the peaceful, familiar scene, but he couldn't put his finger on exactly what it was.

I wonder where we stand, Margo thought as she

gazed at the girl with affection. *I know Sooz isn't angry with me anymore. But will she ever accept me as a second mother?*

From the guest room, they could hear Nell's gentle snores. "We need to come up with a special treat to thank her," Margo whispered. "She's been a wonderful friend to us."

It wasn't until they entered their own room that Seth realized what had been bothering him. Warm feelings flooded them both at the welcome Nell and Sooz had prepared.

Constructed of shelving paper and lettered in red marking pen, a huge Welcome Home banner stretched from one side of their headboard to the other. Sooz's customary bed partner, Bear, was seated regally on Seth's pillow with a red ribbon around his neck and a hand-lettered sign that read Official Hugger and Greeter.

Margo's pillow hadn't gone begging. Propped on it was a framed picture, drawn in crayon by the child she'd learned to love so much. It depicted a man and a woman with their arms around a little girl. The man had red hair, while the woman and girl had been given dark, springy curls. Behind them, the sun was shining. The girl held a baby wrapped in a pink bunting in her arms.

JAYNE ANN KRENTZ

Lady's Choice

Travis Sawyer has a plan for revenge. Juliana Grant has a
plan too—she has picked Travis as Mr Right. When
Travis takes over the resort in which Juliana has invested
her money, Juliana takes matters
into her own hands.

1-55166-270-1
AVAILABLE FROM MARCH 1998

Catherine Coulter

Afterglow

Chalk-and-cheese lovers Chelsea Lattimer and
David Winter finally find happiness after a series
of disastrous relationships—thanks to their
match-making friends.

Afterglow is a wonderful romantic comedy from
New York Times bestselling author Catherine Coulter.

MIRA®

1-55166-472-0
AVAILABLE FROM MARCH 1998

JANICE KAISER

FAIR GAME

Dana Kirk is a rich and successful woman, but someone
wants to kill her and her teenage daughter. Who hates
her enough to terrorise this single mother? Detective
Mitchell Cross knows she needs help—
his help—to stay alive.

*"...enough plot twists and turns to delight
armchair sleuths"*—Publishers Weekly

1-55166-065-2
AVAILABLE FROM MARCH 1998

SANDRA BROWN

THE THRILL
OF VICTORY

Stevie Corbett's life is on the line, but her fate rides on
keeping the truth a secret. Judd Mackie's job is
to uncover secrets. After dogging Stevie for
years, Judd now has the story of the year.
All he has to do is betray her trust.

"One of fiction's brightest stars!"
—Dallas Morning News

1-55166-025-3
AVAILABLE FROM FEBRUARY 1998

HEATHER GRAHAM POZZESSERE

If Looks Could Kill

Madison wasn't there when her mother was murdered, but she *saw* it happen. Years later, a killer is stalking women in Miami and Madison's nightmare visions have returned. Can FBI agent Kyle Montgomery catch the serial killer before Madison becomes his next victim?

"...an incredible storyteller!" —LA Daily News

MIRA®

1-55166-285-X
AVAILABLE FROM FEBRUARY 1998

JOANN ROSS

NO REGRETS

Three sisters torn apart by tragedy each choose a
different path—until fate and one man reunites them.
Only when tragedy strikes again can the surviving
sisters allow themselves to choose happiness—
if they dare pay the price.

"A steamy, fast-paced read."
—Publishers Weekly

1-55166-282-5
AVAILABLE FROM FEBRUARY 1998

'You've found happiness with someone else?'

Katy considered lying, but truth was too important to her.

'I've found a life I enjoy, work I love and contentment, Jake. I was never the risk-taker you were,' she said. 'And that hasn't changed.'

'So, going out with me again, even on an "old friends" basis, would be a risk?' he challenged, his voice full of teasing laughter, as if all his doubts had suddenly been banished.

She tried to work out what she'd said to change his mood, but couldn't find an answer. The temptation to say yes was so strong she felt her lips moving. Then she remembered Julia.

Having pursued many careers—from school-teaching to pig-farming—with varying degrees of success and plenty of enjoyment, **Meredith Webber** seized on the arrival of a computer in her house as an excuse to turn to what had always been a secret urge—writing. As she had more doctors and nurses in the family than any other professional people, the medical romance seemed the way to go! Meredith lives on the Gold Coast of Queensland in Australia, with her husband and teenage son.

Recent titles by the same author:

A FATHER FOR CHRISTMAS

TO DR CARTWRIGHT,
A DAUGHTER

BY

MEREDITH WEBBER

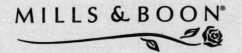

MILLS & BOON®

First published in Great Britain 1998
Harlequin Mills & Boon Limited,
Eton House, 18-24 Paradise Road, Richmond, Surrey TW9 1SR

© Meredith Webber 1998

ISBN 0 263 80731 2

Set in Times Roman 10½ on 12 pt.
91-9802-50244 C1

Printed and bound in Great Britain

CHAPTER ONE

'Hı, GANG! We're back!'

Katy grinned as the children playing in the brightly decorated hospital crèche turned as one, then advanced on Julia with loud cries of greeting and delight. Her heart tripped a beat as she watched Julia's special friend seize her hand and hurry her towards the far corner of the room.

'Come and see what I've made,' he urged, skipping in his haste to 'show' his friend the tower of blocks. 'Look!'

He dragged at her arm until her fingers could touch the vinyl tiles. 'See, there's the floor, and here's my tower. It's a look-out for the castle I'm going to build—a castle for a fairy princess.'

'I know he's an unlikely candidate for a prince,' Nan Chalmers, director of Lake Shore North's childcare service, remarked as she joined Katy in the front entrance to the room. 'But he knew Julia was due back today, and he's been working on her castle all week.'

Katy looked at the little boy, already rumpled and grubby-looking, although she knew he'd have been shining clean when his father dropped him off earlier this morning. Peter Clarke was one of those children who threw themselves wholeheartedly into whatever they were doing, regardless of dirt, dire consequences, or damage to self and clothing.

'He's been more than a prince to Julia,' Katy murmured, watching as the boy guided her daughter's fin-

5

gers up the intricate tower of blocks. 'Peter's a natural leader, and when he accepted Julia without reservations, the other kids knew it was okay to be her friend.'

She saw Nan nod, then shake her head.

'It might have helped,' the director argued, explaining her contradictory reaction, 'but Julia's own nature would have won through even without Peter. I've rarely had to deal with so fearless a child, and other children admire that kind of spirit.'

Katy felt the words tug at the strings which bound her to her child. A fearless sighted child would be bad enough, but for her visually impaired daughter to have inherited her father's reckless streak was something she was trying to ignore.

'So, how was the holiday? You're very brown, and so relaxed you're almost shining. Or is the shine to do with something else? Has John popped the question?'

Nan's words jolted Katy out of the past. It was a long time since she'd thought of Julia's father—since she'd allowed herself to think of him! Yet, she'd slipped back so far—and so quickly—it took her a moment to place John.

'To answer the last question first, no, he hasn't—and even if he had, I'd have said no! I don't love him, Nan. I know he's kind, and good with Julia, and he'd probably make a perfect husband, but...'

'No buzz, huh?' her friend asked, and Katy shook her head.

Definitely no buzz—not that she was looking for the 'buzzing' kind of love.

'We're too different,' she began, trying to explain the idea which had started to crystallise during the month at the beach. 'I mean, on holiday I'm the ultimate slob. I dig in the sand, swim, walk a bit, sleep in the afternoon and eat fish and chips rather than cook.'

'Sounds perfect to me,' Nan sighed.

Katy smiled at her.

'That's why we're friends—both slothful! Anyway, John came up to visit a couple of times and I think he was shocked by such degenerate behaviour. He's more into elegant candle-lit suppers. He seemed to think one shouldn't lower one's standards just because one's at the beach. And the beach bothered him too—so much sand. We've parted, but quite amicably.'

She sighed and shook her head with an undefined regret. He was such a good, steady, reliable man—why couldn't she love him?

'I think he realised it was wrong, too,' she admitted. 'I mean, we've been going around together for six months and haven't progressed past a goodnight kiss. He must have read something into that.'

'I doubt it,' Nan said cryptically, her gaze scanning her friend from top to toe. 'You're looking far too gorgeous for any red-blooded man to resist. Your hair's bleached as light as Julia's and you both tan so well. I can understand Peter wanting her for his princess—'

'And John wanting me for his?' Katy interrupted with a chortle of delighted mirth. 'Sorry, but I'm not cut out to run a castle! Now, if you'll excuse me, I'd better get to work—or the red-blooded male who's taken over the obstetrics department will be firing me on my first day back.'

She whirled across to where Julia was playing, and knelt beside her to kiss her on the cheek.

'See you this afternoon,' she said softly, and Julia's green eyes, so like her own, turned towards her voice.

'Be good, princess!' She touched Peter's reddening cheek and hurried away.

Nan had picked up a toddler and was talking to the child's mother. Katy recognised the woman as the parent of a long-term paediatric patient, and felt a thrill of pride that the crèche she'd fought so hard to establish was being used by both staff and visitors.

'I'll see you later,' she called to Nan, slipping out through the childproof gate that guarded the front entrance.

'I didn't tell you—' her friend called, but she couldn't wait to hear the rest of Nan's news. They could talk this afternoon.

As she walked out of the crèche she paused, as she usually did, to marvel at the transformation the groundsmen had achieved in the last two years. Lake Shore North was a private hospital set in beautiful grounds on the northern end of the lake which gave the city its name.

When the woman who had minded Julia while Katy worked had moved away Katy had begun her campaign for a hospital childcare service. Before tackling the authorities, she'd searched the building for a suitable space and finally found an old storeroom which had looked out over a patch of rough bitumen and three disused incinerators. It had been such an unlikely place to site a crèche her annexing of it had been unopposed.

Now the bitumen had been replaced with grass, and wide sails provided shady areas where the children played. The largest of the incinerators had been cleaned out and converted into a playhouse and the others demolished, their bricks providing the material for the low, zig-zagging balance walls and a creeper-covered mini-maze.

The thrill of pride remained with her as she entered a

side entrance to the building. She hurried along the corridors towards the main foyer of the hospital, nodding greetings to people she knew by sight if not by name. Waiting for the lift to the fourth floor obstetrics wards, she chatted to a nurse who'd just begun her roster in the maternity section.

'Are you enjoying it?' Katy asked, and the girl shrugged.

'It's okay, but I've come from Paediatrics and Dr Gordon is such a sweetie. Copping a perfectionist like this boss straight after him is a bit of a shock. The problem is he simply oozes sex-appeal, so it's almost impossible to keep your mind on the job, then he fires a question at you and—'

'Dan Petersen oozes sex-appeal?' Katy broke in. 'He's nice-looking enough, but sex-appeal? And as for upsetting staff, a more mild-mannered man I have yet to meet.'

'But Dr Petersen didn't take over,' the nurse told her. 'He won some scholarship to study overseas for two months and this Dr Cartwright's filling in.'

The lift arrived and the doors opened.

'Dr Cartwright?' Katy echoed, ignoring more twinges of memory as she tried to place the obstetrician the woman had mentioned.

'At your service!' a deep voice said, and her head jerked upward, shocked into motion by cadences she would never forget. The aforementioned sex-appeal was flowing more freely than an ooze, and Katy could only stare at him, seeing again the slightly uneven balance of his face—craggy features put together in such a way it had a unique attraction—the breadth of his shoulders, the tilt of his head as if he was always listening to something others couldn't hear.

'J-Jake?' she stammered, and watched the lift doors diminish her view of him, so she saw less and less—then finally nothing. She closed her eyes and found the image imprinted on her eyelids. Had he seemed surprised, or had his eyes been laughing at her shock?

'Were you wanting to go up?'

The doors had opened again and he was still there, his face set in a politely enquiring mask. She saw the speculative looks on the faces of staff she knew and spotted the new nurse hovering by his side.

She wasn't trying to get too far away from the sex-appeal, Katy thought bitchily as she stepped into the metal cube.

She had intended finding a corner as far away from Jake Cartwright as the crush of people would allow, but he moved in such a way that the only available space was between him and the nurse.

She wondered if fate might intervene and render her invisible, but fate seemed to be busy elsewhere so she squeezed into the space and breathed in the fresh sharp minty smell of him, a combination of aftershave and toothpaste. She tried to tell herself a lot of people smelled that way.

The lift stopped on 'One' and she was pressed against him as people squeezed their way out and more entered. She could feel the hardness of bone beneath fine wool and muscle and her blood grew hot with embarrassment.

'It's obviously an all-stations,' he said cheerfully, as they were thrust together again on the second floor.

'Change of shifts,' she muttered, battling to overcome the dizzy feeling of faintness swooping through her chest and weakening the bones in her legs. It was more than six years since they'd last met and her body was reacting as if it had been six minutes. Her mind, which should have been producing the neat dismissive speeches she'd practised over those intervening years—practised in the dreams where one day they met again—was paralysed into inactivity.

When the doors opened on 'Four' she practically ran out into the foyer, but, as he followed, she realised there was nowhere to hide. If the nurse was correct, Jake was the new director of obstetrics at Lake Shore North—or the new temporary director.

Which made him her boss!

To make matters worse, as administrative assistant to the director, her desk was in his office—they would be shut away together for at least some part of every day.

She couldn't work with him! Every nerve in her body was screaming its own warning. Could she request a transfer to another department? Immediately?

Would someone swap with her?

She felt his hand close around her arm and turned reluctantly. He would still be in the hospital, she realised, wherever she was working—walking the same corridors, breathing the same air. She gazed at him in despair, noticing the way his hair was touched with grey above one temple—where a scar threaded its way across his skin. The fear she'd felt for him when he'd lain in the hospital, so still for someone who'd always been so active, returned to paralyse her lungs momentarily.

'So we meet again, Katy?' His voice curled around her name in such a familiar way she shivered at the ghosts of yesterday.

'So it seems!'

She blurted out the words, even more unsettled by the all-encompassing scrutiny he was conducting, in full view of the staff passing through the lobby. His eyes, every bit as blue and beautiful as she remembered, took in the sun-streaked hair framing her face, the lemon blouse and vivid yellow skirt she'd chosen because the day was so bright and sunny. His gaze raked her bare tanned legs and lingered on the pale pink-painted toe-nails peeping out of her raffia sandals, then returned to linger on her face.

'And very nice it is to see you,' he said at last.

'I've got to go to work,' she snapped. 'I can't stand here all day, playing out some grand reunion scene with you.'

'Ah, but you're looking far too lovely to be work-ing—like a sunshiny, toasty-tanned, pink-tipped, yellow daffodil.'

'Still honey-tongued, Jake?' she countered, refusing to be beguiled by his words. 'Well, perhaps you can find someone who'd appreciate your flowery compliments. As I said, I've work to do.'

She turned away from him, heading for her office, then her steps faltered—it was *their* office, not just hers!

It gave him time to catch up with her. To touch her so they paused again.

'Imagine my surprise when they told me my assistant would be one Katherine Anne Turner!' he said, and a tiny flicker of apprehension cut through her confusion. The words rang true—but not entirely. There was some-thing else there, something she couldn't quite fathom.

'You were going to be a nurse, not an office girl,' he added, rubbing at his forehead as if to massage his memory. Recognising his uncertainty in the unconscious movement, she wondered if he was as thrown by this unexpected encounter as she was.

But he'd been at Lake Shore North a week. He knew she worked here and would have been expecting her back from her holiday today.

They were blocking the corridor while her mind tried to assimilate too much information at once and her body struggled to understand she didn't want it reacting to Jake as it had in the past.

He was waiting for an answer. What had he asked her?

'Going to be a nurse?' he prompted helpfully, and she guessed he was concealing his amusement behind his bland façade.

'I was going to be a lot of things. Including, at one stage—if I remember rightly—your wife.'

She hadn't known how bitter she still felt until she heard the cutting edge on the words.

'But that's all in the past!' she added, and shrugged as if to show how unimportant it was.

'Of course,' he said quietly, but his hand dropped from her arm in an involuntary flinch and he turned too quickly to walk away.

With a lurch of pain, she saw a slight unevenness in his stride and wondered how a man who'd taken his physical perfection for granted handled even so mild a disability.

She followed him reluctantly,

Impossible to think they could work together!

She stopped again, knowing her shocked brain couldn't cope with physical and mental processes at the same time—and right now she needed to think more than she needed to walk.

It's only for two months, she reminded herself. That's eight weeks of five days. That's forty days. Wasn't forty days a Biblical measure of time—something about forty days in the wilderness?

The wilderness would be okay—it was the company she couldn't handle!

A muffled giggle hovered on her lips. She must be hysterical!

It's not a joke, she told herself severely, but the still unsteady beating of her heart reminded her she had to get through this next encounter whatever way she could—and if joking was the best way, she would use it. Perhaps that was the answer—perhaps if she could keep it light—act unconcerned?

She hesitated outside Ward 'B', considering a quick visit to the nurses' station to say hello to all the staff. But that would only delay the inevitable, and probably make her next meeting with Jake even more difficult. She thought about resigning, but knew she wouldn't. Julia was settled at the crèche and making friends who would go on with her to the primary school just up the road.

Julia! Her fingers pressed against her lips to stop the name coming out as a despairing cry. Until that moment she hadn't considered her daughter in this strange equation of past and present. But Julia was definitely part of it—the factor 'X', the unknown quantity!

And she'd better stay that way, Katy vowed, closing out the panic which hammered in her head.

Thinking of Julia both sobered and strengthened her. She straightened her shoulders, drew herself up to her full five foot seven, and headed down the passage, telling herself she could handle this—just as she'd handled all the other challenges life had thrown her way.

But how she'd handle it she wasn't certain...

As she pushed open the door to their joint office, she saw he was bent over a filing cabinet in one corner of the room. For a tall man, a fraction over six feet, his movements had a particular grace, so he didn't look awkward or ungainly hunched above the drawer.

'Ah,' he murmured, straightening up and glancing at his watch.

'Don't pull that trick on me, Jake Cartwright!' she snapped, forgetting she'd been going to keep it light. 'This hospital owes me more time off in lieu of overtime than it could ever repay. In fact, if I had any brains I'd take the lot—beginning right now!'

'Running away, Katy?'

The challenge was so softly spoken she barely heard it, but it did serve to stiffen her resolve and helped her cross the distance between the door and her desk—a track that took her dangerously close to Jake.

'You've moved the desks!' The words were startled out of her, and she frowned as she considered his re-arrangement of what she thought of as 'her' office.

The previous director had disliked uneven light, so he had placed his desk in the far corner of the large room. He'd sat facing the door and had grouped the four comfortable visitors' chairs in a horseshoe in front of the desk. Katy had angled her desk on the far side of the room, so she could see the door but also see out of the window and feed her soul with the beauty of the lake in all its moods.

'Why should you be the only one with a view?' he responded easily. 'I think this way will work well.'

Jake had grouped the comfortable chairs around a small coffee table, so visitors could discuss things without the barrier of a wide desk between him and them, then he'd set his desk at an angle to hers. They'd be working an arm's length from each other!

She considered the extra leave she was due—more seriously this time.

'Don't you?'

She didn't have to look at him to know there'd be a

glint of mischief lurking in his eyes. But she wasn't going to let him tease his way back into her heart—then turn away from her again.

'Oh, I'm sure it will,' she agreed, letting sarcasm rip along the words. 'Any time you annoy me, I can pick up the brass pelvic frame a kind medical rep gave me and belt you over the head with it.'

His lips twitched but he didn't smile—which was just as well! A smile might have torn aside her thin veil of composure and left her vulnerable to the full force of his appeal.

'I'd thought of other conveniences,' he said softly. 'After all, if one desk is fun, imagine two!'

The heat began in her toes and fingertips, then raced upward through her body until it was flaring in her cheeks and pulsing in her blood. How dared he remind her of that silly escapade?

And how dared her body remember it so vividly?

'Don't even think about it!' She spaced the words to emphasise the threat. 'I'll work with you for two months, Jake Cartwright, but that is it. If you had some crazy idea of renewing an old relationship—if you fancied I'd melt into a little puddle of desire every time you walked through the door—then forget it! What happened between us was over a long time ago.'

Glaring ferociously at him, she added, 'And it was your choice, remember?'

She flicked at an imaginary bit of dust on her desk, but his next words stabbed into her heart.

'Can *you* forget it?' he asked.

Ignore him! her heart shouted.

'Forget the past, Katy?'

The repetition of the words rasped across her skin,

activating nerve-endings so the hairs on her arms bristled to attention.

She opened her mouth to speak but found she'd forgotten how to form words—even if her brain could think of some to say. Her heart was thumping so loudly she was certain he must be able to hear it.

He was studying her face, her lips. She tried to moisten them but her tongue was also dry and she realised she was breathing through her mouth, dragging air into lungs that laboured in her chest. She knew she had to answer his question or lose this battle before it had begun.

'Most of it,' she lied valiantly.

'But not all?' he persisted. 'Not everything?'

He stepped towards her—one pace, then another, and another, and another—until he stood so close she could see his chest rising and falling as he breathed.

'Not this?'

His voice had changed so the words were velvet-smooth. He raised the back of his hand to the side of her neck, sliding it upward towards her ear, lifting the hair that tumbled to her shoulders and hefting it as if testing its weight. She steeled herself against the touch, against the seduction of his voice and the assault she knew would follow as he bent his head and pressed his lips to hers.

She reminded herself of her little daughter, growing up without a father, and told herself she hated him.

His tongue slid along the line of her mouth, then eased between her lips to touch her teeth. How could one man's kiss rouse the blood to tumult when another's left it cold?

Don't think about him. Don't respond, she ordered her body. Don't move, don't flinch, don't let him guess your heart is battering itself to death. Keep your lips closed and your hands still.

Her fingernails bit into the palms of her hands as she resisted the urge to reach up and touch him, while her lips ached with the need to kiss him back, or to part and allow his kiss to deepen. Then, just as she knew she must give in—must fall against his body and let herself feel the magic one more time—he moved away, deep, half-spoken curses rumbling in his throat.

Katy stepped behind her desk and sank into her chair, pleased she'd made it that far before her trembling legs gave out and betrayed her deceit. She opened the top drawer and pulled out the bits and pieces she usually kept on her desk.

Her handbag went into the bottom drawer, then she found the file of notes Jillian, her temporary replacement, had left for her, and the folder with the information on the new maternity unit.

'I'm sorry, Katy!' he muttered, and crossed to slump down in his own chair—still frowning. 'What I did just now—that was unforgivable.'

Jake apologising? He *had* changed!

'Yes, it was!' she agreed, unwilling to let him off the hook too easily. Then an imp of mischief prompted her to add, 'I certainly wouldn't recommend coming on to all your administrative assistants quite that strongly. Not on the first day, at any rate!'

He growled something that sounded quite profane and she knew she had come out on top in this first encounter. She relaxed a little. If she could hide her own turmoil behind a determinedly professional manner she might just survive the next two months!

Determinedly professional! That was the approach.

And don't even think of Julia in case he can still read your thoughts!

'I assume Jillian introduced you to all the staff and showed you around? You've got the schedules for the month,' she began, seeing the note Jillian had attached to her own copy of the list of meetings he was expected to attend. 'You probably realise you won't make half these meetings because you're on call for emergencies or consultations. So I attend all but the department directors' meetings with you—or without you if you're not available.'

He didn't reply, and when she glanced towards him she realised he probably hadn't heard her. He had a puzzled look on his face, as if he'd turned a corner and found himself in a foreign land.

His abstracted demeanour gave her confidence.

'Actually, I could probably run this office on my own, but the hospital seems to think it needs doctors.' She smiled at the feeble joke, realising she was now far more at ease than he was. Surely that would give her an added advantage!

Then he smiled back, and any advantage she'd thought she had was lost. Her heart fluttered in its beat then lurched into a new staccato rhythm, leaving her breathless.

'Spoken like a true administrator,' he said softly.

She stared at him for a moment, afraid of softness from this man, then she turned her attention back to Jillian's other notes and continued to pretend she was totally unaffected by this cataclysmic reunion.

'There's the monthly ward meeting tomorrow,' she reminded him, glancing up but not quite meeting his eyes. Keep it light, instinct reminded her. Play it as a comedy not a drama.

He seemed uneasy—different from the man she'd encountered earlier in the elevator. Or was she imagining
it? The Jake Cartwright she'd known had never had an
uneasy moment in his life. Even when he had lain in
hospital after those two terrible weeks in Intensive Care
he'd been enough in control to tell her she was no longer
part of his life.

She put the thought aside and forced herself to concentrate on work.

'Do you have anything in particular you want to discuss? I'll type up an agenda for you.'

There was a long, tight silence, then he muttered
something that sounded uncomplimentary to all women
and rustled the papers on his own desk. She pretended
she hadn't heard and flicked through the rest of the notes
Jillian had left for her. Patients were being placed in 'B'
and 'C' wings, and 'A' wing should be empty by
Wednesday.

Katy nodded at the note. The hospital had been built
so these wings could be isolated completely. The original idea had been so the various parts of the hospital
could be shut off from each other in case of fire, but it
had proved invaluable for cleaning and pest control pur-
poses. The three utility and storage rooms in 'A' wing
would have to be emptied tomorrow, then the wing
would be ready for its annual steam-clean.

She made a note to check with the ward sister that
staff were available to move the supplies out of these
rooms. She could call in some extra wardsmen if necessary.

She doodled on the paper, thinking ahead. Because of
the chemicals used, it would remain empty for at least
a week. And after that…? Counting today and tomorrow,

she had nine days to convince Jake that the new maternity unit was a good idea. Could she do it?

She looked up again and this time she did meet his eyes. She even smiled.

'Well, boss,' she said cheekily. 'What shall I put on this agenda of yours?'

CHAPTER TWO

FOR a moment Katy thought she'd gone too far, for Jake's frown deepened, but then he shrugged and opened the folder on his desk.

'Jillian's already drawn up an agenda,' he said, his voice so mild she had to dismiss any idea of uneasiness. In fact, he was now as professionally intent as she was trying to be. 'The only item I don't understand is this new maternity unit. She told me it's your pet project and that you'd explain about it.'

'The new unit—' She'd barely begun when he broke in.

'I should tell you I was told fairly specifically that the hospital can't afford to be spending money. Seems every new department director has a pet project he wants to put into place. When Dan Petersen found he couldn't take up his position immediately, the hospital administration was happy to have me come in because I've made a study of cost analysis in maternity wards. A hospital has to run like any other business. It's expected to pay its way—'

'And make a tidy profit for its shareholders,' Katy interjected as a perverse disappointment swamped her. Jake and cost analysis? It didn't seem possible that the wild, brilliant, people-orientated young man she'd known had become a bean-counter. 'Of course, that's more important than patient satisfaction!' she added bitterly, momentarily forgetting her 'keep it light' decision.

He ignored her sarcasm and continued in a bland tone.

'I should also point out that I understood the director's assistant's job was to assist the director, not make snide remarks or instigate changes in the department.'

He sounded so stuffy Katy stared blankly at him for a moment, seeking a sign that he was joking. But no gleam of humour lit his blue eyes! She decided to ignore the jibe and go into attack mode.

'Old Forbes up in the head office has been talking to you. That bit about ''paying its way'' is exactly what he said to me when the board approved the outlay for the crèche. I fought hard for that crèche, but he can't see past the end of a bank statement where change is concerned. He won't even admit it's a success!'

She pursed her lips, dipped her head, and looked up from under lowered brows to imitate the head accountant.

'''It's not your job to worry about such things, Miss Turner!''' she mimicked in a high-pitched whine, then she grinned to show she meant no malice to the old man.

There was no answering smile.

'Well, how do you see your job?'

Katy felt the smile slide off her lips. Maybe the comedy angle wasn't the answer! Yet how else could she hide the dreadful muddle of emotion and anguish his presence was causing?

Concentrate on work—on the new unit. It was vital to get Jake on side if her wonderful vision was to become a reality. Dan Petersen had approved, but she'd often wondered it he'd have the courage and persistence to fight the money-handlers for it, or convince the consultants and medical staff it would work. Now, Jake, as she remembered him, had loved a challenge. Would bean-counting have changed him?

She couldn't tell by looking at him. He just sat there

at his desk, his eyes fixed on the papers he was shuffling as he waited in silence for her reply.

'Oh, assisting the director, of course,' she murmured, and tried another, more tentative smile. 'Doing whatever is possible to make this department run more smoothly and efficiently, also boosting awareness in the community of the services we offer and promoting the good name of Lake Shore North far and wide.'

His lips twitched, and for a moment she thought he might smile back at her. A hollow feeling in her chest reminded her that his smiling back might not be a good idea, but before she had to worry about it the lips had stilled and his brows had drawn together in a frown. She hurried into speech again.

'At the moment everything is running smoothly in the wards, but our obstetric case numbers are dropping.'

'That's happening everywhere,' he pointed out. 'More people are opting for home births or using small specialist birthing centres—'

'Exactly!' Katy told him, leaping into his opening with her argument. 'And there's no reason why women can't see Lake Shore North as just such a centre.'

'See a fifteen-storey pile of steel and concrete as a "small specialist birthing centre"?' he mocked. 'Are you advocating setting up a cabin in the gardens, or pulling down the building to make way for your brave idea?'

She bit back the retort she'd have liked to make and forced herself to continue calmly.

'There's no reason we can't provide what people want within the confines of this building. It's the feel of the place once people come in that we need to change—what's inside that counts, not the external packaging.'

Vague memories stirred, and she remembered another conversation along the same lines. Jake holding her in front of a darkened shop window, 'See how great we look together!' She'd pulled away and made a similarly pompous little speech. He'd laughed at her, agreeing, but pleased with their reflected image all the same. It hadn't been vanity, with Jake, that had made him pleased about their physical appearance, but part of his need to always seek perfection, to strive to be the fastest, highest, smartest, best!

She glanced up to see him watching her as he waited for her to continue. She couldn't let herself begin to think about the past.

'Lake Shore as a suburb is changing demographically,' she said, looking down at the desk as if she needed to read words she knew by heart. 'The wealthy people who once lived here and chose Lake Shore North to have their babies are moving out to houses on acreage and the old houses in the area are being turned into flats—'

'Which should give us more potential customers, not fewer,' he pointed out. 'I know the hospital has an agreement with the government to take public as well as private patients.'

'Exactly what I keep trying to tell Ol—ah, Mr Forbes,' Katy cut in. 'And we're guaranteed no bad debts with the public patients because the government pays. The problem lies in selling the hospital to the newcomers who would make up the bulk of our public patients.'

'Which, as you've so wisely pointed out, is your job. Can't you do it without spending vast sums of money on a new unit?'

Katy bit her lip and took a deep, steadying breath. In the past, Jake had used such crisp retorts to tempt her into argument, delighting in the cut and thrust as he forced her to validate the point she was making. She had grown to enjoy the verbal sparring, but she suspected shock had numbed her brain too much to win a war of words with him today.

'I'm not suggesting we spend vast sums of money,' she said quietly, homing in on the most valid point in her plan. 'There would be no building costs apart from maybe some repainting, which would come out of the maintenance budget anyway. And no new staffing costs because we will still be operating the same number of beds. At the moment we're over-staffed because we're down on maternity case numbers.'

'So, how does a new unit change things around? What are you advocating—offering women whatever choice they want? Underwater births, pseudo-home births, family rooms, or all of the above?'

He turned away from her before she could reply, staring out of the window towards the lake. It was wind-ruffled today, Katy noticed, with the sun flecking the crests of the tiny waves with gold. She loved the lake in all its moods—a love that had begun when she and Jake had first met and walked beside it...

'You've been here a week; you should know we already offer women those choices. The birthing suites were put in for that purpose, and many women do see them as a valid and acceptable alternative to home birth,' she said, dragging her thoughts resolutely back to the present. 'I'm talking about attitude, about taking into consideration the traditions and feelings of women from other cultures.'

'Other cultures?'

His voice seemed to come from a long way off and his face had lost its sternness when he turned back towards her.

'Particularly Asian cultures,' she said, drawn towards the gleam of interest in his eyes. 'Most of the families shifting into the area are from South-East Asian backgrounds. We have interpreters in the hospital, and we can offer Asian food, but we need to do more in training our staff to understand the ways of these people. And we should have a proper antenatal programme for them, not the hit and miss stuff we're doing now. Also, if we can put the women together in one ward, they will be able to speak to each other and should feel less isolated.'

He moved slightly so he was looking out of the window again, but she knew he was listening—listening to and absorbing her idea. She kept talking—quickly—excited by that spark of interest but knowing he could be called away any minute.

'Grouping them together in one ward would help generate informal support networks for when they leave hospital. These women come from a culture where the family is very involved throughout their pregnancy and confinement, especially the woman's mother and the mother-in-law. Most of our patients are immigrants, having their first babies alone in a foreign country without their traditional family support systems.'

He frowned at her and she wondered what she'd said to annoy him.

'We can't discuss this at the ward meeting tomorrow morning,' he told her, shaking his head as if to dismiss the whole idea.

Katy's temper flared.

'And why not?' she demanded. 'If you're into protocol and doing things by the book, then you have to discuss it because it's on the agenda. The ward staff have all had input into the idea and they're keen to try it, and I've already told you it won't cost your precious shareholders much money. What possible reason could you have for not discussing it tomorrow?'

'Because I know nothing about it?' he responded calmly. 'I can't go into a meeting with only the haziest idea of what we're discussing.'

'I've all the information in here.' She waved the fat file at him. 'Including the number of Asian-born women in the area—taken from the Census—and written information on birthing and confinement customs in South-East Asian countries. It's actually the confinement—'

He held up his hand to stop her flow of words.

'I've a ward round in ten minutes, then appointments scheduled through the day. And judging from the names on the patient list I'll be seeing quite a few of your Asian mothers.'

Katy calmed down enough to explain.

'It's the interpreter's day in our outpatients department. We only have her once a month so we schedule most of the Asian women on the day she's available.'

He frowned again.

'I understood the hospital had a number of interpreters. Why do we only get one once a month?'

Katy let out a little sigh of relief. That ready aggression in his voice told her Jake hadn't lost his fighting spirit.

'On paper we have an interpreter once a week,' she told him. 'The problem is it's a man the other three weeks, and the women won't talk through him. It's hard enough to get them to allow male doctors to examine them, but most of them flatly refuse to discuss personal concerns through a man of their own culture.'

'Do you know this for a fact? Did they tell *you* this?'

He emphasised the 'you', as if puzzled by her involvement. After all, he'd already reminded her that a director's assistant should assist the director, not poke her nose into medical business.

'I keep all the department records on the computer,' she explained. 'In the beginning I noticed a number of women not turning up for appointments and when I chased them up I found out why. Now we try to fit them all in on the day when we have Tan here.'

'When *you* chased them up?' Again he allotted a subtle emphasis to the pronoun.

'I took Tan with me and visited the women,' she explained, and saw the flicker of a grin move the corners of his lips. 'Well, I needed to find out,' she added defensively.

'Of course!' He nodded once, then waited as if he expected her to say more, but that slight lessening of the sternness in his face had made her forget what she was saying.

She couldn't let him defeat her with the ghost of a smile! What had they been discussing before he'd begun to talk about today's appointments?

The agenda!

'So we can discuss this tomorrow?' she asked hopefully.

'Is that all the information you have—that the women won't talk through a male interpreter?'

One eyebrow flicked upwards and she shut her eyes against encroaching memories.

'No, I've a file full of information,' she snapped, banging the folder on top of the table.

'Exactly!' he murmured with maddening control. He stood up and walked across to her desk, lifting the sheaf of papers from her nerveless fingers. 'Information I have to absorb before I can consider its value. I'll try to read through it during the day, but I'll need to discuss it with you once I've read it. Perhaps you could have dinner with me tonight? Staying after work is the only way I can see us making sure the item is included in tomorrow's agenda.'

He tucked the file under his arm and walked out, leaving Katy staring, open-mouthed, at the slowly closing door.

She breathed deeply, trying to ease the tension and confusion battling for supremacy in her body.

You can't still love him after the way he treated you, she reminded herself. This reaction is nothing more than shock with a bit of the old physical stuff thrown in.

The words echoed bravely in her head, but it was the 'old physical stuff' causing most concern. Sweaty palms, palpitations and nausea—actual symptoms unrelated to any medical condition.

She tried deep breathing again, and when that didn't work replayed the scene in this very hospital that was etched so vividly in her mind. She and Jake had worked at Lake Shore General, but he'd been brought here after the accident—after they'd argued over his racing his motorbike! She had told him how much the mountain races frightened her and had begged him to stop, had pleaded with him to ride it for pleasure, if he needed the adrenalin rush bike-riding provided, but not to pit himself against professionals.

She'd refused to go and watch, but she'd felt so sick as she waited for him to come home she might as well have been among the crowd of onlookers scattered down the hillside.

The racing professional who'd become his friend had rung to tell her of the accident, to tell her where the ambulance was headed. It had been the first time she'd been in a private hospital and the wide carpeted corridors and almost silent movement of staff as they went about their business had intimidated her.

But not so much that she'd been cowed—or cowardly!

'I don't believe he said that,' she'd railed at his mother that dreadful day.

His parents had been overseas when it happened and had been difficult to contact, and once they'd arrived Katy had been relegated to an extra in the drama—someone who received information second-hand. 'I want to speak to him myself,' she'd insisted.

And eventually they'd let her.

The colour had come back into his skin since they'd moved him out of the ICU and his eyes had been a darker blue than she'd remembered.

'I asked them not to let you in,' he had said, in a cold voice so unlike his own she'd checked to see it really was Jake lying in the bed.

'Why?' she'd demanded.

'Because it's over, Katy.' He had spoken with a calm deliberation. 'It was over before the accident,' he had added, as if he had needed to hurt her more than she'd already been hurting. 'I think we both knew that.'

There'd been a dreadful pause and she'd realised, for the first time, how silence could hammer in the ears.

'I didn't know it,' she'd managed to mumble, her first priority holding back the encroaching tears. There was no way she'd been going to cry in front of him—or let his parents see her grief!

'Think about it, Katy,' he'd said in that same controlled voice. 'Think about it and you'll find you probably did.'

She had turned and walked away, not even pausing when he called her name.

'Thank you for being there when it happened,' he'd

added, and then she'd spun around, because he'd said the words in a tone in which one thanks a stranger.

'It was nothing,' she'd said with a careless shrug, while her heart had pounded its pain and her lips had trembled with the effort of not screaming out the denial which had ricocheted through her body.

She'd tried to believe it had been the accident, that it had been pain making him behave this way—or perhaps the influence of his parents, who had been with him since he'd been moved out of Intensive Care. But when she'd tried to see him again she'd been refused admittance.

Then his parents had had him transferred to a hospital nearer his home in West Australia and she hadn't seen him again. She had written to him twice, all pride crushed by the pain of his betrayal—and by her own fear of and despair for the future—but the letters had been returned unopened and she had finally accepted he'd meant what he'd said.

'Damn the man!' she muttered to herself, staring out towards the lake through a haze of unshed tears.

The little replay had upset her more than it had armoured her.

Relationships ended—falling out of love was as much a fact of life as falling into it. She'd finally accepted that that was what had happened with Jake, finally decided that the argument they'd had before he'd ridden off and nearly killed himself had been a sign that things were over.

For him, perhaps!

It was just a shame she hadn't felt the same way—that they couldn't have parted at some point where the bloom had rubbed off love for both of them.

'Ms Turner to Ward 'B', please,' her speaker phone requested.

The call was like a lifeline back to safety, and she seized it gratefully, hurrying from the ghosts inhabiting the office.

'We've a Vietnamese patient in early labour and can't contact Tan,' Helen Reynolds, the midwife in charge of Ward 'B', told her. 'Dr Spencer tried to examine her but she yelled at him. I sent him out of the birthing suite and she let me take her blood pressure and pulse, but she's objecting to the external foetal heart rate monitor and becoming more and more distressed.'

'I'll try to talk to her,' Katy offered, 'but my Vietnamese is fairly basic. If she understands Chinese, we'll be right.'

She turned and followed the older woman towards the birthing suites, mentally rehearsing the few Vietnamese words she'd picked up in her first lessons.

When she entered the room, the woman was turned away from her. She was so slight and fragile-looking she might have been a child play-acting with a pillow tucked under her gown. Katy could see the shiny knobs of her spine where the hospital gown gaped at the back and made a mental note to find out about the clothing Asian women wore to give birth. Surely not these practical but embarrassing and unflattering gowns the hospital provided for its patients.

'*Chào bà,*' she said, using the traditional greeting to a woman on their first meeting. She'd have liked to add that it was a lovely day to bring a child into the world, but her knowledge of the language was too limited for flowery speeches.

'We need to know when the pains began and where they are.' The deep voice made Katy spin around to see

Jake standing in the shadows near the door. At least he'd had enough sense to keep out of the patient's line of sight.

The woman screamed, apparently alarmed by the sound of his voice, and curled into a tighter ball on the bed. Katy found the movement puzzling. Apart from anything else, it must be uncomfortable to lie that way. Behind her, Helen murmured to Jake, explaining that most of their Asian patients were extremely stoical during childbirth, the Vietnamese women in particular.

Katy sat on the bed and took the woman's hand. Aware of her limitations in Vietnamese, she spoke quietly to her in Chinese and heard a faint response. She spoke again, and felt the waif-like figure relax. When the next contraction began, the woman squeezed Katy's fingers but she didn't scream.

'Try now,' Helen suggested quietly, and Katy asked the questions.

The woman replied quite calmly and Katy translated for Jake, but when Helen approached with the monitor the dreadful keening cry began again.

One word was repeated over and over, but Katy didn't recognise it. She waved Helen away and spoke again in Chinese, repeating meaningless phrases about relaxing, about trying to be calm so the baby wouldn't be upset.

Something buzzed in Katy's brain. She'd read so much about these immigrant women since she'd begun to investigate the feasibility of the special unit that at first she couldn't isolate the thought. She continued talking quietly in Chinese and massaging the woman's hand with her fingers. It was to do with the past...

Memories of her own pain when she'd experienced the flashback of Jake's rejection provided the clue.

When the next contraction finished, she signalled to a

nurse to take her place beside the woman and motioned to Helen and Jake to follow her outside.

'I read a paper on subconscious memory in women from war-torn countries. Although many of the Asian women in this area came out to join family or fiancés, others were refugees who escaped from persecution. Some of them have lived in dreadful conditions in refugee camps for many years while others have experienced torture or saw their parents tortured—'

'So you think instruments we use—say something as innocuous to us as an external foetal heart monitor with wires from the patient to a machine—could bring back memories and even duplicate the pain?'

It was Jake who caught up her vague idea and took it one step further. She could feel his interest quickening and felt a surge of excitement, but before she could speak again he had turned to Helen.

'Take the monitor screen out of the room,' he suggested. 'And anything else that looks harsh or metallic.'

Helen hurried back into the room, and Katy was about to follow when his hand restrained her.

'What else?' he demanded.

She visualised her notes on the new unit and mentally flipped through to the section she'd put together on Vietnamese women.

'The husband isn't present at the birth,' she said. 'It's definitely women's business.'

'Then midwives should handle her,' Jake agreed. 'I'll tell Ron Spencer to keep out, and stay clear myself unless there's an emergency. Will you talk to her while Helen examines her? Can you stay with her until we track down the interpreter?'

He was treating her as a colleague and she responded accordingly. Her heart might still be aching for the magic of the past, but her mind was fully focused on the young woman in the birthing suite.

'At least he's seen at first hand some of the problems we have,' Helen remarked as Katy returned to the patient. 'That should help our push for the special unit.'

While Katy explained to the fearful woman that they needed to know if the baby was close, Helen took the woman's pulse and gently palpated the distended abdomen. Katy knew from her own pregnancy these were Leopold Manoeuvres, and she tried to convey the idea that Helen was checking the exact position of the baby.

'I need to listen to the foetal heart rate after the next contraction,' Helen said quietly. 'Could you tell her I'll use this foetoscope? If she's attended any antenatal appointments she'll be familiar with it, or with an ordinary stethoscope.'

Katy translated falteringly, using her hands and body language to try to explain the technicalities. She was relieved when the woman touched the instrument and nodded. She watched as Helen moved the cone of the instrument over her belly and smiled when the nursing sister nodded reassuringly.

'Ask her if I can take her blood pressure again now. Explain we need to know how her heart is behaving.'

Again Katy translated, pointing to the sphygmomanometer Helen produced from a cupboard.

The patient seemed to withdraw, then flinched as another contraction gripped her belly. When it subsided, Katy mimed putting on a blood pressure cuff and pumping it tight, and the woman spoke freely for the first time.

'Her doctor used the same thing during her antenatal visits,' Katy told Helen, but when she asked the woman for the name of her doctor, the reply was unfamiliar.

'Asian doctor, not Western doctor,' the woman expanded.

'Do you want this doctor with you?' Katy asked, wondering if there were local Asian GPs she might be able to co-opt into her unit.

The woman giggled shyly, and shook her head.

'He man!' she said in English.

The door opened and Tan appeared, bowing slightly to her colleagues before greeting the woman.

They talked for a few minutes, but Katy couldn't follow the fast-paced conversation.

'Can you stay with her, Katy?' Tan asked. 'I've got to sit in on the outpatient appointments with the new boss.'

'I'll stay,' Katy promised, ignoring thoughts of the paperwork and messages she knew would be multiplying on her desk.

The baby arrived three hours later. Helen delivered him and held him so the mother could see the mucus being wiped from his mouth and nose. A Vietnamese midwife who had worked at Lake Shore North the previous year had told them this was important to her people. 'We believe it prevents asthma or emphysema later on,' she'd explained.

Katy waited until the mother had been gently sponged in warm water, then she helped her dress. She watched the woman wrap layers of clothing around herself, then pull a scarf around her head and warm socks on her feet. She shuddered to think how hot their patient must feel, but she knew it was a custom followed in most Asian countries to heat the body after childbirth.

The tiny boy was checked and weighed, then warmly wrapped and presented to his mother. Her eyes were round with wonderment and she sniffed his skin and smiled. Helen grinned at Katy and made a little thumbs-up sign. The maternity ward had already developed the practise of putting ginger root in the water for bathing Vietnamese babies.

'Can you leave her in this room?' Katy asked, and Helen nodded.

'For the moment we can. I've two other suites available for new admissions. Would you ask her if she wants a meal, and, if so, what she'd like to eat?'

Katy spoke to the woman again.

'Hot foods,' she said to Helen. 'The kitchens have a list of what constitutes "hot" and "cold" in this context. If nothing else is available at the moment, she'd be happy with salted rice.'

Helen hurried away and Katy explained to the woman that she must also go. She pushed the baby's crib close to the bed.

'The nurse will stay for a while and she will call me if you need anything. Can I phone your husband or a friend?' she asked.

'My husband is in the big entrance place downstairs,' the woman told her in Chinese. 'He brought me here but could not come up to where babies are born.'

CHAPTER THREE

KATY found the new father—easily isolating him as the nervously pacing young man just inside the front door. He was dressed in a pale grey suit and had a rolled black umbrella hooked over one arm. For a moment she was struck by the incongruity of the couple—the man having adopted such formal European dress while upstairs his wife was swaddled in the clothing her female forebears had worn for thousands of years.

She introduced herself and gave him the good news. His dark eyes gleamed like black onyx and his lips tilted up in a smile that would have taken sandpaper to remove.

He told her his name: Nguyen—the Vietnamese equivalent of Smith it was so common—and she suggested they go back up to the fourth floor where he could see his wife and child. After the struggle to communicate with his wife, she was surprised to find he spoke precise, unaccented English.

'I grew up here,' he explained as they waited for the elevator. 'My wife is Vietnamese-born and was chosen by my grandparents in Vietnam. She was sent out when she was old enough to marry. We had corresponded, of course, but as we learned to know each other our love flourished like roses in a garden. She is learning English, but it is difficult for her.'

Katy was smiling at his flowery tribute when the lift arrived, and once again, as the doors opened, she was confronted by Jake. Her heart reacted skittishly, but her head took control. She introduced Mr Nguyen and explained he was now the father of a fine son.

Jake congratulated him, but he seemed detached. Had his session in Outpatients gone badly?

Katy tried to ignore him, although the restricted space and her physical reactions made this feat difficult. She concentrated on practical matters, turning to the new father.

'Can you stay with your wife for the rest of the day?' she asked him, aware that most Vietnamese were unwilling to take time off work, even for the birth of a baby.

'I have taken paternity leave,' he said proudly. 'I teach in a high school and the system allows me one month without pay. It is more important for my wife to have someone to help her while she does the month than for me to be earning money.'

'That's wonderful,' Katy told him as they all stepped out on the fourth floor. 'And if you can be here as much as possible while she is in hospital, you can explain her needs to the nursing staff and doctors. It will mean we don't have to find a translator every time she is examined, and it could save her from possible embarrassment.'

She showed him into the room and left him with his wife and son, only too aware that Jake was hovering behind her.

'"Does the month?"' he queried as they walked back towards their office.

'It's in the notes,' she told him. 'Although a month is common in many countries, originally in Vietnam the postnatal confinement time was one hundred days. Traditionally, there's a One Hundred Day party, when the child is introduced to friends and family.'

'I haven't a clue what you're babbling on about,' he said crossly, 'and I very much doubt I'll have time to read the notes. I've had a harrowing morning in Outpatients, examining pregnant women by remote control, with some of them unwilling even to supply a specimen of urine, let alone blood! And why I'd need an interpreter when half of them refuse to ask questions, pretending they know everything there is to know, yet looking so fearful and puzzled you'd think I was the devil incarnate...'

His voice trailed away, as if the frustration of the morning was too upsetting to recall.

'Specimens are a problem, as some South-East Asian people are reluctant to give strangers any of their body fluids,' Katy explained. She paused and he halted beside her. 'And Cambodian women in particular hold doctors in such high esteem they're reluctant to bother such great men with questions.'

Her lips twitched with delight as she dropped this little gem of information.

He eyed her suspiciously, aware of the mockery in her voice.

'Go on,' he growled.

'Well, it's because of such wide-ranging beliefs and customs we believe the new unit is so necessary. If we can start with group sessions and interpreters in antenatal clinics, we can explain in the women's own language why we use certain procedures—like taking their blood and urine or performing scans—and let them tell us why they do it differently and what practices they find offensive—'

'Offensive?' he echoed.

'Both sides are offended at times,' she told him. 'The women by some of our ways and our staff by some of theirs. If we can begin to educate them in our system, and learn something of their customs and beliefs well before the actual birth, it should be easier to chart a course for their pregnancy and confinement.'

His pager buzzed and he groaned.

'I'm only here for two months, Katy,' he grumbled. 'Couldn't you put your unit on hold until Dan returns?'

'Once you revelled in a challenge,' she reminded him, and saw a shadow darken his cheeks.

'Once I revelled in a lot of things,' he muttered at her, and walked on down the corridor.

He was on the phone when she entered their office. She'd been called back by Helen to discuss a time for the basic Chinese lessons she'd offered to give the staff. Learning the common courtesies in the patients' language was all part of her grand plan!

As she slipped into her seat she saw the 'New Unit' file open on his desk. Had he read it? She tried not to let her hopes rise too high. A consultant director spent so little time in his office—there was always someone wanting his attention. She sat down and began to respond to the messages on her own desk.

They ranged from leaking taps in shower cubicles to an under-supply of the new muslin nappies they were trialling in the nursery. One by one she dealt with these 'housekeeping' matters, concentrating fiercely in an effort to ignore Jake's presence in the room.

'I'm going back down to Outpatients,' he announced when his phone conversation concluded. 'Page me there if you need me.'

Then her phone rang, and he hesitated by her desk while she answered it.

'The director is busy at the moment,' she said, when the voice on the other end paused for breath. 'Dr Spencer will be doing afternoon ward rounds—' she glanced at her watch. Could it really be that late? What had happened to lunch? '—any minute. You could ask him about the problem.'

She listened to the indignation squawk through the phone. Jake was still hovering on the other side of her desk. She waved her hand to show him everything was under control, but he didn't move.

'It's natural to have difficulties at first,' she assured the distressed patient, 'but I think you'll find the nursing staff far more helpful than the doctor in this matter. Many of them have had children themselves and have experienced the same problems. If Sister has suggested a mild analgesic you can be certain it will be something which won't affect your milk or harm the baby.'

She listened quietly, aware the woman on the other end was regaining her self-control.

'I think the recommended time is forty minutes before each feed, but timing is difficult if you're demand-feeding the baby,' she agreed. 'If you're really against the analgesic, you'd have to put up with the pain. I know it's uncomfortable, but it's a sign your uterus is contracting and getting back into its pre-pregnancy shape.'

Jake had settled himself to wait out the conversation, one hip hitched onto the edge of the desk. He was too close, Katy realised as she continued to soothe the patient. She could see the shape of his thigh muscles against the material of his suit and found she didn't want to think about Jake's thigh muscles. Didn't want to think about any part of Jake!

'If I'd known you weren't busy I'd have sent you down to see her,' she said tartly when the conversation had finally come to an end and she'd replaced the receiver. 'I thought you had appointments in Outpatients.'

'An appointment,' he corrected calmly, shifting slightly so she could envisage more muscled thigh beneath the fine grey fabric. 'It's with the head of the interpreters. He'll be working and will fit me in between patients whenever I get there. Do you field all my calls with such expertise?'

She looked up, trying to gauge his mood from his face, but it was expressionless—remote.

'I try to shield the director from unnecessary complications,' she replied primly. 'That's why calls like that come through to me, not you. Mrs Preston is a patient in Ward 'C'. She's having severe after-pains from contractions when she breast feeds, but—'

'Was concerned over analgesia contaminating her breast milk,' he finished. 'I'm an obstetrician; I gathered that much.'

Katy nodded, ignoring the sarcasm. His closeness was making her breathless, as if he'd drawn all the available air out of the room.

'And nurses are more helpful than doctors?' he pursued softly. 'I know you told me I was redundant earlier, but do you always tell the patients how useless we medicos are?'

She felt a ripple of apprehension. Was he annoyed or merely teasing?

'Of course not,' she said, her eyes defying him to argue. 'I was merely pointing out that the nurses have more experience in some fields—and that includes, strangely enough, nursing care!'

'Did you finish your nursing training?'

The question was so unexpected she knew her involuntary jolt of shock must have been visible to him. No matter how much she loved her present job, she couldn't hold back the spurt of regret that she'd failed to complete her degree.

'No,' she admitted quietly.

'Why?'

She closed her eyes to the image of Julia. Her heart was wrenched with pain. Whatever happens, he mustn't know about Julia.

'I had other things to do,' she muttered.

'Like what?'

The question was so harsh she shook her head—responding to the tone not the words.

'So you gave up, just like that?' he mocked, shifting off the desk so he could straighten up and loom over her. 'The fighter who'd sworn she'd make it although it meant working at menial jobs to pay her way and studying through the night?'

He was goading her deliberately, but she couldn't hold back.

'Maybe I lost interest in it,' she challenged. 'Maybe I decided it wasn't what I wanted. You should understand that, Jake,' she reminded him. 'You made the same decision once yourself—about me!'

She reached out and lifted the receiver. The phone hadn't rung, but she needed to look as if she was dismissing him—as if she had more important things to do than argue about their mutual past.

She pressed the memory button for the crèche, aware that he'd taken the hint and was striding towards the door. She was about to respond to Nan's 'hello' when he turned.

'You've made arrangements for tonight?' he asked, and then, without waiting for a reply, he added, 'I've been given a couple of rooms on the top floor. It's the door on the left as you come out of the lift. Come on

up when you finish and bring the file. We can order a
meal from the kitchen.'

She opened her mouth to object to his orders, but he
was gone before she could think of a valid argument—
or one that didn't involve mentioning her child.

Was she being foolish? Wouldn't he eventually hear
she had a child? It was more than likely! Yet she knew
instinctively that Julia must be protected at all costs—
must be shielded from the pain he'd inflicted on
Katy—that unbearable agony which arose not from love
but from the repudiation of it.

She heard a click as the phone in the crèche was disconnected and remembered what she was supposed to
be doing. For a moment she considered going down to
the crèche to speak to Nan in person and hold Julia in
her arms for a few minutes. But such behaviour would
lead to questions, and at the moment she had no answers.
She pressed the memory button again.

'Nan, it's Katy. Could you take Julia home tonight?
The new boss wants to talk about my pet project, and if
I want it brought up in the ward meeting tomorrow, I'll
have to stay and explain it to him.'

Nan's reply was immediate.

'I'd love to have her. You've no idea how I've missed
her visits while you were both away, and my kids have
been nagging me to have her over as soon as you returned.'

Katy relaxed. Nan's enthusiasm was genuine, and
Julia returned her honorary aunt's affection—so much
so she kept a toothbrush, pyjamas and spare clothes at
Nan's house.

'I'll come down and see her before you go,' Katy
promised, then hung up, her fingers tingling with apprehension now the decision was made.

If she had any sense at all she'd have told Jake it was impossible, but she hated telling lies—and to tell the truth would be unthinkable.

She turned back to the messages on her desk and worked through until four. Jake hadn't returned, and Katy assumed he was seeing his afternoon patients. She slipped out of the office and went down to say goodbye to Julia, then returned via the ward to check on the new Vietnamese patient.

Mr Nguyen must have spread the news, for two elderly women were entering the room as she approached. They carried baskets and cloth-covered parcels so she turned away, not wanting to interrupt when the patient had visitors.

Back in her office, she found a copy of the 'New Unit' file and began to check through it, marking sections Jake might query and mentally preparing her argument in support. She was engrossed in an article she'd included about the use of steam for purification when the fire alarm sounded.

Her first reaction was to race down the fire stairs and check on Julia, but she knew she must see to her own section first. As she hurried into the foyer she recognised the signal as a localised alarm, then the noise stopped.

'That's it?'

She turned to see Jake emerging from the elevator.

'Repeated long blasts signal a major emergency,' she explained. 'That long-short noise indicates the extinguishers have come into operation in one section of the building. When the alarm stops, you know the fire is out.'

As she spoke she heard a commotion in the corridor beyond the foyer, and saw the visiting Vietnamese women emerging from Mrs Nguyen's room.

They were wet!

'Oh, no!' she groaned. 'Not today!'

Leaving Jake in the foyer, she raced towards them, propelling herself past their chattering laments and into the suite.

The new mother was sitting on a chair, her baby held tightly in her arms. A nurse was stripping off the wet bedclothes and a wardsman was mopping the floor. For a moment she thought the woman was as wet as her visitors, then she realised they were tears on her cheeks. Beside her, Mr Nguyen was re-rolling his umbrella, and Katy chuckled as she visualised him calmly using it to protect his wife and child from the downpour while pandemonium erupted among the staff and visitors.

Jake arrived with Helen close behind him.

'What's going on?' he demanded, and Katy pointed towards the small brass urn almost under the bed—now full of sooty water.

'My wife's friend brought it in,' Mr Nguyen explained. 'She believes in the old ways—in the "roasting" after birth. She brought only a small amount of charcoal but it must have smoked too much. We meant no harm...'

He spread his hands and frowned ferociously, as if concerned the debacle might cause his wife's expulsion from the hospital.

Helen looked at Katy and sighed. It had happened once before, and the sprinklers had worked efficiently both times, but it was the worst possible recommendation for the new unit.

'Roasting?' Jake repeated in a weak voice.

'I'll explain later,' Katy told him. A wardsman wheeled in a dry bed, and while Helen held the baby Katy helped a nurse transfer the woman to it.

'We'll take the baby down to the nursery,' Helen told the father. 'He seems dry enough but we'd better check him out. Would you please tell your wife we'll have to move her into the ward while we clean up in here.'

As the young man turned to his wife to explain what was going on Helen murmured to Katy, 'At least there the passing staff can keep an eye on things.'

Katy listened to the flow of foreign words and thought their patient seemed more comforted than upset. Maybe the 'roasting' had been too much for her as well!

'Come along, Miss Turner,' Jake said, tapping her on the shoulder as she bent to admire the baby once again. 'You've got some extra talking to do!'

She followed him back to their office where he pushed the 'New Unit' file to one side and turned his chair so he could look directly at her.

'Now, as you're the local expert on ethnic culture, perhaps you can explain how a visitor damn near set fire to the hospital.'

Katy eyed him warily, unable to judge if he was angry or amused.

'The hospital was never in any danger.' She plunged into her defence with a stout heart. 'The fire alarms are so sensitive even burning toast will set them off.'

'So, do we remove all the fire sensors in the maternity ward when Asian patients are in residence?'

The question was asked with such silky restraint it prodded anger into life.

'Don't be ridiculous!' She flung out her arms in exasperation, knocking over her prized brass pelvis. 'The whole point of the new unit is not a place so much as an approach. I've already said that the hospital needs to set up antenatal clinics for these women which will include group discussions on childbirth and confinement, but it's a two-way street, Jake. We can listen to these women and try to understand what they want, but it also gives us the opportunity to explain the way the hospital works—including the fact that we have fire sensors in all rooms, and that water sprays from the ceilings if smoke is detected.'

He reached out and picked up the fallen ornament, running his fingers over the smooth metal.

'Okay, I take that point. Now perhaps we could go back to today's little disaster and the term they used. "Roasting", wasn't it?'

Katy felt a surge of hope.

'You've got to understand that a great deal of Asian medicine is based on what they call "humours",' she began.

'The concepts of hot and cold, of yin and yang.' He nodded as if he'd heard or read of this.

'That's right,' Katy agreed. 'If you can go along with the concept of hot and cold, then you'll understand when I say most Asian women believe the loss of blood during childbirth leaves them cold. In almost all of their cultures there are provisions for confinement that concentrate on keeping the body warm.'

'Which is why, on a warm day, that woman was rugged up like a football spectator outside on a winter afternoon.'

Katy grinned at him.

'Dreadful, isn't it?' she agreed. 'But that's to our way of thinking. And that's why her friend brought in the little fire-pot. Vietnamese women, in particular, believe the body benefits by lying over a fire. To them, it not only replaces lost heat but it helps dry up the lochia and shrink the woman's tissues back into place. In parts of China it's called "lying in the fire". Some cultures observe the ritual for three days, while others believe you must keep it up for the whole month.'

'Doing the month,' he murmured, and she remembered he had asked about it earlier.

She was wondering where she could begin her next explanation when his pager buzzed and he turned away to press a number on his phone.

He was as quick on the uptake as he'd always been, she realised, listening as he switched from one conversation to the next. She felt pleased the head injury he'd received in the accident hadn't left any lasting legacy, then chided herself for caring what had happened to him.

Professional efficiency, Katy! she reminded herself, and turned the thought to her own advantage.

Surely his intellectual ability should help him grasp the importance of establishing the new unit—although it was a leap of faith to hope he'd understand it all in twenty-four hours. She had been studying the language, customs and culture of these women for two years and still understood so little. How could she explain to someone who had no prior knowledge, had done no background reading on the subject?

'I'll have to leave it till later,' he murmured, slipping his hand over the mouthpiece on the phone while he spoke to her.

She nodded her agreement and turned her attention back to the work that was still clogging the surface of her desk.

Fire report first, she reminded herself, and got up to find the correct form in the filing cabinet. Helen would fill in a similar form, as would the fire officer. Katy smiled to herself. One of her recurring nightmares was of Lake Shore North disappearing under a snowstorm of official forms and duplicated paperwork.

'I'm going down to Cas; there's a pregnant woman who's been involved in a minor traffic accident and the resident on duty is concerned about her. If I don't get back before you're ready to leave, I'll see you upstairs—top floor, first door on the left.'

He touched her shoulder as he walked past and she felt her skin burn where his fingers had brushed it.

You can't still love him, she told herself, despair weighing down her heart. He treated you like some worn-out belonging, to be thrust aside as soon as he was finished with it. Where's your pride, girl? Or your instinct for self-preservation?

By six o'clock she knew she could put off their next meeting no longer. She'd been on the phone to Admin over a hitch in a ward orderly's holiday pay when Jake had come back into the office, picked up the file, and pointed his finger upwards to indicate he was on his way to his temporary abode.

More reluctant than she'd ever felt, she hesitated a moment longer, then rang Nan and spoke to Julia, needing to shore up her defences against Jake Cartwright.

'Been busy?' he asked when she finally pushed open the first door on the left and stepped tentatively into a pleasantly furnished sitting room.

'Always.' She crossed to the window, diverted and delighted by the spectacular view. 'I had no idea the hospital had accommodation up here.'

The wind had dropped and the sun was setting. The flaring colours in the western sky had turned the lake to a gleaming sheet of red, gold, pink and amber.

'Remember rowing into the sunset, Katy?' he asked, and she felt her shoulders curl instinctively forward, as if to protect the soft, vulnerable parts of her body. She'd been thinking of that evening herself, of the soft splash of sound as they'd rowed, and the way the colour had seemed to flow below the surface, following the cuts they'd made as they dug the oars into the water.

'It was like a different world—the hot colours—fire and blood—claimed as ours—as symbols of our passion and our work.'

His voice was husky, tempting her to fall in with this nostalgic journey to the past. Her stomach tightened.

It was one thing to take that walk alone—to remember the good times occasionally. But to do it with Jake? To indulge in an orgy of 'remembers' with him? No way!

'They don't last long, the colours of sunset,' she pointed out, seeing the rose give way to violet, the orange to a burst of red before fading to darkness. Nor does love, she could have added, but instead she said, 'I think I prefer the lake in daytime.' Her voice was far calmer than her intestines. 'Cool colours—blue and green, muted greys and wind-flecked white. That's when the lake looks most beautiful to me.'

'What about silvered by the moonlight, Katy?' he tempted, but she refused to play the game. She closed her eyes against this next intruding memory, then opened them to pick out landmarks in the business district of the city at the southern end of the lake.

'That new tall building is an insurance office,' she said, to make sure he'd got the message that 'let's remember' wouldn't work with her, although her skin and bones belied this thought.

He muttered a reply, but she refused to speculate what it might have been. Instead, she concentrated on standing upright, keeping calm and studying the city lights, which seemed brighter now the sun had gone.

Somewhere beyond the stacked lights of the office towers was Lake Shore General, where she had trained and Jake had worked, and beyond that again the arid suburb where she'd grown up—the rented house surrounded by a straggle of grass she'd once tried to turn into a lawn.

'Do you ever see your father?'

Damn the man. He'd followed her thoughts as easily as if she'd drawn a map.

'No,' she said. 'I tried to once, but he made it very clear he still considers me the cause of all the misery in his life.'

'Still hasn't occurred to him he had something to do with your mother becoming pregnant?'

The words were spoken lightly, but Katy could remember Jake's disbelief when she'd told him of the life she'd lived, caught between two bitter, warring, unforgiving parents and held responsible for their misery.

'It doesn't bother me,' she told him.

'Much!' he teased, and she knew he was probably right. She might have put her childhood behind her, but the experiences of her early years intruded into the choices she'd made as an adult. Especially in regard to bringing Julia up in a single-parent household. Two loving parents might be better than one, but without love…

She shrugged off his intimated doubt.

'I rarely think about it,' she told him—and that was the truth. She rarely thought of anything prior to Jake's advent into her life, and she'd already moved out of that depressing suburb by the time she met him, moving north towards the lake—like going up a kind of domiciliary ladder.

'I live down there now,' she said, and peered downward and to the right. She could almost see the semidetached cottage where she and Julia lived. It was further north again. Not that upward social mobility had persuaded her to buy where she had; she'd chosen the area because it was within walking distance of the hospital and the lake. Paying for it was difficult, but it was the perfect house for her and Julia.

'Can you see your house?' he asked, moving closer.

She stepped casually away from him, pretending she was moving to have a better view. Actually, she'd have needed to be an ostrich to see her place from here, but it seemed a reasonable excuse to edge away.

'No, but I know it's down there.'

She saw him smile and knew he was remembering how possessive she'd always been over having her own living space.

'Shift in with me,' he'd said so often in the past. 'This place of yours is smaller than my bathroom.'

'But it's mine,' she'd argued fiercely. 'My home!'

More of a home than the houses she'd lived in as a child was what she'd meant. And, back then, he'd come to understand.

She turned from the window and walked across to sit in one of the easy chairs.

'Well, tell me what you think of my temporary abode?' Jake waved his hand around his domain. 'They keep the suites for visiting bigwigs—or temporary employees like me.'

He must have walked up behind her while she was reliving flashes of her life, for his words rustled over her shoulder and her skin tingled again with its acute awareness of his presence. But he'd also switched the conversational tone back to purely business, and for that she was grateful.

'Must save Old Forbes a fortune in hotel accommodation,' she replied as lightly as she could manage, shrugging off the potency of his body's closeness.

'Mr Forbes not your favourite administrator?' Jake teased, and she smiled at the question.

'Actually, I quite enjoy our battles, and I think he feels the same way. If the administration in a hospital this size isn't tight, then money that could be providing better patient service is frittered away. And of course there are the factional fights as well!'

She could be as businesslike as he.

'It's the same as any huge organisation,' she explained. 'Every department wants a bigger slice of the pie. Neurology has a top-rate director's assistant. It's a man, and, though I hate to admit it, he's the best in the hospital at wheedling money out of—'

'Old Forbes?' Jake interrupted, and Katy realised she'd been talking too much—probably to hide her nervousness. Surely he couldn't still affect her like this?

Couldn't he what!

'Did you have time to read the file?' she asked abruptly.

He pointed to the pile of papers on a small table beside one of the room's three easy chairs.

'I've read the summary of what you want, but haven't had time to read all the supporting documents. What if we order dinner, then go through the summary and you can tell me why each point is important? That way, if I have to discuss it before I finish the documentation, I'll have some basis for argument.'

He sounded so composed Katy wondered if she'd imagined a different texture in their conversation earlier—a tension fired by one round of 'do you remember?'.

Or was she keyed up because of that unexpected kiss this morning?

Or some hidden hope still lingering in her wishful, foolish heart?

CHAPTER FOUR

THE meal arrived as Katy was explaining the concept of 'hot' and 'cold' foods.

'So "hot" doesn't mean cooked or heated in this context; it means spicy or salty.' Jake poked at his steak as he spoke and grimaced slightly.

'That's right,' Katy agreed, smiling at the expression on his face. 'And in the context of the canteen kitchen, "medium rare" means however it comes off the griller. That's why I always have the sausages. There's not much can go wrong with sausages.'

She thought she'd raise a smile, but he studied her across the table, then frowned instead.

'I should have taken you out for dinner,' he said, surprising her with the vehemence in the words.

'Hey, it's a business meal, that's all.' She spoke casually, to hide the flutter of unacceptable excitement in her chest. 'It's more important to get through the work than to have a gourmet dinner.'

She tackled the sausages and they ate in silence for a while.

'I'm not so sure,' he said grouchily, still prodding at the steak

'I am,' Katy told him firmly, and continued with her explanations. He didn't interrupt, eating absentmindedly while she talked about the adjustments Lake Shore North had already made.

'The food business has been sorted out. We have so many Asian patients in other parts of the hospital it made

57

sense to employ some Asian cooks. We have menus printed in Chinese and Vietnamese and patients can make their own choices.'

Katy cut into a sausage. This eating with Jake had a peculiar intimacy, and she had to struggle to keep her mind on the discussion.

'Menus are easier to sort out than fires under the beds,' he suggested.

'Why?' she demanded, pushing her fork into the cheesy top of the scalloped potatoes. 'I realise we can't have actual fires, but there are air-conditioning controls in all the rooms and all wards. It's impossible to heat a particular room when the rest of the building is being cooled, but the air-conditioning could be turned right down in the new unit. If we can provide the proper counselling during pregnancy, and make certain the staff allow the women to wear their layers of clothing, there'd be no need for fires.'

Her meal was plain but good, and she paused to take another mouthful.

'That's a point.' He finished his steak and pushed his plate away. 'And an argument in favour of keeping these women together in one ward. What else?'

'Showers!' Katy groaned as she remembered some of the battles she'd fought over the showers.

'Showers?' Jake echoed.

She nodded and grinned, her dinner forgotten.

'You've worked in enough hospitals to know how important the daily routines are to nursing staff—particularly the cleanliness routine. Can you imagine the nurses' horror when I suggested something as depraved as not forcing these patients to shower?'

Jake chuckled at her expression of mock-horror. 'Okay, do tell!'

'It's the hot-cold thing again—or it may be to do with body humours—but these women believe water—and especially cold water—is to be avoided during the period after the baby's birth. They think showering or bathing too soon after childbirth will bring on arthritic pains in later life, while hair-washing will lead to hair loss. In some cultures the restriction on bathing and hair-washing only lasts a few days, but in others it is for the whole month. The women keep themselves clean by sitting in steam and wiping the perspiration from their bodies. They use aromatic herbs and spices which they believe helps this purification process, but they don't leap out of bed and have a shower every morning.'

'That must horrify the nurses!'

'And most other patients,' Katy pointed out. 'Some of the women leave hospital days before they should be discharged because they are either intimidated into showering or because the other patients make them feel dirty. It's a difficult position for staff and patients, but, again, if these women could use a particular ward we could set up a portable sauna or steam bath for them.'

Jake shook his head, as if bemused by the extent of her knowledge.

'I can't believe you've gone into it all so thoroughly. What started you on it?'

'When—' She stopped abruptly, aware she'd almost said, When Julia was born. 'I have a Chinese friend who taught me the language. We used to sit and talk in a mixture of English and Chinese, mostly about the hospital and her experiences having her first baby in Malaysia and her second baby here. I was interested in the differences—'

'And began to study them? You've done an enormous amount of work to prepare this file.'

He spoke admiringly but she couldn't take the praise.

'Most of it was organising other people to write papers,' she told him. 'For example, one of the papers is by a woman doctor. She belongs to the Hmong people, a race of Chinese origin spread throughout South-East Asia.'

'She was a doctor in this hospital?' Jake asked, and Katy shook her head.

'I met her when she came to Lake Shore North to have her first baby. She had been educated here, and with her medical training she didn't believe in the old ways. Naturally she didn't ''do the month'', didn't stay quietly at home with her baby as custom dictates, or avoid water, or keep warm. The baby slept in its own room instead of with her, and she actually hired a nanny and returned to work part-time—'

'And her hair fell out?'

It was a gentle tease, not meant to scoff at her explanation, and she smiled at him.

'No, but she wasn't well. Nothing specific—coughs and colds, aches and pains, general debility—'

'Which could be the natural result of trying to handle a new baby and a career at the same time,' Jake broke in.

'Exactly,' Katy pointed out. 'Most customs develop from actual experience. These ancient rules didn't come about by accident. By insisting the woman takes it easy for a month, for whatever reason, it gives her time to recover her strength, establish the baby on the breast and get used to having this little human being dependent on her. Even the bathing restrictions possibly stemmed from a time when the only water in the village could have been contaminated. By avoiding water for a month, the

woman lessened the risk of infection for either herself
or the baby.'

'So what happened to your friend?'

He was leaning forward now, his elbows on the table
and his chin propped in his hands. She could see his
fingers—long and slim, laced together—and if she lifted
her gaze just a little higher she'd meet his eyes.

She looked towards the window instead, afraid of a
growing warmth in the room that had nothing to do with
the temperature or the discussion.

'She had another child almost immediately, but this
time she ''did the month''.' She turned back to him and,
seeing the glint of laughter in his eyes, she smiled.

'No, she didn't roast herself,' she told him, 'but she
did stay at home, she did keep warm and she did eat the
recommended foods. She's a woman brought up and
educated in our Western system, yet she admitted to me
that she hoped by doing it properly the second time she
might undo any long-term harmful effects caused by her
first confinement.'

He shook his head—disbelieving of the theory yet accepting these concepts he didn't fully understand.

'I'll fight for your unit, Katy,' he said, in such a gentle
voice she was suddenly afraid.

'Thanks!' she muttered, rising abruptly to her feet.
'Well, I'll get going now and leave you to read through
the rest of the stuff.'

She grabbed her handbag from the coffee table and
headed towards the door.

'I'll see you tomorrow!'

'Hey, what's the rush? I was going to offer you coffee—I have a very fancy machine supplied in what they
call the ''kitchenette''.'

'I'd better go,' she said, barely hesitating in her forward rush.

'Then I'll see you to your car,' he protested, and she knew she must be imagining the disappointment in his voice.

'I don't have a car—I w-walk!' she stuttered. He was far too close, the room too small—he was taking all her air again!

'Then I'll walk with you,' he said firmly, and his hand closed around her arm as he ushered her towards the door.

They rode down in the lift in silence, but when they crossed the main entrance lobby on the ground floor Katy knew she had to break it. It was constricting her, drawing her closer to Jake, making her feel too familiarly comfortable with him.

As they stepped out through the front door an ambulance siren ripped through the night. Although it was a common enough sound around her work-place, she never heard one without remembering their background chorus, screaming in and out of the A and E entrance, the night she had sat with Jake while they'd fought to stabilise him.

'Do you remember much about being brought here after the accident?' She asked the question unthinkingly —a kind of word-association response. And then wished she hadn't!

'Enough of it, Katy,' he said gravely.

He took her arm again as they crossed the road and made their way towards the path that led through the park to the lake's edge. It was the path she took when walking to and from work, but he didn't know that. He was steering her that way because they'd walked there in the past and because he had more to say to her than, 'Enough of it, Katy'.

Something in his voice, or the tension straining from his body, gave her the warning, but she had no idea how she might deflect him from talking of that time. They reached the lake and he drew her towards a seat that faced the moon-silvered waters.

'You were right, all those years ago, when you accused me of being wild and reckless—of always having to go that one step too far, having to prove something to myself,' he began quietly. 'The wild and reckless bit was tamed, somewhat, but for the rest...'

Pain surfed along her nerves. It was the daredevil in Jake which had appealed to her, for she had felt the same rash determination. Only in her case it was directed towards achievement in her work—an achievement that had come too easily to Jake to provide the challenges he needed.

'I might have criticised you for it, but it was probably the one quality that saved your life,' she argued, remembering his early unconscious state, the severity of his blood loss, kidney damage—the list had gone on and on. 'Sheer bloody-mindedness would have goaded you to prove all the medical experts wrong.'

He chuckled at her words.

'You may be right,' he agreed. 'Although at times I wondered if the fight was worth it.'

'Of course it was!' She leapt to reassure him, for a world without Jake—even a Jake who no longer loved her—would be inconceivable.

He didn't seem to hear her. His eyes remained focused on the water and he shifted, a little uneasily, on the hard wooden seat. She remembered that suggestion of a hesi-

tation in his stride and wondered if his hip still pained
him.

'Of course it was!' he echoed, breaking into her
thoughts of his mangled hip. 'But it took a long time
and then I had to find a job—I hadn't completed my two
years' residency, so the powers-that-be decreed I should
start the second year again. By the time I finished I knew
I wanted to specialise in Obstetrics and Gynaecology.
That took another two years, and then I had a stint overseas for twelve months.'

The night wrapped them in a velvety cloak of grey.
Along the path, puddles of yellow light lay like patterns
in the soft material. The water lapped against the shore,
caressing the shelving sand. Katy absorbed the sights
and sounds unconsciously, taking in the water's voice as
a kind of counterpoint to Jake's story and listening to it
in the silences that fell between his words.

'I came back to a position at a hospital in Perth and
did well there. I was doing some teaching, taking students for seminars, becoming involved with an IVF programme...'

Somewhere in the park a curlew cried, its mournful
note echoing a kind of loneliness she sensed in Jake's
words. She steeled her heart against a stabbing wedge
of pity.

Feel sorry for Jake Cartwright?

Never!

'Well, what happened next?' she asked briskly, as if
his recitation had been simply a statement of facts to
her. 'Did Perth disappoint you? Was the triumphal return
to the old home town not quite what the prodigal expected?'

She stood up so he wouldn't sense her agitation and
began to walk slowly down the path. For some reason

she couldn't bear to think of her carefree, laughing Jake unhappy. He caught up with her and walked beside her, not touching her, until they reached the place where two swans slept, like folded white towels left by the edge of the lake.

If he mentions the swans I'll scream, Katy decided. Enough is enough with this delving into the past!

But he didn't mention the swans.

'Nothing was as I expected, Katy,' he said quietly. 'Or everything and nothing.'

He paused, but she was beyond conversation. The shock of seeing him again, and the continued pressure of his presence throughout the day, had left her feeling quite exhausted. She needed to regroup—to regather the energy she needed to deal with another thirty-nine days of Jake.

She strode ahead, taking the path that cut back towards the end of her street. It led through an avenue of spreading poincianas, their canopies knitted together to blot out the night sky.

'I hope you don't walk home this way after dark,' he said, and his voice had a gravelly sound which scraped along her nerves.

'I rarely walk home after dark,' she said, deliberately distancing himself from his concern. When they regained the road she pointed across it. 'My place is there—the second house along that street. I'll be quite all right from here.'

Her voice was tight with the strain of speaking normally. She wanted to run away, or shout at him to leave her alone—and she certainly didn't want him intruding into her home, didn't want images of his presence left behind like forgotten socks when he walked out of her life again.

She also couldn't risk his seeing the evidence of Julia's existence—the scattered toys, the doll's house they were building out of Lego blocks.

He must have sensed her reluctance, for he paused, then drew her back into the shadow of the trees and turned her so she faced him. In the dim light his face was unreadable, yet she knew his tension was as great as hers. It crashed against her in the darkness, invisible waves pounding on her skin.

'I rebuilt my life from almost nothing, Katy,' he continued, as if there'd been no pause, no conversational shift. 'Bit by bit I put myself back together again—learning first to stand and then to walk again. I retrained my head to read and absorb what it was reading, to think medically and retain knowledge. I worked hard at it and I succeeded, achieving top marks in my specialty exams. I was invited to join hospital staffs, to teach, to be involved in projects. It became a busy life—frenetic, professionally fulfilling—yet as empty as a school during holiday time. The buildings are still there, but there's a desolation about such places...'

She felt his anguish as a burning in her chest, but she shied away from hearing more. She moved, but his hand tightened on her arm.

'Six months ago I began to wonder if it wasn't what I'd won that was bothering me but what I'd lost.'

He leaned forward and pressed a kiss on her forehead. It was as chaste as a child's shy salute, yet it burnt into Katy's skin like a red-hot cattle brand.

Her heart was beating so erratically she could barely breathe, yet she couldn't contain the anger that fizzed and bubbled in her blood.

'*You* broke off our relationship, Jake!' she retorted scornfully. 'You told me it was over, finished, gone and done for—you told me you'd known that for some time, even before the accident. You refused to see me, you returned my letters unopened, you offered me no apology or explanation, just, "It's over, Katy". And now you've got the hide to breeze back into my life and talk about emptiness.'

She resisted an urge to stamp her foot. Instead, she dragged fresh air into her lungs and continued, 'Well, let me tell you this, Jake Cartwright. I know all about emptiness. In fact, I'm an expert on it. And it won't kill you! You can learn to live with it—you can even learn to hide it from yourself.'

'So you don't feel the same? You've found happiness with someone else?'

His voice seemed to be coming from a long way off, but Katy knew it was the echo of her anger roaring in her ears that distanced it. She considered lying, but truth was too important to her.

'I've found a life I enjoy, work I love and contentment, Jake. I was never the risk-taker you were,' she said. 'And that hasn't changed.'

'So, going out with me again, even on an "old friends" basis, would be a risk?' he challenged, his voice full of teasing laughter, as if all his doubts had suddenly been banished.

She tried to work out what she'd said to change his mood, but couldn't find an answer. The temptation to say yes was so strong she felt her lips moving. Then she remembered Julia.

Seeing Jake again had made her realise just how deeply she still cared for him—and that she always would. She knew exactly what he meant about that sense of emptiness, for there was a part of her which would never be complete without him.

But he had said he loved her once before and turned away from her; there was no guarantee he wouldn't do it again. If she'd had only herself to consider, she'd have walked back into his arms—and probably into his bed—and suffered the consequences later. But there was no way in the world she'd risk that happening to Julia, risk her suffering the devastation of loss which was still so vivid in her own mind.

'It would be a disaster, Jake,' she said firmly. 'Believe me!'

'Perhaps,' he said, 'but couldn't we at least find out.'

'Find out I still love you, but that you don't love me?' she demanded, irony icing her voice. 'That would be fun! However, perhaps this time I'll decline. I'll stick to poking my fingers in electric light sockets for my thrills.'

'I had my reasons, Katy,' he said, so quietly she almost missed the words. Or wished she had!

'I've got to go,' she said, ignoring the implied explanation she doubted he was going to give.

He nodded then, and stepped out of the shadows.

'I'll watch you home from here.' He seemed to sense her reluctance to let him encroach any further into her life. 'See you tomorrow.'

And now she, who'd been desperate to get away, found it difficult to move, so he had to half turn her and press his hand against her shoulder when the road was clear and she could safely cross.

She let the touch propel her forward, taking one step at a time with a mechanical efficiency—increasing the physical distance between herself and her Nemesis, but unable to shut out his emotional presence.

There'd been confusion and uncertainty lurking behind his strange confession, and those two characteristics were so foreign to the Jake she'd known it hurt her to think about them.

And why did it hurt her? The question popped into her head as she unlocked her front door.

She slipped into the sanctuary of her home but did not turn on a light. Instead, she leaned against the door, trying to shut out both the present and the past.

Because she still loved him!

Her heart hammered out the answer, then quivered with fear. At least, she hoped it was fear!

She called in at the crèche to see Julia before work, spending half an hour with her daughter before making her way reluctantly upstairs. If the new unit project was approved, she would have an enormous amount of work to do organising it and setting up the programmes she wanted put in place. The two months would be over before she caught breath.

She sighed deeply, only realising it had also been noisy when her fellow passengers in the elevator swivelled their heads to stare at her. The doors opened on Four and she hurried out. The new unit had assumed even more importance now. It would give her a focus, divert her thoughts away from Jake and keep her so busy her body would be too tired to be seduced by his presence.

Her reluctance to face him became impatience. If he was in the office, she'd stress the importance of the project once again.

'We've managed to group five Asian patients together in 'C',' Rosa Williams, the sister in charge of Ward 'C' announced as she caught Katy's arm and halted her headlong rush along the corridor. She led Katy towards the ward.

'They're a bit of a mix—one Cambodian, your Vietnamese friend, a young woman who came over as a student from Malaysia, another Vietnamese woman who's just had her third baby here and an older Chinese woman from Hong Kong.'

Katy smiled as she imagined the diversity of culture and custom in the small group. She followed Rosa into the ward and spoke to the patients, pleased to see that the grouping appeared to be working. All the women were either cradling their babies or had them sleeping in cribs beside them. Not wanting to be separated from their child was another characteristic of the Asian mother.

She greeted them in Chinese and heard the shy replies in a mixture of languages, then the chatter continued. Katy was delighted by the interaction between the women. Although she had no doubt the Chinese woman spoke perfect English, and was obviously wealthy, she was deferring to the older Vietnamese mother, calling her 'younger aunt' as a sign of respect for her experience.

'My mother has been writing to tell me things I should do after the baby is born,' she told Katy, 'but I did not understand why she was so insistent until Auntie explained. What do you think?'

Katy turned the question over to Rosa, but before she could reply a male voice answered.

'I think you must do whatever makes you comfortable.'

Katy knew he was drawing closer, awareness plucking at her skin. She was wrong! No matter how much work she had to do—no matter how busy she kept herself—the two months *wouldn't* be over before she caught her breath. In fact, the way she was reacting to his reappearance in her life, she doubted she'd ever breathe normally again.

'We Western doctors are using more and more techniques from other cultures, particularly ancient Chinese teachings,' Jake continued. 'On a recent visit to Beijing, I saw a Caesarean operation performed on a patient anaesthetised by acupuncture. I'm not saying I'd offer that option to all my patients, but we must work towards providing what is best for each individual.'

The woman from Hong Kong smiled openly at him, but the other women rearranged their bedclothes and lowered their eyes demurely.

It might be their custom, Katy thought, but it was also very effective flirting in a way. Even she could see the appeal of this bashfulness—and she wasn't a male!

'This is Dr Cartwright.'

Rosa introduced Jake and prepared to lead him around the ward. Katy ducked away, pleased the office would be empty and she could restore order to her too-responsive body before he returned.

Which was five minutes before the ward meeting was to begin!

Perhaps he was avoiding her as assiduously as she would like to avoid him. He breezed into the room with a bright good morning, and proceeded to drag his chair across towards the little coffee table.

'So, Katy.' She turned as he dropped a pile of files onto the table. He looked up and smiled at her, and she knew it was probably just a 'friendly co-worker' kind of smile. It was her reaction to it that was the problem. 'You seem to have the ward staff convinced the new unit is a good idea. What's the procedure if this meeting formally endorses it?'

Echoes of the previous night's strange conversation

blotted out her mind for a moment, so when he walked back towards her, she stiffened warily.

'It's up to you to convince the people up top,' she told him. He moved closer, increasing the tension in her body until she jerked away when he touched her arm.

'I need your chair,' he said mildly, but his eyes were laughing down at her as if he knew exactly why she'd reacted as she had.

Hot with embarrassment, she stood up and moved aside, trying to steady the wild beating of her heart.

'Still prefer power points?' he murmured softly, then he stooped and picked up her chair, carrying it across the room to add it to the informal grouping.

She ignored the jibe, staring out of the window to a view hazed by her inward-looking eyes. He was doing this deliberately, she realised. Taunting her with words and touches—as if he needed to prove his power over her.

But why? Was it really to fill the emptiness he claimed he felt—and, if so, for how long would he want her this time? Was it one more challenge for the man who loved a challenge? Or did he simply want to prove the old sex-appeal still worked? Would winning her back—against whatever odds he might perceive—overcome some lingering uncertainty the accident had left in his psyche?

She shook her head, annoyed with her attempts to analyse the man when she should be ignoring him. And even more disturbed by the tiny pinprick light of hope which kept flashing in the darkness of her soul.

What if—?

She slammed the thought away. Surely she'd learnt her lesson where Jake was concerned! She was damned if she'd be used as part of his healing process. And there was Julia, remember...

'So I take it to the top?'

She spun around, frowning as she tried to remember what they'd been talking about—before power points!

'Do you think I'm the man for the job?' he asked. 'Do you think my charm will win the day?'

She knew he was supposedly discussing approval for the new unit, but his intonation underlined another meaning in the words, and the half-smile twitching at his lips sent her heart skittering into the uneven rhythm of a syncopated jazz phrase.

CHAPTER FIVE

KATY was saved from answering by a quiet tap on the door. It opened to admit Helen and Rosa, followed by Ron Spencer and a young woman intern who was doing her O and G term.

'This the lot?' Jake asked.

'Jenny Parish, or someone else from Ward 'A', is still to come,' Helen replied, and then turned as Jenny entered the room.

'I'll get another chair,' Ron offered. 'Seems everyone's turned up to give the new boss the once-over.'

'New temporary boss,' Katy corrected under her breath.

She knew Jake heard the remark, for he winked at her, then, when Ron returned, he waved his hand towards her.

'Katy tells me she could run this office without me, so perhaps I should let her handle the meeting.'

She scowled at him, but produced her agenda and flipped quickly through the early items which were general issues, like rearrangement of schedules with Ward 'A' closed and procedures for dealing with the extra patients in 'B' and 'C'.

When they reached the final item, she asked if anyone had other business to bring up before they discussed the new unit.

'The birthing suites are so popular, I wondered if we might be able to squeeze another one into Ward 'A' if the new unit is established,' Jenny suggested.

Katy watched the pretty nursing sister turn the full force of her charm on Jake and felt a tiny worm of jealousy squirm in her stomach. But Jenny was right. The suites were large rooms furnished to look like fashionable bedrooms. All the paraphernalia of childbirth was hidden away in cupboards behind polished timber doors. The suites were big enough to allow a number of friends or family members to be present at the birth and gave the patient room to move around in the privacy of the suite.

Jenny explained this to Jake and then continued, 'The patient surveys for the last twelve months show six as the maximum number of Asian mothers we've had at one time. Even allowing for an increase once word gets around that we're making a special effort for these women, an eight-bed unit will probably suffice.'

Katy sat quietly. She couldn't argue with that prediction, but she did wonder why Jenny had to swing her shiny dark hair about so much when she was speaking.

'How were the birthing suites set up in the first place?' Jake asked.

'By pinching space from somewhere else,' Helen told him. 'We converted two old labour rooms and closed down one ward to make three suites. It was done about two years ago.'

'Without major upheaval?' Jake asked.

Katy grimaced.

'Hardly! But it's containable,' she said, remembering the chaos while those renovations were completed, 'especially if it's confined to one ward. The worst problem is changing the plumbing for the *en suite* bathrooms. Such refinements hadn't been considered when Lake Shore North was built.'

'Are they necessary in birthing suites?' Jake asked.

'They give the woman an opportunity to take a warm bath or shower during the first stage of labour,' Rosa replied. 'It helps ease the pain of contractions without recourse to drugs. More and more women are seeking drug-free births, so we want to do all we can to encourage them.'

Jake glanced at Ron.

'You have some input?' he asked.

The younger man grinned.

'I know my place in this group,' he said. 'One unacceptable suggestion and they're asking me how many pregnancies I've been through.'

The women chuckled, but Ron was only half-joking. At Lake Shore North there was a move away from specialist attendance at trouble-free births, with the midwives delivering most of the babies.

'However, I have been keeping statistics since I started here six months ago,' he added, 'and, although I wouldn't quote figures outside this room, I'm beginning to believe the literature which claims babies delivered without the use of drugs are more alert and need less intervention after birth.'

The discussion finished with Katy suggesting she contact the hospital architect about plans and Jake agreeing he'd look at the idea when it had been costed.

They moved on to the new unit, and Katy felt a rush of affection for her little team when, one by one, they supported the idea and praised the work she'd done on the proposal.

'I think we should remember that the most important part of the plan is in-service training for the staff,' Jenny reminded them. 'Even if Admin refuse to give the go-ahead, can't we begin to incorporate discussion on the

customs of these women into our in-service programme?'

Jake frowned at her.

'That's not already being done throughout the hospital?' he asked, and she shook her head.

'But you said the hospital has a large number of Asian
patients and the kitchens are organised. Has no one
thought of staff-training?'

'It's not as big an issue for patients in other departments because they're in for medical reasons or surgical
procedures. Geriatrics have been trying to get something
organised because they see a number of patients approaching death—which, like childbirth, has certain customs attached to it,' Ron Spencer explained. 'The culture
clash only occurs when our way of doing things interferes with their traditions.'

'We've all thought of staff-training,' Helen put in,
'but no one person has the knowledge to draw up a staff-
training programme incorporating all the countries involved or all the fields of medicine. It's a one-off project
which would require someone working full-time for perhaps six months, contacting experts in medicine from
the different backgrounds and asking them to contribute.
Considering she has a very demanding job, Katy's done
wonders with our small section, but she can't be expected to do any more.'

Katy turned to Jake and saw he understood the mag-
nitude of the problem. His eyes were grave as he considered Katy for a moment, then he nodded as if he'd
come to a decision he wasn't going to share.

'I'll speak to someone about it,' he said, 'but, in the
meantime, circulate the articles Katy's gathered among
your staff. The more background knowledge they have,
the more tolerant they're likely to be.'

He leaned forward and stacked his folders into a neat pile, indicating the meeting was almost over. He was assuring them he'd seek approval to set up the unit straight away when there was a light tap on the door. Katy went to answer it and found a hospital volunteer standing outside, almost hidden by a huge arrangement of flowers.

'You're Katy Turner, aren't you?' the woman asked, and when Katy, too astonished to speak, nodded, she thrust the arrangement into her arms.

'The delivery man left them at the front desk,' the volunteer explained. 'Must be nice to have someone who loves you that much.'

Katy felt the blood rushing upward to stain her cheeks. Jake used to send her flowers... Surely not!

She backed into the room, wishing she could hide the gift, but the sheer size of the bouquet made that impossible. She sneaked a look at Jake and caught the dark shadow of anger on his face, but then it vanished, replaced by a remote mask.

Jake hadn't sent the flowers!

She dropped them on her desk, too embarrassed to even think of looking for a card.

'That's some floral tribute!' Helen remarked as Katy slunk back to her chair.

'Such lavish attention doesn't look like John's style. Was there a great holiday romance?' Jenny smirked knowingly. She'd gone out with John herself for some time and found his interest in Katy a source of great amusement.

Katy seized the agenda and made some comment about that being all for the meeting. But she was wondering how Jake had reacted to Jenny's words and she could feel the flowers looming behind her like some floral science fiction monster that grew and grew.

'Before we finish,' Jake said quickly, 'I've spoken to the head of the interpreting service and arranged for a second female interpreter—so we can take outpatients from this special group fortnightly. However—'

Whatever he was about to say was swallowed up by the alarm that demanded an immediate response. Katy was the first to the door. She thrust her head into the passageway and saw the blue 'B' flashing on a wall monitor.

'It's your ward, Helen,' she said quietly, and stood aside to let the medical team respond.

As Jenny had surmised, the flowers weren't from John. They were from the support group for the sight-impaired she attended, thanking her for her presidency over the last four years. She'd resigned before her holiday, knowing she'd not have the time required to do the job well if she was getting the new unit under way.

She considered the over-size bouquet and realised Jake would have to continue to assume they were from an admirer—which could work to her advantage! If he thought she had a man in her life, he'd stop the subtle campaign he was waging against her. She stared at the flowers for a minute longer, then carried them out into the passage.

'Here!' she told a passing wardsman. 'If you're not busy, could you take these up to the geriatric ward for me. Tell Sister to spread them around. Most of the elderly patients love flowers.'

The man grinned at her.

'Wrong fellow send them?' he teased, and she found herself blushing—although his guess was as wide of the mark as Jake's had been.

She returned to her desk and typed up the minutes from the meeting, then prepared a title page for the submission to the hospital board. The resolution of the ward meeting was set in block letters in the middle of the page, with the names of those present underneath it. As she typed 'Jake Cartwright' she remembered the first time she'd typed his name.

She'd been working in the office of the public hospital at the far end of the lake. It had been a part-time job which helped pay her living expenses while she studied to be a nurse, and as she'd added the final name—his—to the list of new staff members at Lake Shore General she'd looked up to see a pair of blue eyes twinkling down at her.

'Katy Turner—what a crisp, no-nonsense name!' he'd murmured, reading the name-tag pinned to her white shirt. 'Do you do the guided tours around this place?'

She'd blushed and stammered and known almost instantly that she was in love. It hadn't come on her slowly, as she'd expected love to come—creeping up like fog off the lake's edge. It had slammed against her with the suddenness of an automobile accident, and she'd felt the juddering shock ricochet through her body.

Jake Cartwright!

She studied the name and sighed. She could remember that first meeting so vividly, yet the development of their relationship was hazy. Now, nearly eight years on, it seemed as if they'd been together from that day, yet she knew he'd worked impossible hours and she'd studied when she wasn't either typing in the hospital office or waitressing at night.

Maybe their clashing schedules had made the time they spent together feel more precious, more intense, she decided, unconsciously doodling little daisies around his name. Maybe that was why it seemed, now, as if they had never been apart—back then!

Until after that special Easter break, when they'd both had four days off. They'd camped near the beach at Freshwater Cove, swimming, fishing, walking, sleeping—and making love! The memory was like a precious jewel, tucked away in Katy's mind—not brought out too often in case use might dim its lustre.

They'd come back feeling fit and healthy, ready to tackle whatever the new term had to offer. And with such plans! Jake would finish his residency and she would finish her final year at university, then they'd get married.

She slashed her pen across the daisies. The sense of well-being after the holiday hadn't lasted long. In fact, within a fortnight she'd been feeling tired and sick—her stomach so unsettled she'd bought a pregnancy kit at the chemist and tested herself to make sure that pregnancy wasn't the cause.

Jake's working hours had been even worse than hers, yet his energy had remained undiminished. Her increasingly frequent refusals to join him in some 'fun' had led to a tetchiness developing between them—the first shadows of disharmony in what had been close to perfection.

She sighed and turned back to the computer, tapping out a print command to replace the title page she'd ruined.

The door opened and she looked up to see Jake returning.

'I had Giardia, you know!' she said, and only realised she'd spoken her thoughts aloud when she saw the look of puzzlement on his face.

But now the words were said, she decided to continue.
'Before the accident! When I was sick and you were

so convinced I was either faking it or pregnant and neither option pleased you very much.'

She snatched up the newly printed page, slipped it into a plastic sleeve on the front of the file and shoved the lot across onto his desk. Then she remembered the crisis call and she looked at him again.

He was frowning, but not at her, and she recognised the look as one he wore when he was inwardly scanning his phenomenal memory banks for some hidden bit of information. He probably hadn't even heard her defiant outburst.

'What was the emergency?' she asked, her own past misery forgotten as she worried about the cause of Jake's distraction.

'That woman who was involved in an accident yesterday,' he murmured. Then he looked directly at her and his eyes came into focus once again.

'Katy, there's a paper in Holstead's *Obstetric Text* about concealed haemorrhage in abruptio placentae. Could you find it for me while I change the infusion we're giving her?'

He disappeared through the door while Katy moved towards the bookshelves. She knew enough medicine to know how dangerous it could be for both mother and foetus when the placenta shifted from the uterine wall. Usually the first indication was uterine bleeding, followed by painful contractions.

Did 'concealed' mean there were no symptoms to guide the medical staff?

She found the article he wanted and began to read it. Problems with supply of blood to the foetus, elevated intrauterine pressure, blood clotting factors seriously depleted. The condition meant danger for both the mother and the child. Had Jake mentioned the woman's term? Would the baby survive if they had to deliver it?

He came back into the room as she was wondering and took the book from her without a word.

'Ah, I thought so!' he muttered to himself, then left the room again before she had time to speak.

It was late afternoon when he returned, and she noticed that his shirt, in spite of the air-conditioning, was wet with perspiration.

'Is she okay?' Katy asked, and was pleased when he nodded.

'And the baby?'

The question clutched at her heart. Babies had become doubly precious to her since Julia's birth.

'We've got him in a humidicrib,' he said, slumping down into his chair and resting his head in his hands. 'Is there a counsellor with experience in premature births who can speak to the mother when she's feeling up to it?'

'Of course!' Katy assured him. 'Helen will take care of that, and will also contact the association for pre-term infants. They're a local group of parents who've had pre-term babies. They have volunteers available for either discussion or assistance.'

She spoke calmly, but her heart was beating out its own anxiety. 'How premature is he?'

'She thought she was thirty-four weeks, but I'm not so certain. He's less than two thousand grams.'

Julia had been seventeen hundred grams. A tiny scrap of humanity, she had looked more like a skinned rabbit than a human baby. Katy glanced at Jake, wanting his reassurance that this baby would be all right. But no one could predict his future at the moment, although with new developments in humidicribs, especially in the way of providing warmth and oxygen supplementation, this baby would have a far better chance than Julia had had, even five years ago.

'Was he delivered vaginally?' she asked.

He looked up and frowned, as if perturbed by her question.

'Why are you asking that?' His frown deepened.

Katy shrugged, aware she'd crossed some imaginary boundary between administration and medicine. Still, he had asked!

'A Caesar would mean the woman is going to suffer physical discomfort for longer, and is therefore weaker and less able to cope with the stress and grief and uncertainty related to giving birth prematurely,' she said, then she ducked her head and pretended to be busy sorting the pile of papers on her desk.

'Grief?' It was only one word but it demanded an answer.

She looked up slowly.

'When a family has a child with problems—even if they are only temporary problems—there is grief for the child they had imagined—the perfect child they thought they were going to have. It doesn't lessen their love for the real baby, but the grief is still there. For a long time counsellors ignored that part of the equation, but, since associations like the pre-term births organisations have been formed, counsellors are accepting what experienced people are telling them.'

He shook his head and smiled.

'I did know that,' he murmured. 'We medicos aren't quite the dehumanised beings some people would have you believe. What surprises me is the depth of your involvement, Katy. I know you worked hard on the unit proposal, and I can understand your commitment to that, but this is a different field and you're just as passionate.'

She was embarrassed by the praise she heard in his voice, but also aware she'd drifted dangerously close to personal issues which had to be avoided at all costs.

'It's my department,' she said defensively. 'It's natural I should be interested.'

'Hmm!' He studied her for a moment, his eyes scanning her face as if he might read a different answer on her skin.

'Well, for your information, Departmental Assistant, she did deliver vaginally. That was what I wanted to check in Holstead. With a concealed haemorrhage the blood has to go somewhere. Usually it escapes into the uterine tissues, causing the uterus to take on a bluish or purplish colour. This condition will resolve itself spontaneously, but Holstead believes vaginal birth will bring a better long-term resolution to the affected tissues. I thought it was worth trying to induce her before operating. Having made that decision, there was a period of very nervous waiting, but it worked in this case.'

He paused, then looked around the room, another frown beginning to pucker the skin between his eyebrows.

'What happened to your flowers?' he asked abruptly, and this time it was she who raised one eyebrow. It was a trick which had taken her years to perfect, but it was enough to remind Jake that her personal life was no concern of his.

She bent over her papers once again, determined to finish her work in time to visit Ward 'B' and the nursery before she left. But it was a pretence. Jake's presence in the room disrupted her thought processes and made the nerves in her skin twitch with awareness. It was impossible to think she could work with him for another thirty-eight days—no matter how busy she might be.

Impossible!

She sighed and thought of Julia, and the mortgage on the house, and the down-payment she'd made on the new computer. She sighed again.

Even more impossible to leave!

'If you've done sighing, would you mind taking this submission up to the administration office for me? Leave it with your mate Mr Forbes and tell him I'd like him to have a look at it before the department directors' meeting next Monday.'

She looked into blue eyes which were regarding her thoughtfully.

'But you said—' she began.

'That I'd argue the case for you,' he interrupted. He slid his hand across the desk and touched her on the forearm. 'And I will, Katy, I will. I've already spoken to Mr Forbes and told him how I feel, but it's only fair he gets an opportunity to read through the proposal before it's discussed. He'll also circulate copies to other departments.'

'They already have copies,' Katy protested mutinously. 'But giving Mr Forbes one this early will give him time to find objections. He'll come prepared with little lists of why the thing's impossible.'

The blue eyes gleamed with mischief.

'So we'll have to prepare our own lists,' he said firmly. 'We'll have to go through it word by word and anticipate his objections, then arrange our arguments accordingly.'

'But that would mean hours and hours of work. We actually have a department to run here, which usually takes all my working hours plus another ten or twelve each week. We'd never get it done!'

The problem was, she knew he was right. In fact, she couldn't understand why she hadn't thought of it herself. When she'd pushed the crèche past administrative barriers she'd had powerful support, as three department directors had pre-school-aged children and problems with suitable childcare. There'd been no need for an extended campaign.

Another sigh slipped from her lips. She should have been doing that kind of analysis during her holidays instead of lying on the beach.

'I beg your pardon?'

She turned to Jake, aware he'd been talking while she chastised herself.

'I said it wasn't like you to quit so easily. You know better than most how hard you have to fight for what you want.'

He looked into her eyes, challenging her to deny his words and carrying her back with effortless ease to long-forgotten arguments.

'But *I* can afford to pay your board and tuition,' he'd said, trying to persuade her to give up her crazy schedule of work and study. 'At least let me keep you.'

'I won't take your charity!' she'd yelled at him. 'I was managing just fine before you came along. I can make it on my own!'

He'd cursed her stubbornness, yet she'd suspected he'd admired it at the same time.

'Well?' he asked, and she realised she'd missed another bit of the conversation. She had to stop flashing in and out of the past. Apart from weakening her mental armour against this man, it was making logical, work-related thought impossible.

'Well?' she echoed in a puzzled voice, trying to pull herself together.

'I said, if we don't have time during the week, we'll have to get together over the weekend. Would Saturday or Sunday suit you?'

'I can't do that!' she gasped. 'I'm far too busy!'

And her time alone with Julia was too precious to consider giving up!

'You were never afraid of extra work,' he reminded her. 'Social life taking up all your time these days?' He looked swiftly around the room, as if to indicate he was thinking about the missing flowers. 'Did your fanatical work ethic finally break down when you realised what you were missing? Is that why you gave up nursing? Did it all get too difficult after all?'

He sounded angry, but puzzled as well—and just a little as if he might care what had happened to her, and why!

'My personal life is none of your business, Jake Cartwright!' she said with regal disdain, then she spoiled the whole effect by adding, 'And I'm still not afraid of extra work. In fact, I still waitress every Friday and Saturday nights, if you must know, which is why I don't want to spend what little spare time I get working on this stupid project!'

He looked stunned by her outburst, but she was already regretting it. The new unit wasn't a stupid project—in fact it was very important to her that it succeeded.

'I can go through the papers on my own during the week,' she muttered. 'After all, I'm the one who knows how Mr Forbes's mind works. I'll jot down the things I think he'll object to and you can work out how you want to respond.'

'Why?' he demanded, the belligerence in his voice dragging her eyes up from her paperwork to focus, again, on his face.

'Why do it?' she snapped. 'You're the one who suggested it.'

He waved his hand as if to dismiss her words.

'Not that,' he said. 'Why are you still waitressing? Aren't you paid enough? Should we be concentrating on admin assistants' wages rather than a new maternity unit?'

She almost smiled. Jake was like a truffle hound when he perceived or suspected injustice!

'I'm paid well, but...' She shrugged her shoulders. She couldn't explain that talking computers with raised characters on their keyboards cost only a little less than a space shuttle, nor could she admit that the two nights a week when she worked as a waitress had become a substitute social life for her.

'I like waitressing,' she finished. Let him argue with that!

She was saved by his pager, which buzzed as she finished speaking. He dialled the number shown, spoke briefly, then stood up.

'I'll be in Theatre if you need me. Mrs Carstairs has come in. And before you ask, she's Dr Anderson's patient, remember? All I'll be is an extra pair of hands. It's not up to me to decide on delivery methods.'

Katy tried to look offended, but it was hard when her lips wanted to smile.

'Dr Anderson agrees with me about natural birth whenever possible,' she said primly. 'She's been taken to Theatre because there's enough space there for five humidicribs and access to more emergency equipment if it's needed.'

He shook his head, as if again surprised by the extent of her knowledge.

'Sure you don't want to take my place in the action?' he teased, and her heart raced into its rapid mode as she caught the full force of his smile.

'Definitely not!' she told him. 'I like the theory, not the practical side of things these days.' She hesitated, then added, 'Good luck!'

He'd been walking towards the door, but he turned and smiled again.

'Thanks, Katy,' he said softly, then he continued on his way.

She stared at the door panels for a moment, unable to escape memories of how things used to be between them. Then she remembered their strange conversation last night, her anger with him, and four words he'd said. ''I had my reasons.''

What had he meant?

She shook her head to rid it of such distraction and phoned through to the chief security officer to warn him that their action plan for the arrival of the expected Carstairs quintuplets should begin. The problem of keeping unwanted visitors off the fourth floor would fall to the security staff, but Katy knew any major disaster— like a photographer flashing his camera in the wards or corridors—would upset patients and staff and undoubtedly rebound onto her.

Bill Head assured her he had it all under control and she hung up and dialled Sue Gates in the nursery.

'I'll ring around for extra staff—is there anyone in particular you want?'

'Thanks, Katy, I was about to call you,' Sue replied. 'Two of the nurses on duty today are willing to take an extra shift tomorrow, but the night sister will need at least two extra helpers—three if you can muster them. Once we know how much work there'll be, I'll juggle the staff to suit. I'd prefer to keep the same rota of staff with the babies, so the little mites aren't constantly re-adjusting to different people.'

'Well, I'll find three for tonight,' Katy promised, pulling a list of casual staff from a drawer in her desk. 'Let me know tomorrow if you need more.'

The hospital's 'casuals' were more like members of a private nursing service, with the hospital contracting them to work in patients' homes, medical centres, or even other hospitals when they weren't required for extra shifts in the wards. Katy's list contained the men and women who specialised in maternity and neonatal nursing. She began her phone calls, knowing whoever she found would need time to make arrangements for childcare or to cancel social engagements before they could report for work.

As she finished the calls she smiled. The first three phone calls had been successful. In fact, the three women she'd contacted had all been delighted at the thought of nursing Lake Shore's expected quintuplets. Knowing Mrs Carstairs's love of publicity, they'd probably all get their photos in the paper!

So cynical, Katy?

She mentally chided herself. The Carstairs family would need all the help it could get in the weeks, months and even years to come. If they could sell their story to the press, good luck to them. But selling to the press brought its own problems, as the media outlet who bought the story would demand exclusive rights. And that would leave all the other news hounds baying at the doors, desperate for an unauthorised picture or story. It made the security angle a nightmare!

But that was a mechanical problem she hoped Security could handle. Less solvable was the future of the babies. Katy worried because she was so aware of the increased risk of abnormalities in multiple births. In fact, considering the statistics, shouldn't there be ethical considerations in using drugs which promoted conception but led to multiple conception? It was something that nagged at her, making her wary about the excitement of the coming event.

She shook her head and decided that the pros and cons of IVF treatments weren't her problem. She'd have enough to worry about with the media circus and staff—things which *were* her concern. Even with extra security staff on the fourth floor, some photographer could find his way into the nursery, anxious to take the first shots of the new arrivals. She'd heard stories where such a thing had happened after the birth of a 'celebrity' baby—only the photographer had photographed the wrong child and the parents had sued the hospital!

She tried to shrug off her feeling of apprehension, telling herself to think positively—there was every chance the whole operation would come off without mishap, that their security precautions would work, and, by far the most important factor, that all five of the babies would pull through the long weeks in the nursery.

CHAPTER SIX

KATY thought of Julia, born at thirty-two weeks, but small for her age, malnourished because Katy's own health had been so poor. For the first forty-eight hours she'd seemed all right, although Katy had thought her lips were cyanosed, and her nostrils flaring too much as the tiny mite gasped for breath. At seventy-two hours the specialist had diagnosed RDS—Respiratory Distress Syndrome. The oxygen saturation in the humidicrib had been increased and Julia had recovered.

It had been months before Katy had realised the full extent of the damage to Julia's eyes. Too late to do anything except be grateful her daughter had survived!

She glanced at her watch. She had twenty minutes before she was due to collect that same daughter from the crèche. She'd take the 'New Unit' file upstairs, then pop into the nursery and see the premature baby before she left.

Mr and Mrs Robinson were sitting by their son's crib, gazing at the baby with wariness, despair and fear intermingling in their eyes.

'Hi, I'm Katy. I work here, but I also had a pre-term baby much the same size as your little lad. She's five now, and has reached all the normal milestones in speech and motor dexterity. In fact, although she's still physically slight for her age, she's ahead of most of her peers in other ways.'

93

The couple looked up at her, reaching for each other as if they could now fight together for their son.

'It was such a little accident,' the woman said. 'Phil was distracted by a dog. We just bumped the car in front. We were travelling slowly and there was hardly any damage to either car.'

Katy understood the guilt they were both feeling and hastened to reassure them.

'I'm not a medical person, but I know these things can occur spontaneously. The accident might have precipitated it, but it could also have happened without the accident. It's very important not to waste energy apportioning blame but to get on with the positive stuff. Are you hoping to breast feed? Will you express milk so the little fellow can begin feeding on your milk as soon as possible?'

She knew she'd diverted the woman, but Phil was still looking doubtful so she turned her attention to him.

'And will you help with feeding? You can, you know, when they begin to wean him from the crib. At the moment his skin is very fine, and the tiny blood vessels in it are easily damaged, so the less he's handled the better. The staff will show you how to touch him so he knows you're here.'

She gestured towards the crib.

'They curl him in that little nest to help him breathe and keep him warm. Premmie babies haven't had time to put fat down beneath their skin, so they lose heat very rapidly.'

The man was losing his dazed look and Katy felt a sense of relief wash through her. She knew the staff were too busy to spend much time with new parents, and the hospital counsellor was not always available immediately. That was one of the reasons she tried to see the parents herself, before their lack of knowledge and uneasiness built a barrier between them and the child.

'Someone from a pre term births organisation will probably call in this evening,' she assured them. 'They can help because, like me, they've been through it all and understand how you are feeling.'

The woman smiled at her.

'Thanks for talking to us,' she said softly. 'I think we'll go back to my room now. I feel as if I might be able to sleep for a while.'

Katy watched as her husband helped her to her feet. Would having had someone to lean on have made her time in hospital easier? She'd had Julia in a huge public hospital in a southern city, and the staff had been so busy they'd barely had time to say hello when she'd slipped quietly into the nursery each morning.

Well, it didn't matter now!

She felt her face softening into a smile as she thought of her daughter playing happily downstairs, and hurried from the nursery, anxious now to see her.

They walked home hand in hand, Julia pointing out the flowers on the trees as if she could see them as clearly as Katy could.

'Now we're at the swans,' she announced. 'Are they swimming?'

'They're swimming,' Katy assured her, remembering how Julia had been frightened by the hissing menace of the swans when they'd been nesting. 'And their babies are swimming in line behind them. They're growing some of their white feathers now and don't look nearly as cute.'

'Like the Ugly Duckling in the story,' Julia chortled as they turned into the avenue of poincianas.

Here they walked at the edge of the path so she could

reach out and touch each tree trunk. Katy wondered if she counted her paces between them, for she always knew when to put out her hand so it could slide across the smooth trunk. It was another manifestation of the extra-sensory perception her daughter seemed to have developed to compensate for her loss of sight. It intrigued Katy, and she hoped one day to be able to study the phenomenon in more depth, to work with sight-impaired children and find out if this sensory awareness could be taught like other skills.

There were so many things she wanted to do—one day! Would that day ever come? She doubted it! Her adult life had always been limited by the time she had to give to working to keep herself—and then Julia—alive. Would there ever be a time when she'd be financially secure, so she could stop working for long enough to complete her degree? Or conduct a study into the sensory awareness of sight-impaired children? Or even write a paper on Asian women giving birth in the western world?

Jake had money! The thought insinuated itself into her head.

She wouldn't take it for herself, of course—but for Julia? Her heart beat faster at the implications of the thought, then stilled as she remembered the past.

There was no way she could risk it!

She sighed at the momentary regret.

'You tired, Mum?' Julia asked.

Katy smiled down at her daughter and squeezed her fingers.

'No, love,' she said. 'Just dreaming!'

The jangling summons of the phone woke her from a deep sleep. She glanced blearily at the bedside clock as she lifted the receiver. Nine-thirty! She must have fallen asleep the moment she'd turned the light out ten minutes earlier.

'Hello!'

She tried to make her voice sound alert, annoyed at being caught in bed so early. Julia's fault! Since birth her daughter had been a morning person, and now Katy always woke at five—whether Julia was at home or not.

'It's Jake, Katy. I know I shouldn't be bothering you at home, but I've just got back to the office and needed to talk to someone sane. Fortunately, my predecessor's little book of useful numbers has your home number at the top of the list.'

'Something's wrong?' Her heart was thundering against her chest wall, but she couldn't tell if it was apprehension about work or excitement at hearing Jake's voice on the phone again.

Back when they'd been lovers as well as friends, he'd rung her every evening they'd been apart—rung her to say goodnight and, 'I love you, Katy!'

'Not really!' he said gruffly. 'If you discount Mrs Carstairs's insistence that a film crew be present for the entire delivery, and then Stewart Anderson demanding all but one of them leave and suggesting I help the security men remove them. Then a scuffle with a newspaper photographer in the nursery and one of the security men pulling a gun when the man refused to budge.'

'Oh, Jake! That last bit can't be true,' Katy protested, her voice muffled by the laughter bubbling in her throat. 'The security men don't carry guns, do they?'

She closed her eyes and tried to picture the uniformed men she saw around the hospital each day. But all she saw was Jake's face—older now than her worn images had shown—smiling into the phone.

'Actually, some of them do, I've discovered, but in this case it was a torch. It just looked like a gun,' he told her. 'And the photographer must have thought so, too, because he scarpered.'

'Has it quietened down?'

She heard a shuffling noise, as if he was settling more comfortably into his chair.

'I suppose it's as settled as it can get, with men guarding the main foyer and the fire doors, and all visitors to the fourth floor being screened before they're allowed out of the elevator. But it still won't work, Katy! Someone will eventually arrive to visit one of our other patients and slip away to take whatever snaps they want. Since Mrs Carstairs announced she was having labour pains over talk-back radio this morning, half Australia's media contingent—to say nothing of the usual rush of onlookers and thrill-seekers—have been camped on our doorstep. Most of them arrived before the patient.'

'She announced it on the radio?' Katy echoed. 'I know once a multiple birth had been confirmed she made a great production of the whole pregnancy, much to Dr Anderson's annoyance, but I can't believe she would go that far.'

'Believe it,' Jake told her gloomily. 'She rang the local radio station herself. You must have seen the people gathering outside the hospital when you left. I considered going for a walk—to get some of the air-conditioned air out of my lungs—but when I saw the pack of hounds baying at the main entrance, I headed back up here instead.'

'We go out the back way,' Katy explained. 'I suppose you're lucky you have rooms in the building. The press love photos of the doctors. Poor Dr Anderson will eventually have to run that gauntlet.'

'Not a bit of it,' Jake told her, his voice lightening again. 'He smuggled himself out in an ambulance. Says it happened to him once before. The photographer's flashlight caught him as he was yawning and he ended up with his face splashed across the front page, looking like an incapacitated fish.'

Katy chuckled, remembering the photo Jake described.

'Well?' The single word doused her laughter.

'Well, wh-what?' she stuttered, sensing a shift in the conversation.

'Well, it's your turn to talk, Katy.'

She tried to think of something they could talk about—a conversation which wouldn't stray onto dangerous ground.

'I've started on the list of objections Mr Forbes might have,' she said stiffly, and heard his sigh filter through the airwaves to linger in her ear.

'That's work,' he objected. 'I've had enough of work!'

She knew his voice well enough to know he was smiling as he spoke, although he was pretending petulance. 'Talk to me, Katy, I'm bored' or 'Talk to me, Katy, I'm lonely'. They'd both been common refrains during those other goodnight calls.

The memories were weakening her, and strength was what she needed to deal with Jake.

'We've only work in common,' she told him, hoping she sounded more positive than she felt.

'Not some sharing of the past?' he argued. 'Not memories I haven't forgotten even if you have. What about Freshwater Cove?'

Her stomach shifted uneasily, but she knew she had to make a stand.

'The past is dead and buried, Jake. It died the day you sent me away, but I didn't bury it until my letters were returned.'

There was a silence, then she heard him mutter something indistinguishable.

'I understand how you must feel, how deeply hurt you must have been,' he said more clearly, 'but I don't believe you when you say there's nothing left, Katy. I don't believe it's quite that clear-cut. And I don't believe you believe it either,' he added. 'Goodnight, my love.'

She dropped the phone back into its cradle, blotting the endearment from her mind, turning instead to the puzzle of those indistinct words. She remembered him saying, 'I had my reasons,' yesterday, but she couldn't conceive of a reason with enough validity for him to have cut himself off from her with such deadly precision.

She thought about her own feelings at the time. 'Deeply hurt' didn't begin to cover it! She'd been physically sick, which had added to her devastation, and after the letter telling him she was pregnant had been returned she had told herself she hated him.

But she'd found she couldn't make herself believe it—that she couldn't nurture hate for him at the same time as she was nurturing his baby.

Which didn't mean she'd ever trust him again—whatever he might be trying to make her believe.

She switched out the light and settled down in bed, willing herself to shut out the memories he'd evoked. Willing herself to sleep—not dream of passionate pasts or impossible futures.

The birth of the quintuplets dominated the morning news. Katy turned on the television and saw the pack of photographers camped outside the main entrance to the hospital. Would the security guards have deflected them from the back entrance or would she have to battle through them there as well?

'Can I see the new babies at your hospital, Mum?' Julia asked, tugging at Katy's hand as they left the house.

'They're too little for visitors,' Katy told her, guiding her hopping, skipping daughter safely across the road.

'Someone's waiting under our trees, Mum.'

Julia's remark made Katy pause, clinging to her daughter's hand. They were just inside the boundary of the park, and the avenue of trees was directly ahead of them. In daylight it was a cool green tunnel, and she squinted against the morning glare as she probed the shadows beneath the trees.

He was leaning against the third one along, so still he might have been a part of it. Her lungs felt as if giant hands had squeezed the air from them and she gripped Julia's hand so tightly the little girl cried out.

'Is he a bad man, Mum?' Julia asked, and Katy heard the beginning of panic in her voice. She dropped to her knees and hugged her daughter close.

'No, love, it's a new doctor at the hospital. I didn't see him at first and was startled. How did you know he was there?'

She straightened up, pretending to a normality she didn't feel. She wanted to reassure Julia, not transmit more tension to her.

'He smells like the lemon grass you planted in the back yard.'

Katy sniffed the air. She knew this was another manifestation of Julia's ability to absorb her environment, but she always hoped she might learn to be as proficient with her senses.

There was no trace of lemon grass that she could discern!

'Come on, Mum, we'll be late!'

Julia tugged at her hand and Katy peered warily along the path. Jake hadn't moved—but then, if he'd walked this way to meet up with her, he was probably as shocked as she had been. For the first time since Julia's birth she was glad her daughter was small for her age. At least he wouldn't suspect...

She forced her feet to move, and as she drew closer she even fixed a smile on her lips.

'Good morning, Dr Cartwright,' she said formally. 'This is my daughter, Julia.'

His face looked grey, and she told herself it was the effect of the light beneath the trees. She found she didn't want Jake hurting, no matter what he'd done to her. She turned away, pretending to be looking at the lake, unable to meet whatever emotion might be lurking in his eyes.

Julia reached out and found his hand.

'We're late, Dr Cartwright,' she said, leading them both along the path. 'I told Mum you were under the trees and she thought you might be a bad man.'

Realising she now had two supports, she swung between them while Katy battled the tumult in her body, trying to will herself to behave as if this was a perfectly normal morning. She remembered the major news event with relief!

'How are the new arrivals?' she asked, glancing his way very briefly, then concentrating on the path as if it might have thrown up horrendous obstacles overnight.

'Two are battling—the others should be okay,' Jake replied, and she knew from the strain in his voice that his conversational effort was as forced as her own.

'You've seen the new babies?' Julia asked him,

swinging again so suddenly that Katy snapped at her to stop.

'I have,' Jake replied. 'They are very, very small.'

'I was very small,' Julia confided, and Katy's heart stopped beating. 'But I was only very small, not very, very—wasn't I, Mum?'

'A bit small,' Katy agreed, as casually as she could. She might not be looking at Jake but his tension was transmitting itself in almost visible waves across the top of Julia's blonde head.

'That's why I'm blind,' the child added chirpily.

Katy heard the gasp as it escaped her lips. She knew Jake's footsteps had faltered but she still couldn't look at him. To see pity in his eyes would destroy the last shreds of her composure, and she couldn't let Julia realise how *distraite* she was.

'It was oxy—stuff to help me breathe that hurt my eyes,' Julia added, prattling on as if oblivious to the forces arcing through the air above her head.

'Oxygen?'

Jake offered the word gravely and Julia turned and smiled up at him.

'That's it!' she told him with transparent delight. 'Oxygen!'

But was she so oblivious? Or could she be carrying this conversation to help her mother out of what she sensed was an awkward encounter?

Katy shook her head, unable to think rationally about anything at the moment.

'It's this way,' she muttered when they reached the end of the lake. They turned towards the crossing that led to the road behind the hospital.

'These lights make a noise when it's safe to walk,' Julia confided to Jake. 'First you listen for the cars to stop, then you hear the noise that tells you when to cross.'

She let go of Katy's hand but kept hold of Jake's as she reached out for the smooth metal pole and felt for the button that would stop the traffic. Katy felt a pang of jealousy and told herself she was being ridiculous. Julia had a warm, open, loving nature. She adopted everyone she met as her friend.

'Come on, Mum,' she urged, and Katy took her hand again, scolded her for swinging on the road, then stopped when they'd made the safety of the opposite footpath.

'We go around the back,' she said to Jake, looking directly at him for the first time since they'd met beneath the trees. She hoped her face was as expressionless as his!

'Then you might show me the back way into this place,' he suggested. 'I had to pretend I was a cleaner to get safely through the crowd at the front door. I walked out with a fellow carrying a fearsome polishing machine and tried to look as if I knew exactly how it worked.'

Katy's lips twitched as she imagined the scene and she felt her muscles begin to relax, although she knew their relationship had taken yet another twist. Jake might have spoken lightly but there had been an edge to the words.

'Come on, then.' She led the way along the path towards the back of the old hospital building, where the crèche was situated.

'You mentioned fighting for the crèche,' Jake said as they walked into the brightly decorated yard and Julia was welcomed by her friends and whisked away from them. 'I didn't think!'

He stopped and looked around, and she knew his

mood had darkened with the swiftness of a sudden summer storm.

'I should have figured it out then! Talk about single-minded! Talk about not taking hints! I'm sorry, Katy!'

He sounded angry and upset, yet the apology was genuine.

But for what?

'Sorry, Jake?' she asked, and saw pain and a rueful kind of self-mockery in his eyes.

'Sorry for marching back into your life like this,' he pointed out. 'I assumed—'

He gave a bark of laughter and turned to walk away, but she caught his arm and stopped him.

'Assumed what?' she demanded. He'd already spoilt her morning, tied her nerves in knots and destroyed the fragile web of protection she'd woven around herself and Julia. She wasn't going to let him get away with more.

'Assumed because you weren't married you'd still be single! Stupid, wasn't I? I actually tracked you down, Katy. I phoned the General first and you weren't there. I tried St Christopher's, and then Lake Shore North. I was starting with the places close to your home—and, of course, I was looking for a nurse.'

He paused, but she knew he hadn't finished and she waited, bemused by the passion she could sense in him.

'When I learnt there was an admin assistant named Katy Turner here, I could have cried with relief, and then, when I found which department you worked for, I decided it was meant to be—that maybe I would be granted a second chance. I practically begged Dan Petersen to take that scholarship, and mortgaged my soul to get away from my other job. And all the time I had this weird idea that if I could only see you again, spend time with you, talk to you and try to explain, then maybe...'

Another hesitation, but this time Katy battled hope. If they talked...? If he could explain...?

'But of course marriage isn't everything these days. You found another man, you had a child—no wonder you didn't finish nursing! I assume he's still around, Katy? Assume the flowers were from him? What a bloody fool you must have thought me!'

He spun away again and this time she let him go, not bothering to remind him that he'd wanted to learn the back way into the hospital.

She found Julia and said goodbye to her. Jake had handed her a solution to her problem—a mythical man in her life. She doubted if this ghost would provide the buffer zone she needed between his body and hers, but it would stop his teasing comments and the remarks which suggested he was aware of her reaction to him.

She made her way up to the fourth floor, pausing in the foyer to speak to the security man on duty.

'We're managing,' he assured her. 'One woman reporter sneaked in in a nurse's uniform during the night, but Sister dealt with her. Pretended she thought she was a new nurse on the roster. She took her to the store cupboard, got out an enema tube and bowl and told her to do all the patients in 'C'. The silly nit nearly had a heart attack!'

He chuckled as he related the story, which must have spread through the hospital like wildfire. 'Even I know you don't give enemas any more—well, not *after* the baby's born, anyway.'

Katy smiled at his delight, then turned and made her way reluctantly towards her office.

You have to face him some time, she told herself. So he thinks you've got a lover! So what?

But she didn't have to face him. The room was empty and a note on her desk told her he was doing a postnatal clinic. She frowned at the note. Ron Spencer usually did the public postnatal clinics while private patients saw their own specialists. She made a mental note to ask about it, then attacked the day's work—beginning with a call to the nursery to check on staffing.

'We could do with someone willing to work split shifts,' Sue told her. 'Six to ten in the morning, and four to eight in the evenings. I can take an extra nurse off the wards from ten till four. Could you try Joe Cameron? He's worked with most of these nurses before and I'd like another male voice in the nursery.'

Katy smiled. Sue was adamant babies needed to hear and feel men as well as women tending them. Joe was a most unlikely nurse—a husky six-footer with a deep and unmistakably masculine voice. He was studying for a doctorate in nursing and took casual work to pay his bills.

'I'll try him first,' she promised Sue.

She contacted Joe and arranged for him to start that afternoon then left the office to check the cleaners had begun work in 'A'. She was tempted towards the nursery, but knew there was no real reason for her to go and peer at the new arrivals. And Mrs Carstairs had generated too much fuss for Katy to want to see her.

She spoke to Jenny, who was trying to keep the cleaners' noise to a minimum, then walked back to her office. Still no Jake!

It set the pattern for the days to come. He was out of the office more than he was in it and he treated her with a polite detachment when they were forced to speak

about their work. She suspected he was feeling as much
strain as she was, and was sometimes tempted to say,
There's no one else. But that would lead her back into
the limbo of doubt—the 'Should I? Shouldn't I?' state
of indecision that was as dangerous as an unexploded
bomb.

CHAPTER SEVEN

THEY kept up the pretence of a normal working relationship, helped by the chaos still erupting every day as a result of Mrs Carstairs and her hunger for publicity. As soon as she sensed interest in herself or the babies was dying down, she pulled a new stunt—for example she and Mr Carstairs, drawn together by this great event, reconfirming their marriage vows in the hospital suite, with television cameras and a viewing audience of millions.

'And she had the hide to ask Stewart Anderson to be a witness,' Jake fumed when he passed on this information to Katy.

Katy chuckled, but she was upset the chief medical officer at the hospital hadn't stepped in to stop these wilder examples of excess.

'It's the old story,' Jake said, once again plucking her thoughts out of the air. 'Any publicity is good publicity.'

'Not when it interferes with the running of the hospital and the comfort and security of other patients,' Katy objected. 'This is where private ownership of hospitals breaks down—the situation where service clashes with the profits.'

Jake shrugged.

'I agree, but it's hard to get that point across to the powers-that-be when the name of Lake Shore North is blazoned across the headlines each morning.'

But things did quieten a little after that, and she wondered if Jake had spoken to someone.

On Friday afternoon she handed him the list of objections she predicted Mr Forbes might raise.

'I'll go through them over the weekend,' he promised her, and her heart clenched at the sincerity in his voice. He might be regretting the wild impulse that had led him back to the past, but he would do his best for her.

'Thank you, Jake,' she said quietly, then turned away. She'd have liked to say something else, but Friday afternoons were always hurried. By the time she and Julia had walked home, discussing the day's happenings, then had a play, a bath and dinner, it would be time for Katy to get ready for her other job.

Besides, what was there she could say? Have a good weekend? When she knew he was practically a stranger here. He'd studied in Perth, coming east to do his residency—and back then they'd been a twosome, each to each other, all the friends either of them had wanted or needed.

She left him sitting at his desk, reading through her list. Would he work here for a few hours, then go upstairs to his room and order over-cooked steak from the canteen?

It's not your business what he does, she told herself as she left to collect Julia. Yet her heart ached to think he might be lonely. She thought of what he'd said about a school in holiday time and felt a similar emptiness, like hunger, hollowing out her body.

Julia was asleep by the time Katy said goodbye to Marie, her regular babysitter, and left to catch the bus into town. Leaving her daughter asleep soothed her conscience about working the two nights a week—at least Julia wasn't missing her!

The Baron's Table hadn't changed much in the ten years Katy had worked there. She'd gone south when she was pregnant, needing to get away from both acquaintances and memories, but when she'd returned to Lake Shore her job had been waiting for her, and she'd found a babysitter and slipped easily back into her old routine.

Tonight it was quiet, barely half-full, and she had time to talk to her customers, catching up with the regulars' news and fending off questions about the 'big event' at the hospital.

At nine o'clock a group of eight came in and she was suddenly busy. She had delivered one half of their order and was heading back towards the kitchen for the remainder when someone tapped her on the shoulder.

'Any chance of a medium rare steak in this place?'

She spun around and stared at Jake in disbelief.

'Well?' he prompted.

'Sit down and I'll get someone to take your order,' she gabbled, unable to stop the rapid beating of her pulse or a strange light-headed excitement.

Had he come on the off-chance that she might still work at the same place? Or for nostalgic reasons? Or simply because the restaurant was noted for its quality food?

She sent a young waitress to his table, finished serving her customers, then raced out to the office to find Ben Logan, her boss, and one of the few people who knew Jake was Julia's father.

'He doesn't know,' she told Ben, after explaining about Jake's sudden re-emergence in her life, 'and I'm not going to tell him.'

Ben frowned at her.

'I know he hurt you, Katy,' Ben murmured. 'Heaven knows, I could have killed the bastard with my bare hands he hurt you so bad. But don't you think he deserves to know he has a child? And, from a purely practical point of view, don't you think you could do with a little help from him financially?'

'No and no,' she said firmly. 'I tried to tell him once and he sent my letters back. Now, for Julia's sake if nothing else, it's best he doesn't know.'

Ben shrugged his shoulders.

'I won't say anything, then,' he muttered. 'In fact, I think I'll stay in here, then I don't have to talk to the guy. I might still feel the need to punch him in the jaw.'

Katy chuckled at the image of the short, tubby, dapper little restaurateur taking on the tall, well-muscled Jake.

'Perhaps I can stay in here with you?' Katy asked, only half-joking as she fought the physical effect of Jake's presence nearby.

Ben reached out and touched her hand.

'You'll cope, my girl,' he told her. 'You've the strength of a hundred tigers when it comes to something you really want to do—and a thousand tigers when it comes to that kid of yours!'

'That's what you think!' Katy muttered. 'At the moment a mouse could beat me—and an underfed mouse at that!'

She left the room and returned to her duties, studiously ignoring Jake, who was flirting with the young waitress and apparently enjoying his steak.

And his coffee! Then more coffee.

He was still sitting alone at his table when Katy went through to the cloakroom to change into her street clothes. She wondered if he'd arranged to take the younger waitress out for a drink when she finished work. The thought depressed her as she struggled into her jeans and pulled the zip up so forcefully it jammed and she had to fiddle with it to release it.

'Walk you to your car, lady?'

He was waiting by the door and she flinched away from him as he touched her arm. They walked through the door together, but she hesitated on the pavement. The flashing blue and red restaurant sign was turned off as they emerged and their eyes had to adjust to the shadowy darkness.

'I—I catch the bus,' she stuttered to break the sudden silence. He was suffocatingly close, and now even she could smell the drift of tangy aftershave Julia had associated with lemon grass. 'Just up the road.'

'Oh, for Pete's sake, Katy! Don't tell me you still rely on public transport? How do you get Julia to medical appointments? And don't bother telling me she doesn't have any! I'd have thought even a stubborn, independent woman like you would have realised the difference your own car could make.'

He drew her out of the way of a group of young people heading for the night-club up the road and she leant against the wall, trying to gather the strength to walk away from him.

'You work full time at a well-paid job and waitress at night. Why haven't you got a car?'

She smiled at his vehemence and shook her head as past and present collided again. Jake had wanted to buy her a car to help her cope with her hectic work and study schedule. He had always been infuriated by her determination to be independent.

'Same old arguments, huh, Jake?'

He dragged his fingers through his hair, tugging at it as if it might stimulate his brain.

'Same old lots of things, Katy,' he said soberly. 'I'd always thought desire was something cerebral—you liked someone so were physically attracted to them, as if there were a mental switch of some kind. But if that's the case, a person should be able to turn it off.'

He leaned closer, too close.

'Especially when one realises the object of desire isn't interested. Ridiculous, isn't it, that desire can still exist in such a vacuum? Such an unlikely situation?'

The words brushed across her lips in light puffs of air only seconds before his mouth closed on hers. Their noses bumped and she tilted her head to make the contact easier, forgetting she shouldn't be reacting, shouldn't be kissing him back with all the hunger of her love-parched soul.

Her arms crept around his shoulders, feeling the flesh and bone of him beneath the soft cotton shirt. Her fingers tangled in his hair where it brushed against his collar, then slid upwards to press against his scalp, cradling his head as they slaked their thirst for kisses.

Fine way of showing you're not interested! her mind yelled, while her body moulded itself closer to his. It was so good to be held against him, to feel complete again. Warmth filled her veins, saturating her senses, and a strange lightness made her cling more tightly to Jake, as if to anchor herself in some reality.

'Perhaps not a vacuum!' he murmured, and she shivered as the huskiness in his voice played its own part in her seduction.

His tongue skimmed across her lips, probed deeper, touched and taunted hers, and she stopped thinking altogether and gave herself up to the sensations that came flooding through her body, wave after wave of desire, and heat, and need.

She returned his kisses with a desperation born of six long years of separation. Somewhere in her mind a voice argued that it shouldn't be like this, that the magic shouldn't still be working after all this time! It must be lust! the voice insisted. A frustration-induced chemical reaction! A hormonal rush!

She ignored the voice and pressed closer, her hands conducting their own exploration while her lips tingled with the taste of him and her body throbbed beneath his hands.

'Let's find somewhere a little more private.'

Jake's voice, ragged with emotion, stilled her hands. They were inside his shirt, pressing on his skin, teasing at the whorls of hair and tight, nubby nipples. She withdrew them slowly and patted her own clothes into a semblance of order. She tried to stop the shaking, but no deep breaths or silent common-sense advice could still the raging tumult of her senses.

'Let's not,' she muttered, her own voice as hoarse and rasping as his had been. 'This is stupid, Jake. It can't happen. I can't let it happen!'

She pushed away from him and clutched her hands against her chest, hoping pressure might calm the turmoil surging beneath her skin.

'Why not, Katy?' he asked, his fingers smoothing her tangled hair back from her face, touching her skin with the lightness of love.

But was it love? Or that far more inconvenient emotion, passion? Hadn't she mistaken passion for love once before, then felt the fury of the flames as it had burnt itself out?

'Because of Julia's father?' he demanded gruffly.

'N-no!' she stuttered, then registered who Julia's father was and amended her answer to a frantic, 'Yes!'

'You can't love him and respond to me as you did!' Jake growled, clasping her shoulders as if he'd like to shake some sense into her. 'If you're sticking with him for Julia's sake, it's a big mistake, Katy. You, of all people, should know that. Think what happened in your life because of misguided choices.'

Her own childhood was the last thing she wanted to consider at the moment. Jake's anger was as potent as his kisses—because it made it seem as if he cared! She shivered in the darkness as he spoke again.

'And what is he? Some worthless scum who can't afford to keep you? He bloody well can't think much of you to let you work the hours you work—and as for letting you travel on public transport at this time of the night—!'

'Hear, hear!' a male voice responded, and Katy spun around.

Jake's complaints, growing louder with each grievance, had attracted the attention of passers-by so they now had a small crowd of onlookers.

'Well, I can't take public transport tonight,' she pointed out. 'You've made me miss my bus!'

Her voice was shaking as much as her body, and she leaned back against the wall and tried deep breaths again.

'Drive her home, mate!' one of the strangers encouraged, and Katy, infuriated to find she'd become a bit of sidewalk entertainment, turned on Jake.

'I'd rather walk!' she snapped, and whirled to face the spectators. 'And the show's over, so you can all go home!'

'We're not going home!' one of the girls said. 'It's only one o'clock. We're going to the Night Owl—why don't you come along? A few drinks—bit of dancing—sort out your problems in a civilised atmosphere.'

Someone giggled and Katy realised their audience had already had a few drinks—enough to mellow them, to let them think they could solve the problems of the entire world.

The anger trickled out of her as she remembered feeling that way herself, then she felt Jake's arm reach out and draw her close.

'Not tonight,' he said gruffly. 'But I hope you all enjoy yourselves.'

Katy swallowed, trying to banish silly tears that had welled up at this new memory of the past—and of the dark, underground club where she and Jake had danced till dawn the evening of the day they'd met. It had become 'their' place, frequented on the nights when they didn't have work commitments or early-morning schedules.

'Come on,' he said when the group had wandered off. 'I don't have a car to run you home but I'll put you in a cab. I'll even pay for it, as I've made you miss your bus!'

He sounded tired but his arm still held her close. As he steered her along the footpath she didn't pull away from him but relished the warmth of his body against hers—even if it was only as far as the cab rank.

'Will you go up to the Night Owl on your own?' she asked. 'Or there's a new place near City Square called Four Bells. A lot of the hospital staff go there—I believe it's very nice.'

'You sound like a tour guide,' he said gruffly. 'I don't need entertainment or night-clubs or social meetings with other staff, Katy. I'll put you in a cab and take the next one on the rank straight back to the hospital.'

'That's ridiculous,' she protested. 'If we're going the same way we can share a cab.'

She felt the movement of his muscles as he shrugged, then his arm dropped from her shoulders as they reached the first cab in the rank. He leant forward and opened the door for her, told the driver to head along Lake Shore Drive towards the hospital, then dropped into the darkness beside her. Without thinking, she reached out and took hold of his hand.

They sat in silence as the cab left the city. Jake's fingers lay passively in hers yet she fancied she could feel the blood running through them, keeping his precious flesh alive. She brushed her thumb across his skin, warm, satiny skin, and remembered how his chest had felt—the coarseness of the hair.

She'd splayed her fingers in it in the past, reaching out before she went to sleep as if the physical connection with Jake would keep her safe throughout the night. In the morning, she would feel him move, and wake to turn into his arms...

'Turn here. It's the second house on the left,' she told the cab driver, shunning the memories.

The security light above her front door flashed on as the cab registered on the sensor.

Katy hesitated, reluctant to leave the cocoon of darkness, then, obeying instinct rather than common-sense, she leaned sideways and kissed Jake softly on the lips.

'Goodnight!' she murmured, then she opened the door and slid out before she did anything else she was certain to regret later.

Marie was awake, head bent over books and papers spread across Katy's dining table.

'Busy night?' she asked, without raising her eyes from her work.

'Not bad!' Katy told her. 'Want tea or coffee?'

Marie shook her head, and Katy remembered her own absorption with study when she'd been Marie's age. She and Jake would begin together, but his brain worked faster than hers and he'd finish his allotted amount of work and then pace around the room, trying to tempt her away from her set task.

She shook her head, remembering the feel of his fingers in her hair, his lips on the nape of her neck—then the shivering torment as she tried to deny the effect he had on her!

'I'm going up to bed. Don't overdo it!' she said, as she always did. She was halfway up the steps before her words registered with Marie, who called a belated goodnight in an abstracted voice.

Katy reached the landing and turned towards Julia's room. Her daughter lay face-down, flung across the bed as if sleep had caught her by surprise and tossed her there. Katy smoothed the golden hair and pulled a sheet over the slight body. She turned down the covers on the second bed. Marie would creep in later and sleep through half the day, relishing the quiet of Katy's home.

Thinking about the luxury of sleeping in made Katy yawn. She tiptoed out of the room and headed for her bedroom. Julia would be shaking her awake in less than four hours—sleep-ins existed only in her dreams!

Their Saturday morning routine involved getting several loads of washing onto the line—a task that was becoming increasingly difficult as Julia grew older and insisted on helping. That done, the two of them headed for the shops, Julia dragging the wheeled trolley on the way there, and Katy pushing it, full of groceries, on the way back.

After lunch they walked down to the lake, where they fed the swans and played games identifying people by the way they walked, or through snippets of the conversations which reached their ears.

It was a good game because Julia insisted Katy close her eyes. This meant she could lie on the blanket, put her hat over her face, and doze between passers-by.

'It's the new doctor from the hospital,' Julia hissed, rolling over on the blanket so her lips were close to Katy's ear.

'You can't know that,' Katy told her, too tired to stir.

'I do, I do!' Julia insisted, then she moved away and Katy, reaching out and not making contact, sat up with a start.

'Good afternoon, ladies!'

Katy felt her spine stiffen and tiny tendrils of delight flicker in her blood.

'It can't be!' she wailed, watching as he bent and touched her daughter on the shoulder.

'Can't be me? This park private?'

His eyes were wary, gazing down at her over Julia's tumbled curls. Such lovely eyes...

She shook away the fancies. This intuitive process of Julia's was becoming too unsettling for her to be thinking of blue eyes.

'I can't tell how she knows!' she told him, while Julia tugged on his hand, urging him to join them on the blanket.

Which wasn't that good an idea, Katy realised, as the blanket shrank to pocket handkerchief size.

'Other senses compensate,' Jake reminded her, taking Julia in his arms and settling her on his knee.

'You try it! Go on! Lie down and close your eyes and listen to the footsteps of people going past. What can you tell about them?'

'Yes, do it, Dr Cartwright,' Julia urged, standing up so she could push at his shoulders and force him backwards.

He gave in to her insistence, making her gurgle with delight when he tumbled over, pretending he was too weak to resist her.

His head came to rest on Katy's thigh, but when she tried to move she found her muscles wouldn't respond to her command, so he lay there, eyes closed, allowing her to study his dear, familiar face. Strong-jawed, harsh-profiled, it was a manly juxtaposition of features that was uniquely Jake—uniquely charming, and very, very sexy.

She clenched her hands, feeling her fingernails biting into her palms as she resisted the urge to run them across his smooth, tight skin and feel the ridges of bone that shaped his looks.

'Someone's coming,' Julia warned, tucking her body close to Jake's and taking his hand in hers.

'It's a man,' Jake guessed. 'And he's plump and most important because he walks with short, strutting kinds of steps. I think he's wearing a red waistcoat, yellow tie, blue suit and carrying a red and yellow umbrella.'

Julia clapped her delight.

'Is he right, Mum, is he right?' she asked, squirming with excitement.

'Almost right,' Katy told her, as an elderly man in grey shorts and a blue shirt ambled by. 'Except his waistcoat's blue and the umbrella is purple.'

'Not true!' Julia declared. 'He smelled like onions, and I'm sure an onion man wouldn't carry a purple umbrella.'

Jake sat up slowly, and Katy was fairly certain he was sniffing the air.

'How often is she right?' he asked, his fingers stroking Julia's arm absent-mindedly.

'If it's someone we know—'

'Like my babysitter, Marie, or Nan, or her family, or Helen from the hospital—' Julia interjected.

'Almost always,' Katy finished. 'She told me you were here, but, as she's only met you once, I didn't believe it. I keep wondering if she might be... If I should...'

Her voice trailed away a second time. She couldn't voice her concerns in front of Julia, but if she could talk to Jake about the possibility that her child was especially gifted he might be able to advise her on whether it was important to have her tested.

'Are you working tonight?' he asked, and Julia replied for her.

'Mum's always working!'

Katy knew the disapproval in her voice was a bit of child-parent manipulation, but she couldn't help defending herself.

'I don't leave till you're asleep,' she pointed out. 'It's not as if you're missing out on special time with me.'

'But you're tired next day,' Julia continued, obviously pleased to have a new audience for her complaints.

'Enough!' Katy told her. 'We've been through all this before.'

'But I haven't,' Jake objected. 'I'm with Julia. I'd like to know why you have to work nights—why you're still pushing yourself so hard?'

He sat up and turned so he was facing her, and she found it difficult to meet his eyes.

'We're paying off the house and Mum's saving for my new computer,' Julia answered, before Katy realised her daughter was still involved in the conversation. 'Mum says she's sure a spaceship would be cheaper, but a spaceship wouldn't be nearly as much fun for me as a computer that talks.'

Katy saw Jake's eyes darken with anger and she could read the unspoken question.

Does her father provide nothing? he was silently demanding, but, 'Why, Katy, why?' was all he said.

Julia decided the question was meant for her and launched into a list of the virtues of her computer. Katy turned away, looking out across the lake to where the two swans glided, their growing brood holding a straight line behind them.

Soon the park rangers would take the young swans away. Would the parents assume their children had willingly left the nest? Taken off because it was time to go? Her own experience of family was so bizarre she found it hard to judge even the feathered variety.

'Swans stay together for ever.'

Julia's clear, childish voice, adopting a different subject but one still close to her heart, brought her back to earth with a jolt.

'The mother and father, that is,' she added. 'The children leave home when they're old enough, but the mother and father stay together.'

Katy knew the heat she felt must have turned her cheeks to scarlet. So many conversations coming back to haunt her! Jake had told her about the swans and she'd argued from her own experience, using the words he'd repeated to her last night, that staying together wasn't always so good.

'It's because they love each other,' her parrot of a daughter added. 'It only works with the love bit, Mum says.'

'Does she, pet?' Jake said lightly, but Katy could hear the pressure of her own tears in his voice.

'We've got to go!' she announced, standing up so

suddenly her calf muscles cramped and she stumbled awkwardly.

Jake reached out to steady her, and, looking down, she saw more questions in his eyes. He rose to his feet but she couldn't bring herself to step away from him, so their clothes and skin brushed against each other and tremors of excitement fluttered in her lungs.

If she touched him now...

If he took her arm...

'Can I run?'

She caught back the drifting, dangerous thoughts and turned towards her daughter, poised at the junction between the two paths.

'As far as the shadows,' Katy told her, and watched the slender figure dart towards the trees.

'I make sure there are no pedestrians to be knocked over,' she explained to Jake, her voice as hoarse as if it were never used.

'Has she enough sight to tell where the shadows begin?' he asked, damping down her erratic reaction with the practicality of the question.

'I don't think so.' She gathered up the blanket and walked towards her waiting daughter. 'I think she can tell by the change in temperature on her skin. I don't like to probe too much in case...' She hesitated, wondering how she could explain her reservations. 'When you were a kid, did you ever wake up in the night and think you'd forgotten how to breathe? It's such an automatic action no one analyses it, yet when you start to think about it, you find it difficult.'

His footsteps slowed, as if he knew she would want to finish this conversation before they reached Julia.

'You're afraid if she starts to think about how she senses things, she'll lose the knack?'

'Exactly! So I bumble along, wondering about it, trying desperately to train my senses in the same way—to find some clue of how things work for her.'

'It would be an interesting study—the degree of sensory perception in sight or hearing-impaired children.'

'Wouldn't it just?' Katy agreed fervently. They reached Julia and she took her by the hand. 'It's one of my dreams,' she confessed, adding, in almost inaudible tones, 'One day!'

She felt Jake's attention shift, and wondered if he was thinking of a similar dream she'd shared with him. I'll be a nurse—one day! She straightened her shoulders, arguing silently against an imagined reminder. Just because one dream had died, it didn't mean you held a wake for all the others!

He walked with them to the end of the avenue of trees.

'We're going swimming in the hospital pool tomorrow morning,' Julia told him, while Katy wondered why she'd spent so much money on speech therapy because she'd been worried about Julia's verbalisation skills. At the moment she could see unlimited advantages in having a non-verbal child! 'Because you're a doctor, you could come.'

'That would be lovely,' he said gravely. 'If I'm not working, I'd like to join you.'

'And have lunch with us afterwards in the canteen?' Julia urged, and as Jake raised that questioning eyebrow at her Katy shrugged.

'She especially loves their mushy beans on toast—prefers the canteen to McDonalds.'

He looked horrified—probably remembering the steak—but he made a noise that could have been a yes, then touched his new admirer lightly on the head.

'See you in the pool, Julia,' he said. 'Be good.'

'I'm always good,' she told him indignantly. 'I'm my Mum's one and only best, best girl!'

Katy saw Jake straighten and his eyes met hers. Her heart thundered as she realised how many 'Jakisms' she had unconsciously passed on to Julia, including 'You're my one and only best, best girl'. Would he remark on it? She waited, feeling the silence, like the sunshine, on her skin.

'I'm on call, and the place is still a mad house, so I'll be at the hospital if you want to talk to me,' was all he said, then he turned and walked away.

What did he mean—want to talk to him? Surely he couldn't have picked up anything about her single state from Julia's prattling conversation. For one horrible moment Katy had thought Julia might blurt out the information that her father hadn't loved her mother, which was why, unlike the swans, her parents had parted. But she'd been diverted in time, so it couldn't be that!

CHAPTER EIGHT

JAKE wasn't at the pool, but Helen was enjoying the use of the hospital facilities and she filled Katy in on the latest drama being played out in the main building.

'Happened in the early hours of this morning,' she began, settling herself on the edge of the pool where Katy sat to watch Julia swim back and forth across the width. 'Post-partum haemorrhage! You can imagine the scene. Mr Carstairs, who's usually very meek and mild, screaming hysterically at the sight of blood, and Mrs Carstairs—predictably—threatening to sue everyone from the hospital shareholders to the security guards.'

'Was Dr Anderson available?' Katy asked, and saw Helen shake her head.

'When's a specialist ever around when you need him? He was at his daughter's wedding down the coast, but Jake Cartwright was on call and fortunately lives in the hospital. He appeared within minutes and told Mrs Carstairs he'd let her bleed to death if she didn't stop her nonsense.'

Katy whirled on her friend, shock jolting her upright.

'He couldn't possibly have said anything so stupid! "Never make even light-hearted threats to patients!" That's rammed into every nursing and medical student from the time they start to study.'

'Well,' Helen said, 'he didn't quite use those words, but I think he got the message across that if she continued to make a fuss, things could get worse. Anyway, according to the night staff, she settled down.'

Helen kicked at the water, sending an arc of droplets into the air. 'Mind you, I suspect that man could charm the flowers off wallpaper if he set his mind to it,' she added.

'What was the problem?' Katy asked, hiding the strange scrunchy feeling she felt inside when Helen spoke of Jake.

'Well, it could have been retained placental material or uterine atony—the uterus not contracting properly after the birth. Usually that shows up sooner, but it wouldn't be surprising after the stretching it must have had during Mrs Carstairs's pregnancy. She'd been given the usual dosage of oxytocin in IV fluids after the placenta was delivered, and the staff had been massaging her when she'd allow it—'

'You mean when she wasn't busy giving interviews or getting remarried!' Katy had seen the list of 'appointments' Mrs Carstairs had arranged through her publicity managers.

Helen laughed, agreeing that the whole procedure had been stage-managed throughout.

'Anyway, Dr Cartwright told her if it was that, there were two options: drugs or surgery. You can imagine how she reacted to any suggestion of surgery! He palpated her abdomen and decided it was boggy enough to need dealing with first, so he increased the infusion rate, added Methergine sequentially and everyone waited.'

'Methergine?' Katy repeated the unfamiliar word.

'It'll usually produce really strong uterine contractions—some specialists use it, some prostoglandin. I've known them to use both in quite a few cases. I think Dr Cartwright was a bit doubtful about the effectiveness of drugs, with the patient's abdomen the way it was and the possibility that the haemorrhage might have been caused by something else. Anyway, she's got blood replacement flowing into one arm and the IV cocktail into the other, and she must have felt a bit better because she demands we get the photographer and video cameraman back in to record this bit of the drama for posterity.'

'I don't believe you,' Katy gasped. 'She must still have been feeling dreadful—why would she want anyone taking films or photographs?'

'Why would she do any of the things she's done?' Helen asked. 'I'm just glad I wasn't on duty! Evidently Dr Cartwright blew his top and told her she was a seriously ill woman and he was going to invoke hospital regulations to prevent anyone other than her husband entering her room.'

'Can we do that? *Are* there hospital regulations which give us such power?'

'Ron Spencer asked him that when they walked out of her room, and Ron says Dr Cartwright said he'd make some up if necessary, but he was damned if he was going to lose a patient because some press hound wanted one last photo. Seems he sent people flying in all directions—wanted new blood tests for a coagulation profile, ultrasound for retained placental material or blood-clots—'

Julia swam back to where the two women sat, bobbed her head above water, grabbed Katy's ankle and demanded, 'Where's my doctor?'

'She's met Dr Cartwright,' Katy explained to Helen, then she touched Julia on the head and said, 'He's very busy today.'

Seemingly satisfied, Julia felt along the edge of the pool beside where Katy sat, finally locating four thick plastic hoops. She positioned herself carefully, her back against her mother, and dropped them into the water so they formed a semi-circle around her feet on the bottom of the pool.

'Now, I'll dive for them,' she announced.

'She's showing off for you, seeing "her" doctor isn't here,' Katy explained to Helen. She watched Julia's legs thresh above the water as she duck-dived to the bottom, but her mind was on Jake and the problems he'd been having.

'What did the scan show? Did he take her back to Theatre for a curette?' she asked, reaching out to take the first coloured hoop from Julia. 'Very smart!' she told her daughter, and watched her dive again.

'Unfortunately it was unclear. No nice line showing the uterus had contracted, and little sign of anything else. He suggested a curette, in case that was the problem, but she refused to consider his performing even such a simple operation. She wanted Anderson or no one, and refused to give consent.'

'Poor Jake!' Katy murmured, taking the second hoop from Julia.

She felt a shift in Helen's attention and heard a hint of added interest when she said, 'You sound as if you really care!'

'I care about any doctor who's given a hard time by a patient. When things go wrong, they have to cop both the patient's blame and their own uneasiness that they might have been able to do more. In cases like this, the doctor is in a rotten situation.'

'I guess!' Helen murmured, but she didn't sound as if she was thinking about Mrs Carstairs.

Julia picked up the last two hoops.

'Time to get out, kitten,' Katy said to her. 'You're getting waterlogged.'

'Once more, over and back,' Julia pleaded.

'Okay, see how quickly you can swim.'

'She's so fearless,' Helen remarked. 'She splashes into people, then gets going again as if she can actually see the other side of the pool.'

'I know she can distinguish light and dark,' Katy explained, 'but I'm beginning to wonder if she can also detect some difference in the texture of the light. So the other side of the pool might have a particular appearance she can recognise.'

'Have you had her tested?' Helen asked, and Katy shook her head.

'You and Nan!' she muttered. 'You're both as bad as each other. What if I do have her tested and it proves she's in the group they class as "talented and gifted"? What's it going to prove? The special clubs and programmes they have are for sighted kids.'

'As long as I've known you, Katy, you've never treated Julia as if she's sight-impaired. Why would joining one of those groups make a difference?'

'I can't explain,' Katy told her. 'I haven't said I *won't* have her tested—I'm still thinking about it.'

She knew she sounded defensive, but she remembered Jake telling her about the club he'd attended. His intelligence had made him 'different' from the other kids at his school, and he'd had to play harder and fight tougher and continually prove himself as 'normal' as any of his peers, again and again.

And Julia was already 'different'.

She helped her daughter out of the pool and wrapped a towel, cloak-like, around her, wishing she had the power to provide a cloak of emotional protection as easily.

'See you tomorrow,' she said to Helen, herding Julia towards the changing rooms. They'd have lunch in the canteen then walk home, and, with any luck, Julia would sleep for a few hours and she could lie down and relax herself. Her quiet Sunday afternoons were precious—a time when she was just herself, not an administrator, or a waitress, or Julia's mother.

James Carlyle, the chief medical officer at the hospital, put paid to that plan. The phone was ringing when they reached home.

'Can you come in to work, Katy? There's all hell breaking loose in this place and I need someone to man the phone on your ward. Three of the staff have already been reduced to tears after they refused to give out information and the switchboard operators are threatening to quit if they have to handle all the calls themselves.'

He sounded tired and harassed.

'I've spoken to Nan Chalmers from the crèche and told her we need you here. She suggested you take a cab and drop Julia at her place. Charge it to the hospital, of course.'

'Okay, James,' she agreed. 'I'll get there as quickly as I can.'

Given Mrs Carstairs's propensity for publicity, she didn't know why she was surprised to hear that this latest dramatic development had been made public. No doubt the woman would milk it for all it was worth.

Julia was playing on the floor, rolling balls with one hand and catching them with the other.

'I've got to go to work for a while, pet. Would you mind if I dropped you at Nan's place?'

Silly question! Julia loved going to Nan's—in fact, her enjoyment of the rough and tumble she shared with Nan's kids sometimes made Katy feel guilty about her daughter's only child status.

She phoned for a cab, then, leaving Julia playing, raced upstairs and threw some clean clothes for her daughter into a small backpack. Nan would keep her for the night if Katy was held up at the hospital, and the supply of clothes already at Nan's might not be enough.

She thought about changing out of her shorts, then decided no one would be worried about how she looked. She'd be a voice on the end of the phone, nothing more.

Nan was waiting on the footpath outside her place when the cab drew up. Katy kissed her daughter and handed her over, then climbed back into the vehicle.

The cab driver refused to be intimidated by the crush of people outside the main entrance to the hospital. He put his hand on the horn and blasted his way through towards the door.

'Charge it to the hospital, love?' he asked, and Katy agreed, giving him her authorisation number. She opened the door and leapt out, hoping she'd be taken for a normal visitor.

As she hurried past the security men who held the crowds at bay, she heard whispers of the stories that had swelled their ranks.

'Mother's dying...'

'Could be dead already...'

'Three babies gone...'

'Adoption...'

'No, all the babies are okay—the father says he'll bring them up himself. Someone's raising money...'

How do these rumours start? she wondered as she showed her identification to a policeman who was on duty in the main foyer.

James must be panicking to have brought in the law!

She found another policeman on the fourth floor and wondered what effect this circus was having on their other patients. And what did the Asian mothers, who turned shyly away from fuss and attention, make of it all?

She reached her office and phoned through to the switchboard to let them know she was there.

'Before you start directing calls to me, I'll need to speak to a doctor so I know exactly what I can and can't say,' she explained.

'Dr Anderson's not here yet, although I believe he's on his way,' the operator told her. 'I'll see if I can get on to Dr Cartwright or Dr Spencer.'

A few minutes later Ron Spencer knocked on the door.

'Thank goodness you're here, Katy. Maybe you can provide a bit of sanity in this madhouse.'

He perched on the edge of her desk, where Jake had sat.

The phone rang and she reached out to silence it.

'Could you hold for a minute?' she said politely, then flipped a switch so soothing music would play in the caller's ear. 'What's happening, Ron? And how much do we make public?'

'She's still bleeding, blood pressure's low. Jake's beside himself and someone is keeping sections of the media up to date on every move we make.'

'Can't we remove the phone from her suite on the pretext she's too sick to take calls?'

'We've done that,' he told her. 'There's another leak somewhere.'

'So what do we do?' she asked him.

'Take the calls and say she's stable. You can repeat that there's been some post-partum problems which are being handled in the usual manner.'

She lifted her eyebrow and he laughed.

'You'll think of something to keep them happy,' he assured her.

'I'll try,' she promised. 'But if word's leaking out somewhere else, you might put someone on to finding where. The rumours circulating downstairs are unbelievable.'

'I'll see what I can do,' he promised, and turned to leave.

Katy was about to switch back to the caller when she remembered the babies.

'What's the status of the kids?' she called after him, and he swung back towards her and shrugged.

'Go with "stable", Katy,' he said quietly. 'The neonatal specialist is still worried about two of them, and you know how dicey it is to predict outcomes for any pre-term baby.'

Katy watched him leave, then turned her attention to the caller. It was a reporter from an international newsgathering service who thought her charm and persistence would find a weakness in Katy's carefully worded statements. Katy fended her off, but she was relieved when the call was over. Until the next one came in! The switchboard must have had a backlog of them, for no sooner did she hang up than the phone would ring again.

Someone brought her a cup of tea, and Ron poked his head in at one stage to say there was no change but Stewart Anderson had finally arrived. A wardsmaid brought her a sandwich and she ate it while she talked, repeating over and over again the limited litany of facts.

At seven o'clock, James Carlyle came in.

'Come on, Katy, I'll drive you home.'

She'd been warily eyeing the phone, wondering why it hadn't rung for three minutes, and she looked up in surprise.

'Siege over?' she asked.

He nodded.

'I've given orders to the switchboard to tell all callers that this hospital will issue a news bulletin at seven tomorrow morning and no further information on the Carstairs' family is available until that time. I've also instructed the people on duty to hang up if a caller persists.'

'Good for you!' Katy applauded, knowing how wary James usually was about taking a firm stand with the press. He hated to think anything he said or did might dim the shining reputation of 'his' hospital.

'Yes, well...' he said, looking a little embarrassed by her mild praise. 'We discovered Mrs Carstairs's sister, who's been with her since she was admitted, has a cellular phone. She's the one who's been relaying all the information, slipping into the bathroom to make her calls. We can't stop her visiting her sister, nor can we prevent her using her own phone, but let's see what happens when word leaks out that she's the only contact. My guess is, she'll turn the damn thing off.'

Katy smiled at him.

'And will word leak out?' she asked.

'Just about now, I would say,' James told her, and moved towards the window. 'We can't see from here, but Jake Cartwright is about to do his "cleaner" routine and walk out muttering about how impossible it is to get work done in the place and fancy having to phone Miss Johnson's mobile to get access to the Carstairs room. As Miss Johnson featured largely in the television presentation of the birth, it shouldn't take the media people too long to work it out—or find out the number.'

'I could print it on a placard and hang it out the window if you like,' Katy suggested, wondering if Jake had thought of the plan to relieve pressure on the hospital phone lines.

James smiled at her.

'Let's hope that won't be necessary,' he said. 'Now, shall we go?'

For a moment she hesitated. While she'd been in the office there'd always been a chance Jake would call in for a few minutes and she'd see him. Now she was stupidly disappointed because he hadn't. She wouldn't even see him in the corridor or ward foyer if he was parading downstairs in disguise.

'Okay,' she agreed, hoping James didn't sense the reluctance in her voice.

Jake rang at nine, his voice a husky murmur over the phone, as if all his energy had drained away and the sounds were being formed by memory, not effort.

'I heard you'd been seconded this afternoon, but by the time I came up to see you James had whisked you away. Did you handle it okay, Katy?' he asked, his voice so flat she guessed he was depressed as well as tired.

'My job was the easy part,' she told him. 'How are you coping?'

'Just!' he muttered.

There was a pause, and then he said, 'Talk to me, Katy?'

She knew then that he'd rung because talking to her had, in the past, helped him think things through. He wouldn't talk about his problem right away, but would order her to talk while his mind sorted it into order. She began to speak, telling him of their trip to the pool, of Julia's diving for the rings.

'You were going to ask me something about her yesterday—about her sensory perception,' he reminded her. 'Want to ask me now?'

She would have loved to talk about it now, but would discussing Julia's abilities and reminding Jake of his own 'special' status link him to her in such a way he'd suspect their relationship? Just at the moment she couldn't think through all the implications of that particular discovery!

'No, I'll sort it out. She missed you at the pool,' Katy added, and heard him sigh.

'And you, Katy? Did you miss me?'

'Helen was there,' she said, skirting the question. 'She told me of your fun and games so I knew what was going on before James rang.'

They'd come full circle now. Was he ready for questions? She took a deep breath, then asked anyway. 'How's Mrs Carstairs?'

'Stewart Anderson is back, thank heavens,' Jake replied. 'He's with her now. The drugs weren't working and surgery is the only answer. He'll try tying off blood vessels, but, given the suspected severity of the atony, he may have to opt for a hysterectomy. He mentioned that possibility to Mrs Carstairs, and she's dug her heels in and refuses to allow him to take her to Theatre.'

'Is a hysterectomy such a problem? She's got five babies—surely that's enough for any woman?'

Another sigh filtered into her ear.

'You'd think so!' he said. 'Unfortunately I rather suspect she's had so much fun with all the publicity she wants to do it again. Although with new guidelines about fewer fertilised eggs being implanted the possibility of another multiple birth is unlikely.'

'But no one would put her on another IVF programme,' Katy protested. 'It would be...'

'Unethical?' he suggested. She could almost see the shrug which would have accompanied the word. 'The problems of ethics and IVF are so immense we haven't begun to sort them out. There are ethical and legal battles raging in countries all over the world over the destruction of frozen embryos. And, if you consider that a doctor should do his best to comply with the wishes of his patient, would it be so unethical to put Mrs Carstairs on another course of fertility drugs?'

'Yes!' Katy replied without the slightest hesitation. 'The programme was initiated for couples who had problems conceiving. There are waiting lists of people wanting to get on to the programme at Lake Shore North. If it had been a single birth, then fair enough—put her on the bottom of the list and let her work her way up to the top for a second child—'

'Hey, I happen to agree!' he interrupted, and his voice had lost the strain she'd detected earlier. In fact, he was probably laughing at her vehemence. 'But Mrs Carstairs still has the right to refuse surgery—for whatever reason—and so far that's exactly what she's doing.'

Katy groaned with disbelief.

'I'm glad I'm not a doctor,' she said. 'How can you hold back when you know the patient may die if you don't operate?'

'With a great deal of difficulty, Katy!'

There was a moment's silence, then he went on, 'I'll have to go back down to the ward and see what's happening. Thanks to you, my best, best girl, at least I feel halfway normal again.'

Her heart contracted, but she knew she couldn't let him get away with it.

'I'm not your girl, Jake,' she said quietly, denying her heart.

'No, Katy?' he murmured. 'Are you quite sure of that?'

'I have to be sure,' she told him sadly. 'Good luck!'

She turned on the television news next morning and learnt, with the rest of the population, that Mrs Carstairs had experienced some post-partum problems, had had some minor surgery and was resting comfortably. All five babies were progressing in a satisfactory manner.

James Carlyle had faced the cameras himself, and his calm demeanour had come across more strongly than the media's emotive questions, defusing much of the hype that had been associated with the Carstairs' family since before the birth.

Katy headed for work, hopeful that sanity would have been restored. She wanted the upperlevel powers in the hospital to be thinking about her new unit today, not about quintuplets. As she walked along beside the lake she hid a sense of disappointment that Jake hadn't come to meet her. It was stupid to feel that way, because she knew how hectic his weekend had been.

But he was in the office—standing just inside the door! She jolted to a stop and stared at him, transported back to Saturday night, when they'd kissed. Memory fired her blood.

'Still not my best, best girl?' he murmured, then he moved so his foot kicked the door closed. His hands grasped her shoulders and his lips met hers in a kiss of such hunger she gave herself up to the reaction she'd denied him a week ago.

Every cell in her body came to life—completely, joyously, throbbingly alive. She moved so their bodies fitted, complementing yet completing each other, and when the emotion he aroused began to drain the strength from her legs she let him ease her back against the closed door and hold her, so her body seemed suspended in the same unreality as time.

Then the phone rang, his pager bleeped, and her speaker phone told her she was needed in 'B'. Somehow the combination of demands broke through the spell and they released each other slowly, moving automatically to silence the ringing and buzzing.

She answered the phone, assured Sue Gates she could keep the extra staff and was heading for the door to answer the call to 'B' when Jake spoke.

'You can't love him, Katy!'

She turned back and frowned, wondering what on earth he was talking about.

'Julia's father!'

Oh, but I do, she thought, and panic began to shiver through her body.

It was like standing on the edge of a landslide—feeling that first downward slip and knowing if you turned around, if you tried to go back, half the hillside was likely to come tumbling down on top of you. Only it was Julia's happiness which could come tumbling down!

'I've got to go,' she mumbled, and hurried from the room.

Helen wanted some information on a patient dredged up from records. The woman had given birth in the hospital eight years ago and the records were no longer in the computer's data bank.

'I hate to ask you to do it, but the woman's in labour now and she's sure she had some problem last time but can't remember what,' Helen said. 'I rang Records and they've three staff off with the summer 'flu that's going around, and because it's a manual search they won't be able to get the information to me until later in the day.'

'I'll go down and see what I can find,' Katy told her, taking the slip of paper Helen handed her with the patient's details on it.

She made her way down to the records room in the basement of the newer part of the building. She'd worked here when she'd first come to Lake Shore North, so was familiar with the quiet surroundings.

The rooms were well sealed and air-conditioned, the temperature and humidity maintained at a set level to protect the records. They were stored on disk here, although Katy knew abbreviated hard copies were also kept in a second room.

She found the disk she needed, popped it into a computer and scanned it for the information she wanted. Information was cross referenced, so you could follow up an admittance date, a name, or even a condition. She used the search command and found the woman's name.

She was right when she said she'd had problems! There'd been a secondary arrest of dilation during her active labour, when dilation of the cervix had ceased for three hours. The doctor in charge had diagnosed inadequate uterine contractions rather than malposition of the foetus or foetal disproportion. He had allowed the patient to rest, then augmented the labour with oxytocin and the patient had delivered vaginally.

Katy typed in a 'print' command, and while she waited for the machine to spit out the information for Helen she studied the disk cabinets lining the walls—each year with its own divisions into departments. Obstetrics, Gynaecology, Neurology, Orthopaedics.

Orthopaedics! Jake had been in this hospital—his record would be in there.

Why should she care?

She couldn't answer, but knew she wanted desperately

to see his name, to read the medical description of that time of such great pain.

She glanced towards the printer, which was still chattering busily, then crossed to the file drawer for the year of the accident. She found the disk and slipped it into a second computer, again using 'search' to find Jake's name. As the bare clinical details rolled down the screen she recalled the shock and pain—even the sterility of the air in the ICU.

Head wound, mangled hip, fractured left femur, tibia and fibula, spinal cord compression, lacerations—

Spinal cord compression?

She went back and found the reference, demanding more information. Paralysis of lower limbs, word after word that meant little to her now, descriptions of tests carried out, of the lack of response to stimuli.

And three final words—'possible outcome paraplegia'.

'I had my reasons!'

Jake's voice echoed in her head, but the anguish she'd felt for him back then was blown apart by anger. She shut down the program, slammed the disk back into place, tore the reams of patient information from the printer and raced out of the room. Then she remembered the second disk and returned, telling herself to calm down. With shaking fingers she exited the program then returned the file.

Helen thanked her for her help, but Katy barely heard the words. She wanted to get back to her office and confront Jake Cartwright—confront him with his cowardice. For that was how she saw his action in cutting her off from him.

He wasn't there, and she remembered he would be at the directors' meeting. A note on her desk confirmed that fact and a string of messages kept her busy for the next few hours.

He'd have seen it as the 'right' thing to do, she realised, when she allowed herself to think about the new revelations. Bathing himself in a rosy glow of nobility while he broke her heart! The anger seethed and burnt within her, but she had to push it back—to think about work, not Jake.

Impossible!

She did what she could, but the rage persisted, and when he opened the door, walked through it and smiled hesitantly at her, it was ready to erupt.

'I'm sorry, Katy, but we didn't have time to discuss the new unit.'

'Didn't have time!' The banked fires blew upward in a cataclysm of flame. 'No doubt there were far more important things to discuss! Well, I wouldn't want you putting yourself out for me—or for the people I feel are important. It's what you think that must come first— your perception of what's important and what isn't!'

She was nearly crying with rage, but the stunned look on Jake's face brought its own satisfaction.

'I'm going to lunch!' she added, grabbing her handbag and storming past his immobile figure and out the door.

He caught up with her as she waited, toe tapping in seething impatience, for the elevator.

'Would you mind explaining what that little outburst was all about?' he asked, speaking in a breathy undertone that whistled out through gritted teeth.

'No!' she snapped. 'Why should I? Since when did anything I think matter to you?'

'That's nonsense, Katy!' he argued, loudly enough for the little group of hopeful passengers to hear. 'Do you think I'd have disrupted my life like this if what you thought and felt didn't still matter to me?'

The lift arrived and the doors slid open.

'It didn't matter what I thought six years ago,' she flung at him, heedless of the onlookers. She plunged into the compartment as his pager sounded again. He began to follow her, then turned away to answer the call.

CHAPTER NINE

KATY headed for the crèche, intending to collect Julia and take her across to the park to eat their lunch by the lake. She forced herself to relax, to put Jake and the past right out of her mind before she saw her daughter.

'She's asleep,' Nan greeted her. 'My fault, I suppose, I let her stay up a bit late last night to watch a video with my kids.'

As she left the building on her own Katy's disappointment was diverted by thoughts of how often 'sight' words were used in conversation. 'Look at this.' 'Watch me.' 'Do you see?' Although Julia followed television by listening to words and sound effects, even she talked about 'watching' it.

Katy reached the park and found a seat by the lake. The sun burned into her skin but she relished its warmth—hoping it might banish her inner coldness.

The enormity of what Jake had done made it too difficult to consider logically. Earlier she'd reacted with anger over something else—but now it blotted out all thought processes, so she ate her sandwiches and stared out over the water.

The office was deserted when she returned, but a messenger came down from Admin only minutes later with the typed notes of the department directors' meeting.

She flicked through the printed pages. Jake had obviously had a legitimate excuse for not raising the new unit—the entire meeting seemed to have been devoted

146

to discussing ways and means of handling 'celebrity' patients.

She turned to the last page and saw a recommendation that new procedures be put in place. Among the suggestions was one for a public relations office to be set up, headed by a person experienced in dealing with the media. Katy liked the idea. It would take pressure off units already under siege because they were housing the 'celebrity'.

And an official bulletin would be released at a specific time each day—which might stop the press from camping outside the front entrance hoping for a lucky photograph or a snippet of gossip.

The list continued and Katy could see sense in all of it. Bigger hospitals might already have such precautions in place, but Mrs Carstairs had been Lake Shore North's first experience of a media feeding-frenzy. At least the powers-that-be had learned from the experience.

She worked through the afternoon, her disappointment about the new unit very real—but blunted by thoughts of Jake's diagnosis, by wondering what she would have done if their situation had been reversed.

A sick feeling in her stomach told her she should understand his actions, but that didn't make them acceptable.

With a conscious effort, she set aside all thoughts of Jake. Her last duty for the day was always pleasurable, a quick visit to the wards to collect roster sheets and discharged patient files, and check there were no problems requiring her attention.

The doors to 'A' were tightly closed, and she experienced a pang of disappointment that her plan wasn't being put into action immediately. Having the empty ward would have made it so much easier to rearrange beds and patients.

Helen greeted her in 'B'.

The ward looked different, and Helen explained they'd brought in extra beds from 'A', although they weren't in use.

'We decided we'd put any new arrivals in here, even if it meant being a bit crowded. I've nabbed the extra staff from 'A', so staffing's no problem. Rosa has enough on her plate with Mrs Carstairs in one of her birthing suites and the Asian mothers in the ward area. It's worked out well. In fact, like the women in my ward, they've been most unimpressed by the fuss she's making and have withdrawn into their own exclusive little group. I think Mrs Carstairs would have preferred a bit of awe and admiration from her fellow patients, but she's certainly not getting it from those.'

'But if she's in a suite she wouldn't see much of the other patients,' Katy objected.

'No?' Helen said, and smiled at her. 'Before the latest incident, she'd taken to parading up and down the ward, talking about ''my babies'' in a loud voice. Sometimes Mr Carstairs followed her, but Rosa put a stop to his accompanying her, saying it was violating the other women's right to privacy.'

Katy shook her head, unable to believe the excesses of their famous patient.

'I'm glad Rosa was firm,' she said. 'Another belief among some of these women is that the baby shouldn't see too many strangers early in his or her life.'

'That stems from common-sense, really,' Helen agreed. 'The more people in contact with the baby, the more chance of someone passing on an infection of some kind.'

'The more I read of their customs, the more sense it all makes to me—apart from not showering!' Katy replied. She smiled at Helen. 'And what about Mrs Carstairs's health? Was the surgery successful? Has it calmed things down a bit?' she asked.

'Go see for yourself,' Helen suggested.

'I suppose I'll have to,' Katy said reluctantly. She walked on down the corridor and into 'C'. A nurse she didn't know was at the station, so Katy introduced herself and asked for Rosa.

'She's ducked out for ten minutes,' the young woman explained. 'I think she's probably on the fire stairs letting out great howls of frustration. It's been one of those days!'

'More trouble?'

The girl smiled and shook her head.

'Actually, a lot of the fuss has died down, and Mrs Carstairs hasn't been feeling well enough to think of a new sensation, but Mrs Robinson definitely wants to breast feed and she's been having trouble expressing milk. Rosa has spent a lot of time with her, trying various breast pumps, but we suspect the milk's not coming in because she's getting more and more distressed about it.'

'And the baby was pre-term, remember. All the proper signals weren't in place in her body.'

'That's true,' the nurse agreed. 'Actually, there's someone from the pre-term births association in there with her now. She's always more cheerful after one of their visits.'

'If her visitor leaves, I'll pop in and see her before I go.' Katy collected the roster sheets and patient files, then walked on into the ward. Her Vietnamese friend had been discharged that morning. Katy had no fears for her—her sensible husband would look after her well while she 'did the month'.

The woman from Hong Kong beckoned her, and Katy walked across and sat down in her visitor's chair.

'This is an excellent idea,' she told Katy, 'putting we Asian mothers together.'

Again Katy was struck by the differences more than the similarities between the women. Mrs 'Hong Kong', as Katy thought of her, was wearing an embroidered silk negligée with what looked like a white angora wrap thrown around her shoulders to keep her warm. Gold jewellery shone against her pearly skin—fat rings with glowing diamonds, heavy linked chains on her wrist and slung around her neck.

'It means we can do things in the old way and talk about the customs of our ancestors, but you need a steam room—and arrangements should be made about placentas for those who wish to know it has been properly treated.'

Katy tried not to shudder. She knew some South-East Asian people believed the placenta should be salted and buried outside their home to ensure a safe and happy life for the child. She hadn't included any suggestions about this custom in her file on the new unit because she couldn't see how the hospital could legally regulate such unorthodox disposal of what constituted waste product.

She ignored that issue and began to explain that the hospital was hoping to set up a special unit.

'Eventually, we hope to be able to offer far more than just grouping the patients,' she said.

'But I can do it now,' the woman said. 'You tell me how much it will cost and I will fix it.'

Katy felt her jaw drop. Until that very moment she'd always regarded the expression as ludicrous, but she had felt her jaw definitely slacken, no doubt leaving her mouth agape with shock.

'It's more involved than money—' Katy began to explain, but the woman waved away her objections.

'Work it out!' she ordered in a crisp, peremptory tone. 'I am staying here until Wednesday; tell me by then.'

Katy mumbled something soothing, spoke briefly to the other women and departed. Mrs 'Hong Kong' was obviously used to getting her own way—but if she wanted to give some money to the hospital, it was up to Katy to work out how best they might spend it. Perhaps a steam room would be possible after all!

She'd spoken to Sue Gates several times during the day, so she bypassed the nursery—although she'd have liked to have checked on the Robinson baby, and sneaked a quick look at the quins!

Back in her office, she tried three firms listed in the Yellow Pages as supplying steam baths and saunas, but all were closed. It was too late to do any more today and Julia would be growing impatient. Although the crèche remained open until after evening visiting hours, and even provided an overnight service to staff on night shifts, Julia believed five o'clock was 'going home time' and tended to nag when Katy was late.

Perhaps the money would be better spent on a language programme of some kind, she thought, and then, as she took the lift back to ground level, decided that the staff all managed quite well with sign language and the interpreters' help.

She collected Julia and listened to her chatter on about her day, grateful to Mrs 'Hong Kong' because considering her suggestion helped keep thoughts of Jake at bay.

Until he loomed up on the path in front of them and was greeted with great delight by Julia!

She seized his hand and began to swing, but Katy's warning growl was enough to convince her that it wasn't a good idea.

Julia chattered to Jake and Katy let her take control. She certainly couldn't have carried on a normal conversation. Her anger at Jake was still storming through her blood, but his presence prompted so many other responses her body felt at war with itself. His appeal—for her at least—was like a force-field of electrical currents, zapping constantly at her skin, her nerves...

'So you'll come?' Julia finished.

Come where? Katy wondered wildly. Where were they going in the near future? Where had Julia invited him?

'It might not suit your mother,' Jake said quietly, glancing towards Katy with a strange expression on her face.

She frowned, trying to think whether she'd promised Julia they'd go somewhere special, then her daughter answered for her.

'Oh, Mum never minds another one for dinner. Marie often comes, because it's on her way home from uni or she needs to study and her house is too noisy. But she won't come tonight because she's going to a rock concert.'

Ordinarily the information that the quiet, demure Marie was going to a rock concert would have diverted Katy, but she'd caught on to the question now.

Julia had invited Jake to *dinner*!

Tonight!

'Katy?'

So, he wasn't going to come unless she asked him—at least that was something.

'Please, Mum, please say yes!'

She looked down into the lovely sightless eyes and knew she couldn't disappoint the excited child.

'Of course you can come,' she said coolly, keeping any hint of welcome from her voice.

She had some chicken schnitzel—Julia's favourite food—in the freezer. She'd pull it out as soon as they reached the house. Her heart was thudding against her ribs, but she kept her mind on the practicalities of dinner. Thinking of chicken schnitzel stopped her thinking of electric currents.

He was the perfect guest.

He played with Julia while Katy fixed dinner, he cut Julia's schnitzel, and unobtrusively slid the pieces of chicken under her fork as she felt for them. He washed the dishes while Julia had her bath, then gave in to the child's pleas to read to her before she went to sleep.

Katy made a pot of coffee while he was upstairs. She didn't want him staying for coffee, but she had to do something to keep her hands and mind occupied. He had, as she'd suspected he would, invaded her house like an invisible fog—taking possession of its atmosphere with effortless ease.

If she closed her eyes, she could see him sitting on the floor, guiding Julia's hands as she fitted blocks together, pushing toys within reach so she didn't have to scramble for them. And as her heart ached for what might have been she forgot the past and felt her rage beginning to dissolve, washed away by the memory of a child's joyous laughter.

'She's waiting for her goodnight kiss.'

Jake's voice startled her out of her dreams.

'I'll go straight up,' she said, and hurried past him.

She realised—too late?—that the anger had been a barrier, some slight protection against his magnetic appeal.

'So, Katy?'

The words greeted her as she came cautiously down the stairs. He was sitting in the living room, his coffee poured and the cup clasped in his lean, tanned fingers.

'So what, Jake?' she muttered.

'So what was all that fury about this morning?' he said, his voice calm but implacable.

Fortunately she felt a flicker of the heat and fury return, and she procrastinated—hoping the flicker would strengthen into flame. She poured herself a cup of coffee, then sat down opposite him. Her house—quite adequate for two—seemed smaller now, and the sitting room felt more like a closet than the spacious room she'd once thought it.

'It was about something you said to me last week. "I had my reasons", you said, Jake.' She tried to listen to her voice, to see if she sounded as calm as she was pretending to be, but subtle nuances were beyond her. 'I saw your hospital records this morning.'

'Hospital records are confidential, Katy.'

His quiet, slightly reproving tone broke through her thin veneer of control.

'So report me and have me sacked,' she raged. 'What "reasons" did you have, Jake? That you were going to be crippled? What kind of a person did you think me, that you could possibly decide I'd be upset by that?

'I loved you, Jake—loved you so much it almost hurt to breathe—and you put me through hell because of your stupid pride. Because that's all it was, you know! You couldn't bear to think of yourself as less than perfect. You couldn't cope with me seeing you that way. I didn't hate you then—I couldn't—but I hate you now, Jake, hate to think you thought so little of me you could cut me off the way you did.'

Her fingers were shaking so much the hot coffee slopped over them. She reached out and put the cup down, feeling in her pocket for a handkerchief, blinking furiously to keep her tears from falling.

'It wasn't pride, Katy.'

He spoke into a silence that had seemed so complete she might have been alone.

'It was a lot of things but it wasn't that.'

She'd found her handkerchief and wiped her fingers. She blew her nose, then sniffed back a few more tears. She wanted rage, not tears!

'Well, don't stop there!' she snorted. 'What was it if it wasn't pride?'

He set his cup down carefully on the side table, then leaned forward. He was close enough to touch if she reached out. She pushed her body back into the chair—denying the urge!

'It was you,' he said softly. 'You and your damned independence! Honestly, Katy, you were the most stubbornly independent person I had ever met. You refused help from your friends, from people like Ben Logan, who would have done anything for you, and, most of all, you refused help from me—someone you supposedly loved!'

He looked up and she saw pain and grief in his eyes—recognising it because she'd seen it in her own eyes so often.

'So how do you think I felt when they said I'd probably never walk again? How do you think I felt when I realised I was going to be dependent on someone for the rest of my life—and, if we stayed together, dependent on the world's most independent person? It was great stuff, Katy, believe me!'

His voice was hoarse with the memories of that time and she could hear the pain he must have felt.

'But I wouldn't have cared,' she yelled at him. 'Don't you understand that? Didn't it enter your thick skull that I loved *you*? Not an outer shell which could or couldn't walk, but the person inside that shell—the bit of you that laughed and cried and argued and helped me with my studies and held me when things got too much to handle. You could have kept doing all those things with legs that didn't work.'

'I know you wouldn't have cared, Katy,' he said gruffly. 'That was the problem. You'd have kept loving me and bullied me to get better and taken me up as yet another burden on your slim shoulders. But I cared too much to let you do that. I loved you too much to diminish you that way, to have you give up your studies to look after me, give up your dreams...'

His voice faded, then he added, 'But you did that anyway,' in a tight, hard voice, and leaned back in the chair, as if saying the words had drained the last remnants of his strength.

Katy could see his reasoning, could almost hear the things he'd left unsaid. Caring for a paraplegic was costly. She'd have had to accept hand-outs from his family, and her pride, not his, would have been ravaged in the process.

'But we'd have made it,' she argued. 'We'd have worked our way through it all.'

'Would we?' he asked.

She shook her head. No one could say for certain. She'd seen so many relationships break down and die when too much outside pressure was brought to bear, and the pressures both she and Jake would have had to endure would have been enormous.

'You could have given me the choice!' she muttered, the old wrong not righted, the old pain still tender to the touch.

'I couldn't give you the choice,' he replied. 'You know how you'd have chosen. And I didn't want your love to turn to pity, our passion to die because I was a "duty". You'd have grown to resent me, to remember I went into that race against your wishes—wildly and recklessly brought the accident on myself! I couldn't take the risk—I couldn't give up what last shreds of self-respect I had. I couldn't let myself become dependent on you!'

His voice deepened with the strength of half-forgotten convictions, then softened as he continued, 'You, of all people, should understand, Katy. Would you have let me care for you if the positions had been reversed?'

Probably not, she thought, remembering she'd considered that question earlier today. But she wasn't going to admit it. The positions hadn't been reversed.

'You're walking now!' she pointed out, knowing he would understand all the things she hadn't said.

He bowed his head, and she saw his chest rise as he drew in a deep breath, then heard the sigh of its release.

'My parents flew me home from here. They called in more specialists and refused to accept the doctors' verdict—'

'You parents, Jake? Not you?' she interrupted, not willing to believe he'd been a passive patient.

'My parents,' he confirmed. 'I didn't care what happened to me, Katy. I'd lost you, lost my strength and nearly lost my mind! I'd lost too much to care about anything—and I was only too aware that the whole blighted mess could have been avoided if I'd had one shred of common-sense, so I had a load of guilt to bear as well.'

'Go on,' she told him, feeling in her heart the deep agony of regret which must have haunted him.

'They took me to America—to a specialist in the United States. I went through barrages of tests again and he decided it wasn't my back but my hip.'

'Weren't both legs paralysed?' Katy asked, drawn into the medical aspect of the problem in spite of herself.

'They were, but this doctor decided it was sympathetic paralysis in the right leg. He operated and released pressure on the sciatic nerve caused by the way the pelvic bones had knitted together and he did a nerve repair of a kind that hadn't then been tackled in Australia. It still took time—two years before I was walking properly—but—'

'And it didn't occur to you even then to write and say, "I'm better, Katy". To tell me how you'd felt and why you'd acted as you did. You had to wait another four years, then smash your way back into my life—into my house…' She was crying now in earnest, the tears rolling down her face faster than she could wipe them away. She bent her head so he couldn't see how deeply his story had affected her.

'I did write!'

Her head jerked upward and she peered at him through the blurred veil of sorrow in her eyes.

'When?' she demanded, hope and despair jostling in her heart.

'In December of that first year,' he said. 'I sent you a Christmas card from America with snow and robins on it, because we'd always laughed about Christmas cards like that out here, when it was ninety degrees in the shade. I told you what was happening—why I'd lied to you that day and sent back your letters when I thought all hope was gone.'

In December she'd been in hospital, a thousand miles from Lake Shore. She'd been admitted, sick and weak from the prolonged diarrhoea of Giardia, at the beginning of the month. The trouble she'd assumed was persistent morning sickness had finally been diagnosed and she'd been treated, but it had been too late to save Julia from the effects of placental insufficiency. She'd been born on Christmas Eve, six weeks before she was due.

'I didn't get a letter,' Katy whispered, trying not to consider what such a letter would have meant to her at that stage.

'I know. It was returned to sender.'

'I moved in August,' she told him. Moved south and found a small flatette that faced the morning sun and would be suitable for a baby.

'I wrote care of the university, care of the hospital,' he added, 'and I even wrote to your father. The university and hospital letters came back, but your father didn't reply.'

Katy wrapped her arms around her stomach. She felt physically sick, as if all the lost years, the unhappiness and regret, were churning inside her.

She'd stopped her degree course when she'd realised it would be very hard to nurse and raise the baby on her own. The irregular hours and roster system would make her time with the baby too erratic, and the demands of the job would be physically draining. She'd brushed up her secretarial skills and worked from home instead, typing students' assignments and theses until Julia was twelve months old.

'Katy?'

One word, but a thousand questions.

He stood up and moved to stand beside her, his fingers trailing lightly down her hair.

'Go home, Jake,' she pleaded. 'I need to think about all this.'

He was silent for a moment, then he bent and kissed her on the cheek.

'Take your time, Katy,' he murmured, touching his lips against her temple. 'It took me over six years to come to terms with it—you're entitled to all the time you want.'

Then he knelt so he could look into her face and his eyes proclaimed a love so blinding she had to look away.

'You're also entitled to send me away—to say, Thanks, but no thanks Jake. I'd understand that—I wouldn't like it, but I'd understand—because what I did to you must seem close to unforgivable, and it would have to be forgiven before we could begin to recapture what we had.'

She wanted him to kiss her—wanted it so badly she trembled with the force of her desire—yet she knew he wouldn't. The next move would be up to her, and she wasn't so lost in dreams of hope and love that she could make it yet.

'Please go,' she repeated, and watched him stand up, hesitate, then touch her lightly before he moved away. She heard him fiddle with the front doorknob and knew he was setting it to lock behind him.

'Goodnight, Katy,' he called, then the door closed and she was alone with ghosts and images and reasonable-sounding if emotive explanations.

His story rang true—the tragedy of it all lying in the letters he'd written when she'd moved on into a different phase of her life and her whole being had been concentrated on her child—not forwarding addresses!

It had been deliberate, not leaving her new address when she'd shifted, not telling the hospital because she hadn't wanted to be found. She had cut herself off from all their acquaintances, at first to avoid their sympathy over Jake's accident and desertion, then to hide her pregnancy.

She'd moved away from Lake Shore, seeking anonymity in a bigger city further south, then returned when Julia was two and she'd heard of a special programme for sight-impaired children at Lake Shore North.

By the time she'd returned the programme had closed through lack of funds, but Katy had decided it was so good to be home she had found a job at the hospital and stayed.

So, Katy?

Her head repeated his words, but she couldn't make it think logically. It kept reminding her that what had happened once could happen again.

Another accident? desire argued sardonically.

Improbable!

But could some other change of direction provide a similar excuse for him to turn away?

She felt his parting touch as clearly as if his fingers still lingered on her skin, and recalled the shaft of longing that had pierced her at his soft caress. Her body ached for him in a way she would have thought impossible a week ago, yet she couldn't take that next step—that decision which would alter all their lives.

The phone rang while she was still sitting in the chair. She knew it was Jake and hesitated before reaching out to prevent the noise waking Julia.

'I know I said I'd let you think, but I need to know one thing.'

She didn't ask him what—couldn't speak for the joy fluttering in her throat, the joy just hearing his voice had set free.

'There's no other man, is there, Katy?' he demanded. 'I found it hard to believe you were still working so hard—' He broke off and she heard a husky mutter. 'Who am I kidding? I told myself there couldn't be— that my instinct about your reaction to me couldn't be that far out! And if that makes me sound conceited, I'm sorry—I don't mean it that way. It's a belonging kind of thing, Katy, a knowledge that comes from deep within that you and I are meant to be together.'

He paused, but she was too unexpectedly moved by his words to reply.

'Of course, I had other clues. Julia talked about her babysitter but never of her father. So tell me, Katy, make it definite. There's no one important in your life, no one you care about now, at the moment?'

She shook her head.

Only you, was the answer. There's only ever been you, she could have said. But she wasn't ready to tell him that yet, so she whispered her reply.

'There's no one else, Jake.' And she was about to hang up when he spoke again.

'And the flowers? And the "John" Jenny mentioned?'

He's jealous, she thought with an unfamiliar feeling of joy. Should she tease him?

She smiled to herself.

Not Jake! She'd never been able to hurt Jake, any more than she'd been able to hate him.

'The flowers were a thank-you from a support group I led for some years and John was a friend who never became more than that,' she told him, and heard his sigh of relief.

'For what it's worth, I love you, Katy,' he said quietly, and it was he who disconnected the call.

CHAPTER TEN

JULIA woke Katy in the morning. She was still dressed, still sitting in the armchair.

'You haven't been to bed,' her daughter accused.

'I must have fallen asleep in the chair,' she muttered, and made a joke of her silliness. But it was hard to laugh when her emotions were in tatters and her body ached from a cramped, uneasy sleep.

Another working day! She put out Julia's clothes, pleased the little girl insisted on dressing herself, then hurried into the shower. Warm water cascaded over her, so refreshing she tilted her head to let it flow over her hair as well. If she towelled it off it would be nearly dry by the time she'd walked to work.

She poured shampoo into her hand and lathered it into rich suds. Memories of Jake intruded. Jake washing her hair under the shower, letting the lather run all over her body—the lather and his hands...

'I'm ready for breakfast,' Julia called.

Julia? How would she adapt to another person in her life? Not another person—a father! She liked Jake well enough, but she was too young to understand what had happened between her parents. Would she hold his earlier desertion against him?

Katy dried herself and wrapped a towel around her wet hair. She dressed for work, then fixed breakfast for them both, eating hers at the kitchen bench while she made their sandwiches for lunch.

'Will Dr Cartwright come tonight?' Julia asked.

'I don't think so, pet,' Katy replied, and then she told herself the decision might be easier if she saw more of him outside working hours, and her heart missed a beat as she amended her reply to, 'Maybe!'

She left Julia playing downstairs while she combed out her hair and skimmed a sun-screening moisturiser across her face. She added a touch of green shadow above her eyes and emphasised her lips with a soft coral-pink lipstick. Her hair was damp, and she fluffed it out around her shoulders. She would brush it and confine it with a ribbon when she reached the crèche.

'Let's go, kid,' she called to Julia as she hurried down the stairs. She picked up Julia's backpack and her own handbag and they were ready to tackle another day.

'Dr Cartwright's waiting for us,' Julia announced when they reached the park.

This time Katy wasn't surprised by Julia's percipience. Knowing Jake, she'd guessed he would be here. He might say it was up to her to make the next move, but he'd never been one to stand back and let destiny run its course.

Well, not if he could give it a little nudge in the direction he had chosen!

They walked beside the lake, its placid surface a pale silver-blue reflection of the morning sky. Julia chatted companionably to Jake, and Katy was reminded of the 'X' in the equation. It would be so easy to give in to the love Jake professed, but at what stage in the proceedings did she introduce the subject of Julia?

Before they made love again?

Directly after, when he'd be relaxed and loving and—hopefully—understanding?

And what would she say? By the way, you have a daughter...

Her stomach flipped at the thought.

'You seem preoccupied this morning?' His voice slid into her consciousness and she turned to see his eyes gleaming with delight. He was so certain he had won, so sure she still returned the love he claimed had lived on in his heart.

Which she did!

She turned away without answering. She'd responded to his kisses, she'd admitted there was no other man in her life—it must seem so simple from his side.

They said goodbye to Julia at the crèche and Katy took Jake through the maze of corridors leading to the main lobby. He walked beside her, close, but not touching her, yet she could feel his presence as vividly as if they were standing naked together. Perhaps the mythical man in her life *had* been a protective barrier for her, or had Jake held back the full force of his attractiveness when he'd thought she was involved with someone else?

The feeling intensified when they crowded into the elevator and their clothes and skin brushed accidentally. By the time they exited into the fourth floor lobby Katy's nerves were twisted into a skein of torment, her body hungering for Jake's in a way she had never experienced before.

Six years' chastity, she reminded herself as she smiled and nodded to passing staff, hoping she looked more in control than she felt.

She made it to the office and slumped against the wall inside the door.

'You too?' Jake murmured gruffly, then he took her in his arms and held her close.

'Hell, Katy, what's happening to us?' he muttered, after they'd stood together for what seemed like hours. 'I felt so randy I could have thrown you down in the corridor in front of all those people, ripped the clothes off you and ravished you.'

'I wouldn't have fought you off,' Katy muttered, detaching herself shakily from his arms.

He ran his fingers through his hair and she saw the strain in his face give way to humour. 'Willing victim, huh?' he teased, and flicked one finger against her cheek.

'Willing, but stupid,' Katy told him, crossing to her desk and sitting down so she could at least pretend to be working.

'Stupid?'

She looked up at him.

'We're rushing into this, Jake,' she said. 'Going far too fast because of some hormonal thing that's battering at both of us.'

'Perhaps we'll think more clearly once we've given in to it,' he mocked, stepping very deliberately towards her. 'But I agree we should attempt to at least get through the day before weakening.'

He was standing on the far side of the desk and it was as if invisible threads bound her skin to his, tugging her towards him.

'I—I think that would be best,' she stuttered, wishing she felt more confident that getting through the day was possible.

He crossed to his chair and sat down, reaching out for his phone. She was thankful he'd begun to concentrate on work. Her phone rang and Katy seized it gratefully, hoping a sensible conversation would dispel images of the time she and Jake had made love on a desk—

'Hello!' she answered, dragging her mind back to the present.

'Are you on the pill, Katy?' a voice murmured in her ear.

She turned towards him and saw him smiling at her. She could feel heat colouring her cheeks, flowing through the most hidden parts of her body.

She tried to answer, but no words came, so she shook her head, remembered she hadn't tied her hair back tidily, stared at her brass pelvis, then dropped the receiver back onto its cradle.

Her hands were shaking—in fact her whole body was shaking! She rather suspected her mind was in similar turmoil, or had given up functioning. Through a haze of inconvenient emotion, she heard Jake's pager buzz, then he was on his feet, touching her lightly on the shoulder, and disappearing through the door.

He'd told her where he was going, but she hadn't made sense of the words—her usual cool efficiency and composure destroyed by a libidinous excitement.

She pulled out her diary and considered the day. No ward meeting—thank goodness! A note about steam rooms and saunas reminded her of the patient's offer. Doing something different might distract her, so she'd start there.

By lunchtime she had tackled all her regular jobs, and also had a list of three different portable units they could use within the hospital building. She'd checked with the hospital electrician and plumber to make certain the units could be installed safely and had quotes for the installation. The morning had gone more smoothly, she realised, because Jake had not reappeared.

Pleased with her efficiency, she decided to take a full hour for lunch. She collected Julia from the crèche, and walked with her to the lake. She deliberately blotted all thoughts of Jake from her mind while she enjoyed the time alone with her daughter. Jake might be impatient with destiny, but she'd gone beyond rational thought and was content to let fate take its course—for a while, at least.

When she returned Julia to Nan's care, she remembered another decision she'd taken and asked Nan to make arrangements to have Julia assessed. If it was done within the familiar preschool environment, her daughter would be more relaxed.

And if her daughter proved particularly gifted?

She shook her head, reluctant to confront that question. In fact, she half hoped the tests would show her daughter within the 'normal' range—whatever that might be!

A note on her desk told her Jake was in Outpatients if she needed him, but he'd be off duty by six and would like to take her and Julia out to dinner. 'I can borrow a car so be ready by six-thirty,' he'd written, and she could hear the peremptory tone he'd have used if he'd spoken the words to her.

Was dining with him—even with Julia as a safety valve—letting destiny carry her too far?

Probably!

But after the way she'd reacted to him this morning, destiny had already carried her past the point of no return.

She told herself that making love need not affect the choices she must make, although her heart knew a physical reunion could alter everything.

They went to dinner with him, Julia delighting in Jake's vivid description of the classy restaurant. Closing her eyes and listening to his words, Katy could see the sparkle of candlelight reflected off the silver cutlery, the drop of water on the rose petal in the silver bud vase on the table. She could feel the crispness of the linen napkins, and smell the rich medley of perfume and aftershave in the air around them.

'You asleep?' Jake murmured, and his fingers touched her thigh, electrifying her nerve-endings and starting a quiver of unfamiliar delight through her body.

'I often try to "see" it as Julia does,' she explained, opening her eyes to see the blazing message of desire he'd hidden behind the laconic words.

She knew her eyes were answering, but she'd known where this evening would end from the moment they'd left Julia at the crèche this morning. She just hadn't wanted to admit it—even to herself.

Somehow, she survived the meal. She was sure it had been delicious, but couldn't remember what she'd eaten. She knew Julia had kept the conversation going and hoped her daughter hadn't been too brash or cheeky. She'd responded—appropriately, she hoped—when someone spoke, and smiled a lot, for the conversations she had taken in had been amusingly different.

But destiny was sweeping her along—a leaf in a tide-tugged stream.

'Okay, we'd better take your mother home,' Jake said. 'I know she looks as if she's here, but she isn't with us.'

'Perhaps she's asleep,' Julia suggested, giggling with delight at the thought of a mother who'd slept through dinner.

'Perhaps she should have been,' Jake murmured in Katy's ear as he took her elbow and helped her up from her chair.

It was like waiting for exam results, Katy decided. A stomach-wrenching mixture of anticipation and dread. She made an effort to be sociable as they drove home, but it was hard to pretend it was a normal outing.

Julia fell asleep in the car, half woke as Jake carried her inside, then went straight back to sleep when Katy had undressed her, slid a nightdress over her head and tucked her into bed.

'Coffee?' Jake suggested when she made her way slowly back down the stairs.

She shook her head, too tense to speak, then stepped towards him as he came to meet her, his arms outstretched, his face alight with messages of love.

For a while they simply stood, letting their bodies absorb the secret scent and texture of each other, then Jake bent to kiss her and the room spun wildly.

'Shall we go upstairs?' he whispered, stroking the words against her skin.

She was beyond replying but she let him guide her upward. He knew Julia's room, so guessed the other would be hers, opening the door and sweeping her into his arms to carry her over the threshold.

Her heart was banging against her ribs and her breath fluttered in her lungs. Jake dropped her on the bed and looked around, his eyes gleaming with delight.

'Single bed? How virginal, my love.'

He knelt above her and began to undo the buttons of her dress, pushing back the material, his fingers lingering on the lacy bra she had beneath it.

Back to the buttons, each one so slowly extricated from its hole. Her body trembled with the prolongation of desire, this teasing dalliance that was heightening her need and sharpening her desire.

'So slim! So pale!'

His hand trailed across her stomach, then lingered on the lacy scrap of material below it. Heat surged between her thighs—remembered heat, remembered pulses of desire.

She was no longer able to stay passive, to take the feasting of his eyes and teasing of his fingers without response. She reached up and drew him down so he lay across her body, and while they kissed her fingers slipped his buttons free and pushed his shirt aside so skin met skin and sensory delights could multiply and magnify.

The kiss deepened, drawing out her air, her heart, her soul. She heard her own capitulation in a whimper of hunger, a sighing cry of yearning. They scrabbled their clothes aside, hands urgent now, felt for each other's bodies, drawing closer and closer, arms straining, fingers biting into flesh, pressing together to try to ease the pain of the aeons they'd spent apart.

Katy felt the heat of Jake's body transmitted into hers, felt the aching sexual emptiness which only he could fill. She arched towards him, lifting her body to invite him to take it and make it his once more, to work the magic of that wondrous release when the earth stopped turning and only she and he existed in the universe.

He hesitated, then she felt him press against her, his fingers teasing her to readiness before he entered her body and thrust inside her, timing his movements so the sensations twined and twisted, rising higher and higher, until they levelled off into a kind of suspended wonderment and then, at the next stroke, peaked and flew her far away, tendrils of delight rippling through her body, strangling her with potent magic.

Jake's shuddering groan matched her cry of triumph and she held him as he slumped against her.

'I love you, Katy—please love me again!' he muttered, his lips pressed to her ear so she couldn't miss the words.

Her arms tightened around his back but she couldn't

speak—too full of joy and wonder to think beyond this instant.

Until his hands began to move across her skin, and nerves which should have said, Enough, roused themselves again.

This time it was a different seduction. The lure of a worshipper, the intense delight of being praised, with hands and lips smoothing at her skin, teasing and tormenting, suckling at her breast, sliding up her thighs, fuelling the fires of her passion until she joined the game herself and, touch for touch, brought him to full arousal, then carefully raised the stakes a little higher, finding the protection he'd brought along and sliding it on while he groaned and threatened all manner of kinky punishment. Then she moved to sit astride him and watched his face as she made love to him.

'This bed is impossible,' he said, a long time later.

'It's fine for one,' Katy pointed out. Some vestiges of sanity were returning and she was faced—again—with the two great mountainous subjects still unresolved between them.

Would he go away again? was one. And Julia the other!

'I should go anyway,' Jake murmured, causing a momentary heart-stoppage with words that echoed her fears. 'Julia might not be ready to find me in the house at breakfast time!'

'We've got to talk,' Katy muttered, but he silenced her with a kiss.

'Isn't this better than talking?' he teased, and she found it was.

She must have fallen asleep, because she woke at dawn to find him gone. Her body was heavy with the aftermath of love, and pleasurably tender in parts. She sighed and rolled over, intending to go back to sleep for another hour, but her conscience reminded her that things were far from resolved between them, so she sat up in bed and worried for an hour instead.

He kissed her when she walked into the office and his hands flowed over her, as if to mark her with an invisible brand.

Mine! they said, and she would have revelled in the touch, but the problem of Julia was looming larger and larger.

'I'm on call tonight, but I could borrow the car again, then come to your place and be back at the hospital within minutes if I'm needed.'

She knew he was trying to arrange things now because who knew what emergency would arise to keep them apart for the rest of the day? But this headlong rush into a renewed relationship increased her uneasiness and she pulled away from him, flustered and embarrassed—and too intoxicated by his presence to think straight.

'It will be okay,' he assured her, as if he could feel her doubts and confusion. 'I know you must be concerned about Julia, you must have doubts about the future, but—' He caught her in his arms again and tilted her chin so she had to look up into his face. 'You can't deny what we do have going for us, Katy, or tell me you don't believe in my love for you.'

He kissed her again—a gentle, sweet, non-sexy kind of kiss that still lit fires beneath her skin. She was about to kiss him back when there was a tap on the door and Helen walked in. They sprang apart, too late to hide their closeness but quickly enough to underline their guilt.

'Well, well!' Helen remarked to the air between them.

'That was quick work. I can come back later, if you like.'

Katy stumbled into denials, explanations and excuses, but Jake reached out and slid his hand across her mouth.

'We're old friends,' he said smoothly. 'Now, did you want me or Katy?'

'Both, as it happens,' Helen told him, her eyes gleaming as she absorbed the value of this new bit of hospital gossip. 'I was bringing these requisition forms to Katy, so I became the message girl. Dr Anderson would like you to meet him in the lobby, Dr Cartwright, and Rosa wants to speak to Katy.'

Katy took the sheaf of papers and dropped them on her desk. She was mortified by her unprofessional behaviour—and by being caught in Jake's arms. She followed Jake and Helen from the room, trying to regain the enthusiastic efficiency with which she usually approached her work.

'Mrs Li would like to speak to you,' Rosa told her, using Mrs 'Hong Kong's' real name. 'I said you couldn't make the decision about the new unit, but she seemed to think she might be able to bring influence to bear somewhere if you explained your idea.'

Katy groaned. She was already behind in her morning's work—thanks to Jake's insidious influence—and now another hour or two would be lost as she set out the details of her plan for Mrs Li.

Still, if the woman was willing to make a donation, and if she did have influence in the district, maybe...

She entered the ward and took the visitor's chair beside the new mother.

'I've found out about steam baths and saunas,' she

began, and went on to explain how things stood at the moment.

'Yes! Now you have explained, I understand how important it is to do this properly,' Mrs Li said later. 'Especially in the antenatal stages. Perhaps I could organise some friends to talk to other Asian mothers and undertake some research into the various customs. We could begin with the women I have met in here. Younger Auntie knows much, and my new Cambodian friend has a book printed in her country on the ways of childbirth and confinement. Leave it to me!' she ordered, with a wide sweep of the jewelled hands. 'First I get the information, then I pay someone to collate it all. We will get your unit started without the hospital permission.'

Katy felt she'd been dismissed. She thanked the woman and left the ward. She'd meant to talk to Jake about this offer of financial help, but somehow it had slipped her mind last night!

'I wonder why?' she muttered to herself.

'Tonight?' Jake asked as they passed in the corridor a little later.

Katy shook her head, then nodded, not knowing what she wanted to do. He'd said he'd give her time, but she knew she couldn't bring herself to demand it. Already she was thinking about this evening, about their lying together in her narrow bed as soon as Julia had gone to sleep!

Julia! The still-unknown! Panic skittered in her heart and she forced it back, but in the end it was Julia who precipitated the confession. Julia, showing off to Jake later that evening, counting to one hundred, adding and subtracting, challenging him to give her harder sums.

'Not bad for a cheeky kid who's only—what?' he

said, taking her in his arms and tossing her gently into the air. 'Three and a half? Four?'

She was squealing with delight and so breathless she had difficulty answering.

'No, no, silly,' she squealed. 'I'm not a baby. I'm five—and this Christmas I'll be six.'

Katy heard the silence stiffen into something hard and awkward.

'Five!' Jake echoed. 'Six at Christmas!'

He didn't need his special gifts to do the sums, nor did Katy need a translator to tell her how he felt.

Across Julia's blonde head he looked at her, his eyes dark and hard with anger and disbelief.

He put Julia down with exaggerated care—bent and kissed her on the cheek.

'I'll see you soon, little one,' he said softly, then he turned and walked towards the door.

Katy held her breath and waited. Surely he'd turn back—say something! Anything!

She shivered in the warm night air and watched him fiddle with the catch, setting it to lock behind him.

She tried to call to him, but her lips weren't working, so she watched the door open, then close behind him, and she wondered if he'd cut her out of his life for a second time.

CHAPTER ELEVEN

JAKE didn't phone to say goodnight—although that didn't surprise Katy. Nor was he in the office when she arrived for work, and she wasn't certain if she was pleased or sorry. The strain was plucking at her nerves, making concentration difficult.

At ten he came through the door and glanced towards her as he said, 'I'd like you to sit in on this meeting, please, Katy.'

No smile, no blazing message of either love or desire in his blue eyes.

A strange, leaden feeling filled her chest, but she couldn't begin to guess what he might be thinking. He wouldn't give up Julia now he knew he had a child—but would Katy be included in the package?

Ron Spencer had followed Jake into the room, now Helen entered, and with her Stewart Anderson.

Jake settled them in chairs and Katy grabbed a note-pad from her desk and dragged her own chair across to join them. She didn't look at Jake but she knew every time he shifted in his chair, and her fingers remembered the shape and feel of the scars his accident had left on his body.

'I want to run through a few ideas I've been mulling over about the new unit and the care of mothers from South-East Asia,' he said crisply.

Katy dragged her mind away from thoughts of his body and tried to concentrate on what was being said.

178

'I know you don't see many of them, Stewart, as they're mostly public patients—'

'Don't you believe it,' Dr Anderson interjected. 'More and more of my patients are Asian women. In fact, I'm trying to learn basic Chinese at the moment, although I miss half the classes because I'm called out.'

Jake nodded.

Katy thought she could detect a greyness in his skin, as if he hadn't slept well. Work, or worry? she wondered, and felt a twinge of guilt that she should be adding personal concerns to his burden of responsibility at the hospital. I shouldn't have let him walk out like that! she thought. I should have made him stay and talk about what had happened.

But Julia had been awake, and he'd been hurt—upset...

'Good—you'll understand where I'm coming from,' Jake continued, and again Katy tried to focus on the present, not the past. 'Although the board hasn't yet approved a unit, as such, I've been wondering if we can't organise outpatient visits along the lines Katy's outline suggests. Most of the Asian women come on the same day as it is, so could we have a "clinic" approach, with a group session early in the day, then individual appointments later?'

'I could see Nan at the crèche and make certain she has a Chinese-speaking aide on duty on those days,' Helen suggested, 'so the women could leave their pre-school children there. The main reason women don't like to be away from home too long is because of shaky childcare arrangements.'

'Gran will mind the kids for two hours, but if you're any longer she gets upset!' Ron put in, and Katy smiled. He and his wife, a GP in a small practise near the hospital, had three children under five, so he understood the problems.

'That's a good idea, Helen,' Jake applauded, then he looked at Katy. 'What's the best way to tackle educating these women in our ways?' he asked, as a colleague not a lover—perhaps not even a friend. She recalled discussions she'd had with her Chinese friend about this subject.

'I think if we had leaflets printed in Chinese, Vietnamese and Cambodian for a start—explaining why women should see a doctor during their pregnancy, what each visit will entail, how to know when it's time to come to the hospital for the baby, what to bring and what will happen when they get here...'

'But they might find our ways so offensive they avoid us,' Jake argued. 'Hasn't that been the problem in the past?'

Katy nodded, but Helen answered for her.

'I think the leaflet should emphasise that this is how we, as Westerners, do it, but that every effort will be made to fit into the patient's way. It should point out that one of the reasons it's important for them to attend antenatal clinics is so we can find out their customs and how they would like things done.'

'You could be quite definite about it,' Dr Anderson said. 'Say something like, "It will be hard for us to do things your way if you don't help us learn the customs."'

Everyone nodded and Katy felt a little surge of excitement break through the lump of dread and worry in her chest. Perhaps it was time to mention Mrs Li.

'A patient in Rosa's ward at the moment is willing to help financially.' She explained about the sauna and steam baths. 'I think a sauna might be better, because it

comes as a unit that can be fitted into a shower stall and
the patient can sit in it and cleanse herself in the traditional way.'

She went on to tell them of Mrs Li's idea of research-
ing the customs and collating them into a form which
could be used for staff training. Her concern over the
mess in her personal life was pushed aside as she concentrated on work.

'That's great,' Ron said. 'Well done, Katy! And
when's the sauna being installed? I've often thought I
could do with a steam clean after a big night out!'

Katy smiled at him.

'It's the installation that might be a problem,' she said.
'Since Helen, Jenny and Rosa have managed to group
the Asian women together in 'C' this week, I've been
wondering if the unit has to be a special space. Couldn't
it be more of a concept?'

'I've been thinking that myself, Katy.' Jake glanced
her way but didn't really look at her. No half-smile, no
secret gleam of light in his eyes! 'Do we have to make,
say, 'A' Ward, the ward for Asian women? Or could we
simply keep them together in whatever ward has the
beds. That way they're not completely isolated from the
other mothers and the cross-cultural influence can go
both ways.'

'That's what I'd thought,' Katy agreed. 'And with a
more flexible approach it might be better to get a steam
bath which can be relocated to whatever set of ward
bathrooms the women are using.'

Helen muttered about extra work, but Jake silenced
her.

'Would they really mind walking a little further to
have their sauna?' he asked. 'I've been thinking about
Jenny's suggestion for more birthing suites. I have to

study the figures, but I've noticed the three wards aren't used to full capacity, so we could probably fit two birthing suites and a special sauna room into 'A', which would solve the problem of shifting things around.'

There was a moment's silence while they pictured the changes.

'It could work,' Helen said, 'because the suites are large enough to take two beds. If we did get busy, we could use them as double rooms.'

'So we begin by getting information printed?' Jake asked. Helen and the two men agreed, Helen offering to adapt and extend their English-language leaflet to include all the necessary information before passing it on to the interpreting service for translation.

'Why wasn't all this done earlier, Katy?' Jake asked as the others left the room.

She was pleased his mind was still fixed firmly on a work-related topic, because she wasn't ready for a confrontation yet.

'The influx of Asian migrants is fairly recent,' she explained. 'Two years ago a new manufacturing business was set up on the outskirts of the city. It makes metal fittings for heavy machinery. A number of Asian families moved in as both men and women were needed for jobs on the assembly line. Then a big food chain set up a distribution centre here, and there were more jobs available, and last year a computer software business began operation—more jobs, but this time for skilled workers and technicians. The owners are a group of Australian-Chinese businessmen who decided the area had more growth potential.'

'So the immigrant population has mushroomed in a very short time,' he said, crossing to the window and staring out towards the lake.

'And we've been slow to catch on to the change,' she admitted. 'A big organisation like this, that's doing well enough, doesn't change direction quickly.'

'Unless someone stirs them into action,' he said. 'A fighter like you!'

He turned back towards her and she knew the moment had arrived.

'Is Julia my child, Katy?' he asked.

She frowned at him. She'd expected many questions, but not that one.

'Of—of course she is,' she stuttered. 'You worked out the dates! What did you think? That I'd been having an affair with someone else while we were lovers? Is that why you were so upset last night? Is that why you walked out? How could you possibly believe such a thing?'

Her anxiety had peaked and she let the words lash out at him, hoping they were hurting him as much as his shock assumption had hurt her.

'You weren't pregnant,' he pointed out. 'We did the test. You were sick, but you said the other day that it was Giardia...'

The words faltered. She couldn't see his eyes but knew they'd be dark with the pain and confusion she could hear in his voice.

'We made love that morning, before you left, if you remember...'

Now her own voice stuck, because it had been a strained, sad-angry kind of mating and she'd always felt children should be conceived in love.

She tried again, remembering the theory she'd worked out—months after the accident—when she'd begun to suspect there were two changes occurring in her body, not just one sickness that came and went, draining her energy and dulling the pain of Jake's loss.

'I'd been sick on and off for weeks. It must have affected the barrier effect of the pill I was taking.'

Her body was stiff with tension. She didn't want to handle this alone, to remember her despair and fear, and the dragging debility of an undiagnosed condition. She looked at Jake but he'd turned back towards the window, heedless of her silent calls for him to hold her in his arms.

'You should have told me!' he said harshly. 'You must have known it would have changed things.'

'Made you love me again when you'd said it was all over, Jake? I didn't think so!'

Why was she hesitating? Why hold back because the truth might hurt?

Because she loved him!

'It was my right to know!' he objected, and she knew she'd have to tell him, however much it hurt.

'I did write,' she said bluntly. 'Twice! You sent the letters back!'

She saw his head bend to touch the window and his shoulders slump forward.

'Oh, Katy!' he said, the words a groan dredged up from the depths of his being. 'Oh, Katy, what did I do to you? To Julia—my own child?'

She crossed the room, needing to touch him, to offer the physical support she'd wanted earlier, but the phone rang and she remembered they were both at work, and a ten-minute lull—though it had seemed like an hour—was a rare occurrence in their work-day lives.

'You're needed in Theatre,' she told him, her heart contracting at the ravaged look of grief on his face.

'Can you forgive me? Is it possible we can start again?' he asked.

'Let's talk about it later, Jake,' she said quietly, still conscious of the hurt his doubt had dealt her.

She turned back to her desk and went on with her work, but even the excitement of knowing they could begin to put her plans for the Asian patients into action failed to stop the nagging uneasiness after their unresolved conversation.

She didn't want Jake feeling guilty about the past. She wanted him making positive moves towards the future—helping her think through the implications for Julia, discussing how best they should handle it.

Her heart told her the future would include Jake, that they would be a family, but there was one last fence to jump and she couldn't do that on her own.

She didn't see him again that morning, but he phoned at two to say he would be finishing early and could he walk them home.

'Of course,' she said, because the messages of pain had diminished in his tone and the sound of love was softening every consonant.

'If I don't get back to the office I'll meet you at the crèche—five-thirty at the latest.'

He paused, and she wondered where he was and who was listening, for his *I love you, Katy* seemed to echo through the silence—unsaid, but deeply felt.

'I love you, too,' she murmured, pleased to have the words said at last.

She thought she heard him smile before the click told her they'd been disconnected, and the afternoon flew by as she anticipated seeing him again.

'Let's sit a while and talk about the swans,' he said, when they'd walked beside the lake in a silence broken only by Julia's demands and chatter.

They reached a bench overlooking the lake and Jake took Katy's hand and held it, even after they were seated. Julia climbed confidently up and settled on the other side of Jake.

'You holding Mum's hand?' she asked suspiciously.

'I am,' Jake told her. 'That's what I want to talk to you about.'

'Is it love stuff?' Julia asked, and Katy blushed at the precocious tone.

'Very much so,' Jake replied, his voice edged with laughter. 'What do you know about "love stuff"?'

There was silence while Julia considered the question.

'Nan's kids talk about it all the time,' she confided in the end.

'They're teenagers!' Katy added, by way of explanation.

'And I know about the swans,' Julia told him. 'They love each other.'

'They do,' Jake agreed, in a husky voice. 'What I want to tell you, Julia, is that I knew your Mum a long time ago and we were very much in love.'

'Did you live at Lake Shore then?' Julia asked, as if she needed to get the setting for this story straight.

'I did,' he told her, slipping an arm around her shoulders so her head rested against his chest. 'I came here to work at the General Hospital and your mum was the very first person I met! Oh, we had some fun!'

Katy found it hard to breathe. Jake was doing very well, so far, but how would he introduce himself as her father?

'We were going to get married, only then I did something very, very stupid and I hurt myself—'

Julia pushed away from him and turned towards the sound of his voice.

'You had an accident!' Julia shouted, anticipating the next part of the story. 'You're my father?' she cried. 'My really, truly father? Oh, Dr Cartwright, can I feel what you look like?'

Katy swallowed the lump of tears and watched through watery eyes as Julia scrambled onto Jake's knee and ran her tiny fingers over the planes and angles of his face. She could see the tears in his eyes, too, and feel his tension in the fingers biting into the flesh of her hand.

Then Julia sighed and relaxed against Jake's body, and his arm drew her against his chest and held her close. He turned to Katy, a thousand questions in his eyes, but she answered only one.

'I think she's got your IQ as well,' she said, and tried to smile.

A long time later, she stood with Jake beside Julia's bed and watched their daughter sleep.

'I have to thank you, Katy,' he said gruffly as they left the room and walked back down the stairs.

'Why?' she asked, heading for the couch where they could sit together. She felt drained by all the emotion of the last twenty-four hours, wanting just to relax and let the tumult in her world die down.

'For not turning her against me,' he said, sitting down beside her and kissing her gently on the cheek. 'What had you told her that she made the leap from accident to father?'

His hand found hers and he held it, lifting it to his lips and kissing her fingers one by one.

'I said you'd been so badly hurt you'd had to go away and learn to walk again.'

She looked at Jake and saw he understood now the depths of the pain she'd endured—understood she hadn't had the courage to cut him out of her life completely, and, most important of all, knew she'd never hated him!

He leant forward and kissed her on the lips.

'I didn't deserve your unselfish kind of love,' he muttered. 'I was too young and full of myself to realise how rare and beautiful it was!' He kissed her again, a silent pledge, then straightened up.

'So, she always thought I might come back?' he asked, and Katy frowned.

'I didn't want her thinking that,' she told him. 'In fact, I tried to make it sound as if you would have if you'd been able but it was impossible.'

'But you didn't let her hate me, Katy!' he said, his voice full of wonder and relief.

'How could I, Jake?' she asked, and this time she turned and kissed him, on the cheek. 'I couldn't have my daughter hating the only man I'd ever loved—ever would love, could love, will love!'

'Are you sure of that, my darling?' he murmured, taking her in his arms and looking down into her eyes. 'Quite, quite sure, my one and only best, best girl?'

She smiled and kissed him again, this time on the lips, then drew back for long enough to say, 'I'm certain!' before she let her lips find his and felt the blood flow swiftly through her veins, carrying sweet messages of love throughout her body.

JANICE KAISER

FAIR GAME

Dana Kirk is a rich and successful woman, but someone
wants to kill her and her teenage daughter. Who hates
her enough to terrorise this single mother? Detective
Mitchell Cross knows she needs help—
his help—to stay alive.

*"...enough plot twists and turns to delight
armchair sleuths"*—Publishers Weekly

1-55166-065-2
AVAILABLE FROM MARCH 1998

Catherine Coulter

Afterglow

Chalk-and-cheese lovers Chelsea Lattimer and
David Winter finally find happiness after a series
of disastrous relationships—thanks to their
match-making friends.

Afterglow is a wonderful romantic comedy from
New York Times bestselling author Catherine Coulter.

1-55166-472-0
AVAILABLE FROM MARCH 1998

JoAnn ROSS

NO REGRETS

Three sisters torn apart by tragedy each choose a
different path—until fate and one man reunites them.
Only when tragedy strikes again can the surviving
sisters allow themselves to choose happiness—
if they dare pay the price.

"A steamy, fast-paced read."
—Publishers Weekly

MIRA®

1-55166-282-5
AVAILABLE FROM FEBRUARY 1998

HEATHER GRAHAM POZZESSERE

If Looks Could Kill

Madison wasn't there when her mother was murdered, but she *saw* it happen. Years later, a killer is stalking women in Miami and Madison's nightmare visions have returned. Can FBI agent Kyle Montgomery catch the serial killer before Madison becomes his next victim?

"...an incredible storyteller!"—LA Daily News

She knew he was going to kiss her...

Her mouth was waiting for him and her eyes were already beginning to close as his lips touched hers. The kiss was hard and sweet, hungry.

'Catherine, Catherine...' Keir covered her face in burning little kisses, before taking her mouth again in a deep, long kiss that made her want more. She found herself straining into him, her hands clinging to his shoulders.

Keir was the sort of man who only happened once in a lifetime. But he had been married and widowed, and the last thing he would be looking for was serious involvement.

So...why had such a man looked at her twice?

Helen Brooks lives in Northamptonshire and is married with three children. As she is a committed Christian, busy housewife and mother, her spare time is at a premium, but her hobbies include reading, swimming, gardening and walking her two energetic, inquisitive and very endearing young dogs. Her long-cherished aspiration to write became a reality when she put pen to paper on reaching the age of forty, and sent the result off to Mills & Boon.

A MAN WORTH WAITING FOR

BY
HELEN BROOKS

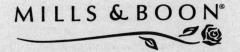

MILLS & BOON®

MILLS & BOON and MILLS & BOON with the Rose Device are registered trademarks of the publisher.

First published in Great Britain 1998
Harlequin Mills & Boon Limited,
Eton House, 18-24 Paradise Road, Richmond, Surrey TW9 1SR

© Helen Brooks 1998

ISBN 0 263 80732 0

Set in Times Roman 10½ on 11 pt.
91-9802-57461 C1

Printed and bound in Great Britain

CHAPTER ONE

'LOOK, tell me to mind my own business if you like, but you look as though you've been in some sort of accident. Do you need help?'

Catherine heard the deep male voice but had difficulty in focusing for a moment as she raised her eyes from the hard wooden bench on which she was sitting, the big figure standing in front of her merely a dark blur. 'I...' Her voice petered out, and she tried again, taking a deep breath and trying to co-ordinate her jumbled thoughts. 'I don't know,' she whispered weakly. 'I do feel strange, but I can't remember... I'm not sure where I am.'

She wasn't making sense—she knew that—but the cotton-wool muzziness in her head and dull throbbing at the back of her eyes were overpoweringly strong.

'You must be going somewhere.' The figure crouched down in front of her, and a pair of keen stone-grey eyes held her frightened blue ones. 'This *is* your suitcase, isn't it?' He patted the big brown case at her feet as he spoke.

'Yes, but...' Again words failed her.

'Are you with anyone?'

'I don't think so.' The drumming in her head intensified as she tried to think. 'No, I'm sure I'm not, but I'll be all right,' she said as firmly as she could. 'I just need to rest a while, that's all.'

He said nothing for a moment, and then, 'You've a nasty cut on your forehead so I guess you've had a bang on the head in the not too distant past. Can you remember if you fell, or were knocked over—anything like that?'

5

'No.' She was beginning to feel frightened, the fuzzy sensation intensifying moment by moment. 'I can't remember anything,' she said a trifle desperately.

'Perhaps your name?' he suggested softly, his deep voice soothing. 'Think a minute; it will come to you.'

She stared at him helplessly as she searched in the fog of her mind, her senses registering, even in the midst of her turmoil, that he was dark and powerfully built, and handsome in a very masculine, intimidating way, with a strongly chiselled bone-structure. Thick black hair cut uncompromisingly short indicated he was a man who had little time for personal vanity, a man who knew who and what he was and exactly where he was going.

'Catherine.' She wasn't sure how she knew, but suddenly the name was there. 'My name's Catherine, and…' Just for a second something flashed across her mind, but before she could catch it it was gone. She rubbed her hand bewilderedly across her forehead and then flinched when it came away sticky and red.

'Well, Catherine, I would say you have a slight case of concussion.' He stood up as he spoke, and for a blindingly frightening moment she thought he was going to walk off and leave her.

She felt as though she had been sitting in the tiny park all her life, helplessly watching the world go by, sights and sounds registering with a strange dream-like quality before becoming merged in an overall blur that she was powerless to alter. 'Concussion?' She forced the word through the thickness in her head. 'But don't you go unconscious with that?'

'Not always.' He surveyed her with narrowed eyes, his hands thrust deep in the pockets of his jeans. 'I'm meeting my sister for lunch shortly, and I think she ought to take a look at you,' he continued firmly. 'She's a nurse so she knows what she's talking about…on medical matters,' he added drily.

'I…I don't know.' Part of her wanted to go with

him—he was the only solid thing in a world that had suddenly become an alien environment—but how did she know she could trust him? she asked herself faintly. In this day and age one didn't wander off into the unknown with a complete stranger.

'It's all right; I'm not a mad rapist or serial killer.' He seemed to know instinctively what she was thinking, and she flushed hotly at the slightly caustic note in the deep voice. 'Neither am I so desperate for female company that I would have to spirit one away against her will,' he added softly.

She could believe that at least. She gazed up at the tall, relaxed frame in front of her on which there wasn't an ounce of superfluous flesh. Oh, yes, she could certainly believe that, she thought again as the mocking, smoky-grey gaze held hers.

'Well?' He eyed her unblinkingly. 'The restaurant is just a stone's throw from here, and I've no intention of leaving you sitting here like a little waif and stray; it would spoil my lunch. I'd prefer you to walk—my carrying you kicking and screaming might damage my reputation somewhat—but either way we're going to get that head looked at. I've a nasty idea it might need a stitch or two.'

'I...I'm sure I'll be all right, thank you.' She wasn't, but she didn't know what frightened her more—the thought of going with him or the thought of him leaving her. 'I can't seem to think straight at the moment, but it will clear...won't it?' she finished somewhat pathetically.

'Come on.' He settled her indecision by the simple expedient of bending down and picking up her suitcase, before raising her firmly to her feet. 'I'm not leaving you here. Everyone has to trust someone some time, and this is your time, like it or not. My name is Keir Durrell by the way; I'm the local vet.'

What was she doing, allowing a complete stranger to

take over like this? The thought was there, but now she was on her feet it was taking all her powers of concentration just to put one foot in front of the other.

She was very aware of the height and breadth of him as he led her from the tiny square of park that was little more than a thoroughfare between the two main roads in the old Yorkshire village. Also that he had an air of command and authority that was entirely natural and very powerful—but her head was pounding unbearably now and lucid thought was not an option.

'The restaurant is just over here.' As they walked through a cobbled market place, its venerable stones ancient and warm under the hot June sun, he indicated a small square building of mellow old bricks. 'Janice should be at our table by now so you'll be quite safe.'

It was said with that same touch of dryness that had been present in his voice before, but she couldn't answer; keeping on her feet was taking everything she'd got, and waves of nausea were making the woolliness worse.

He opened the heavy, squat oak door and ushered her through, his hand at her elbow, and as he did so a tall, dark-haired girl half rose and waved in their direction from the back of the room. 'Keir? Over here.'

Catherine was overwhelmingly thankful to be able to sink into a seat, closing her eyes as she fought back the sickness. She could hear Keir at the side of her, and the general hum of lunchtime conversation and clinking of glasses, but it was remote, unreal, like a half-remembered dream in the first moments of waking.

'Catherine?' A light touch on her arm brought her eyes open, and she saw Keir's sister had moved her chair to her side. 'I think you've been involved in an accident of some kind. Would you mind if we had a look through your handbag to see if we can find a name and address or something? It might jog your memory. And I really think we ought to take you to the local hospital and get someone to have a look at your head; it's a nasty cut.'

'Here.' Catherine moved the bag off her shoulder and onto the table as the room spun. 'Please look.'

'Catherine Prentice—does that ring a bell?' Keir asked a few moments later as he fetched out an envelope from the depths of her cloth bag.

'Yes.' Catherine tried to focus on the hard male face, but it was difficult. 'Yes, that's me.' She could hear her voice from a great distance, the sound echoing in her mind.

'Okay, I think we'd better get you to a doctor right now,' Keir said grimly as she swayed in her seat. 'And stay still; I'm going to carry you.'

It was the last thing she heard before a thick, consuming darkness took over and drew her into its black void, and then she was falling, falling, the pain in her head overpowering.

'Catherine?' She could hear someone speaking her name, and struggled to respond, forcing her eyes open and then shutting them immediately as a bright light sent sharp jabs of pain stabbing through her head. 'I'm going to give you a little injection,' the voice continued in the sort of tone one normally used with very small children. 'And then you can sleep again, all right? Just relax; that's it.'

She felt a pinprick in her arm but didn't attempt to open her eyes, sinking gratefully back into the layers of darkness, and down, down, down to the peace and tranquillity of oblivion.

The next time she surfaced all was quiet and still, and as she opened tired eyes there was none of the bright light of before, just a soft and comforting semi-darkness that bathed her senses in a feeling of restfulness. She made a slight movement and immediately a figure at her side stirred, followed by the same voice as before, saying, 'You're awake, dear; that's good. Would you like a little sip of water?'

'Where...?' Her tongue seemed too big for her mouth, but she forced the words out after licking her lips. 'Where am I?'

'You're in hospital, dear.' A motherly, middle-aged face bent over her, grey hair shining in the muted light. 'You had a little bang on the head, remember?'

'Keir.'

'That's right, dear.' From the soothing note in her voice it was clear the nurse didn't have the faintest idea what she, Catherine, was talking about, Catherine thought tiredly, but she just as clearly wasn't going to challenge her on anything right now. 'Now, you shut your eyes and sleep a little more; you're over the worst now. I'm sure you'll be as right as rain in the morning. There's a bell by your hand—' Catherine felt the fingers of her right hand pressed on something hard '—so if you need anything you just ring and we'll be here straight away, all right?'

She wanted to say more, ask questions, but it was all too much effort. And as the thick blanket of sleep claimed her again she was aware of murmuring that name once more before she allowed herself to slip into the warm darkness.

'Cup of tea here for you.'

The clatter of crockery and the cheerful voice in her ear brought Catherine's eyes wide open at the same time as someone opened a blind, sending white sunlight spilling into the small room.

'Oh, thank you.' She struggled into a sitting position in the narrow hospital bed, and took the cup of tea one of the two orderlies handed her, relieved to find the terrible headache was a thing of the past. 'I must have slept the night through,' she said tentatively as the two young women smiled at her encouragingly.

'You've been asleep ever since they brought you in, love,' one of them responded buoyantly. 'Best thing for concussion. How you feelin' this mornin', then?'

'Better, much better,' she said weakly.

'That's right.' They nodded at her reassuringly.

'Had an accident, did you?' one asked brightly.

'An accident?' And then she remembered, with a rush of thankfulness that her mind was her own again. 'Yes—yes, I did. Just after I left the train station, I fell down some steps.' She stared at the two women as her mind replayed the scene. 'Someone had spilt something, and I slipped and hit my head on the edge of one of the steps,' she said slowly. 'I think I cut it.'

'You certainly did, love. Bruised yourself a bit too, I'd say. Still, all's well that ends well, eh? Lucky someone had the sense to bring you here—you could have wandered about for ages in the state you were in, and although most folks round here are okay you never know these days. Anyway, you enjoy a nice cup of tea and we'll be back with your breakfast a bit later, all right?'

'Thank you.' She smiled somewhat bemusedly, and they beamed back.

She spent the rest of the morning dozing in between having her temperature and pulse checked every half hour, and answering a whole host of questions that a brisk and very efficient sister read to her from an official-looking form.

'It's good to see you so alert,' the sister said as she stood up to leave. 'We thought it was a simple case of concussion but you seemed absolutely exhausted, which didn't help. Have you been ill recently?'

'Yes.' There was no way she was going to elaborate further, and she added quickly, 'Pneumonia. But I'm better now. I actually came to Yorkshire for a few weeks' holiday. I thought the air here would be more bracing than London's city fumes.'

'I can guarantee it.' The sister smiled approvingly.

'Well, you rest now; the doctor will be round shortly, and we'll see what he thinks of you.'

It was just after lunch when the knock sounded at her door and she sat up expectantly, thinking it was the doctor or one of his minions. But the tall, dark man who entered the room was definitely neither. 'Catherine.' It was the deep, slightly husky voice she remembered, the voice that had haunted her dreams for the last few hours. 'How are you feeling?'

'Fine.' The ugly hospital nightgown put her at a distinct disadvantage, she thought weakly, as did her pale face devoid of even a scrap of make-up, and the massive bruise that covered half of her forehead. *And he was so gorgeous.* Even yesterday, in a state of semi-consciousness, her senses had registered he was something of a hunk. But seeing him today, with mind and intellect working on full throttle, the impact of that big, lean body and devastatingly male face increased a hundredfold.

He was deeply tanned, his hair blue-black and gleaming, with a virility even the severe hairstyle couldn't diminish. And, although the handsome, classical features and hard bone-structure would demand a second glance from any female from sixteen to sixty, there was something more to him than just good looks. He had an assurance, a cool confidence that added an extra dimension to the arrogant maleness, and was powerfully attractive.

'You don't remember me?' he asked quietly. 'My name is Keir—Keir Durrell. My sister and I brought you to this hospital late yesterday morning.'

'Oh, yes, yes, I remember.' She was inexpressibly thankful he had mistaken her wide-eyed stare for confusion. She couldn't remember a time when she had ever ogled a man so blatantly, and the knowledge brought hot colour sweeping into her face. It was the knock on the head, she told herself desperately; that was what it was. She wasn't quite as well as she'd thought. 'I... Thank you—thank you so much,' she added stumblingly. 'It was very good of you—'

He swept her thanks aside with an abrupt wave of his hand. 'Anyone would have done the same,' he said dismissively. 'I just happened along, that's all. So, the memory is back, is it? That's good. The sister tells me you have a recollection of falling down some steps.'

'Yes, outside the station.' She had never felt so tongue-tied in her life, and forced a smile she hoped came across as natural before continuing, 'Silly, wasn't it? I should have been more careful—'

'What are your parents doing, letting you wander about the country on your own?'

'What?' She stared at him in amazement.

His tone had been curt, and now she was sure the dark glitter at the back of the stone-grey eyes was tightly held-in disapproval. This seemed to be confirmed when he said again, his voice cold, 'I asked you what your parents were thinking of to let you wander about alone.'

'I'm not wandering about.' Her chin rose a notch, and now the colour staining her pale, creamy skin was due to annoyance rather than embarrassment. 'And I answer to myself, no one else.'

'Do you indeed?' He came fully into the room now, walking over to the bed and looking down at her with narrowed eyes, his whole stance one of irritation and censure. 'And exactly how old are you, Miss Catherine Prentice? Fifteen, sixteen? And I want the truth, mind,' he added warningly. 'If you've run away from home now is the time to confess it.'

'If I've…?' She stared at him in absolute amazement, her anger wiping away any feeling of intimidation and putting fire in her violet-blue eyes as she hissed, 'I am twenty-one years of age. *Twenty one*, got it?'

'I don't believe you,' he said flatly, his gaze moving over the ethereal slimness of her, the fine-boned hands and pale, silvery blonde hair that framed the small face. 'You aren't a day over sixteen. Now, then, admit it.'

'I... How dare you?' All her life she had been dogged by looking far younger than her age, and normally she could take it quite well. But for him to think she was a *schoolgirl*...

Her spluttering was brought to a halt as he said, coolly and without the slightest shred of doubt, 'And a show of outrage won't wash either. If you're as old as you say you are I assume you can prove it?'

'*Prove it?*' Her voice was too high, and she lowered it a tone as he winced. 'I shouldn't have to prove it, but yes, I can,' she shot back furiously. 'Pass me my bag, would you? It's by the chair.'

'Certainly.'

He still thought she was trying to bluff him, she thought with a mixture of fury and wonder as he bent down with a lazy assurance and picked up her big, baggy cloth bag from the floor, dropping it onto the bed without a change of expression, and continuing to watch her with narrowed, hooded eyes while she rummaged about in the cavernous depths. 'Driving licence do?' she asked caustically as she fished it out from the back of her large leather purse and presented it to him with a flourish.

'Driving licence?' For the first time a touch of uncertainty showed.

'It's a document that entitles one to drive a car,' she said bitingly, 'and I've had one for nearly four years, okay?' Her headache was beginning to return, and it was all his fault! 'I'm not a runaway, or anything else you might have dreamed up,' she added tightly. 'I'm here... I'm here on holiday.' Well, she was...in a way, she told the sudden, sharp jab of conscience.

'I see.' He eyed her again after studying the driving licence. 'Then it would appear I have made a mistake; I apologise. If you would like to give me the telephone number or address of where you're staying I'll explain the circumstances of you being a day late to them, and ask them to hold your accommodation.'

'That won't be necessary.' He knew, he just *knew* she hadn't booked anything, she told herself irritably. She could see it in the hard, arrogant face and alert eyes. 'I haven't actually arranged anything yet,' she continued tightly. 'I thought I'd sort it out when I got here.'

'Did you?' It was said in the sort of patient tone one used when dealing with a recalcitrant child who was being ridiculous. 'Towerby isn't a bad size for a Yorkshire village,' he said smoothly, 'but in the middle of the holiday season, and when the weather has been good for weeks, a bed for the night isn't always on tap. However, there are plenty of other villages and towns dotted about—'

'I wanted to stay in Towerby,' she interrupted firmly. 'I'll try there first.'

'Why Towerby? One Yorkshire village is very much like another—'

'Nevertheless, I'll try there first,' she said tightly.

'Persistent little thing, aren't you?' he drawled easily, his eyes on her strained face. 'Are you always so determined?'

She shrugged warily; it hadn't been a compliment, but she was blowed if she was going to explain why Towerby was so important to her, especially to him. And she had thought she *liked* him...

'Be it on your own head.' He glanced at her hair as he spoke, its pale silveriness almost luminescent in the light from the window. 'But you could be walking the streets for hours,' he warned quietly.

'I don't care.'

She looked about twelve, sitting there in that horror of a nightie with her hair all tousled and her eyes flashing, never mind sixteen, Keir thought grimly. The urge to shake some sense into her was paramount. She was going to leave this place and tramp about Towerby look-

ing for somewhere to stay? The girl was brain-damaged!
How she'd got to twenty-one years of age was a miracle
in itself.

'I'd better be going; I'm on my way to a farm the
other side of Kilburn, but I had to pass here and I
thought I'd call in and see how you were.' He kept his
voice quite expressionless. 'I'll call by later this afternoon on my way back, if I may?'

'I might be gone by then,' she said carefully, 'but
thank you again for all your help. Thank your sister for
me too, would you?'

She thought she'd hit the right note of polite dismiss-
iveness until she glanced into his face and saw the sardonic gleam in the stony eyes. 'Don't like to be told
you're acting like a fool, do you?' he murmured with a
calmness that was more aggravating than any show of
annoyance as he walked towards the door. Once there,
he turned to survey her once more, and added before she
had a chance to speak, 'Goodbye, Catherine.'

And then she was alone again and calling herself
every sort of name for not firing back with some cutting
retort that would have put him in his place... whatever
that was, she thought bitterly. She had met some arrogant, self-opinionated men in her time—London was full
of them—but he took the biscuit; he really did.

Her thoughts continued to run along the same lines as
she replayed their conversation over and over in her
mind, getting angrier by the minute, until, when the doctor finally arrived, her cheeks were burning, her pulse
racing, and her temperature was a couple of degrees
above normal.

'I definitely want you here for another night of observation,' the doctor said when she asked him how soon
she could leave. 'That was a nasty bang on the head,
young lady, and you were pretty much out of it when
you got here. I understand you're on holiday?' She nod-

ded without speaking. 'Where are you staying?' he asked quietly.

Oh, no, not another one. She took a deep breath before saying, 'I haven't actually arranged anything yet.'

'I see.' The doctor was about thirty years older than Keir, but his face portrayed the same disapproval when he said, 'You think that was wise? I understand you don't have transport.'

'No—no, I don't,' she admitted tightly.

'And Sister tells me you've been ill recently—pneumonia. Was that all it was?' he asked intuitively.

'I don't understand what you mean,' she prevaricated quickly, flushing hotly as she stared back into the wise old eyes.

'I think you do.' His voice was gentle, but possessed of a firmness that told her he was prepared to dig for the truth. 'The concussion in itself wasn't too serious, but the way your body reacted to it suggested complete exhaustion of body and mind. Have you had some sort of a breakdown?' he asked with a directness that took her by surprise.

'I...no...yes—' She stopped abruptly. 'Not exactly,' she said after taking a deep, calming breath. 'I *was* ill for a time with pneumonia after a severe attack of flu, and then I had some bad news.' She gulped hard before she continued, 'I hadn't really recovered physically, and I found I couldn't cope too well for a time, but it wasn't as serious as a breakdown; nothing as definite as that.'

'I see.' He hadn't taken his eyes off her as she had spoken. 'Well, a holiday is probably just what the doctor ordered,' he said with a warm smile that completely belied the somewhat austere image. 'But it will have to begin tomorrow, if you are well enough to leave then. And we will have to do something about arranging accommodation, Miss Prentice. You are probably going to feel a bit shaky for a couple of days, and I really couldn't

countenance you roaming the streets looking for somewhere to stay.'

'Right.' She suddenly didn't feel like arguing. In fact
all she wanted to do was to lie back among the covers
and go to sleep.

However, once the doctor had left she found her mind
was too active for sleep, and she lay curled up in a tight
little ball under the thin sheet, staring at the tree-tops
through the window, the June sky clear and vividly blue
and devoid of even the merest wisp of a cloud.

The last few months had been hard... She closed her
eyes and drew her knees up to her waist, clasping her
legs under the thin white sheet as she lay hunched in the
bed. So hard. Why had everything happened to her? It
wasn't her fault, none of it, and yet she was the one who
felt lost, alone, abandoned. Here she was, twenty-one
years old and supposedly grown up, but she didn't know
who she was, and she certainly wasn't the person she
had thought she was all her life. And no one, *no one*
cared...

'Oh, God, help me.' It was a prayer she had whispered
almost every day over the last few months as she had
sought to draw on a power outside herself to get through.

She had always been conscious of the fact that she
was unloved and unlovable, she thought now as she
opened her eyes and stared blindly across the room. Her
parents were not demonstrative people—even with each
other—but nevertheless displayed some sort of affection
towards her brother and sister that was totally absent in
their dealings with her.

When she was younger she had occasionally made the
odd outrageous bid for their approval, but in time, as the
long, lonely years of her childhood had come and gone,
she had faced the fact that they simply did not like her.

She had wondered at times if her appearance was the
cause of their dislike—her brother and sister were tall
and dark like their parents, with brown eyes and unpre-

possessing features, and Catherine's tiny build and ethereal fairness was a stark reminder that she was different,
the cuckoo in the nest.

Why hadn't they *told* her when she was a child? she
asked herself for what was probably the hundredth time
as the memory of that night four months ago swept in
with searing clarity.

She had been working hard the preceding months,
holding down a demanding job as secretary to a sales
executive in a busy London office, and attending night
school four evenings a week in order to obtain the further qualifications needed if she was going to advance
up the career ladder. Her delight in hearing she had ob-
tained excellent grades on the course had been damp-
ened by a vicious attack of flu, which had resulted in
complications and an admission to hospital for three
weeks with pneumonia and pleurisy.

She had returned home low in both body and spirit,
and with the bitter knowledge that not one of the family
had visited her in hospital. If it hadn't been for the loyalty of her friends and workmates she would have been
quite alone.

It was that same evening the row between herself and
her mother had begun, soon to flare into a bitter
exchange that had devastating consequences.

'Don't "Mother" me!' The words were spat into her
white face, her mother confronting her with hands
clenched into tight fists at her sides. She had bent her
body at such an angle that she appeared for all the world
like an enormous bird preparing to peck at the ground.
'There is no blood of mine running in your holier-
than-thou veins, I can tell you. You dare to judge me
because I haven't danced attendance on you the last
three weeks? Why should I? *Why should I?*'

'What do you mean, there's no blood of yours in me?'
Catherine had been sitting hunched over the small fire
in the pristine-clean, cold little lounge, but now she rose

sharply, her eyes narrowing. Her mother continued glaring at her without speaking, her sallow skin turkey-red, and when it was apparent she wasn't going to reply Catherine turned to her father who was standing in the doorway. 'What does she mean?'

'Why can't you keep your big mouth shut?' Her father flashed an angry glance at his wife before turning to Catherine. 'Ignore her; forget it,' he muttered irritably.

'Tell her, George—go on, tell her.' Her husband's censure seemed to tip the other woman over the edge. 'She's twenty-one in a week or so's time; she'll find out one day so it might as well be now. Tell her what she is, where she came from.'

'You tell her—I want nothing to do with this.' His face was now as red as his wife's. 'I said all along it was daft to take her on, and dafter still not to tell her. You're the one who's always had the answers—you tell her!' So saying, he stomped off, slamming the door violently behind him.

'You aren't our child, girl.' Her mother's voice—or the voice of the woman she had thought of as a mother all her life—was merciless. 'We adopted you when you were a baby because we thought we couldn't have kids of our own. You're my sister's child.'

'I don't believe you.' Catherine stared at the other woman even as a tiny segment of her brain acknowledged this was the answer to the questions that had haunted her for years. 'You've always said you have no family, that when your parents died—'

'*I know what I said.*' The plain, middle-aged face was pinched with spite. 'But I'm telling you now it wasn't true, all right? When my sister was seventeen, she got engaged to a boy who turned out to be a real bad lot.'

'She was my parents' darling, spoiled rotten from when she was born.' The words were little more than a snarl. 'She couldn't believe it when she got pregnant and he upped and left her; she thought everyone would always dance to her tune.' There was a throb in her mother's voice that went far beyond maliciousness. 'After you were born she had no money and no job, and she wanted to get rid of you.'

She was enjoying this, Catherine thought numbly as she stared into the beady brown eyes; she was actually *enjoying* it.

'She was going to put you up for adoption when she was still in the hospital, so George and I decided we'd have you. It seemed like a good idea at the time.'

'Then you're my aunt?' Catherine asked dazedly. 'Is that what you're saying?'

'No, I told you, you're nothing to do with me.' The other woman sucked in her thin cheeks as she contemplated the small, pale girl in front of her, and there wasn't a shred of compassion or pity in her face or voice as she continued. 'I was adopted myself, you see, for the same reason George and I took you on. But then your mother arrived seven years later and from that moment I might as well not have existed. Everything was given to Anna—new clothes, toys—she only had to ask for something and she got it.'

'And you hated her,' Catherine said flatly, her body shrinking away from the venom in the face in front of her.

'Yes, I hated her.' She was spitting out the words now, a deep bitterness grooving the lines more markedly round her eyes and mouth. 'She was beautiful, very beautiful, something my parents never let me forget for a minute. It was all Anna this, and Anna that—'

'Then why did you help her?' Catherine asked bewilderedly. 'If you hated her so much why did you take me?'

The older woman's eyes flickered and then fell from hers as she turned and walked over to the narrow window at the far end of the room, her back stiff and straight. 'Because it suited us,' she said tightly without turning round. 'You have had a roof over your head for the last twenty-one years, haven't you? I can't see you've got anything to complain about. You're lucky—luckier than most in your position.'

Her voice rose as she turned to face Catherine, her eyes narrowed and gimlet-hard. 'That's what my parents told me,' she bit out through thin lips, 'every time they pushed me away or took Anna out without me. I had to be grateful, understand my position. Well—so do you.'

And then Catherine understood. This woman was so caught up with resentment and bitterness that she had taken her sister's baby in order to work some twisted idea of vengeance on her, to make Anna's child pay for all the misery she felt she had suffered in the past. That was why Catherine had always been brushed aside, shown no physical love or affection, ostracised in her own home.

And circumstances had played right into her adoptive mother's hands by presenting her with two children of her own. That really must have seemed like the icing on the cake, Catherine thought numbly. The whole exercise had been a cold-blooded plan of revenge. How could someone be like this? She stared at the woman she had always called mother as shock and horror kept her dumb.

'Well? Cat got your tongue?' the vicious voice continued.

'My real mother?' Catherine asked dazedly. 'Where is she?'

'I don't know and I don't care,' the other woman answered sharply. 'She moved away from London once the formalities were completed, and we've never seen her since. Good riddance to bad rubbish—'

'Where did she go?' Catherine asked again. 'I know you know; I can see it in your eyes.'

'Oh, can you, little Miss Clever-Pants?' The mockery was callous and fierce. 'Such a bright little thing, aren't you? Just like your mother. She was always top of the class at everything, always the best, but she got her comeuppance just like you'll get yours.'

'Where did she go?' Catherine persisted weakly. The malevolence was frightening.

'Yorkshire—a little place called Towerby—but that was nigh on twenty-one years ago.' The thin shoulders shrugged tauntingly. 'She'll be long since gone if I know anything about Anna.'

Catherine stumbled from the room then, her head feeling as though it would explode, and cried for hours in the questionable comfort of the tiny box-room she called her bedroom. She didn't sleep that night, the searing misery that was ripping her apart unbearable, but by the time the first tentative pink fingers of dawn were stealing across the night sky she had come to several irrevocable decisions.

As soon as she was well enough she would leave this house and never come back. And she would find her mother, her real mother. And when she did…she would ask her how she could possibly have abandoned her baby into the care of someone so cruel and twisted, so *wicked*, and she would make her listen to the life she had endured at the hands of her adoptive family.

And then… She gazed unseeingly at the charcoal-streaked sky, her eyes dry now and burningly bright. And then she would tell her that she hated her, that she would never forgive her, that as far as she was concerned she had no mother, and she would walk away without a backward glance. *She would.*

CHAPTER TWO

'IN A better mood now?'

The deep, cool voice brought her head jerking upright. She had been engrossed in her thoughts and hadn't heard the door open, but now she saw Keir framed in the doorway, his dark face unreadable. 'I wasn't... I'm not... What are you doing back here?' she asked tightly. 'I thought you'd got a farm to go to?'

'I have.' He eyed her sardonically. 'And please try to restrain your enthusiasm at my presence, it's quite embarrassing.'

The none too subtle reminder that she was being exceptionally rude brought hot colour into her cheeks, but in the next moment he stepped into the room again, speaking in a lazy, relaxed manner that nevertheless grated on her overwrought nerves.

'I thought I'd make a few enquiries regarding accommodation before I left,' he said easily. 'See if anything was available. So I phoned all the possibilities in Towerby.'

'Yes?' Say something, say you're grateful, thank him, *something*, she told herself desperately, but her mind seemed to have totally seized up.

'And there's nothing.' He came to a halt by the bed and reached out for the straight-backed chair at the side of it, hooking it with two fingers and swinging it round so that the back was against his stomach as he sat astride it, his face on a level with hers. 'Zilch.'

'Oh.' Why hadn't she brushed her hair, put on one of her own nighties from her suitcase in the corner of the room, since he'd been gone? she asked herself weakly.

24

She must resemble something even the cat wouldn't drag in.

'So I had a little word with Janice and we've got a proposition for you,' Keir continued smoothly. 'Something for you to think about over the next twenty-four hours.'

'Oh, yes?' Say something other than 'oh' or 'yes', please; you're not stupid, you're quite intelligent—and you certainly aren't the silly little schoolgirl he took you for either, she told herself helplessly.

'Well, in a nutshell, you're looking for a place to stay for a couple of weeks, and we happen to have a spare room that's recently been vacated by the veterinary student who's been staying with us for the past twelve months,' Keir said quietly. 'If you've really set your heart on a holiday in Towerby, it would seem the ideal solution, yes?' The grey eyes were narrowed and piercingly intent on her face. 'But think about it. You might decide somewhere else would do just as well—here in Compton, perhaps.'

'Oh, I couldn't impose—'

'Think about it.' He interrupted her hot-faced mumbling with a cool-eyed nod, his voice brisk and devoid of expression. 'The doctor tells me you're here for another twenty-four hours at least. There's no rush; the room's not going anywhere.'

'Keir—'

'And now I've really got to go.' He stood up, looking very masculine in black denim jeans and a denim shirt that was unbuttoned at the neck, showing just a smidgen of dark, curling body hair that drew her eyes like a magnet.

Help... The thought was there, but what exactly the silent cry meant she wasn't sure.

'I'll call by later, okay?' He didn't wait for an answer, walking to the door and then turning to survey her with smoky-grey eyes. 'And sleep the afternoon away; you look as though you need it.'

Charming, absolutely charming! The door had already shut as the import of his words hit home. And he thought she'd take any favours from him? She'd rather die first. She sprang out of bed as though on a spring, and then had to wait for her head to catch up with the rest of her as the room swam and dipped.

She had never met such an infuriating, arrogant know-it-all in her life, she thought caustically as she padded to the loo and back, her legs feeling as though they belonged to someone else. Not that her knowledge of men was particularly profound, she acknowledged wryly as she climbed gratefully back into bed and waited for her heart to stop pounding.

She had had the odd boyfriend since leaving school, but nothing serious. This was partly due to her parents making it clear her friends were not welcome at the house, but also because she hadn't met anyone who had remotely stirred her interest beyond platonic friendship, and her job combined with her college course had left little time for fun.

All work and no play... Was she dull? She twisted restlessly in the bed as the thought hit home. Oh, what did it matter? What did anything matter but finding her mother, the person who had betrayed her so heartlessly? All the rest was dross, nothing. She turned over, burying her face in the pillow as the tears flowed, hot and acidic.

The afternoon passed slowly, very slowly. She spent most of the time gazing out of the window at the view stretching away in front of her. The hospital was built in a wonderful position on an incline overlooking an old Yorkshire town of craggy grey stone, and with rich, swelling moorland behind it that carried the scent of a thousand summer flowers. One of the nurses had told her the hospital serviced all the villages hereabouts, including Towerby, which was some miles away over the fells.

There was a winding river in the distance, meandering its way through tranquil countryside dotted with grazing sheep, and on the far horizon what looked like the ancient remains of an old castle, crumbling now after years of relentless attack by the elements.

It was peaceful. She continued to gaze out of the window as her thoughts moved on. Peace was what she so desperately craved at the moment. Would she ever feel happy again? She shook her head slowly. Had she ever really felt happy in the first place? She couldn't remember a time when she hadn't been aware that something was missing, and that she was searching, searching for something that always just eluded her.

But now an inner certainty told her this was her time to be strong and follow the desires of her heart, wherever they led her and whatever heartache ensued. She *had* to find her mother—it wasn't a whim, it was an overwhelming conviction that seemed to come from something or someone outside herself and grew stronger every day.

She was lying in bed idly flicking through a magazine one of the orderlies had brought in when Keir returned later that evening. This time he had Janice with him.

'Hi there.' Janice bustled into the room in a flurry of starched uniform and neat black shoes, her hair pulled into a severe knot at the back of her head and her pretty face preoccupied. 'I can't stop—I'm late already and Sister'll kill me—but I just wanted to see how you are and say you're more than welcome to stay with us, you know. It'd be great to have another woman about the place, actually.'

'It's very kind of you, but I couldn't, really. It's not your fault I didn't have the sense to book something before I came.' It was easier to admit she'd been wrong to Janice, much easier. But she was aware of Keir on the perimeter of her vision as she concentrated on the other woman, and didn't dare turn her gaze on the figure leaning nonchalantly against the far wall. 'I don't want to interfere with your lives—'

'Don't be so silly; there's no question of that.'

Janice smiled sunnily, her grey eyes—which were a softer hue than her brother's—dancing as she surveyed the pale, slim girl in the bed, and her mouth turned up at the corners, revealing pearly white teeth. Catherine found herself wondering what their parents looked like to have produced two such exceptionally good-looking children, and her thoughts prompted her to say, 'But your parents—wouldn't they mind a total stranger suddenly invading their home?'

'The aged ones don't live with us,' Janice returned cheerfully. 'But I'll leave Keir to explain about that. I really must dash; I'm on nights on the men's surgical ward this week and they always keep us on our toes. Men are such babies, aren't they?'

She swung round and was out of the door while a goodbye was still on Catherine's lips. At his sister's exit Keir levered himself off the wall and walked lazily to her side, hooking the chair as he'd done before and sitting astride it before he spoke. 'Convinced?' he asked drily.

'What about?' She knew of course, but needed the time the prevarication bought.

'That the room is going begging and you're more than welcome to use it,' Keir said easily. He'd changed since lunchtime; now the tall, lean body was encased in loose grey cotton trousers and a thin charcoal shirt that made the broad shoulders seem even broader in the small white room. 'I tend to work all hours—vets do,' he added wryly. 'And Janice normally sleeps when she's not working or out with her fiancé. You could have a key and do your own thing.'

'And your parents?' she asked bemusedly, her senses registering the faint but delicious smell of aftershave and the sheer *power* of him in a way she could well have done without.

'They live down south—Cornwall to be exact; they moved there two years ago,' he said quietly. 'My mother came from Bude originally so there are still plenty of relations in that neck of the woods, and for years my father has suffered with arthritis which has been getting progressively worse. The doctor thought the milder climate would help him; the winters are pretty rough here, and very cold.'

'Has the move helped him?' she asked carefully when he paused a moment.

'On the whole, yes.' He smiled slowly and her heart stopped beating, and then raced at a furious pace at the transformation of the handsome and very male face, at the way his features mellowed and softened. 'He's still as irascible as ever. He drives my mother to distraction half the time, but they are quite devoted to each other.'

'Are they?' The words produced a dart of such painful longing that she changed the subject quickly. 'So are you and Janice in the old family home?' she asked quietly.

'No, that was sold to buy the property down south. But I had already taken on the veterinary practice in Towerby some months before when the old vet retired, and was living in the flat above the surgery premises. Janice and I decided it was logical for her to move in—she was in the midst of her training, added to which she had just decided Michael was the one for her and didn't want to leave Yorkshire.' He shrugged easily, the big shoulders bunching under the thin material.

'The flat's a decent size. It has three bedrooms and a kitchen and lounge so we're not on top of each other at all. Janice finished her training twelve months ago and secured a job here, and the practice has come on in leaps and bounds, so there's no reason for anything to change until she marries Michael.'

'You seem very sure of what you want.'

It was unreasonable, but his confidence and cool self-possession grated on her. Something of what she was feeling must have come over in her voice, because his face was straight when he replied, 'And that's a bad thing?'

'I didn't say that.'

'You didn't have to.' He eyed her grimly for a moment. 'You don't like me much, do you, Catherine?' he asked in a deceptively soft voice that masked the portent of his words for a second.

'I...that's ridiculous; I don't know you.' She knew her face was flaming—she could feel the heat burning her cheeks—but she had never felt so embarrassed in all her life. He had rescued her when she was ill—behaved like the original white knight in shining armour, if she thought about it—and then offered her the use of a room in his home, and all she had done was to act as though he were the Marquis de Sade personified, she thought, horror-stricken.

But he was right...in a way, although she wasn't sure if she actually *disliked* him. It was more...he disturbed her, unsettled her, she thought weakly. He was too determined, too virile, too...male.

'No, that's true, you don't know me,' he said quietly, standing up as he spoke, and looking down at her with that intent, perturbing directness she had noticed more than once. 'And I've an idea you intend to keep it that way—or are you going to accept the offer of a bed for a few nights until you can find something else?'

Put like that it sounded so reasonable, so practical, that she really couldn't think of a reason to refuse. Besides which, he had made it clear that to say no would be churlish in the extreme. But she didn't *want* to form any link, however tenuous, with Keir Durrell, so it was with some amazement that she heard herself saying, 'Thank you, that's very nice of you. I'll find somewhere elsc as soon as I can...so you can have your home back to yourselves,' she added hastily as the dark eyebrows rose sardonically.

'Of course.' His voice was very dry, and her cheeks burnt even hotter, if that was possible, as he walked over to the door and turned to survey her with that devastating grey gaze. 'I'll ring the hospital tomorrow morning and see if you are going to be able to leave,' he said quietly with very little expression in his deep voice. 'And if so I'll pop across and fetch you after morning surgery.'

'There's no need for that,' she said quickly. 'I can get a bus or a taxi; I'm used to looking after myself.'

'Nevertheless...' He opened the door and glanced across once more. 'I'll fetch you.'

'I don't want—' But he had gone, the door swinging shut behind him and cutting off her voice as she stared exasperatedly across the room, already bitterly regretting her decision, but without really knowing why.

The sun was sailing high in a cloudless blue sky when Keir arrived just after lunch the next day, striding into the quiet little hospital room with the force and energy that were an intrinsic part of the man, and dispelling the hushed hospital atmosphere as he did so.

Catherine was feeling incredibly nervous, and furious with herself for allowing her nerves to be so affected, so her smile was a little strained as she looked up from the book she had been trying to read for the last half hour.

'All ready?'

Tell him—tell him you aren't coming, that you've changed your mind, that you'll be quite happy staying somewhere other than Towerby, she told herself fiercely. She'd been rehearsing a little speech while she'd been pretending to read, but somehow, with Keir Durrell very much in the flesh in front of her, words failed her. In fact—and the knowledge was galling, incredibly galling—she didn't dare.

With his earlier comments in mind, she had dressed simply but not too casually, knowing that the jeans and big baggy tops she usually favoured enhanced the impression of a young schoolgirl. Her tailored trousers and close-fitting waist-length blouse in soft blue were quite elegant, and with her hair in a loose knot on the top of her head and a careful application of light make-up she felt she could pass for at least eighteen, if not her true age. Anyway, she felt more in control like this, she reminded herself firmly, and she had an idea that wouldn't be a bad thing around Keir Durrell.

'This is really very good of you.' She found she was practically trotting at his side in an effort to keep up with his long strides as they walked out of the hospital and into the hot car park. 'I'm sure I'll get something else in a few days and be out of your hair—'

'Catherine.' He stopped abruptly, putting down her suitcase and turning to take her arms in his hands as he faced her, his deep voice holding a dark quality that silenced her more effectively than any show of annoyance would have done. 'The room is yours while you stay in Towerby, all right? Just let it drop now.'

'I was only saying—'

'I know what you were saying, and *I* said let it drop.' She was like a wisp of thistledown in his hold, he thought as his stomach muscles tightened at the contact—so fragile, a breath of wind could blow her away. 'The room is there; it's ridiculous for you to pay for something else.'

'But I must pay you.' She stared at him, aghast. 'I can't possibly—'

'You can possibly.' His eyes were narrowed against the piercing white sunlight, his jet-black hair and the vivid whiteness of his shirt a startling monochrome against the different shades of green in the view spread out before them. Again something gripped her heart, causing her to jerk from his hold with more haste than finesse.

'I'm here on holiday,' she said stiffly. 'I expect to pay for my accommodation.'

'Then it can be in kind.' His voice was flat and without expression, but she knew her reaction had registered from the grimness of his face. 'The phone rings incessantly, especially in out-of-surgery hours and in the evenings; it would be a great help to have another pair of hands to answer it and take messages, especially if I've been called out already and the matter is urgent and I need notifying. And there are other little things that will become apparent. Not that any of this would be expected of you.' He let go of her now, walking over to a smart Land Rover and opening the passenger door for her to climb in. 'But if you happened to be around and could help it would be appreciated. So, quits, eh?'

'But it doesn't seem fair,' she protested once he had shut her door and joined her in the Land Rover, his big body and long legs suiting the large vehicle. 'You don't really benefit from the arrangement.'

'And you think the only reason we should do something is if we personally benefit from it?' he asked smoothly, making no effort to start the Land Rover as he turned sideways in his seat to face her, his dark face expressionless, and one arm on the back of her seat.

'No, no, of course I don't,' she said sharply. 'That's not what I meant.'

'What *did* you mean, Catherine?' The deep voice was still cool, with a thread of steel underlying the silkiness.

'Just... Oh, it doesn't matter.' She raised her head slightly and stared at him out of big violet eyes, her whole body language expressing the fact that her defences were up and remaining up.

'Have you contacted your family since you've been

in hospital? Presuming you have a family, that is.' It was straight for the jugular, and she flushed violently before tearing her eyes away from his to look out of the window. This man was too perceptive by half, she thought painfully. He knew there was something wrong and he was digging, but she'd rather die than reveal her past to him.

'No.' She thought briefly about lying, but decided she would set the record straight now; it would stop any pertinent questioning in the days ahead—hopefully. 'My family aren't interested in what I do or where I am,' she said tightly.

'You don't live with them?' he asked softly, his eyes on her pale profile as she stared through the windscreen.

'No.' The memory of that last, bitter farewell was hot and caustic in her mind; the savagery in the eyes of the woman she had called mother had been frightening as she had screamed her venom into Catherine's face. She had been living on a powder keg of hate all her life without knowing it; how could she have been so *blind*? she asked herself for the hundredth time. And the man she had known as a father had made no effort to stop his wife as she had hurled abuse at Catherine, and her brother and sister had seemed to actually enjoy the scene. And she had thought they were her *family*.

'No, I've a flat in London,' she said quietly as she dragged her mind back from the degradation and pain. 'With some friends.' She hadn't, but she balked at admitting she was homeless on top of everything else.

Anyway, it was only a half-lie, she told herself reassuringly. Some of the girls she used to work with shared a house in Kensington, and they had said she could move in with them. But she had decided on a clean break, handing in her notice and severing all ties with London, intending that once she had settled her business down here she would move somewhere quite different and start again—Manchester, perhaps, or

Birmingham—anywhere big and impersonal. She had enough money in her building society account to live quite comfortably for some months; there was no rush.

'And you don't want to let your friends know you're all right?' Keir persisted softly.

'No.' No one cares, can't you see that? she screamed at him silently. No one cared, and she was going to make sure she didn't care about anyone either in the future. If you didn't get close to anyone they couldn't hurt you—simple.

But she wouldn't be able to rest until she found out about her mother—where she was, *who* she was, why...why she hadn't been able to love her. What was the matter with her that her own mother had given her away and walked out of her life without a second thought? And, worse, given her to the person who had reason to hate her.

'Catherine?' She became aware he had spoken her name more than once, and turned her head quickly, a brittle smile on her lips. 'What's wrong?' he asked quietly.

'Nothing.' Everything. 'Shall we go?' she said brightly, turning her head to look through the windscreen again. Go—go now, she prayed tightly, before I break down and say something silly or howl like a baby.

He said nothing for a long moment, and then started the engine abruptly, his face set and cold and his mouth grim. They drove right through the old Yorkshire town without speaking a word, the atmosphere in the Land Rover taut. But when they left the houses behind, the warm June air and the beautiful scenery soothed her agitation, and she found herself saying, 'I...I do appreciate you coming to fetch me, Keir; I know you must be very busy.'

He shrugged, the movement offhand and very male, and again the sheer power in his dark masculinity rose up and caused her breath to catch in her throat and her stomach to flutter nervously. She should never have agreed to stay in his house, she thought desperately. It was crazy, madness, because somehow, however she tried to explain it away to herself, she felt threatened by him.

She'd met handsome men before, fascinating, charismatic men—one often did in the big cities—but she hadn't met anyone like Keir Durrell. And it wasn't his darkly chiselled good looks, or the lean, honed body, or even the authoritative self-assurance and control he exerted as naturally as breathing. It was something beyond all that—a magnetism, an overt sexiness that scared her half to death, much as she hated to admit it. If he wanted a woman he would take her. Her eyes opened a little wider at the thought, and hotness invaded her limbs as she pictured his sensual mouth. And when he took her it would be...wonderful.

Oh, what was she doing? She almost wriggled with irritation and disgust, and stopped herself just in time, sitting straight and stiff in the seat. What did she know about the act of making love anyway? Apart from in the odd torrid novel, that was. He could be useless in bed, cold, impotent, even... She glanced from under her eyelashes at the hard, sculptured face, her gaze dropping to the big, firm hands on the steering wheel. But she doubted it. She certainly doubted it.

'It's not too far to Towerby.' She jumped visibly as he spoke and hoped he hadn't noticed. 'We're going over the fells; it's a pretty route,' he said easily, apparently quite relaxed while she was turning inside out, she thought ruefully, as nervous as a kitten. Still, men like him didn't get hot and bothered around *schoolgirls*—his words had rankled more than she would have liked—and he had made it plain that was exactly how he viewed her.

But then, as the journey unfolded, she forgot all about her confusion and pique in her delight at the vista spread out before them. The hot summer sun was beating down as they drove higher into the clean, pure air, the road ahead deserted as the vehicle climbed into a remote landscape where the sweet perfume of warm grass and wild flowers hung heavy and redolent in the stillness.

Rocky streams, the water crystal-clear, and enchanting miniature waterfalls seemed to appear around every corner, the wide open spaces with the great expanse of blue sky overhead captivating. For the rest of her life Catherine was to remember that journey as something set apart from real life, a breathtaking introduction to the beauty of the Yorkshire Dales.

'I was down at that farm most of the night.' As he spoke he gestured to a little doll's house far below them that was surrounded by grazing sheep—little dots of white wool on the green hillsides. 'A difficult foaling,' he continued evenly, 'but it ended well, with a whopper of a colt, and the mare forgot all her troubles the minute he was born. However many times you see it, it still continues to amaze, that fierce mother love.'

'Yes.' The pain that pierced through her was so acute she couldn't say any more. Even the creatures of the fields got it right, so why not her mother?

It was just after two o'clock when they drove into the quiet little village of Towerby, passing the thirteenth-century church and old coaching inn before pulling off the road and driving through wide-open large wooden gates into a small cobbled yard. 'We've arrived.' Keir glanced at her as the engine died, and the twittering of birds became apparent in the sluggish air. 'I'm taking you in the back way; the front is used mainly by patients and their owners.'

'Right.' He had already left the vehicle as she spoke, walking round to her side and opening her door before lifting her down onto the sun-warmed round stones.

'Welcome, Catherine.' His voice was very deep and his hands were warm around her waist as she stood in front of him, her face lifted up to his, and then, as their eyes caught and held, the moment lengthened. Her heart began to thud as he bent his head, but not to capture her lips as she had feared—*feared?*

No, the brief touch of his mouth on her forehead was the sort of chaste kiss one bestowed on maiden aunts or budding teenagers, she thought snappily as he released her immediately and walked over to a six-foot wooden fence that bordered what was clearly the end of a long terraced garden.

'Mind the cobbles.' His smile was easy and his voice cool as he turned with his hand on a small door cut into the fence. 'Don't twist your ankle. These cobbles look attractive enough, but they are renowned for keeping the local doctor busy.'

'Really?' She tried to keep all trace of testiness out of her voice, and smiled brightly as she joined him, stepping through the open door and into a long walled garden containing numerous fruit trees scattered about a thick green lawn. The high stone walls were covered in vibrant green ivy, and a narrow path wound and curled towards the house some hundred yards away, past the odd flower-bed full of gaily coloured blooms.

'It's lovely,' she breathed softly. It was. The melodious drone of busy insects was faint on the still, warm air, and a host of velvet-petalled wallflowers perfumed the air with the scents of summer. 'So peaceful.'

'Not when the surgery is in progress,' he said drily, taking her arm as he led her towards the house. She was vitally aware of his body, not least the easy animal grace with which he moved, and again she found it bothered her. Not that she wanted any attraction between them, she told herself sharply. Of course she didn't—just the opposite in fact. But he was one of those men whose masculinity couldn't be ignored, and it was...unsettling.

'We seem to have had an influx of bad-tempered cats

and dogs lately—the hot weather getting to them, no doubt—and it sounds like a circus most days.'

She nodded, but didn't answer. This *was* peaceful, whatever he said. No harsh words, no snide comments, no poisoned little darts to wound and smart. Animals she could take; it was human beings she had trouble with.

They entered the house through a heavy oak door, and she found herself in what appeared to be a long, narrow corridor, the floor stone-flagged and the walls painted white. 'Come and have a look around before surgery,' Keir invited. 'Meet a few of the patients. You do like animals, I take it?' He clearly didn't consider it a possibility she might not.

'Very much so,' she said at once.

'I thought as much.' His voice was warm and satisfied.

'What would you have done if I'd said I didn't?' she asked curiously, glancing up into his dark face as she spoke.

'Changed your mind.'

She felt the arrogance in the statement was typical of him, and frowned quizzically. 'And if you couldn't?' she persisted, determined not to let it go. 'What then?'

'I always do what I set out to do.' He eyed her mockingly. 'If I want something bad enough I don't take no for an answer, however long it takes.'

The caustic reply that sprang to her lips never had the chance to be voiced, which was probably just as well, because in the next moment he opened the nearest door and pushed her through ahead of him. 'This is the recovery room,' he said quietly, 'complete with residents.' He indicated the stack of blanket-lined cages that dominated two walls, several containing sleepy patients who eyed them dozily. 'The room's wired so that we can hear any sound from here all over the building if so required.'

'Are any of them very ill?' An engaging little puppy

occupied one cage, and she gestured at the small dog who had one leg encased in plaster. 'Him, for example?'

'He'll be fine.' Keir drew her out of the room and back into the corridor as he spoke. 'Although his owner's purse will be a good deal lighter in the process. He was left alone with a couple of older dogs who decided they'd use him in a tug-of-war contest. Fortunately the owner heard his squeals and rescued him before too much damage was done, but the case is typical of owners who don't understand animal behaviour. The lady was visiting a friend and thought it would be nice for her puppy to get to know the other dogs, so they shoved them all in a room together and went off to the kitchen to have coffee.'

His tone was scathing, and Catherine felt a moment's sympathy for the unfortunate owner; she had a feeling Keir wouldn't mince words in such a situation.

'Here's my operating theatre.' He opened another door a little further on, and she saw a clinically clean white-washed room with all the necessary equipment and paraphernalia associated with a hospital theatre.

'The surgery kitchen.' He opened yet another door. This room too was immaculate, and smelt faintly of antiseptic and carbolic. 'Used mainly for preparing the animals' meals and so on. Some of them are on very special diets, and the preparation can take some time.'

This was more than just a promising career to him. She glanced at the hard, dark face from under her eyelashes as he led her to the end of the passage. The fervent note in his voice, his pride in his little empire...this was his life's blood. He really *cared* about the animals, she thought wonderingly, with a force of emotion she wouldn't have thought this self-assured, somewhat formidable man capable of.

As they left the passageway the area widened into a large square hall, with black and white tiles on the floor and the front door directly before them. Keir gestured to a room on the right. 'The main waiting room with the reception area. There are three consulting rooms beyond that,' he said briefly, 'and also a storeroom. As you can imagine, our patients range from the big beasts on the farms right down to pet hamsters, so we cover a vast range of animal life.'

'I can imagine,' she agreed meekly.

'And—' He stopped abruptly, turning to glance down at her suspiciously from his considerable height. 'Are you laughing at me?' he asked slowly.

'No.' And she wasn't, not really—in fact his enthusiasm made her feel anything but amused, generating as it did a reluctant tenderness at his vulnerability that she could well have done without.

'Good.' The grey-eyed gaze held hers for one moment more before he turned to the left, his hand on a door beyond which muffled whines had been steadily building as they had been talking. 'And now you'd better meet Muffin and the gang—brace yourself,' he warned just a second before the door opened and a flood of animals surged into the hall, to the accompaniment of high, joyous barking and deep, throaty woofs.

'Are they all yours?' She had crouched down on her haunches to say hello to the dogs, which ranged from the biggest, most powerful long-haired German shepherd she had ever seen to a tiny, diminutive Yorkshire terrier who kept leaping into the air as though on invisible springs. 'How many are there?'

'Yes, they're all mine, and there's six of them.' He spoke a sharp word of command and the pack melted into an ingratiating circle at his feet, tails wagging frantically. 'This is Muffin, the indisputable boss,' he continued quietly, patting a soulful-eyed cocker spaniel. 'She was my mother's dog originally, but my mother decided she couldn't separate her from the others when she went to Cornwall.

'Sally, her best friend and ally—' he gestured to the

Yorkshire terrier '—and James and Josh. They are cross-bred beagles my father found abandoned in a disused caravan some years ago. Megan is a whippet who was used as a breeding machine until we got hold of her, and the German shepherd is the youngest of the lot. I've had him from a pup, and he's two now. He was an indulgence, considering we'd already got five dogs in residence, but I'd always promised myself a long-haired German shepherd.'

'He's magnificent.' She eyed the powerful dog warily.

'He's the softest of the lot,' Keir said ruefully. 'They all boss him about, especially the little Yorkie.'

All this love. She stared at him for a moment as something gripped her heart so tightly it hurt, and it was her inner turmoil that caused her voice to be sharp as she said, 'I always thought vets had a rule not to become involved with their patients, and certainly not to take in waifs and strays.'

'Did you?' His voice was cool, almost expressionless. 'Then perhaps you've been involved with the wrong sort of vets.'

'I haven't known any,' she returned indignantly.

'Then how could you possibly make a statement like the one you just did?' he countered evenly.

'I...I've read books, articles, that sort of thing,' she admitted in feeble defence of her criticism.

'Ah, I see.' The dark face told her more eloquently than words exactly what he thought of her reading material. 'I always prefer my opinions to be made first-hand,' he continued drily. 'That way I've no one but myself to blame when I fall flat on my face.'

She felt her colour flare at the none too subtle rebuke, and the defence mechanism she had employed for years to deal with jibes from her family sprang immediately into place. 'I'm sure you never fall flat on your face,' she said with a honeyed sweetness that curled at the edges with biting sarcasm. 'You know so much about everything, you're so wise.'

'Thank you.' He bowed slightly, his eyes infuriatingly amused at her attack. 'That's the nicest thing anyone has ever said to me.'

'Oh, I can't believe that.' She heard herself continue with a feeling of dismay, but somehow she couldn't stop, couldn't betray any vulnerability in front of this big, arrogant, *together* individual. 'Girlfriends, for example—they must have been complimentary now and again?' She smiled brightly. 'Assuming you've had girlfriends, of course,' she added sweetly, bending to fuss one of the dogs as she spoke.

'Not recently.' If she had been looking at him she would have noticed the change in his face.

'Oh, but—'

He stopped her blundering on any further with a touch on her arm, his face closed and expressionless as he said, his voice quiet, 'My wife died just over eighteen months ago; she had a degenerative blood condition that was incurable. I haven't dated anyone since.'

'Oh...' She straightened slowly, her eyes wide with horror. 'I didn't know—I'm sorry, I'm so sorry... I...I don't know what to say.'

He had been married—*married*? But, of course, she might have known a man like Keir Durrell wouldn't have remained single so long, that he would have been snapped up. And his wife had died...

'There was no reason you should know.' His voice was cool, remote, and as he ushered the dogs back into the room she stood quite still, her mind racing. Of course there was no reason she should have known, she told herself painfully. No reason at all. She was here for two or three weeks, that was all, and only because he considered her a waif and stray in much the same way he did the animals he took under his wing.

He had extended a hand of condolence, pity, shown

charity to someone he clearly considered young and foolish and incapable of looking after herself—and it was nice of him, very nice. She realised she was wringing her hands together, and unclasped them abruptly. Very nice...

CHAPTER THREE

'COME and meet Sandra, my receptionist, and then I'll take you upstairs to the flat and show you your room.'

She brought her head, which had been drooping forward, sharply upright as Keir turned from shutting the door. As he saw the look on her face he stopped abruptly, his smoky gaze holding hers.

'I'm sorry, Keir.' She had to say it now, properly, before she lost her nerve. 'About your wife—what I said—'

'Catherine—'

'No, please listen.' She took a deep breath, her hands clasping again without her being aware of it, although the big, dark man looking down at her was aware of every movement she made. 'I... You've been so kind, helping me and then offering me a place to stay, and it's just that—' Oh, how did you explain the unexplainable? 'I'm not used to people being kind,' she murmured helplessly. 'I know I'm prickly—'

'Hedgehogs have the sweetest faces.' His voice was like thick silk, and held a note that made her nerves quiver. 'Have you ever noticed that?'

'Hedgehogs?' For a moment the metaphor didn't register, and then she blushed furiously.

'And it's all right—really.' It wasn't, but she felt her tension and confusion drawing him up and away from her as he recognised her distress. 'Forget it.'

'Forget it?' It was like a slap round the face. Did he really think she was so shallow that she could push to one side the pain and grief that must have accompanied his statement 'My wife died eighteen months ago'? Did

45

he think she was so wrapped up in herself that she couldn't recognise another's agony? 'I can't, and I am grateful—'

'I don't want you to be grateful.' The silk had been torn aside and there was steel underneath for just a second before he said, 'That's not necessary, Catherine. Just enjoy your holiday, okay?'

'Keir—' Her mouth was open to say more, to tell him that this was not a holiday, that it was a mission, a mission to find someone who didn't want to be found, someone who had betrayed her, cast her aside. But then the door to the reception area opened and the moment was lost.

'I thought I heard voices.' The girl was pretty, very pretty, with a heart-shaped face and big green eyes, her luxuriant hair the sort of ash-blonde colour that owed its attractiveness to a bottle but was none the less stunning for it. 'I was just checking everything was all right.'

'Thanks, Sandra.' Keir's voice was easy now, warm even, and Catherine could see why. Sandra had the sort of looks and figure most models would be proud of. 'I was just bringing Catherine to meet you, as it happens—you remember I said she'd be staying in the flat for a while?'

'Yes, I remember.' The green eyes were as clear and cold as glass as they met Catherine's although the rosebud mouth smiled prettily. 'How do you do, Catherine? Fully recovered from your little accident?'

She made it sound as though she were a child who had fallen down and cut her knees, Catherine thought uncomfortably as she forced herself to smile and take the proffered hand. 'Yes, thank you. I feel fine now,' she said as naturally as she could, although there was something in the other girl's gaze that made her feel awkward. 'I'm just sorry to have caused such a fuss.'

'Yes...' The word could have been one of sympathy for her predicament, but somehow Catherine didn't think so. 'Keir?' Sandra's face mellowed and softened as she turned to him. 'I'm afraid there's a list of calls for this afternoon, including one at Beck's Farm; that cow still isn't feeding her calf and it's been a few hours.'

Keir nodded slowly. 'We've had trouble with that particular cow before, but an injection will set her to rights. Once she gets going she's a good little mother. I'll just check my bag while you finish showing Catherine around, okay?' His gaze swung to Catherine. 'And then I'll take you up to the flat and you can take it easy for a bit,' he added absently, although it was clear his mind was already at Beck's Farm with the cow and her calf.

'Come on through.' Sandra dragged her eyes from Keir's departing back with obvious effort, turning to walk back into the reception area without waiting to see if Catherine followed, and talking in a flat monotone as she showed her the consulting rooms and dispensary.

'So...' As they returned to the waiting room Sandra's eyes flicked over Catherine's face, and again she felt their chill in the little shiver her nerves gave. 'How long are you staying in Towerby, Catherine?'

'I'm not sure,' she said quietly. 'I don't want to impose on Keir and Janice; they've already been so good.'

'Oh, Keir's a great one for picking up strays.' Sandra laughed lightly, but the sound wasn't pleasant. 'I'm talking about animals, of course,' she added mockingly as Catherine's face straightened. 'He's a target for every lame dog in the county.'

'Is he?' Catherine stared hard at the other girl's scornful face. She had lived with dislike long enough to recognise it instantly.

'His work is his life, of course.' Sandra's eyes had narrowed on Catherine's face. 'Especially after the tragedy with Marion.'

'His wife, yes, he told me.' Thank you, thank you, *thank you* that I didn't have to ask what she was talking about, Catherine prayed silently; Sandra would have loved that. 'It must have been a terrible time for him—for everyone.'

'Yes, it was.' Sandra flicked a long lock of hair off her shoulder as she spoke, but her gaze remained locked on Catherine's face. 'I was a close friend of Marion; that's partly why I took the job when she became ill. She was Keir's receptionist too, you see. Do you work?' she asked abruptly.

The manner of asking, rather than the question, was undeniably impertinent, but Catherine forced herself not to overreact to the other girl's antagonism. She was Keir's receptionist when all was said and done, and any unpleasantness between them might be picked up by him. Besides which, she didn't want to make an enemy in her first few minutes in his home.

'I'm between jobs at the moment,' she said carefully. 'And as I'd got some money put by it seemed a good idea to take my holiday just now and have a good break before I look for something else.'

'Why the Yorkshire Dales?' Sandra managed to suggest anywhere else would have been a better idea.

'Why not?' Catherine countered lightly.

'Well, there's no nightlife for a start,' Sandra said tightly. 'And coming from London I'm sure you know how to have a good time,' she added with biting intent.

Whatever had she said or done to incur such wrath? Catherine paused a moment before she said, 'I do like to have a good time, and that's exactly what I intend to have here—plenty of long walks in the fresh air, peace and quiet, and some time to please myself.'

'Oh.' Her definition of a good time clearly didn't sit well with Keir's receptionist. 'So you're a country girl at heart?' Sandra asked flatly. 'Is that what you're saying?'

'I suppose so, but—' Catherine's reply was cut short as Keir reappeared, his dark face preoccupied, and

Sandra turned away from her to smile a smile of sickly sweetness at him which he didn't appear to notice.

'Ready?' he asked Catherine, before glancing at Sandra and handing her a sheaf of papers. 'Type those onto the surgery records, would you?' he asked absently. 'And I'll be back about four, okay? You've got the list of visits in case you need to make contact before then, haven't you?'

He didn't wait for a reply before taking Catherine's arm and ushering her firmly into the hall and up the stairs situated to one side of the front door, stopping on a large, uncarpeted landing and gesturing with his head to the stairs that continued upwards. 'Just attics and spiders up there,' he said shortly, 'along with the junk of several vets from over countless years.' He opened the heavy oak door in front of them with a key which he then handed to Catherine. 'This is yours, incidentally. If you lose it there's a spare for emergencies hanging up in the dispensary by the window. Come and go as you please.'

'Oh, right.' The speed with which he was dealing with her tied her tongue.

'Your room is the one at the far end of the hall, but explore where you like,' he said as he drew her into the flat and pointed to the end of the passageway. 'I really must go, but help yourself to food or coffee or whatever.'

'Yes, thank you.' Her voice was cautious, quiet.

He caught sight of her somewhat guarded expression just as he turned to go, and stopped, swinging round to face her again and looking down at her with narrowed, unreadable eyes. 'Don't look so scared,' he said softly. 'You might be in the wolf's lair, but he can be quite civilised when he feels like it.'

'What?'

'You weren't imagining I was going to leap on you at the first opportunity?' he queried drily.

How could he say such a thing? She was mortified. 'No, of *course* not.'

'No?' He clearly didn't believe her, and her embarrassment grew in a hot flood that stained her face and neck deep pink.

'No—I've told you,' she stammered desperately. 'I didn't think… I don't…'

'Then why are you so nervous around me, so defensive?'

'I'm not.' Oh, this was awful—*awful*.

'I think you are.' His voice was soft, gentle even, but its silkiness was embracing steel. 'Have you been hurt by a man, Catherine? Abused, perhaps?'

'No!' Her voice was too high, and she tried to moderate it as she said, 'I haven't—really.' Not in the way you mean, and not by a man, she added silently. Perhaps that would have been easier to come to terms with than having to accept that the people she had thought of as her family for twenty-one years were strangers, that they had never wanted or loved her, that her whole *life* was a lie.

'Okay, okay.' The relief that filled him was knee-trembling in its intensity. But there was something—he knew it—something that was eating her up inside. If it wasn't a man, then what the hell was it?

'You…you said you had to go,' she said shakily.

'I'm going.'

Catherine wasn't aware of the pain that had turned her violet eyes almost black; she just knew this conversation had to stop. He was being kind; she was another of his stray lambs, wasn't she? As Sandra had so pointedly made clear, he felt sorry for her. 'I…I hope you find the cow well.'

She saw him suddenly bite his lip. A husky, strangled sound escaped from his throat, and it was a moment or two before he said, with a careful lack of expression that

spoke its own story, 'I'm not going to have tea with her,
Catherine.'

He was laughing at her! She stiffened, her outrage
evident in every line of her body, but in the next moment
he leant forward to touch her face gently with the palm
of his hand in a gesture she was sure was meant to be
just comforting, but which she found...disturbing.
Especially as his nearness forced her to acknowledge the
faint, male smell of him, the broadness of his chest, the
way the sprinkling of silky black body hair revealed by
his open shirt collar suggested a hairiness that was positively threatening.

'Relax.' He had noticed her physical withdrawal at
his closeness; she could see it in the sudden tightening
of his mouth and the narrowing of his eyes. 'Like I said,
I can be quite civilised when I feel like it.'

She didn't doubt it, but what he didn't realise was that
it was not *his* control she was worried about. For some
reason her hormones seemed determined to go haywire
around Keir Durrell. She didn't want it, she certainly
didn't *like* it, but she had to face the fact that he exerted
a sexual attraction he was quite unaware of and which
was as powerful as a nuclear bomb—relatively speaking,
of course, she qualified with a touch of self-derision at
the analogy. It was making her jumpy, ridiculously so,
and it had to stop.

She took a deep breath, raised her chin and forced a
smile. 'Shall I come back with you to the Land Rover
for my suitcase?' she asked brightly, deciding it was
better not to continue a conversation in which she was
totally out of her depth. 'Then you can shoot straight
off—'

'It's already in your room; I brought it in when you
were talking to Sandra.' He stepped out of the flat as he
spoke, pausing on the square sunlit landing to say,
'Janice is still asleep, but she'll be up soon; she'll want
to have a shower and something to eat before she leaves

for the hospital. Her room is the one next to yours, incidentally.'

'Right.' She was fiercely grateful that there would be more than one thin wall separating them, which again was quite absurd but nevertheless how she felt. Somehow the thought of perhaps being able to hear him moving about, preparing for sleep, getting *into* bed, was shattering, humiliating as it was to admit it to herself. It didn't help to acknowledge that she was behaving just like the giddy schoolgirl he had taken her for either, or that her imagination seemed to run riot round this man. Oh, *why* had she accepted his offer of a room? She hadn't wanted to.

She was still pondering the thought when she realised he was halfway down the stairs and she hadn't returned his somewhat cool farewell.

The flat was surprisingly large, bright and airy, with a magnificent view over the surrounding village from the large picture window in the lounge. The small kitchen was compact and sparkling clean, with every modern appliance known to man squeezed in its tiny frame, and she was entranced to find a huge cast-iron bath in the gleaming bathroom with quaint bow legs and ball-and-claw feet. But it was when she opened the door to the room that would be hers that she really fell in love with the place.

The room wasn't large by normal standards—although compared to the tiny box-room that had been her bedroom for twenty-one years it was enormous—but it was the huge window that took up most of the far wall, and the view beyond, that made it utterly enchanting.

She stepped across the sunlit room, the colour scheme of pale lemon carpet and walls and ivory furnishings and curtains reflecting every scrap of sunshine, and leant out of the window, reflecting that it seemed as though half of Yorkshire was spread out before her. 'Beautiful...'

She breathed in the sweet, moist air for a few heady moments. 'Just beautiful.'

From her eyrie she gazed out over distant green fields of grazing sheep, the smaller bodies of still young lambs running to their mothers now and again, and gazed still further to a sweeping crescent of tree-covered hillside that rose up and up into the endless blue of the sky.

She could smell myriad scents on the warm June air, her nostrils teased by the intoxicating fragrance of flower-dotted hillsides, newly cut grass and the pulse of summer as she drank her fill of the vista. To think that people lived and worked in such surroundings every day—people like Keir...

The name broke her tranquillity and she turned abruptly, glancing across at the big suitcase on the bed.

What would he say if he found out she was up in his part of the world to confront a woman she had never seen, a woman who most definitely would not want to see her, a woman who had ignored her existence for twenty-one years? she asked herself agitatedly. Mind you, she had no reason to think her mother was still living in these parts. The reminder was one she had given herself over and over again in the last few weeks, but somehow it didn't bear weight with the conviction deep inside that her mother *was* here. She didn't know how she knew, she just did—or perhaps it was merely wishful thinking?

'Oh!' The exclamation was angry and sharp. She had to stop this perpetual cross-examination when she was alone; it was driving her mad.

She would unpack, and then just lie down on the bed for a few minutes until she heard Janice stir. It was amazing how tired she felt, considering she had been lying in bed for two days...

She awoke to a room filled with the mellow, soft shadows of dusk, the heat of the day having settled into a mild, balmy warmth that was gentle on her skin. She lay cocooned in a relaxation of mind and body that she hadn't felt in years, just watching the sky turn darker outside the window, the accompaniment of quiet baaing of sheep in the distance and the odd night sound from the village soothing.

She could be happy here. The thought was there before she had time to deflect it, and it brought her abruptly from the bed. At almost the same moment she heard Keir's deep voice rumble somewhere outside the room, Janice's softer tones less distinguishable. Her heart fluttered and raced, and she made a sound of annoyance in her throat at her weakness.

Keir wasn't in the least interested in her, and that was good—*it was*. She was going to have to concentrate all her time and energy on discreet and very careful enquiries about a woman who had moved to these parts twenty-one years ago, and the odds were heavily stacked against her succeeding, too. Romantic complications she didn't need. If her quest was fruitful she would certainly have to leave Yorkshire immediately after seeing her mother; anything else would be too embarrassing and difficult for everyone concerned. If it wasn't, then she would have to leave anyway, to continue the search. Either way, Yorkshire was closed to her.

She ignored the jolt her heart gave, and walked across to the small dressing table, sitting down and brushing out her hair so the silky, silvery waves hung free about her shoulders. Then she carefully removed every scrap of make-up so that her face had a shiny, freshly scrubbed look and contemplated her reflection in the mirror for a moment. Yes, she did look about sixteen, she reflected flatly, but that was all to the good, considering her mission.

And Keir? a quiet little voice in her head questioned slyly. What about him thinking you look young, gauche and unpolished?

A gentle knock at the door interrupted her thoughts, bringing her head swinging round as she called, 'Come in.'

'Hi.' Janice was already dressed for work as she came into the room, carrying a cup of tea. 'You've slept the afternoon away, which is exactly what I'd have prescribed.' She grinned cheerily. 'Keir's preparing the dinner, but I'd go and keep an eye on him if you don't want to be poisoned.'

'Aren't you eating?' Catherine asked anxiously, the fluttering returning tenfold at the thought of a cosy dinner for two with Keir as she accepted the cup of tea with a smile of thanks.

'Nope, I've had a sandwich, and that's all I can take when I'm on nights.' Janice grimaced, her nose wrinkling. 'It plays havoc with my digestive system. I've got to dash; Michael is on nights too, so he's picking me up in a couple of minutes.'

'He works at the hospital?' Catherine asked interestedly, putting the disconcerting matter of dinner with Keir to one side for a moment.

'He's a doctor.' Janice's face glowed. 'But that's not where we met, if that's what you're thinking. I've known him for years—all my life really.' The sound of a car horn brought the conversation to a close as Janice swung round with a quick, 'That's him; must dash,' and left the room in the same pell-mell fashion that Catherine was beginning to learn was characteristic of Keir's sister. They might be alike in looks, but that was all. Janice had none of Keir's cool authority and formidable, almost cold control.

'Feeling better? You looked all in earlier.' The quiet voice issued from the door to the kitchen as she walked through the hall after drinking the tea and changing her crumpled clothes for comfortable old jeans and a long, baggy top. The earlier resolution to look grown-up and sophisticated had gone, washed away by a heavy dose of common sense that told her she wouldn't be able to keep it up. She was what she was.

'Yes, thank you.' She paused in the doorway, her senses receiving the usual jolt at the sight of him. He was standing at the small, compact breakfast bar busily slicing mushrooms, a tea-towel tucked into the waistband of his black denim jeans and the sleeves of his shirt rolled up to reveal muscled, sinewy arms covered liberally with short black hairs. The contrast of domestic familiarity and sheer sex appeal was heady, and she felt her toes curl.

'Good.' He looked up briefly, the devastating grey eyes taking the whole of her in before they dropped to the task in hand. 'I hope stir-fried chicken and salad is okay with you?' he said easily. 'My culinary skills are somewhat limited.'

'Yes, but I ought to be doing that; I mean—'

'Don't tell me you are one of those rare females who feel a woman's place is in the kitchen?' he asked mockingly. 'That really would be too good to be true.'

'No.' It was a snap, born out of the agitation and unease she always felt around this man, but she qualified the sharpness by quickly saying, 'I just meant that in view of everything that's happened the least I can do is cook dinner.'

'What's happened?' He shrugged nonchalantly, the movement bringing her eyes to the dark shadow under the thin material of the shirt which spoke of thick body hair, and doing nothing to lessen her nervousness. 'We've a spare room and you need a place to stay for a while,' he said with magnificent simplicity. 'Nothing could be more straightforward. Here, pour us both a glass of wine if you insist on being useful; it's open.'

In her haste to obey she spilt a little of the deep red liquid, but he didn't appear to notice, taking the glass she offered with a word of thanks as he continued to stir the delicious mixture in the huge wok.

Now she was actually in the kitchen it seemed rude to leave, and so she perched on one of the two long-legged stools at the end of the breakfast bar, acutely aware that the limited space brought him uncomfortably close with every movement he made.

'Tell me a bit about yourself.' It was casual, easy, but it was what she had been dreading, and for a second her thought processes froze.

'There's nothing much to tell.' The wine was mellow, fruity, and she took a big gulp before she continued, 'I was born and raised in London, I'm twenty-one years old—' he acknowledged the statement with a wry lifting of his thick brows which told her he hadn't forgotten their earlier conversation '—and I'm up here on holiday, that's all.'

'That's all?' His mouth twisted in cool disbelief. 'What about family, friends, your job?' he asked softly. 'The things that make up real life?' He turned to face her, his eyes penetrating.

Right, you knew it was coming, so just deal with this with an economy of truth, she told herself firmly. Just enough to satisfy that razor-sharp mind. 'Family consists of my parents and a brother and sister,' she said flatly. 'And—'

'Hey, hang on, hang on.' He reached out and touched her arm, and she felt the light contact in every nerve and sinew. 'Do you see much of them? Are your brother and sister older or younger than you—?'

'Younger.' She cut him short before he could ask more. 'Quite a few years younger, but there's only a year between them so they argue like cat and dog. My parents—' she took a deep breath and prayed for control '—are not like me—' thank you God, *thank you God* '—and we've never really got on.'

'I see.'

He didn't, but she didn't give him a chance to ask more. 'Friends are numerous, job is secretarial, and I think the stir-fry is burning,' she finished, still in the same matter-of-fact tone.

It took a moment for her words to register, and then he leapt to the wok, salvaging their dinner before any harm was done, while she blessed the fact that her guardian angel had been on the ball after all.

Soon after, they ate together—Catherine taut with a nervous energy that kept her from appreciating the food—at the old wooden table in one corner of the lounge, the big windows open to the scented night air, and the village lights beginning to twinkle on, one by one, as night drew a dark mantle over the world outside.

Keir chatted easily as they ate, but although his voice was calm and his manner relaxed Catherine felt the curiosity he hadn't voiced, and knew that sharp, agile brain was ticking away on quite a different level as he kept her entertained with amusing stories about his work. But as long as he didn't *ask* her it would be all right, she told herself tightly. And if he did she would have to prevaricate about her past life; there was no other way.

'Apple pie and cream okay?' He stood up as he spoke and reached across for her empty plate, the movement causing her nostrils to flare as the faint, tangy smell of his aftershave touched her senses for a fleeting second.

'Could I just have coffee?' she asked quietly.

'No.' Her eyes sprang to his dark face, and she saw his mouth quirk at her expression of surprise. 'You're far too thin; you need feeding up,' he stated firmly. 'If you don't like apple pie there's chocolate-chip ice cream or fruit cake.'

'I don't want anything.' She had stiffened at the criticism, and her cheeks were burning. 'Thank you,' she added a few seconds later, forcing the words out through gritted teeth.

'Not that you aren't lovely the way you are,' he continued as though she hadn't spoken, his eyes considering as they moved over her frame and his voice thoughtful, almost analytical. 'But you definitely need a few extra pounds.'

'Now look here—'

'So which is it to be?'

'*Keir*—'

'Two apple pies?' His voice was still quiet, but exerted a force of will she really didn't feel up to challenging.

'Oh, all right,' she muttered ungraciously. 'If you insist.'

'I do.' His voice was soft now, dark. 'I told you before I don't take no for an answer if I want something, didn't I?' he said gravely. 'And...' He paused for a moment, bringing her eyes to his. 'My profession helps me to recognise when someone's been unwell, and you've been unwell.'

It was a statement, not a question, but she nodded anyway. 'Not that I was a two-ton Tessie before that,' she said acidly, still smarting from his fault-finding. 'Not every girl has huge—' She stopped abruptly at the raised eyebrows. 'Is curvaceous,' she finished weakly.

'Who said anything about curvaceous?' he said mildly. She had the sort of beauty any red-blooded man would take a second look at, and yet the inferiority complex was as big as a house. What the hell had gone on in her life to make her so nervous, so wary? Who had bruised that delicate ego so badly that she was like a cat on a hot tin roof most of the time? He felt his stomach muscles contract as darker possibilities flashed hotly through his mind for one caustic second before he thrust them away.

No, she was an innocent; he'd bet his life on it. He'd seen too many of the other sort in his life to doubt the naive artlessness which in itself was unwittingly seductive. But nothing about her present situation added up. Girls like her didn't holiday by themselves, or if they did it wasn't in a small village in Yorkshire.

Catherine was standing at the window when he returned with two plates of steaming pie, her back to the door, but she turned quickly, almost guiltily, at his entrance. 'I...I was just looking down at the village,' she said jerkily. 'It's not very big, is it? Everyone must know everyone else very well.'

'Must they?' His voice was bland, uninterested, as she scuttled back to the table, but if she had been looking at his face she would have seen the keen dark eyes were focused and intent. 'Is that good or bad?'

'Neither, just a fact.' He had moved her chair away for her to sit down again, and now pushed it under her jean-clad bottom as she sat down.

Nice bottom, he thought appreciatively—tight and rounded, and just the right span for a man's hands to cup...

'Was your wife from these parts?' She acknowledged far too late that she'd said it partly as protection against the intimacy of their meal for two, but also because she really wanted to hear about her. But once the words were out she was aghast at her tactlessness. 'Oh, I'm sorry, I shouldn't have asked; I didn't—'

He stopped the torrent of words with a cool but unrevealing voice as he said, 'Why not? Marion was not a local girl, as it happens. In fact she came from London, like you, initially. We met at veterinary college.'

She watched him as he returned to his own seat, sitting down and proceeding to eat a mouthful of pie before he spoke again. 'And you? Any broken hearts pining at your absence?'

'Me?' To her chagrin she blushed hotly at the perfectly acceptable question. 'No, no, there's not.'

'Right.' There was an inflexion in his voice, just something that made her glance into the dark face searchingly, but the hard, male features were remote, implacable, as he stared back at her.

She shouldn't have agreed to stay here. Again the

thought sprang to mind, but this time it was strong and fierce and possessed of an urgency that made her nerves quiver. She couldn't begin to work him out—he made the word 'enigma' sound positively commonplace—but one thing she was sure of: *she should never have agreed to stay.*

CHAPTER FOUR

CATHERINE slept deeply that night, only once waking briefly at the sound of a telephone ringing somewhere, followed a few minutes later by a creaking door, footsteps and then the front door closing. She glanced sleepily at her tiny alarm clock on the side of the bedside cabinet. Two o'clock in the morning; it had to be a night call for Keir, she thought, moments before she snuggled down under the covers again and fell immediately asleep.

The next time she opened her eyes it was to a room full of early morning sunlight, and although it was only six o'clock she found it impossible to go back to sleep again, her mind fresh and alert and raring to go.

She pulled her thick towelling robe on over her nightie and padded along to the bathroom. Keir and Janice's open doors bore evidence to the fact she was alone in the flat. It couldn't be much fun to have to turn out in the middle of the night, she thought reflectively, although no doubt the soft summer nights were far better than the stark chill of winter on tired bones. Keir worked too hard, though; it had been evident in the lines of tiredness etched round his mouth as they had talked last night—

She caught her thoughts abruptly. It was no business of hers how long or hard he worked, she told herself grimly. None at all. He had offered her a room because it was vacant for the moment and she had been in need. He had his own life which seemed to suit him just fine; she would be nothing more than a passing shadow in the overall scheme of things.

She ventured into the kitchen, making herself a cup of instant coffee and taking it into the lounge where she curled up in a big, comfortable easy chair close to the window, her eyes on the sleeping village as she sipped the hot, fragrant liquid. A small milk-float was making early morning deliveries among the winding streets far below, and she watched its progress idly, her tiny feet tucked under the folds of the robe and her hands cupped round the warm mug.

Her mother could be down there somewhere, breathing, talking, laughing, *living*, without any knowledge that her own flesh and blood was just within reach. How would she react when the daughter she had hoped to get rid of confronted her? With anger that she had been found out? Embarrassment? Confusion? Shame? Fury? There was a pain like a knife turning in her heart, and she took a big gulp of the burning hot coffee, shutting her eyes tightly for a moment as though to blank her mind.

She wasn't going to cry again, she told herself fiercely. She was past all that; *she was*. If she had learnt anything from the last twenty-one years it was that the old cliché 'Laugh and the world laughs with you; weep, and you weep alone' was painfully true. And yet... Her eyes were drawn to the village again... She had always felt there was someone looking out for her, keeping her, giving her the strength to follow through on her own convictions and desires, and that certainty had never been so strong as in the last few weeks. She *had* to do this, and now was the time.

The sound of a key turning in the lock brought her out of her reverie and quickly to her feet, just as Keir walked slowly into the lounge, his hard face slightly grey with exhaustion and a grim line to his mouth.

'Good morning.' Her voice was a little breathless, and she heard it with a dart of exasperation. 'Hard night?'

He nodded abruptly. 'Distressing more than tiring,' he

said flatly. 'A case that was doomed from the start.' He rubbed at his nose to hide his emotion, and the curiously boyish gesture from this big hard man hit her in a way she didn't like, causing her to be momentarily lost for words. 'I know in my head that I can't win them all,' he continued quietly as he passed her to stand at the window, his back to the room, 'but that doesn't always help.'

'No, I don't suppose it does,' she agreed carefully. 'Can…can I get you some coffee?'

'Coffee?' He turned as he spoke, his face shadowed and dark in contrast to the brilliant light behind him, and his clothes bearing evidence that he had been out to one of the farms; a smudge of something grisly was on one muscled forearm.

'And something to eat?' She hadn't intended to say it—she had made up her mind last night that the less contact she had with Keir Durrell the better after that intimate dinner for two—but somehow the words popped out of her mouth of their own volition. 'While you have a shower,' she added with a wry smile. There was a definite odour of farmyards beginning to permeate the air.

'That would be great.' He tried to hide his surprise but didn't quite succeed, and to her chagrin she found herself blushing as furiously as if she had suggested something obscene rather than fixing breakfast. 'But only if you eat with me,' he said quietly, his voice devoid of expression now.

She scuttled away without giving him an answer, her face flaming, and once in the small kitchen leant against the soothing coolness of the sky-blue tiles for a moment before opening the fridge.

What had made her suggest she fix him breakfast? she asked herself weakly, pulling bacon and mushrooms out of the well-stocked fridge and reaching for the basket of eggs on the breakfast bar. And when she'd smiled at him had he thought it was in a come-hither fashion, or just the smile of a friend? 'Oh...' She groaned at the possibility of the former, slumping against the wall before jerking sharply upright at the sound of his voice just behind her.

'You haven't done anything wrong, you know.'

'What?' She spun round, her colour surging again at the thought that he had read her mind.

'By being relaxed enough to treat this place as your own for a few moments and offer a starving male sustenance,' he said quietly. 'Both Janice and I want you to feel at home while you stay, I told you that; there's no need to stand on ceremony.'

He just thought she was embarrassed at giving the impression she had taken over, she realised faintly. She would have died if he'd guessed she was attracted to him. *Attracted to him?* The sudden knowledge was alarming.

'And I will have that shower; I guess I don't smell too good.' He was already turning as he spoke, and when in the next moment she was alone again she leant against the stove as a little whoosh of air escaped her lips.

Okay, so she was attracted to him, she admitted to herself silently. So what? Most women would be. It didn't *mean* anything. He had more than his fair share of sexual magnetism, and if her body chemistry responded to the age-old appeal it was purely due to a seduction of the senses, and as such could be controlled. Mind over matter. Simple.

The bacon, eggs and mushrooms were ready to be served, the ground coffee was percolating and the fresh orange juice and toast were already on the table some minutes later when his voice arrested her from the doorway. 'That smells delicious.'

She turned, a polite smile already stitched on her face, and then breathed deeply as her gaze took in the hard, lean body encased in black denim jeans and a pale blue shirt tucked into the narrow waistband, his short black hair still damp from the shower and the very masculine stubble on his chin indicating he hadn't taken the time to shave. He still looked tired, she thought weakly, but that only added to his appeal rather than detracted from it.

He was the type of man who would still look good at seventy, and just at the moment she found that fact distinctly irritating—especially as she was still in her robe with her hair tousled and loose and her face flushed from the stove.

'Can I help—?'

'No!' She interrupted him so emphatically it was insulting, and she hastily qualified her vehemence with a quick, 'There's not room to swing a cat in here; you go and sit down and I'll come through in a minute.'

He made no effort to obey, surveying her with narrowed grey eyes for a long moment before he said, 'I make you nervous, don't I? Is it me or all men? What has happened in your life that you view the world with such distrust?'

'I don't.' She stiffened as he walked the few feet separating them and reached out, but it was only to take the spatula out of her unresisting fingers and place it gently on the work surface.

'You're like a nervous little fawn, ready to bolt at the first sign of danger,' he said softly, so close that her fine body hairs prickled at his male warmth. 'I still find it hard to believe you've been in this big, bad world for twenty-one years.'

It wasn't so much what he said as how he said it that caused her to flush in protest, her back straightening and her chin thrusting out as she stared up into his dark face. So he thought she was some pathetic little helpless female, did he? The sort of woman who wouldn't dare to say boo to a goose? 'Well, I have.' Her voice was militant, abrasive. 'And appearances can be deceptive, you know. I'm more than capable of looking after myself; I've been doing it for most of my life.'

'So you're worldly-wise, a nineties woman?'

He was mocking her, and suddenly it made her hopping mad, loosening her tongue and prompting her to speak before she could check herself. 'Exactly.' She eyed him angrily. 'I know as much about life as you do—more, probably.' Being brought up in the tender bosom of my family saw to that, she added silently.

'I see.' He wasn't mocking her any more; the piercing grey eyes had fastened on her flushed face with an intentness that was disturbing. 'And it hurts?'

'Hurts?' Too late she realised that smoky gaze had seen far more than she would have liked. 'I don't know what you mean,' she lied shakily.

'No?' The last of the mushrooms that were still waiting to join the other food on the two oven-warmed plates were beginning to resemble pieces of charcoal, but neither of them noticed. 'I think you do, Catherine. There was a chink in the armour there for just a moment, wasn't there—?'

'Keir, please. I don't know what you're thinking but I can assure you—'

This time it was her voice that was cut off as he lowered his head, and the kiss was no chaste salutation to a maiden aunt like before, it was a hot, sweet fusing of their mouths that took her completely by surprise.

In the moments before she jerked away she was conscious of the smell and feel and taste of him, the broadness of his frame as he towered over her, the complete dominance and power with which he exerted his maleness over her soft femininity. But then she stepped backwards sharply, hitting her hip on the side of the breakfast bar without even being aware of it.

'Don't.' She couldn't believe the sensations that had exploded through every nerve and sinew at the brief embrace. 'I don't want this.'

'Catherine, I'm not going to hurt you—'

'I mean it.' She couldn't take the gentle, even tender side this big, hard, assured individual was displaying. It was dangerous—far more dangerous than any aggressive battering down of her defences, and she suspected he knew it. 'I don't like being pawed about.' It was deliberate…and unforgivable.

'*Pawed about?*' In any other circumstances the sheer outrage and indignation on the dark, handsome face would have raised a smile—she doubted if any other woman had ever reacted to him in this way—but as she faced his fury there was nothing to laugh about. 'Paw… I kissed you, woman, that's all. What the hell is the matter with that?'

'I didn't ask you to—'

'You normally *ask*?'

Put like that it sounded ridiculous, but she knew he knew what she had meant. Her voice, shaky though it was, was firm as she said, 'Keir, this clearly isn't going to work out; I think it would be better if I looked for somewhere else and moved out today.'

'Because I kissed you?' he asked incredulously.

'Because… Oh, lots of reasons,' she said painfully. 'I'm not here to get involved, to start… I just wanted a peaceful holiday before I moved on, that's all.'

'Don't you mean go back?' he asked swiftly, seizing on her gaffe with devastating perceptiveness.

'I mean… Look, I don't have to explain what I mean to you or anyone else.' She gathered the torn pieces of her dignity about her with formidable determination as she felt herself backed into a metaphorical corner.

'True.' He had folded his arms across the solid wall of his chest as he stood looking down at her, his feet slightly apart and his big body relaxed, almost lazy. The anger had gone, along with the initial outrage at her accusation, but the calm, expressionless façade was more disturbing than any show of temper, hiding as it did the relentless astuteness of a razor-sharp mind. 'I just don't like to see anyone running away from something, that's all.'

'I haven't said I'm running away.' And she wasn't, if he did but know it, she thought with painful wryness. In fact she had run *to* her problem—or where she thought her problem was, she qualified silently.

'You don't have to.' He gestured to the black, charred remains that were smoking ominously. 'Perhaps it would be a good idea to turn the gas off now? I'll carry the plates through, shall I?'

It was a statement, not a question, and as she hastily put the frying-pan under water before following him into the lounge her head was spinning. Had he accepted she was leaving? she asked herself shakily, trying to bring her whirling thoughts under control. She had made it plain...hadn't she?

He was sitting at the table waiting for her, his back to the window and his hair blue-black in the white sunlight. She padded over to her seat, feeling ridiculous in her bathrobe with her feet bare, but as she opened her mouth to speak, he was there before her, his voice deep and dark and suspiciously humble.

'I'm sorry I frightened you, Catherine—'

'You didn't—'

'It was a gesture of comfort, nothing more.' He had continued as though she hadn't spoken, and the sheer force of his will closed her mouth with a little snap. 'Janice would be somewhat upset if you left now. And your departure might be a little difficult to explain to Sandra and any others who know you are staying here,' he said in such a reasonable tone that she found herself nodding in agreement before she checked herself. 'This is an excellent breakfast,' he added mildly. 'I normally make do with toast and coffee.'

'I...' She was being charmed, sweetly railroaded into doing what he wanted, she thought helplessly. But it *might* look bad if she suddenly decided to leave; she hadn't considered that. And perhaps he *had* just meant the kiss as a gesture of comfort? The thought brought hot colour into her cheeks. Maybe it was her awareness of him as a man that was the trouble, leading her to think there was more behind his friendliness than was actually the case.

Whatever, she had made more than a fool of herself, she thought miserably, jumping away from him like a scalded cat and practically accusing him of attempted rape! He must think she was some sort of nutcase.

'Can I pour you some orange?' he asked smoothly.

'Orange?' She stared at him as though he had spoken in a different language, and then nodded quickly, 'Oh, yes, thank you.'

'What are your plans for today?'

She nearly said, Plans? in the same gormless voice as before, but managed to pull herself together and reply fairly coherently. 'I was just going to have a look around, perhaps take a packed lunch and explore a little,' she said hesitantly, keeping her eyes on the orange juice he had just handed over. 'But about what I said earlier—'

'Take a couple of the dogs with you if you go hiking into the hills,' he said easily.

'What?' She was honestly bewildered.

'Yorkshire is probably safer than the big city—I appreciate that—but a couple of the dogs, or all of them if you feel so inclined, is the best protection I know. They often escort Janice, and they know the drill; they wouldn't let anyone touch you.'

'Keir, I can't impose on you and Janice in this way,' she said quickly before she lost her nerve or he interrupted her again. 'Whatever you say, to have someone come and stay with you is an inconvenience.'

'Is it?' His eyes moved slowly over her flushed, earnest face, the wide violet eyes and silky, shimmering mass of silver-blonde hair, the slim but perfect figure hidden under the thick towelling robe. 'Funny, but I don't see it that way, Catherine.' His voice was deep, husky even, with a smoky, soft element to it that made her toes curl into the carpet.

She drew in a quick breath. He was being kind, just kind, she told herself firmly; she mustn't let her imagination run away with her again.

'If you weren't here I'd have had a solitary breakfast of toast and coffee,' he continued quietly, his voice in its normal cool, remote mode again. 'So you've already done your good deed for the day, okay? So relax now, enjoy your exploring, and I'll think of another good deed for you to satisfy that martyr complex tomorrow.'

'I haven't got—' She stopped abruptly at the mocking amusement in his grey eyes. Why did she let him get under her skin? Why couldn't she be composed and self-assured, exchanging light, careless banter and amusing cross-talk? No wonder he had likened her to a hedge-hog—an enormous, great porcupine would perhaps have been more apt.

'All right. Thank you.' She finally admitted defeat gracefully. His will was stronger than hers, and this morning had only re-emphasised the conviction of last night that the less she had to do with Keir Durrell the better. She didn't have the background, the experience, *anything*, to meet him on equal ground.

Keir tucked into his breakfast with every appearance of enjoyment, but although Catherine managed to clear her plate it was an act of will, her appetite completely subdued by his presence. She was painfully conscious of every tiny movement he made, every tilt of that dark head, every muscle in those powerful arms, and it *infuriated* her... But she couldn't do a thing about it.

She had had enough thrown at her in the last few months, hadn't she? she argued silently. Her illness, the shocking revelations by the people she had always con-

sidered her parents, the consequential decision to leave
all she had ever known and take a great step into the
unknown, the knowledge that she was preparing to face
someone who didn't want her, would probably be horrified at her appearance in their life—ashamed, disgusted
even.

She forced down the last mouthful of food as her
stomach trembled. A further complication she just didn't
need, she told herself tightly. But why, when her head
knew that quite distinctly, did her body seem to have a
mind all of its own around this man? And why had he
been the one to find her? Why couldn't it have been a
grey-haired old man with a fat little wife and countless
grandchildren?

She immediately felt guilty at her ungratefulness, and
stood up at once to do penance. 'I'll get the coffee,' she
said quietly, reaching for his empty plate, 'and do the
washing up while you try and catch a couple of hours
of sleep.'

'No chance of that.' He stood up with her, big and
self-assured, and she knew there was no way on this
earth she could squeeze into the small kitchen with Keir.

'Well, you can relax for a while at least.' Her smile
was nervous, quivery, and again he felt that dart of burning curiosity to know more—but now was not the time.
He had dealt with enough frightened and jumpy patients
to know when he could push it and when he couldn't.

'If you're sure.' As he sank back into his seat she
knew a moment's blinding relief that was out of all proportion to the circumstances, and just nodded quickly
before leaving the room for the sanctuary of the kitchen,
placing the plates on the breakfast bar then pouring two
cups of strong coffee with shaking hands.

From now on she would make sure she was never
alone with him, she told herself firmly, inhaling the fragrant aroma in a bid to steady her nerves. Not that she
thought he would look twice at her, what with his wife's

death and his busy job that was more or less a twenty-
four-hour one from what she could make out. No, it
wasn't *his* control that was of concern. She bit her lip
hard. It was hers, galling though it was to have to admit
it.

The more she thought about it, the more she realised
it was her own guilt about her feelings towards Keir that
was revealing, even making problems. The kiss hadn't
been rapacious—she ground her teeth slightly as she
picked up the other mug of coffee—it was her sordid
mind that was reading more into his actions than was
there. The thought that had materialised before breakfast
solidified. So...she wouldn't put herself in a position
where she could embarrass herself, or him, again.

He didn't look particularly embarrassed when she
walked into the lounge; in fact he looked quite pleased
with himself as he took the coffee from her with a nod
of thanks, his voice lazy as he said, 'Help yourself from
the stuff in the fridge for your packed lunch, and we'll
eat dinner about seven, okay?'

'Oh, no, don't worry about me; you and Janice eat
when you want to and I'll sort myself out,' she said
quickly.

'If you say so.' He eyed her somewhat sadly from
under black brows, the grey gaze holding mild disappointment. 'I was just hoping you might be around to
help cook dinner. I've a devil of a day in front of me
and this morning hasn't been too good a start, rising, as
I did, at two. But if you're going to be busy...'

She immediately felt horribly selfish.

'Of course, I understand this is your holiday—'

She interrupted the generously understanding voice
uncomfortably, a little uneasy at his carefully bland expression but telling herself she was imagining things
again. He wasn't manipulating her; how *could* she think
such a thing? And it would be outrageously mean to
refuse to cook them dinner in the circumstances

wouldn't it? 'I'd be glad to cook dinner; I didn't realise—'

'Brilliant.' The winsome little-boy-lost façade was gone in a flash, and the air of satisfaction was strong as he said, 'Seven, then, if that suits you? There's a couple of steaks in the fridge, and Janice is picking up some groceries on her way home so there'll be plenty of salad and so on. She'll sort herself out, incidentally; she doesn't like a big meal before she starts work.'

'Oh, right.'

'Do you prefer white wine or red?' His voice was smooth and matter-of-fact, and she had answered before she thought about it.

'Red, but—'

'Fine. I'd better go and check on a few of the animals before morning surgery. I'll just have a shave first so I don't frighten the patients.'

He stroked the stubble on his chin, the movement bringing her eyes to his face, and the flagrant masculinity that was all the more devastating for being utterly natural made her weak. 'Yes, of course. You go ahead; it's your bathroom.' She was gabbling, she thought desperately, and she *never* gabbled.

Once he was downstairs in the surgery she fairly flew about the flat, washing and dressing in record speed and throwing a couple of apples and a Cornish pasty into her old cloth bag, along with a light romance from the dozens in the bookcase with Janice's name scrawled in the flyleaf.

She crept downstairs quietly, her heart thudding although there was no good reason for it to do so, and didn't dare take a deep breath until she had slipped stealthily out of the back door and sprinted down the garden towards the little door in the fence.

The morning was warm and sunny, the heady scents of summer heavy in the air as she walked briskly through the village of Towerby and out into the undulating countryside, following the winding river for some time. Its banks were starred with thousands upon thousands of tiny white daisies and gleaming yellow buttercups, busy insects going about their business of taking pollen as she walked, and she stood for a while in one quiet bower on the river bank, watching the fish darting in the shallows, London feeling a million miles away.

This was another world. She glanced at the hills that were beckoning in the distance. And she had all day, and days after that, to explore it.

For the first time in months a dart of happiness pierced the confusion and darkness, and she breathed in the perfumed air in great gulps as she stood with her eyes lifted to the hills and her shoulders thrown slightly back. She was alive, she was young, and just for the moment that was enough.

She ate her meagre lunch in a small gully where a secret little waterfall splashed its busy way over smooth, ancient rocks and boulders, its water crystal-clear and icy cold. She cupped her hands and took thirsty mouthfuls, the sun warm on her face, before climbing still further. Dry-stone walls stretched in a timeless pattern before her, and the sweet smell of thick moorland grass teased her nostrils as she plodded along, the silence of the windswept fells broken only by the distant bleating of sheep far away.

This was where Keir lived and worked, she thought longingly, in this breathtakingly awe-inspiring landscape. A soul could breathe up here, find itself, *belong*. The word mocked her immediately she thought it. Belong? She shook her head as she gazed up into the clear blue sky. She didn't belong here; she didn't belong anywhere. Her own mother hadn't thought she was worth having, so why should anyone else want her?

She felt the darkness begin to descend and thrust it away angrily. She wouldn't think now, not now; she didn't want this one day to be spoilt by demons from the past. Thinking could come tomorrow and the days after that. For today she would just *be*.

It was getting on for late evening by the time she retraced her footsteps into Towerby, and the air was mellow, soft, the heat of the day slowly draining from warm stone walls and the old, uneven pavements.

She had to walk over an ancient pack-horse bridge to enter the village, under which the water gurgled and splashed over sun-washed stones. She stood for a moment in the dusky air, her nostrils teased by the sweet, timeless scent of woodsmoke as she looked towards Keir's house set in a row of old properties that were above the main village.

'I *will* leave here.' She spoke out loud as though denying a previous statement. 'This is just temporary, that's all; none of this matters.'

She turned and looked back the way she had come, at the great expanse of hills now clothed in the misty blue of dusk. 'And I will manage by myself,' she said defiantly. 'I don't need anyone, anyone at all.'

Tomorrow, or perhaps the next day, she would begin to make discreet enquiries about a young woman who had come to these parts twenty-one years ago. Anna Mitchell. Or perhaps her mother had come here under a different name? It didn't matter; if she was here she would find her—and then? Then the skeletons would be out of the cupboard, she thought painfully, her heart suddenly raw and heavy as she began to walk on. And her mother's cosy little life in this tranquil part of England would never be the same again. She would make sure of that at least.

She found the thought brought her no satisfaction at all.

CHAPTER FIVE

THE concerted barking of several dogs interrupted Catherine's reverie, and as she lifted her head she saw Keir at the entrance to the lane that led up to the row of houses, the dogs bounding round his feet.

She hesitated and then waved, unsure of what to do, but it was a moment before the big, dark figure responded, and then it was just a cursory nod of his head as he waited for her to approach.

'Hello.' Her voice was soft, breathless, and she didn't want it to be. 'I...I'm not late, am I?' she asked suddenly as the thought occurred to her. In her panic to get out of the house before she saw him again this morning she had left her neat little wristwatch on the dressing table in her room.

'Yes, you are late, Catherine.' He was angry. Although his voice was cool and controlled she somehow knew he was angry. 'An hour and a half late.'

'Oh, I'm sorry; have you eaten? Shall I—?' She was gabbling again, and stopped herself abruptly. So she was late, she thought defiantly, but it wasn't the end of the world, was it? He was quite capable of getting himself something to eat, after all. 'Have you eaten?' she asked again, this time quietly and slowly.

'No.' He eyed her without blinking.

'I'll see to the dinner when I've changed.'

'Damn the dinner.'

Yes, he was definitely angry, in spite of the almost conversational tone of voice.

'Look, I couldn't help it—'

'Why didn't you take the dogs with you—or a couple,

even one?' he asked evenly. 'Was it an act of defiance against me because I rub you up the wrong way, or just plain stupidity?'

'What?' And then she remembered what he had told her, and he recognised the dawning awareness in her eyes.

'You forgot, didn't you?' It was a flat statement, but not without heat. 'You go tramping off without letting a soul know in which direction you're going—no one has seen you all day—and then you are nearly two hours late back. You could have fallen down somewhere, brained yourself, been attacked—anything—and no one would have been any the wiser.' His voice was rising, she noticed bemusedly, dark colour staining his cheekbones as he struggled to keep his temper in check.

'Don't you read the papers?' he asked grimly. 'Or is there some divine intervention on behalf of you that the rest of us know nothing about?'

'There's no need to be sarcastic.' There was a strange feeling deep inside her, a painful ache that was slowly twisting her guts into knots. He had been worried about her, he'd made enquiries, he'd *cared*. The realisation was one of anguish, frightening. She couldn't handle it, and the fact made her voice sharp. 'I'm not answerable to you or anyone else.'

'You've already said that line once and I don't buy it twice.' This time the deep voice was steel-hard. 'You're not a stupid woman, Catherine, so don't act like one.'

'I beg your pardon—?'

'And I don't buy the self-righteous indignation either,' he continued relentlessly. 'Not when we both know I'm right. If you want to take a hike and get away from it all that's your prerogative—you can walk your feet off for all I care—but you take the dogs with you, okay?'

'No, it's not okay.' She didn't know why she was defying him like this, but she couldn't stop. 'It's far from okay.'

'Tough.'

'Now look here—'

'*Catherine.*' It was just her name, but it stopped her angry voice like the crack of a whip. Not that he shouted; he didn't have to. There was something in the deep tones that was more effective than any show of rage. 'Stop this,' he growled softly. 'You may not care about your safety but others do; leave it at that.'

And then she did the unthinkable. One moment she was facing him angrily, her chin tilted for battle and her stance militant, the next she had horrified him and herself by bursting into tears. And not gentle, feminine tears either, but great, anguished wails that silenced the dogs as though by magic and caused Keir to freeze for one shocked moment before he reached out and pulled her into his body, settling her against the hard wall of his chest as he murmured soothingly into the soft silk of her hair, his chin nestled on her head.

She couldn't hear what he was saying—her gasps and splutterings had filled her nose and ears and mouth—but she was aware of the gentle rumble above her and the warm comfort of his body as he held her close.

Too aware. As her sobs subsided her senses took over, and along with the awful knowledge that she had just made the most terrible fool of herself was a warm, pleasurable, throbbing ache in the core of her that had nothing to do with her distress and everything to do with Keir.

'I...I'm sorry.' The fear that she might give herself away was stronger than her embarrassment when she looked into his face, but as she leant backwards and tried to move out of his arms his hold tightened.

'Why? Because you forgot yourself long enough to show weakness? To let the real Catherine through?' he asked softly. 'Is that so terrible?'

Yes, it was terrible. It was terrible when it started the sort of chain reaction that was happening in her body, she thought desperately. She had never, in all her life, understood how women could supposedly be swept away by the force of their emotions when making love. Or how girls—and plenty of grown women too—could fling themselves at the object of their devotion, be it a pop star or lover or whatever, and beg to be taken. But she was understanding it now, and he hadn't even *kissed* her. What was she, some sort of repressed nymphomaniac? She groaned silently. What on earth would he say if he could read her mind?

The thought stiffened her still more, but again he wouldn't allow her to break free.

'Well? Is it so terrible?' he asked again, his eyes narrowed on her flushed, tear-stained face.

'Yes.' She wriggled a bit, but he appeared not to notice. 'At least crying all over you for no reason is,' she amended quickly as one dark eyebrow quirked.

'I take it that's a polite way of saying you don't intend to tell me what's wrong,' Keir said drily.

'There *is* nothing wrong.' The absurdity of the statement, considering her tear-drenched face and swollen eyes, hit her a second before he shook his dark head slowly.

'Catherine, Catherine...' Her name was like a warm caress, and she shivered before she could help herself. 'You really shouldn't attempt to tell lies, you know,' he cautioned gravely. 'Not with a face like yours.'

'What's wrong with my face?' She tried to sound coolly dignified, but it was difficult with the reality of his maleness all around and his muscled arms holding her fast.

'Let me see.' He was aware he was stringing this conversation out for his own gratification. He had known she would feel good pressed close against him, so he could enjoy the curves of that small but beautifully proportioned female body, the soft round breasts and fragrant sweetness of her skin. He just hadn't realised *how* good, he acknowledged wryly as he felt his loins stir.

'Do you want a detailed list or a few throwaway comments?' he murmured softly.

'Neither.' The dogs had recovered their equilibrium after her outburst, and had now gathered in a noisy and enquiring huddle round their legs, tails wagging frantically and brown eyes inspecting their faces as first one, then another, would jump up to make sure everything was all right. 'Look, the dogs don't like this,' she said nervously. 'They're worried.'

'Silly dogs.' But he let her go, stepping back a pace and smiling that devastating smile she had seen once or twice that had the power to take her breath away, before taking her arm and turning her in the direction of the house. 'Come and eat,' he said evenly. 'You must be starving.'

Easy, easy, Keir, he cautioned himself as they walked slowly up the incline surrounded by gambolling dogs, the ache of his arousal hard and hot. He hadn't been wrong when he had likened her to a nervous little fawn, and it shouldn't be too hard to display the same sort of patience he would use in dealing with a fearful, tense animal. It shouldn't be...but it was. What he wanted to do— He shut the lid on what he wanted to do.

'Go and have a soak while I finish off the meal.' As they entered the flat Keir's voice was brisk, impersonal. 'Take a glass of wine with you if you like.'

'Oh, I must help.' She followed him uncertainly to the kitchen door, noticing with renewed guilt a prepared bowl of salad on the breakfast bar, and the two, as yet uncooked, steaks under the grill. He had been working hard all day—and that day had started at two in the morning—and she hadn't even been home in time to prepare dinner.

It wasn't *home*. The reprimand was sharp and fierce in her mind. And it wasn't up to her to look after him in any way, shape or form either, and she had better remember that. She could be here a matter of days or a matter of weeks, depending on how quickly her enquiries bore fruit, and when she had gone he would forget her immediately.

'No need.' He poured two large fluted glasses of red wine from the uncorked bottle at his elbow and handed one to her, before turning away to the chopping board where a batch of large-domed mushrooms were waiting to be sliced. 'Everything's under control; go and freshen up.'

Everything's under control? she thought ruefully. She wished.

Once in her room she surveyed her tear-stained face and bedraggled hair with a feeling of despair. What a mess; *what a mess!* She shut her eyes briefly, but the reflection hadn't improved when she opened them. And this was her first day here too; he must wonder what on earth he had taken on. She nipped at her lower lip as hot embarrassment flooded every nerve and sinew, and then took several gulps of the fruity red wine to ease the ache in her throat.

Well, from this moment on she would be the model of decorum—she *would*. No more displays of prickly nerves or agitation or tears, whatever she was feeling inside. She had had years of practice at keeping her feelings hidden—twenty-one in fact—and normally she managed perfectly well.

She was well aware that among her colleagues at work and few close friends she had always been regarded as something of a closed book—reserved, cool even. It had been the only way to get through sometimes when the hurt had been so sharp, after some family upset or other, that she had felt the very essence of her was bleeding slowly, raw and vulnerable.

So why, she asked herself now as she stripped off her sticky clothes quickly and reached for her bathrobe, couldn't she maintain that self-protecting restraint around Keir Durrell?

She opened the door and fairly sped to the sanctuary of the bathroom, feeling horribly exposed at the knowledge of her nakedness under the robe. But once in the warm, perfumed water she found herself relaxing as the soft bubbles eased away the dust of a day spent outdoors.

After a five-minute soak—she really didn't feel she could spend longer in the water with Keir working in the kitchen—she washed her hair under the shower and hurried back to her bedroom, dressing quickly in white leggings and a long jade-green shirt, before rubbing her hair almost dry with the towel. A few silky silver tendrils curled about her face, as they were apt to do when her hair was damp, but she left it lose, applying just a touch of green eyeshadow to her eyelids before padding out into the hall.

'Refill?' Keir gestured at the empty glass in her hand as he turned at her entrance into the kitchen. 'Help yourself; the steaks need browning a little more.'

'Thank you.' She glanced uneasily at the broad back as he reapplied himself to their dinner. The wine was delicious, but potent; two glasses would more than suffice. She needed all her wits about her tonight.

'So, what do you think of Towerby now you've had a chance to look around?' Keir's voice was bland, his body language relaxed, and she tried to make herself answer naturally, the way someone would if they were visiting for a few days on holiday.

'It's very pretty.' He nodded, but didn't answer, and she waited for a moment before she added, 'I didn't see many people, but those that were about seemed friendly.'

Keir was in a better position than most to know who was who in the surrounding district, she thought with a shred of excitement, but he was too astute by half. She would have to tread carefully if she was going to learn anything.

'It's a working community.' He turned briefly as he spoke. 'Pass me those plates, would you?'

She passed the plates and watched as he deftly served the two beautifully cooked steaks, heaped with mushrooms and onions, before gesturing towards the lounge with his head. 'Shall we go through?'

They had almost finished the mouth-watering blackcurrant cheesecake Keir had produced for dessert—'Not home-made, I'm afraid,' he had admitted with a wry twist of his mouth that was undeniably sexy—before she was able to bring the subject of Towerby's population into the conversation again. It was one of Keir's amusing stories about a somewhat eccentric old farmer he had visited that day that gave her the necessary opening. 'He's never been out of Yorkshire in his life,' Keir finished with a wry smile. 'So perhaps his mistrust of new gadgets is understandable.'

She nodded before saying carefully, 'I expect most folk round here are Yorkshire-born and bred?' Her heart began to thump painfully. It seemed almost...deceitful to be questioning him like this about friends and acquaintances he had known all his life—but she had to *know*, she reassured herself firmly. It was what she had come here for, after all.

'On the whole.' She hadn't been careful enough. 'Why do you ask?' he asked expressionlessly.

'No reason.' A blob of blackcurrant sauce landed on her white leggings as she felt herself flush. Lying had never been one of her strong points; even the tiniest fib had always left her red-faced and mumbling. 'It's just...you must have summer visitors, like me, and people buying holiday homes, things like that?'

'Yes, we do.'

He wasn't making this very easy, she thought irritably. 'And I'm sure some of them fall in love with the place, like I have.' She smiled brightly.

'Have you, Catherine?'

'What?' She was concentrating so much on the real thrust of the conversation that she lost the thread.

'Fallen in love?' he returned blandly. 'With Towerby.'

'Yes, yes, I have.' This wasn't going to work; perhaps she would learn more from villagers, shopkeepers, people like that?

'That's good.' His voice had a brooding quality to it now, his eyes very dark as he stared at her across the table before rising abruptly. 'Coffee?'

Well, so much for detective work. 'Thank you.'

It was almost dark outside, the sky a dense charcoal streaked with pewter-grey, and the lighted windows from the village below giving a cosy, chocolate-box feel to the night. She was standing looking down at the slumbering houses when he returned with the coffee tray, her eyes examining each lighted window and trying to reach beyond to the people inside. She was here—her mother was here. Catherine just knew it.

'Come and sit down in a comfortable seat.' He ignored her hasty return to the table and walked over to the other side of the room where the big, comfy three-piece suite sat, placing the tray on a coffee table in front of the sofa. 'Those dining chairs are hard on the rear end after a time.'

'They're fine.' She avoided the seat next to him on the sofa, and sat down on the carpet behind the coffee table on the pretext of pouring the coffee. 'You've done more than enough,' she said, her voice a little too bright. 'I'll pour, shall I? Black or white?'

'Black, as you would expect,' he murmured cryptically.

She passed him his coffee, taking care their hands didn't touch, but nothing could cushion the disturbing aura of powerful masculinity, the magnetic attraction in the cool, closed face and menacingly lean body. He was the sort of man who would have women turning cartwheels in a bid for his attention and not even notice, she thought painfully. What had his wife been like?

As though in answer to the unspoken question her

eyes alighted on a big embossed photo album at the side of the CD player, which had obviously been there some time, judging from the thin layer of dust on its cover.

'A photo album; would you mind if I had a look?' she asked quickly before she lost her nerve.

'What?' It was clear he hadn't noticed it, and still more clear he wasn't pleased to see it there, judging from the frown—swiftly hidden—that coloured his grey eyes stormy dark. 'Not at all.' Politeness won. 'Janice must have left it out some time; probably she was showing Michael the regulation baby snaps,' he said expressionlessly. 'She insisted on putting an album together when our parents decided to move—nostalgia at its most painful,' he added somewhat heartlessly.

He had been a serious baby and a serious little boy. Catherine glanced through the carefully arranged plastic sleeves as her heart lurched and thumped. And wickedly handsome even then. Janice looked just the same, and their parents seemed a jolly, smiling twosome, often laughing into the camera along with Janice, while Keir stared steadfastly into the lens, his face reflective.

And then she turned the page and there she was, as Catherine had known she would be—Keir's wife, Marion, on what was obviously their wedding day. She wasn't dressed in white, but in a chic pale pink suit and tiny little hat complete with veil that sat on top of her glossy dark hair like the icing on a cake. Her face was lovely, wide-eyed and heart-shaped, and her body was model-thin, her slimness accentuated by her considerable height which was just a couple of inches shorter than Keir's.

So he liked his women tall and dark, did he? Catherine thought painfully. The very antithesis to her, in fact.

'This is your wife?' She had to say something. She was burningly aware of his sombre gaze on her face as she looked at the photographs, and the moment had become charged with tension. It must hurt him when he was reminded of all he had lost like this, she thought wretchedly. She really shouldn't have instigated the situation, but it was too late now.

'Yes, that's Marion,' he said quietly, moving from his seat on the sofa to sit down beside her on the carpet, looking over her shoulder at the album she had placed on the coffee table.

It wasn't a move she would have suggested. There they were, looking at a photograph of his dead wife on what must have been the happiest day of their lives, a day that had promised a long future together which had been snatched away by the cruel hand of fate. And, in spite of the tragedy of it all, all she could think about was how good he smelt, how close he was...

'That photo was taken on our wedding day, of course,' he said softly, reaching out and flicking over the page. His breath was warm on the back of her neck, his torso touching hers briefly as he leant forward, and she felt a tight congestion in the pit of her stomach that was positively painful. 'This is Janice and Michael—he was my best man. You haven't seen him yet, have you?' he continued quietly.

'No.' She was having difficulty in seeing him now; all her senses were tuned into the warm, tough, male body behind hers, and nothing else seemed real. She forced herself to concentrate on the photograph of Keir and his bride, with Janice and Michael at either side of the happy couple. 'He looks very nice,' she managed fairly naturally as her eyes took in the somewhat small, chunky man smiling into the camera.

'He is.' Keir shifted slightly and she tensed, but the hard frame didn't touch hers. 'But what's even better is that he understands Janice through and through, and manages to curb her excess of enthusiasm when appropriate,' he said with dry, brotherly satisfaction. 'Her heart rules her head most of the time.'

'Does it?' She couldn't tear her eyes away from the tall, elegant figure in pale pink.

'But she was a tower of strength for Marion,' he continued softly, almost as though he could see where her gaze was directed.

'So you were only married for a short time...?'

'Twelve months.'

Twelve months? *Twelve months?* However had he coped?

'But we had known each other for some time before that. Marion... Marion decided to leave college and marry me instead of qualifying; she felt being my receptionist was the next best thing to being a vet herself.' She couldn't quite place the note in his voice, and would have given the world at that moment to see his face.

'She must have loved you very much,' Catherine said quietly, keeping all expression out of her voice by a superhuman effort. She had started this particular ball rolling, she thought numbly; it wasn't his fault it hurt so much.

'Yes, she did.' His arm reached over her again and shut the album with a little snap, and for a moment there was absolute stillness in the room. She didn't dare move; she felt almost as though something momentous was about to happen, ridiculous though that was. But when in the next second the telephone rang shrilly in a corner of the room the disappointment was shattering.

'Excuse me.' As he stood up one hard thigh brushed against her shoulder, and the brief contact was electrifying.

The call signified an emergency at one of the farms, and Keir left within minutes after apologising about leaving her with the washing up.

'No problem.' She smiled at him quickly. It wasn't. The problem would have been both of them squeezing into the small kitchen and sharing such a cosy domestic chore.

Once she was alone she cleared the debris off the table, washed and dried the dishes and restored the small kitchen to gleaming order, and, after pouring herself another cup of coffee from the percolator Keir had switched on, she walked through to the lounge again.

The photograph album suddenly seemed to have become an entity in itself, pulsing gently in the corner of the room as her eyes were drawn to it.

It would do no good to open it again, she told herself firmly. No good at all. She didn't want to gaze at his wife again, look into that lovely face and try and decide what it was about this particular woman that had captivated Keir enough to ask her to spend the rest of her life with him, to wonder how he had felt when Marion had been snatched from him.

She had no right to go poking about in his home anyway, and he had made it clear, by that abrupt closing of the album, that he hadn't liked her curiosity. She was here as a temporary guest, and only because circumstances had thrust her on him and he had felt obliged to help her out. It wouldn't be right to take advantage of that.

She opened the album.

It was nearly an hour later before she closed it again and walked through to her room, her heart as heavy as lead and her face sombre.

She wished she hadn't come here. The thought was savage and strong, and she stood for a long time at the window, looking out into the darkness beyond before pulling the curtains and getting ready for bed, only to lie in the warm blackness for what seemed like hours as her mind churned and spun.

It was stupid—*she* was stupid—to think she could find her mother after all this time. She obviously hadn't wanted to be found; there had been no contact in twenty-one years after all. She was the proverbial needle in a haystack. The best thing Catherine could do was pack her bags tomorrow and leave Yorkshire at once, make the new start she had promised herself. There was nothing for her here—nothing—and she didn't want there to be, she added fiercely.

Yes, she would leave tomorrow. She curled into a tight little ball under the covers, willing the hot tears that were stinging the back of her eyeballs not to fall. Her mother didn't want her? Well, she didn't want her either. She didn't want or need anyone; she could survive on her own. The ache in her chest worsened, becoming a physical pain, and her pillow was damp when at last she drifted into a troubled, restless slumber full of nightmarish images and jangled, elusive half-dreams.

It was two weeks later, and Catherine was still in Yorkshire. She had awoken the morning after the dinner with Keir determined to tell him she was leaving, but somehow the day had come and gone and there hadn't been a right moment, and then the following days had settled into a pattern all of their own almost without her being aware of it.

She rose early every morning, only leaving her room when she heard Keir go downstairs to the surgery. And, after a hasty breakfast, she fixed herself a light packed lunch that included a large bottle of water in her knapsack, rounded up the dogs, and left for the hills.

And so it was that the seven of them spent warm, sunny day after day in the pure Yorkshire air, usually without seeing another living soul, exploring wooded valleys, shallow, crystal-clear rivers, rich, scented moorland and the odd beautiful monastic ruin that Catherine stumbled over in her wanderings.

The dogs were wonderful companions, and were soon quite devoted to this new friend who had obviously been sent from doggy heaven as a ministering angel completely in tune with their needs, from roaming the countryside each day to snacks of biscuits and chocolate when the opportunity arose, as it did fairly frequently.

And gradually, imperceptibly, as her clear, soft skin took on the golden, honey-toned hue of long hours spent in the hot sun, her mind and body began to relax, enabling her to sleep deeply at night and wake refreshed and rested each morning.

After that second evening Janice had finished the night shift and was now back on days, so dinner was a threesome—something that Catherine was inordinately thankful for. She normally escaped to her room fairly quickly after the meal, pleading, quite truthfully, exhaustion.

Not that Keir seemed to notice if she was there or not. It had rankled at first—the distant, almost cold way he had of treating her since that night they had looked at the photograph album together—but she had come to terms with it now; she'd had to. She had wanted him to keep out of her way, she'd told herself over and over again in the ensuing days, so she couldn't very well take umbrage when he did just that, could she? He was a busy man, and more so at the moment as he was waiting for his new assistant—a local lad who had been away at veterinary college but now needed a job—to arrive.

No, she really couldn't complain. But it was just that—ridiculous though it sounded when she tried to identify the feeling that gripped her—the flat, the village, even the countryside seemed to *breathe* Keir. She never really felt as though she could get away from him. He was constantly in her thoughts, popping in at any odd moment she didn't guard her mind, and then staying tenaciously there, obstinately resisting all her attempts to cast him aside. It was more than a little disturbing—and distracting—and consequently she hadn't followed through on any further enquiries about her real mission here.

But she had to nerve herself to set the ball rolling.

She knew the success of her quest would be purely down to her determination, and so, one morning, when she had been in Towerby just over two weeks, she found herself opening the door of the village shop with tentative fingers.

'Hello there, lass. Another grand day again, isn't it, eh?' The little old lady behind the ancient counter, who resembled a small round robin as much as anything, smiled at her cheerfully. 'You're the young lass who's staying with the veterinary, aren't you?' She bobbed her head and flattened down her apron like a bird smoothing its feathers.

'Yes, Keir and Janice.' Janice had already told her that her arrival in the small community would have been noted and discussed since day one. 'I'm here on holiday for a week or two.'

'That's right, lass. Well, you enjoy yourself. Nothing like good Yorkshire air for putting roses in your cheeks.'

She was treated to another beaming smile before the little woman continued to slice a joint of fresh home-cured ham, a half-filled box of groceries at her elbow indicating she was completing an order for someone.

Catherine wandered to the back of the shop, glancing idly at the well-stocked shelves. It was like stepping back in time here, she thought wonderingly as she took note of the old-fashioned layout and big wooden counter complete with a large, archaic till. She had grown up in London with supermarkets and high-rise flats at every corner, a hundred different take-aways within reach at any one point—even the odd corner shop that remained in the metropolis was streamlined and run by sharp-eyed businessmen.

But here, with the delicious smell of ham and bread permeating the shop, and a glass cabinet displaying cheeses, cold meats and little pots of home-made pickles, she could hardly believe she was in the twentieth century.

She reached for a bar of chocolate and walked back to the counter, deciding she would stock up the fridge in the flat with some ham and cheese and salad stuff before she went for her walk today. Keir wouldn't let her pay anything for her board and lodging, although she had already decided she would leave a healthy cash thank-you when she left. *When she left*. She thrust the sudden, sick feeling aside and made her requests known to the little shopkeeper.

'It's lovely round here, isn't it?' She wondered how she could bring the conversation round to the real point of her visit. 'The scenery is quite magnificent.'

'Aye, it is that, lass, although it's the same old story,' the small woman said cheerfully. 'Them's that are born and bred here see the other side of things. The winters are hard; we're snowed in for weeks hereabouts in the worst of it.'

'Are you?' Catherine saw her opportunity and took it. 'But you still get people moving here, so I guess it doesn't put everyone off. I seem to remember my parents saying someone they knew moved to this very village some years ago.'

'Oh, aye? When was that, then?' The little shopkeeper put the pound of ham she had sliced into a greaseproof bag and reached for the slab of creamy white cheese Catherine had selected, cutting and weighing a generous portion on the gleaming old scales.

'About…' Catherine licked suddenly dry lips and aimed for nonchalance. 'About twenty, twenty-one years ago, I think; something like that. Her name was Anna.'

'Anna?' There was a quick shake of the bird-like head.

'Well, I've been here all me life, lass, and I don't remember no Anna. The only Anna I know is Mrs Brown's little 'un, and she's five.'

'I think it was Anna; Anna Mitchell,' Catherine said carefully.

'Well, you could be right, lass; there's some that's come and gone who I don't remember too clearly. Perhaps she didn't stay long?' the small woman said brightly. 'Not all of 'em do.'

'No, I don't suppose they do.' Catherine opened her mouth to say more, but in the next second the door was jangling open again and a young woman with two small and very active toddlers entered, shopping list in hand, and the moment was gone.

Once in the street again, her packages in two carrier bags, she stood for a moment or two lost in thought, and then almost jumped out of her skin as a deep voice behind her said, 'You look weighed down, Catherine; can I help?'

'Keir!' Her heart was still thudding painfully seconds later. 'You're supposed to be at Major Gregson's place.'

'I was.' He grimaced ruefully. 'Earning myself a nasty kick between my shoulderblades from a less than grateful patient. That big stallion of his is a bad-tempered brute at the best of times, and me sewing up a gash on his hind quarters didn't appeal for some reason. I went from one end of the damn stable to the other.'

'The horse kicked you?' She was horrified, and it showed. 'But it must have hurt!'

'Somewhat,' he murmured drily. 'The more so because the stablehand is a girl, and the relief of being able to express my dissatisfaction vocally with the animal was therefore denied me. Anyway, I thought I'd better pick up some of my tried and tested standby in this situation—' he indicated the package in his hand that bore the local chemist's name '—before I continued with the rest of the calls. I've learnt by experience you can't apply the stuff too soon.'

'What is it?'

'A special embrocation that's something of a witch-doctor's brew, but works like magic.' He took the carrier bags from her unresisting fingers. 'You're going home with this lot?'

'I'm going back to the flat.' If he noticed the deliberate clarification he didn't comment, merely walking her over to the Land Rover parked at the side of the road and opening the passenger door, taking no notice of her protestation that she could walk.

'You're going home, I'm going home,' he said smoothly once he was inside the vehicle and she still continued to object. 'Okay?'

It wasn't. He was too big, too close and too... everything, she thought weakly, but she could hardly say so. 'Fine.' She nodded brightly, and thought she saw the hard mouth curve slightly, but he said nothing, starting the engine and driving the few hundred yards back to the surgery without further comment.

They entered the house from the long rear garden as normal, but once in the hall Sandra was there as though by magic, big green eyes taking in the carrier bags Keir was holding and Catherine's flushed face. She homed in on him like an anxious mother with a wayward child, Catherine thought with dark amusement, but there was nothing maternal in Sandra's feelings for her handsome boss; she would dare bet her life on that.

'Back so soon?' Sandra's voice was a little too sharp and brittle—a fact the beautiful blonde must have picked up herself, because the tone was blander when she added, 'Anything wrong?'

'No.' Keir didn't pause as he rounded the corner, his hand on Catherine's arm, and began to mount the stairs. 'I've been to Gregson's, incidentally, but the rest will have to wait a while. I'm leaving again in half an hour or so; if anyone calls in the meantime take a message and put it on the list of calls if they can't make a surgery visit. I'll check with you before I go.'

'Right.' Sandra obviously wanted to say more but Keir gave her no chance, opening the front door of the

flat as he finished speaking and ushering Catherine
through before shutting it firmly behind him.

She saw him wince as he lifted the carrier bags onto
the breakfast bar for her to unpack, and the thought that
had been bothering her since their conversation—namely
how he was going to reach the middle of his back without assistance—intensified. If it had been anyone
else—*anyone else*—she would have offered to help, but
Keir... Why couldn't the horse have kicked him on the
leg? she thought unsympathetically. Or his arm, his
chest? Anywhere but the most unreachable part of his
anatomy!

Oh, for goodness' sake! The flood of self-disgust was
hot. She was sure this small, simple gesture of help
wasn't beyond her, especially in view of all he had done
for her. She was acting like the worst sort of prude, and
it wasn't like her. He probably wouldn't accept the offer
if she made it anyway.

He did, with an alacrity that gave her no chance to
change her mind.

'It doesn't smell too bad.' He walked through to the
lounge, Catherine trailing awkwardly behind him, and
placed the bottle on the table before beginning to undo
the buttons of his shirt.

Oh, help, he was taking his clothes off! Not his
clothes, the other part of her mind answered soothingly,
just his shirt. Just his shirt? Her breathing quickened as
he shrugged the material off very wide male shoulders,
the strong muscles in his neck and arms and his hair-
roughened chest causing her to acknowledge that just his
shirt was more than enough.

'Right.' Her voice was squeaky in spite of her efforts
to sound businesslike and controlled, and she struggled
with the cap of the bottle for humiliating seconds before
he reached across and took it out of her weak fingers.

'Allow me.' There was a smoky amusement in the
deep voice that brought her eyes sharply to his face, but

he stared back at her innocently as he handed back the opened bottle, his face suspiciously blank.

'Thank you.' She aimed for dignity, sternly refusing to blush. 'Now where, exactly...?'

'Here.' He turned, the movement causing muscles to ripple across his smooth, tanned back. But it wasn't his body that caused her to catch her breath this time, but the severe bruising—already a nasty deep blue at the centre which was two inches wide—that covered the whole area from shoulderblade to shoulderblade, and was swollen and angry.

'Oh, Keir.' Her voice was faint but so shocked, he turned again, the self-deprecatory smile at her reaction to his injury fading as he saw the real horror in her eyes.

'Hey, it's not as bad as it looks—if it looks as bad as I think it does from your face.' He was aiming for lightness, but for the life of her she couldn't respond.

'You could have been killed—if he'd kicked your head...'

'He didn't.' His voice was very soft.

'You ought to see a doctor—'

'No way.' That was adamant enough.

Quite when in the conversation the bombshell hit her she wasn't sure—even afterwards, when she dissected every word and intonation of their voices—but suddenly she knew, without a doubt, the reason she had been avoiding Keir from almost the first moment they had met. She had sensed that here was a man she could fall in love with...and she was more than halfway there.

'Catherine, I'm all right, really,' he said gently—so gently that she immediately suspected he knew her shameful secret and was embarrassed by it. He must have women throwing themselves at him all the time, she thought wretchedly. Sandra for one, and Janice had hinted there were more who would like to comfort him in his widowed state.

Well, he might take a bit of comfort—most men

would, she admitted honestly—but it wouldn't mean anything to him beyond a brief, pleasurable interlude. She had seen that his work was his life now; he was almost ruthless about his commitment to the practice, and he clearly didn't have time for any emotional involvement even if he wanted it—which he didn't.

'Catherine?' He reached out to touch her but she moved so sharply his mouth tightened, his arm falling back to his side. 'I can get Janice to put the ointment on later if you like,' he said quietly. 'Being a nurse, she's used to far worse than this.'

'No, no, I'm fine.' Control, Catherine, control, she told herself grimly; it's all in the mind. 'I just wasn't expecting it to be so sore, that's all.'

'He's got a powerful body,' Keir said flatly as he turned again.

He's not the only one. Catherine's stomach clenched but she poured a small amount of the pale green creamy liquid onto her hand and took a deep breath as her legs trembled. Oh, he was gorgeous, she thought with a kind of numb painfulness as she tentatively stroked the embrocation over the hard-planed contours of his back, standing on tiptoe to do so. His skin felt warm and silky-smooth under her fingers, his flesh brown and vibrant and alive, with a fresh, lemony smell that was quickly obscured by the faint medical odour of the ointment.

She was unprepared for the rush of sensation that exploded within her, and eternally grateful he couldn't see her face. Her hands moved slowly over the surface of his skin, her touch gentle and rhythmic, especially on the heart of the bruising, and she was shamefully aware of little tremors of pleasure at the feel of his body beneath her fingers.

Unlike some naturally hairy men Keir's back was as smooth as his chest was hairy, his muscled shoulders wide and firm with not an ounce of superfluous flesh to be seen. He leant forward slightly as she worked, his

arms outstretched and his hands resting on the edge of
the table, his head bent downwards.

She wanted to ask him if she was hurting him but she
didn't trust her voice. She had never dreamt in her wildest dreams that the feel of a man's body could be so
erotic, so primitively sexy; she was in very real danger
of losing control.

And Marion had been *married* to him. The thought
was piercingly painful. They had worked together, eaten
together, *slept* together, done all the hundred and one
intimate little things that made up married life. Had she
known how very lucky she was? Catherine thought
dumbly, and then felt quite shattered that she could think
such a thing about a woman who had died so tragically
young.

'Is that enough?' She forced the words through dry
lips, but even to herself she sounded feeble.

'Would you mind doing the area on my backbone a
little more?'

His voice was strange, husky, but then he was in an
uncomfortable position, Catherine thought shakily, du-
tifully pouring a little more creamy liquid onto one palm.
And his back must be aching like mad.

There was something aching, but it wasn't Keir's
back. The shy and tormentingly erotic caress of
Catherine's nervous massage was responsible for a tide
of passion that was causing his blood to surge through
his veins like fire, his arousal hot and hard and his
breathing ragged. What was the matter with him? he
asked himself now. He wasn't a masochist by nature, so
why the hell was he prolonging this suffocatingly sweet
torture?

'Does…does this sort of thing happen often?' She had
to say something to break the lascivious nature of her
thoughts.

'What?' His voice was startled, and then she felt him

take a deep breath before he said, 'Oh, the stallion, you mean? No, not often.'

'I still think you should see a doctor.'

'I don't want to see a doctor, Catherine,' he said quietly as she took a step backwards and began to screw the top on the bottle. He flexed his powerful shoulders as he spoke, turning to look at her with narrowed grey eyes for a moment before he added, 'Thank you; that's helped.'

'Good.' She would die if he guessed anything—shrivel up to nothing and disappear, she thought wildly. But unfortunately, especially in view of the way she felt, her legs had no strength to move, and her eyes were hopelessly riveted on the alien hairiness of his naked chest. She didn't want to act like the naive young schoolgirl he had first accused her of being; she just couldn't help it.

She knew he was going to kiss her a moment before he bent his head—well, she had all but begged him to, hadn't she? she savaged herself painfully. But although the sensible thing would have been to move away, to turn her head, *anything* to preserve the last remnants of her dignity, her mouth was waiting for him and her eyes already beginning to close as his lips touched hers.

The kiss was hard and sweet, hungry, and as he pulled her roughly against him she could feel his heart slamming against the solid wall of his chest, his maleness overwhelming. He moulded her softness against the primitive thrust of his body, his powerful arms crushing her into him as though he would envelop her, eat her up. And along with a shred of panic at the hitherto unknown force of his blatant arousal was a fierce, eager exultation that he wanted her—badly.

'Catherine, Catherine...' He covered her face in burning little kisses, each one like hot, sweet honey, before taking her mouth again in a deep, long kiss that made her want more. She found herself straining into him, her hands clinging to his naked shoulders and her feet almost off the ground as he held her close.

And then they both heard it—the frantic ringing of the doorbell, followed by loud voices, distraught wails by what was obviously a child, and then Sandra's feet flying up the stairs to the flat.

Catherine had jerked herself free at the first ring, the strident note cutting into her tumultuous emotion, and Keir was already at the door, shirt on but unbuttoned, when Sandra knocked.

'There's been an accident.' As Keir opened the door Sandra blinked rapidly, but continued speaking with a composure Catherine envied. 'A car mounted the pavement in front of Sarah Matthews and little Toby. Toby's okay—he was in the pushchair—but the car took the lead out of Sarah's hands and Bingo went under the front wheels—'

Catherine didn't hear any more as the door banged shut and two pairs of footsteps hurried down to the surgery, where, within a few minutes, the wails stopped and all was deathly quiet.

CHAPTER SIX

It was a full half hour before Catherine could pull herself together sufficiently to venture downstairs, and then she found the front door was locked and Sandra was obviously assisting Keir in the operating theatre. There was no sign of the said Sarah Matthews and little Toby, so she assumed Keir had sent them home to await further news on their pet.

She couldn't have described how she felt to anyone. Part of her was raw inside at the terrifying realisation she had fallen in love with someone who was as far out of her orbit as the man in the moon. Keir was the sort of man who only happened once in a lifetime, and if she recognised the fact it was a sure-fire certainty the rest of the female population did too. Females like Sandra—beautiful, self-assured, with no skeletons in the cupboard and no hang-ups to cripple any emotional relationships.

Add to that the fact that he had been married and recently widowed—a devastating blow for any man—and the last thing he would be looking for was serious involvement after such a tragic, searing time.

He had a career that was much more than that to him—it was a way of life, an integral part of him, a foundation that even the death of his wife hadn't rocked, something rewarding and substantial. So...why had such a man looked at her twice? There was only one answer—she was available, and she had thrown herself at him.

She stood in the hall, shutting her eyes tightly and clenching her fists against the red-hot shame that covered her skin in a warm flush and sat in her stomach like a great, heavy stone.

What must he think of her? She opened her eyes quickly as though the thought were going to conjure him up out of thin air. She didn't really want to know the answer to that one, did she? she thought with scathing self-disgust. He would think what any other man would think in the circumstances—that she was into casual relationships, a good time, whatever. He wasn't to know that he had hit her like a ton of bricks, that she had never felt this way before and couldn't imagine doing so again.

To him the facts alone would speak for themselves. She hadn't even known him three full weeks and yet she had allowed— Well, it wasn't so much what she had allowed, she corrected herself miserably. Nothing had actually happened of any earth-shattering importance, but only because poor Sarah Matthews' little Bingo had been run over. Otherwise... She cupped her hot cheeks in her hands. Otherwise things might well have had a very different conclusion...

She had to get away and think. She rounded up the pleased dogs—who knew the routine by now and stood obediently waiting for the requisite collars and leads to be put on—and left quickly, without even stopping to fix herself a packed lunch. She could buy some chocolate or something, she told herself as she hurried down the garden and let herself and her eager cohorts through the gate, and a packet of biscuits for the dogs. She didn't feel like eating anyway; she felt sick to the heart of her.

However, a day spent in touch with nature and the peaceful solitude of the rolling countryside restored her equanimity sufficiently for her to be able to tell herself that she had blown the incident with Keir out of all proportion as she walked homewards in the quiet of the balmy evening.

Nothing had happened, she told herself firmly as her eyes were drawn up to the row of houses on their incline above the main street of the village, and nothing was going to. This feeling that gripped her—her mind balked at the word 'love' now—would diminish once she left Yorkshire. The last few months since she had found out the truth about her beginnings had been devastatingly painful, confusing, and that was colouring her thoughts and emotions; that was all it was. That was all she would *allow* it to be.

Nevertheless, by the time she let herself into the back of the house her heart was thudding wildly and she felt weak with a mixture of apprehension, excitement and panic.

'Catherine...' Keir was just leaving the recovery room as she stepped into the corridor, and she felt light-headed—dizzy, almost—at the sight of him. 'Are you all right?' he asked softly.

'Fine.' She forced a bright, brittle smile, keeping her voice expressionless as she asked, 'How's Bingo?'

'Bingo?' He stared at her blankly for a moment before saying, 'Oh, Bingo; he'll pull through. Fortunately the car wheels missed his body and just caught one of his back legs, but the break isn't too serious and he's a young dog. It was shock and loss of blood from being dragged that was the initial problem, but that's under control now. Catherine—' He paused and took a deep breath. 'About what happened earlier...'

'I'd prefer to forget it.' It was the tack she had decided to take as she replayed the incident over and over in her mind earlier that day, deciding the only way she could come out of this with any dignity at all was to be cool, calm and composed. The main thing to let him know was that he was off the hook, that she understood without a word being said exactly how things stood.

She had thrown herself at him and he had momentarily responded as any red-blooded male would have done, especially one who had been used to an active sex life that had abruptly stopped eighteen months ago. She couldn't blame him, but she couldn't let him continue to think that a light affair, a brief dalliance, was what she wanted either.

He would expect her to go cheerfully when her holiday was ended, no strings attached on either side, but this...feeling she had for him wouldn't allow that if she got close. So she didn't get close—in fact she took a great big hefty step backwards.

'Forget it?' His eyes narrowed as his mouth hardened. 'What exactly does that mean?'

'Just what I said.' The brightness of the smile intensified until she felt her face would crack, and the light airiness of her tone would have done credit to any acting school. 'It was nothing, after all; we both know that. And I'd hate anything to spoil the friendship I have with you and Janice.' A nice touch, a caustic little voice in her head whispered maliciously. That should settle the matter. 'I'm so grateful for you taking me in when I needed help—'

'Grateful?' His face had whitened, and now his mouth was a grim line in the taut skin. 'You mean you were being grateful?' he asked incredulously. 'You thought I was asking for some sort of payment this morning?'

She opened her mouth to deny the outrageous conclusion her words had led him to, but he gave her no chance to speak, swinging round on his heel and walking ahead of her past the other doors and into the hall at the end of the passageway, the dogs surging round him as he walked.

'Keir, please, listen—'

'I think we've both said enough tonight.' His voice was icy, his face more so, and her sense of desperation increased when Sandra appeared from the reception area like a beautiful genie out of a bottle.

'I thought I heard voices.' That seemed to be her stock line, Catherine thought painfully. 'Mrs Matthews is on

the telephone, Keir; could you speak to her?' the other
girl asked sweetly.

'Sure.' Keir glanced at Catherine, his eyes stony and
cold. 'Feed the dogs, would you? It might appease those
feelings of gratitude a bit.'

'Certainly.' She didn't betray, by her voice or expression, how deeply the sarcasm had cut her, acting as
though she had taken the words completely at face value
and as though everything were fine. 'I'll take them
through—'

'I've already got their meals prepared, actually.'
Sandra smiled at Keir as she interrupted Catherine. 'I
was waiting for Catherine to bring them back, but everything's ready.'

'Good girl.' He didn't look at Catherine again, walking through the door into Reception and banging it shut
behind him.

'I see to the feeding of the animals, *got that*?'

Catherine was still staring at the shut door, her senses
stunned, and for a moment the import of the softly hissed
words didn't register.

'What…?'

'The dogs.' Sandra made no effort to hide the hostility
in her voice and face, the sea-green gaze lethal. 'I see
to all that side of things. Keir's far too busy as it is, as
anyone with eyes to see would know. We don't need
someone else coming in and upsetting the routine.'

'Sandra, *he* asked *me* to feed them, not the other way
round,' Catherine said bewilderedly, taken aback by the
sudden attack. 'And I can assure you the last thing I
want to do is upset your routine. I should imagine Keir
was trying to save you time.' She could hardly explain
the truth. 'You always seem to be rushed off your feet.'

'I don't mind that.' The green gaze didn't mellow an
iota. 'It's my job—*my* job,' Sandra added aggressively.

'I know.' Catherine tried very hard to keep cool and
calm, but it wasn't easy.

'Just as long as you do. This is a working practice, not a holiday home.'

'Now look, Sandra, it was Keir's idea I stay here for a while, not mine—ask him if you don't believe me,' Catherine said stiffly. She was all for keeping the peace, but enough was enough. 'And considering I'm out for most of the day I hardly think my presence is an intrusion into the smooth running of the practice.' She raised her chin slightly as she spoke, meeting the other girl's hard gaze head-on.

Sandra stared at her for a full thirty seconds without speaking, her green eyes slanted and calculating and her mouth pursed with barely concealed contempt, before she flounced round, calling the dogs into the kitchen in a hard, sharp voice that made their headlong dash for food a little more tentative than normal. As the last one disappeared through the door it was slammed shut with such force that a framed print on the wall in the hall rattled before shuddering back into place.

That was all she needed. Catherine stared at the closed door for a few moments before turning and climbing the stairs to the flat, her stomach churning at the sudden confrontation. If she didn't know better she would think Sandra had some claim on Keir, from the way she acted. There had been something in the other girl's face that went far beyond the actual words voiced. But did she know better? The thought hit her between the eyes, and she fumbled with the key before opening the door with shaking fingers.

'Hi there.' Janice was just entering the kitchen as Catherine stepped into the hall, the fact that she was still in uniform evidence that she hadn't been home long. 'I'm just going to have a coffee—fancy one?'

'Thank you.' If ever she'd needed a dose of caffeine it was now.

As Catherine followed her into the kitchen Janice

turned and smiled sunnily. 'Keir told you the good news yet?' she asked briskly.

'Good news?'

Catherine's voice was wary, but Janice didn't appear to notice as she poured two cups of coffee and handed one to Catherine before continuing, 'About Martin, the new assistant. He can start tomorrow—earlier than expected—which should take some of the workload off Keir, thank goodness. The practice is too big now for one man to cope. Being a local lad, Martin knows everyone too, and having just qualified he'll be all bright-eyed and bushy-tailed!' She grinned at Catherine as she spoke.

'Eager to prove himself, you know? You'll like Martin; he was always something of a comic, and I don't suppose he's changed much—got worse if anything, I expect. Sandra had her eye on him at one point, but then—' Keir's sister stopped abruptly and turned a little pink.

'But then?' Catherine asked quietly, trying to keep the burning curiosity that had flooded her system out of her voice.

'Well, I shouldn't say really—it sounds dead bitchy—but...' Janice paused uncomfortably and then rushed on. 'Oh, I'm not going to be hypocritical, and it's what I think. Sandra was all over Martin until Marion died, and then she dropped him like a hot brick once she thought Keir was in the running again. She's always liked him and made no secret of the fact; I'm sure that's why she wormed her way in here as receptionist. She'd got a brilliantly paid job in Compton, and Keir can't pay her half what she was earning there.

'Anyway, that's what I think,' Janice said again, obviously flustered, 'but I could be wrong, of course.'

Oh, no, she wasn't wrong. Catherine's face was thoughtful as she began to prepare the dinner after encouraging Janice to shower and change. And how did

Keir feel about the beautiful blonde? she asked herself flatly, her heart thudding. But then he'd given her the job, hadn't he? Surely that spoke for itself?

Dinner was a painful affair despite Janice's bubbly presence. Keir was icily polite, his manner one she hadn't seen before and which was overpoweringly intimidating, making it a herculean feat to swallow every mouthful of food. Eventually Keir's grim face and forbidding presence subdued even Janice, and, although Catherine was aware of her searching glance on their faces and the puzzlement she couldn't quite hide, Keir's sister was too well bred to pry.

Everything in Catherine wanted to fling herself on Keir's hard, broad chest and hold him while she explained the truth—that he had misunderstood her words earlier, that her feeling for him was tying her up in knots, and emphasising that she couldn't bear to be a ship that passed in the night, that she wasn't someone who went in for brief, physical affairs. But perhaps it was better this way, with this wall between them. In a strange sort of way it was protecting her against herself.

All day she had tried to convince herself that what she felt for Keir was mere infatuation. She was particularly vulnerable at the moment, she had told herself time and time again as she'd tramped the fells. Her physical illness followed so sharply by the searing revelations about her birth had made her raw and bruised, open to all sorts of strange notions and ideas. It was natural she would search for love—her emotions were sensitised, susceptible; she desperately needed an anchor.

But it wasn't that, she realised now. She forced down the last mouthful with a feeling of relief that the dreadful torture of trying to appear normal could finish, and she could escape to her room. She wished, oh, she *wished* it were that simple, but the bald truth was, the more she had got to know this big, dark, capable man, the more she had discovered things to love about him.

Right from that first meeting he had disturbed her in a way she couldn't explain to herself—or perhaps wouldn't admit, she corrected painfully. If she had found him to be brutal, cruel, cold, would she still feel the same? she asked herself now. But if he had been like that this certain something deep inside wouldn't have responded with such intensity anyway. It was as if her heart had immediately known him, and it was frightening, unnerving, without logical explanation.

First her mother, now this. What was happening to her? Why had it happened? It wasn't fair... Her eyes were burning with tears she didn't dare let fall, her throat and chest tight with a despair that gripped her heart like an iron band. She was all alone, and perhaps this search of hers was self-destructive, but still the fundamental urge to find her roots was paramount. She didn't have the faintest shred of hope that her mother would want to be faced with the product of her teenage mistake, but even that searing knowledge couldn't deflect her from her purpose.

She had to know, had to *see* the person she had come from—hear what she had to say, make some sort of impression on her even if it was painful and caustic for them both. It wasn't a decision born out of logic or commonsense, but a primeval *sine qua non* for her having any basis for a future life.

Oh, she was a mess. She gave a little unconscious shake of her head at herself which a pair of keen stone-grey eyes across the table didn't miss. She couldn't blame Keir, or anyone else, for wanting simple, uncomplicated beauties like Sandra who were all sweetness and light for the man they adored. And Keir had had enough trauma of his own in his recent past to steer clear of involvement and ties—

'If you wouldn't mind...?' She came out of her dismal

thoughts to the embarrassing realisation that Keir had been talking to her and she hadn't heard a word.

'I'm sorry?' Her face was hot as she met the cool grey gaze.

'I asked if you would mind helping with one of the patients,' Keir said calmly, with no inflexion in his voice and his face expressionless. 'Janice has been on her feet all day and she's bushed. But of course if you've something else to do she can—'

'No, no, of course I'll help.' She was just amazed he'd asked her, considering how grim and silent he had been all evening, and it was clear from the look on Janice's face that the brotherly consideration had surprised her. 'I told you before, anything I can do to help. I'm only too pleased—' She stopped abruptly. She was gabbling again and it just wouldn't do.

'To express your gratitude...? Quite.'

Her eyes shot to meet his, but she could read nothing in the hooded gaze beyond a smooth blandness which in itself was suspect.

'Is it Bingo?' Keir opened the front door of the flat and allowed her to precede him down the stairs, and she was vitally aware of the big figure behind her before she reached the silent hall and turned to face him.

'No, it isn't Bingo.' His voice was quiet and deep, the slight huskiness which was intrinsic in it causing a secret little shiver to tremble down her spine.

'It's a little bitch I operated on this afternoon—emergency case of severe pyometritis, a bad infection in her womb. She's not a young dog and her heart isn't all it could be—added to which she had a bad experience as a puppy with her first owners and consequently doesn't like men. Normally it's not a problem, but in a case like this anxiety or distress can labour the heart, and she isn't too good yet. I won't require you to handle her as such, merely to talk to her and soothe her while I do what's necessary. Okay?'

'Fine.' If he'd caught the quiver in her voice she hoped he would assume it was due to apprehension at the forthcoming business with the dog, rather than the effect his nearness was having on her fragile composure.

The little dog was sleepy but undeniably nervous, her brown eyes wary as they fixed on Keir's big frame. But once Catherine began a reassuring dialogue, stroking the small head and bending close to her while Keir silently checked her over, she seemed to relax.

Keir didn't speak until he had finished his ministrations and fastened the cage again, and then his voice was soft and careful. 'Good; she's doing better than I expected. Her pulse is strong and she's more alert than I'd hoped for. If we can keep the post-operative shock to a minimum I think she'll make it.'

'I'm glad.' Why, oh, why did her body persist in remembering what it had felt like to be held close to that flagrantly male, hard frame? she asked herself desperately. There he was, as cool as a cucumber and as formal and distant as the man in the moon, while she was shaking like a jelly inside. 'Can I do anything else?' she asked stiffly as she forced herself to meet Keir's piercing gaze.

'Is that a serious offer?'

It wasn't what he said, or even how he said it, that caused her to become pink and flustered. But, even though she told herself it was her own reprehensible imagination that conjured up the dark mockery in his eyes, it didn't help. The trouble was, the heady aphrodisiac of power and gentleness combined, along with the clean, elusive scent of his aftershave and total control of that strong body and formidable intellect, had reduced her to jelly.

'Of course, I told you, I'm—' She almost said 'grateful,' and stopped herself just in time. 'More than willing to help,' she finished weakly.

His handsome face was perfectly serious now as he

surveyed her with narrowed grey eyes, his arms crossed against his broad chest and his legs slightly apart. It was a stance that did nothing for her efforts to get her racing heartbeat under control. 'And you don't think dealing with the animals would distress you?' he asked softly. 'Unfortunately they aren't always pleased to be under my tender loving care.'

Under his tender loving care. It took more determination than she had known she possessed to banish the picture that had flashed unbidden onto the screen of her mind and reply fairly normally, 'I don't like to think of anything being in pain or confused and bewildered, but I know it's in their best interests to be here. You don't want to hurt them.'

'But it's sometimes necessary to be cruel to be kind.' It was a flat statement of fact, and she somehow felt he wasn't referring to the animals now. 'One has to get to the bottom of the trouble, however painful,' he said grimly. 'Anything else is weakness in the long run.'

'And you're never weak?' she asked feverishly, looking up at him with great, drowning eyes as he moved closer, unaware she had backed to the wall until she felt its hardness behind her back.

'Not now, not in the things that matter. I've learnt the hard way—' He stopped abruptly as she went to move away, both arms coming up to either side of her shoulders to brace the wall, effectively trapping her within his hold, but without any part of him touching her.

'I've learnt the hard way it doesn't pay,' he continued softly. 'Marion knew there was something badly wrong months before she went to the doctor, but she wouldn't face it. She had the idea that to do so would make whatever it was a concrete certainty. We can do that in whatever area of our life we're struggling in—work, health, our emotions. It's running away, Catherine, plain and simple.'

'But not everything is black and white,' she protested

shakily, vitally aware of his male warmth, the sensual pull of the powerful muscled body and large hands that could work with such skill and expertise when needed, but were now securing her as firmly as a rabbit in a snare. She moved restlessly, but he didn't release her, leaning forward slightly so his body was just an inch or so away from hers, his head bent and so close that she could see the tiny black hairs of his beard breaking through the hard-planed line of his jaw.

'Not everything, no,' he agreed softly. 'Was it only gratitude you felt when I kissed you, Catherine?' he asked suddenly, noting the start she gave as his words registered. 'Or something more? Something pleasurable, satisfying?'

'Don't...'

'Why? Why shouldn't I kiss you when we both want it so much? It's the most natural thing in the world to give and receive pleasure; the animals know that without ever having to be told.' Desire thickened his voice and sent trickles of fire down her backbone.

'Keir—'

'I like it when you say my name.' His breath was warm and sweet on her face, and she felt almost faint as she looked into his eyes and saw her need reflected in his. This Keir was so different from the cool, controlled man of daylight hours; this was the side of him Marion must have known night after night as he transported her into the heavens... The thought hurt, but not enough to give her the strength to push away.

'And you needn't be frightened of me; I don't want to hurt you,' he murmured persuasively. 'Just relax into the moment, Catherine.'

'I can't.' But her voice was husky and trembling, and quite without conviction.

'You can.' He just stroked her lips at first, his arms still at either side of her shoulders and his body a breath away from her softness. His mouth was warm and knowing, and she shuddered as the kiss deepened, aware that his arms were holding her now, crushing her against his hardness as he explored, almost leisurely, the hidden depths of her mouth, slowly fuelling and increasing her response to him until she was trembling helplessly in his arms.

His lips moved to her closed eyelids, her cheeks, her throat, one hand holding her firmly against him as it splayed the small of her back, and the other caressing the honey-smooth silkiness of her arm before stroking down the length of her torso, his sensual touch causing her body to tighten and swell with an alien warmth that was all sensation.

'You see?' His voice was deep and throaty. 'You see how it could be?'

Oh, yes, she saw all right, she thought frantically as she caught at some thread of reason to fight the desire that had turned her fluid in his arms.

Perhaps if she had come from a happy, secure background and were here on holiday as Keir thought, if she had no dark secret that could well cause a miniature explosion in this quiet little community, if she hadn't fallen in love with him—which would make it impossible to walk away when the fun was finished—perhaps then she might have gone with the flow and given fate her hand whatever the consequences.

But there were far too many perhapses.

She jerked aside, the movement so sudden and fierce it took him by surprise, and she seized on his momentary disadvantage by taking another step backwards away from him, feeling safer once she was out of arm's reach. 'Please, Keir, I just came down here to help you.'

She tried to speak calmly, as though her heart weren't pounding in her throat so hard she felt it would choke her, but her white face and over-bright eyes spoke their own story to the man watching her so closely.

'You did—help me, that is,' he drawled mockingly,

the lazy amusement in his voice covering white-hot frustration. What was it about him that she found so threatening? he asked himself angrily. Or was it all men? She had been there with him for a minute—he had felt it, tasted it, damn it!

'This is Bingo.' He broke the unbearable tension by turning and indicating one of the cages where a mournful-looking mongrel was lying with one leg stretched out in plaster. 'He'll be going home tomorrow. And this is Mopsy; most of her problems have been caused by an over-indulgent owner who persists in treating her as a human rather than a cat and feeding her all the wrong things…'

He continued to talk about each occupant of the blanket-lined cages, his manner easy and light, and Catherine found herself staring at his profile as anger was added to the pain and turmoil raging in her breast. How dared he, how *dared* he be so nonchalant and unmoved when she was being torn apart inside? Their embrace had clearly meant nothing to him, had been just a brief flirtation, an indulgence of a physical attraction that could obviously be turned on and off like a tap as far as he was concerned.

She found she was biting her lip so hard there was the salty taste of blood in her mouth, and she quickly schooled her features into blankness as he turned to face her, her voice flat and even.

'Janice tells me your new assistant is starting tomorrow?' Two could play at this game, she thought painfully. There was no way on earth she was going to betray, by word or gesture, how much she was hurting. 'Martin?'

'And not a day too soon.' He indicated for her to leave the room as he continued, 'Hopefully I might find time to pick up some sort of social life again; I haven't had time to breathe the last few weeks since the other guy left.'

And I bet I can guess who will be first in line to help you relax, she thought tightly as Sandra's beautiful, feline face swam over the screen of her mind.

'All work and no play?' Her voice was too bright; if she could hear it so could he.

'Exactly.' He was just behind her as she climbed the stairs to the flat, and she had never been so conscious of her body, almost stumbling up the last few. 'Perhaps you might like to come out one night for a meal?' he asked casually as they reached the dusky landing and he opened the door. 'We could catch a film first, or go for a drive—see a little local colour?'

'I don't think so.' Her smile was brittle as she faced him. 'I'm normally exhausted from a day exploring; all I want to do when I get back is have a hot bath and go to bed.'

'As you wish.' The ice-man was back in an instant, the distant formality he did so well settling over him like a cloak and masking all expression, the ardent lover of a few minutes before a million miles away. 'I'm sorry to have delayed you tonight; it won't happen again.'

'Oh, I didn't mean...' But he had already passed her after shutting the front door, walking into the lounge without bothering to see if she followed.

She stood irresolutely in the hall for endless seconds, and then walked slowly to her room, shutting the door behind her very quietly and then falling onto the bed in a paroxysm of weeping that was quite silent, but none the less agonising for it.

CHAPTER SEVEN

'SO YOU'RE the mysterious Catherine I've been hearing about. I'm very pleased to meet you.'

Martin's introductory speech caused Catherine to stare at him intently, seeking some veiled meaning behind his words, but the good-looking, blond-crowned face was without guile as he grinned at her, and she realised it was just an opening line, nothing more.

'Hardly mysterious.' She smiled back. 'I'm sure you get hundreds of holidaymakers down here in the summer.'

'Perhaps, but they don't all look like you do.' The sky-blue eyes were frankly appreciative. 'You've caused quite a little stir along the local lads,' he continued, before Keir's cool voice interrupted him, the tone icy.

'If you're ready, Martin?' He indicated the door leading to the reception area and consulting rooms. 'There are some points I'd like to go over before morning surgery.'

'Right.' Martin seemed quite unperturbed by his new boss's high-handedness, but Catherine stiffened, her hackles rising. She had waited in her room this morning, after rising early from a troubled, restless sleep and watching a warm, pink-edged dawn banish the black shadows of night, until she heard Keir leave the flat and go downstairs.

She had thought her departure from the house would go unnoticed, but as luck would have it Keir and Martin had appeared from the recovery room just as she'd reached the bottom of the stairs with a view to rounding up the dogs.

118

Her first impression of Martin had been something of a surprise; he was good-looking—very good-looking— with thick blond hair and vivid blue eyes, his broad physique and warm, easy manner undeniably attractive. But he had hardly said two words before Keir had intervened, she thought now, almost as though she wasn't worth talking to. It shouldn't rankle but it did—unbearably—and she had just determined to say something more when the front door opened to reveal Sandra standing in the aperture, her right hand and arm swathed in bandages, made all the more noticeable by the sleeveless dark blue dress she was wearing.

'Sandra?' Keir was immediately at her side although Catherine noticed Martin hadn't moved. 'What on earth...?'

'I fell down the stairs at home.' Keir was treated to a brave, winsome smile before Sandra continued, 'Silly, I know, but I caught my foot in a loose stair rod. I'm afraid I've torn some ligaments and so on, so it will be a few days before I can work as normal—'

'You mustn't work at all,' Keir said firmly. 'You should never have come in. Go home and rest; we'll manage here.'

'Oh, no, really, I'd prefer to be here.' Sandra managed another valiant little smile. 'I thought perhaps, if Catherine doesn't mind, she could work with me for a day or two—do some of the typing and the things I'd find difficult. It won't be for very long—' she turned to Catherine now with a gentle little appealing gesture as though Catherine had already refused '—but it would mean things could carry on more or less as normal, and this is such a busy time for Keir.'

'Of course I'll help.' Catherine tried desperately to conceal her amazement that Sandra had suggested it in view of what had transpired the day before, not to mention the other girl's seething antagonism from day one. 'I'd love to, really.'

Keir was frowning, his eyes narrowed. 'There's no need. I can call Mrs Napier; she is always available to stand in for Sandra if necessary—'

'She's away on holiday at her sister's.' Sandra's voice sounded almost satisfied, and again Catherine found herself studying the other girl's face. If she didn't know better she would have thought Sandra *wanted* her in the surgery, but that was ridiculous. It was only last night she had been warned off in no uncertain terms. 'And we're terribly busy at the moment, Keir.'

He didn't want her, he clearly didn't want her, Catherine thought with a stab of pain in her heart region. But it was the original catch-22 scenario, and other than being downright rude there was no reason to refuse her help.

'So, two new employees all in one day.' Martin's voice was jolly, with the sort of brightness that was meant to cover an awkward situation. 'Hello, Sandra.' He moved in front of Catherine and nodded at the beautiful blonde. 'You're still working here, then?'

'As you can see.' Sandra smiled, but it was totally without warmth, and it dawned on Catherine that her helping Sandra wasn't the only difficult situation within these four walls. The other girl had thrown Martin over for Keir, and surely Martin was aware of that? She felt a moment's deep sympathy for Keir's assistant, and wondered if he still cared for the beautiful young woman looking at him with such cool composure. She hoped not; he seemed too nice for the shallow blonde.

The next few days were strange, surreal, although Catherine couldn't put her finger on what was troubling her so much. Martin was now a regular fixture in the practice, and was already taking a load off Keir's shoulders. He was cheerful, understanding with both the patients and their owners, and had a wicked sense of humour that lightened Catherine's day more than once.

He treated Sandra with a friendly impartiality that showed no signs at all of a romantic attachment, and which made the working day easy, even pleasant.

Sandra, on her side, seemed all sweetness and light to both men and, more surprisingly, to Catherine. She was seemingly grateful for Catherine's assistance, and displayed none of the covert hostility that had been characteristic before her accident.

And yet... There was something. Catherine's brow wrinkled as she walked down the stairs to the surgery on her fourth morning. It wasn't the fact that Keir had clearly washed his hands of her, much as she had to admit it hurt. No, it was tied up with Sandra somehow, something...menacing, threatening even—like a disaster just waiting to happen.

Oh... She shrugged irritably as she reached the hall. What did it matter? What did any of it matter? she asked herself bitterly. All her careful enquiries as to the whereabouts of a young woman once called Mitchell had proved fruitless, and Keir could hardly bear to look at her and obviously wanted her gone at the first opportunity—what could Sandra do to make things worse?

She was to find out in the next ten minutes.

'Feeding time? I'm starving myself.' Catherine was busy preparing bowls of special food for the patients in the recovery room from a list pinned in front of her when Martin joined her in the surgery kitchen, sniffing appreciatively at the five bowls of pungent-smelling food. 'Got any of that stuff to spare?'

'Don't be revolting.' She laughed and pushed at him with the flat of her hand as she wondered, for the umpteenth time, how she could feel so easy and relaxed with him, whereas Keir created a whole host of different emotions, along with an ache of tense, churning excitement that never seemed to fade. If this agony was love she never wanted to feel it again, she thought painfully.

'Revolting?' He stretched his face in simulated disapproval. 'How can appreciation of good food be considered revolting, I'd like to know? It's easy to see you've never been a struggling veterinary student eking out your last two pennies,' he added with a sorrowful shake of his blond head.

'Neither have you.' He had already told her his parents had more than amply supported their only child through university and veterinary college.

'True. Perhaps I am revolting, then,' he said laughingly. 'Why don't you come out with me one night and find out? I bet—'

What he would have betted she never knew, because in the next instant a cold, hard voice from the doorway interrupted them with all the softness of a razor-sharp blade.

'Martin, Catherine, could you come through to my office, please?' Keir asked grimly, his eyes sweeping over Catherine's flushed face for one heart-stopping moment before he turned and led the way through Reception and to the consulting rooms, beyond which the tiny cubby-hole that housed the large old-fashioned safe and Keir's desk stood. She had never heard Keir refer to the tiny room as an office, but then she had never seen such chilling coldness on his face either, she thought nervously as her heart thundered in her chest. Something had happened—something...awful.

Martin was clearly of the same opinion, his silent grimace and surprised raising of his eyebrows his only comment as they followed Keir into the small room where Sandra was already waiting, her face expressionless but her green eyes bright and sharp.

'Keir? What—?'

Keir cut off Martin's voice with a raised hand, seating himself on the edge of the desk before levelling his gaze on each of their faces. 'Sandra informs me there is a considerable amount of cash missing from the safe,' he said slowly. 'Have either of you borrowed some money and forgotten to put an IOU in the safe?'

'What?' Martin's voice was blank with shock. 'Are you joking?'

'I presume I can take that as a no,' Keir said calmly. 'And the same goes for you, Catherine?' The grey gaze was dark and forbidding, like a stormy winter sky.

'Yes—no—I mean...' Catherine took a deep breath and forced herself to speak rationally. 'I haven't borrowed any money,' she said shakily. 'I wouldn't do that without asking.'

'No, I didn't think you would.' It was said quietly, and Catherine felt, rather than saw, Sandra stiffen at her side.

'Keir—'

'And you have no idea where the money is?' Keir interrupted Sandra's indignant voice smoothly, his tone still measured and steady as he looked straight at his receptionist.

'Of course not—at least...' There was a moment's pregnant pause. 'It doesn't take the brain of Britain to work it out, does it?' Sandra continued, with a meaningful glance at Catherine's white face.

'No? Enlighten me,' Keir said with deadly calm.

'Well, it's obvious, isn't it?' Sandra said tightly, her narrowed gaze making her appear even more like a dangerously beautiful cat. 'Martin's worked for you on and off in the holidays and such like for ages while he's been at college, and I've been here for about eighteen months and nothing like this has happened before. So...' She turned and glanced at Catherine again, a gleam of something malevolent showing briefly in the feline gaze before it was quickly veiled.

'So?' Keir asked expressionlessly.

'Well, because of my arm Catherine has been using the safe, of course.' Sandra was rattled at her boss's slowness, and it showed. 'As far as I'm concerned, there's only one conclusion to be drawn,' she said hotly.

'Ah, I see.' Keir's voice was quiet, even soft now as he kept his eyes on Sandra's flushed face, which added to the sense of unreality pervading the room. Catherine's gaze travelled to Martin, helplessly searching for she knew not what, but his blue eyes were wide with shock, and something else—a wariness, a suspicion—as he looked back at her. He believed Sandra, Catherine thought with a touch of horror; he thought she had stolen the money.

'How is your arm, Sandra?'

It seemed ridiculous in the circumstances that Keir was enquiring about her injury, but as he did so Catherine was aware of Sandra's eyes swinging to his face, and it was a moment or two before she replied, 'It's...it's much better, thank you.'

'Would you mind showing me?' Keir asked coolly.

'What?'

'I would like you to remove the bandages,' Keir said grimly. 'Surely you have no objection to that?'

'I... Well, yes, I have, actually.' Sandra's other hand had gone instinctively to the bandaged arm. 'I...it's still so bruised, sore—' She stopped abruptly, her chin lifting as she bit out, 'Anyway, what's my arm got to do with anything? We're here to catch a thief, aren't we? There's over two hundred pounds missing as well as some cheques, and I know who's taken it even if you don't.'

'Oh, but I do—'

'Keir, I didn't take the money,' Catherine said desperately. 'I can't prove it, but I didn't take it.' This was a nightmare, a living nightmare, she thought frantically as she looked into the handsome, cold face. What could she do? What could she say?

'I never for one moment thought you had, Catherine.' It took a moment or two for Keir's words to sink in, spoken as they were in a calm, matter-of-fact tone, but then she looked at him—*really* looked at him, without fear and panic clouding her vision—and saw he meant what he said.

'Th—then who…?' she stammered numbly.

'Call the police, Martin.' Keir's voice was like liquid ice. 'I think Sandra will be able to help them with their enquiries; this has gone far enough.'

'*Me?*' Sandra's voice was a screech of outrage, and in that moment she looked anything but beautiful. 'You accuse *me*, when I've worked for you all these months and she's just arrived? Aren't you even going to search her things? Well, I will; I'm not being accused like this—'

'*Sandra!*' Keir's voice was like a pistol shot, and all three of them jumped. 'Not another word unless it's the truth. Make that call, Martin.'

'You're mad.' Sandra had gone as white as a sheet, her green eyes standing out like darkly glowing emeralds in her pale skin. 'If you search her things you'll probably find the money, and that's the main thing. The police don't need to be involved, surely? As long as she leaves—'

'The decision is mine to make and I've made it,' Keir said grimly. 'There's nothing more to be said. A couple of those cheques that have disappeared were handled only by me; I'm sure the police will be able to find some fingerprints to tie them up with the culprit—unless gloves were worn, of course.'

'Gloves?' Sandra's face had a grey tinge to it now, and her voice was croaky. 'I… You can't… *No!*' As Keir signalled for Martin to leave the room Sandra caught hold of the younger man's arm. 'No, stay here,' she said wildly.

'You didn't wear gloves, did you, Sandra?' Keir said with an icy softness that sent chills down Catherine's spine as she watched Sandra's eyes fly to his face. 'Careless, very careless.'

'I…I didn't take the money for me, to keep,' Sandra said desperately, still gripping Martin's arm. 'It wasn't like that.'

'I know what it was like.' Keir's voice was relentless. 'This whole business of your fall was pure fabrication from beginning to end, wasn't it? You resented Catherine being here, you felt your job was threatened, and so you determined to get rid of her.'

'And why shouldn't I?' Any vulnerability fled as Sandra swung round to face Catherine, her eyes blazing. 'I've worked here for eighteen months and everything was fine until you arrived, with your Keir this and Keir that; you make me sick! You might pull the wool over everyone else's eyes, but not me; I know you've got your eye on the main chance—'

'That's enough.' Keir didn't shout, but the tone of his voice was enough to cut Sandra's voice dead. 'So you admit taking the money?'

'I didn't *take* it—not in that way—I always intended for it to be found,' Sandra ground out between clenched teeth. 'It's in Catherine's room, under her mattress.'

'How—?'

Catherine stopped abruptly as Sandra turned to her again, her tone contemptuous as she snarled, 'With the spare key, of course; it was hardly difficult.'

'No, I don't suppose it was,' Keir said softly. 'Not when someone was trusted as you were. Martin, make that call, please.'

'You can't.' For the first time something akin to fear showed in Sandra's face. 'I've told you, I didn't take the money to keep—'

'You did something far worse.' Keir's voice was curt and cold, and quite without mercy. 'You set out to destroy someone else's reputation with a ruthless disregard for the consequences that was criminal.'

'I don't believe this.' Martin sat down very suddenly on a box of tinned dog food which was standing to one side of the door, his amazement at the unfurling tableau plain as he rubbed a shaky hand cross his face. 'How did you know it was Sandra?' he asked Keir bewilderedly.

'Because it couldn't be Catherine,' Keir said simply. 'She isn't capable of anything like that.'

Oh, Keir, don't, *don't* make me love you even more... Catherine felt his words stab her heart, even as they pierced the icy horror of Sandra's malevolence. No one had ever believed in her before and she dared not trust that it was real. The sudden self-knowledge was more shattering than Sandra's vindictive hatred, and she felt its impact right down to her toes. If he had the sort of faith in her his words had implied that might mean what he felt for her was more than a momentary fancy, and it terrified her.

It would mean opening herself up, becoming vulnerable, *trusting* someone, and she couldn't do it. That was what she had been running away from since she had first met him, not Keir himself.

'Keir, don't call the police.' Sandra's voice was small now, and quiet. 'Please, I'll do anything...'

'I don't want the police involved,' Catherine said quickly before Keir could answer. 'There's no need. We know where the money is, and Sandra's admitted what she's done. Can't we just let the matter drop?'

'Is that what you really want?'' His eyes were deep, dark pools as they held hers, and she trembled at his power over her. 'You realise what the possible consequences could have been if we hadn't discovered the truth?'

'Yes.' She drew a deep, steadying breath and forced herself to speak calmly through the thundering in her ears. 'But we did discover it—' you did, *you* did, my darling; oh, I can't bear this '—and it was an act of malice rather than stealing; I don't think it's a police matter.'

'I disagree, but as you were the target I accept it's your ultimate decision.' Catherine felt a fresh riot in her stomach region at the gentleness in his voice, the tone of which altered dramatically as he turned to the sulky-looking blonde.

'You'll be out of here in five minutes flat, understood? And I suggest your next job is in Compton, or even further afield, if you don't want the result of this day's work to become general knowledge. If you come within a hundred yards of Catherine, for whatever reason, I'm going straight to the authorities. I mean it, Sandra,' he added grimly. 'I don't make idle threats.'

'Oh, I'll go all right.' With the threat of the police gone the bumptiousness was back, and Sandra's voice was loaded with venom as she added, 'But you'll see; you'll see what she's like. There's more to her than meets the eye; you see if I'm not right. She might fool you, with her dewy-eyed look and little-girl-lost approach, but you're in for a surprise, Keir Durrell; just you wait and see.'

So saying, she flounced round, yanking open the door using her bandaged arm—with a force that confirmed Keir's theory as to the 'accident' was right—and leaving with her head held high and her eyes blazing.

'That did all just happen, didn't it?' In any other circumstances the look on Martin's face would have been comical. 'I didn't imagine it all?'

'Unfortunately not,' Keir said grimly. 'Are you all right, Catherine?' His voice softened on her name, jerking her to life.

'I...I think so.' She mustn't cry, mustn't give way now; she had to get away and sort out the turmoil in her mind, she thought frantically. Sandra's vindictiveness, Keir's faith in her honesty and the trauma of the last few minutes were all muddled in her mind with the knowledge that Sandra was right—she wasn't all she seemed; in fact she didn't know who or what she was. It had been hate that had driven her to this quiet little village, that and a desire to confront the woman who had given her life, to force her mother to acknowledge her existence whatever havoc it might wreak in her life, and suddenly she didn't like this side of herself.

Keir was different from any other man she had met, and not just in his physical appearance, impressive though it was. He was strong, straight as a die—what would he think of her if he knew the truth, that she was living a lie? She almost shut her eyes as hot misery swamped her.

But her own mother had wanted to be rid of her— she'd counted as nothing to the person who was supposed to love her the most—and rightly or wrongly she couldn't rest until she found her. But Keir wouldn't understand—no one could understand—how this thing was eating her up inside. She was no good to anyone like this; perhaps she never would be.

'Catherine, look at me, please.' She had been vaguely aware of Martin leaving the room moments before, and now the note in Keir's deep, slightly husky voice made her tremble as she raised her eyes to his. 'This whole episode has been a shock to the system—it is all right to show emotion, you know.'

But it wasn't, it was far, *far* too dangerous, she thought numbly. In fact nothing about her being here in Yorkshire was right—not the situation that had arisen with Sandra and the money, nor her secretly seeking her mother with this burning resentment colouring every minute of every day, and especially not her feelings for this cool, handsome man in front of her; none of it was right. It couldn't be more *wrong*. Things had somehow run away with her, become complicated and horribly tangled, and now on top of everything else she had lost Keir his receptionist at one of his busiest times of the year.

The thought opened her mouth. 'What are you going

to do, now Sandra's gone?' she asked shakily. 'How will you manage—?'

'*Damn Sandra!*' The explosion was sudden and fierce. 'And damn the practice too. I'm not talking about that, woman, I'm trying to find out how you *feel*; is that so wrong?'

'No—'

'Then *talk* to me, Catherine. Shout, Scream, cry, if you want to, but for crying out loud break out of that damn ivory tower you inhabit most of the time,' he said angrily. 'I want—'

As he took a step towards her she instinctively stepped backwards, terrified of what she might reveal if he touched her, and he froze immediately, his dark eyes raking her white face as he visibly fought for control. 'What is it about me that you find so hard to take?' he asked bitterly. 'I mean, I'd really like to know. I thought at first it might be all men, but I've seen you with Martin—seen you laugh, joke, even flirt a little—'

'I've never flirted with Martin,' she protested vehemently.

'No? Then what was that little scene I interrupted earlier?' he ground out tightly. 'Are you trying to tell me you weren't making a date with him?'

'It wasn't like that.' He was obviously furiously angry, and she couldn't think why, unless he was more put out by Sandra's sudden departure than he'd admitted. 'He was just messing around, being funny.'

'Was he?' There was a thunderous pause. 'And you like your men in clown costumes, is that it?' he asked with grim sarcasm.

'Now you're just twisting my words,' she said stiffly.

'How can I, when you never *say* anything?'

'Keir—'

'No, that's enough.' A moment after he pulled her into his arms, his mouth came down on hers with a violence that spoke of intense frustration. But almost in the same breath the assault mellowed, his lips warm and persuasive as they stroked hers apart, his tongue exploring the inner sweetness with a terrible knowledge of what it was doing to her.

His thighs were hard against hers, his arms forcing her against his male frame so that her softness seemed to merge with his masculinity, and she could feel his heart slamming against his ribcage, the solid wall of his chest pounding with the beat.

She drank in the smell and feel and taste of him, her body ripening and becoming moist as sensation upon sensation shivered ripples of pleasure into every nerve and crevice, her blood singing through her veins as he systematically set out to break down her resistance. If she had been capable of rational thought she would have drawn back, made an effort to still the fire that was burning so fiercely, but her arms were wrapped around his neck, her body straining against his as his hands moved feverishly over her slim frame.

The madness had to end—it was early morning on a busy working day—but as they heard Martin's voice calling from beyond the tiny room Keir seemed loath to let her go, pulling her even harder against him for one brief moment before raising his head and looking down into her soulful eyes.

'You see? You see how it would be?' he growled triumphantly. 'Now tell me you don't want me like I want you.'

But wanting wasn't enough. Even if everything else was all right—and it wasn't—physical need alone wasn't enough, she thought helplessly. Her mother had discovered that the hard way. Whatever Keir might say, in the final analysis there was no substitute for love.

'Keir, please.' She drew herself up and away from him, but he wouldn't let go of her completely, keeping her loosely within the circle of his arms. 'I can't—'

'No, don't say anything—not if it isn't what I want

to hear.' He stopped her with a finger on her lips. 'You're coming out with me today on my rounds; I'll show you more of the real Yorkshire.'

'I can't.' His finger left her lips and trailed caressingly down her throat, brushing her breast and one taut nipple on its journey, making her tremble helplessly. 'Sandra's gone—'

'Mrs Napier is back from her holiday; she's used to standing in when it's necessary. She likes the extra money, and Martin is here to hold the fort. You need a day in the fresh air after this morning's trauma; it'll do you good to meet some of the farmers and their wives.'

'No... No, I—I can't,' she stammered weakly. 'You must see—'

'I promise to behave myself.' He let go of her now, and for a moment she felt quite bereft. 'I can't say fairer than that,' he added with a wry huskiness that caught at her nerve-endings, his eyes dark with self-mockery as he looked down at her.

'You do?' She hadn't seen him in this darkly sexy, teasing mode before; it was as different from the powerfully contained, cold ice-man who had confronted Sandra as chalk from cheese—and dangerously attractive.

'Hand on heart and hope to die,' he said softly. 'Will that do?'

She was playing with fire here—she knew it—so why was she nodding her agreement? she asked herself silently.

'Good.' He smiled, his eyes a brilliant grey in the tanned darkness of his face, and she caught her breath at the sheer, sensual pull he exerted as naturally as breathing. 'I'll contact Mrs Napier, and once she's here you pop upstairs and fix a picnic lunch, okay? We'll leave after morning surgery. And perhaps you'll retrieve the treasure in your bedroom and return it to the safe?'

He twitched an ironic eyebrow. 'Unless you'd like me to come and help you search, that is.'

'I don't think that will be necessary,' she said primly, ignoring his muttered 'Spoilsport' as she left the room.

'You okay?' Martin eyed her anxiously as she walked into the reception area a few moments later, Keir staying in his office to lock up the safe. 'I still can't believe Sandra did that.'

But you believed I'd done it at once, she thought. It struck her anew that but for Keir's discernment the morning's happenings could have had a very different outcome. But she hadn't time to dwell on it; morning surgery was due to start in ten minutes, and until Mrs Napier arrived she was going to have to stand in the breach.

It was just over half an hour later when a small, stout, middle-aged woman bustled into the waiting room and over to the reception desk where Catherine was working. 'You must be Catherine. I'm Mary Napier; how do you do?'

'Oh, hello; please come round. Keir phoned you, then?' The morning surgery had been so busy, she hadn't seen Keir since the episode in his office, and now she wished she'd checked to find out what he had told the little Yorkshire woman.

'That he did, lass.' The bright blue eyes examined her carefully. 'Bit of a do, eh? Don't worry, Keir knows I can keep me mouth shut. And I've always thought Sandra was no better than she should be—too many airs and graces with that one—and it wasn't the job that brought her here in the first place, if you get my meaning?' Her voice was low and conspiratorial. 'Still, there's an end to it now, and I can't say I'm sorry. I've never liked working with madam, as Keir well knows, but least said soonest mended. You plan on staying in these parts long, then?'

It was clear plain speech was the order of the day,

and as Catherine mumbled her way through an explanation that she was here on holiday for a few weeks, she was aware of the blue eyes searching her face.

'You remind me of someone, lass, but I can't think who. You got any relatives in these parts?'

Catherine's heart stopped, and then raced on at a tremendous rate, and it was a moment or two before she could manage to say, 'I think a member of the family—a woman—moved here twenty years or so ago. Her name was Mitchell—Anna Mitchell.'

'Mitchell?' Mary shook her head slowly. 'No, that don't ring no bells, lass, but it'll come to me in time.'

'When it does, let me know.' Catherine strove with all her might to sound casual. 'If it is the same woman it might be nice to meet her before I leave.'

'You definitely planning to leave, then? Keir tells me you're going out with him today round the farms.' It was said as if one thing cancelled out the other, but mercifully the conversation was brought to an abrupt end as a sudden influx of owners and animals arrived and claimed Mary's attention.

Catherine escaped gratefully upstairs and set about preparing the picnic basket, finding cold chicken, hard-boiled eggs, home-grown tomatoes and creamy white cheese in the fridge. She made some ham sandwiches and added two crisp green apples to the feast, along with a bottle of lemonade and the requisite plates, glasses and napkins. And all the time, in spite of telling herself Keir's inviting her along meant nothing, absolutely nothing, her heart was singing.

She could take this one day, couldn't she? She glanced at her reflection as she changed quickly into figure-hugging jeans and a sleeveless white top, brushing her hair until it shone in gleaming waves and fixing it in a silky ponytail on the top of her head, with a few curling tendrils softening the style. She had made it plain she wasn't in the running for a light holiday fling or brief affair, after all; if he wanted to give her a change of scene after the dreadful start to the day it was nice of him, very nice, she told the warning little voice in her mind.

And now she had the lead from Mary Napier as to her mother's whereabouts, after all the weeks of nothing. And it *was* a lead, she was sure of it. She nodded to the wide-eyed girl in the mirror as her stomach turned over. Something was happening, things were being worked out; she could feel it in her bones...

'Catherine?'

Keir's voice broke into her thoughts and she sprang up quickly from her seat at the dressing table, before forcing herself to walk slowly from the room, rather than gallop to his side as she felt like doing.

He was waiting in the hall, picnic basket in hand, his dark blue jeans and denim shirt making him appear even larger in the light-coloured setting, and causing her breath to catch in her throat as the enormity of her love for him overwhelmed her again with a feeling of sheer panic.

Fire. She had been right; she was playing with fire. And if she wasn't very careful she was going to get fatally burnt, she thought nervously, walking to join him on legs that were suddenly leaden, the smile that had been on her face wiped away as though by magic.

CHAPTER EIGHT

'DOES the soul good, doesn't it?' Keir's voice was deep and soft and he didn't open his eyes as he spoke, his long, lean body stretched out on the big checked car rug and his hands resting behind his head, emphasising his broad, muscled chest in a way that Catherine was finding hard to ignore.

The remains of the picnic had been devoured in seconds flat earlier by the dogs, who were now cavorting in play in a deep grassy hollow beneath the idyll on top of a hill, where a vista of gently roving fells broken by a glinting river winding tantalisingly among great, spreading tees and ancient stone walls could be seen in the distance below them.

Yes, it did the soul good. Catherine glanced at the dark man lying by her side and wondered why, in the midst of such beauty and with Keir so close, she wanted to cry and cry and cry. Perhaps because catching a glimpse of heaven and knowing it wasn't for her was too much to take. She wanted him. She wanted him so much she ached with it, but she was too much of a coward to follow her heart and let the consequences take care of themselves. If he rejected her too—a week, a month, a year from now—she wouldn't be able to stand it. And why wouldn't he? Everyone else in her life so far had. Why should Keir be any different?

She hugged her knees tighter to her chest as her eyes returned to the dogs, engaged in a crazy game of tag, but she knew the second that Keir opened his eyes and lay watching her.

'You're so beautiful, you know. You do know, don't

you?' he asked softly. 'With your sapphire-blue eyes and hair like spun silver, I can't think of anything else but you. You're getting in the way of even the most mundane things I do. I think I'm concentrating and then you're there in front of me, with your tiny, perfect shape and shy smile. There's times I think I'm going mad.'

'Keir, don't—'

'I can't help it. I'm not even sure if you like me.' He rolled over and raised himself on his elbows, his chin propped on his hands as the devastating grey gaze raked her face. 'Oh, I know you are attracted to me—physically, that is—but you've fought that every inch of the way, haven't you? Why? What are you so frightened of?' he asked huskily. 'I'm not a monster, Catherine.'

'I'm not frightened.' It was a lie, and not even a convincing one. 'And I'm not trying to fight you, Keir.'

'I think you are.' The softness had gone, his voice a low growl. 'Is it because we both know that if I started to make love to you, *really* make love to you, you would turn to fire in my arms and there would be no thought of holding back? You want me, Catherine; your body tells me so every time I so much as touch you.'

It wanted him now, her breasts ripening and her skin growing hot at the naked desire in his voice. It was her weakness that made her voice sharp as she said, 'And you think that's enough? Physical attraction, lust, call it what you will? Even certain segments of the animal kingdom operate better than that.'

'No, I don't think that is enough, but we're talking about you, not me,' he said with soft intent.

She stared at him, willing herself not to fall prey to the dark sensuality reaching out to her. How did she manage this, him, *herself*? He had been married, and no doubt he had had other women before his wife. He had a sexual knowledge she knew nothing about. She had no skill, no sophistication; she knew nothing about the little tricks women like Sandra would use to keep a man interested once the initial craving had been satisfied. All she had was herself, and it wouldn't be enough to hold him; she knew it wouldn't. It was the only thing she *was* sure about.

He had said he wanted her, that she was driving him mad, that he thought she was beautiful—but not once had the word 'love' been mentioned, not even as a gesture of convention when he was making love to her.

'You said...you said you wouldn't—'

'Make love to you?' he interrupted roughly. 'But I'm not, am I? I'm talking to you, that's all. But of course if you've changed your mind...'

'I haven't.' She frowned at him, her eyes wary.

'Pity.' His smile was sardonic, brooding, and the tilt of his mouth brought a tingle to her own lips, almost as though he had kissed her. 'I'm learning that with you it's better to act first and ask questions later; you need to be taken by storm.'

'I don't need to be taken any way.' She tried to sound severe, but like several times before his mood had undergone a lightning change, and the wry amusement evident in the handsome face was hard to resist. Manipulation? It could well be...

'We'll have to differ on that point, but for the moment this...interesting interlude will have to take second place to Frank Marley's young heifers.' The transformation was complete. He had gone from ardent admirer to angry lover, followed by a dose of dark, self-mocking amusement, and now it was the authoritative, cool figure of working hours that faced her, his dark gaze unreadable as it held hers and the hard angles of his face attractive but remote.

How could he turn on and off like that? she asked herself with more than a touch of testiness. Was it due to an impressive single-mindedness? Or was his pursuit of her merely an amusing and interesting diversion for a short while? She didn't know. She didn't have a clue what made him tick, and—

'Come on.' She realised too late he had stood up and was offering her his hand, his grey eyes narrowed against the white sunlight sweeping the fells and his hair blue-black in the brilliant light. 'And stop frowning; it won't do my reputation any good if you spend the afternoon with a face like a wet weekend.'

'And you have one? A reputation, that is?' she asked tartly, letting go of his hand as though it had burnt her once she was on her feet and pretending to brush imaginary grass from her jeans.

She hadn't expected a serious answer to what was only a somewhat astringent retort on her part, but he straightened from picking up the car rug, purposely blocking her route to the Land Rover as he said, 'I did have, once; you're bound to hear about my wild youth sooner or later so it might as well be sooner.' His voice was cool and mocking, and she wasn't really sure if he was teasing at first.

She eyed him warily, her face expressing her uncertainty, and he acknowledged her unease with a wry shrug of his wide shoulders. 'Of course, it wasn't as bad as people liked to make out,' he said smoothly, one dark eyebrow quirking mockingly as it dared her to disagree.

'Oh, of course.' Her voice was waspish, but she couldn't help it—the thought of him with other women had the little green-eyed monster dancing crazily in her chest.

'Yorkshire is the same as anywhere else. People always love to put two and two together and make ten,' he continued evenly as though she hadn't spoken. 'I had a wide circle of friends at university, male and female, and inevitably different ones would visit from time to time and come home with me for breaks and a taste of home cooking.'

'Male and *female*,' she repeated with scathing sweetness.

'Just so.' The grey eyes were laughing at her, and she could have hit him. 'The gossips had a field day; it was a bit of interest for them after all, and something aside from the normal daily routine. But if I'd slept with all the girls accredited to me I'd be worn out by now... And I'm not.' The pregnant pause accompanied by the smoky amusement in the dark gaze had her stomach muscles clenching.

'Really?' The word carried a dignified coolness. 'I don't know why you are telling me all this, Keir.'

'I think you do.' The amusement had gone. 'That little brain of yours has enough weighed against me without more being added to it. I don't like promiscuity in either gender—I never have; neither have I slept around. Do you believe that?'

'It's nothing to do with me—'

'Do you believe it, Catherine?' he asked persistently. 'A simple yes or no will suffice.'

He wasn't going to let it drop, and as she stared back at him, her eyes wide and steady, she knew it would be fatal to let him see how much this conversation was hurting her. She didn't want to think of him with other girls, women—and that included Marion. It was unreasonable to feel jealous—ridiculous, in fact—but she couldn't help it.

'So you're whiter than white?' She hid behind a light smile and a casual shrug.

'I didn't say that,' he said calmly. 'I've never pretended to be an angel, just an ordinary man with my own moral code and my own set of ethics which I endeavour to live by. There are some things in my past I'm not proud of, but hopefully they've made me wiser.'

'I see.' She didn't have the nerve to ask what they were.

'You don't sound too sure.' He stared at her a moment

longer, and then turned and walked over to the Land
Rover, opening her door and helping her inside before
saying, his voice lazy, 'But don't worry; I don't turn
into a werewolf at the stroke of midnight.'

The dogs came immediately Keir called them, like the
well-trained animals they were, and once they were on
their way again Catherine pretended to look out of the
window as her mind buzzed with all that had been said.
He was being honest with her—very honest. What would
he say if he knew the reason for her being here was one
great big lie? Should she tell him? Her stomach churned
at the prospect, and she shut her eyes tightly before
opening them to gaze at the blue expanse of sky above.
She couldn't; she just couldn't.

He would be surprised and disappointed she had kept
up the deceit for so long, and worse still, he might just
pity her too. That really would be the last straw. As
things were now, if he remembered her at all when she
had gone it would be as someone he'd liked, wanted,
been attracted to, and that image was one she desperately
wanted to keep intact. To have it tainted with pity…she
wouldn't be able to bear it. If she couldn't have him, to
be remembered as the one who had got away, forever
desirable, was all the comfort she would have through
the long, lonely years without him.

Was that awful, wicked? She breathed deeply to control her racing heartbeat. She didn't know—perhaps it
was—but it was the way she felt. She was a mess inside,
muddled, hurting, but he didn't know that, and that was
the way she wanted it to remain. It might be foolish and
proud, but it was all she had.

She glanced at him now out of the corner of her eye,
unaware that he had noticed her peeping until he said,
his voice very dry and sardonic, 'Catherine, I'm sure it's
unintentional, but you're making me feel like the worst
lecher this side of the channel—which is severely testing
the old adage about honesty being the best policy. The

farm's up ahead; could you do us both a favour and relax?'

Frank Marley's farm was small and compact, and Catherine stayed in the Land Rover while Keir went into one of the big barns to inspect the ailing heifers. The grimy farmyard had clearly had animals housed on the big flagstones prior to their arriving, and there wasn't a clear path to tread through the muck and grime, the prevailing odour overpowering.

By comparison, the next farm they visited was a grand affair, with pristine buildings, neat, smart pens outside, and a general air of prosperity that sat well on the big cheerful owner and his attractive grey-haired wife.

'These are my godparents, Martha and Bill Alton,' Keir said in a low undertone as he drew up outside the impressive-looking stone farmhouse, where the middle-aged couple were deep in discussion with a couple of burly farmhands. 'They'll expect to be introduced to you.'

'Will they?' But she had no time to ask more before Martha and Bill were at their side. Introductions were brief; there were a large number of sheep penned and waiting to be inoculated. Whilst Keir, Bill and the two farmhands dealt with the animals Martha insisted on making Catherine a coffee in the gleaming, surprisingly high-tech farmhouse kitchen.

'I understand you're stayin' with Keir and Janice, lass?' Martha said over her shoulder as she bustled about, preparing a tray for the men. 'Grand young man, is Keir, and a brilliant vet. My Bill wouldn't have anyone else to see to his stock. You known him long, then?' It was the sort of direct approach Catherine was getting used to in Yorkshire, where everyone said exactly what they meant and flowery speeches were unheard of, but as she explained the circumstances that had led her to Keir's home she found herself becoming acutely uncomfortable under the older woman's tight scrutiny.

'So you're just here on a visit, then?' Martha deftly cut a giant fruitcake into large slices as she talked, before adding it to the tray along with four mugs of coffee.

'Yes.' Catherine sensed criticism but was powerless to understand why. And although the conversation progressed fairly naturally once the farmer's wife had returned from taking the tray to the men the feeling persisted that Martha wasn't happy to see her with Keir, making her stammer over her words and fumble her replies.

'Bad business with Marion.' It was straight out of the blue; they had been discussing the good works of the Women's Institute, of which Martha was a stalwart member, moments before. 'You know he cared for her himself at home right up to the end?'

'No, I didn't; I don't know too much about it,' Catherine said uncomfortably.

'Marion was petrified of hospitals.' Martha's body language expressed disapproval which was confirmed by her next words. 'Put a tremendous strain on Keir, with him having taken on the practice and all. Between Marion and the surgery he wore himself into the ground. But there you are; he wouldn't have it any other way. He can be very stubborn, you know.' She looked straight into Catherine's eyes now. 'But we think the world of him, me and Bill. I wouldn't like to see him hurt again.'

'No...' It dawned on Catherine that she was being warned off, in no uncertain terms, and for a moment she didn't know whether to be angry, offended or just plain hurt that Martha obviously found her so wanting. She settled on a mixture of all three. 'I'd hate to see him hurt too, Martha.'

There was an inflexion in Catherine's voice, of which she was completely unaware, that had the older woman's eyes sharpening on her face. It was a full thirty seconds before Martha said, her voice soft now and quiet, 'That's good, lass, because I've got an idea—'

What Martha's idea was Catherine never discovered, because in the next moment the kitchen door opened with gusto as Bill and Keir entered, and within minutes she and Keir were seated in the Land Rover again and on their way.

'What's wrong?' Keir's voice was flat, and Catherine realised she had said nothing for the last five minutes, having drifted off into a world of her own as she worried at all Martha had said like a dog with a bone. Having lived with condemnation and discouragement all her life, it took little to make her doubt herself, and now she found she couldn't throw off the weight Martha had placed on her shoulders, try as she might.

'Wrong? Nothing's wrong,' she lied brightly. 'I was just enjoying the beautiful scenery—'

'Did Martha say something to upset you?' He refused to accept the weak prevarication with a firmness that was formidable. 'She can be a little...forthright at times, but her heart is as big as a house.'

'Is it?' Catherine responded doubtfully. Be that as it may, she had the feeling that the door to that house was very firmly closed to her.

'Okay, let's have it.'

'Have what?'

'Catherine...' His sigh was very deep and pointedly patient. 'You aren't an easy lady to deal with; in fact on a count of one to ten you rate at something minus zero. I've asked myself more than once why I keep coming back for more.'

'Have you, indeed?' She drew herself up, aiming for a stately hauteur that would put him in his place—the effect of which was totally spoilt when he laughed out loud, causing her to flash back with, 'You needn't bother; you know that, don't you?'

'If only that was true.' There was undeniable amusement in his voice now which rankled even more. 'But somehow, somehow, you've got under my skin and there's nothing I can do about it. You turn me on, Catherine, but you're in here too.' He tapped his brow with a rueful hand. 'You drive me crazy at times, you test my patience to the limit, and I've never had so many cold showers in my life since you've come to the scene, but...I want you.'

'Keir—'

'But back to Martha and Bill.' He interrupted her panicky voice with a cool aplomb she envied. His words had aroused a sweet enchantment that was painful in its intensity, and she was alarmed at her vulnerability.

'Let me give you a little background history on them so you can understand better where Martha is coming from.'

'It doesn't matter—'

'It does to me.' This time she knew when to keep quiet, and she turned in her seat to watch his face as he talked. 'Martha and Bill were childhood sweethearts,' he said softly, 'crazy about each other from the cradle. They married when they were just nineteen, and both sets of families were from the farming community, but the top end of the market, so to speak. A lot of the farms round these parts were little more than smallholdings in those days, but their families were wealthy, very wealthy, and it looked as though their future was a rosy one when their wedding present was their own place. They had each other, two close and supportive families; they had it made in most folk's eyes.'

Hers too, Catherine thought with a fierce stab of envy that took her breath away.

'Martha had always wanted a big family,' Keir continued quietly, his eyes on the road ahead. 'But after a few months of marriage she had a miscarriage, followed by another six months later, then another, until the pattern was repeated year in and year out. They went everywhere, did everything, but still the miscarriages kept coming.

'Martha got desperate. It began to affect her mind and she wouldn't see anyone, shutting herself away on the farm and refusing all offers of comfort from friends and relations, until, twelve years on, the marriage was all but on the rocks. It can happen, you know...'

He turned to glance at her intent face with dark, narrowed eyes. 'You can home in on what's wrong, to the exclusion of everything else, until it becomes an obsession.'

He wasn't talking about Martha now, and they both knew it. But before Catherine could say anything he continued, 'Then she came to a crossroads when everything was at its worst, and the way she told it to my mother the choice was clear-cut—she could lose Bill, the farm, perhaps even her sanity, or she could look away from her own disappointment and pain and go with what she *had* been given rather than crying for the moon.'

'And so she did that, fell pregnant and everything was all right?' She didn't mean to sound cynical, but she had seen the photographs on the massive kitchen windowsill of Martha and Bill with their rosy-cheeked babies, little tots in school uniform, and later ones of smiling teenagers.

'Not exactly,' Keir said expressionlessly. They had been travelling along a fertile valley floor for some minutes, on a road that was little more than a rough dirt-track linking the farm to the outside world, and now he pulled in under a large, spreading elm tree and cut the engine, before climbing down and letting the dogs out from the back of the vehicle.

He walked round to her side of the Land Rover, where she was still sitting, and leant one muscled shoulder against the door, looking straight ahead down the valley as he talked through the open window.

'She began to talk to Bill, like she'd done in the years before the obsession got a hold, and they acknowledged they were wealthy, healthy, with a huge farmhouse that just begged for children but no foreseeable hope of ever filling it naturally.

'They decided to go in for the long-term fostering of problem kids—kids who had been through the mill one way or another—rather than adopting very young babies. Martha felt it was her way of making up for all the wasted years. They did that for several years, and then felt they wanted to do more, so they arranged with the social services to run a summer holiday home at the farm for under-privileged kids.'

'She hasn't any children of her own?' Catherine asked slowly.

'Not in the biological sense.' He was quite still, his arms folded across his chest and his voice even and almost without expression. 'They had six long-term foster children of their own, and then groups of other kids for a month or so through from May to September right up to a couple of years ago, when Bill suffered a mild heart attack. Of course their own foster children are often around—four live in the area and have kids of their own now—and many others come down for a visit on a regular basis to see their adopted mum and dad. They've straightened out a lot of lives in their own way.'

'And if they had had their own children none of that would have happened; that's what you're saying, isn't it?' Catherine said flatly. 'That it was the best thing—'

'No, that would be terribly presumptuous of me.' He put his hand through the open window, turning her face to meet his eyes. 'I'm sorry they didn't have the desire of their heart,' he said softly, 'but I admire them for playing the best they could with the cards they'd been dealt—*that* is what I'm saying, Catherine. Life isn't always fair; it can kick us so hard in the teeth that we think we'll never get up from under it, and some people don't. It makes them bitter, inward-looking; the chip on their shoulder becomes so heavy they're bowed down under the weight of it.'

She didn't want to hear this. She stared back at him, her shadowed eyes defensive and her chin jutting with painful defiance. She *had* to hold onto the consuming anger against the woman who had abandoned her—it was all she had. If she let go of that, if she allowed herself to feel any trace of longing, any hope that when she met her her mother might be glad to see her, even want her, she would become frighteningly vulnerable and exposed, and dangerously wide open to a last, final rejection.

This way she was safe. It would be *her* that would walk away with her head held high and her back straight. She wouldn't ask for anything, and she wouldn't expect it either. Not from her mother...and not from Keir.

She was grateful he hadn't believed Sandra's lies and she was touched by his faith in her, but she mustn't allow herself to run away with the idea that it meant more than it did. He was recovering from his wife's tragic death, a wife he had only had for a short time and whom he had, of course, loved—and Keir wasn't the sort of man to give his love easily.

Almost as though he had read her mind, he straightened, opening the door of the Land Rover and offering her his hand to alight. 'I want to talk to you, explain something, and it will be easier if we're walking,' he said flatly.

She stared at him for a moment as panic gripped her throat again, and then forced the feeling under control. 'All right.' But she didn't take his hand as she jumped down from the vehicle in one quick, light movement, thrusting her own hands deep in the pockets of her jeans and keeping her eyes on the gambolling dogs some fifty yards ahead.

Keir expelled a deep, silent breath. This wasn't going to be easy, but then he had never expected it to be. 'There's a stream down there among those trees; we'll walk the dogs that way and they can have a drink.' He glanced at her beautiful, pure profile with narrowed eyes. She looked scared to death, damn it, and it inspired such a mixture of emotions in him he had trouble distinguishing just one, except the frustration of continuously walking on egg shells. Enough was enough.

He didn't speak again until they reached the little copse of trees, and then his voice was magnificently matter-of-fact when he said, 'I wasn't in love with Marion when I married her.'

'What?' She couldn't believe she had heard right, her eyes huge as she stopped dead in her tracks and stared up into his dark, expressionless face.

'Not in the man-woman, romantic sense,' he continued evenly as though she hadn't spoken, taking her arm and forcing her to walk on at his side. 'There was a group of us at university, a few lads and girls, who got on well, were great mates, that sort of thing, with no physical intimacy clouding the friendships. We all had partners who came and went and were outside the circle, but it was an unwritten pact that we never moved in on each other—something we never discussed, but just knew.'

'And Marion was one of the girls?' she asked weakly. It was the last thing in the world she had expected him to say, and shock had numbed her reaction.

He nodded slowly. 'It was only the two of us out of the group who went to veterinary college but we continued to be there for each other, nothing heavy—or so I thought. But then Marion started to be ill all the time, one cold after another, that sort of thing. Looking back—' He stopped abruptly, shaking his head, his face drawn. 'Looking back I should have made her seek medical advice, but she just said she was low, that she'd get a tonic or something. A tonic!' His voice was tight and full of a raw self-contempt that caught at Catherine's heartstrings.

'Keir, it wasn't your fault; you didn't know.' She forgot all about self-protection and caution in her desire to comfort, catching hold of his arm as she spoke, her voice urgent. 'How could you have possibly guessed?'

He turned to face her, his eyes black with harsh self-condemnation. 'I should have known, Catherine; I was the only one who knew her that well. I knew she was terrified of medical people, hospitals, the whole caboodle. She had a phobia about it that was a result of an accident in her childhood, and it was like a ten-foot wall in her mind—unsurmountable. But I was working like mad, and she hid it so well—'

'You couldn't have known,' she said again, her voice soft and tender. 'You couldn't.' She was holding both of his arms now, the ridges of muscle hard beneath her fingers as she looked up into his face.

There was a long moment of silence as he gazed down at her, his body completely still but taut with tension, and then he took a deep, shuddering breath as he fought for control. 'We found out when she collapsed during one of the final examinations,' he said huskily, 'but by then it was too late—far too late. She felt so ill she thought she was going to die straight away, and so she told me—' He shook his head, his voice ragged. 'She told me that she loved me, that she'd always loved me, right from the first week of university years before.'

He turned away from her then, the movement harsh and abrupt, and stood with his back to her as he continued, 'But with the drugs they gave her she began to get better. Oh, we knew it was borrowed time. They were talking about nine months, twelve at the most, and probably a good proportion of those in hospital—which had the power to send her to hell and back every time she thought of it. Do you know what it's like to see someone you care about suffer like that?' he ground out grimly.

'No.' He had cared about Marion but he hadn't *loved* her. The thought was beating a tattoo in her head. Not in the way a man usually feels about the woman he marries.

'I pray you never will.'

'And so you married her,' she said quietly.

'And so I married her.' He turned to face her again. 'And it was a real marriage in every sense of the word,' he said evenly. 'Marion wanted it that way.'

It took more will-power than she had known she possessed to just nod quietly, the anguish that streaked through her soul at his admission shocking her with its intensity. Not that she resented Marion finding strength and peace in his arms to face the inevitable, she thought painfully; it wasn't that. It was the knowledge that if she could have swapped places with the tragic brunette, taken just a year of being his wife and having him close in exchange for the rest of her life, she would have done so.

'I'm sorry, Keir—for Marion, for you—'

'I didn't tell you for that.' His eyes were steady as he reached for her, holding her arms in much the same way she had held him a moment or two earlier, before pulling her closer to within a breath of his body, his face dark and handsome as he looked down into her troubled gaze. 'Do you have any idea how I feel about you?' he asked thickly. 'Any idea at all? I don't want to scare you off, I've told myself over and over that I've got to tread carefully, but damn it all, Catherine, I've never felt this way before, and it's killing me.'

'Keir, don't.' This was the ultimate irony in the snarled mess that made up her life, she thought desperately. She had known, even before the revelation about Marion, that what he felt was more than just a physical attraction. And it had terrified her; she had to admit it. It was the thing she had been fighting against every day she had been living under his roof, working with him, seeing him, loving him.

'I love you, Catherine.' The world went very still as

he said it, and for a moment everything was picked out in painful detail—the look on his face, the angle of his body, the trees behind and the blue sky above. 'I've never said that to any other woman—'

'No!' He didn't love her; she wouldn't believe it. This feeling he had for her might be more than just physical need but it wasn't love; she didn't, *couldn't* believe that. It would make the rest of her life too hard. Because she knew, suddenly and without the slightest measure of doubt, that she was too much of a coward to believe him. She couldn't believe he would continue to feel the same, for weeks, months, years. *She didn't trust him*; she didn't trust herself.

The mental abuse that she had suffered day in, day out from a tiny child right up to the moment she had walked out of the only home she had known for twenty-one years had savaged all the normal expectations—girlish dreams of a home and family, and settling down with one man who loved and adored her—clean away.

She knew that one day he would tell her it was over. She didn't know when, or how circumstances would unfold, but she would be waiting for that moment when she had been weighed in the balance yet again and found wanting. It had happened from the moment she could toddle, time and time again, and had eaten away at her self-perception and her confidence like a darkly insidious and avaricious black worm.

'Give me a child until he is seven and I'll have him for life'. The old phrase the Jesuits had used flashed into her mind. The woman she had called mother had had her for much longer than that...

'Catherine?' He gave her a gentle little shake, but his voice was tight when he said, 'This time I'm not going to allow you to escape and bring down the shutters, do you hear me? I don't care what's happened in your past—you could have been the worst sinner in the world before the day you came into my life and it won't affect how I feel. Your life started from the day I picked you up off that bench; that's what's real. And don't tell me you don't feel something for me because I won't believe it. And however little it is I'll build on that.'

'Stop this.' She wanted to scream and shout and wail with disgust at her own cowardice, tell him he didn't know her, that he didn't have a clue what she was really like, and that he'd run a mile if he did. But to do so would be to open the lid of Pandora's box, and she couldn't risk that. 'I don't want any sort of relationship with you or anyone else, Keir—'

'Yes, you do.' She had lowered her face as she spoke, and now he cupped her small jaw in his hand, forcing her tremulous gaze to meet his.

'No.' She shut her eyes, but still the glittering grey gaze was there in front of her closed eyelids, burning its way into her brain. 'It wouldn't work. Surely you see that?' she said desperately. 'We've only known each other a few weeks—'

'So we'll get to know each other better. I can be patient when I have to be.' She felt him take a deep breath. 'Open your eyes, Catherine. Look me full in the face and tell me you don't feel a thing for me,' he said softly, 'and then I promise I won't bother you again.'

She shook her head, keeping her eyes stubbornly closed.

'What are you so frightened of?' he asked huskily. 'That I might do this?' He kissed her slowly, and the thrill of sensation that shot through her tiny frame brought her jerking away from him, only to be pulled back into his hard body with a passion that told her his control was only skin-deep.

'You only have to tell me you don't want me,' he taunted gently. 'But properly, so I believe it.'

Her eyes were open now, the turmoil she was feeling reflected in their bruised blueness, but although she opened her mouth the words wouldn't come.

'I love you, Catherine,' he said again. 'I mean I *really* love you. I want you living with me, working with me, sharing the good times and the bad times, I want happy ever after—'

'There's no such thing,' she said weakly, forcing the words through the painful tightness in her throat.

'Yes, there is. I'll prove it; I'll give you a taste of it right now…' His hands cupped her face as his mouth took hers, the kiss hungry and possessive and frighteningly sweet, but although she could feel the fierce tension in his body, the control he was keeping on his desire, he was touching her gently, tenderly, as though she was something precious. And it was her undoing.

She kissed him back, straining into him as her love blanketed the fear and panic, and he froze for one infinitesimal moment before gathering her against him so closely she could feel the tremors sweeping through his muscled frame, and the pounding thud of his heart. How could she live in a world where he walked and talked and breathed, and yet be far from him? The thought seemed impossible as his hungry mouth stroked her tiny ears, moving on to the silky smoothness of her throat and neck, creating shivering rivulets of fire wherever it touched.

She was vaguely aware of the little inarticulate cries floating on the warm air, but ignorant of the fact that they came from her own lips, her whole being lost in a flood of sensation so strong, the rest of the world had ceased to exist. The hairy warmth of his skin, the muscled strength of his body, the wonder of what his mouth and hands were doing to her—they were the only real things in this world of colour and light and touch and taste into which she had plunged.

She was only conscious that they had slid down to the ground when the heady summer perfume of thick warm grass and wild flowers pervaded the sweetness. But then, as she felt the length of Keir's body against hers, it was all sensation again, his hard, male toughness fascinatingly at odds with the trembling of his body.

He kissed her slumberous eyelids, tasting their velvet silkiness with his tongue, before trailing feather-light, tantalising kisses to her mouth which was already open and waiting for his touch. He bit gently at her lower lip before teasing her tongue as he explored her mouth in an erotic arousal that turned her limbs liquid.

He was good, he was so, so good at this, she acknowledged faintly. But although the thought should have been a warning she couldn't respond to it.

Her hands were linked at the back of his muscled neck, and she could feel the silky bristles of his severe haircut as she ran her hands up into his hair. She loved him, she wanted him; she couldn't believe how much she wanted him...

'Now tell me again you don't believe in happy ever after,' Keir whispered huskily, his teeth nipping sensually at her ear. 'Tell me you don't believe I can make you happy. You're in my life, Catherine, like I'm in yours. There's no going back. Trust me; let me in.'

It was the one thing she knew herself to be incapable of. He felt her stiffen, her body freezing beneath his, and he couldn't believe she was doing it again—retreating into that formidable ivory tower and slamming the door shut.

He felt a hot surge of the rage and frustration he had felt on other occasions, but this time he didn't give her the space she silently demanded. He was *damned* if he was going to...

'If I wanted to I could take you right here and now and you know it,' he said grimly. 'If I cut the talking, did away with trying to find out what's going on in that head of yours—'

'Why don't you, then?' She tried to push him away, but the broad chest didn't move an inch, his muscles like iron. 'If you think it's that simple, why don't you?'

'Because I'm not an animal, Catherine, and I want more than your body.' He rolled away, sitting up in one swift movement and watching her with unfathomable eyes as she smoothed her clothing into place. 'I *will* have you. But it will be all of you, and not a hasty coupling in a field either. It will be slow and sweet, and you'll be there with me every inch of the way, mind, soul and body. It wasn't chance that brought you to Towerby. You might not be able to accept that right now, but it's the truth.'

He would never know the irony of those words. She raised her head and glanced across at him, and the pull of the sexual magic that pulsed from the big body was so tangible she could taste it on the air.

She had to end this now. She didn't quite know how things had gone so far, but if he ever guessed at his power over her she would be lost. She didn't *want* to love him, she didn't want to love anyone; love meant betrayal and pain and disillusionment, and she had had enough of that to last a lifetime.

She should never have come to Towerby. It had been a mission of revenge, and how could anything so flawed deserve to succeed anyway? She was no better than the woman who had brought her up in following through on this quest for retribution and reprisal against her natural mother. She didn't want to hurt anyone... The tears were stinging hot at the back of her eyes, but she dared not let them fall.

'It wasn't chance that brought me to Towerby,' she agreed dully. 'I planned to come here.'

The sudden elation he felt that she was going to open up to him was quenched by the look on her face and the deep desolation in her eyes. 'Catherine—'

As he made to move close to her again she jerked away so sharply he was immediately still, sensing she was at the very limit of her endurance.

'Some months ago I was ill with flu which developed

into pneumonia...' As she continued to talk, her voice flat and monotonous, he listened quietly, outwardly calm but inwardly burning with rage against the people who had so damaged the spirit of the woman in front of him. It took all of his considerable will power not to take her into his arms, but he knew now was not the time. She had to say it all first, open the wound and let the poison out.

'And you still have no idea who your real mother is?' he asked softly as she finished talking and shut her eyes, her body limp and drained. 'No clue at all?'

'No.' She shuddered at the tenderness in his deep voice. She had expected scorn at what she saw as her feebleness, disgust perhaps at her deceit, certainly a touch of self-righteous anger that she had been less than honest with him all the time she had lived under his roof. She could have coped with all those things, they didn't threaten her; she had lived with their twins all her life. But gentleness, consideration...they were dangerous—sweet little demons to undermine her resolve.

'Come here.' His voice was husky, deep with concern and desire, and her eyes shot open as her back straightened. She knew what she had to do now; she should have done it weeks ago.

'No, Keir.' It was difficult to look into the face she loved so much and say what she had to say, but she managed it—just. 'I've told you about my mother, my past life, so you'll understand my leaving has got nothing to do with you—'

'Leaving?' He didn't shout, but the tone of his voice made her stomach churn violently. 'You think I would let you leave?'

'You have no choice in the matter,' she said steadily, her voice firmer than it had been all day. 'You don't own me.'

'Yes, I do, in here.' He clenched a fist against his heart, the anger and frustration he was trying to conceal narrowing his eyes into dark slits. He had never looked more handsome, or more unattainable, she thought miserably, but she had to carry this through. He deserved better than her. He needed an eager young wife, strong in body and mind, to work alongside him and share the load, make a family life, bear him children.

If, by some miracle, he didn't cast her aside once he really got to know her, she would still be like a millstone round his neck. She would never be able to live up to his expectations and one day, *one day* those devastating grey eyes would ice over, his heart would grow cold, and she would have ruined his life as well as her own.

'I'm leaving, Keir.' She lifted her head proudly. 'I mean it.' She stared at him, holding his gaze with her own.

'What about your mother?' he said quietly.

'That doesn't matter any more.'

'You came all the way here, gave up your job, your friends, and you say it doesn't matter?' he said tightly. 'That was only a few weeks ago—what the hell has happened to make you change your mind?'

You. 'It was stupid, a pipe-dream, to think I could find her,' Catherine said wearily. 'And even if I could I realise now the only person I would hurt is myself. I might cause her a few problems in the life she's made for herself, make her angry, embarrassed, but I couldn't bear—' She stopped abruptly and then forced herself to go on. 'I couldn't bear to see her face when she looked at me.'

'She might be glad you'd found her,' Keir said softly, the searing pain in her face gentling his voice. 'Have you considered that?'

'She left me when I was a few weeks old, and she hasn't been in touch once. She knew where I was; she could have made contact at any time, but she didn't want to.' She drew a shaking hand across her face. 'Those are the facts.'

'And you hate her for that?'

'I don't know what I feel any more,' Catherine said huskily. 'I just know she's out there somewhere, somewhere close—I feel it in my bones—and she doesn't know me. I could walk past her in the street and I wouldn't know she was my mother. I keep looking at every woman about the right age, searching their faces, and the stupid thing is I don't even know what I'm looking for. I can't carry on like this,' she whispered painfully, her voice struggling. 'I don't want to.'

'If you run away now, you'll be running all your life. You know that, don't you?' he said grimly. 'Forget us for a moment; that aside I still think you should stay. I know people round here; I could make careful enquiries that your mother, if she's here, will never know about unless you want her to. I can help—'

'I don't want your help, Keir.' The well of loneliness that had always been a part of her, even from a tiny child, increased a few thousand feet. She steeled her heart as well as her voice, and said, 'You might think you love me, but you don't, not really. You don't know me. What you feel—'

'Don't tell me what I feel, Catherine.' He was angry and it showed, and when she would have taken a step backwards he caught her wrist, forcing her to remain still. 'I can accept you don't feel the same...yet,' he added deliberately, 'but give me the credit for knowing my own heart. I'm thirty years old, damn it, not some young teenager still wet behind the ears. I know what I want.'

'And I know what I want.' She stared at him, her eyes enormous in her white face, and lied like she'd never lied before. 'And it's not Towerby, or village life, or—'

'Me?' he finished grimly, dark colour flaring across his hard cheekbones.

'Or you.' She had to do this, make him hate her, or that tenacious streak in him would drag the truth out of her. 'I want a career in one of the big cities; the examinations I was working for when I became ill were to that end.' The touch of fact in the statement was enough to give a ring of genuineness to her words, and she saw the narrowed gaze flicker as he continued to search her face.

'I want my own flat, nice clothes; I don't want to have to be answerable to anyone other than myself.' If ever a picture filled her with horror it was the one she had just painted for herself. 'I want to see life, have fun.'

'I don't believe you.' He shook her slightly, the anger and frustration he was keeping under iron control causing his eyes to glitter and burn. 'I don't believe you're like that.'

'Like I said, you don't know me.' She dredged up a conciliatory smile from somewhere and forced herself to speak lightly. 'Of course, I shall always be grateful for all you've done for me, and I'm very honoured you want me to stay—'

'To hell with your gratitude.'

His eyes held hers for a moment more, and she was tempted, terribly tempted to fall against that muscled chest and tell him she loved him, adored him, that she'd do anything for him...

'Get in the Land Rover.' He had mastered the sudden explosion of rage. His voice was expressionless now, his face closed and cold, and once he had whistled to the dogs, and they were all safely in the back of the vehicle, he slid in beside her without saying a word, starting the engine immediately.

It was finished.

CHAPTER NINE

THE rest of the afternoon was a nightmare of endurance. Catherine and Keir visited two more large farms, neither of which was as prosperous or grand as the Alton premises, before driving right to the very top of Peak Fell to attend to a sick pig. The Robinsons' premises consisted of a small wind-blown farmhouse and several ramshackle outbuildings, and were situated in an exposed position where the grass was constantly flattened by the northern wind that blew with furious intent in the winter, a fact that the few spindly bent trees surrounding the buildings bore evidence to.

Keir hadn't said a word that wasn't absolutely necessary during the last hour and a half, and now, as he parked the Land Rover, he glanced at her briefly, his eyes remote and hooded. 'I won't be long.'

She had remained in the vehicle at the other two farms, but now something rebellious flared into life at the unspoken order that she stay put. 'Can I come?' she asked carefully. These were the sort of memories she was going to have to feed off for a long, long time once she was gone as she pictured him going about his daily work. 'I need to stretch my legs.'

His shrug was careless. He clearly didn't care one way or the other, and she really couldn't blame him, she thought miserably.

The patient was a huge sow with beady little eyes and wicked yellow teeth, but although she raised her head at Keir's entrance into her pen she made no effort to rise from her prone position. Keir's large hands were gentle but firm as he examined the animal, his manner reassur-

ing to the anxious little smallholder who kept up a
monologue of comforting baby talk to the pig whilst
stroking the big, spiky head, in much the same way one
would fuss over a pet dog or cat.

'She's going to be fine, Bob.' Keir smiled at the distraught man as he patted the sow's huge rump. 'She's
got a touch of erysipelas; I'll give her an injection of
serum right now, and you'll find that high temperature
will rapidly come down. She'll be on her feet in twenty-
four hours and ready to fight the world again.'

'Oh, I don't mind her bad temper,' the little man murmured equably. 'Me and Daisy understand each other,
don't we, lass?' The mean little eyes glanced his way as
one big ear flapped lazily, and Catherine couldn't help
wondering what the smallholder saw in the animal to
inspire him with such devotion. The pig was clearly
more of a pet than a farm animal.

It was after five o'clock when they began the journey
home, the late-afternoon sunlight highlighting the endless stone walls patterning the dales, and the gently dying heat of the day bringing the scents of thick moorland
grass and wild flowers into the vehicle.

Had he believed her when she had outlined what she
wanted for her future? Catherine asked herself painfully
as she sat steeped in silent misery at Keir's side. She
hoped she'd lied well. It would be fatal to let him guess
that her heart and soul would always be here, that she
would never stop aching for what might have been if
things had been different, if *she'd* been different.

The long garden was gently dozing in the warmth as
Keir opened the gate and stood aside to let her pass
through, his big body distant and remote, his face closed.
One wall was covered with pale yellow velvet-petalled
rambling roses in full bloom, and the thought came that
she would never be able to smell that rich, heavy per-

fume again without experiencing the grinding anguish she was feeling now.

Keir went straight into the surgery after leaving the dogs in the garden with bowls of cold water, and as Catherine climbed the stairs to the flat she found her head was pounding, the events of the traumatic day having given her a thudding headache. She would have a bath and stay in her room tonight, she thought wearily as she opened the front door to the flat, and then tomorrow she would pack and leave whilst the morning surgery was in progress. Keir had Martin and Mary Napier now—even her usefulness was finished.

'Thank goodness you're back!' Janice leapt out of her room as she heard Catherine's key in the lock. 'You'll never guess what I've done. Is Keir with you?' she added anxiously, glancing behind Catherine. 'I need to talk to him too.'

'He's downstairs.' Catherine tried to muster some enthusiasm in her voice as she asked, 'What's the matter?'

'I'd forgotten, I'd *totally* forgotten that Michael's mother has invited us all over for a meal tonight,' Janice said agitatedly, running her hand through her dark hair so it stuck out in every direction. 'She mentioned it a week ago and I meant to clear it with you and Keir, but I just forgot. And then when Michael reminded me today I didn't have the nerve to say I hadn't told you, especially when she's got everything in. He's always moaning I'm not organised enough, and we've already had one row on the subject lately when I double-booked us at the weekend, if you remember?'

Catherine did remember. Janice and Michael had gone to dinner with some newly married friends when another couple had arrived at the flat to take them out for a drink. As it was the third time in as many weeks that Janice had done something similar Michael had been less than pleased, and things had got pretty heated for a time, until

Janice had promised faithfully she would write everything down in her diary in future.

'You aren't doing anything, are you?' Janice asked anxiously. 'Please say you aren't.'

What could she say? Catherine stared at the other girl as she understood, for the first time, how Janice's haphazard approach to life could so infuriate Keir and Michael. How could she possibly endure an evening in Keir's company after everything that had happened that afternoon? It would be hell on earth for them both, and all because Janice had forgotten to mention Michael's mother's invitation. But she would have to go; it would place Janice in an impossible situation with Michael again if she didn't.

'No, I'm not doing anything, Janice,' she said quietly, her headache intensifying at the thought of the evening ahead. 'But I don't suppose Keir can drop everything without any warning; there's a couple of new patients from this morning in the recovery room that need careful monitoring. I'm quite happy to come with you and Michael, though, if Keir can't make it.'

'Perhaps Martin would stand in?' Janice suggested hopefully. 'If not I'll have to say there was some sort of emergency, but I bet Michael will guess the truth. He knows me too well.'

Say you can't come, Keir, say you can't come. Catherine continued to send silent signals all the time Janice was downstairs, but when the other girl popped her head round Catherine's door a few minutes later her smiling face told its own story.

'No problem,' she beamed happily. 'I got another lecture, but Keir could see it wasn't fair on Michael's mum not to come. You'll love her, Catherine, she's such a pet.'

'Is she?' Catherine stopped listening as the other girl prattled on. Well, this was certainly going to be an evening to remember, for Keir as well as her! She still couldn't believe what he felt for her was love—how could a man like Keir love *her*?—but whatever it was she had caused him embarrassment and pain, hurt his pride and dented his male ego.

Oh... She came to herself again to find she was alone, Janice having left to get ready. How could she bear it? How could she leave and never see him again? The thought made her feel physically sick, and for long, searing minutes she took great lungfuls of air, willing the nausea to subside.

And if she left this place she would never see her mother. She knew it, just as she knew she was close somehow. It wasn't a knowledge born of logic, but it was as hard as concrete, a sixth sense that had been awakened by something outside herself. And she wanted to see her...

She walked across to the door and shut it very quietly, before flinging herself down on the bed and crying as though her heart would break. Just once, *just once* she wanted to look into the face of the woman who had given birth to her, to see what her own flesh and blood looked like, to hear her speak. And it wasn't because she hated her, or wanted to spoil her life—nothing like that. She brought her hands across her chest as the pain became too much to bear. Perhaps it never had been. She just wanted to know if there was any chance that her mother had regretted what she'd done, had thought about her sometimes, wished she could see her...

'Oh, God, help me.' She groaned the words through such an anguish of soul that it had her screwing herself up into a tight little ball, the pain unbearable. 'Do something, show me; I can't go on...' She had made such a mess of everything; it had all gone from bad to worse like a runaway train that was out of control. And now she had hurt Keir, and she had to spend a whole evening pretending to be someone else, someone who had their heart set on a career and the high life.

She continued to pray, in fits and starts, for some time, her thoughts spiralling round and round like a huge roller coaster, until gradually she became quiet, a sense of peace pervading her troubled mind and blanketing her soul.

'How could someone do that to a little baby?' She spoke out loud into the quiet room, rising off the bed and walking across to the window, her eyelids heavy with weeping. She felt so sorry for the little baby she had been, but this time when she thought of it there was none of the bitter anger that had coloured such thoughts before, just a deep sense of sorrow and regret.

She didn't understand, she thought sadly, her eyes following a lone bird as it soared in the sky outside, its wings making good use of the warm air currents. And perhaps she never would. But if she was ever going to build some sort of a life for herself, learn to fly above the misery and despair of her early years and soar in the warm air currents of life, she had to let go of the crippling resentment and rage, justified though such emotions were.

Perhaps that was why she had been guided here? She continued to watch the carefree bird in the light-washed sky as dusk slowly put fingers of pink and mauve into the scene outside the window, other birds joining the first one as they feasted on insects the warm evening had brought out. Perhaps she had never been meant to find her mother. Maybe she'd had it all wrong from the beginning.

She was ready when Janice knocked on her door at eight, her careful use of cosmetics hiding the utter exhaustion that seemed to have taken her over. As she joined the others in the hall she felt as though she was in some kind of vacuum, a suspended void in the gallop of time that was surreal, dream-like.

The strange serenity took something of a knock when she looked at Keir. He seemed to fill the light-coloured hall, the black trousers and charcoal-grey shirt he was wearing making him seem even bigger than usual, the muscled strength of his powerful shoulders and chest very evident under the dark material.

He looked back at her, the sharply defined angles of his face hard and handsome and his stone-grey eyes expressionless as they took in the small, slim woman in front of him, dressed simply in an ankle-length full-skirted dress in white cotton, the plain colour relieved by a vivid violet-coloured belt that exactly matched the colour of her eyes.

'You look very lovely.' Catherine couldn't quite determine the tone of his voice, but she was aware of Janice's gaze darting between them, and then, as the moment stretched and became painful, she tore her eyes from his.

'Thank you.' He could have been carved in granite, she thought helplessly; she couldn't read a thing from his sombre face. 'So do you—look nice, that is,' she added hastily as her cheeks began to flame. 'And you, Janice.' She managed a quick smile at Keir's sister who still hadn't said a word.

'We'll bring the mutual admiration society to a close and get moving, shall we?' Keir drawled lazily. 'Mustn't let Michael's parents think we've forgotten, eh, Janice?'

It was below the belt, but in the circumstances all Janice could do was smile sweetly, although she obviously found it painful. 'Keir, you won't... You won't let on...?'

'My lips are sealed.' He glanced across at Catherine, the devastating grey gaze lingering on her mouth. 'How about yours?'

'I... Yes—I won't say a word, Janice.'

He was doing this on purpose, Catherine thought tightly as she followed Janice out of the flat, sailing past Keir with her nose in the air—the effect of which was spoilt by the brilliant colour staining her cheeks. He was trying to make her feel uncomfortable, embarrassed, because of this afternoon. *This afternoon...* The memory of how it had felt to be crushed close to that big, male frame suddenly obliterated the last of her fatigue, producing a rush of adrenaline that was more effective than any number of black coffees.

Well, she would get through this evening without rising to his subtle bait, and once they were in the car driving home, with Janice as chaperon, she would tell him that she was leaving in the morning. She ignored the savage thud her heart gave, and concentrated on putting one foot in front of the other as she walked down the stairs, acutely aware of Keir just behind her when she reached the bottom.

'This way.' As both women made to walk along the passage to the back of the house Keir unlocked the front door, before calling through into the reception area, 'Martin? We're off now. See you later, and thanks for holding the fort at such short notice.'

'My pleasure.' Martin's voice drifted through from the other room. 'Have a nice time.'

'A taxi?' Janice stood still on the top of the steps as she stared at the taxi-cab waiting in the street outside.

'Well spotted.'

'But we don't usually have a taxi.' Janice obviously didn't appreciate the brotherly sarcasm, as her terse tone made clear.

'Perhaps I'm trying to convince Catherine that we aren't quite the heathens we appear to be, and that even in the deep, dark wilds of Yorkshire we have the refinements of modern living,' Keir said pleasantly but with lethal intent. 'Besides which, I've found that Ian's taste in wine isn't to be frowned at, and I'm rather in need of some fortification tonight.'

'Oh.' Janice had clicked on to the fact that all was not well. 'Bad day?' she asked carefully.

'I've had better.'

Michael's parents lived on the outskirts of the next village, which was a bare five miles away, but, seated next to Keir in the back of the taxi, his hard thigh pressed close to hers and his arm stretched along the back of the seat in a manner that looked casual but which she just knew was meant to keep her fully aware of him, it seemed like fifty.

Dusky golden sunlight was slanting onto the roof of the beautiful thatched cottage when the taxi nosed its way through wrought-iron gates and onto a large rectangle of pebbled drive surrounded by a big, riotous border of boisterously unrestrained flowers. Hollyhocks, lupins, blue larkspur, brilliant scarlet snapdragons, the trumpet-shaped fragrant pink and white flowers of naked lady, Michaelmas daisies, clusters of lavender-blue Queen Anne's lace and feathery white baby's-breath all jostled for space, along with candytuft, lovely white anemones and the brilliant gold of faithful little marigolds.

It was breathtaking, an English garden at its best, and Catherine stood for a long moment in the dying sun once she was out of the car, breathing in the rich perfume of a host of gillyflowers as the peace she had felt earlier stole over her again.

'A little touch of English village life for you to see.' Keir's voice was deep and soft behind her, and when his hand closed over her bare elbow she felt the contact right down to her toes. 'If we can provide the fun too that's half of your criteria for a successful evening met.' His tone was sardonic as it stated he hadn't forgotten her words from the afternoon, and as she spun round to face him her face tightened.

'That's uncalled for—' she began furiously, only to stop abruptly when he placed a warning finger on her lips as Janice joined them.

'Look, is anything wrong?' Janice was clearly out of her depth as her eyes moved from Keir's mocking face to Catherine's angry one. 'I'm sorry I sprang this on you tonight—'

'No problem.' The taxi had swung round in a semi-circle, and just as it left the heavy oak door to the cottage swung open. 'And here's your beloved, right on cue,' Keir continued easily, raising his hand to Michael who was standing in the doorway, with an older couple just behind him.

'What *is* the matter?' Janice asked testily as they walked towards the others, but there was no time to answer as Michael stepped forward, his face wreathed in a smile of welcome, and introductions commenced.

'Catherine, these are my parents.' He stepped to one side as he waved at the couple behind him. 'My mother—another Catherine, I'm afraid, so forgive any confusion tonight—and my father, Ian.'

'How do you do?' Catherine smiled politely, but it was an effort. Whether it was due to the fact that Keir's hand had now snaked round her waist and she had been drawn very firmly into his side, or that Michael's mother wasn't at all what she had expected, she wasn't sure. She was very small—her doctor husband towered over her by a good nine inches—but it was her face that had arrested Catherine.

She knew Michael was the same age as Keir—thirty—and she had expected his parents to be around the fifty mark, probably going grey, but tanned and robust like most of the people hereabouts. But his mother was tiny—ethereal was the word—and although her face

still bore evidence of what must have been great beauty
in her youth her hair was pure white, utterly devoid of
colour.

How old was she? Catherine found she could hardly
tear her eyes away from the other woman's face. She
could be any age from forty to sixty, her skin still fine
and translucent, but the web of lines radiating from her
eyes and mouth and the deep sadness in her eyes suggesting a tragedy in her past that had ravaged her beauty
almost cruelly. It was a gentle face, a tragic face, and
Catherine felt herself drawn to it without knowing why.

'Catherine, please come in...' Michael's mother made
a little fluttering gesture with her hand that suggested
nervousness, and as Catherine felt Keir's arm tighten
round her body she glanced up into his face and saw he
was looking at the other woman with something akin to
shock darkening his eyes.

'Keir?' As they followed the others into the cottage—a vision of olde-world charm—he seemed determined not to let go of her. 'What's the matter?'

'It's not possible.' He was talking as though to himself, but with his eyes on her face. 'Catherine, you said
your mother's name was Anna—Anna Mitchell?' he
asked urgently.

She nodded, frightened by the expression on his face.

'Then how—?' His murmur was cut short as they
joined the others in the beautiful little Victorian summer
house attached to the dining room at the back of the
house, where a trolley of drinks was waiting.

There was a strange atmosphere prevailing as everyone was settled in big, comfy cane chairs with their
drinks. Ian kept very close to his wife, his eyes constantly darting to her face, which was as white as lint,
and even Michael seemed to sense that something was
wrong, his glances at his parents troubled as he mixed

and deposited drinks, and offered round the little tray of hors d'oeuvres.

'Michael tells us you live in London, Catherine.' It was a relief when Michael's mother engaged her in conversation—even the normal banter between Michael and Janice had been stilted and forced. 'You're down here on holiday, I understand?' she asked gently. 'Recuperating after an illness?'

'Yes, in a way.' She had already told Keir, so there was no point in perpetuating the lie. 'I've actually left London, and I'm having a break before I move on to Birmingham to live and work.' One city was as good as another, and she had decided on Birmingham that afternoon as she had watched Keir come and go about the farms.

She felt him stiffen at her side on the small cane sofa for two where he had deftly sat them, but he said nothing, and she didn't dare look at his face.

'You've family in London?' It was a perfectly reasonable question, but the look on Michael's mother's face was making Catherine feel uncomfortable.

How did she answer that? She had no family in London—the people who had brought her up had never been a family to her—but polite pre-dinner conversation didn't lend itself to the truth. 'I'm adopted.' She saw the words register in the other woman's eyes like a blow. 'And my adoptive family and I don't get on, so I don't really have any ties there, if that's what you mean.'

Her heart was beginning to pound, and the feeling that she had met this woman before, that she knew her in some way, was growing. But there was a chilling numbness holding part of her brain, the part that had hoped and prayed and groaned for the last few months since she had found out the truth about herself.

'What's your surname?' As Ian moved to put his arm round his wife's shoulders, she was aware of Keir doing exactly the same to her, but the icy trickles that were shivering down her spine were holding her transfixed.

She stared at the woman in front of her, utterly unable to speak, her heightened senses taking in Michael and Janice in one part of the room—clearly bewildered by what was happening, as their unnatural stillness showed—the evening bird-song beyond the open door of the summer house where the large garden stretched, the blue sky through the windows, the shadow falling across her mother's face... *Her mother's face.*

'Prentice.' It was a whisper.

'And you are twenty-one years old, and you have a tiny birthmark on your thigh in the shape of the moon... Catherine, oh, Catherine...'

'You're my mother.'

'And you're my baby, my precious, precious baby.' How she came to be clasped in her mother's arms she wasn't sure; her eyes were blinded by tears, but the arms holding her were strong for all their fragility, and the embrace was soft and warm and perfumed, and went on and on.

She was aware of muted hustling and bustling at the sides of them, but she was incapable of pulling herself together for long minutes, and when eventually she did raise her head it was to see her mother sitting beside her on the sofa—and she realised they were quite alone. Her mother's face—the face she recognised was so like hers now she knew—was drenched in tears, but lit with an inner light that told her all she wanted to know.

'You don't mind that I've found you?' Catherine whispered brokenly. 'I thought...'

'*Mind?*' Her mother shut her eyes for a second and her face crumpled as she said, 'I've lived for this moment for twenty-one years—dreamed it, breathed it. Without believing that one day we would be reunited I wouldn't have remained sane.'

'But why—?' Catherine stopped abruptly.

'Why, feeling like that, did I give you up?' her mother said softly. 'Can I tell you, explain from the beginning? It won't excuse what I did—nothing can do that—but if you just understand how it was…'

Catherine nodded without speaking, her mind still stunned by the enormity of it all, and her mother gathered her close for one minute more, as though she couldn't bear to let her go, before drawing away and composing her face, which was awash with tears again.

'I was very confused when I met the young man who was your father—confused, lonely and unhappy. I was just seventeen, my parents had been killed in a horrific accident I'd witnessed, and the effect on me was very traumatic. My sister, my adopted sister, was already married and I'd been placed with her. We didn't get on, but I knew lots of siblings who were the same, and she was the only family I'd got. But she treated me badly, and when I met Alan…'

Her voice trailed away, and she took a deep breath before she continued, 'When I met Alan I fell for him hook, line and sinker. He…he told me he loved me, that he'd look after me, that we'd get married and I could leave my sister's home, and then…then I got pregnant.'

She raised her head and looked Catherine full in the face. 'He left the same week,' she said bleakly. 'My parents had always been very protective, and I was painfully naive for my age—not that that excuses anything. I was offered an abortion but I couldn't, I just couldn't, and so I continued with the pregnancy although my sister made each day an ordeal.

'But, when I saw you, it was all worth it. You were so beautiful, so perfect; I loved you instantly. I named you Catherine Joy—Catherine because that's my second name and Joy—because of the joy I felt when I first saw you and knew you were mine.'

'And then?' Catherine found she was holding her mother's hands in her own. 'What then?'

'It was a hard birth, and I was ill—physically and mentally—afterwards. I brought you home and all my sister did was go on at me—that I was unfair, how you would suffer without a father, the cruelty other children would subject you to, the things I was depriving you of—on and on and on. She said she could give you everything and I could give you nothing, and in the end I cracked. I became very ill in my mind.'

She shook her head blindly. 'The loss of my parents, Alan's desertion, the pregnancy and the birth, and then the pressure from her afterwards—it was just too much, I suppose. And so I gave in. She couldn't have children, and she wanted you so much. I knew with them you would have a normal family life, that they could give you everything I couldn't.'

Oh, the irony of it all. Catherine looked at the pain-ravaged face in front of her and knew she couldn't tell her the truth—not now, perhaps not ever. There were some things love had to carry.

'My sister was adamant I couldn't see you again, that it had to be a complete severance or else she wouldn't feel you were hers. I could understand that, in a way, but it was the hardest thing of all. If I could just have stayed on the perimeter of your life, seen you occasionally...'

'And so you came to Yorkshire,' Catherine said gently, the knowledge that her mother had suffered even more than she had through the years wrenching her heart in a way she would have considered impossible just days—hours—ago.

'I came as housekeeper to Ian after answering an advertisement.' Her mother brushed a wisp of white hair from her brow with a trembling hand. 'I told my sister where I was, that if at any time—*any time*—in the future

she would let me see you I would come straight there...
But I knew she wouldn't. My one hope through the years
was that you would try and find me when you were old
enough to do so.'

'And you married Ian?' Catherine asked quietly. And
became Michael's mother. It hurt; she couldn't help it.

'When I came up here I was on the verge of a nervous
breakdown, and leaving you tipped me over the edge.
Ian was so good; instead of me being housekeeper to a
nine-year-old boy and his father, they looked after me
for months and months until I began to recover. I told
Ian everything; he's a very good man.'

Her mother shook her head slowly. 'He asked me to
marry him twelve months later, and he understood I
could never give him a child. I felt that to do so would
be a betrayal of you in some way, and he accepted that.
Michael loves me, as I do him, but perhaps because of
my illness in the early days it was not the traditional
mother/son relationship. He is very protective, but looks
on me more as an older sister, I think. And you—you
are my only child, Catherine, my precious only child.'

She reached out a shaky hand and touched Catherine's
face. 'I've looked at your photo every day we've been
apart.'

'Did you know, when you asked me here tonight?'
Catherine asked quietly, her heart thudding when she
realised how easily she could have missed it. 'Did you
know I was your daughter?'

'I wasn't sure. Janice had mentioned you, of course,
and the name, the age, the fact you were from London
all seemed right. But she said you were on holiday—'

'I wasn't. I came looking for you,' Catherine said
quickly. 'But for Anna—Anna Mitchell.'

'I used my second name when I came here—it was
the only link I had left with you—and then of course I
married Ian so my surname changed...' She stopped and

they both looked at each other for a long moment, the wonder of it all reflected in both faces. 'I thought you might hate me for giving you away,' her mother said softly with a little catch in her voice, her eyes expressing far more than the words said.

'I love you,' Catherine said just as softly. 'You're my mum.'

CHAPTER TEN

'CAN'T sleep?'

Keir's voice was soft and deep, but Catherine still nearly jumped out of her skin as he came up behind her in the dark lounge. It had been two in the morning before they had got back to the flat, after an evening containing so much gruelling emotion, Catherine had thought she would fall asleep on her feet. But once alone in her room she'd found her mind was buzzing with a thousand images, a thousand words, a thousand fragmented scenarios, and try as she might she couldn't stop pacing the floor.

At four she had given up any notion of sleep, opening her door quietly and padding out into the hall in just her nightie and towelling robe to make herself a cup of coffee in the silent kitchen.

Once in her favourite seat in the shadowed lounge—in a big easy chair overlooking the sleeping village below—she had curled her feet beneath her, and with her hands cradling the coffee mug had allowed her thoughts to roam at will.

She had found her mother, and never in her wildest dreams had she allowed herself to imagine she would be loved, wanted, *needed* so very much. Ian had taken her aside at one point during the evening to tell her, quietly and very gently, that he believed the crucifying grief his wife had felt over leaving her daughter behind had turned her hair white when she had come to Yorkshire. 'There hasn't been a day since I've known her that she hasn't spoken your name,' he'd said softly, his arm round her shoulders. 'I can't tell you what it means to both of us to have you here, Catherine. We've prayed for this day for twenty-one years.'

Yes, there was no doubt that she was loved and wanted, that the doors to her mother's heart and her home were wide open. So why, when everything had turned out so incredibly, so miraculously well, did she feel as though she had missed something somewhere? Since she had prayed yesterday evening she'd felt she was being shown something, but she hadn't grasped it, and the feeling was even more urgent now, since she had found her mother.

She turned in the chair now to look up at Keir, and her heart gave a giant lurch at the sight of him, big and dark, just behind her. He was still in the clothes he had worn earlier in the evening, and she said the first thing that came into her mind. 'Haven't you been to bed?'

'No.' He walked in front of her, settling one thigh on the broad windowsill as he looked back at her, the bright moonlight making the room a stark contrast of clear shapes and dark shadows. 'I've been in the garden since we got back...thinking.'

'Oh.' She hardly dared breathe.

'Do you know what about?' he asked softly, the expression on his face making her heart thud still harder and her mouth go dry.

She had to lick her lips before she could speak, and his narrowed gaze followed the action, the sensual gleam in his eyes making her hot. 'No.'

'You. You, my hard-hearted little sprite.'

'I'm not hard-hearted!'

Her very real indignation caused his mouth to curve in a wry, crooked smile. 'No?' He let his gaze run over her face, her eyes, her lips, her throat, and she felt its impact as though he were actually caressing her, her skin growing pink and her breathing quickening.

'I don't have to touch you, do I? I don't even have to

touch you and you melt for me,' he said thickly. 'And you're talking about leaving here.'

'That's just sex.'

'The hell it is.' He glared at her before shaking his head and saying more softly, 'The hell it is. I love you, Catherine. I love you more than I ever imagined loving a woman, and there is no way I'm going to let you walk out of my life.'

'Keir—'

'No, cut the "Keir"'s and the "I can't"'s,' he growled slowly. 'I'm not being kept at arm's length by them any more. I know you, Catherine; I know you in here.' He thumped the front of his chest angrily. 'I know the sort of woman you are, and there is no way you would respond to me like you do unless you felt something for me beyond the desire for a quick tumble in bed.

'And I'll tell you quite frankly—' a touch of chagrin entered the grim voice for a moment '—if I hadn't needed more from you than an easing of my body you'd have been bedded weeks ago. Because I *want* you, Catherine; physically I want you very much indeed. The things I imagine doing to you—' The twist of his mouth expressed dark self-derision. 'Believe me, you would be in no doubt that I want you.'

She loved him, oh, she loved him, but she didn't dare believe what he felt for her would last. Something of what she was feeling must have been written on her face, because he reached out for her, pulling her up and into his arms before she could move. 'I'm not letting you go, Catherine; get that into your head first of all,' he said in a smoky, thick voice that made her quiver. 'If you leave here I'll find you and bring you back; it's as simple as that. Besides which, you have family here now; you can't escape me.'

She didn't want to; there was nothing she wanted less. 'It wouldn't work.' She pushed against his broad chest, feeling the thud of his heart against her hand and realising he wasn't as calm as he was acting.

'The only way you can convince me of that is to say you feel nothing for me,' he stated softly. 'Me as a person. Tell me, Catherine—tell me I just turn you on, that there is nothing else there at all, and if I believe you I'll leave you alone. I promise you that.'

'Keir, this is ridiculous—'

'Tell me. Tell me you just want fun with no emotional ties, that you are hell-bent on climbing that career ladder to the exclusion of any personal commitment. I wouldn't stop you having a career if that was what you wanted, Catherine.'

He took her face between his big hands, the grey eyes that could appear so cold glowing like sun-warmed stone. 'Of course I want a family, children, one day. But it can be years from now, decades, if that's what you want—'

'It's not my career. Don't you *see*? It's me.' The words were torn out of her, the emotional roller coaster of the last few hours breaking down all her defences. Fear was like a thick mist, choking her, strangling her, panic at her own inadequacy so real she could taste it, bitter and tart, on her tongue. 'I can't be what you want, Keir. It would all go wrong and you...you'd be disappointed.'

'What are you talking about?' He stared at her with very real amazement on his face. 'Is it something that's happened in your past? Is that it? I don't care; I told you when you met me the slate was wiped clean.'

'It's not anything that's happened—not in that way. I told you everything yesterday. I've never...I've never gone with a man. It's just that you could have anyone,' she whispered dully.

'But the one I want is a silver-haired girl with eyes I

could drown in,' he said softly. 'I don't want anyone else; I never will.'

'You think that *now*—'

'Catherine, what do you want from me?' His hands moved to her shoulders and he shook her gently. 'I'm turning myself inside out here—'

'But that's part of it, don't you understand?' she said urgently, jerking away from him and shaking her head wildly. 'You want someone uncomplicated, easy to be with, someone who can make you happy.'

'Stop playing the martyr!' The words, and the tone he used, were like a bucket of cold water over her head, and she froze in shock, her eyes enormous as she stared into his angry face, before stepping forward and hitting him once, very hard, across the face.

'How dare you? How dare you say that to me?' she spat furiously . 'I hate you—'

'No, you don't, you love me.' He had both her wrists in one hand now, his other arm moving her struggling body against his, where she continued to twist and turn, her breath sobbing in her throat. 'And I love you, and I'm not going to let you throw away the one chance of happiness we both have because of what's happened in your past. I could kill your family for what they've done to you, but they are your past and I'm your future; do you hear me?

'When I saw you next to your mother yesterday I could've kicked myself for not realising who she was before, but when I've looked at Ian's wife in the past all I've seen is a sad, tragic figure who has always been something of a recluse.'

She had stopped struggling now, and he put her to arm's length whilst keeping hold of her shoulders. 'I'm not going to let that happen to you, Catherine, however much you fight me. Together we are going to beat this thing; you are not going to let that maniac who brought you up wreck your life too. I can't promise you I'll always be the perfect husband. I'm human; I make mistakes—I get too wrapped up in my work and take too much on, I'm untidy, I leave the top off the toothpaste. But one thing I can promise you...'

He paused, pulling her against him and holding her face with his hand. 'I'll always love you, always be there for you, always need and want you, till death and beyond.'

She hadn't realised she was crying, silently, until he bent forward and took her salty lips in a long, deep kiss as his hands moved over her body in an intimate caress.

'We are going to build our *own* life, with our *own* family, and you'll learn to believe it—I promise you that too,' he said shakily after long, sweet minutes of love-making. 'You'll see your children playing with their grandmother and you'll heal her mind too, give her back the years that the locust has eaten. It *will* happen, Catherine, I promise you.'

'All these promises...' She tried to smile, but the tears flowed again.

'But first you have to say you love me; you never have, you know,' he said huskily, and just for a moment she saw a flash of uncertainty, of a desperate need for reassurance in the face of this big, controlled, authoritative man she loved so much, and it melted the last of her resistance.

'I do—I do so much—but I can't help being frightened...'

'That's fine.' He held her so tightly she thought her ribs would crack. 'I can deal with that. I've got all the time in the world, the rest of our lives, to convince you of how much you're loved.'

It was said with such arrogance—that same arrogance

that had so got under her skin when they had first met—that she wanted to smile, but he had captured her mouth again and her soul was flying.

EPILOGUE

THE only place they could have considered being married was the ancient little thirteenth-century parish church in the middle of Towerby, and it seemed to Catherine that the whole of the village had turned out as she walked up the long, winding path to the church door on Ian's arm.

Keir had wanted a December wedding, telling her that the best Christmas present in the world would be to wake up beside her on Christmas Day. And Mother Nature had conspired to add her own touch of magic to the occasion, draping the trees and hedgerows with a brilliant, glittering mantle of frost beneath a clear winter sky of deep cloudless blue, creating a white, diamond-studded wonderland.

'All right?' As they reached the top of the path and Catherine turned round to smile at Janice behind her, resplendent in her bridesmaid's regalia of wine and ivory, Ian's quiet voice at her side brought her eyes snapping back to his.

'I think so,' she said shakily.

The girl in the mirror who had stared back at her just a few minutes before leaving her mother's house hadn't looked familiar, the frothy satin and lace ivory dress and fur-lined cape and hood edged in wine silk giving her an ethereal beauty that was quite breathtaking and a little awe-inspiring, her skin a delicate, translucent cream and her hair like spun silver.

'I think he's waiting.' Ian smiled at her, and she felt a surge of love for this quiet man who had been a tower of strength to her mother since the day they had met,

185

and who had accepted her into his family as his own daughter without a second thought, becoming the father she had never had as easily as if she were his natural child.

As the strains of the Bridal March began Catherine felt a little fluttering of panic, and then she was walking through the small arched doorway, Ian's comforting bulk at her side, and beginning the walk up the aisle. Every pillar, every windowsill of the beautiful old church was festooned with flowers, their fragrance filling the building. But she only had eyes for the tall, dark man standing with Michael in front of the altar.

Would she make him happy? Could she forget the past and reach out to the future? And then he turned, while she was still a few feet away, and smiled at her, and she knew she had nothing to prove to Keir, and never would have. He loved her; he loved her more than she had imagined herself ever being loved.

His parents were smiling at her on her right, a bevy of uncles and aunts beaming their approval in the seats behind, and then she caught sight of her mother's face in the pew opposite, her eyes sparkling with tears of joy and happiness and her face alight with love.

She was covered in love, deluged with it, wrapped in its delicious warmth as she floated to Keir's side and Ian placed her hand in his, Michael grinning at her from Keir's other side.

'A few minutes more and you're really mine.' Keir's voice was low and deep, and for her ears only.

'I'm yours.' She smiled at him, her tears of happiness glittering like diamonds in the deep blue of her eyes. 'I've always been yours.' She was home.

JAYNE ANN KRENTZ

Lady's Choice

Travis Sawyer has a plan for revenge. Juliana Grant has a
plan too—she has picked Travis as Mr Right. When
Travis takes over the resort in which Juliana has invested
her money, Juliana takes matters
into her own hands.

*"Jayne Ann Krentz is one of the hottest writers
in romance today."*—USA Today

1-55166-270-1
AVAILABLE FROM MARCH 1998

Catherine Coulter

Afterglow

Chalk-and-cheese lovers Chelsea Lattimer and
David Winter finally find happiness after a series
of disastrous relationships—thanks to their
match-making friends.

Afterglow is a wonderful romantic comedy from
New York Times bestselling author Catherine Coulter.

MIRA®

1-55166-472-0
AVAILABLE FROM MARCH 1998

JANICE KAISER

FAIR GAME

Dana Kirk is a rich and successful woman, but someone
wants to kill her and her teenage daughter. Who hates
her enough to terrorise this single mother? Detective
Mitchell Cross knows she needs help—
his help—to stay alive.

*"...enough plot twists and turns to delight
armchair sleuths"*—Publishers Weekly

1-55166-065-2
AVAILABLE FROM MARCH 1998

SANDRA BROWN

THE THRILL OF VICTORY

Stevie Corbett's life is on the line, but her fate rides on
keeping the truth a secret. Judd Mackie's job is
to uncover secrets. After dogging Stevie for
years, Judd now has the story of the year.
All he has to do is betray her trust.

"One of fiction's brightest stars!"
—Dallas Morning News

1-55166-025-3
AVAILABLE FROM FEBRUARY 1998

HEATHER GRAHAM POZZESSERE

If Looks Could Kill

Madison wasn't there when her mother was
murdered, but she *saw* it happen. Years later, a
killer is stalking women in Miami and Madison's
nightmare visions have returned. Can FBI agent
Kyle Montgomery catch the serial killer before
Madison becomes his next victim?

"...an incredible storyteller!"—LA Daily News

1-55166-285-X
AVAILABLE FROM FEBRUARY 1998

MIRA®

JoAnn ROSS

NO REGRETS

Three sisters torn apart by tragedy each choose a
different path—until fate and one man reunites them.
Only when tragedy strikes again can the surviving
sisters allow themselves to choose happiness—
if they dare pay the price.

"A steamy, fast-paced read."
—Publishers Weekly

1-55166-282-5
AVAILABLE FROM FEBRUARY 1998